THE
BLOODY
HOAX

Jewish Literature and Culture
Series Editor, Alvin H. Rosenfeld

THE BLOODY HOAX

BY SHOLOM ALEICHEM

Translated by Aliza Shevrin
Introduction by Maurice Friedberg

INDIANA UNIVERSITY PRESS
Bloomington and Indianapolis

Translated from the Yiddish, *Der Blutiger Shpas* (Warsaw: Kultur-lige, 1923).
English translation © 1991 by Aliza Shevrin
Introduction © 1991 by Maurice Friedberg

The paper used in this publication meets the minimum requirements of American
National Standard for Information Sciences—Permanence of Paper for Printed
Library Materials, ANSI Z39.48-1984.

∞ ™

Manufactured in the United States of America

Library of Congress Cataloging-in-Publication Data

Sholem Aleichem, 1859–1916.
    [Blutiger shpas.   English]
    The bloody hoax / by Sholom Aleichem ; translated by Aliza Shevrin
; introduction by Maurice Friedberg.
       p.   cm. — (Jewish literature and culture)
    Translation of: Der blutiger shpas.
    ISBN 0-253-30401-6 (cloth)
    I. Title   II. Series
PJ5129.R2B5413   1991
839'.0933—dc20   91-11717

2 3 4 5   95 94 93 92

For Howie,
husband, friend, partner

Introduction

In October 1990 I attended in Moscow a performance of *A Memorial Prayer (Pominal'naya molitva)*, a stage adaptation of Sholom Aleichem's tales of Tevye the Dairyman. The musical *A Fiddler on the Roof*, which is based on the same tales, was then playing in another theater in the Soviet capital. Banned in the USSR only a few years earlier, as were nearly all plays with a Jewish theme, each was now a commercial success and tickets were hard to come by, even on weekdays.

As the evening progressed, a curious inconsistency became increasingly apparent. Neither the largely Jewish audience nor the actors on the stage seemed in the least familiar with Jewish customs and religious observances. Sholom Aleichem's Tevye wore a prayer shawl on a Friday night, his wife lit a Hanukkah menorah, women were banished from the Sabbath table while blessings were recited over wine, and Tevye prayed on his knees together with a Christian neighbor—details as incongruous as would be a Christian on a prayer rug facing Mecca or a Moslem crossing himself. Only a part of the audience appeared to recognize the single Hebrew text, that of the memorial prayer *Kaddish*. On the other hand, there was an eerie silence in the auditorium during the scene of the pogrom and at the end of the play when Jews were being expelled from their ancestral village in the Ukraine. Clutching their meager possessions and trying to calm frightened children, Sholom Aleichem's Jews of prerevolutionary Russia embarked on a long journey to the Promised Land of America.

It then dawned on me that here in a Moscow theater I was witness to what Edmund Wilson called the shock of recognition. Like their ancestors of nearly a century ago, Soviet Jews of 1990 lived in fear of pogroms (I personally have seen leaflets and graffiti threatening Jews with physical violence) and the number of Jews leaving for America or for Israel was approaching a thousand a day. Like those on the stage, they included young and old, learned and simple, prominent and obscure, onetime fighters for a revolutionary utopia that would obliterate ethnic distinctions, and even converts to Russian Orthodoxy with their Gentile spouses. A classic chronicler of the Russian Jewish past, Sholom Aleichem was also uncannily relevant to the Soviet Jewish present.

Readers of Sholom Aleichem will not be surprised by this observation. Great writers of all nations shed light on the human condition. Sholom Aleichem, the greatest Yiddish author of all time, shed light on a seemingly permanent trait of the Jewish condition, namely, its singular vulnerability to irrational racial and religious hatreds. There is, in fact, some confirmation of the writer's apparently conscious desire to emphasize, as it were, this Jewish universality. Born in 1859 in Imperial Russia, Sholom Rabinovitch, bearer of a classic Jewish name (to this day, Jewish protagonists of Russian jokes are usually called Rabinovitch), chose for his *nom de plume* the common Jewish greeting *sholom aleichem*—"peace unto you." Indeed, in *The Bloody Hoax*, when two young men agree on a prince-and-pauper exchange, a Russian nobleman undertakes to live for a time as a Rabinovitch, while the real Rabinovitch is allowed to enjoy for a time the tranquil life of a Gentile squire named Popov. Other main characters in *The Bloody Hoax* are similarly endowed with such common Jewish names as Hurvitch and Shapiro. They are thus all Jewish Everymen.

But then, Sholom Aleichem—the man as well as the writer—was in many ways quintessentially turn-of-the-century East European and Jewish. His life illustrates, and his works reflect, the clash of tradition and modernity, of the various strains of Jewish nationalism and the internationalist Jewish Socialist Bund, of Jewish distinctiveness and integration into Gentile society. A secular writer, Sholom Aleichem described religious rituals and observances with genuine warmth. (Indeed, he even served for a time as a state-appointed rabbi, a post that required commitment both to Jewish tradition and to modern learning and values.) A Zionist, he wrote but little in Hebrew, the language Zionism promoted, and became famous for his writings in Yiddish, the language on which Zionists frowned. Moreover, he ultimately settled in America, not in Palestine. And notwithstanding his understandable grievances against both state-sponsored and popular Russian anti-Semitism, he much admired Russian culture, literature above all.

A pragmatist, Sholom Aleichem sought an accommodation that would allow the Jewish spiritual legacy to adjust to societal change, and championed acculturation without assimilation. His ideological stance was consistent also with the sad and gently comic flavor of most of his writings. He showed no hatred even of the haters, and his most pointed satires are remarkably free of rancor. "Laughter," he wrote, "is good for you. Doctors recommend it." Sholom Aleichem was not the only Yiddish author of his time to enjoy critical acclaim and popular esteem, but he was by far the most beloved, in part for the kindness, tolerance, and good cheer that his writings exude. When he died in New York on May 13, 1916, there was an unprecedented outpouring of popular grief among the city's largely immigrant Jews. The sewing machines in the sweatshops of the garment district went silent, and hundreds of thousands joined in the funeral procession.

A singularly prolific author, Sholom Aleichem, as Chekhov once said of himself, wrote everything except poetry and denunciations to the police. His novels were serialized in newspapers, his short stories were printed and reprinted wherever Yiddish was spoken, his plays were important in the Yiddish theater's repertory, but it was in the semi-journalistic genre of the feuilleton that Sholom Aleichem truly reveled.

To Chekhov, the feuilleton served as a literary exercise that enabled him to produce his later, serious novellas and plays, much as Czerny's compositions help train future concert pianists. Not so with Sholom Aleichem. As Dan Miron notes, it was feuilletons that earned him his enormous popularity. Some have, in fact, become part of Yiddish folklore. Feuilletons, in Miron's estimation, afforded Sholom Aleichem "complete freedom to present fragments of stories,

descriptions, reflections, cynical and sentimental outpourings, jokes and character sketches, spicing them with quips and trick devices in the manner of Lau-
rence Sterne."* Sholom Aleichem's limitations are those of his favorite
European author, Charles Dickens. He is, for example, distinctly uncomfortable
with romantic motifs—but is delightfully at ease portraying children. He prefers
descriptions of physical and social realities to explorations of the human psyche.

With all that in mind, of Sholom Aleichem's broad canvases of Jewish life in
Imperial Russia one might say what Friedrich Engels once observed about Bal-
zac's novels. They are a wondrously realistic social history. Even of details of
economic life one learns more from them "than from the books of all the experts
of that time—the historians, the economists and the statisticians—taken together." It may well be that the co-founder of what became known as "scientific
Marxism" succumbed here, of all things, to the hyperbolic allure of poetic li-
cense. Still, there is no disputing the fact that Sholom Aleichem's writings
enrich the scholarly histories of Jews in czarist Russia—such as those of Simon
Dubnow and Salo Baron—with sound and smell and color. They make their dry
bones live. And none more so than *The Bloody Hoax* (1912–13), a novel that
portrays Jewish life during the final decade of the Romanov Empire, and one of
Sholom Aleichem's last books.

Jews have lived in Russia since that nation's dawn of history. They were not
very numerous at first, and from the very beginning they were subjected to
persecutions. The invasion of the Mongols in the thirteenth century and the
nearly three hundred years of their rule were a period of great suffering. The end
of the foreign yoke, however, brought little relief. In the sixteenth century Ivan
the Terrible ordered that Jews refusing to convert to Christianity be drowned in
the river. The seventeenth century was marked by the Bogdan Khmelnitsky
massacres in the Ukraine, which were followed by mass murders of Lithuania's
and Byelorussia's Jews by Muscovite armies. And in 1742 Empress Elizabeth
ordered the expulsion of all Jews residing in her domain.

Unbelievably, fifty years later Russia's Jewish community was the world's
largest, a distinction it continued to hold until World War I. Not that Russia
suddenly became hospitable to Jews. The three partitions of Poland—those of
1772, 1793, and 1795—and the subsequent annexations of the rump Polish
Kingdom and areas in the southwest, extended the Romanov Empire to territo-
ries densely inhabited by erstwhile Polish and Lithuanian Jews. By the middle of
the nineteenth century the country's Jewish population was estimated at close to
two and a half million. Fifty years later, notwithstanding considerable emigration to America, to Western Europe, and a modest one to Palestine (the Jews of
the United States are predominantly descendants of these emigrés), the number
of Russia's Jews exactly doubled.

Of the many disabilities suffered by the Jews of the Russian Empire, most
notorious were the limitations on places where they were allowed to reside.
Originally the Pale of Settlement (*cherta [postoyannoi evreiskoi] osedlosti*, "the

Encyclopedia Judaica, vol. XIV (1971), p. 1279.

Pale [of Permanent Jewish] Settlement") corresponded to similar restrictions
on the freedom of movement of Russian townsmen, merchants, and, above all,
peasants. By the mid-nineteenth century, however, these were all relaxed, particularly after the abolition of serfdom in 1861, two years, incidentally, before
Lincoln's Emancipation Proclamation. By contrast, rules and regulations per-
taining to the Jewish Pale of Settlement became, if anything, more rigid. According to the census of 1897, ninety-four percent of the country's Jewish
population, 4,899,300 men, women, and children, were confined to an area of
less than 400,000 square miles between the Baltic and the Black Sea, compris-
ing, roughly, Lithuania, Byelorussia, the Ukraine, Bessarabia, and a part of Poland, including Warsaw and Lodz. Jews permitted to live outside the Pale, and
also in some cities within the Pale itself, included the wealthiest merchants,
university graduates, dentists, nurses, and several categories of artisans. The
other privileged exceptions were the few army veterans who, after twenty-five
years of service (these were the "cantonists" kidnapped into the army at age
twelve or so), remained Jewish, most having been forcibly converted to Eastern
Orthodox Christianity; and, endearingly, Jewish prostitutes. These were the Jews
entitled to a precious residence permit, the *"pravozhitelstvo"* that is mentioned
so often in the pages of *The Bloody Hoax*. By the end of the nineteenth century
hundreds of thousands of young Jews were clamoring for admission to Russian
secondary schools *(gimnazii)* and universities, but only a small number were
admitted under the rigid quotas, the notorious *protsentnaya norma*. (This helps
explain many American Jews' suspicions of quotas in admissions to colleges). Of
course, there was an "easy" way to avoid all anti-Semitic discrimination. Under
the tsar, Jewish converts to Christianity became full-fledged citizens. (Earlier, in
Poland, they were automatically ennobled as well!) We meet one such convert in
Sholom Aleichem's novel.

According to the 1897 census, fully ninety-nine percent of Jews in the Pale of
Settlement spoke Yiddish (though many, to be sure, spoke some Russian as
well) and, as a rule, Jewish children received only a religious education. Because
most Jews were forbidden to reside in villages, only very few engaged in agricul-
ture. The majority lived in small towns that were often almost exclusively Jewish
or else formed large minorities in the bigger cities of the Pale. Some forty percent
of gainfully employed Jews were tradesmen, and over thirty percent were artisans, most often tailors and shoemakers. Not a few were *Luftmenschen*, literally
"people of the air." Their lack of permanent occupation was no bohemian
affectation. It bespoke extreme poverty. These men and women were the Jewish
Lumpenproletariat. Some of Sholom Aleichem's most memorable characters belong to this group of petty traders, beggars, middlemen, and ne'er-do-wells. A
few appear in *The Bloody Hoax*. Yet even their more prosperous neighbors were,
for the most part, only marginally better off. It was this cutthroat competition
among impoverished artisans and shopkeepers which, together with the anti-
Jewish legal restrictions—to say nothing of bloody pogroms—fed the constant
stream of Jewish emigration from Russia to America and Western Europe. The
Pale of Settlement continued to exist to the bitter end of the Empire. It was

abolished in March 1917, together with other discriminatory legislation directed at ethnic and religious minorities, by Russia's democratic Provisional government. By the time of the Communist coup d'etat of November 7 of that year, thousands of Jews from the Pale had already legally moved to Moscow and to Petrograd.

Sholom Aleichem's *The Bloody Hoax* is justifiably subtitled "an extraordinary novel." A part of it is, quite literally, a chronicle of a current event. Not of a historical event, but of an unfolding, ongoing courtroom drama—and one, moreover, that could affect the destinies of virtually every one of Russia's five million Jews. Many pages of *The Bloody Hoax* are thinly fictionalized summaries of newspaper accounts of the Beiliss blood-libel trial printed while Sholom Aleichem was at work on his book.

Charges that followers of a minority religion's faith use human flesh and blood for ritual purposes go far back in history. "We are said to be the most criminal of men, on the score of our sacramental baby-killing, and the baby-eating that goes with it," lamented a writer in the second century A.D. The writer was Tertullian, a Church Father, and he cited the "glory" of a pagan Roman magistrate "who had brought to light some Christian who had eaten up to date a hundred babies." In the centuries that followed, Jews were frequently accused of the same crime by Christians, despite the fact that they were repeatedly exonerated of the charge and that blood libel was condemned by no fewer than three Popes, Gregory IX, Innocent IV, and Clement XIV. Exoneration of the accused, however, was no cause for rejoicing, since the prisoners were often tortured and the trials themselves inspired anti-Semitic violence. While in medieval Europe blood-libel trials occurred mostly in Western Europe, in modern times their center shifted to Russia, where the sinister myth became a staple of general anti-Semitic propaganda. While out-and-out anti-Semites were ready to believe that all Jews require Christian blood for the baking of Passover *matzot*, the "moderates" were inclined to agree with Nicholas I, who declared that "there are among the Jews savage fanatics or sects requiring Christian blood for their ritual." At least two major cultural figures subscribed to this view, the eighteenth-century poet Gavrila Derzhavin and the folklorist and lexicographer Vladimir Dal'.

It is against this background, then, that we should consider the fictionalized account of the Beiliss trial in *The Bloody Hoax*. Except, of course, for the mistaken identity of the accused Popov-Rabinovitch suggested by the logic of the novel's plot, Sholom Aleichem's account is closer to the factual record than the later American novelistic treatment of the story, Bernard Malamud's *The Fixer*, and the motion picture of the same name. The following is a summary of the actual events.

On March 12, 1911, a mutilated body was discovered on the outskirts of Kiev. The victim was identified as Andrei Yushchinsky, a boy of twelve. The many wounds on his body inspired the local anti-Semitic newspapers to declare that the boy was murdered by the Jews for ritual purposes, and at Yushchinsky's funeral leaflets demanding vengeance on Jewish murderers were distributed by the Union of the Russian People, a rabid anti-Semitic organization known as a prime instigator of pogroms. A police investigator, however, traced the murder to a gang of thieves associated with a local woman with a long criminal record. The anti-Semites proved influential enough to have the police investigator fired and his findings disregarded. Acting on instructions from the anti-Semitic minister of justice I. G. Shcheglovitov, the Kiev district attorney instructed the police to keep looking for a Jewish connection. Eventually, a witness testified that, on the day of the boy's disappearance, he had seen him playing with two other boys in the yard of a Jewish-owned brick factory and that the boy was then kidnapped by a Jewish employee. It was on the basis of this testimony that Mendel Beiliss, the factory's manager, was arrested on July 21, 1911. He was to remain in prison for two years.

It was apparent to all that just as in Captain Dreyfus's case in France a few years earlier it was not merely the defendant's fate that was at issue. The stakes, moreover, were much higher in the trial of Mendel Beiliss. Anti-Semites wished to prove that Beiliss, and by extension adherents of Judaism, committed ritual murder. Jews and proponents of religious tolerance both in Russia and abroad hoped Beiliss would be exonerated. In the course of the trial the principal witness for the prosecution confessed to having been coached by the police, and a Catholic priest with a criminal record who testified as an expert on the Talmud was discredited by the defense. Ultimately, a jury of Ukrainian peasants declared Beiliss not guilty. Russia's Jews, however, never quite recovered from the frightening experience. Besides, World War I broke out within a year of the trial, and three years after that came the two Russian revolutions and a new wave of pogroms.

The first decade of the twentieth century was marked by remarkable changes within the Pale of Settlement. Foremost among them was rapid linguistic acculturation. Whether in schools, from private tutors, or simply by reading newspapers, hundreds of thousands of Jews learned Russian. Among the younger Jews of more affluent background, Russian became the language of choice and little if any Yiddish was spoken. While anti-Semitism persisted, contacts between educated young Jews and Gentiles became more frequent. Jews became voracious readers of Russian literature, and a number of Jewish authors began to publish in Russian. Indeed, a Russian-speaking Jewish intelligentsia came into being. Religious observance declined, and secular political movements grew in influence and in numbers of adherents. Because anti-Jewish discrimination—indeed, physical violence—was of prime concern to every Russian Jew, all of these movements first and foremost addressed those issues. The Socialists, whether from the general Social Democratic movement or from the specifically Jewish Bund, insisted that anti-Semitism would disappear together with other forms of capitalist injustice. The Zionists were more pessimistic. Jews, they believed, would find safety only in a state of their own. And then there was emigration. Only ordinary, quiet assimilation was out of the question because it required formal conversion to Christianity, a step most of the Jews were unwilling to take.

All of this, understandably, resulted in a chasm between generations. The conflict was more visible at relatively tranquil times, and muted in periods of danger, such as the years of the Beiliss trial. Still, one detects in *The Bloody Hoax* an appeal for moderation, much as in Turgenev's *Fathers and Sons*. Traditional observance is portrayed with sympathy, while ostentatious piety is satirized—as is the apostasy of a young Jew who jettisons ancestral faith to further his career. Infatuation of educated young ladies with fashionable Russian authors is ridiculed, though primarily because they show no interest whatever in Yiddish writing. (Significantly, the women who are so ashamed of Yiddish are daughters of an ultra-Orthodox wealthy Jew.) And in an obvious parallel with Turgenev's novel, the model young couple harmoniously blend Jewish tradition with Russian modernity. Betty Shapiro is at home in Yiddish as well as in Russian. Benny Hurvitch, for his part, is thoroughly modern but is also steeped in Jewish learning. He is also, significantly, a friend and admirer of Popov-Rabinovitch. On one issue, however, Sholom Aleichem remained adamant. He unquestioningly admired the obstinacy of his stiff-necked people, who insisted on survival against all odds. And that, when all is said and done, is the quintessence of Jewish history.

This is the first-ever English translation of *The Bloody Hoax*. We are fortunate that Aliza Shevrin undertook such a Herculean task (the Yiddish text is liberally sprinkled, not just with Hebrew, but with garbled Russian as well) and produced a fine English rendition. She thus made this important novel accessible to readers interested in Jewish or, for that matter, Russian history, to devotees of Sholom Aleichem's melancholy humor, and to all those who enjoy fiction that bears on seemingly timeless social issues.

Maurice Friedberg

Translator's Note

In late fall of 1982 I was fortunate enough to have a fellowship at the Rockefeller Foundation Bellagio Study and Conference Center on magnificent Lake Como in northern Italy. During my stay, Steve Lavine, then Associate Director of the Humanities of the Rockefeller Foundation, had arranged a five-day conference called *Continuity and Transformation: Jewish Literature since World War II*. It was attended by such widely acclaimed writers as Yehuda Amichai, Aharon Appelfeld, the late Arthur Cohen, Cynthia Ozick, Grace Paley, and A. B. Yehoshua, as well as by the outstanding critics and essayists Maurice Friedberg, Dan Miron, and Ruth Wisse, among others. At the time, I was completing the translation of a Sholom Aleichem novel, *In the Storm* (G. P. Putnam, 1984), and was wondering what my next project ought to be. It was the noted authority on Sholom Aleichem, Dan Miron, who suggested I might take on the daunting *Der Blutiger Shpas* ("The Bloody Hoax"), a two-volume Sholom Aleichem novel that had been made into a popular Yiddish play produced in New York in the 1920s under the title *Shver tzu zayn a yid* ("Hard to be a Jew") but had never been translated into English as a novel. He warned me it might be difficult to locate a Yiddish copy, as it had not been included in the twenty-eight-volume collected works *(Alle Verk fun Sholom Aleichem)* found in most university libraries and in many personal collections and as it had originally been published in Warsaw.

His warning was prophetic. Library and personal searches failed to turn up any trace of the book. But a visit to the YIVO library in New York and the able assistance of the all-knowing Dina Abramowicz proved successful. She located one copy in the stacks in such poor condition that she could not allow it to be removed or even handled. Luckily there was a microfilm of the book and a copy was made and sent to me. Before I could find out whether it would be a feasible project, I had to spend many long days in the University of Michigan Graduate Library copying, page by blurry page, black on white, sometimes white on black, more than seven hundred sides! It took an entire summer to read through the book, at which time I decided to go ahead with it.

It proved to be a daunting task indeed, taking more than three years to complete. The novel anticipates in its main plot two much later American novels, *Gentleman's Agreement* by Laura Hobson and *The Fixer* by Bernard Malamud. Two young men, one Russian, one Jewish, decide to trade places so that the Russian can experience what is is like to be a Jew. Figuring prominently in the plot is a blood libel, based on the infamous Beiliss case actually in progress in Kiev at the time the novel was being serialized. I often had the feeling that, when the trial itself might have lagged or there was a delay in the proceedings and Sholom Aleichem still had to produce a new chapter for *Heynt* ("Today"), the periodical in which the novel was originally printed, he would use the lull to be didactic or to embroider the more romantic aspects of the plot.

The Bloody Hoax differs from Sholom Aleichem's earlier works in that, in contrast to their *shtetl* settings with their Talmudic references and highly idiomatic speech, this is a thoroughly modern, big-city novel, but one whose characters are no less persecuted than Tevye and his family. Moreover, Sholom Aleichem provides a portrait rarely found in Yiddish literature of the everyday lives of wealthy Gentiles.

The problems of translation were not so much in finding equivalents for idioms or biblical references as in translating Russian official and military terms and titles. Sholom Aleichem transliterated the Russian terms into Yiddish, not always correctly, thereby bewildering the Russian native speakers whom I asked for help with those terms.

Since I began working on this translation, the political situation for Jews in Europe has gone through enormous, world-shaking changes. Notwithstanding the inherent value, outlook, and message of this work, it is at the present more timely and applicable than one would ever have imagined. The threat of re-emerging anti-Semitism in the Soviet Union and Eastern Europe, for example, reminds us that what was considered unthinkable for so long, blood libels and pogroms, now are, alas, again within the realm of possibility. One hopes Sholom Aleichem's history lessons in this novel will not go unheeded.

The triple length of this book required not only triple the time to translate it but triple the patience and encouragement on the part of my family. Born during this period were three grandchildren, who I hope will one day read their grandmother's translation. Many thanks are in order. In particular I wish to thank my Russian friends, Basya Genkina, Luci Lemberskaya, and Sara Kupershmidt, Professors Serge Shishkoff, Zvi Gitelman, Shoni Guiora, and Anita Norich, Rabbi Robert Dobrusin, Bel Kaufman, Joan W. Blos, and my daily walking companion, Rivka Rubinfeld. Even more than always, my husband, Howie, to whom I dedicate this book, was an active page-by-page collaborator. We brainstormed each chapter, literally translating the English back into Yiddish to ensure that nothing had been overlooked. His writing talent was avidly exploited at not inconsiderable expense of time and effort on his part. I cannot adequately express my gratitude. I could not have done it without him.

Aliza Shevrin

PART ONE

PART ONE

the first chapter

LET'S CHANGE PLACES

It was long past midnight.

In a private room of an elegant restaurant, The Elephant, under recently invented electric lights, amid loud music, chitchat and laughter, a dozen or so young men barely out of their teens were carousing—drinking, smoking, arguing, bantering, and joking while someone was banging away at a piano.

It was the celebration of a group of classmates who had just completed *gymnasium*—secondary school—and were enjoying one last evening together before bidding one another farewell for a long time, perhaps for good. In a few days each would be heading home, and only God knew if they would ever meet again.

The thought of never meeting again was so new to each of them, so alien that they had to imagine it could only be a dream. For eight years they had been as one! In those eight years, not a single day had gone by without their seeing one another. And now suddenly they would all be going their separate ways, and who knew where or when they would meet again! . . .

"And that's why, my friends, we have to down another glass of wine!"

Another glass of wine and another glass, and after each glass cheeks flushed deeper, eyes grew drowsier, foreheads glistened with sweat. It was time to begin parting in earnest.

"More wine!"

"Champagne!"

"Champagne! Champagne!"

For the tenth time they sang the traditional student song:

Gaudeamus igitur
Juvenes dum sumus . . .

This was sung in a fine baritone voice by a cheerful, dark-haired young man with rosy cheeks and lively eyes, and the rest of the delighted young men joined him:

Post jucundam juventutem,
Post molestam senectutem
Nos habebit sumus . . .

"Hey, Hershke! Why so downhearted? Why that hangdog look?" the cheerful, dark-haired young man with the rosy cheeks called out to another young man who was sitting by himself off to the side staring down at his feet, making it impossible to see his face.

"Leave him alone, Grisha, he's a goner. He really polished off a couple of good ones!" one of the bunch exclaimed to the dark-haired young man.

"You're an ass!" the fellow called Grisha cut him off, "Hershke can't be drunk. He belongs to a people who stay sober on principle."

With those words, the dark-haired Grisha went over to the solitary young man called Hershke, who belonged to that sober people, and tapped him lightly on the head. The other one lifted his face. None of his features were at all Semitic. On the contrary, the cheerful, dark-haired young man who called the other one Hershke and was himself known as Grisha looked more like a Jew and more likely to be called Hershke because his hair was dark and his eyes too lively. He was also endowed with a small bend to his nose. But only on the real Hershke's pale forehead were to be found a few more wrinkles than one would expect for his twenty years, and his eyes revealed a suppressed, ever present sorrow, a sadness which carries over among our people from generation to generation on which only a Jew can be an expert because a Jew feels more with his heart than he perceives with his eyes . . .

"What's the matter, Hershke?" Grisha asked him, pulling up a chair and seating himself close to him while the rest carried on—drinking, smoking, laughing, making an uproar and reveling merrily.

The young man named Hershke made an effort to smile weakly and the two boys started to converse.

"Nothing's the matter, Grisha. It's just that my head hurts a little."

"You're lying, you're worried about something. I've been noticing it all night. You can't fool me, Hershke, I know you too well."

"I'm glad you know me. But I wish you knew me a little better. If you did . . ."

The rest was expressed with a gesture and Grisha asked him,

"Then what?"

"Then you wouldn't have to ask me. Then you would know that I'm not like the rest of you. I can't celebrate as you do."

"Why?"

The young man named Hershke smiled, gesturing with his hands expressively. "For the reason that when you celebrate, you celebrate with your whole being, with every part of your body and all your senses."

"And you?"

"And I? I don't dare . . . I can't . . . Before my eyes there is always the *memento mori*, reminding me that I am a Jew . . ."

"That's ridiculous!"

Grisha pushed his chair back from Hershke, looked him directly in the face and said warmly, "Hershke! You certainly can't accuse any of us. We, your friends, who . . ."

"Don't be a fool! Who's taking about you and our friends? Do you really think this is the way the world is? Outside the *gymnasium* is the real world. There are other people out there besides you. You don't know what kind of hell is out there. If you were in my shoes for just one year, then you would know, then you would feel . . ."

The young man known as Grisha was thoughtful a while. Then he tossed his dark hair back and said, "Do you know what I'm going to tell you, Hershke?"

"What are you going to tell me?"

"Let's change places."

The two of them burst out laughing at the notion. Then Hershke said to Grisha, "It's easy for you to make jokes, but if your name were Hershke, not Grisha . . ."

"Let's trade places," Grisha said again, seriously now, but Hershke wasn't listening and continued, "You would, for example, have to be subject to the quota system."

"You're talking nonsense, Hershke. What quota? What system? You've won a gold medal. What do you care about quota systems?"

"Some reasoning! Do you know how many of last year's medalists are without jobs no matter what they try to do about it? They sell their last pair of pants to scrape up enough money to send off a wire to the minister, a whole song and dance, full of heartrending feelings, crying out to the heavens."

"Nu?"

"Nu-nu."

"What 'nu-nu'?"

"Fool that you are! They don't even get an answer. Yids sending wires! Those pushy people! Lucky they don't get themselves arrested! They get off easy if they're just driven out of the city and their residence permits revoked. And the same thing will most likely happen to me."

"You're wrong! It won't happen to you. You won a medal."

"Again with the medal? What an ass! You can't get that medal out of your head, can you!"

"That's why I'm telling you—let's change places."

"The whole problem is that you aren't really hearing what I'm saying. It's going in one ear and out the other."

"Go to the devil! I've worked myself into a sweat over this."

Grisha mopped the perspiration from his forehead and with a laugh moved closer to Hershke, taking his arm.

"Listen carefully to what I'm say to you, Hershke. Let's trade places!"

Hershke finally heard what was being said to him and seemed to wake as from sleep.

"What do you mean 'trade places'? What can you possibly mean by that?"

"We can switch diplomas. You give me your diploma with those top grades of 'fives' and your medal and I'll give you my diploma with its 'threes.' You'll be Grisha and I'll be Hershke. Has that gotten through to you yet, or not?"

"Have you gone mad? Or are you pulling my leg?"

Grisha crossed himself and Hershke burst out laughing. Then they both began laughing together, and finally Grisha said to his comrade in all serious-ness, "You said that I should try being in your shoes for a year. And I'm telling you that the devil himself isn't as bad as he's portrayed. We're not changing places forever, just for a year. Why not! You be Grisha Popov, and I'll be Hershke Rabinovitch. Do you understand yet or not? We'll exchange diplomas and names and passports. I'll be you and you'll be me. Why are you looking at me that way? I'm not joking with you. I'm being very serious." (And Grisha put on a serious face for his friend.) "I'm well acquainted with you and with other Jewish students and all I ever hear from you is: 'Jews . . . Jews are a tragic people,' and other such statements. I don't understand it. My brain registers it but I can't say I really know what it means. Do you understand that or not? I want to be in your skin for a little while. For one year I want to be a Jew and feel what it's like to be a Jew, understood? Let's shake hands on it and give our word before all our friends that whatever may happen during this year will be past and forgotten and not a soul must know that you are you and I am I, I mean, that I am I and you are you—Hell! I mean, that I am you and you are me. So is it agreed?"

Grisha offered his hand as Hershke rubbed his forehead and looked at his comrade like a person who isn't sure whether the other one is a bit crazy or whether he himself is in his right mind. Nevertheless, he put his hand out to his friend, and his friend Grisha helped him to his feet, led him over to the rest of the group, who were still caught up in their revels. With one hand he slapped the tabletop so hard that the bottles and glasses clinked together loudly and with his other hand pointed to Hershke, who was standing in a state of confusion, and cried out at the top of his lungs in his rich baritone voice, "Silence, comrades! Be quiet! I don't want to hear a pin drop!"

Suddenly it did become quiet. All eyes turned toward Grisha and at his apprehensive friend, Hershke. Grisha assumed the stance of an orator and began to give a speech.

the second chapter

THEY CHANGE PLACES

"Friends!" Grisha began in a quiet voice, hooking his thumb in his vest like an experienced speaker, his eyes looking downward at first. Then as he raised his head slowly, his voice grew louder and louder. "Friends! At this very moment, the man you see before you is not your friend Grisha Popov, but your other friend, Rabinovitch. Don't think I am out of my senses or that it is the wine speaking. I assure you I have all my wits about me and I swear to you that I have never been as sober as I am at this moment.

"I shall clarify what I mean in a moment. Our comrade, who was known as Hershke Rabinovitch and who will now be known as Grisha Popov—you will soon see why—belongs to a people which the world does not love and which is persecuted almost everywhere on the face of the earth. We don't know the whys or wherefores of this powerful hatred and it is not our task at this time to decide which party is more to blame—the oppressors or the oppressed, the persecutors or the persecuted. Possibly both sides are in the right according to their points of view, or perhaps they are both in the wrong. We only know that the stronger of the two brings down every evil on the heads of the weaker, accusing them of every sin, while the weaker protests that these are all lies and that they are no worse than others and perhaps even better. For better or worse, this is not a matter easily settled and I don't know who has the right to settle it.

"I can believe one way, you another. I myself believe that both sides have exaggerated their positions. For instance, I am convinced that we, as Christians, don't hate the Jews nearly so much as the Jews imagine we do, and I am of the opinion that the Jews don't suffer nearly so much as they would have us believe. True, it isn't pleasant to be persecuted and hated by the whole world. But there remains a certain satisfaction, a special pride, one might say, a kind of sweetness, in the word 'martyr.' It is more convenient to believe I am being pursued for no reason than to believe I am pursuing someone else for no reason. In any case—the devil is never as bad as he is portrayed. I expressed this opinion to my friend Hershke here . . . pardon! our friend Grisha, and he answered that it was easy for me to say because I have never been a Jew. If I were to find myself, he says, in his skin for at least a year, then I would, he says, know what it's really like. That gave me an idea. Perhaps he isn't entirely wrong. One has to be in another's place in order to really experience what it's like and only afterward can you judge, either blaming or justifying . . . And so with this idea in mind I suggested to my friend Hershke that we exchange diplomas, names, and passports for no more than a year. In other words, at this very moment, this is no longer Grigori Ivanovitch Popov who is speaking to you, but Hersh Movshovitch Rabinovitch, and he, Hershke, is no longer Hersh Movshovitch Rabinovitch, but Grigori Ivanovitch Popov. He will leave here with my documents and will enter the university, and I will leave here with his documents. He insists that with his documents it will be difficult for me even to be admitted to the university because he is a Jew, and I say, nonsense, with a medal I can laugh at the whole world."

"Bravo!" the boys shouted as one, and began to applaud enthusiastically. But Grisha didn't let them applaud long. He raised his hand for silence and went on.

"Comrades! I have entrusted you with a secret, a deep secret, and I am asking two things of you: first, that you congratulate us both for our new exchanged roles. And second—quiet! Hold on, I haven't finished yet. And second—give me your word of honor and swear that no other human being alive besides us here will know of this, not now, or later, even when the year is up. The whole plan has to be, I insist, a secret, a holy secret that we must take with us to our graves!"

"We swear! We swear!" they cried out in many different voices, and Grisha ended his speech.

"I swear you to secrecy by all that is holy to all of us. He who bares this secret to an outsider will be considered a traitor and a criminal. Friends! I propose we fill our glasses and drink a toast to our new-born comrade who was once called Hershke Rabinovitch and today will be called Grigori Ivanovitch Popov. Let us all wish him good luck. Long live Grigori Ivanovitch Popov! Hoorah!!!"

*   *   *

The excitement and enthusiasm that this totally unexpected toast aroused among the young classmates cannot be described. That they all took it upon themselves to keep the holy vow without wavering—of that there was no question. And that they all agreed with the sentiment of the toast was evident from the way the glasses were emptied to the last drop. The crowd was so taken with the idea that a Hershke had turned into a Grisha and a Grisha into a Hershke that they made the two of them exchange not only their documents but their clothes as well right in front of their eyes. And once they had changed clothes, there was such glee among the group that they proceeded to embrace both of them, their voices ringing to the rafters. Then one of them sat down at the piano and started to play a waltz, to which they all danced. And when they had had their fill of dancing, Hershke Rabinovitch, now known as Grigori Ivanovitch Popov, stood up and spoke to the crowd.

"Friends! Our comrade Grisha Popov, or, as he is now called, Hershke Rabinovitch, started out with a joke which has now turned serious. We can't be so clever as to know in advance how this joke will turn out or what terrible consequences may come of it. Furthermore, it is obvious which one of the two of us will profit more (as the former Hershke, I can't restrain myself and must use the word 'profit'). That much I know, as you must also be well aware of if you have any brains at all. And if you don't realize this, then it's not my fault. But I must make one request of you, my dear friends. Since our friend Grisha, I mean Hershke, has taken a vow and has made me take a vow for a year that he will be me and I—him, and since we cannot know in advance what can befall us in our new lives into which we are now entering, I therefore wish to state a condition, that should one of us come out of this looking badly, that is . . ."

"No conditions!" called out the former Grisha Popov, now Hershke Rabinovitch, springing up from his seat, "No conditions! It's decided and no going back!"

"No going back!" echoed the rest of the crowd.

"*Byt posyemu*—So be it!" added the new Hershke Rabinovitch.

"So be it!" repeated the crowd.

When our new Grigori Ivanovitch Popov realized he was being out-voted, he stood up from the table, went over to the former Popov, now Hersh Rabinovitch, and with a smile on his lips put out his hand.

"Remember now, Hersh Movshovitch Rabinovitch, no regrets."

"Regrets?" the former Popov replied forcefully and with pride. "The Popovs, I mean the Rabinovitches, know no regrets. I come from a people, *chort vozmi*, which has gone through fire and water! My forefathers kneaded clay in Egypt, built the eternal pyramids, erected the famous cities of Sodom and Gomorrah . . . pardon! I mean Pitum and Ramses, suffered until they settled in the land of Canaan. And when we settled in the land of Canaan, there came Balshazar . . . Tphoo! I mean Nebuchadnezzar, who burned down our holy temple and dragged us off in iron chains, brought us, together with our sisters and children, to the idolatrous Babylon, and from there—I am taking a giant leap, my friends, and leaving out Haman and Ahashueros and other such fine folks because it's already daylight outside—and from there they chased us to Spain, to that accursed Catholic Spain where the Inquisition was awaiting us. Just bear in mind, my friends, what my blessed ancestors suffered in the Inquisition! They were burned at the stake; on the scaffold they were slaughtered, stabbed, axed, drawn and quartered! . . ."

"Bravo, Hershke, bravo!" burst out the entire group of youths, the true Hershke Rabinovitch among them, applauding loudly and laughing even louder, so impressed were they with their comrade Grisha Popov, who had entered into the role of Hershke Rabinovitch so skillfully and so naturally that one wanted to embrace and kiss him. "An artist, a true artist! Look how his eyes light up! And how do you like that serious face? He doesn't allow so much as a smile. Would you be able to tell, even if you had the brains of a genius, that this is Grisha Popov, not Hershke Rabinovitch? No, look at his Jewish face, his Jewish eyes, even his nose seems to have bent into a Jewish nose, ha-ha. Bravo, Hershke, bravo! Bis!! Bisss!!! . . ."

* * *

It was already broad daylight when the classmates left the elegant restaurant, The Elephant, and seated themselves in droshkies which took them off in different directions. Grisha and Hershke boarded the same droshky, Grisha in Hershke's clothes, Hershke in Grisha's clothes. Even though Grisha Popov was now Hershke Rabinovitch and Hershke Rabinovitch was now Grisha Popov, they had much to talk about. They had to give one another personal information, background, and family history before each would go his own way, assuming his new role. In truth, it was the beginning of the great hoax.

the third chapter

A ROOM TO LET

A pleasant excitement prevails in a large university town as the end of summer approaches and before the fall semester begins. Vacations are drawing to a close, and the *gymnasiums*, the polytechnicum, and the university itself prepare to open their doors for the new semester.

From nearby cities and towns, and places well beyond, parents with their offspring in tow arrive in the university town, some ready to begin a new grade and some to take entrance examinations in order to qualify for the temples of enlightenment and learning.

A special anxiety stirs the parents, even more than in the excited offspring. Young mothers, dressed in the latest fashion, beat down the doors of the directors' secretaries, administrators, and teachers. They are prepared to fall in a dead faint or throw three hysterical fits because their "Volodka" or their "Sashka" wound up with only a "two" on the entrance examination.

The booksellers and stationers display their latest and best selections, which they have prepared for the young people's delectation. They are ready to do business, to make a bit of money, to exchange old books for new ones—in a word, to serve the culture of the fatherland with integrity and loyalty like good, honest patriots.

The tailors and clothiers are also no mean patriots. They display in their show windows the finest and most up-to-date fashions they can muster, from elegant uniforms with shiny buttons to stylish trousers which seem to plead: "Come put us on and show us off!"

The hatmakers and milliners display entire collections of peaked caps and hats decorated with all varieties of white and yellow ornaments, eagles, bars, and decorative gold braid. In the luggage and variety shops, even the smallest satchels are given their place; they too are on display along with spats, galoshes, candy, and cigarettes. And the sausage makers—who are certainly not to be found anywhere near the august Ministry of Public Education and who don't hold much by learning, but who also wish to partake, however distantly, in the culture of the fatherland—display in their shop windows thick, juicy slices of sausage and ham, meat pies and beef so fresh and redolent of garlic that the best student can quickly forget all about culture and the fatherland when hunger comes upon him and he takes a good whiff of that aromatic pork.

The hotels and inns, the restaurants and cafeterias are packed full with the newly arrived guests, fathers and mothers and children of all sizes. On the windows of almost all the houses are attached notices advertising "*Komnata Vnayom*—Room To Let."

Those who put up the notices know beforehand who will be occupying the rooms. It will be either a single male student who possesses but one pair of trousers, two shirts, and a mountain of books; or it will be a female enrolled in special courses, one who once wore her hair bobbed and now fancies short, tight frocks which in Paris are called "culottes." At any rate, each little room contains no more than one iron bed, hard as the notorious bed at the gates of Sodom, one iron washstand, which will not tolerate one's standing too close to it while washing, as it suffers, may such an affliction not be visited upon you, from a rusty rheumatism in its legs since the day it was brought from the factory.

The little room also contains a table and a chair, which have their good points and bad points. The little table can serve as a desk or as a place to eat or, for that matter, for whatever else you might wish. Those are its good points. The one bad point of the table is not to be blamed on the table itself, but on its drawer. Once you open the drawer, it doesn't want to shut; and once it is shut, under no circumstances can you open it—not from the front, not from the back, not from the sides. You can yank it as hard as you wish and the table will simply drag right along with you. Do you want to outsmart it and try to pull the drawer out from underneath with both hands? Go ahead and try. I can tell you ahead of time what will happen: the back legs will lift up and the whole table, with its books, inkwell, and carafe of water, will wind up together with you on the floor. So? What have you accomplished? You had better get along without a drawer. Where is it written that a table must have a drawer?

And what about the chair I was telling you about? A chair like any chair, this is one of those chairs called "*Wiener shtuhlen*—Viennese chairs." They are lightweight, strong, and comfortable to sit on because their seats are woven of straw—flat and smooth and soft. Those are the virtues of "Viennese chairs" in general. But the chair which is found in the room we have described has not one of the enumerated virtues. Suffice it to say we will share this secret with you— the chair lacks a seat. That is, it has a seat, but without straw, that is, it once had straw, when the chair was a chair. But let's not waste any more breath on this poor excuse for a chair. Let's talk about the landlady who was letting the little room, her husband, their daughter Betty, and about the person who came to rent this room—much more important matters.

Sara Shapiro—that was the name of our landlady—was still a young woman, pretty with attractive, dark features. She was standing at the stove, her sleeves rolled up, preparing lunch, while her daughter, Betty, a true beauty with a fiery temperament, about eighteen to twenty years old, was sitting reading a Russian newspaper when the doorbell began to ring loudly.

"It must be another *shlimazel* for the room!" the mother announced to her daughter, indicating that she go open the door.

Unenthusiastically, the daughter laid aside the newspaper and ran down the three flights to open the door. In two minutes she returned with a clean-shaven young man carrying an almost empty satchel who wished to look at the room to let.

Carefully looking over the newcomer with the almost empty satchel, the mother quickly determined that he must be a poverty-stricken student from the hinterlands who couldn't rent the room in any case and consequently told her daughter in Yiddish to overstate the rent. The daughter obeyed and told the young man the rent. The young man didn't blink an eye and asked to see the room. At that point Madam Sara Shapiro laid aside her cooking, rolled down her sleeves, and went along to show the young man the room.

As they entered the previously described room, our guest carefully looked over the landlady and her daughter much more than he did the room and its furniture. After a short deliberation, he declared that, good, he was satisfied. Madam Sara Shapiro again found it necessary to remind him of the price. The visitor said the price was fine. If that were the case, Madam Shapiro felt she had to tell him that he had to pay for the first half-month in advance. The young man said he wouldn't mind paying a whole month in advance.

At this Madam Shapiro became a bit wary: what sort of customer was this? He comes along, takes one look, doesn't bargain; you tell him he has to pay half a month's rent in advance and he's willing to pay a whole month's rent! Who knows what kind of fly-by-night he is? She and her daughter exchanged glances. When she took a good look at the young man she noticed how fixedly he was staring at her Betty. This made her mistrust him all the more and she decided on what she had to do.

"Please don't be offended, but we have to be very strict . . . You understand, the police . . . if you wouldn't mind showing me your documents . . . Your passport . . ."

"Oh, my passport? . . ." Our young man withdrew his papers from a side pocket and with a gentle smile handed his passport to Madam Shapiro and then started to open his wallet.

But at that moment something occurred that stopped the young man from taking his money out. Madam Shapiro looked at the passport and read aloud: *Shklovskii Meshchanin Hersh Movshovitch Rabinovitch*, telling her he was a resident of Shklov and, from his name, a Jew. She gave her daughter a quizzical look, then said to the young man, "Please don't be offended . . . I'm not sure you can stay here. I didn't know that you were a . . ."

With a little smile the young man turned toward Madam Shapiro.

"That I am a what?"

"That you are one of ours . . . a Jew."

"And if I am a Jew, what of it?"

The young man put his wallet back in his pocket and the three of them looked at one another wordlessly.

the fourth chapter

THE POWER OF A MEDAL

Up to that point the conversation had been carried on in Russian. But now that it became clear that he was a resident of Shklov whose name was Hersh Rabinovitch, well then, what would be the harm if they were to converse in "our" language? And Sara Shapiro directed herself to him in plain Yiddish.

"I'm surprised at you. You look to me like a worldly young man and yet you don't know that a Jew has to have a residence permit."

To this compliment the worldly young man had no response as he had understood not one word spoken to him. He answered Madam Shapiro in Russian, blushing a little.

"Excuse me, I'm afraid I don't understand Yiddish."

Madam Shapiro could no longer contain her laughter.

"A Shklov resident with the name of Rabinovitch and you don't understand Yiddish?! . . ."

Betty, who till then had been standing off to the side seemingly uninvolved, interrupted the conversation to come to the aid of the young man who had rented the room. She addressed her mother in Russian.

"There aren't enough young people nowadays, children of Jews, who don't understand any Yiddish?"

Then she explained to the young man, briefly and to the point, what they were speaking about: a Jew was forbidden to live in that city unless he had a special residence permit. If anyone were to allow a Jew to live there without that permit, they would be severely punished: their residence permit would be taken away and they would be sent from the city within twenty-four hours. "Now do you understand?"

All this was said with so sweet a smile and with so much charm that were her mother not by her side, the young man would have thrown his arms around her and kissed this enchanting young woman who was capable of such sweet and yet such mischievous smiles. And even though the regulation about residence permits was only vaguely known by our hero—he *had* heard that there were cities where Jews must have permits to live but he remembered it quite dimly—nevertheless, he acted as if he were well aware of it and said with a smile to the charming young girl, "I do know all about the permit regulation even though I'm not from these parts. It's a regulation they should have gotten rid of a long time ago together with all the old trash. But I wish you could explain one thing to me—why did they require me to leave all my documents at the university?"

The word "university" burst upon both mother and daughter like a sudden bright ray of sunshine. Their faces lit up and the mother slapped herself on the thighs.

"Is that so? Are you really a student at our university? Why didn't you say anything until now?"

"Didn't say anything? It seems to me that all three of us have been talking quite a bit," the student said smiling, all the while gazing at the daughter, not at the mother. The mother continued her interrogation.

"Does that mean you're already admitted?"

"Just about . . . I have a medal."

"Ah! You're a medalist? Is that so? Hear that?"

The last sentence was addressed in Yiddish to the daughter, with a sigh. But she quickly collected herself and said to the medalist in Russian, "I was saying to my daughter, she has a brother, that is, I have a son who is a *gymnasium* student, in the third class, and I've been badgering him for almost three years, every morning and every night, 'A medal, a medal, a medal!' Does he listen to me? A Jew without a medal is like a . . . like a . . ."

Madam Shapiro looked around the room for something she could use as a comparison for a Jew without a medal, but there was nothing in the room that had any resemblance to a Jew with or without a medal. Her daughter Betty felt this was entirely beside the point. Why did a stranger need to know whether her brother would earn a medal or not? She said to the student, indicating his half-filled satchel, "Is this all you have or do you have more?"

"What more do I need?" he answered, looking directly into her lovely, luminous eyes so intently one could interpret his look as saying, "What more do I need when you have such beautiful, kind, intelligent, lustrous eyes and such adorable dimples in your cheeks? . . ."

The mother, whose sole life's objective was to have her son win a medal, interceded for the new tenant and said to her daughter, again with a deep sigh, "He's absolutely right. What else does he need? If he has a medal, he needs nothing else. Nothing else!"

The words "nothing else" she clipped as with a knife. She suddenly became very attentive to the medalist tenant and asked him in a most friendly manner, "Do you have a father and mother?"

To our hero this question was so unexpected that for the moment he quite forgot whether Hershke Rabinovitch had a father and a mother or only one or the other. He was quite unable to answer the question. Luckily Betty again came to his rescue. She turned to her mother.

"That's enough cross-examining our roomer. It might be better if you asked him if he'd like a cup of tea."

And to the new tenant Betty said with a lovely little smile, "My mother likes to talk a little too much . . . You can order a samovar if you'd like some tea. Your rent includes two samovars a day."

"Why only *two* samovars a day?" her mother interrupted, "—three samovars. In the morning, in the afternoon, and at night."

"That's because you have a medal," Betty added with a laugh, and said to her mother in Yiddish, "Come!" And both daughter and mother left the room, leaving the medalist alone with his half-empty satchel and with his thoughts, which were revolving around the power of his medal, and even more, about the charm of the lovely girl with the pretty, clear, intelligent eyes, mischievous smile, and dimples in her cheeks.

THE SHAPIRO FAMILY

As satisfied as the new lodger was with his lodgings, Madam Shapiro was even more satisfied with her new lodger. He was a lively young man, very modest and quite affable—a gem.

From the very first day he had shown an interest in her son, a third-year *gymnasium* student, helping him prepare for his examinations as well as taking it upon himself to work with the lad on his daily lessons. Madam Shapiro had been planning to find a tutor for him, if she could find the right student at the right price. She couldn't pay a great deal and she wondered what her new roomer might charge.

She turned her full attention to him, the thought passing through her mind, "Wouldn't it be wonderful if this young man refused to take any money!" And so it happened—as if she had been a prophetess. Not only did the young man refuse any payment, he dismissed the question out of hand. How could he possibly take money from her? For what?

"So? What did I tell you?" the happy mother teased her daughter.

"What *did* you tell me?"

"You've already forgotten? Didn't I tell you right away that he's a decent sort?"

"You said he was a decent sort?"

"What then did I say?"

"You said he was a *shlimazel*—a fool," the daughter reminded her.

"I said he was a *shlimazel?*"

"Who else said it! Me?"

"Betty! Are you starting in again with your old tricks, talking back to your mother, making me out to be a liar?"

"Who's making you out to be a liar? I'm just saying that you don't remember what you said. You say you said he was a decent sort and I'm saying you said he was a *shlimazel*."

" 'I said—you said! You said—I said'! Tell me, will there ever be an end to this?"

As these words were uttered, the head of the household, David Shapiro, entered. He was a flustered man, quick in his movements, hurried, a man who did everything quickly. He spoke quickly, ate quickly, walked quickly—everything was done quickly, in one breath.

At work—he was a bookkeeper in a large firm—he impressed people as a retiring person, submissive, without pretensions and without fuss. But in his own home he played the part of a stern taskmaster and something of a tyrant although no one really minded him. His wife ridiculed him to his face, calling him "my lord of the castle" and "speed demon," or simply "express train."

The children also paid little heed to him. They knew they meant the world to him, that the sun rose and set with them, and that they could do no wrong in his eyes—why not? He had but two children: an only daughter, Betty, a fiery girl, and an only son, Syomke, whose Russian nickname derived from Shloyme by way of Shlyomke, a youngster in the third class who never did his lessons unless his mother first paid him a tenner for each lesson. From his father he was awarded in addition, for every grade of four he brought home from *gymnasium*, another tenner, and for a grade of five, four tens.

"What's the sense in that? How come a four gets a tenner and a five gets four times as much? How do you figure that?" So queried his wife, Sara Shapiro, and was put down for it smartly. David Shapiro was in the habit of good-naturedly ragging his wife, although it happened frequently that she herself gave more in return than she received. No one really came out ahead in their squabbles.

"Whose fault is it if you're a numbskull," David said with a little smile, "you don't begin to understand the difference between a four and a five in *gymnasium*."

"Well, yes, how should I know what the difference is between a four and a five?" Sara answered him with a bitter smile, and the children listened to how their parents sparred and exchanged sharp words. "Only a genius like you can understand such things. After all, a 'lord of the castle.' Your only fault is that you're a little too speedy and fly around too fast."

"You *should* know. Here, let me show you why you don't begin to understand. For example, according to you, the difference between a four and a five is how much? One? Really? But if your head were screwed on right, you would know there's another way to figure it. Take your Syomke, for instance . . ."

"If that isn't the limit! What kind of example is that?" Sara cut him short. "A speed demon is talking, flying off like an express train and doesn't hear what he himself is saying! What's this abut *my* Syomke? He's as much *your* Syomke as *my* Syomke."

"All right, your Syomke, my Syomke. But let's suppose your Syomke has taken his final exam and receives all twelve fives. Twelve times five is how much? Sixty. Divide by twelve, how much is that? Five. So that means he has a gold medal."

"Amen, may it turn out to be true, God in heaven!" exclaimed Sara, raising her eyes piously heavenward, only to receive a new put-down from her David, who was now looking for support from his daughter.

"Nu? Can anybody talk to her? I'm trying to explain something to her and she lifts her eyes up, that mother of yours, and gets into a conversation with God!"

"All right. Figure, figure. Who's stopping you, my dear 'lord of the castle'?" Sara said to him in a tone that made David more indignant so that he spoke even more rapidly and with more fire.

"So, with twelve fives he has a gold medal. But how would it come out if he took the exam and got eleven fives and one four? If we multiply eleven times five, we get fifty-five. Plus four? That's fifty-nine divided by twelve. How much does that come to? That's over your head, because that's called, you should know, fractions. All together, it comes to no less and no more than four and eleven-twelfths. And since he's still short one-twelfth, he can't get a gold medal, only a silver one."

"Let it be a silver one," said Sara with a sigh, and David glanced at his daughter.

"Did you ever see anything like it, a woman doesn't let you talk? Let me go on. So, how would it figure if he should get, let's say, seven fives, which is thirty-five, and five times four is twenty: thirty-five and twenty is how much? Fifty-five. Divided by twelve? We have apparently four and how much left over? Seven-twelfths. No tragedy, he can still get a silver medal. But do you know when you have to worry? If it should happen, God forbid, the other way. What if he should get, let us say, five fives and seven fours—Ah! Then we're in trouble! Why? A simple calculation: five times five is twenty-five. Four times seven is twenty-eight every time. Put it all together, it comes out to be, exactly as if measured on pharmacy scales, fifty-three. Divided by twelve, it comes to four and five-twelfths. Less than a half. And if your Syomke finishes *gymnasium* with five twelves, they'll give him a fig, not a medal, and if he doesn't have a medal, he might as well stay home."

"Bite your tongue!" Sara exclaimed. David spat, quickly got up and flew off to his bookkeeping job.

And Sara remained standing as if someone had slapped her face. Not because her husband had spat—everyone knew he was a Shapiro and all the Shapiros were like that—a family of madmen. No, Sara was upset about something else. Sara was afraid that maybe, heaven forbid, her Syomke would lack a twelfth. But no! She wanted nothing to do with such calculations: seven-twelfths, thirteen-twelfths—her Syomke had to have a medal, and would, with God's help, assuredly get a medal—unless there was no God in heaven!

the sixth chapter

WE HAVE A GREAT GOD!

Without cause had Sara Shapiro doubted God. For was it not God who had answered her prayer at a time when her Syomke was in the third year and needed a tutor as one needs life itself and there was no spare money to hire one because although her David was that rarity, an honest man and an outstanding bookkeeper and worked in one of the largest firms in the city, for the finest people who considered themselves high-flown aristocrats, but who nevertheless were not ashamed to demand of him that he be at work from eight in the morning until nine at night, and recently, when he had asked for a raise, had informed him that there were at least ten young men eager for his job, better trained, recent graduates with medals! Luckily Sara Shapiro did her own cooking and housework, even though she was not accustomed to doing these chores in her own parents' home. And when necessary, her daughter Betty also helped out with the cooking and cleaning even though she was an only daughter and a pampered one. So how could one even think of paying a tutor? But there is a God in heaven and what does He do? He manages to deliver to them a student, a *shlimazel* from Shklov.

"Betty," the mother called to her daughter, who had been sitting all the while studying. "Betty! Isn't that *shlimazel* back yet?"

"See, Mama, I caught you! And you said you never called him a *shlimazel!*"

Sara Shapiro, preoccupied with but one thought—"What a great God we have,"—did not hear what she had just said herself. She stared at her daughter as if she were babbling nonsense.

"God be with you, Betty! When did I say the word '*shlimazel*'?"

"Mamanyu!" the daughter laughed. "What's happening to you? You just asked, 'Isn't that *shlimazel* back yet?' "

Sara looked at her daughter with a faint smile on her face.

"Betty, are you asleep? Or are you running a fever?"

"No, Mamanyu, you're running a fever, not me."

Mother and daughter exchanged wordless glances, both on the verge of bursting out laughing. Then the mother said to her daughter, still thinking about how great God was, "Betty, you're getting more and more insolent every day, really. It's getting hard to put up with you. Is that the way you talk to a mother? Ay, Betty, Betty! We have a great God, do you hear . . . What did I want to tell you? Yes. I remember now. Why don't you ask that *shlim*—I mean, that student, if it might not be such a bad idea for him to toot the both of you, you and Syomke."

"Not 'toot,' 'tutor,' " the daughter corrected her.

"Let it be as you say. Do you understand what I'm saying? You can't find a better tooter than him. Since he started working with Syomke, the child no longer brings home fours, but only fives. If he would agree to toot the two of you . . ."

" 'Tutor,' " the daughter again corrected her as the mother continued.

"Let it be as you say . . . I wouldn't charge him any rent."

"Really? Do you mean it? That's quite a bargain you want to strike, Mama. You forget that he's a poor student who depends on his pupils for a living and every minute is money for him. You can't just exploit everyone."

The mother felt the daughter was right, but she was resentful that she was teaching a mother how to behave and that she was lecturing her about exploitation. She wanted to ask the daughter, while she was on the subject of exploitation, why she didn't talk about the way they were exploiting her poor father, the bookkeeper, whom they kept working thirteen hours a day like a slave, making him so nervous and crazy that you couldn't say a straight word to him? But she didn't want to involve herself in a long discussion with her daughter, not only because of her insolence, but even more, her superior understanding. "She has her father's head on her shoulders. God grant me her brains. What a clever face!"

So thought Sara Shapiro, gazing lovingly at her daughter and saying softly, "You stick up for the whole world but not for your mother. It bothers you if a student from Odessa might lose, God forbid, a minute from his tooting, but for your poor mother, who wants her children to be able to learn and can't afford it, you don't care one bit, God help me. Not so much as a drop. No. How come?"

Both mother and daughter sat silently for a moment. But Sara had in mind to push forward with her plan and so she said to her daughter as if for the first time, "Listen, Betty! I've thought it over. As soon as he starts tooting the both of you . . ."

" 'Tutoring,' not 'tooting.' "

Sara Shapiro jumped up, shouting angrily.

"Why do I deserve this punishment from God this morning! Whatever I say and however I say it, it's wrong! Enough, let it be as you say! As soon as he starts tooting the both of you, I'll throw in meals too. He can eat with us at the same table."

"Don't you think it's enough that he has to sit in his little room and listen to you and Papa arguing day and night?"

"*I* argue with your father day and night?"

"Who then? *I* argue with him? Who does Papa call 'numbskull' and 'fool' and 'silly' at the dinner table?"

"Betty! You had better shut up. It would be much better for you, I mean it! Really shut up!"

"For good? Does that mean, Mama, you want me to become mute or die?"

Sara Shapiro wrung her hands, "May the enemies of the Jewish people become deaf and dumb! How do you like that! She says I want her to die! Bite your tongue, daughter mine! You can't say a straight word to her anymore! May God not punish her for these words!"

One could hear tears in the mother's voice. And the daughter's heart softened.

"What *do* you want, Mamanyu?"

"I don't want anything. Enough."

The mother had become quite angry and she ceased talking, but the daughter snuggled up to her, caressed her and kissed her until they both began to laugh.

"Will you tell him?"

"Tell him what?"

"You forgot! I just asked you to suggest to him that if he toots both of you, he won't need to pay room or board. Tell him that . . ."

"I'll tell him, I'll tell him. Let him get settled. Let him first get admitted to the university. Today's the last day to find out."

"The last day?"

"The last day."

The downstairs doorbell rang.

"Oh! It's him!" said Betty, blushing a little. She ran down the steps so quickly that she almost tumbled head over heels, alarming her mother. But Sara Shapiro soon returned to her previous thoughts, saying to herself with a sigh, "We do have a great God! . . ."

the seventh chapter

DAY OF RECKONING AT THE UNIVERSITY

While the conversation about the new tenant was going on at the Shapiros, the tenant himself was at the university finding out what his fate was to be.

This was the final day—the day of decision for Jewish students. Only a few vacancies remained for over a hundred candidates, among them more than twenty medalists. They had all gathered in a separate group in a large corridor of the university, as nervous as recruits about to be conscripted into the army. It was not yet known which of them would serve and which would not. It was sheer luck, a lottery.

Our eager hero—who through the caprice of a boyish prank had been transformed from a happy, carefree, self-assured Grigori Ivanovitch Popov, born a Russian nobleman, into Hersh Movshovitch Rabinovitch, an outcast resident of Shklov, was gradually realizing the true meaning of "*Atoh b'khartonu mikol ha'amim'*—You are chosen from among all peoples." It meant having to go every single day to the administrative office of the university, having to gaze into the pale, dried-up face of the secretary who hated Jews, although he hid this fact, and having to listen time and time again to the same empty, polite rebuff: "Mister Hersh Movshovitch Rabinovitch, I'm sorry I can't give you any good news, even though I wish I could." Still, he could not feel his disappointment with the same depth as his real Jewish friends, who were wandering about like shadows between those great high-windowed walls. Their frightened faces conveyed something he could not understand. The lost look in their sorrowful Jewish eyes could have spoken to him could he but have understood their language. He would have been able to read on each face the story of that person's life: a sad, tragic story of a spirit which from childhood had been seared on the slow flame of poverty, loneliness, and want, tormented by needless racism, every kind of humiliation and insult, venomous and poisonous.

Among these lonely and humiliated young men—these "recruit-candidates"—Rabinovitch had two acquaintances: Tumarkin and Lapidus.

He had become acquainted with Tumarkin a few days earlier, at that very same place, in the university forecourt. Tumarkin's expressive face, his vivacity and garrulousness had appealed to him immediately. On his pale, open face there always hovered a half-smile. His eyes, although overcast with sorrow, were constantly alive with good humor. His black, shiny hair curled like that of a young lamb. Even his newly sprouted sparse beard was curly and he had the habit, when he spoke or was in deep thought, of rapidly twirling each hair with his slender, white fingers. Add to this a small, bent nose, a badly curved back, a cardboard collar, a faded tie, a shabby jacket, worn-out shoes, and a crumpled hat—and you have the complete portrait of this tragicomic figure.

The first time Popov-Rabinovitch saw him, he felt great pity for him. He thought he was Yosski, the cigarette hawker with the slender fingers, the only Jew he had known in his non-Jewish town.

Realizing he was being stared at, Tumarkin approached him, stuck out a thin, white hand, and with a smile introduced himself.

"Tumarkin."

It was then that Popov-Rabinovitch realized he had made a mistake. He quickly introduced himself.

"Rabinovitch."

On hearing the name Rabinovitch, Tumarkin's face lit up and he began talking to his new acquaintance in Yiddish.

"You're one of us? *Sholom aleichem.* Where does a Jew come from? Where are you on the list?"

"Excuse me, you're speaking a language that . . . that I don't understand."

Tumarkin was taken completely aback.

"But you are a . . ."

"A Jew? So, that's obvious. If I weren't a Jew, I wouldn't be here. I would have been up *there* a long time ago."

He pointed to a wrought-iron staircase up which a long line of fortunate, recently admitted students were running, some of them already carrying books under their arms. He again had to invent a lie, saying that because he had studied in a Russian city, far from his parents, he had altogether forgotten how to speak Yiddish. As he said this, his face turned red, which Tumarkin took to mean that he was ashamed of having forgotten how to speak Yiddish. He began to console him, saying, "Look! Our Jews wind up all over the world. But who cares whether you speak Yiddish or you don't speak Yiddish? So long as you're a Jew, you're an alien and must bear all the pains we've been condemned to bear."

Rabinovitch felt his face burning and Tumarkin continued consoling him.

"Nonsense! You don't have to be ashamed because you don't understand the *mame-loshen,* Yiddish. I can well imagine that you were born in a Gentile city and grew up among Christians without your parents. As I see it, what is there to bind you to your Jewishness, except your name Rabinovitch? And yet, I think more highly of you than of those who can't handle temptation and throw themselves into baptismal water with closed eyes, fleeing from the tormented to the tormentors. Oh! Those are the ones I despise! I could tear them limb from limb! Do you see that dandy, the one with the fancy walking stick? Lapidus is his name. He is one of those damned turncoats who run off at the first sign of danger, who are prepared to sell their conscience, their people, their God for the sake of their careers. Quiet! He's coming over here to you, it seems. Do you know him? Let me advise you to keep your distance from him, because besides being a candidate for conversion, he is, I'm afraid, a bit of a stool pigeon."

the eighth chapter

TUMARKIN AND LAPIDUS

No sooner did Tumarkin leave when Lapidus, the dandy with the ornately decorated cane, appeared in his place.

"What's new with you, Rabinovitch? Still no news? I hear that even with five twelves not one will be accepted. What was that fanatic talking to you about?"

"What fanatic?"

"That black-haired creature with the curls . . . I can't stand them, those Zionists!"

"What do you have against Zionists?" Rabinovitch asked him, himself not exactly sure what "Zionists" were.

"You don't know them? You don't know that they're chauvinists who insist that everyone believe the same as they do? . . ."

Although Rabinovitch had met him only recently, rather casually, still Lapidus grabbed him by the lapel in a very Jewish manner and began to rage against Tumarkin and all Zionists, attributing to them every possible evil, not excluding Haman's grudges.

"I can't stand them, those hypocrites, those self-appointed apostles of God who take on the Lord Almighty's battles here on earth. Is it their business that a few unfortunate students had themselves baptized so they wouldn't have to spend the rest of their lives hanging around here like you and me? I ask you, why are we suffering, and for what purpose, you and I, hee? And how long do we have to hang around on the outside looking in, you and I, hee?" He ended every sentence with "hee?" which must have been his way of saying "heh?" He was elegantly coiffed and coutured, with blue eyes, arched eyebrows, a small, pointy blond beard, white teeth, and a delicate, puckered mouth. That was Lapidus. He was not in a good mood that particular morning. He had been looking for someone upon whom he could vent his rage, and so he was pleased when he saw

Tumarkin, the Zionist, leaving Rabinovitch's side. In truth he was not so worked up over Tumarkin or the Zionists, who had done him no harm. His anger came from another source. Lapidus had cause to be upset. For one, he didn't have a medal. For another, he hadn't been admitted to the university. And for those two reasons, he knew he had to convert, but couldn't take the step because of his mother, who would not be able to bear it—that was a certainty. In the end that's what he would have to do. Poor Lapidus was looking for someone to whom he could pour out his heart and came upon his recent acquaintance, Rabinovitch, who appealed to him because, although he looked Jewish, he didn't have the Jewish habit of crawling into your guts, boots and all.

"You're lucky, Rabinovitch, you have a medal and are sure to be accepted. But try to put yourself in my place. I have an old mother and a younger sister and both are dependent on me. Their entire fate rests on whether or not I graduate someday and become a doctor. In the meantime the three of us have to live on what I make from giving one hour a week tutoring a rich Gentile. That has to be a secret because if they should ever find out in the *gymnasium* that I was doing this against the rules, and for a Gentile at that—all hell would break loose! I don't know if someone else in my place, let's say even Tumarkin, wouldn't convert and who would blame him? What would you say about that, hee?"

What could he say about that? He himself didn't know. He was simply standing by and observing all these Tumarkins and Lapiduses whose lives seemed to depend on having a medal. They all desperately desired medals. Even his landlady, Madam Shapiro, was constantly dreaming of a medal for her Syomke, and only a gold one at that—what a strange people! It was as if there was nothing in the world that held any interest for them except *gymnasium,* medals, and universities—as if the whole world ended on the other side of the university—a strange, strange people! . . .

And Rabinovitch reminded himself that when he was still Popov, he had a different idea of these people. He had heard that for the Jewish people there existed but one thing sacred in the world—money!

Suddenly the group of candidates—medalists and nonmedalists—leaped up as one and rushed toward the door of the admissions office. What was happening? The secretary had just arrived. Today was the day of reckoning. Today they would know exactly who would be admitted and who would not. Confusion and tumult reigned. A hundred or more Jewish young men from all walks of life packed themselves into the crowded room, all of them pressing forward toward one person, the poor secretary of the university, a pale fellow, his face dripping with perspiration. They might soon tear him limb from limb. Everyone had something to ask and everyone wanted to know first.

Our Rabinovitch was one of the last who was able to reach the secretary. The secretary, with his perspiration-soaked face, his eyes looking down, asked him, as he did all the others, curtly and impersonally, "Your name?"

"Rabinovitch."

The secretary riffled through a stack of papers and said with a groan, "Rabi-

novitch Hersh Movshovitch? Do you want to take your papers now or do you
want the police to deliver them?"

"The police deliver them?" Rabinovitch repeated excitedly, as if he hadn't
understood what was being said to him.

The secretary's pale, perspiring face looked even more exhausted and he muttered, "What do these stubborn Yids want from me?" As gently as he could, the
secretary gave him to understand that he could take his papers back because his
number hadn't come up. Acceptance on the basis of the Jewish quota was
over . . .

"Do you understand, Mister Hersh Movshovitch Rabinovitch?"

When he received no reply, the secretary turned to another student, also a
Jew.

"Your name?"

And to Rabinovitch he said over his shoulder, "You can go. Your papers will
be delivered by the police . . ."

the ninth chapter

THIRTEEN MEDALISTS

At first, when our Popov-Rabinovitch found out that he had
been left hanging in midair, he felt oddly free. He had not yet had time to
evaluate the situation properly and to take full account of his new circumstances
when he came upon his recent acquaintances, first the flamboyant Lapidus,
then the tragic Tumarkin.

"So?" Lapidus stopped him with a bitter laugh, grasping his sleeve and looking at him as if he already knew that Rabinovitch had not been accepted, and as
if he were greatly pleased by this news. "What did I tell you, hee? Was it really
worth struggling for eight years, earning a medal? No, that's not for me. I'll get
even with them! No matter what they do, I'm going to be a student! And in
addition to admitting me as a student in the university, they'll have to admit
another Jew on account of me, maybe even you, Rabinovitch. What do you
think of that, hee?"

Lapidus could tell by Rabinovitch's expression that he didn't begin to understand how Lapidus could help him get into the university. He drew closer to him
and began to expound his theory about the quota system.

The sense of it was as follows: there was a ten percent quota for Jews admitted
to the university. For every nine non-Jews, a tenth must be a Jew. And since he,
Lapidus, had found out they were short one Christian in order to admit a Jew as

the tenth, he, Lapidus, would be that ninth Christian so that Rabinovitch could be the tenth . . .

This ingenious calculation so pleased Lapidus that, with a slap to the forehead, he complimented himself on his cleverness.

"That's some brainstorm, hee?" he asked Rabinovitch, and didn't receive an answer as Rabinovitch was distracted by his other acquaintance, Tumarkin, who was standing in a circle of young men and was winking at him from across the room to come over to him. Rabinovitch excused himself and went over to Tumarkin, who introduced him to his friends.

"Here you have another victim, and also a medalist. I wholeheartedly commend him to you. A warmhearted fellow, even though he doesn't understand a word of Yiddish, never mind his Jewish name, Rabinovitch."

"A true phenomenon!" said one of the group, a fellow from Pinsk with an energetic, intelligent, pimply face whose summer suit matched neither the season nor his face. "Did you hear that! A Jew named Rabinovitch who doesn't understand a word of Yiddish is unique enough to rent him out or sell tickets to see him. You can bet anything you want that you won't find among a hundred and thirty million Gentiles one Gentile named Popov who doesn't understand a word of Russian, unless he was born deaf."

The Pinsk fellow's joke was wasted as no one was in a mood to laugh. At that moment each one's thoughts were focused on quotas, medals, vacancies, and the university, always the university.

If there was anyone who was surprised by the joke, it was Rabinovitch, and not so much because of the joke, but because his real name had been used as an example. What ever made him use the name Popov and not Ivanov or Sidorov?

But he wasn't allowed any time to ponder this question. Tumarkin informed him that there remained only one recourse—all the medalists had to chip in and send off a strong telegram of protest to the minister, and the sooner, the better.

"Jews! How many are we here?" Tumarkin asked, and began to count heads with his slender, pale fingers. "Not one, not two, not three, not four . . . nine, ten, eleven, twelve, thirteen. Thirteen medalists!"

"Thirteen?" the fellow from Pinsk interjected. "Not a lucky number! I'm afraid one of us, do you hear, will have to convert . . ."

This joke was wasted as well. No one rewarded him with so much as a smile. Sending the minister a telegram was not a bad idea but it would take some doing. The majority of the group were in such dire straits that they could hardly afford a cup of coffee, much less a telegram.

"How much will it come to and how much will it cost each of us?" asked one of the young men with a hungry look and frightened eyes.

"I'll pay for it all myself!" Rabinovitch cried out, and turned red because all twelve pairs of eyes turned toward him curiously, and the fellow from Pinsk couldn't contain himself, looked at him, and had to crack a joke.

"Listen, which Rabinovitches are you related to? Are you related to the banker, Lev Brodsky? Which capital shares pay the highest dividends and which bank do you recommend for me to open an account?"

Luckily all these jokes were said in Yiddish, in the tongue Rabinovitch didn't understand, otherwise he would have been embarrassed.

"It's not important how much the telegram costs or who pays for it," said Tumarkin. "Whoever can, will pay, and whoever cannot, his friends will pay for him. More important is what kind of telegram to send and where we should meet. I suggest we all go straight to that inexpensive vegetarian restaurant we like so much. Friends, what do you say to that?"

"To the vegetarians, to the vegetarians!" they all joined in, and our thirteen medalists took off for their favorite vegetarian restaurant.

the tenth chapter

AT THE VEGETARIAN RESTAURANT

After enjoying a fine repast and receiving the bill, they realized that the principle of vegetarianism was worthwhile promoting throughout the world, not only because it was opposed to the eating of flesh—which in itself was commendable—but because the food was more tasty and digestible than meat. They composed a strong telegram of over a hundred words to be sent to the minister. And then Tumarkin, the ringleader of the thirteen medalists, stood up, and with a grand gesture poured himself a generous beaker of water and held forth, in Russian, while rolling his r's, which we translate here into our Yiddish language word for word:

"My friends! When thirteen medalists who have been left out in the cold and who have not been allowed to enter the temple of learning only because of the great sin of counting among their ancestors Abraham, Isaac, and Jacob—when such thirteen heroes, I say, come together in a vegetarian restaurant to eat well, I can permit myself to drink a toast with the kind of liquor you can never get drunk on no matter how much of it you drink.

"I wish to say that this homely beaker and this sober drink symbolize the humbled status of our people, that sober folk to which all thirteen of us belong and from which we do not wish to be separated, even though we have suffered because of it and have endured affliction and adversity, grief and even disgrace, one can truly say, from the day we first opened our eyes until this very day. No! We will never leave our people! And I go further! I say we cannot leave, even if we wanted to.

"I could put before you, my friends, a whole catalogue of evidence and many

examples of how we have maintained our Jewishness. But why need we look further when we have an example right in our midst? Here among us thirteen medalists we have a comrade from the heart of Russia, a Jew who doesn't understand a word of Yiddish, although he has a Jewish name, I would even say too Jewish a name, for what can be a more Jewish name than Rabinovitch? Go ahead, ask him exactly what holds him to his Jewishness. What stops him from taking that one step, just one step, that would rid him once and for all, in one day, of all affliction, adversity, and disgrace? I'd wager he himself couldn't give you a clear, rational explanation!

"Would you like me to tell you *where* this power lies? Would you like me to show you *where* this strength that binds us so powerfully together over so long a time can be found? This power, I'm afraid, does not lie *within* us, but *outside* us.

"That we are all so stiff-necked and drive ourselves to imbibe from the well-springs of Torah, enlightenment, and knowledge, and that we insist on being cultivated—all that is not *our* fault, but the fault of those who will not allow us near, those who thrust us away, who drive us off with clubs. But let them open the doors wide and you will see how our eagerness for enlightenment will flag. Just let them force us to study and you will see how quickly our ardor will cool.

"You can interpret my words as paradoxical and you can laugh even harder than you are laughing. But I tell you again—the passion to study exists only because it is forbidden to us.

"There is a joke going around, a very banal joke, but bitterly true: If an edict were to be issued that from the first of January Jews would not be allowed to convert, on the evening of the thirty-first of December the world would be deluged with converts!

"Friends! It's a joke, a banal joke, a silly joke, but the bitter truth! Just see how our brothers are racing to convert this year more than ever before. Do you know why? Because there have been rumors of decrees affecting converts. They're afraid that it will soon be disallowed and there might be a quota on converts.

"Comrades! When I speak of those people who have abandoned everything that is holy, those who are prepared to sell their own souls, a fire ignites in me and I haven't enough words with which to damn them! Some talk about fanaticism. They mention the word compassion. They wish to absolve these people, to justify their actions, to find some way to defend them, as it is written in our Talmud: 'Judge not thy friend, until thou hast stood in his place.'

"To that I will give you this answer. If those who desert us at such a bitter time in their own self-interest or to further their careers do sometimes deserve our sympathy, their apologists who defend them are not worth the earth they walk on! And if our downtrodden, rebuffed people is obliged to maintain its Jewishness even more strongly in such bitter times, then we, the youth, are certainly obliged to do so!

"Therefore we must speak out unequivocally against those comrades who desert us in the battlefield where we wage war against malevolent forces. We are not deterred because our numbers are dwindling. If we decrease in number, we increase in spirit. We will wage our battle with even more pride and renewed courage than we have till now. We will not lay down our arms under any circumstances!

"Our shield has always *been* and always *will be: the Book.*

"I drink, comrades, to our eternal shield, to the Book and to our heroes, who do not cower and do not submit and who do not lay down their arms.

"Long live the Book! Hoorah! HOORAH!"

the eleventh chapter

ALL THREE ENJOY A LAUGH

Although the thirteen medalists had drunk water with their vegetarian meal, not wine, our hero Rabinovitch came home feeling strangely elated, his head spinning and his ears buzzing, a state produced by observing and listening to his new friends the last few days, all of which he had not fully digested. He had witnessed many extremes, had heard many different views, various pronouncements and speeches, but felt it was still premature to come to any conclusions.

One thing was clear to him—he had not been admitted as a student. They had promised the police would return his papers . . . Good. But then what?

That question, which bored deeply into the brains and very marrow of the other Jewish candidates, not permitting them to eat or sleep, merely aroused curiosity in him. He simply wanted to know what would happen next. And, too, he wondered how this comedy, in which everyone thought he, Grisha Popov, was not Grisha Popov but Hershke Rabinovitch, would end? He frankly had not thought himself capable of playing his role so cleverly, so artfully and consistently.

Quite pleased with himself, he rang the doorbell of the apartment and prayed that the door would be opened by Betty, the charming, dark-haired, lovely Betty with her intelligent, clear eyes and mischievous dimples. Moreover, he resolved that if Betty would open the door, he would take it as a sign that she loved him . . . but if someone else opened it? . . .

Before he could complete his thought, the door opened. There stood Betty, beautiful Betty, looking at him with her lovely, intelligent eyes. "Does this mean she loves me?" was the first thought that flew through his mind. "Yes. She loves me, as I love her," he answered himself, walking up the stairs with her.

When she saw the lodger, his cheeks glowing and his eyes shining, Betty immediately assumed she would soon be hearing the good news that he was now a university student. In her mind's eye she could already picture him in his student uniform with shiny gold buttons, and she wondered how he would look in his new outfit.

"So? How did it go?" Betty asked him, gazing into his happy eyes as they were climbing the stairs.

"Very well! Exceptionally well!" the lodger replied, unable to drink his fill of her bright face and her lovely, intelligent eyes, all the while thinking how the lucky omen, the sign he had hoped for, had been granted him.

"May I congratulate you?" Betty said to him amiably, offering him her hand.

"For what?" he asked, taking her soft, warm, tender hand.

"For being admitted to the university . . ."

The lodger greatly regretted having to release that beloved hand and he delayed answering her. But finally he had to tell her the truth. It was still too soon to congratulate him about the university because . . . because the acceptance of Jews had closed that day and they had promised that the police would return his documents.

"What's that?" Betty cried, and clapped her hands together so loudly that her mother, Sara Shapiro, ran in from the kitchen, her sleeves rolled up, beside herself with fear.

"What's the matter? What happened?" she demanded to know, looking from one to the other with such alarm that the daughter had to calm her.

"Nothing, nothing happened . . . You know, Mama, they didn't accept him into the university," she indicated the lodger with the kind of stricken expression she might have had on her face in reporting that he had been hit by an automobile and had lost a leg.

"Oy, what a thunderbolt!" Sara Shapiro exclaimed in Yiddish as she looked at her roomer as if he had lost, not one leg, but both legs and both arms. "What will happen now? Woe is me!"

In a split second three different thoughts raced through her mind, one worse than the other: What would he do without a residence permit? What would now happen with the room? And most important of all, what would they do without a tutor?

"God pity me and my terrible luck that doesn't end!" Sara kept repeating, wringing her hands as she looked at the lodger, lamenting his plight like a devoted mother. And though the roomer did not understand a word she was saying, he could tell by her sorrowful face, by her mournful voice, and from the way she wrung her hands that she was unhappy for him. He clasped her hands in his, desiring to comfort her.

"Calm yourself, *Matushka*, calm yourself . . ."

But Sara Shapiro didn't want to be calmed. She turned, not to him, but to her daughter.

"What's this with *Matushke*? Who is *Matushke*? Better ask him, the *shlimazel*, what he's going to do now without a *pravozhitelstvo*."

The lodger understood only one word of the question she had just posed: *pravozhitelstvo*—residence permit.

"*Pravozhitelstvo, Matushka, nichevo*—it doesn't matter!" he said, which evoked a smile from all three while he patted her on the back.

"Can you figure him out?" the mother said to the daughter, again in Yiddish, with tears standing in her eyes, "Nu? And you were annoyed at me because I called him a *shlimazel* . . ."

"*Chto eto znachit 'shlimazat'*—what does '*shlimazat*' mean?" the roomer asked the daughter, apparently thinking it had something to do with residence permits.

The word *shlimazat* called forth a gale of laughter from the mother and daughter, and the lodger, admiring Betty's small, white, pearly teeth, wanted to show that, although he spoke no Yiddish, he could somehow understand every word.

"If we have to resort to *mazat,* then we'll do so," he said, demonstrating how he would grease another's palm, the meaning of *mazat* in Russian.

That threw mother and daughter into such fits of laughter that the roomer burst out laughing at the sight of such hilarity.

"What's this laughing all about?" demanded the head of the household, David Shapiro, in a characteristically stern voice, sweeping into the house like a whirlwind, "Why all this celebration? Does he get a *mazel tov?*" he said to his wife and daughter, indicating the lodger.

All three were enjoying a good, hearty laugh. And David Shapiro stood looking at them as if they were mad, not granting them so much as a single smile.

In a few words the daughter brought him up to date on the misfortune that had befallen their roomer. David Shapiro grabbed his head and could not believe his ears. After all, a medalist!

Then he turned to his wife. "Now do you see? And all you talk about day and night is 'Medal! Medal!' Now you see where a medal will get you!"

And without waiting to hear Sara's response, he scratched himself behind the ear, wrinkled his brow, and said to himself, "Ay-ay! Ay-ay! Ay! Tighten your belt, David. You have a burden to carry! A very heavy burden!"

the twelfth chapter

THE TRUE MEANING OF RESIDENCE PERMITS

In matters concerning residence permits, our Shapiro deserved high praise, for he was a specialist in the subject, one could almost say a genius. It was this same Shapiro who, with great energy, undertook to provide for his lodger Rabinovitch a residence permit, complete and perfect in every way.

"A young man with a diploma from a *gymnasium* and with a medal on top of it," so said David Shapiro to him after the police had delivered the lodger's documents, during which visit Shapiro's teeth were chattering with fright much more than the roomer's. "Such a young man, I say, should have no problem getting a residence permit. I'll bet on that, ten to one! Where is it written that Hersh Rabinovitch has to become a doctor of medicine? And if he becomes a doctor only of teeth, would he be worse off?"

With these words he went off with the lodger straight to a dental school, where, in no time at all, he made arrangements to enroll him as a dental student, one-two-three.

That sounds easy to say—no time at all. Much, much, however, needed to be done—papers, papers, and more papers! But David Shapiro was not intimidated by red tape. David Shapiro was a veteran who had worn out his teeth on such matters. As he said of himself, he was like an old beaten dog. What he had been through since settling in this blessed city till he had obtained a perfectly legal permit, and then only because his son, Syomke, was a *gymnasium* student, is not possible to describe.

"It's a pity you're so weak in our language," he said to the lodger as they went together from the dental school to the police, where they had a great deal of trouble because the police had already stamped his passport in red, *"Na vy" ezd v dvadtsat' chetyre chasa*—Ordered to leave the city within twenty-four hours." "Eh! If you only understood our language and could write Yiddish, about *my* residence permit, you could write a book this big," and with his hand Shapiro motioned from the floor almost to the ceiling. "That's what it would take for someone to write it all up."

And even though the lodger was terribly weak in "our language" and could never write such a book, Shapiro nevertheless did him the favor of filling his ear with such horrifying stories, wild tales, comic episodes, dreadful events, and amazing happenings that had it not been for Madam Shapiro and, especially, their daughter, Betty, sitting nearby and confirming these accounts, the lodger would have been correct in thinking his landlord was fantasizing, talking nonsense, or inventing things that were entirely untrue. For how was it possible to believe that one man, he may even be a Goliath, or a Samson, could survive so great a burden of woes, cruel regulations, and persecutions over so short a space of time without showing so much as a gray hair?

How many times, do you think, had David Shapiro been expelled from Petersburg and Moscow and other Russian cities? How many times, do you imagine, had he been transported under guard, shackled together with all kinds of thieves, bandits, and cutthroats? In how many prisons had he been a guest, and with what sort of criminal had he not become acquainted? And for what reason, do you suppose? For one and only one transgression—his grandfather was stubborn enough to refuse to change his religion. And here! Right here, in this blessed city? How many times, do you reckon, had he been in immediate danger of being expelled? And who was to say, I put it to you, that he was still not in danger, that this very night they couldn't come, wake him up from his sleep, and ask him please to be so kind as to "take a little trip to Berdichev," as had happened so many times before in Petersburg and Moscow and other cities?

Shapiro went on telling one amazing story after another about residence permits as the lodger listened and thought, God Almighty! What kind of a people is forever being persecuted and chased like dogs and never protests? Shapiro was not unique, his whole people was like that. If one man cries out, his voice is lost in the wind, but if a people, an entire people, should raise its voice, it would seem the cries would reach from one end of the world to the other! The very heavens would tremble! A strange people! Here sits a Jew, Shapiro, a human being like all other human beings, who has to struggle for the right to live someplace, a right due, not only every human being, but every living creature, even a cow in the field! No, he can even find in himself the spirit to talk in a mocking tone, "Please take a little trip to Berdichev!"

"How is it possible," he asked Shapiro, "how is it possible that they could expel you? And where is *your* residence permit?"

"My residence permit, ha-ha-ha?" Shapiro broke out laughing. "What do you mean *my* residence permit? How can I say, for instance, *my* hand? Or *my* foot? The hand is mine so long as I write with it, or eat with it. The foot is mine so long as I walk on it. And should God want to take away this hand or this foot from me, whose would they then be? That's exactly the way it is with my residence permit. So long as there is an edict which permits parents to live in the city while their children are studying in *gymnasium*, well and good. But what would the situation be if some so-called legal expert were to come forward and prove that the edict says explicitly that only those children can study in *gymnasium* whose parents already have residence permits? Do you understand the sense of that? Ay, but then we come to another question: how can I have a residence permit before I have obtained a residence permit? Do you understand or not? Now listen and put your mind to it. It would be as if you were to ask me how I could have been born before my parents were on this earth! Our Talmudists ask the same question: how was the first pair of iron tongs made when you need iron tongs to hold the tongs in the fire? Do you see how profound this is? So? Why are you so quiet?" the landlord said to the roomer, poking him with his elbow.

What could the roomer possibly say to all this? He listened with mouth agape. What a remarkable contrivance, this residence permit. It came along with a strange philosophy having to do with anatomy—a hand and a foot, and Talmudic argumentation about iron tongs. He was left absolutely speechless! And incidentally, sitting there across from the table was Betty, the lovely, dark-haired, adorable Betty, pretending to read a book, but he was as sure as two times two is four that although she was looking at the book, she was well aware that he, Rabinovitch, was gazing at her, and she knew quite well he was thinking about her because that very morning, in passing, he had said, "Betty, I have something to tell you." And although he had not as yet said anything to her, because her mother had at that very moment appeared and had informed him that her Syomke had brought home two fives from *gymnasium,* still what he had said had been enough to make her face glow like a spire in the sunset. And our Betty was smart enough to realize how much Rabinovitch loved her and how dear she was to him.

Not only Betty, but Betty's mother, Sara, had endeared herself to him at that moment of meeting. That morning Sara had told him other news which was even more welcome than Syomke's two fives in *gymnasium.* Sara Shapiro had taken advantage of her daughter's absence to tell the lodger she had a proposition for him.

"Such as?"

"Such as I would like you to toot" (Betty wasn't there to correct her mistake!) "my daughter just as you have been tooting my son. I can't pay you. But I can give you lunch and dinner free."

Rabinovitch was stronger than iron to be able to contain himself and refrain from throwing his arms around the landlady and kissing her for the wonderful news! Two pieces of news: First, that he would be teaching Betty. Second, that he would be eating at the same table with her! No, the world doesn't have too many landladies like his landlady. Forget all the other landladies and all the other women in the world!

Rabinovitch took the landlady's hand and thanked her warmly and sincerely, assuring her that he accepted her proposal with pleasure. With pleasure! With great pleasure!

"Wait a minute. There's one condition," Sara insisted.

Rabinovitch's heart skipped a beat.

"Like what?"

"Tea and sugar are at your expense."

Rabinovitch felt as if a thousand pounds had been lifted from his soul.

"That's understood, my expense! That's understood!"

At that point Betty came in. With one glance she took in the situation. She reprimanded her mother in Yiddish, "Couldn't you wait till I made the suggestion?"

And to the lodger she said in Russian, as a sweet smile played on her lovely lips and a blush spread across her dimpled cheeks, "When it comes to her children's education, my mother becomes all business."

"Ah! Dear, dear Betty!" thought Rabinovitch, taking her in with his eyes. "Only an angel like Betty could have such a mother! And only a mother like Sara Shapiro could have such a daughter!"

YEHUDIT

We may have certified David Shapiro as a specialist and genius in the law and commentary on residence permits too soon. A few days after his lodger, Rabinovitch, enrolled in dental school, a catastrophe struck Shapiro's house, in fact, a not uncommon occurrence in those times; it happened almost every night in the university town in which our extraordinary story takes place.

It was already well past midnight in the Shapiro home when the doorbell rang loudly and continuously, loud enough to waken the dead. Another in Shapiro's place would surely have fallen out of bed or jumped out the window. But Shapiro was, as we already know, a veteran, well acquainted with that kind of ringing. He knew they only rang a doorbell like that when the house was on fire and they had to rescue the inhabitants, or when they were making a police roundup of Jews. In police language it was called "rounding up unregistered residents."

Call it what you will, police roundup, house search, they ring until you open the door. And when you open the door, in burst your guests: the chief of police and his aides and anyone else you can think of. They politely request that you wake up the entire household, young and old, big and small, and ask for everyone's papers. The papers are then examined and stamped, the occupants thoroughly checked out and counted, and if everything is in order, they give you clearance and depart. After that you can do whatever you wish: put up the samovar for tea or, if you can, go back to sleep—perhaps to have sweet dreams . . .

But should your papers not be in order, heaven forbid, or should they find illegal merchandise, contraband, or, to be more precise, a Jew without his residence permit, then they will ask you to be so kind as to dress, the quicker the better, and do them the favor of accompanying them to police headquarters. There you will be investigated thoroughly and they will stamp your documents in red, *"Na vy" ezd v dvatsat' chetyre chasa*—Ordered to leave the city within twenty-four hours." Or they will escort you with great honor to the city of your birth where you can visit all your aunts and uncles whom you haven't seen for ages . . .

David Shapiro, although an old hand in these matters of police roundups, found he had nothing nice enough to wear to greet his uninvited guests; however, it would be no tragedy if he were to entertain them without a smoking jacket. He didn't linger too long over it, threw a short jacket over his underclothes, stuck his bare feet into his slippers, and began trying to strike one match after another, which stubbornly refused to ignite, until finally Sara Shapiro sat up in her bed.

"Madman, what are you rubbing there?" she said to him, tearing the matches from his hands. "Rubs and rubs! Can't wait! Express train! The devil won't take them if they have to wait outside and ring a little longer!"

With these words, Sara lit a small lamp with a smoky glass as David ran down to open the door. Soon one heard the sound of many feet running up the stairs and the Shapiro home became as lively as a party, all brightly lit up, so brightly that no matter how hard Sara Shapiro tried to wrap herself in the blanket she had hastily thrown around her, she could not quite succeed in totally covering herself, so that one could glimpse either her naked breast or her bare feet, never mind her hair, which had loosened and tumbled over her bare shoulders. And whose fault was it if not the "express train's"? If only he hadn't been in such a hurry to open the door, she could have arranged her hair or put something on.

"How many are you here?" demanded a tall, broad-boned officer with sensuous, thick lips and with bloodshot, drowsy eyes as he gave a long, loud yawn like a healthy person in need of sleep.

Screwing up his courage, David Shapiro answered, "We are three," though his teeth were chattering, and like the veteran he was in these matters, he didn't wait till they said the word "potchport," but went over to his long coat hanging on the wall, unbuttoned the breast pocket and drew out the passport, residence permit, and other necessary papers, brought them over to the officer quite smartly, accompanying the delivery of the documents with an elegant clicking of the heels, like a cavalier, apparently forgetting that he was barefoot and wearing nothing more than a short jacket over his white underclothing.

"Three, you say?" the half-asleep officer said, staring with his bloodshot eyes at Madam Shapiro as he stuck a glaringly bright lantern close up to her face. She didn't know what to do about her messy hair, her bare bosom, and bare feet. Suddenly she realized that her husband had said something that was terribly mistaken. What does he mean that we are three when we are obviously four, and with the lodger, we are really five! Her terror made her forget they were not alone and she reached out to her husband with her bare arm, speaking to him in Yiddish.

"David! God be with you! What kind of three? Did you forget we're five?"

David rubbed his eyes as if he had heard the strangest news.

"Five? How do you figure five?"

"Mathematician mine! You and I are not two? Betty is not three? Syomke is not four?"

David slapped his forehead, spat to the side, and said to the officer, "I completely forgot. We're not three, but four. There are four of us."

"Not four," his wife shouted, "not four, but five!"

"Why five? How do you figure it?"

"Did you forget the roomer? Or do you just want to bring down a catastrophe on your head?"

"Devil take it!" Shapiro honored himself with another slap to the forehead and spat. Then he spoke to the officer with a deferent smile.

"I'm all mixed up. We are not three and not four, but five."

"Is that so!" the officer drawled, all the while admiring Sara Shapiro's black hair, which had tumbled onto her pure white, still youthful bosom. "Five, you say? Maybe six? Maybe seven? And maybe even more? All right, let's take a look."

And the officer with the sleepy, bloodshot eyes winked to his aides, ordering them to make a house search, and the aides fell to their task with zeal. Beds and bureaus, tables and chairs were examined several times over. They pulled Syomke's blanket off him and shone a bright lantern directly into his face, which elicited an embarrassed giggle from the youngster. They were about to repeat this procedure with Betty but she sprang out of bed angrily, wrapped herself in a sheet, and remained standing face to face with the half-asleep officer with the lascivious lips, whose bloodshot glance shifted from daughter to mother and from mother to daughter, apparently trying to decide which one he would prefer.

"The devil take them if I know which is the prettier!" he thought. "They're both beautiful, but the young one is exciting . . . Venus . . . Juno . . . Aphrodite . . ." His mind was beset with tangled memories of names he had read in novels. But of all the names, he forgot one name which at that moment would best have suited the lovely Betty with her clear, pale face with its perfectly shaped nose, her beautiful, dark hair, her thick eyebrows, and her large, luminous eyes which burned with the flame of grief and sorrow.

That name was Yehudit.

the fourteenth chapter

HANDS OFF!

Had our Rabinovitch been the real Rabinovitch and not Popov, and had the real Rabinovitch not been admitted to the university despite his medal, surely the real Rabinovitch would not have slept so soundly as our Popov-Rabinovitch did that night. Not only didn't he hear the frightful ringing or the stamping of many feet and loud shouting, he didn't even hear his landlord, David Shapiro, who was standing over him and tugging his blanket, trying to waken him in a voice growing louder and louder, "Rabinovitch! Rabinovitch! Rabinovitch!" Rabinovitch was off who knows where! Off somewhere sledding downhill over the snow, and not alone but with someone else, with Betty, who was embracing him, her face close to his, pressing her soft cheeks to his lips, and he was kissing her, kissing her, kissing her, and she was laughing, pulling away from him, laughing as he kissed her and kissed her and drew her closer. "Where are you taking me?" "Come, darling! Come, Betty!" "Where to?" "There, there, to the church." "To the church? Ha-ha-ha! What will we do in the church?" "There we'll get married. There I'll take you. There you'll be mine, mine, mine!"

"What are you babbling about—mine, mine, mine?" the landlord exclaimed, and pulled off his blanket. "Get up, the police are here! Rabinovitch! Rabinovitch!! Rabinovitch!!!"

"What's this Rabinovitch? Where is there a Rabinovitch here?" the roomer said to the landlord, pulling the blanket back with one hand and rubbing his eyes with the other. "What is it? What's happening?"

"Police are here. A search, a roundup, I mean, a search."

"What the devil are you talking about? Police? What search? The devil take it!"

"God be with you, Rabinovitch! What are you saying? *Pravozhitelstvo*—residence permit . . ."

That last word finally worked better than anything else.

"*Pravozhitelstvo*? Aha! Now I know. So where is she?"

"Who?"

"The *pravozhitelstvo*, for crying out loud!"

"Damn it! If you weren't a Jew I'd say you were drunk. You're not talking like a sober person. I'm telling you the police are here, there's a roundup, I mean a search, they're asking about your residence permit, and you're asking me where *she* is?"

Only after hearing these words and seeing a police officer at the door did it begin to dawn on Rabinovitch what was going on and he began to remember who he was supposed to be and where he was. Nevertheless, he kept cursing under his breath till the landlord helped him to his feet and led him into the other room, where he came upon the landlady wrapped in a blanket and Betty in a sheet, and opposite them, the officer with the sensuous lips.

At first he couldn't altogether figure out what was happening. All right, a search is a search. But why did the two women have to stand there half-naked? And why was that creature looking at them like that?"

He felt the heat rise in him because he had come in at the very moment when the officer with the thick, sensuous lips was asking Betty her age.

"Eighteen," the mother replied for her daughter, but the officer cut her off.

"I'm not asking you, I'm asking her."

"Eighteen," Betty now answered for herself.

"You're lying, *dushenka*," the officer said with a little smile on his thick lips, and tried to pull the sheet down a bit from Betty's shoulders. The lodger suddenly came fully to his senses and thundered out so loudly that all were startled.

"*Ruki proch!!!—Hands off!!!*"

For as long as the officer had been an officer and had conducted house searches, he had never known a Jew to raise his voice to him so loudly. He stood stock still a moment and stared at the young man, unable to speak, so taken aback was he. When he regained his composure, he went to work on the fellow.

"You . . . Who do you think you are?"

"You can't speak to me like that. You be more polite!"

The officer's arms fell to his side with surprise and a crooked little smile crossed his thick, lascivious lips. He simply glanced at his aides and ordered, "Take him!"

"You don't have to 'take' me, I'll go by myself," Rabinovitch said firmly, and, accompanied by the aides, went to his room to dress and prepared himself to go wherever they would lead him.

The officer with the lascivious lips, who a moment before had been full of lust for the two half-naked women, and especially for the younger one, who seemed to him like a fresh fruit, a fragrant, ripe peach still covered with dew, was speechless with the rage burning in him, not only because of the Jewboy's audacity, but also because his exciting fantasies had been dashed to the point where he almost forgot what he had just been imagining.

"Ah!" he quickly reminded himself, casting a last glance at Betty, who at that moment, wrapped in a white sheet, resembled a beautiful statue carved out of marble. "Ah! Venus . . . Juno . . . Aphrodite . . . An *apetitnaya zhidovochka*—a sexy little Jewess—no doubt about it, what a shame! Instead of this contemptuous fellow, I'd much rather be taking her away, this Venus from the Jewish Street."

A deep sigh issued of itself from the depths of his heart. For this elemental man it was truly a great loss.

How could he have foreseen that this rare beauty, this Venus from the Jewish Street, would sometime in the future again fall into his hands, and under what circumstances indeed?!

In the meanwhile, time wasn't standing still and there were things to be done. The officer urged his aides to hurry the young man, but the young man had plenty of time. He had to get dressed. David Shapiro, who wished he could have interceded for his lodger, decided against it since the roomer did have a legitimate residence permit, would that *he* had such a piece of gold! So what was the problem? The problem was that the permit was still at the dental school. The officer pushed Shapiro aside, turned to his aides, who were helping Rabinovitch get dressed, and called out in a loud voice, "Why are you fumbling around there so long? What the devil is going on? We're wasting time! There's plenty of 'contraband' left to ferret out among these children of Israel on this Jew Street! Step on it! Move! Ready! March!"

A SLEEPLESS NIGHT

No one in the Shapiro household slept a wink that disrupted night, even though they had more or less calmed down, gone back to bed, and extinguished the lights in preparation for sleep.

But no one was able to sleep.

David Shapiro and his wife were planning for the following day. With God's help, first thing in the morning, David said he would dash off to the chief of police.

"To the chief of police?" Sara interjected. "Why are you dashing off to the chief of police, my 'express train'? First you have to go to the dental school, and then . . ."

"It's a good thing you reminded me!" David added sarcastically. "Without you, I probably wouldn't know what to do next. When it comes to residence permits, you can leave it to me."

"Is that so? Well, if you're such an expert, how come you didn't make sure his residence permit was in his pocket, my 'lord of the castle'?"

"Why do I waste my time talking to an idiot? I thought I told you seventy-seven times over that he's just a kid, a kid, a kid. No matter how many times I lay it out for him, again and again, that a Jew without a residence permit in his pocket is like a person without air, like a fish out of water, he pays no attention to me at all—in one ear and out the other . . . A strange person, this Rabinovitch! What made him lash out at that officer and raise his voice so loud? I almost fell over dead. He has in him, I tell you, some very un-Jewish traits! I don't understand what kind of a Jew he is! He isn't afraid of anything, not of the police, not of the devil, not of anything!"

At this point the daughter, who could no longer tolerate such talk, interrupted and reprimanded her father for calling something a fault that was a virtue.

The mother stood up for her husband but also received a good scolding from the daughter. Thus the night was passed in endless wrangling, the possibility of sleep entirely out of the question.

Even young Syomke, who had grown up in constant fear of these checks by the police, could not fall asleep again.

The fact that they had suddenly taken away his teacher in the middle of the night was not what bothered him. Probably his permit was not exactly in order. What was keeping him from sleep was worrying about his *gymnasium* ranking. Without the tutor he would no longer bring home those fives, of that he was certain, and without fives, his father wouldn't reward him with those forties. And without those forties, where would he get the money for the cinema?

He also felt a bit sorry for the tutor himself. A pity—what if they sent him away, with whom would he do his lessons? With Betty? He hated to study with Betty. She had a quick temper—like a match! It was much different studying with the roomer. Studying with him was a pleasure. He liked the roomer and he knew the roomer liked him. The roomer liked all of them: him and his mother and Betty. Betty more than all the others, that he knew for certain. Why else did he, this Rabinovitch, stare at his sister that way when no one was looking? And why did he drop his eyes when his mother saw him looking at his sister that way?

And the sister also really, really liked him. Why else did she turn so red whenever he looked at her? And what did the two of them always write to each other on the blackboard, using those letters from a book which, even if you were a genius, you couldn't make out? A pity on his sister if she remained without her teacher. Was it possible he really wouldn't come back? From whom could he find out? From Betty? Betty was angry. She was quiet but he knew she was angry. Father and mother were wrangling. They were wrangling and arguing. He was calling her 'idiot' and she was calling him 'express train'—ha-ha-ha! But listen! Betty has also gotten into the middle of the argument. I must hear what Betty has to say.

And Syomke overheard what Betty was saying.

"I can't listen to this anymore. I feel I'm going to burst!" she said. "What did you expect him to do, let himself be stepped on like you? Crawl on all fours like you? They won't talk down to him like they do to you, you can be sure!"

"A lot of good it did him!" her mother called out from her bed, with the voice of a person who is desperate to sleep even a little bit but cannot. "They won't talk down to him! Some triumph! They'll say to him, 'If you please, go in good health, back to Shklov.' "

"Look at you, you're talking just like a woman!" David cut her off. "They won't send him back to Shklov. You can depend on me. A law is a law. Dental school is as good as the university. Just let it be morning, I'll dash off to the chief of police."

"Again to the chief of police? Don't you mean the dental school?" Sara interrupted him.

"Yes, of course. First to the dental school, then to the chief of police. The chief of police will have him released. You can be sure of it!"

"Let's hope so, God in heaven!" Sara sighed. "From your mouth into God's ears . . ."

"Oh, thank God!" thought Syomke. "If that happens, we can still do our lessons tomorrow. We don't have any mathematics or geography tomorrow. So what do we have tomorrow?"

And Syomke's thoughts returned to his lessons, the *gymnasium*, mathematics, and geography and he no longer heard his sister's arguing or his parents' name calling. He turned his face to the wall, covered his head with the blanket, and was soon sleeping the sound, blessed sleep which is possible only during one's young, carefree, childhood years.

the sixteenth chapter

JAILED

When they wake you up in the middle of the night during your soundest sleep and take you for a stroll through dark streets, uphill and downhill, making you slog through the autumn mud in the custody of a band of soldiers who prod you, along with other captives, like cattle, and you hear shouts and curses you have never heard before, and they bring you to a place which is so thick with smoke and stench it is impossible to see the light of day, and they throw you in together with drunks and thieves and God-knows-what-else, and you want to sit down but there is no place, unless on the bare, filthy, slippery floor, and if you want to protest, there is no one to protest to but the four walls—if you manage to get through all this, you discover you've lost your courage, and you start to dwell on things you have hardly ever thought of before.

As much as our hero tried to keep his spirits up, to take heart, marching like a cossack on sentry duty: one-two, one-two—promising himself to be strong to the bitter end, in fact, feeling that night even stronger and prouder than ever, nevertheless, when he was brought to that place, he had to admit that writing about one's life in a book was a lot easier than living through it, and being a Jew was, apparently, a lot harder than one could have imagined.

What he saw and heard while detained and what he carried away from that one night was certainly more than he would have carried away from an entire year of freedom.

Every few minutes the jail door would swing open and a new transport of prisoners would be led in, mostly Jews, frightened as rabbits, miserable, terrified, stunned, and dispirited. What interested him most was that the other prisoners greeted each transport of Jewish prisoners with mocking glee, with jeers and stinging comments, occasionally accompanied by a curse, a grinding of the teeth and a jab in the side. "*Zhidovskaya morda, psiakrew, sobaka nevirnaia*—Jew bastards," they cursed in Russian, Polish, and Ukrainian.

And what truly amazed him was the fact that all those frightened, miserable, dispirited people simply stood there and absorbed the jeers and curses indifferently, as if they were not the objects of the derision!

One of them, a wrinkled Jew carrying a sack almost twice as big as he, was the recipient of a blow to the side from a tall, big-boned fellow, a tough-looking man in rags, who knocked him down and rolled him over and over together with his sack. The old man merely stared into the big boned fellow's face as if he wanted only to know what was going on. Rabinovitch gathered from the way in which the other Jews attacked the fallen man with the sack and began shouting all at once that the man was likely being punished for not going where he was supposed to, or for dragging such a big sack around. And it astonished him that one's own brothers did not come to the defense of one of their own. "Where is their solidarity?" he thought. Where was that sense of community, that loyalty of which he had read many times in *Novoye Vremya—The New Times*—and in other newspapers that were considered to be right-wing? "What kind of a people is this?" he asked himself after he had sat down at the end of a bench which a prisoner with a black eye had vacated. "What kind of a people is this that can exist under such conditions, eat, drink, and sleep, do business, study, go to theaters and concerts, dance and rejoice while at the same time the authorities can come into your home in the middle of the night, raid the premises as if you were ordinary thieves or wild animals, and treat you in a manner violating all the rules of humanity and godliness? Where does this remarkable secret lie hidden? And where is the source of this hatred of all toward one? There must be a reason for it, a root! It simply isn't possible that everyone should be against them for no reason at all, without any cause! Probably there is something about the Jews, something, something that drives everyone away."

At that moment the door opened and a new transport of prisoners was led in. These were again mostly Jews who talked all at the same time and so loudly that one of the old prisoners began to mimic them, "Yak-yak-yak." And the crowd broke out laughing.

That forced the Jews to lower their voices, but the prisoner with the black eye was still dissatisfied and complained that the Jews were whispering together, telling secrets, engaging in dark dealings. He vented his rage with an obscenity and a curse very popular among that crowd which society had labeled "hooligans."

"They beat them for a reason!" called out one of them, whose face could not be clearly seen through the smoke.

"Beating isn't enough," added another, whose speech indicated he was something of an intellectual. "They should expropriate their wealth and they themselves should be slaughtered like sheep."

Our hero rose to his feet. He was most eager to look into the face of that intellectual. But he soon forgot why he had stood up because he found himself gazing instead into a pair of familiar eyes, which immediately recognized him also.

the seventeenth chapter

AN ENCOUNTER

The eyes belonged to the lad from Pinsk with the pimply face and the white summer suit, one of the thirteen medalists who had signed the telegram to the minister.

"*Sholom aleichem!*" the lad from Pinsk greeted him in a Yiddish singsong, extending his hand to Rabinovitch. But he quickly caught himself and began talking in Russian. "Bah! I forgot you're that phenomenon who understands every language but his own mother tongue. So, does this really mean you don't have your residence permit, Mr. Rabinovitch?"

"Still making jokes?" Rabinovitch replied. "What are *you* doing here?"

"What am *I* doing here? Ha-ha, because of the same ancestral privileges as you . . . A night of police roundups. But I scoff at them, do you hear? What can they do to me? They'll stamp my documents in red and tell me to go home to Pinsk? So I'll go to Pinsk. Feh! May they have as many boils as I have the wherewithal to go! Do you know who I feel sorry for? For my sister, because they picked me up at her house and they can take away her residence permit. Her husband is a craftsman, a bookbinder. Well, and where did they pick *you* up?"

"Me? Why are you standing? Sit down," Rabinovitch said to him, and looked around for a place for his acquaintance to sit down but realized that he himself had been left without a seat. When the group of prisoners had found out he was called Rabinovitch and was conversing about roundups and residence permits, they lost all regard for him. The same man with the black eye who had just before so politely offered him his seat now made himself at home, stretching himself out full-length and placing his bare feet on the bench. Beside him a streetwalker smelling of whisky and iodoform had seated herself and the two were engaged in a discussion about Jews, of course, and how it was impossible to put up with them. Wherever you went and whatever you did, there they were underfoot!

"There's no getting rid of them!" the odoriferous streetwalker added as she sat admiring her elegant shoes, which peeped out from her tight dress.

"Real microbes!" the intellectual spoke up. "The nature of microbes is such that the more you try to get rid of them, the more they thrive and multiply. Read *Znamya*, and you'll know what you're dealing with."

The intellectual continued his lecture on the subject as the entire group listened intently, except for an occasional interruption to interject a piquant word or a pointed curse which would evoke guffaws. Involuntarily, our two candidate-medalists had to listen to this litany.

"What will you learn from these people, that a dog barks?" the lad from Pinsk said to Rabinovitch quietly, and drew him off to the side where he questioned him about how things were going for him, how life was among the dentists, and what had ever happened with their telegram to the minister?

"You'll have to ask Tumarkin about that," Rabinovitch answered, and then proceeded to ask the lad from Pinsk what he was doing and how he was managing. "Ech, please don't ask!" the lad from Pinsk replied with a wave of the hand and a bitter smile. "I manage, if you call that managing! They've dashed all my brightest hopes, lay waste all my golden castles! My mind is buzzing with all kinds of new medical discoveries. I wanted to study chemistry. I was always drawn to the chemistry laboratory. The way I see it, chemotherapy will revolutionize medicine entirely. Since Ehrlich discovered his new remedy for syphilis, I can't get it out of my head. I am positive, as sure as two and two are four, that if we continue working along the lines of Ehrlich's work, we will find the cures for cancer and tuberculosis and who knows how many other diseases and afflictions that destroy mankind. Long live our Ehrlich! Did you know he was one of us?"

"Who?" asked Rabinovitch, gazing at the young man's high, white forehead.

"Who? Professor Ehrlich. He's one of us," the lad from Pinsk answered him with some disappointment.

"What do you mean by 'one of us' "?

"It means he doesn't have a residence permit, like you, like me, like all of us, ha-ha! And if, God forbid, he were to come here and if they rounded him up, listen to me, he would be sitting exactly in the same place we are, listening to that one lecturing on microbes. He's lucky he's over there, living among the wretched Germans. As you can imagine, he also knows the taste of exile, what it's like to be a Jew."

"Is all that true?"

"Of course it's true. Really! Haven't you been reading the newspapers? Aren't you interested? Aren't you a Jew?"

"No!" said Rabinovitch but quickly caught himself. "I mean, yes. I am a Jew. But lately I haven't had time to read. What do they write about him?"

"What do they write!? The whole world is excited! At first they didn't know who this Ehrlich was, some unimportant little Frankfurt professor. Listen, now they know. First of all, that he's one of us, one of our faith, a friend; and second of all, the poor man had to beg to get into Berlin University, had to plead for a position, a chair, his own laboratory, and a few students. So, what did they tell him? No, with a capital N! Go to the devil!"

"Why?"

The lad from Pinsk laughed out loud. "Why! Because it's Saturday! You heard what that fellow over there was ranting about: microbes, parasites, exploiters, ha-ha-ha!"

*   *   *

The information the lad from Pinsk had recounted to him about Professor Ehrlich led him to reflect still more deeply on the question that gave him no rest. It still was a mystery: what could the source be of this burning hatred on the part of the whole world toward this small clump of people who call themselves Jews?

And he remembered that the very same words he had just heard about microbes, parasites, and exploiters he had heard countless times in his own home and had read about in *Novoye Vremya* and in other so-called right-wing newspapers. But he had never before stopped to think about it. Now that he was among Jews, he had to find out the truth. Now he had the opportunity to study the question at its source, at its very root, to observe, to explore, to investigate. And he was glad to have such an opportunity, so glad that he almost forgot where he was, and he hardly realized how quickly the night had passed.

In the morning it was impossible to tell from his happy, refreshed face what a difficult night he had endured and what humiliations and insults he had suffered. He was called to go upstairs.

He stepped into the office with renewed resolve, prepared to raise a scandal. But he was left speechless when he was greeted quite courteously and was informed that they had just learned by phone from the chief of police that his residence permit was in order and that he could leave.

"Shapiro!" flew through his mind, and soon after Shapiro, Betty's name came to mind. And he felt a strange warmth spread from his heart into every one of his limbs.

"Is this really getting serious?" he thought as he jumped into a droshky and ordered to be taken to the Jewish Street. "But where will this all lead? What will come of it? What will come of it?"

The question "What will come of it?" he had lately been asking himself frequently. Sooner or later, he would *have* to reveal his secret, who he was and what he was. How would he tell her? How would she take it? And what would happen afterward? Afterward?

Like a whirlwind these questions spun through his mind as the droshky sped that fresh autumn morning over the badly paved streets, creating a deafening noise of iron rims over the irregular cobblestones.

He leaped from the droshky, rang the doorbell, and saw Betty. All his questionings ceased. And though Betty did not throw her arms around his neck, she greeted him in a friendly enough fashion, even in a bit more than friendly fashion. Her eyes, however, told him much more than the warmest words. He arrived at the Shapiro home as one would arrive at one's own home, and he greeted the Shapiros as one would greet one's parents. Food was served, the mood was gay as each one recounted his experiences: the roomer, how he had spent the night in prison, and the landlord, David Shapiro, how, after eagerly awaiting the morning, he had immediately gone off to the dental school and from there to the chief of police.

"He went off immediately?" the landlady, Sara Shapiro, cut in, glancing at her daughter. "I told him, it must have been ten times, 'David, first you have to go to the dental school and *then* to the chief of police.'"

"What do you say to that?" David said to the daughter. "She says she told me . . ."

"You said, she said!" the daughter cut them both off and turned to the roomer. "I'd rather hear you tell us what happened in the morning when they called you upstairs."

The doorbell rang. It was Syomke, home from the *gymnasium,* his cheeks red from the cold, huffing and puffing from the stairs, his schoolbag on his back. He went straight to his teacher. Student and teacher embraced and kissed one another.

AFTER THE POLICE ROUNDUP

That one sleepless night our hero spent in jail, where he had endured much worry, aggravation, and heartache because of all that he had witnessed, did not leave his health unaffected and he became ill. He complained his head ached, he felt feverish, and he retired early to his room, where a large, warm comforter was thrown over his usual covers so that he would sweat.

The comforter belonged to the landlady and the sweating was also her idea. She made him drink his fill of dried raspberry tea, covered him well, and prepared a concoction of vinegar and alcohol so that when David came home from work, he would rub the lodger's body down and then he would really be able to sweat properly.

Sara Shapiro had wanted to send her daughter for the doctor immediately, but the roomer was adamant, saying it wasn't necessary.

"What do you care if the doctor sees you?"

"It isn't necessary."

"We know this doctor, a friendly person."

"It isn't necessary."

"He doesn't charge much, as much as you give him . . ."

"It isn't necessary."

"What a stubborn mule!" Sara Shapiro said to her daughter in Yiddish and then spoke to the roomer in Russian.

"Listen, I want to ask you something. Are all the Rabinovitches like you or are you the only one like this?"

"They're all like this."

"No better than the Shapiros?"

"Worse."

"If that's the case, you deserve to be congratulated."

To this the roomer made no reply. He simply glanced at the landlady's daughter, who was standing next to her mother beside his bed, and both of them broke into such gales of infectious laughter that the landlady also began to laugh as she rolled up her sleeves, preparing to return to the kitchen to put up a pot of soup made from a quarter of a chicken for the roomer.

"All right, you don't want a doctor. But you'll certainly eat some soup made from a quarter of a chicken, won't you? For God's sake, where do such people come from?" the landlady exclaimed again in Yiddish and vanished into the kitchen as her daughter and the roomer broke out into fresh laughter.

Since the previous day's events, they had been feeling particularly cheerful and would start laughing for no special reason. They were laughing because they were both young, full of energy, healthy and vital, and a strange power, of which they were not aware, was drawing them together since the moment they first set eyes on one another. They imagined they had always known each other, and though they hadn't put it into words, except for a few hints, they both realized full well what they were feeling toward one another.

The few "hints" were these: One time the roomer was sitting at the table working on young Syomke's lessons with him. The mother was in the kitchen and her daughter was seated at the opposite end of the table reading a book. Suddenly Betty got up, straightened her dress, smoothed her hair, and was about to leave. Rabinovitch picked up a notebook lying on the table and quickly scribbled a series of initials: W.A.Y.L.? . . . and pushed the notebook toward Betty. Betty looked at the letters and blushed. She understood that the initials meant "Why are you leaving?"

She then took the pen from him and wrote under his letters, also in initials: I.T.I.W.D.Y. . . . ("I thought I was disturbing you.")

Answering her, Rabinovitch quickly wrote the letters H.C.Y.D.M.? O.T.C.! . . . ("How can you disturb me? On the contrary! . . .")

To this Betty made no response. She merely sighed and sat down to read her book again.

Another time he had been sitting and working with Syomke. Betty was not seated at the table this time but was in her small room, dressing to go for a stroll. Her mother was seated nearby, getting enormous pleasure from observing her only son, who was studying so hard, and from the teacher, whom God had sent to them, directly to their house, and a real bargain at that. "May the One Above help him, give him long life . . . May he remain in the dental school a year or two; then let him go to the university and stay four more years. Meanwhile my Syomke will finish all eight grades with a medal . . . But then what? Here this *shlimazel* himself has a medal—and where has it gotten him? Never mind! By the time Syomke finishes *gymnasium,* the Messiah could come!"

At this point Betty emerged from her room all dressed up and turned to the roomer. "What time is it?" Rabinovitch, before looking at his watch, snatched up his notebook and wrote down a series of initials: W.A.Y.L.W.M.? ("Why are you leaving without me?")

Betty put on her gloves, glanced at the notebook and added a few initials: I.W.F.Y.D. ("I'll wait for you downstairs"), and left.

Rabinovitch was sitting on pins and needles. As if out of spite, his student was finding the lesson difficult. Syomke was distracted and had not been listening to what was being said to him. He gnawed at his pen and stared at the notebook, at the initials. The teacher noticed this, removed the notebook, erased the letters, and told his student to continue doing his lessons on his own for the time being. Later, when he returned, he would sit down with him again for another hour.

"Now that's what I call a tooter!" Sara Shapiro thought after the roomer had gone. "Not a roomer, but a treasure! A blessing from God!"

*   *   *

The chicken soup which Sara Shapiro had prepared for the lodger, although made from a mere quarter of a chicken, was, as Sara herself expressed it, "paradise itself, fit for royalty."

That was also the opinion of the roomer, who experienced paradise itself not so much from the taste of chicken soup as from the fact that Betty was sitting near him, and not merely sitting but holding the soup bowl and making sure he finished every drop, not leaving anything over. Ach! To be sick and to eat chicken soup served from Betty's own hands—for that he would gladly sign his life away! The only problem was that they were never left alone for so much as a minute. Either Sara Shapiro herself was constantly coming in with another reprimand, or she was sending Syomke in to join them, or else in barged the landlord—and that was the end of that!

David Shapiro rushed into the house, as usual, unexpectedly. "What's going on here? Is the roomer sick? What's the matter with him? Has he a fever? Why don't you call the doctor?"

"Look who's here, the express train!" Sara welcomed him in her usual way. "How do you know we didn't want to call the doctor?"

"You *wanted* to call? Why *didn't* you call?"

"Go ask *him!*"

David Shapiro disliked long explanations, wasted words. He knew that if a person was unwell you called the doctor. And without being overly concerned about any protestations, he threw on his overcoat and personally brought back the doctor, to the great regret of the roomer. At the very instant the doctor arrived, the roomer was sitting and leaning on an elbow, his thick hair disheveled, barely having had time to say just a few words to Betty as he squeezed her hand with his feverish hands, wanting desperately to bring that hand to his even more feverish lips.

Sara Shapiro was correct in describing the doctor as friendly, perhaps a bit too friendly. He called all of them by their first names, pinched Betty's cheek and asked her if she had a boyfriend, patted the landlady on the back, and lay Syomke over his knees and gave him a friendly spank. Then he turned serious, told David to keep quiet, and began to question the roomer, asking him more about who he was and from which Rabinovitches he came than about what ailed him. He merely felt his pulse, put his ear to his heart, and pounded him on the back. "Well, may every sick person be as sick as he is and may all Jews have such strong hearts and lungs!" the doctor said to the Shapiros. And to the patient he said in Yiddish, peering at him carefully through his thick spectacles, "Young man! Have you ever studied in a *kheder?*"

When the doctor found out from the Shapiros that their lodger understood not a word of Yiddish, he sprang from his chair, studied the patient, removed his thick eyeglasses, put them back on again, and, with a strange expression on his face, looked wordlessly from one to the next. Then he gave them directions for the patient's care and began to take leave of his patient, who had managed to push a coin in his hand. The doctor would under no circumstances accept payment and argued with the patient until in the end the coin remained in the doctor's hand.

"*Shut gorokhovoy!*—What a clown!" the roomer complimented the doctor behind his back, hating him for having interrupted his tête-à-tête with Betty.

"What are you saying?" Sara came to the doctor's defense. "A diamond of a doctor! He takes as much as you offer."

"What a strange roomer you have!" the doctor said to David Shapiro and to Betty, standing at the door and dropping the roomer's coin into his trouser pocket. "Strange. An odd person, a mystery! . . ."

the nineteenth chapter

A MYSTERY

Rabinovitch was a mystery to everyone he met: who he was, his behavior, his appearance, his ideas, and his mannerisms raised questions in people's minds because they seemed so contradictory. Think about it. How could it be—a Jew who didn't understand a word of Yiddish! His face, it would seem, was one of ours; it had a bit of Jewishness it it, yet one saw not a single Jewish expression on it. Not a hint of Jewish curiosity, Jewish ambition. Often naive as a small child, his questions would cause you to laugh out loud. And he often was shocked at things the smallest child took for granted.

For instance, when they had tried, with difficulty, to get through his head so simple and basic a fact as a residence permit, he would on no account believe that in the city where they lived were streets where Jews were permitted to live and other streets where they could not.

"How is it possible?" he had insisted, "Are we in ancient Rome? Or in Spain? Or living in the fifteenth century? Or . . ."

"What a fool!" David Shapiro cut him off. "Like talking to a kid! You say one thing and he says another! My dear man, how come we have right here in our city a street where on one side Jews are allowed to live, and on the other side, they can't, no matter what!"

Rabinovitch could not accept this until one day, on a Sabbath, the landlord deliberately took him for a walk on that very street where on one side, the left, it was legal for Jews to live, and on the other side, the right, it was forbidden.

Afterward David Shapiro had story after story to tell. He ridiculed the roomer right to his face.

"You wouldn't believe what a strange character this Rabinovitch is! Just imagine—he thought a Jew could not walk by on the right side of the street, couldn't even set foot there, ha-ha! We aren't, as you say, in Rome, Mr. Rabinovitch, or in Spain, and we don't live, as you say, in the fifteenth century!"

"What's the difference?" the roomer argued, and was amazed at the landlord who was speaking so glibly about such things, "What's the difference between the fifteenth century and now if I can live on one side of the street and I can't on the other?"

"There's a big difference!" cried David Shapiro, who could not abide anyone disagreeing with him. "A big difference! Take you, for example. Did your grand-father ever dream that his grandson would someday graduate from the *gymnasium* as a medalist, study to be a doctor, get a permit to live anywhere in the country, even in Petersburg and in Moscow, and perhaps be selected as a repre-sentative to the Parliament to participate in enacting laws?"

"God help us with those laws!" the landlady tried to get a word in, only to be put down by her husband, in Yiddish.

"Who asked you to butt in while people are talking?"

"People? And Mama isn't a person?" Betty came to her mother's defense. But it did no good. When David Shapiro began talking, he was oblivious to every-one; he went on.

"Or, for example, take my Syomke. Can I predict what this little squirrel will grow up to be some day? Maybe a professor of mathematics or a *gymnasium* teacher? And maybe even a finance minister? Syomke! Come over here and tell us what you would like? . . ."

"A bicycle!" cried Syomke, who until then was striding across the room recit-ing lines from Pushkin by memory, rolling his *r*'s as he chanted and waved his arm to the beat:

> Kak nyne sbikhayetsya veshchii oleg
>   Otomstit nekhazumnym khazakham . . .
> As Oleg the Wise was getting ready
>   To wreak vengeance on the foolish Khazars . . .

Another time the roomer and the landlord became embroiled in a heated discussion about Jewish matters known only among Jews. As an example, we'll take *kahal*—the community of Jews.

Rabinovitch knew beforehand that he would never come out ahead of his landlord. And he was exactly right. Shapiro flared up, gesticulated, translated the word *kahal* into Russian as *obshchestvo*—community—and if there was once a *kahal*, today it no longer existed.

"Where can you find any trace of true *kahal* today?"

Rabinovitch heard him out and asked him a new question, more to tease him than out of curiosity; the roomer enjoyed seeing the landlord work himself up.

"So what's this we read in the papers about a worldwide *kagal*?"

"What are you talking about, *kagal-shmagal*? Where did you read that?"

"Everywhere . . . All right, let's say I read it in *Novoye Vremya* . . ."

When Shapiro heard that name, he grabbed his head and tore around the room.

"What? You're citing me evidence from *Novoye Vremya*? That's good. Very nice. Did you hear that? Don't even *mention Novoye Vremya* to me, do you hear, don't even *mention* it!"

"Why?"

Shapiro stopped dead in his tracks.

"Why—he says! My dear fellow, who doesn't know that *Novoye Vremya* is a business, a big business, a business dealing in Jews? Now Jews are in the news, so they're running a series on Jews and they're all preoccupied with Jews! Tomorrow the Poles will be in style and they'll take after the Poles. Jews, Poles, Gypsies— all they are is stuff for articles. Now *we* happen to be the hot news item of the season."

"Nevertheless!" Rabinovitch tried to contradict him. "You can't deny altogether that you don't have any special, well, let's say, interests . . ."

Now Shapiro really became angry at the roomer and assailed him furiously.

"First, tell me, sir, who is this '*you*' you're talking about? What's this '*you*'? And who are *you* then? Aren't *you* a Jew too, just like me, just like all of us?"

Rabinovitch realized he had slipped and tried to extricate himself, but Shapiro wouldn't allow it. Shapiro hated to let anyone else have the floor.

He loved to do the all the talking himself. On he went.

"A Jew talking about 'special interests'! What kind of special interests do we have except making a living, residence permits, and the children in *gymnasium*? How's that for special interests!"

The landlord went on and on, citing evidence supporting what an unfortunate people we were; it was each one for himself, there were no shared interests, not a drop of unity among Jews!

The roomer looked at him wonderingly. Can this really be true? And where was that Jewish clannishness he had read so much about in those newspapers? And what about how close a community Jews had and what about all those Jewish organizations? Was it all just a dream? Was it really a made-up story with the aim of creating hatred of one people against another?

"Will there ever be an end to this, or not?" the landlady intruded, and called everyone to the table to eat.

It was also a mystery to the Shapiros why the roomer never wanted to talk about his home, his parents, or his family. He never spoke to anyone about his childhood or early years. Nor did they know where he went every day, who his friends were, or how he was able to support himself. At first, they assumed he was living on the money he made tutoring students, but that proved not to be the case. Except for teaching the Shapiro children, he had no other students.

Moreover, David Shapiro had recounted that he could swear he once saw the roomer leaving a branch office of the Moscow Commercial Bank. What does a student and a medalist who is studying dentistry have to do with a bank?

"So why didn't you ask him?" Sara came back at him.

"How do you know I *didn't* ask him?"

"So what did he say?"

"That he had to go there."

"Is that all?"

"What else did you want?"

"Couldn't you ask him *why* he had to go there?"

"I'll leave that for *you* to ask."

"Of course I'll ask him. Why not?"

"Why must you ask him? What's this habit of prying into other people's business?" interrupted the daughter. "What business is it of ours to know other people's affairs? I never . . ."

No one, however, wanted to solve this mystery more than Betty herself, as it touched her more closely than the others, especially since that night after the police roundup when with hints and half-spoken words he had given her to understand that she meant everything to him and he was prepared to reveal to her his innermost secret! . . .

If not for the doctor, whose arrival had interrupted them, he would have told her his secret then and there. But after the doctor's departure, his temperature had risen and he had fallen asleep, tossing and talking feverishly the rest of the night. David Shapiro, who had gotten up several times during the night to check on him, had related that the roomer had been muttering strange words all night, not making any sense at all. But Shapiro would under no circumstances reveal the exact words he had heard no matter how much they begged him.

"Do you really expect me to tell you what a sick person babbles when he is running a fever! So long as it turned out all right and now he's well and he has a residence permit in his pocket. What else matters?"

Rabinovitch was thankful that he hadn't said anything more to Betty, to whom he had almost blurted out the truth about his real identity . . .

the twentieth chapter

SARA SHAPIRO'S DISCOVERY

The roomer was to remain a mystery for a long time. But the secret of where he was getting his money was quickly revealed to the Shapiros, thanks to the landlady, Sara Shapiro, who afterward had the right to boast to her husband and daughter.

"So? What did I tell you?"

It happened some time after the police raid when the three of them were sitting together just before supper—the roomer, the landlady, and her daughter. It was right in the middle of winter.

The landlord was at work, Syomke at the *gymnasium*. Betty was sitting at the table over a book, as usual, and her mother was knitting a pair of warm socks for Syomke. The roomer had just arrived from dental school and was pretending to warm himself at the stove, but in truth he wanted to sit and gaze at Betty.

The roomer told them that Chaliapin was singing at the theater and if she, Betty, wanted to hear Chaliapin, she could hear him. He had been promised two tickets . . .

The daughter asked her mother with her eyes whether she might go with him to hear Chaliapin. The mother hesitated. She wasn't so much fearing anything bad as wondering how it would look for her daughter to be going to the theater with a student. What would people say? Another thing kept bothering her: where did he get the money, this *shlimazel*?

She had long had it in mind to talk to him about money matters, and had actually attempted to bring it up several times. But each time he had managed to put her off with a clever word or by making a joke, and she still didn't know where he was getting his money.

Now the opportune moment had arrived.

"You want to take my daughter to the theater?" she said to the roomer, averting her eyes. "I hear that tickets are very expensive. This Chaliapin is very popular . . ."

"*Pus-tya-ki*—Ri-di-cu-lous!" the roomer drew out the syllables. "Who is telling you such nonsense?"

"Why is that nonsense!" Sara Shapiro said. "Money doesn't seem important to you. I suppose someone is sending you a monthly allowance?"

"Well, yes, an allowance," the roomer replied.

"Where from? I suppose from home?"

"Well, yes, from home."

"How much are they sending you?"

Betty could stand it no longer and interjected, "What are you, Mama, a court investigator?"

"What did I say?" the mother defended herself. "I just wanted to know where he was getting his money from."

"What does it matter to you? He steals it—" the daughter said, and she and the mother started to laugh, as did the roomer because he was beginning to understand a little Yiddish, not much, but a few words he heard frequently in the Shapiro household. And in order to placate the landlady, who was insisting on knowing where he was getting money, he made up a story about having a rich aunt and told her this on the condition that she tell no one else.

Sara Shapiro swallowed it whole and said to him, "A widow or a divorcee?"

The roomer didn't hesitate a moment and answered, "A widow."

"Has no children?"

"No children."

"Didn't have any, or they died?"

"Died."

"Every one of them?"

"Every last one of them."

Sara Shapiro sighed, "Bless her soul! Why didn't she remarry?"

"For God's sake!" the daughter again broke in, barely able to sit still. "What kind of interrogation is this?"

"Quiet! Why does it bother you? Is it costing him anything to tell me? Will it hurt him?" Sara Shapiro said sharply to her daughter and then turned her attention to the roomer, all the while knitting away at Syomke's sock.

"What else did I want to ask you? Ah, yes. How is this aunt related to you? Is she your mother's sister, or was her husband your father's brother?"

"She is my mother's sister."

"Is that so? Her sister? An older or a younger one?"

"An older one, I mean, a younger one, no, actually older . . ."

Sara Shapiro looked first at the roomer and then at Betty, who couldn't take another minute of this. She got up, took her book, and went to her room. This bothered Sara not at all, and she resumed her cross-examination, like a practiced investigator.

"Was he a rich man?"

"Who?"

Sara Shapiro stared at the roomer.

"Whom are we talking about? About your uncle, no? I'm asking if he was a rich man."

"A rich man."

"A very rich man?"

"A very rich man."

"Give me an idea, what do you call a very rich man?"

The roomer didn't know what to answer her. The landlady helped him out by explaining.

"Jewish wealth . . . when you come right down to it—doesn't amount to much! We have a saying: It doesn't cost anything to exaggerate about other people's wealth or one's own children . . . I mean, how much was he worth?"

"Who?"

"Again who!"

Sara Shapiro glared at him and he caught himself. "Ah, how much my uncle was worth? That I don't know."

"You don't know! Who then should know? I'm not asking you exactly to the penny. I just wanted to ask how much your uncle had before he died?"

The roomer thought a while.

"I guess about a million."

The sock and knitting needles fell from Sara's hands.

"How much did you say? A million? A whole million?"

"Almost a million—more or less . . ."

Sara Shapiro moved a little closer to her roomer and began scratching behind her ear with a knitting needle she had just retrieved.

"Please answer this question I'm going to ask you. Since the other children have all died, as you say, and there aren't any other heirs besides yourself, isn't it better that she didn't remarry?"

"As a matter of fact, why not?"

The landlady lowered her head and looked at the roomer quizzically. "Tell me something, please, are you acting stupid on purpose or are you really so dumb?"

The roomer gazed at her with laughing eyes. "What's the matter?"

"What's the matter, he asks! What do you mean, what's the matter? If that's so, in a hundred and twenty years it will all be yours!"

"In a hundred and twenty years? Oho!" the roomer cried out amazed, unaware of that phrase's meaning to Jews, and the landlady laughed so hard that Betty came running from her room.

"What do you say to our roomer, Betty? He's a real Gentile! I tell him that in a hundred and twenty years he'll inherit his aunt's money and he doesn't understand what a hundred and twenty years means, ha-ha-ha! . . . This belongs on the stage! Just like my Aunt Riva from Proskurov, who willed a cow to her two daughters, specifying that in a hundred and twenty years they should sell the cow and divide the money between them. They went to court and at the trial the wise judge ruled that they couldn't sell the cow because the will specified in a hundred and twenty years, and legally that meant exactly that, ha-ha! Talk about a *goyisher kop!*"

Betty had to take it upon herself to explain to the roomer not only the story about Aunt Riva's will but what a hundred and twenty years meant, and all three had a good laugh. Soon the landlord, David Shapiro, came home for supper. As usual, he was sullen and restless.

"What's all this laughing about again!" he said to no one in particular.

"It belongs in the theater! It's worth printing in the newspapers!" Sara exclaimed to her husband, and related to him the whole story about the hundred and twenty years that the roomer hadn't understood, and at the same time she wanted him to know where the roomer was getting money from and about the inheritance which was awaiting him.

"A million! Do you understand? A whole million! And maybe even more than a million!" Sara Shapiro concluded, her eyes sparkling and her cheeks flushed as she seemed to grow younger. Even her voice changed.

"I don't know about that! Jewish millions, what are they worth?" David cut her off, like a person who wanted to show he was more knowledgeable when it came to money than anyone else, and, rolling up his sleeves, he went off to wash up before eating.

Sara Shapiro looked as if someone had poured cold water over her. She felt like strangling her husband or at least making a scene, as he well deserved, but her eyes met her daughter's sharp glance warning her to keep quiet. She bit her lip, postponed the scene for another time, and began serving supper.

THE HAPPY MOTHER

Before David had returned home and while Betty was still in her room dressing for the theater, Sara Shapiro stepped into the lodger's room on the pretense she needed to check if the little stove was heating adequately. But she was really there to resume her conversation about the aunt, the millionairess. She even knew her name—she was called Leah (wouldn't you know that *shlimazel* pronounced it "Leeahh," not "Layeh," as we do)—and that his uncle was called Abram Abramitch.

Sara stared at the roomer. "How is that possible? How can a Jew have a father called Abram and the son also be called Abram? That's only possible among Gentiles, where the father can be Ivan and the son Ivan . . . Ivan Ivanovitch . . ."

Rabinovitch looked at Madam Shapiro sensing that he was being accused of something when he had no idea what sin he had committed. But luckily Sara herself came to his rescue, saying, "Unless your uncle happened to be born after his father died?"

Rabinovitch grabbed hold of this like a drowning person.

"That's true, you're absolutely right. My uncle died before his father was born—I mean his father was born before my uncle died. Tphoo! What a tangle!" And both broke out laughing.

"May your enemies get tangled up for you," Sara said to him but wouldn't let him off the hook.

"What exactly, was your uncle?" Sara asked, no longer looking at him but at the ceiling, and received an answer from the roomer.

"What was he? He was a person."

"I know that," Sara said, still staring at the ceiling. "I know he was a person, not an animal. I mean, what did he deal in?"

Rabinovitch, before he was Rabinovitch and was still Popov, had always heard that Jews dealt in old rags, so he decided to say, "What did he deal in? He dealt in odds and ends."

Sara clapped her hands together in surprise and turned her eyes toward the roomer.

"What are you talking about? Odds and ends? How do you become a millionaire from odds and ends? *Vey iz mir!*"

The roomer realized that the more he said, the worse it got; he was sinking into a morass. He hastened to correct himself and to explain.

Before Rabinovitch was Rabinovitch, but Popov, he had heard that Jews became rich by being economical, by saving their kopeks. He used this explanation and she seemed to accept it because she was now wringing her hands, saying to the roomer, "What a story! What a story! Then he must have lived to be as old as Methuselah. He had to be a very old man and she must have been his second wife?"

"You guessed right."

"Of course I guessed," Sara Shapiro said. "I always guess right, because I use my head. I may not be that old, but I'm pretty wise. My husband is, as you yourself can see, a bit hasty, he does everything in a hurry. And most of all, he doesn't believe good things about other people. You heard what he said, 'Jewish millions.' He thinks that if he doesn't have anything, neither does anyone else. Even Rothschild. Don't listen to what he tells you! And Betty, what does she know about such matters, she's a mere child? I'm smarter than all of them put together. That's why you should listen to what I'm going to tell you. It's none of my business, but if you ask *me*, you should be writing more often to your aunt. After all, an old widow and all alone. When do you figure on seeing her?"

Rabinovitch thought it over.

"I figure . . . if not Christmas, then Easter . . ."

"What kind of Christmas do Jews have? And what kind of talk is this about Easter? I've noticed many times how all our holidays have Gentile names for you. *Chanukah* you call Christmas, *Passover*—Easter. It doesn't matter to me, but many times, I've wanted to call it to your attention, to tell you it isn't right, it simply doesn't look good for people. Everyone who sees you and speaks a few words to you can't believe you're a Jew . . . Wait! Take our doctor, for example. Just the other day he told me again that if your name weren't Rabinovitch he would never in this world say you were Jewish . . ."

"Did he really say that?" Rabinovitch said with an embarrassed laugh.

"Did he really say that? What do you think? I'm making it up? And another thing. You have a bad habit: when you want to say something about Jews, you don't say 'by us,' but 'by them.' Really an unpleasant habit. It's none of my business, but you really should try to get rid of it. I'm a good friend, that's why I'm telling you this . . . Here's Betty!" She turned toward her daughter, who was standing in the doorway all dressed up and wearing a long, cowled, hooded fur cape which covered all but her lovely, clear eyes, her thick eyebrows, and the tip of her nose. "I was just saying to our roomer that he should be sure not to let you go from the theater straight outside when you're all perspired. You should cool off first. Do you hear what I'm telling you? I beg you, Rabinovitch, in the name of God, take good care of her, she shouldn't catch cold, God forbid, your Chaliapin shouldn't cost us."

"Rest assured, *Matushka*, you can rely on me!" she was comforted by the happiest of all roomers as, together with Betty, he ran down the steps, whistled to hail a sleigh in the Moscow style, "Eh, Vanka!" . . . Three Vankas rushed up with a whoop and a clattering of wheels. They seated themselves in the sleigh; he covered her with the warm fur blanket and put his arm carefully, slowly around her shoulder as one would protect a fragile object or a statue that might fall and shatter. He ordered Vanka to fly like the wind! Vanka obeyed, whipped his horse, and the sleigh shot forward like an arrow from a bow.

The snow crackled on both sides, spraying their faces with icy drops. The stars in the clear, frigid, winter sky shimmered, outshining the widely spaced, dim street lamps. And Sara Shapiro stood at the window, her nose pressed against the pane, and watched as the sleigh carried them away, her heart pounding, though she could not tell why. Was it out of great happiness? Her eyes saw what only a mother, a happy mother, can see, and her heart felt what only a mother's, a happy mother's, heart can feel, and she thought, "Who knows? Maybe it's fated, it was meant to be, maybe it's a match?" And the happy mother followed them, in her mind, right to the theater. And, in her mind, she walked into the theater with them, sat in the seat next to them, followed their every step, listened to their half-spoken words, saw them squeezing one another's hands, saw them gazing into one another's eyes. Ah, she knew what those gazes signified. She was an expert on those half-spoken words. Had it been so long since she herself was a young girl and her David a young man? . . .

And Sara Shapiro remembered that happy time, wasn't it just yesterday, when her David, a bright young man, mature, knowledgeable, with all fine qualities, was dogging her every footstep, writing her passionate love letters, swearing he would take his life if they wouldn't let him marry her! And Sara's father, a *Chassidic* Jew, permeated with his rabbi's religious zeal, wanted neither to see nor hear of this David Shapiro because he was a working man, even though he had a wealthy father who would pay any amount in order to have Sara as a daughter-in-law! It had gotten to the point where the young couple had decided that David would marry Sara in front of only the two necessary witnesses or move away altogether from their small town to a large city and marry there . . .

Ach! It seemed it was just yesterday, this dream, and there she was now, standing at the window, watching her daughter speeding through the snow on a sleigh with a strange young man, perhaps her intended!

And she begged God, this happy mother, that if this were indeed her intended, he should be what she, Sara, hoped he would be. He seemed to be a fine young man. The One Above had already provided him with an inheritance, may it happen to all Jewish children. Let's hope he really was what he appeared to be. After all, her Betty deserved both a fine bridegroom and a million. A million?! It was so easy to say a million! Just a word—million! A whole million! Obviously, it wouldn't be too terrible to have a daughter who was a millionairess . . .

"Where is Betty? Where's the roomer? What a burning frost out there!" David Shapiro entered, as always, without ringing, frozen to the bone, with bits of ice hanging from his moustache. When he discovered from his wife that they were at the theater hearing Chaliapin, David suddenly went wild.

"What is this going to the theater alone all of a sudden?"

"*Mazel tov*, look who's here!" his wife said indignantly. "I told you that they had tickets for Chaliapin and that they were going to the theater, so why are you huffing and puffing away like an express train?"

"What's so great about Chaliapin!" David continued to rage and pace about the room, warming his frozen, numb feet. "No, I never would have allowed them to go to the theater alone. Never! On no account! Who ever heard of going to the theater alone? No. I'm getting dressed and going straight there. Just let me warm up a little . . . Chaliapin!! You can keep your Chaliapin!" . . .

"All right? Are you finished?" Sara said, walking over to him, and standing close to him, she looked into his eyes and spoke to him in a new gentle tone.

"David!"

And not another word . . . David immediately stopped raging and pacing about the room and said plaintively to his wife, "But I don't know who he is or what he is . . ."

"David, what are you saying? What more do you need to know? A brilliant young man, a gold medal, a wealthy aunt worth almost a million, and he is her only heir . . ."

"Good. But he himself, who is he? What is his father? I don't know a thing about him!"

"David! And what if my father *did* know who your father was?"

"You're bringing *that* up? How can you compare the two? You call that a logical comparison?"

"*Papasha!*" You owe me a twenty!" Syomke announced, running in from the small bedroom, with a chewed pen and black, ink-stained fingers. The father asked to be shown on paper why he deserved twenty kopeks as Sara carried in a steaming samovar, which was bubbling merrily, spreading a soft warmth through the room; soon the aroma of fragrant tea could be smelled.

the twenty-second chapter

AT THE THEATER

When they arrived at the theater, they first went to the cloak-room to remove their wraps. Betty threw off her white, full-length fur cape, revealing a simple black cashmere dress trimmed with black beads, which sparkled on her beautifully shaped figure. Her simply coiffed hair, which encircled her clear, smooth face, so enhanced her charm that people in the theater immediately singled her out from among the other beauties that evening, and many eyes gazed at her with admiration. Many lorgnettes and binoculars focused on where this young couple had sat down. The couple was aware of this attention and both appreciated that the lorgnettes and the binoculars were all trained on them—a pretty girl and her young escort, who could either be her brother or her fiance or simply an acquaintance. Bathed in this attention, Betty's radiant cheeks with their characteristically charming dimples deepened in color, becoming like ripe peaches, rendering her even more exciting and attracting even more the eye of the public which had, because of Chaliapin, packed the loges and the galleries and the orchestra from top to bottom so that not even a single seat was unoccupied.

Only when the curtain rose did the lorgnettes and binoculars move away from the newly arrived Betty and all eyes turn to the stage, awaiting the appearance of the world-renowned opera singer, the beloved idol whose name had filled the theater that evening.

Betty, too, had come to the theater on account of the great Chaliapin, and was soon deeply engrossed, along with the entire audience, in what was about to happen on the stage. Betty had not come merely for appearance's sake, as had many of those for whom it was fashionable to attend the theater, but had wanted with all her heart and soul to hear the famous singer and performer, Chaliapin.

But if Betty's heart and soul were up on the stage, her escort's were right there in the orchestra seat, next to her, close to Betty, on whose account he had arranged the Chaliapin evening. For him, the singer was far from his thoughts. He had brought Betty there for the sole purpose of being alone with her in order to reveal to her at least the secret he had planned to tell her that morning after the police roundup. And if there had been any delay in doing so, it had only been because he himself had not yet been ready. He had not been entirely sure how serious his feelings were for her. But lately he had become utterly convinced that he could not live without her and that this whole comedy, this hoax in which he had changed identities with his friend, was no more than an act of fate, predestined in order for him to have met this girl, to fall desperately in love with her to the very death, and to bind himself to her forever! . . .

True, he knew full well there loomed ahead of him many obstacles. He knew full well what a battle he should have to wage at home with his unpredictable father and even more so with his deeply Russian family, which would surely consider it beneath their dignity that he, Grigori Popov, would marry a Jewish girl! He was well aware of all of this, had considered it many times, had examined it from every angle a thousand times, and had concluded there was nothing to be afraid of, he would overcome everything. His father would forgive him. The family would forget. He wasn't the first, he wouldn't be the last. Wasn't there a prominent minister in our country whose wife was of Jewish ancestry?

But one difficulty remained: where to begin? Should he first reveal who he was, or should he begin by asking her what she would do if she were to fall in love with a Christian and would have to change her religion because of that?

On another occasion he had posed just such a question to her and she had answered him quite seriously that it was no problem as it could never happen.

"Why couldn't it ever happen?" he pressed her, becoming a bit uneasy.

"Because. It could never happen," she had answered, "that a Christian could really fall seriously in love with a Jew given the present mood in our country and the current nationalist friction in the world in general."

Was that all? Was the implication, then, that it all depended on how deeply the Christian had fallen in love? Thank God if that were the case, because how much more deeply in love could one be than he was in love with Betty?

And that Betty was in love with him—of that he was absolutely sure. The smallest child could see it. Even her mother knew it, and if her mother knew it, then so did her father, and it didn't appear they had any objections. But then again, they had no idea who he was or what his background was. But that was minor. Let them but find out who his father was!

And he began to imagine various scenes, one livelier than the next. One was how David Shapiro would be astonished when he heard the name and rank of his father, with his high ranking title, *Yevo Prevoskhoditelstvo*—His Excellency— and possibly in time he would become even higher in rank, *Yevo Vysoko-Prevoskhoditelstvo*—His Exalted Excellency—ha-ha-ha! And Sarah? Ah! What would Sara Shapiro say when she found out that, in addition to rank and titles, his father owned land and forests in T____province that were worth much more than a million, these millions which so impressed her, ha-ha-ha!

He took it for granted that Betty would be delighted to discover who the man was that her heart had chosen! . . .

And he was already picturing how her face would glow with pride and how her eyes would shine with happiness. Then he pictured how they would travel to his home in T____province, how he would bring her before his father, what his father would say to him, and what he would say to his father. And though his father was unpredictable, nevertheless he was really a goodhearted, gentle person; all he would have to do was look at his chosen one and speak two words to her and he would immediately forgive her origins because no one in the world had Betty's bearing. She could truly hold her own, as her mother, Sara Shapiro, had said, "in the Czar's palace."

And he turned his eyes upon his chosen one sitting next to him at the theater. She had not an inkling of the joys that awaited her . . .

The first act had ended and our happy couple rose from their seats and went directly, along with the others, to the vestibule for an intermission stroll. There he would be able to speak freely with her. There he would finally disclose the holy secret he had been carrying in his heart, the great hoax, how, for a year's time, he had from a Popov been transformed into a Rabinovitch, why this had been done and what had come of it. No more. Now was the time to do it.

the twenty-third chapter

TWO ENCOUNTERS

No sooner had our young couple emerged from the orchestra and stepped into the vestibule, where the crowd was milling about, than they immediately noticed a tall figure with broad shoulders, reddish eyes, and thick, sensuous lips. The man was standing with his arm clasped behind him, taking them in with his eyes.

They both immediately recognized him as the officer of that night raid who had arrested Rabinovitch. At that time he had been dressed in his police officer's uniform, and although he was now wearing the long, black coat of a civilian, he remained standing in one spot, as if on guard duty, while casting his gaze right and left over the crowd passing by.

Rabinovitch and Betty were greeted with a particularly penetrating look from those reddish eyes. Betty keenly felt that look, which passed through her like an electric current.

"Is that him?" she asked her escort, not quite sure why her heart was suddenly pounding as she instinctively grasped the hand he had offered her.

"What if it is?" Rabinovitch answered her, wishing to calm her fears while in his own heart he cursed this creature. He was convinced this meeting did not bode well.

And sure enough, as soon as they stepped into the resplendent grand foyer, where it was possible to find a place to sit close together and discuss things quietly and intimately, God blessed them with another encounter—this time with an elegantly appareled student, sporting a new uniform moments from the tailor's needle: gold buttons, a tight blue collar, a gilt sword at his side, snow-white gloves, his chest thrust forward like an officer on parade. In a word, it was one of those extravagant student-fops who were dubbed the "White Satin Linings."

"Hello, classmate!" he called out to Rabinovitch, and a sugary-sweet smile appeared on the student's red face with the little yellow pointed beard which peeked out from his tight blue collar.

It was not at Rabinovitch the student was smiling, but at the lovely woman with the pert nose who was holding onto the arm of his "classmate."

"Don't you recognize me, hee?"

Hearing that "hee," Rabinovitch now recognized who this was.

"Oh? Lapidus?" he drew out the words, offering his hand, thinking, "What evil wind brought *you* here? May he break his neck, this . . ."

Rabinovitch had absolutely no use for Lapidus, although at the same time he felt sorry for him. He turned up too often, this blond young fellow, filling his ear with protestations about how hard it was to be a Jew—how it wasn't fair, it wasn't convenient, it wasn't smart, and it wasn't logical . . . Why? To what end? To whom do we need to prove something? Who will reward us with a pinch on the cheek?

"I know, believe me, I know, why you don't give up your Jewishness, hee . . . You don't do it out of cowardice, you're afraid of your father or your mother—" so Lapidus had tried to persuade his friend Rabinovitch, all the while grasping him by the lapel.

"You are mistaken," Rabinovitch had tried to tell him, but he wouldn't let go of his lapel and burst out laughing, greatly irking Rabinovitch.

"You say I'm mistaken, hee? I never make a mistake. If your father weren't a manufacturer . . ."

"My father isn't a manufacturer," Rabinovitch had said, trying to extricate himself from the conversation.

"If he's not a manufacturer, then he's a banker . . . If your father weren't a banker, and if you weren't going to inherit his fortune, may he live to a hundred and twenty, as we say in Yiddish, hee-hee, and if you had a poor mother and a sister as I do, you would do the same thing I plan to do, what many other bright young men are doing." Suddenly Lapidus stopped talking and changed his tone. "How about making a bet with me?"

"On what?"

"That a year from now you will be a Christian . . . How much do you want to bet, hee? You're not saying anything? Aha! Hee-hee-hee! . . ."

And so Rabinovitch had relented and begun to laugh, which Lapidus had taken as acceptance. After that time, whenever they met, Lapidus would ask, "Well?" But at that moment Rabinovitch had no desire for Lapidus to remind him of their bet and he was fervently hoping that this boor would leave. But one can't be rude and he felt he had to introduce Betty. Lapidus was gazing at her much too avidly. Quite courteously Rabinovitch introduced him to Betty, and the constantly smiling Lapidus could not keep his eyes off her, and now that he had been introduced to this beauty, he refused to leave their side. There was no use trying; the three of them had to stroll together through the foyer—Betty in the middle, Rabinovitch and Lapidus on either side.

There was no curse Rabinovitch did not wish upon this nuisance, this plague of a "White Satin Lining," Lapidus. Wasted, he thought, a whole intermission. He would not have the opportunity to have a tête-à-tête with Betty about what was in his heart, but what could be done? He had to put on a friendly smile and join in the conversation as well. And what was he talking about, this fop, may the devil take him? He was prattling on with such foolishness, such empty banalities, boring nonsense, enough to make one ill! Look at him, all dandied up, dressed as for his own funeral, and thinks he is the cock of the walk!

Rabinovitch was eager to ask him how it had been possible for him to afford a student uniform. But his heart wouldn't let him utter the words. He remembered their conversation and unwillingly felt a pang of sympathy for this poor, blonde young man who had the burden of supporting a poor mother and sister. Contemplating his happy, shining face, with its little yellow goatee, and the respectable-looking figure he cut, Rabinovitch forgave him for usurping an entire intermission. "What the devil, the poor fellow, let someone else give him a difficult time, not me," Rabinovitch said to himself, appreciating what a dear price this poor *schlimazel* had had to pay for his fine, blue student uniform with the white satin lining, how high the cost for donning this uniform. He was reluctant to remark on this delicate matter, afraid to hurt him where he was perhaps vulnerable. But Lapidus himself opened the wound. He suddenly stopped, looked carefully at the way Rabinovitch was dressed, not as a student, and said to him, "So, my dear classmate, what's going to happen now, hee? I already know. For that you have to thank your Tumarkin, who thinks he is doing you a great favor; in the end he's causing you, and others like you, a lot of harm. Really, I have a great deal of pity on you."

Rabinovitch broke out laughing. "I'm very grateful to you for your pity."

Lapidus was chagrined at Rabinovitch's laughter and said to him, without allowing his gaze to leave the lovely girl, "It's easy for you to laugh! What do you care if you're a student or not? Your father is a banker or a manufacturer, but a bourgeois in any case, who can support you year after year. But try being in my place and having to support an old mother and a poor sister whose lives depend on you so that your fate is their fate, your pain their pain! In short, how can you possibly know what I'm feeling?"

Betty broke in, "How do you know that Rabinovitch can't feel what you do? And who told you his father is a banker or that he doesn't have an old mother and a poor sister exactly like you?"

Lapidus straightened his back, raised his shoulders, and said to Betty, "Who told me? No one! But one knows. Oh! One knows! Who doesn't know the Rabinovitches? A famous firm! . . . But that isn't important. Just tell me this: what would he do, yes, this Mr. Rabinovitch, if he were in my shoes, with no medal, without a banker for a father, with a permit to stay here for no more than twenty-four hours, with a sick mother and a poor sister? Do you have any idea what I'm talking about?"

"Then according to you, any Jew who has an old mother and a poor sister— and which Jew doesn't have an old mother or a poor sister?—should, on account of them, do what you have done, as I understand it?"

"Absolutely!" Lapidus answered her with a little laugh, proudly thrusting out his chest, showing off the uniform on which the tailor had expended so much effort.

Betty bestowed on him a radiant glance with her lovely, clear eyes and, smiling faintly, said softly. "You are to be envied. How easily you have solved such a painful dilemma, over which hundreds of generations have allowed themselves to be trodden up, driven out, burned, and tortured! I daresay, you are to be envied."

A forced smile appeared on Lapidus's lips. He grinned broadly, displaying his white teeth.

If this woman weren't so excitingly beautiful, her eyes so lovely and clear, her voice so musical, her figure so classic, her entire appearance so sympathetic, and her whole being crying out, "Love me!" our talkative Lapidus would have found a way to respond to her irony. But as Betty had entirely dumbfounded him, he turned to her with a smile.

"Don't be offended, Miss . . . Miss . . ."

"Miss Shapiro," Rabinovitch reminded him.

"Pardon! Don't be offended, Miss Shapiro, at what I will ask you. It may seem to you beside the point, but it does pertain to what you just touched on. You say a hundred generations were driven out, burned, and tortured. Those are all fine stories of old. That's what we call 'history,' to which we doff our hats. Very fine.

But what would you say to this fact? Not to history, no—but to life itself, an event which actually happened right here not too long ago, right here, in our city? Let me tell you about it. It's an intriguing story, I daresay, and a tragic one . . . If I were a writer, I would surely write it up for a newspaper, so that people would know about it. Never mind, you would do well to hear it."

And Lapidus, pleased with himself and savoring his raconteurship and the fact that he had the ear of so pretty a girl, began to recount his "intriguing" story in a tone which conveyed that he was a man very taken with himself.

"Now then, dear lady," Lapidus began, clearly directing his words to Betty rather than to Rabinovitch. "Now then, dear lady, this story is a true story which, I would say, is 'one of many' because these are daily occurrences. Such stories occur often in recent times, very often.

"To get to the point, I have a good acquaintance, a friend, a good friend, his name isn't important—and my good friend has a sister. A young girl. Actually a fine girl. Notice I'm not saying she is outstanding, not a beauty. Beauties are very rare . . ."

These words, accompanied by a lingering glance at Betty, were meant by Lapidus to convey to her that *she* was one of those rare beauties. Betty let this pass, but Rabinovitch had a strong urge to grab this impertinent Lapidus either by the point of his little blond beard or by the lapels of his admirable blue uniform, white satin lining and all, and say to him, "Look here, get on with it!" but he held himself back and with a slight smile said to him, "So, you have a good friend, and your friend has a sister. Then what?"

Lapidus took Rabinovitch's remarks to imply he was resentful that he, Lapidus, was such a fine raconteur and so, reserving his gaze for Betty alone, he continued.

"So then, dear lady, as I was saying, my colleague has a younger sister, a fine cultured girl who wants to study, to make something of herself, to achieve something, do you understand me? Well, she arrived in this city from a small town to take the examinations in order to get in wherever she could, whether midwifery or dentistry, so long as she could study, so long as she could get a diploma.

"So far, so good. She arrived at her brother's. Her brother is, as you probably have guessed, a student. She arrived—very fine, a guest, nothing unusual about that. But it turns out they won't allow her to stay. They won't allow her to stay even one day. Why? I don't need to tell you. You must have figured it out yourselves: residence permit. The poor girl pleaded: just let me pass my examinations and get admitted and then I'll have my residence permit. But it turns out that in order to take her examinations, she must bring her residence permit with her. Ha-ha! Do you get the point?

"In a word, it's bad! What to do? The examination is coming up and here's the official saying, 'Either you show your residence permit or be so kind, little girl, as to go back where you came from. Take a little ride to Berdichev, hee!'

"Somehow, who should turn up but a good friend, a wise Jew, and he gives her the idea . . ." (Lapidus leaned close to Betty and lowered his voice) "that

she should register . . . she should take out . . . a thousand pardons . . . that
she should make out a yellow residence card they give to prostitutes! . . . Do you
get what I'm saying?

"I almost went out of my mind when I heard that. And from whom, do you
think, did I hear it? From her own brother! Picture it, he didn't try to keep it
from me! He received quite a tongue-lashing from me. 'God in heaven,' I said to
him, 'how can you bring those words to your lips? How can you even think of
such a thing?' So, I ask you, isn't it smarter, a thousand times smarter and more
respectable and more practical and more honest to renounce oneself once and
for all rather than *that* way, to sink so low, to be so amoral? Let's say it—to allow
oneself to fall into the abyss? Hee?"

Rabinovitch, who had become quite absorbed in the story and who was in
agreement with Lapidus, tried to open his mouth to say something, but Lapidus
silenced him with a motion of the hand as Betty had started to speak at the
same moment. She turned to Lapidus, not looking directly at him but at the tips
of her shoes, but nevertheless there was no doubt about the intense anger
evident on her face.

"So, what happened to your friend's sister? I mean, what did she . . . what did
she do?"

Here Lapidus stopped walking, clasped his hands over his heart dramatically,
and said to her with a bitter laugh, "That's what I'm asking *you*! What is *your*
opinion? Hee? Whose advice should she have taken?"

Betty also stood still and, now looking directly into Lapidus's eyes, she answered him sharply, and one could hear the anger in her reply.

"I greatly regret your acquaintance's situation . . . your acquaintance's sister.
And if you sincerely wish to know my opinion, I must tell you that I in her place
would certainly *not* have taken your smart, practical, and honest advice!"

The word "honest" was so pointed and spoken so emphatically that Lapidus
well understood her meaning and bit his lip although he tried to look as if he
were laughing.

"Is that what you say? Hee?"

"That is what anyone in my place would say who has the least sense of honor,
who has in him a free spirit, not an enslaved one—in a word, anyone who
cannot be bought either for money or a midwifery diploma or for any diploma in
the world!"

Betty spoke these words with such seriousness and with such fire that Rabinovitch began to admire her all over again, unable to get his fill looking and
listening to her. He saw her in a completely new light, not the charming girl with
the dimples in her cheeks and with the coy smile that had attracted him when
he first came to rent the room. He had never seen her so beautiful, so magnifi-
cently beautiful as at that moment. Her ever smiling eyes excited him. Her
cheeks, which had just been blushing like newly ripe peaches now turned
strangely pale. Her upper lip trembled.

Lapidus, who was also avidly admiring her face all this time, envying Rabinovitch his companion, said nothing. He simply pretended to laugh, thrust his chest out even further, raised his shoulders higher, and said to Rabinovitch, "How about that? I thought Tumarkin was the only chauvinist. I guess I was wrong. Listen! The bell is ringing," he said and bid farewell to them without shaking hands but with an elegant bow of the head and clicking of the heels, officer-like, and vanished into the great mass of the strolling audience now returning to their seats.

From what Betty had just said, our hero realized it was no longer of any avail to speak to her about what he had been planning to say; there was no use in disclosing his secret. No. Her opinion of his plan was now obvious to him. All the castles in air he had built suddenly began to topple. All the golden dreams he had been nurturing suddenly began to disperse like smoke . . .

Is it possible? he asked himself as they walked back to their seats with Betty at his side holding his arm, feeling the warmth of her skin, is it possible that because of such a small matter, he was in danger of losing such a treasure? Is it possible all is lost? No, he answered himself resolutely, no! It *cannot* be! It *must* not be! It *will* not be!!" . . .

the twenty-fourth chapter

A BLACK CAT

Upon leaving the theater, our young couple beheld a breathtakingly beautiful night, one of those spectacular, cold but gentle, white wintery nights when the snow spreads out like a freshly ironed sheet, the frost nips at the nose, the stars, reddish-blue, sparkle like diamonds, and as far as the eye can see, all is white.

"Why don't we walk?" Rabinovitch suggested to Betty.

"That's fine with me," Betty answered, bestowing upon him a look which for him equaled the brilliance of the stars. She placed her hand in his and they started downhill, sliding more than walking. And though the sky was clear, a few snowflakes fell from above, wafting like feathers in the light of the street lamps, spinning and swirling and slowly settling on the fallen, well-trodden snow.

It was almost warm. At least, so it seemed to our young couple as they slid downhill hand in hand, slipping, laughing loudly as they came close to falling several times. And each time they almost fell, Betty pressed closer to her escort, who had to master the impulse to sweep her up in an embrace, draw her face close to his, and kiss her cheeks, all rosy from the frost.

At those moments Rabinovitch forgot entirely what he had so recently heard her say in the theater. Simply to talk to her, to be close to her, to feel her body against his, made him forget everything else. What difference did it make to him now—Jew, Christian, religion and all the rest, when her hand was in his, when he could feel her breathing, could hear her heart beating! Away, away, all ideas, all thoughts! He was sure of one thing only: he loved her and she loved him—that was as plain as that clear sky above them, as that pure snow beneath their feet. No! He had to be stronger than iron to keep from throwing his arms around this beautiful girl, drawing her face close to his, and covering her frost-reddened cheeks with kisses.

And possibly he might indeed have lost control of himself that night had not Betty suddenly burst out laughing, throwing her head back, and exclaiming, "What a clown!"

"Who?"

"That Lapidus of yours."

He froze in his tracks.

"In what way?"

"In every way. He and that story he told. Ha! Ha! Ha!"

In a split second he had fallen from the highest heaven. Her strident laughter disappointed him. Is it possible that the only thing this tragic story aroused in her is ridicule?

Unbidden, his old thoughts about Jews returned, and he wondered, What a strange people! So little compassion they have for one another. Apparently they are so accustomed to misfortune that nothing bothers them any more. A strange people!

The beauty of that rare night suddenly vanished. A black cat scurried across their path. He could not keep silent. He had to tell her what he was thinking. He sought the words with which to convey as gently as possible his reaction to her laughter so that she wouldn't feel insulted. One had to be very careful—she was a sensitive girl.

"Don't you have a bit of pity in your heart for him? A little compassion?"

Betty wasn't looking at him but at the star-filled wintery sky.

"Pity? Compassion? For whom? For that yellow-haired, common, ugly little creature who has betrayed us, who has abandoned us, who has sold his God and his people for a blue uniform with a toy bronze sword? Ha-ha-ha!"

No. Betty's shrill, angry laughter on that superb winter night harmonized not at all with the mood of our hero, who, a moment before, was prepared to throw himself at her feet and beg her to be his, his forever. Was all lost? Was it over? Nonsense! There was still time—and now was the time—he must tell her what had been in his heart for so long. There had to be an end to it, if not today, then tomorrow—the truth had to come out!

He gazed into her eyes and spoke gently, quietly.

"Betty, I must ask you something. You say that Lapidus sold his God for a blue uniform. How would it be if he did it for another reason?"

Betty turned to him,

"What other reason?"

Rabinovitch stopped, took Betty's hands in his and looked searchingly into her eyes,

"For instance, how would it be, if I loved you and you loved me, and you found out that I . . ."

Betty looked straight into his eyes and it seemed to him an ironic little smile played across her lips.

"Why are you so hesitant about saying it? You want to know what I'd do if I found out you wanted to do what your friend did?"

"No, not that! Not that! Worse!" he wanted to blurt out, and clasped her hands even tighter. She tore herself from his grasp and ran off, he in pursuit.

"Betty! Miss Shapiro! Berta Davidovna!" But no matter how loudly he called after her, no matter how hard he pleaded with her to stop for a moment, that he had something to say, one word, no more, it was to no avail. She wouldn't stop and wouldn't listen to what he had to say, covering her ears with her hands, and in this state they arrived home, flushed, upset, and exhausted.

"Shh . . . God in heaven," Sara Shapiro greeted them, putting her finger to her lips as people were already asleep. "Why were you running so, as if someone were chasing you? And why did you walk home?"

Betty removed her hat, drew off her gloves, and forced a laugh, but her face was ashen and her eyes shone with a strange fire.

"Who said we were running, Mama? And how do you know we walked home?"

A fine question—how Sara knew! How could she be expected to sleep soundly! Didn't she hear them running across the snow? She wasn't her husband, who downed his supper and fell dead asleep as soon as he returned from work.

Not that this was altogether true. Sara had not planned to go to bed at all. She had sat by the window in her night clothes for a long time looking out for the children, anxiously awaiting their return. And when they did return and she had looked into her daughter's eyes, she knew immediately that something had happened between her and the roomer. The happy mother had assumed that in the theater, or on the way home, he had declared himself to her daughter.

"Betty, what happened?" she asked her daughter after the roomer had quietly said goodnight to them and tiptoed to his room.

"What could have happened?" the daughter answered curtly, as usual. "Nothing happened. Good night."

"Good night. Sleep well."

Sara knew that it was a waste of time. The more she would question her, the less she would find out. She cracked her knuckles and, hope singing in her heart, went to bed, all the while thinking that when God willed it, He would deliver it right to your doorstep.

A HEART FULL OF TROUBLES

That God had sent to the Shapiro's house good fortune in the form of a wealthy roomer, a student who was courting their daughter, was common knowledge on the Jewish Street. All the neighbors, good friends as well as acquaintances, were forever talking about it.

Sara herself had spread the good news all over town, arousing the envy of her good friends. Naturally, she didn't say it was a settled matter. She was no fool. But she did drop a word here and there about the wonderful lodger God had sent her, a roomer and a boarder and a tutor all rolled into one. "A sensitive boy, comes from a rich family."

Here she would bend over and whisper into the ear of each one separately, in half-hints and allusions:

"A rich aunt . . . sends him heaps of money! . . . What do you think? . . . A widow, a millionairess, without children . . . just he alone . . . the only one! . . ."

The last words were spoken out loud, her finger held up to indicate just one, her eyes glowing, and her face shining like the sun in summer.

And those "good friends" would hear her out with a friendly smile, and when she would leave, they would say to one another, "Nu? Do you have to be smart? You just have to be lucky. If you're lucky, good fortune waits for you right on your doorstep. The Shapiros could never have imagined such a bridegroom! But a bridegroom first has to sign engagement papers and break a dish, as God intended. I'll tell you something. Many times you think you've landed a bridegroom, and when you get right down to it, nothing comes of it."

Such was the talk on the Jewish Street, even among those who had nothing against the Shapiros, who didn't, God forbid, wish them harm but simply resented the fact that such ordinary folk had become lucky. And so easily! Painlessly!

"How do you know they're that lucky? Come on, I'll bet you anything the whole story with the aunt and the inheritance is all made up."

"Ha-ha, say, there's an idea!"

"If that's the case, then it's a pity both on the Shapiros and on the daughter."

"What can you do about it? It's up to God . . ."

But this was all said behind the Shapiros' backs. In their presence, they were as good friends ought to be—visiting one another on an occasional evening for a game of Sixty-six, or coming by on a Saturday afternoon for a glass of tea. Sometimes the Shapiros would be asked to bring along their roomer. "Why should he stay home by himself?"

After a while, the good friends began to ask, "What's taking so long? Why aren't we hearing any announcements about a celebration, a party, a *mazel tov?* What's going on?"

The Shapiros listened with forced smiles as if it were already a settled matter, when in truth they knew exactly as much as anyone else, if not less.

"What can you do with today's children? Do they tell you anything, or will they allow you to question them?" Not to mention that after that evening in the theater, Betty had been behaving strangely. Heaven help her if Sara could begin to comprehend what was going on with her daughter.

One time she tried to start up a little conversation with her, a casual "So what's new with you?" Betty had given her back a "So what's new with you" to remember!

"Mama!" she had snapped so angrily one would have thought she wanted to kill her. "If you ask me one more time about that, you'll see what will happen!"

"Sha-sha! Look at her! I touched a sore spot! Can't even say anything! Exactly like her father! David Shapiro sends his regards!"

"How come you're talking about David Shapiro all of a sudden, tell me?" David demanded, entering the room quickly, as usual, without warning and just when his name was being mentioned in vain.

Sara sought for a way out, but David knew it was simply an excuse and there ensued between them a protracted discussion punctuated by their customary insults and name calling with which they honored one another. He to her, "Cow!"—she to him, "Speed demon!" He to her, "Silly Goat!"—she to him, "Windmill!" He to her, "Blabbermouth!"—she to him, "Shapiro!" Although the name "Shapiro" was obviously a source of pride to both of them—David claimed he was a descendant of the real Shapiros, the Shapiros of Slaviteh—Sara's tone conveyed that David was a descendant of the Slaviteh Shapiros as you and I might be descendants of King David. This slight to his ancestry inflamed David's rage to the point where he wanted to tear her limb from limb. He demolished his meal in minutes, slammed the door, and sped off to work.

But this was an ordinary domestic scene. Husbands and wives quarrel and make up. But problems with children transcend everything else in importance. Sara Shapiro's heart was burdened with worries she could not relieve. As she herself opined, Sara was an expert at sniffing out trouble. She wasn't blind. She could see very clearly that her daughter and the roomer were carrying on a serious but unspoken romance, and an unspoken romance is of no use to anyone. Sara Shapiro was convinced, and no one on earth could tell her otherwise, that nothing good can come of an unspoken romance. One had to see to it that the mute acquire language and that the silent start to talk. But how to bring it about?

Sara Shapiro had tried several times to initiate a conversation with the young man about this and that, but nothing had come of it. If she could at least have spoken to him in Yiddish, she could have set him on the right path, but if one's tongue is in exile, it is impossible!

And to convince her husband to have a talk with him was as likely as drawing heaven and earth together. A stubborn mule. What can be worse than a proud man? It would be beneath him, he said, even if he knew the entire million were to fall right into his pocket! Here David patted his breast pocket for emphasis. He didn't want anyone to think he was selling his daughter for money. He was content to wait till the young man would come to him and say, "*Gospodin*, Shapiro, I want you to know I love your daughter and your daughter loves me and we ask your blessing."

"May it be so, God in heaven, from your mouth into God's ear!" said Sara with a deep sigh, cracking her knuckles, suffering silently inside. There was no one to whom she could bare her heart.

She knew her husband was suffering in his own heart the same pain as she, but he would never let on because he was, after all, a Shapiro, one of the Slaviteh Shapiros, no small matter!

the twenty-sixth chapter

TWO MOTHERS

There was, in fact, one person to whom Sara could occasionally bare her soul—her sister-in-law, Toibe Familiant, David's older sister, a pious woman who wore a wig and whose neck was heavy with pearls.

Although she was not as pious a woman as she appeared, she maintained a strict *Chassidic* household, as befits a *Chassid*'s wife, and because she was the wife of a rich man and David's elder sister, she felt she was entitled to give advice to her brother, David, and his wife, Sara, on how to raise their children. Whether it helped or not, she took it upon herself to point out faults and to moralize without end.

Into the bargain God had granted this Toibe the face of a *rebbitzin*—a rabbi's wife—with tightly pursed lips and the voice of a skilled speaker—a soft, quiet, honeyed voice.

David didn't like his sister and she knew it; he always referred to her as "the *rebbitzin*." Betty hated her aunt, if only because her forehead was too shiny. If one had to tolerate her unctuous sermonizing and moralizing and if one had to visit her every Sabbath and holiday, it was only out of duty, because she was the richest in the family.

Only Sara could get along with her, because they were both mothers who had problems with their children and knew what lay in each other's heart. Toibe knew that Sara knew that Toibe's younger daughter was once in love with a drugstore clerk and that Toibe herself, as a young girl, had carried on a romance with a boy who later turned out to be a womanizer and a scoundrel, and against her will they had sent her to a *Chassidic* home, where she became indoctrinated in *Chassidism*. And Sara knew that Toibe knew that she, Sara, had once considered eloping with Toibe's brother, David.

Now they were both mothers who took great pains seeing to it that their children not stray from the beaten path, God forbid, who expected them to obey their fathers and mothers and meet people their parents approved of and fall in love only with those their mothers would accept.

There was no more touching scene than when these God-fearing women, honest, devoted mothers, engaged in a conversation full of oys, ays, achs and dear hearts, darlings, my loves.

"So what's new, Sara dear?"

"Oy, what should be new, Toibenyu, dear heart! It's still the same . . . Nothing has moved so much as a hairbreadth."

"Not good, Sara, not good. You are a mother and you have to know one way or the other, either yes or no."

"Aye, Toibenyu, my darling, how can you say that? You yourself have children, you yourself have two daughters."

"What can they say about my daughters? About my daughters they can say nothing. My daughters, God bless them, are not involved with students and don't go with strange young men to the theater . . . Sha! You don't have to get insulted, Sara, my dear. I don't, heaven forbid, mean any harm. I know your Berta is a good girl, a devoted Jewish daughter. She comes from the Shapiros, from the Slaviteh Shapiros. And that young man, that Rabinovitch I mean, really made a good impression on me, as I told you many times already. Just one thing, though, he's a little weak in Yiddish. My Shlomo says he's extremely weak! Still, my Shlomo thinks very highly of him. He had a chance to talk with him several times and he says he's a very likeable fellow and a devoted Jew. I mean, he's not close to Jewish life, but he's a very passionate patriot. You should see to it, Sara darling, that by *Pesach* it should be definite, and seven weeks later, by the *Shabbos* after *Shevuos*, God willing, some thought should be given to setting a date for a wedding."

"The Sabbath after *Shevuos*—the Feast of Weeks? Oy, Toibenyu, dear heart, I would be satisfied if it would happen by the middle of Elul in the fall or by a year from Chanukah! Just let me live to hear the good news from him or from her. But the problem is they don't talk and they don't let anyone ask."

"It's your fault, it's your fault all around! God helps him who helps himself. As you sow, so shall you reap. We have to take matters into our own hands. A person has to act and God has to help. If you wouldn't mind taking my advice, I would, Sara dear, tell you what to do."

"Oh, on the contrary, Toibenyu, my dear, please give me some good advice!"

"My advice, Sara darling, is simple and straightforward, nothing can be more straightforward. I'll talk it over with my Shlomo. My Shlomo is, praise His name, a person who can talk about worldly matters to someone even though he may wear the gabardine of a *Chassid* and the large *tallis*. So, now that we're approaching the holidays, we only have a few days until Purim, and all of you will certainly be coming here for the Purim feast with your roomer, I'll take no excuses. You must all come, we should all live and be well until that time! And my Shlomo will take the young man quietly off to the side and tell him, 'This is the way it is, young man, you understand?' "

"Oy, long life to you, Toibenyu, my love! But I'm just afraid of one thing. Oh, I'm not worried about the young man—he doesn't have a mean bone in his body. May I have such a good year if he isn't the finest young man! You can do whatever you want with him, he's so good-natured. But Betty—what will you do with *her?*"

"Why worry about her? In the first place, who's asking her? And in the second place, are you a mother or not?"

"Oy, Toibenyu, Toibenyu! How can you say that? You yourself are a mother. You have two children."

"Children? What can they say about my children?"

Here ensued a complete replica of the previous conversation, and both mothers were prepared to continue their dialogue on and on when suddenly little Syomke burst in from outdoors, wailing that Volodka had hit him. He was playing nicely in the snow with Volodka and they had a fight.

"Oh, that awful Volodka!" said Sara, hugging and kissing Syomke.

"Who is this Volodka?" Toibe Familiant asked her sister-in-law.

"The last straw!" answered Sara, wiping Syomke's dirty hands. "We have a neighbor woman in the next courtyard, a Gentile, Kirilikha they call her. She has a brat from her first husband—his name is Volodka."

Toibe Familiant said nothing. It would have been far better had she said something; instead, she pursed her lips and became silent, with a look one gives to people who are beyond hope. Sara Shapiro understood that silence and replied in her own defense, "He may be a problem for my Syomke, but he's a very good child, this Volodka. Our roomer can't praise him enough. He's studying with him now, for free naturally. He says the poor boy, even though he's riffraff, has a Jewish head on his shoulders. The problem is that his stepfather is a drunken Gentile who beats him, it's a pity on the creature!"

Toibe Familiant kept her lips tightly pursed and looked with pity at her sister-in-law. But once Sara had started to talk about the neighbor boy, she had to continue.

"One time the drunkard beat him so badly, the whole courtyard filled with neighbors—I and my daughter and our roomer were among them—and we barely tore the boy alive from his hands. From that time on, he's been studying with Rabinovitch."

Sara became quiet and the pious Toibe Familiant opened her pursed little mouth slightly and began with her unctuous voice to lecture her younger sister-in-law.

"Nu, I ask you, Sara dear, how can your daughter respect you when you yourself . . ."

At that moment Betty walked in and the pious Toibe put on an innocent face.

Sara said, "Oh, speak of the Messiah! Your Aunt Toibe was just asking if you still have a cold."

Betty knew full well from her Aunt Toibe's innocent-looking face that her mother had just told a lie, and she turned all colors.

the twenty-seventh chapter

OUR HERO DANCES

The wonders our hero witnessed when the Shapiros took him along to their wealthy relatives' Purim party he would be recounting for years to come. It was all entirely new to him; he was in a state of constant amazement. These people greatly interested him because he had learned they were *Chassidim.*

"What will be going on there?" he kept asking his landlord and had received an irritable retort from David Shapiro.

"What do you think will be going on there? Haven't you ever been to a Purim celebration? Or maybe your people don't consider Purim a holiday or Haman a villain!"

"No, that's not what I meant," the roomer protested, but made things worse. "I'm just asking because they're *Chaseedim.*"

"*Chaseedim!*" David Shapiro mimicked him. "So what if they're '*Chaseedim,*' what's the difference?"

"But aren't they a kind of sect?" Rabinovitch tried to justify his question, but Shapiro was becoming quite testy and agitated.

"What kind of sect? What are you talking about? Some sect! What have Jews to do with sects? Where did you grow up? Among Jews? Or in a forest?"

Sara Shapiro was a great deal more gentle with him and responded to his questions more considerately.

"It's going to be very festive," she said, "There'll be eating and drinking, singing and dancing, clapping and merrymaking, the way *Chassidim* usually carry on. I assure you that you won't be sorry to get to know them a little better, especially my brother-in-law, Familiant. He's a very wise Jew. You really should listen to what he has to say. He doesn't just talk lightly, every word, you can say, is worth a commentary . . ."

Sara had her own reasons for believing this and was, understandably, looking forward to this holiday as one does to the Messiah.

And when Purim arrived, Sara Shapiro's holiday attire far outshone her daughter's. She looked more like Betty's sister than her mother. David also donned his best suit and cast off his customary sour expression for one that was more pleasant. Syomke wore his school uniform buttoned to the top, his sparse sidelocks were combed out, and he was warned a thousand times not to dare to remove his hat for so much as a minute at his Uncle Shlomo's house, because the pious Jews at the party disapproved of going without a hat, a terrible sin. "Do you understand, little squirrel, or not?"

Although those words were directed to the "little squirrel," they were intended for the roomer so that he would not forget and remove his hat.

When the Shapiros arrived at Shlomo Familiant's home, they found the entire family already gathered around a long, white-bedecked table, surrounded by a large group of guests, Jews in long kaftans wearing all shapes and sizes of hats and caps.

Seated at the head of the table in a large chair was the head of the family, Shlomo Familiant, a tall Jew with a thick red beard beginning to turn gray, and with bushy red brows above his nearsighted eyes. His reddish gray sidelocks were fashionably turned under. He wore a starched white collar and a broad silk cravat on his ample velvet vest adorned with a gold fob watch chain. A braided sash encircled his expensive black silk jacket covering his generous stomach. All this, in addition to his large bent nose and his pure-white hands, extending from his broad sleeves, gave him the appearance of a patriarch. At least, so he seemed to our hero, who was amazed by everything he saw, finding in each detail a particular charm.

For one, he was taken with the Familiants' two daughters, one more attractive than the other, and both of them elegantly dressed as only young girls can be. And though they carried themselves in a dignified way, remaining quite still and poised, their eyes spoke more than they could ever have expressed in words. Looking at them and at their mother, one could see that the apples had not fallen very far from the tree. Their mother, Toibe Familiant, now a matron no longer young, must once have been a beauty. She still looked lovely in her custom-made clothes, which were offset by her pearl-entwined hair. The pendant diamond earrings and pearl necklaces on her clear-white throat still suited her and were evidence that she was once an attractive woman with graceful hands. Even now she had fine, large blue eyes, and it was a pity she kept them lowered and always pursed her already thin lips.

What greatly impressed Rabinovitch was how all eyes looked with enormous respect at one person, at the patriarch with the reddish-gray beard. He was also impressed by the huge, saffron-colored Purim *challah*, kneaded with raisins and sprinkled with almonds, which the patriarch teased apart with his aristocratic, white hands after making a blessing over it. The other men in their long kaftans repeated the blessing, dipped the *challah* into salt, and uttered phrases that to the Shapiros' roomer might as well have been Turkish.

Soon after, the patriarch rolled up his wide sleeves, winked at the guests, and as one, the guests began singing a tune which emanated, it seemed to Rabinovitch, not from their throats, but from somewhere in their beards and collars.

While singing, they all kept their eyes shut and occasionally threw their heads back, one hand held at the throat. The master of the house also sang with eyes shut, head thrown back, sleeves rolled up to the elbow, and fingers snapping in rhythm. The men clapped along to the beat, their faces suffused with joy and a special holiday harmony. On the host's face, one could say, rested the Divine Presence.

Delicious, peppered, gefilte fish, saffron-colored in honor of Purim, was served. After the fish, the wine glasses were filled, and the crowd, sipping the wine, began to exchange toasts which, except for the single word, *l'chaim*, Rabinovitch had never heard before.

"What are they saying?" he asked his landlord, who replied testily.

"What should they say? They're not really saying anything. They're just making a *l'chaim* and wishing that each live till next year and be good Jews."

"Is that all?" said Rabinovitch, who could not see the sense to this kind of toast—to hope to live till the next year and remain good Jews? Was there nothing better to wish for?

After barely touching the wine to their lips, the crowd seemed to become intoxicated and lively. The singing and clapping became louder and louder. The men joined hands to form a circle and began dancing. Sara Shapiro's roomer had never seen so strange a dance. Eyes tightly shut, each dancer bobbed his head and kicked his legs, all the while singing, "*Tatenyu! Gotenyu!*" The host himself, Reb Shlomo Familiant, entered into the middle of the circle, clapping his hands and urging the dancers on.

"Lively now! Jews! Lively! Lively! How fortunate we are! How happy we are to be Jews! We have a great God! Lively! Lively!"

Sara Shapiro's roomer couldn't control himself and again had to turn to his landlord to translate what Familiant was saying.

David Shapiro translated each word, but again, his roomer, for the life of him, could not understand why being Jewish was a source of happiness. Are these the "*Chaseedim*," he wondered, that sect of wild people he had read about in *Novoye Vremya*? What a strange people! Even the drunkards behave differently. They barely touch their lips to the wine, hardly drink a drop, and look how happy they become! True, it's another kind of happiness. They're happy, apparently, because they're Jews! They're satisfied, even grateful to have a God! See how two of them over there are embracing, kissing each other like real sots, their eyes full of tears! They're both jabbering about something—but about what! About God! A strange, strange people!

He caught a glimpse of two *Chassidim* suddenly pulling his landlord into the circle, and before long, Shapiro was dancing energetically with the rest in the circle. "Will they pull me into the ring too?" our Rabinovitch was wondering when a pair of hot, sweaty hands grabbed him and pulled him into the ring before he had time to finish the thought.

"Young man! You're a Jew like the rest of us, so don't make a fuss and join the dance!"

The circle expanded and the frivolity grew like yeast. Little Syomke and the other children also pushed their way into the ring, where they began prancing about in their own way.

Joyousness grew by the minute, spreading contagiously without benefit of words. The whole room erupted in celebration, feet seemed to be flying on air, dancing, dancing, dancing.

Thus was our hero, Rabinovitch, or Grigori Ivanovitch Popov, drawn into the spirit of the Purim dance. Together with all the *Chassidim* he stomped his feet, leaped and cavorted as light as a feather, barely feeling the floor beneath him. And since he couldn't sing the *Chassidic* melodies and he did so want to sing, he hummed a Russian tune,

> *Propadai moya telega*
> *Vse chetyre kolesa!*
> May I lose my cart
> And all its four wheels!

and, surprisingly, no one knew the difference.

the twenty-eighth chapter

A TRIVIAL EVENT

It was an ideal plan. As soon as the Purim party was over, Sara Shapiro's brother-in-law, Reb Shlomo Familiant, would take her roomer aside into his study, offer him a seat and a cigar (Shlomo Familiant smoked expensive, aromatic cigars), and engage him in casual conversation, during which he would bring up the Shapiros and their daughter, a fine girl, a capable person with many talents, but, alas, without money, but herself worth more than gold; the man who would win her would be lucky. And, as they talked, he would skillfully elicit the young man's intentions. He would advise him, as an older man, not to waste too much time but to make up his mind. By no means was she a bad catch, God forbid; there were plenty of others interested in her. And if it were yes, why should one hesitate? It took but a few words to arrange a marriage and *mazel tov!* And here and there he would throw in an interpretation of *Gemara*, a sacred verse, or parable as only he knew how! You could depend on it. Although a pious Jew with long kaftan and large prayer shawl, Shlomo Familiant could talk you into anything. He was a worldly merchant who dealt with rich Gentile landowners daily. Was it any wonder he was on intimate terms with the governor himself?

Ah! How Sara Shapiro was building her hopes on her brother-in-law, even though her David was against this plan. He did not approve of his sister's husband. The long kaftan and large prayer shawl were no more than affectations. His visits on Passover and *Sukkos*—the fall harvest holiday—to the *Chassidic* rebbe, without whom he claimed he wouldn't make a move, were only for show so that the *Chassidim* would flatter him for his piety, pay their respects on holidays, while stuffing themselves on his food, guzzling, and dancing at his celebrations.

"The world has all kinds of pleasure-seeking idolatry!" So David expressed his cynical opinion of Shlomo Familiant to Sara. How her David could carry on! Here was a man whom nothing pleased, who found fault with everyone, a Shapiro! May God bless her if she didn't have a better head for business, even though he was a man and considered himself an expert.

No. It was an ideal plan. But it wasn't fated to be carried out as she had wished because of a trivial event over which one would ordinarily not have spent so much as three minutes. But it was Sara Shapiro's luck that this trivial event would result in an uproar that would bring her no end of trouble. This is how it all started.

Right at the height of the revelry, when the circle was growing and the tipsy crowd was dancing with fervor, suddenly two strange creatures appeared at the door: a short Gentile woman with a red face and glazed eyes and behind her, standing at a little distance, a *vergelyetz*—a Gentile youth—carrying a long whip and wearing a peaked cap.

It became quickly evident that the red-faced Gentile woman with the glazed eyes was searching for someone in the crowd without success. The youth with the whip and peaked hat appeared to be her escort, or perhaps a witness, or someone who might protect her if that proved necessary.

The appearance of those two strangers at that very moment was so unexpected that the crowd of Jews, who had just been in such high spirits, turned stone sober. They stopped dancing and looked, first at one another and then, to a man, at the patriarch, Shlomo Familiant, who had gone over to the Gentile woman, peered at her with his nearsighted eyes, and asked her in Russian whom she was looking for.

But the woman didn't so much as glance at him. She kept searching the crowd with her glazed eyes till she spotted the one she was looking for. Among the women she located Sara Shapiro and ran toward her excitedly.

"Oh! Madam Shapiro! *Ahdeh moya dytyna?* Where is my child?"

Sara Shapiro stood up, responding to her question in Russian. "What child?"

"My Volodka."

"Your Volodka? How should I know?"

The woman's glazed eyes clouded over even more, and staring at a distant point, her lips barely moving, she began relating in an endless monotone a long tale about how her Volodka had disappeared, vanished as if into thin air. From yesterday morning on, when he had left home with his schoolbooks, she had waited for him, hoping he would be home by nightfall, but he hadn't returned. By this morning, he still had not come home, nor by afternoon nor by evening.

She had just gone to the Shapiros' house and was told that Madam Shapiro was here, and so she had come to ask her where her child was.

"How should I know?" Sara repeated, and the woman began retelling her whole story from the beginning in every detail.

"What do you say to this pain in the neck?" Sara said in Yiddish, turning to the crowd, which was standing in shocked silence and listening, not beginning to understand what was going on. "Maybe you can tell me what on earth I have to do with her Volodka? That's her child. He's called Volodka."

With a wave of a hand to the woman, she said, "Leave me alone! How am I supposed to know? Leave me alone! Go!"

And it's possible the Gentile woman would have obeyed and left with no more than she had come, had not little Syomke jumped up and said to his mother, "She's looking for Volodka? We played together today, Volodka and I. Well, maybe it was yesterday. We played together yesterday."

"Where did you play with him?" his mother asked.

"Where we always play, outside," Syomke answered, pointing outdoors.

Hearing Volodka's name, the woman refocused her glazed eyes on Syomke. "Where's my child?" she said, and again, "Where's my child?" and once again, "Where's my child?"

Who knows how this scene might have ended had not Shapiro's roomer interceded at this point. He approached the mother and placed his hand on her shoulder.

"*Matushka!* Go home to your husband. He and he alone will tell you where your child is . . ."

Those words were spoken in the tone of one who knows what he is saying, and that was enough for the Gentile woman, who turned toward her companion, and after exchanging glances for what seemed a long time, they left.

Not till after they had departed did the crowd suddenly come to life. The men began to speak, asking one another about what had just happened. What was going on?

"Who is that *goyeh*?" Shlomo Familiant asked his brother-in-law, David.

"I haven't the faintest idea!" David answered, looking angrily at his wife.

"Who is she?" Familiant now asked Sara, avoiding her eyes, as a *Chassid* should.

"She's a neighbor of ours," Sara replied. "They call her Kirilikha. Her husband is a drunkard. Volodka is her son from her first husband."

"So?" said Familiant.

"So, the stepfather beats him to within an inch of his life."

"So?" Familiant pressed her.

"So, the boy apparently disappeared."

"So?"

"So, she came looking for him and wanted to know if I had any idea where he was . . ."

"Why did she come to you? What does her brat have to do with you and what does Syomke have to do with him?"

"Nothing. If you're neighbors, it happens that children play together," Sara answered, feeling guilty that Syomke played with a non-Jewish child.

Shlomo Familiant was obviously not too happy to have been interrupted right in the middle of his party, his celebration ruined. He thrust his hands into his trouser pockets, stuck out his prayer-shawl-covered fat stomach, shrugged his shoulders, and muttered to himself, "Fine thing! Little brats! Neighbors! Gentiles! Non-Jews! Volodkas! Whoever heard of a Jewish child playing with such trash! That's what comes of your *gymnasiums*, your students and universities!"

In vain did his wife, Toibe, try to calm him, to quiet things down. *Shh*-ing and *shaa*-ing, she bade the crowd to return to the table, ordering the servants to serve the food. All in vain. Shlomo Familiant showed himself to be the master and the rich man, and began to attack today's children and today's parents, who lead their children to the sacrificial altar just as our Father Abraham led his one and only son, Isaac. He continued to strike out left and right as if he were railing against people in general, but it was all intended for his poor relatives.

And the poor relatives had to hear out their rich relative's diatribe to the very end. Only Betty, who had always despised her rich uncle, rose up quickly and began to put on her coat. Neither her mother's entreaties nor her aunt's disavowals that her uncle wasn't referring to them, God forbid, but was just talking in general, could stop her. Betty said, "Happy holiday," and left the house. Rabinovitch followed after her quickly—how could he let a young girl go out in the middle of the night alone?

Thus came to naught the plan Sara had conceived. And because of what? Because of a trivial event! Because of a foolish trivial event!

Sara Shapiro almost wept with heartache and vexation as she accompanied her husband home. As if that weren't enough, David rubbed salt into the wounds.

"An ox," he told her, "has a long tongue but can't blow a *shofar*. Did you have to tell stories to that *Chassidak*, that false Messiah, that Sabbatai Zevi?"

"Big mouths don't always say wise things," Sara repaid him with another proverb. "He's *your* brother-in-law, not mine!"

"I'll give him to you for free, if you want."

"Thanks for nothing!"

the twenty-ninth chapter

TROUBLE LOOMS

When it came to her children, Sara Shapiro was not one of those mothers who let anything stand in her way. Now that the opportunity offered by her brother-in-law, Familiant, was lost, she sought other means. And she did find someone she could rely on more than anyone else, a person she could trust with her secret because he was thoroughly honest. He might, in fact, have been *too* honest.

Sara's confidant was no other than her roomer's friend, Tumarkin, the last of the thirteen medalists who had waiting so long for a response from the minister to their urgent telegram. One by one they had been caught like fish in a net and sent packing from the city.

Only Tumarkin had managed to escape. He eluded the authorities by making sure to spend days where he didn't spend nights and spending nights where he didn't spend days. He carried his knapsack from acquaintance to acquaintance, greased the palms of the head gatekeepers, worked a deal with the local police-men, lay shivering in attics in the coldest frost—in short, walked a tightrope and, thank God, survived the winter as did so many other Jews in that blessed city.

It was almost comical to observe how that poor soul, with his black curly hair, was always on the move, seeking all over town for a sanctuary for the night, a place where the police had already made their house search the night before. His wanderings brought him to Sara Shapiro's roomer, who was his savior more than once late in the night after Zionist meetings.

"What are we to do with this *shlimazel?*" Sara had said to her husband, ready to defend him even though he *was* a *shlimazel.* "You can't throw him out in the street on such a cold night. Why don't you go take care of the gatekeeper, David, slip a little something into his grimy hand, may he choke. You're the only one who can handle him."

Those last words were said as a compliment, intended to mollify David Shapiro, who was furious at her for endangering their residence permit. But in the end he went down together with the roomer to the head gatekeeper and they settled with him quietly for the night. The *shlimazel* stayed in the lodger's room, where Sara had made up a bed for him out of three chairs. She wished them both a good night, and she herself hardly slept a wink lest someone come and discover him, proving David right after all.

"How did you sleep? Sara asked Tumarkin in the morning, pouring him a glass of tea.

"Wonderfully!" Tumarkin lied. Aside from the fact that the chairs kept mov-ing apart so that he felt in danger of falling through at any moment, he hadn't slept a wink all night, mainly because he had been engrossed in conversation with his friend, Rabinovitch, who had worn him out by constantly cross-examin-ing him on the nature of Jewishness.

Whenever the two came together, sparks flew. Both spoke at the same time, both became impassioned. One would argue: make up your mind, one way or the other. Either convert as Lapidus did, or else all of you, young and old, get together and settle in your historic land, in the land of your fathers. Show you are a people, a people that wants to live and can live, a people that can do for itself, not just for others.

"Sha! Enough, enough!" the other shouted him down. He could no longer tolerate what he was saying because he wasn't talking as a Jew should talk. "In the first place, what's this '*your* people'? What kind of talk is this about '*your* land,' '*your* fathers'? And secondly . . ."

"Are you two ever going to shut up?" the landlady banged on the door. "What a *shlimazel*! Enough! He can't find a place to sleep and he doesn't let anyone else sleep!"

Tumarkin had no other name to Sara than *shlimazel*, but as she thought the world of her roomer and he was her roomer's friend, Tumarkin's stature grew in her eyes. She greatly desired for him to strike up a conversation with Rabinovitch in which he could feel him out on that subject closest to her heart: what were his thoughts, what were his feelings, what were his intentions? By no means should he inquire directly, but in carefully chosen, courteous hints because it was, after all, a delicate matter.

"Do you understand? A very delicate matter."

With a sniff and a special look, Sara conveyed just how delicate a matter it was. And though Tumarkin had no idea yet what Madame Shapiro was referring to, he still nodded his head, twisting his black curls as Sara moved closer to him, wanting so much to whisper her secret in his ear, when Betty arrived. She stood still a moment, trying to grasp what her mother was saying to Tumarkin, then said to her mother, "Mama, do you know what's happened? There's trouble. They've found him."

"Who did they find?"

"They've found Volodka."

Sara sprang up. "They've found Volodka! Thank goodness! Where was he?"

"Where he was? No one knows, but now he's here, right near our own courtyard, dead."

Sara almost fell backward.

"Dead? Volodka dead?"

"Not just dead. Murdered."

Sara began to tremble.

"Murdered? They murdered Volodka. Oo-va! He was a fine boy. Who murdered him?"

"No one knows. They found him murdered . . . Slashed and stabbed . . . Apparently he was murdered some time ago because his body was beginning to decay."

Sara turned her face away and spat. "Heaven protect us from such things! Where did they find him?"

"I'm telling you, not far from here, near our courtyard. The whole street is full of people, Jews and Gentiles, doctors, police."

Hearing the word "police," Sara, who had altogether forgotten about the *shlimazel*, glanced at Tumarkin.

"Oh, my God, police!"

Tumarkin, on whom the word "police" had had almost the same effect as on Sara, realized her fear was on account of him. They must not catch him without a permit in her house . . .

"Don't worry," he calmed her down with a laugh. "First of all, it's not night-time. Daytime isn't as dangerous as night, and second of all, I was about to leave anyway, ha-ha. You can't be surprised. You must know me by now."

"Go, go, but go quickly and quietly. Don't let anyone see you. Or better still, go slowly and do let them see you, but hold your head up proudly like a person who actually has a legitimate residence permit, do you understand?"

"Of course I understand."

Sara accompanied Tumarkin down the stairs, quietly telling him at the door to be sure and return tomorrow to spend the night, when they would have a chance to talk in private since it was a delicate matter.

"A delicate matter," Tumarkin repeated, not hearing what he himself was saying.

"A very delicate matter!"

"A very delicate matter . . ."

the thirtieth chapter

GONE MAD

Sara Shapiro had not been mistaken in placing her confidence in Tumarkin as her one hope to feel out her roomer. Other than a matchmaker, who else would underatake such a "delicate matter"?

As soon as Tumarkin heard all the details from Sara Shapiro, his eyes almost popped out. He began twisting his black curls nervously and reassured her he would talk to Rabinovitch exactly, exactly as she wished.

"But delicately, subtly," Sara admonished him at least twenty times, "and quietly, so no one will hear."

"Subtly, subtly!" he agreed, not quite hearing what he was saying. He was raring to get down to the task at hand immediately, that very instant. But Sara held him back, again and again giving him the same instructions about what to say and how to say it. It was no trifle, it was a delicate matter.

"A delicate matter," Tumarkin repeated each word, quite loudly.

"Shh—don't speak so loudly. Why are you shouting? Where do you think you are!" she silenced him. "Remember now, whisper, so not a soul will know!"

Tumarkin repeated every word and prepared to go. "Not a soul will know."

"No one at all!"

"No one at all."

"What kind of habit is this of yours," Sara scolded him, "repeating every word like a parrot?"

"Like a parrot," he echoed but caught himself and reassured her. "You can trust me. You can be sure. It will turn out all right. It will work out well. Wonderfully well!"

And Tumarkin went off to talk subtly to Rabinovitch.

Of late, the two had become so close that hardly a day passed without their seeing one another.

"Listen," Tumarkin spoke as soon as he entered the room, finding Rabinvitch seated at his wobbly desk, writing a letter. "Listen to what I'm going to tell you. Put down your work, shut the door tightly, sit down in your chair right here next to the window. I'll sit on the bed opposite you so I can see your face, because I have to talk to you about something very important, a secret . . ."

Rabinovitch went pale when he heard the word "secret." He immediately thought, "They've found out who I am," but as he was by nature not someone easily frightened, he rose, shut the door, tossed back his shock of hair, and seated himself face to face with his friend.

"A secret? Speak, so we'll both know."

Tumarkin began riffling the pages of a book he was holding nervously, as was his habit, because when he spoke he had to have something to do with his hands. He came right to the point, without any introduction.

"I'm going to ask you something and I want you to answer me. You love the landlady's daughter and the landlady's daughter loves you, so why are you dragging your feet?"

Beneath him, Rabinovitch's famous chair with the woven seat known as a "Viennese chair" made a scraping sound as he tried to spring up, but Tumarkin held him down with both hands, looking him straight in the eyes.

"Sit still. Why have you become so red in the face? You don't have to stand on ceremony with me. You can talk straight. Tell me what's eating you?"

To our Rabinovitch, this was so unexpected that for a moment he lost his ability to speak. He could not fathom how one could talk that way about a matter which was to him the holiest of secrets, a matter over which he had wracked his brain. And second of all, how did Tumarkin know? Could she herself have hold him? And a confusion of feelings and thoughts took hold of him, raising him from his seat, and he began to pace back and forth across the room. Then he stopped.

"Listen to me, Tumarkin, you are an honest, trustworthy person. I recognized this immediately. Just tell me one thing. How do you know about this?"

"What business is it of yours how I know, so long as it's true? It is true, isn't it? You won't deny it."

"It's not that, I mean something else. I want to know if she herself told you. I have to know."

Tumarkin stood up and then immediately sat down again.

"Are you mad? I can see you really are a great fool! As well as I know her, and I know her a lot less than you, she isn't that kind. She would rather have both her hands cut off before speaking to a stranger about such a matter."

After hearing these words, Rabinovitch understood whose idea this had been, and he wasn't pleased. He would have preferred to have heard that it had come from Betty, because ever since he had known her, loved her, following her every footstep, he had never heard so much as a word of encouragement from her. He had declared himself to her many times, if not outright, then in hints and suggestions, but she had not uttered a word in return. True, he could see she treated him differently from others. He felt with his whole heart that he was special to her. He would love to hear that from her own lips, but no! Everything else was possible—chatting, teasing, joking, talking, going for walks—as much as one would want. But not that one word he longed for. And especially since that evening at the theater, after their meeting with that fop of a Lapidus, she could become so distant that he could not figure her out. One moment she was cold as ice, the next she was affectionate, soft, lively, happy. And then suddenly she was again serious, distant, inscrutable as a sphinx, unresponsive as a statue. No, he didn't begin to understand this girl.

"Betty," he had once said, "you are a riddle to me."

"There is no greater riddle than you," she had responded and changed the subject, slipping out of his arm.

"So you've lost your tongue," Tumarkin said to him, nervously riffling the book lying on his knees, page after page. "I want to hear you say something."

"What can I say?" Rabinovitch answered, again pacing, deep in thought. "I can't tell you anything."

"Why not?"

"Because there are certain things one can't talk about even with one's closest friends. There are certain things . . ."

Tumarkin tossed the book aside. "Yes, yes, there are certain things, there are certain things . . . I know what you mean!"

Rabinovitch stopped pacing.

"What do I mean?"

"You mean that between the two of you there is an abyss, because she is a poor girl and you are a prince, the only heir of a millionairess aunt. I know, I know everything. And if so," Tumarkin stood up from the bed and looked Rabinovitch right in the eyes, "if so, I must call you by your right name: you are a scoundrel!"

The effect of his words was not what Tumarkin had expected. Instead of his friend springing up like one singed, becoming infuriated or defending himself, Rabinovitch bent down almost to the ground, doubled over, grabbed his sides, and erupted into laughter as if a hundred devils were tickling his ribs. Finally he collapsed on the bed and rolled back and forth, laughing harder and louder until the door flew open and in burst Sara, followed by Betty, both frightened out of their wits.

"What's the matter? What is happening here?"

"Your roomer has gone mad!" Tumarkin told them angrily, grabbed his book and his cap, and left for good.

From that time on, neither the Shapiros nor their roomer ever heard from Tumarkin again.

"The *shlimazel* is gone, vanished into thin air!" Sara lamented, and no one missed Tumarkin so much as Sara because he had carried away with him one of her dearest and deepest secrets.

the thirty-first chapter

THE COMING OF PASSOVER

All outdoors announced the coming of Passover.

It smelled of Passover time. The sun shone with the special glow of Passover. The entire Jewish Street took on that special busy look that always preceded Passover. No matter how Jewish the street might be, no matter how teeming with the children of Israel, it was still located in a Russian city and not every Jew could have the privilege of spending the night there.

Observing the run-down houses, the shabby Jewish inhabitants, the overworked women with their half-naked children, and listening to the din rising like a cloud from the houses, from the shops, and from the whole Jewish quarter, you might surely believe you had found yourself in the very depths of the Jewish Pale, where police, official gatekeepers, and residence permits were unknown.

Here were the same exhausted, desperate Jewish faces, the same worn-out, pregnant women, the same forever-hungry children; the same hurrying and scurrying as in the blessed Pale; the same scrambling and scraping for a groshen, for a crust of stale bread, for a dank, fetid corner in which to rest one's head; the same cut-rate shops, lean-to stands, and pushcarts. How their owners survived was God's secret.

You encountered the same *Luftmenschen*, pinning their hopes on miracles, the same idle, footloose young people, the same buxom women wandering the streets with empty baskets, the same naked, barefoot children dashing about aimlessly in the streets because their houses were squalid and cramped, and outdoors there was the open sky and the welcome sun.

Even the *kheders* and study houses were the same—old, dreary *kheders* with dark, sweaty walls. The same dismal study houses, bare and mournful with impoverished, wretched students—exactly the same as in the old Pale, not changed so much as a hair.

And, as in the Pale, with the arrival of the Passover season, the quarter came to life and began to stir. Furnishings and household goods were moved out of doors in order to be cleaned, aired out, renewed, refreshed. Everywhere a hubbub and commotion, everywhere a hustling and bustling—it was the week before Passover!

There was greatly increased activity in the factories which housed the large furnaces temporarily devoted to the baking of matzos. What pushing and shoving, what an uproar and rushing. Everyone wanted to have his matzos baked first.

This year Sara Shapiro was late in getting her matzos baked. And because of whom? Because of her husband, because he was a Shapiro, one of the real, Slaviteh Shapiros, and he felt it beneath his dignity to accept anything less than having his matzos made in the first baking of the day. Sara herself desired this, but needled him nevertheless.

"He compares himself to Shlomo Familiant. There's nothing worse than seeking honors and not being able to afford them. Make up your mind. If you're poor, don't make demands. In this world it's 'put up or shut up.' "

"All right! What do you want from my life?" David cried in exasperation. "You want to bake matzos, go bake matzos!"

But Sara wasn't letting him off the hook so easily. "What do you mean, bake matzos? I thought you had to have it in the first baking or nothing!"

David gave his daughter a look reserved for those occasions when Sara drove him over the edge, and Betty came to his rescue.

"Mama! Enough talk about matzos! Since Purim that's all we hear—matzos, matzos, and more matzos!"

For an entire week, indeed, all one heard in the apartment was "Matzos and matzos! Matzos and matzos!" Finally the roomer became curious about what matzos were.

That during Passover Jews ate a food called matzos, or *mazzah*, as the Russians pronounced it, he had known for a long time. But what kind of food it was and how it was eaten, he genuinely wished to know.

But there was something he wanted to know even more: he had heard and read, where, he could not recall, that to this Jewish mazzah Jews added blood, Christian blood. He himself had little belief in this nonsense, but he was curious to learn how these stories had arisen.

He was embarrassed to ask any of his friends. Talk to Shapiro? Impossible! A madman! For a question like that, he would chop you up into mincemeat. After Kirilikha's son, Volodka, was found murdered, Rabinovitch read in a local newspaper a few days later about whisperings in the city that it was likely Volodka had been murdered by local Jews, his veins opened and all his blood drained from him while he was still alive for the sake of their *mazzah*, which they would soon be baking for Passover.

The roomer read this news item aloud while sitting at the table but didn't get to finish the article because David Shapiro snatched the paper from his hand, spat on it, and flung it out the window.

"Is he out of his mind!?" Sara exclaimed. "Has he gone crazy?"

"I did him a favor!" David defended himself. "Why should a Jew read such trash?"

The following morning our Rabinovitch went out of his way to buy a copy of that same paper and secretly read what was written about Volodka's mysterious death.

He himself knew full well whose work it had been. Soon after Volodka had disappeared, he had immediately thought that his stepfather must have been responsible, as he had long wanted to be rid of the child. Rabinovitch himself had frequently rescued the boy, more dead than alive, from his stepfather's hands. But he was puzzled by the brutal way he had murdered the boy. Why did he have to stab him so many times? Forty-nine stab wounds had been counted on the body, according to the papers. Why exactly forty-nine? Why that number?

We can understand why our hero had become so interested in the matzos and wanted to see for himself how Jews baked it.

"I've never seen how they bake mazzah," he confessed to his landlady.

"First of all, it's not 'mazzah,' Sara corrected him. "In Russian it's mazzah but in our language, in Yiddish, it's called matzos. That's one thing. And second of all, if you'd like, why don't you come along with me to the foundry tomorrow or the day after and you'll see how it's done. But I must tell you beforehand, they won't let you stand around without helping out. You wouldn't feel comfortable, either, looking on with your arms folded while everyone else was working. You'll have to pitch in and help out."

Rabinovitch was elated. "Help bake mazzah? Ah!"

"Not mazzah, matzos!" Sara corrected him again. "I've told you a thousand times not to talk like a Gentile."

"Well, all right, khorosho, matzos, matzos. What will I have to do there?"

"They'll tell you what to do," Sara said, pleased at the thought that her roomer, a student, a medalist, and a millionaire, would be working side by side with all the poor people, ha-ha-ha!

Sara was beaming at the prospect and laughed out loud.

"What's the laughter about, Mama?" Betty asked, coming in from her room, her face aglow, ready to share her mother's pleasure. Still laughing, Sara told her about how the roomer wanted to help out with the baking of the matzos, ha-ha-ha!

"So what of it?" Betty said to her in Russian. "I also want to go. They say it's quite lively."

"And me too!" cried the schoolboy, Syomke, putting away his books, paper, and paraphernalia. He had no idea what was going on, but hearing that his teacher and sister were going somewhere lively, he wanted to come along too. This delighted the adults.

"Khorosho, good! You too, you too," Rabinovitch promised him and gazed with gratitude and love at Betty for understanding him without words.

MATZOS

This time David had his way. He prevailed on his wife to bake his matzos, though on a later date, in the first baking of the day. It was beneath him to have his matzos baked at the same time as the poorer people. Sara attempted to change his mind with a few well-chosen words.

"Crazy fool that you are! Stubborn mule! Isn't it all the same, the first baking or the last? Matzo is matzo . . ."

It did no good. His mind was made up. A Shapiro, one of the true Slaviteh Shapiros, heaven protect us!

Nevertheless, Sara herself was pleased that it had worked out; let the other wives envy her. Sad to say, there was little else to stir envy, at least let it be for that.

In the morning, Sara rose early, engaged a carriage to help her deliver the sack of flour to the foundry, prepared Syomke's lunch to take to the *gymnasium*, made sure he said his morning prayers (medal or no medal one has to say one's prayers!), and was about to leave. To her surprise, in came her daughter and the roomer, fully dressed, ready to go along.

"What are you doing? Are you out of your minds?" Sara laughed as she looked with pleasure at the young pair, wishing to herself, "May these two soon become a real couple. Please, God, may it be so."

"What? You're really serious about going to help bake matzos? I thought you were joking. All right, good. Come along then, I hope you won't regret it. That's no place to stand around and look. There you have to work!" said Sara, chuckling to herself at the thought that her roomer, a student, a medalist, and a millionaire besides, that he—ha-ha! Oh, how to keep from laughing out loud!

And the three of them seated themselves in the carriage and were off to the foundry to bake matzos.

The morning turned out to be one of those rare clear days with a blue sky, a warm sun, and a soft breeze, a pre-Passover day that tells you it is time to throw off, along with melancholy, your warm winter clothing and to don your light summer garb because Passover is on the way—dear, beloved Passover.

Oh! Passover! Passover! Who loves you more than the poor Jewish Street, than the poor needy children? Like little worms, they poke their heads out from their dark, dank holes into the world outside, into the open air, into the sunlight after having barely survived the long, cold winter. There it is, the beloved outdoors. There it is, God's sky. There it is, the beautiful, the bright, the warm sun. Come out, children, come out! Don't be afraid because rivulets of water are running down the street. Roll up your trouser legs, that's the way, and come, all of you, let's go see what's doing there on the other side of the street. Just see how many people! Ay-Ay! So many Jews, like stars in the sky! Like grains of sand! People walking, driving, housewives taking sacks of flour in carriages to the foundry to bake matzos. Do you hear me? Matzos! Matzos!

And the poor but happy children from the poor Jewish Street rolled up their trouser legs above the knee and with bare red feet ran down the hill of the Jewish Street, greeting each passerby with delight, with joy, and each carriage with a hoorah! They ran alongside, even ahead of the horses, leaping and prancing—it was good, it was warm, it was pleasant, it was the day before Passover!

Our Shapiros and their roomer were greeted by a band of children with a loud fanfare and a fine hoorah all the way up the hill, almost to the door of the foundry.

It was the first time our hero had seen so many Jewish children—poor, half-naked, barefoot children with pale faces and hungry-looking eyes, yet happy, lively, excited. He found it difficult to comprehend the source of their happiness. Intellect alone was inadequate to the task; one had to feel it. And in order to feel it, one had to have been a Jewish child from the Jewish Street, to have been born and raised and to have grown up in the same poverty and wretchedness, in the same misery and want.

"Good, there's the foundry!" Sara said, climbing out of the carriage, and after her, the roomer and her daughter.

A wide courtyard. A high, red brick wall. A tall chimney—an iron foundry. Below in the cellar, down a long flight of stairs, a huge, deep oven burning like an inferno in a large, gaslit room. Along the walls long tables covered with new, bleached-white tablecloths. Men wearing yellowed prayer shawls, women wearing white aprons, young girls with sparkling, smiling eyes. The heat, like a steambath; a babble of voices, like geese; a din, a tumult, a commotion, as at a fair. Here was where the matzos were baked.

"It's a good thing you came, Madam, or else we would have started baking someone else's matzos," Sara was greeted by Pesach-Hersh, the baker, a Jew with a perspiring face, dull eyes, a round chin jutting out too far and too sparsely bearded, his lower lip twisted to the side so that one didn't know whether the man was laughing or crying.

"You wouldn't have heard the end of it from my husband!" Sara replied. "You're forgetting my husband is a Shapiro, one of the true Slaviteh Shapiros."

"I know all too well. I haven't forgotten, I have a good memory!" Pesach-Hersh, the baker, answered and began to instruct the assemblage in baker's language and in rhyme:

Hey, women and girls! Tuck in your curls!
Save your chatty ways for other holidays!
Water in the bowl, flour in real fast,
Matzos in the oven, matzos out at last!

Reb Zalman-Ber, come over here!
Frume-Beile, don't bake a failure!
Boruch-Zeidel, spin like a dreydl!

And so on.
"Let's get to work," said Sara, and rolled up her sleeves.

the thirty-third chapter

SHALKHA-NARAKH

Our Popov-Rabinovitch, who had come to see how Jews baked matzos, had another aim in mind. He began to pay close attention to every detail. He had promised himself, you understand, that once and for all he had to find out the whole truth! The *mazzah* must open his eyes, drive away the clouds, and forever put an end to that nightmare, to that stupor in which he had found himself since the terrible events surrounding the murder of Kirilikha's son, Volodka.

Volodka had been found in such a ghastly state that one had to assume something had occurred which could only take place once in a hundred years. Popov-Rabinovitch had also read everything in all the newspapers about the hideous atrocities that Jews committed against Christian children exactly at the time just before Passover for the sake of their matzo.

"It is as clear as day that Jews killed the unfortunate Volodka!" certain journals kept repeating that same old song. "Not just killed him, but first tortured him, drained his blood from his veins from forty-nine wounds, and then pierced his heart with an awl while he was still alive and forced to stand up."

Other, cleverer troublemakers claimed they were well-versed in Talmudic law. "According to Jewish law," they wrote pompously, "according to *Shalkha-narakh*" (by this they meant the *Shulkhan-arukh*, the 613 Jewish laws of conduct), "Jews must have Christian blood for their Passover *mazzah*, at least a few drops. It sufficed, therefore, for all the Jews of the world to kill just one healthy Christian child with plentiful blood in his veins. Not one Passover goes by without one's hearing that somewhere a Christian child has disappeared. The *Shalkha-narakh* states specifically that it is necessary to use only children no younger than five and no older than fifteen."

So claimed these clever authorities; they went on to describe in lurid detail the solemn ceremony that took place when the Jews found their victim, how rabbis, scholars, ritual slaughterers, and cantors intoned certain biblical verses

and chants, how all the Jews rejoiced, sang and danced in ways strangely similar
to savage African natives or wild Patagonians.

These were the articles our Rabinovitch had been reading constantly from
Purim to Passover, devouring every word and not believing any of it: these
"tales" from the *Shalkha-narakh* seemed to him too simple-minded, too crude,
too outlandish, too much resembling fantastic old-wives' tales, stories of a-
thousand-and-one-nights, plainly having the sole purpose of sowing hatred between one people and another. He was genuinely pained and deeply ashamed of
his Christian brethren, the perverted minds who thought up such beastly accusations, as well as the ignorant masses who believed such idiotic nonsense. Still,
a worm of doubt gnawed at him relentlessly, impelling him to go, to see for
himself, to convince himself with his own eyes. And as he now had the chance
to visit the foundry where they were baking Jewish matzo, why let such a rare
opportunity be lost? What harm would there be in observing, in listening? And
as he was already in the very place where the matzo was being made, he would
see, you can be certain, all there was to see! No detail would escape his eyes!

This was what our Grigori Ivanovitch Popov told himself he would do, and
this is what he saw at the baking of the Jewish matzo:

The assembled group took to its task in a lively and cheerful manner. In the
twinkling of an eye the sack of flour was untied. From a large, brand-new,
wooden pitcher, water was poured into a sizable copper basin. Two women,
sleeves rolled up above the elbow, kneaded a soft, white dough with their clean,
white hands. The soft, white dough was then divided into many smaller portions
among the younger women and girls, with their smiling, clever eyes, who distributed the pieces of dough on the smaller, white, cloth-covered tables. With clean,
brand-new rolling pins, the balls of dough were flattened as thin as cigarette
paper. A wiry lad appeared, his head cocked to the side, in his hand a small,
brass perforating cylinder, which he quickly rolled across the length and width of
the dough—one batch of matzo was now ready to bake!

Meet Boruch-Zeydl, Boruch Zeydl Fliam they called him, a soldier serving in
the infantry who still had two and a half years to go before he would, with God's
help, marry his fiancee, Bluma Karshuk. You might as well meet her too, she was
also there in the foundry, a healthy girl, attractively dark-skinned, with the large,
full breasts of a nursing mother. After Boruch-Zeydl's ministrations, the perfora-
ted matzos flew to Zalman-Ber on a long, white paddle and from him to Pesach-
Hersh himself, who had the honor of shoving them into the oven, which burned
like an inferno. Within a minute, one could already detect an aroma, the delicious, wonderful aroma of good, baked, dry matzo, which Rabinovitch could
imagine crumbling and crackling between his teeth, eating it exactly as the Jews
had once eaten it in the desert.

Is that all? Where is the ceremony? Where are the rabbis, the scholars, the
ritual slaughterers, the cantors? Where are the songs, the dances, and all the rest
of the *Shalkha-narakh*? And he felt ashamed, because even though he knew
beforehand that it was all a fabrication, nevertheless he had to come to watch
for himself, to investigate in order to convince himself.

"Why are you standing there like that, I ask you, looking like a relative at the wrong wedding?" said Sara Shapiro, who was helping to roll out the matzos. "You'd do better to roll up your sleeves, if you don't mind, and make yourself useful instead of standing idly by. We talked about this, didn't we?"

"What should I do? Tell me . . ."

"What should you do? Help pour out the flour, and Betty will pour the water, ha-ha-ha!" Sara was amused, not because her daughter, a seventh-year *gymnasium* student, would join all the women to make matzo, but by the thought that her roomer, a medalist student and a millionaire, would be . . . ha-ha-ha!

Sara Shapiro was happier on this day than usual. She was not alone in this; everyone was happy and in a holiday mood. This contagious mood finally infected Shapiro's roomer as he began to roll up his sleeves.

"Not like that, like this!" said Betty, herself in a better humor than ever before, and she began to roll up his sleeves for him. Rabinovitch felt ecstatic; every touch of her delicate fingers on his bare arms ran through him like an electric current which stirred and warmed his heart. He could smell her hair and feel the warmth of her body so close to his. His head was spinning, and he thought, "How long? How long can this hoax go on? How long can we continue to play out this comedy? I'm going to throw myself at her feet this very minute . . ." But his eyes met hers, her lovely, intelligent, clear eyes, which appeared to be both friendly and stern, conveying, "Not now, not here."

And he was aware of many eyes looking at him—at him and at her. The pretty girls and the curious women were casting their knowing looks at the pair while poking each other with their elbows, meaning "This had to be a twosome meant for one another."

The older women whispered into Sara's ear, "A match? May God grant it be so."

Sara didn't say yes or no, but responded with a little smile and with a soft sigh as she thought, "May it be so, God in heaven! From their lips into God's ear." And before she knew it, she was finished with her matzos.

The carriage was waiting outside. In the meantime, a gang of poor but happy Jewish children from the Jewish Street had gathered and were driving the carriage. That is, they were playing at driving the carriage. One boy sat up front, hands folded, head high in the air like a wealthy gentleman. Another held the reins, pretending to urge on and whip the horse. "Giddyup! Giddyup!" he smacked his lips and whistled. Luckily the horse was tied to a fence and was eating his lunch from a bag of oats hung over his head or there might have been a catastrophe. The driver, also a Jew (Sara Shapiro wouldn't hire a non-Jewish driver before Passover, especially for matzo baking!), had slipped into the foundry and, standing with his whip leaning against the door, hat tilted back, was observing the procedures and deeply envying everyone involved—the bakers, the workers, the helpers. "What a wonderful way to make a living," he thought. "A warm and happy way to make a living."

"Reb Ezriel, time to go!" Sara winked at him, and Reb Ezriel (though he was dressed in a regular Russian coachman's uniform, he was still called Reb Ezriel) ran out to his carriage, and when he saw the gang of boys, he shouted at them, first in Russian, and then slipping more naturally into Yiddish.

"Hooligans! May the devil take you! Wait till you get a taste of the whip! I'll teach you all a lesson!"

They were not about to stand around waiting for Reb Ezriel to teach them a lesson. Before he could raise his whip, they were gone, like frightened mice, not a sign of a Jewish child . . .

With great speed and agility, Pesach-Hersh grabbed the baked matzos and carried them ten at a time to the carriage and loaded them so adroitly that not a single one was broken.

While the matzos were being transferred to the carriage, Sara paid the baker and the helpers, who wished her a kosher Passover, much happiness, and a speedy engagement while casting glances at her daughter and the handsome young man standing next to her, both already dressed to leave.

"You children go on home. I'll bring the matzos back myself." Sara said the word "children" so softly, so gently, and with so much motherly love and devotion that both her daughter and her roomer felt a special warmth. Their eyes met and their faces reddened with sudden emotion.

"Shouldn't we ride together with your mother and the matzos?" Rabinovitch said to Betty and she laughed.

"Mama, do you hear what he said?"

"I hear. He doesn't know you're supposed to walk alongside the matzos."

"All right, whatever you say," he said, not taking his eyes off the matzos, watching carefully as they were carried, stacked, and covered with a clean linen cloth. He kept his eyes glued to them until they were brought home, removed from the carriage, and placed in a clean Passover drawer lined with white paper.

When the drawer was filled and Sara began to lock it, she noticed her roomer staring fixedly at the matzos and she laughed.

"Why are you staring at the matzo like a cat at cream? Maybe you'd like a taste? Tell the truth!"

Oh! He would love to tell her the whole truth if he weren't so ashamed . . . a terrible, awful shame! How could he, a cultured man of the twentieth century, have believed for even a second such crazy nonsense? If he could believe such an outlandish fabrication as the *Shalkha-narakh*, then what was the difference between him and those evil fanatics who, several hundred years ago, believed that Christians used human blood to poison wells, and other such drivel? And in order not to raise her suspicions about why he was staring so hard at the matzos, he confessed to his landlady that she was right, he wouldn't turn down a taste of the matzo.

"Is that right?" Sara said to him with a happy laugh. "You can't wait till the Passover seder? At the Passover seder you'll get a taste. What are you—a Gentile? Don't you know you're not allowed till then?"

And laughing and jingling the keys, Sara Shapiro locked the matzo drawer.

ALL BY HERSELF

Sara Shapiro was no *rebbitzin* and couldn't be compared to her sister-in-law, Toibe Familiant, who, it was said, put socks on the cat's paws lest it carry *khometz*—leaven and other contamination—into the rooms already set aside and prepared for Passover. Nevertheless, at Passover time Sara became another person. Without servants, it fell to the poor woman to do everything herself, from the matzos to the Passover borscht; she cleaned the house, koshered the meat, scoured, washed, scrubbed, shook out, polished, chopped—in short, ushered the *khometz* out and welcomed the Passover in—all by herself. Was it any wonder she was constantly worked up and touchy so that one took one's life into one's hands to approach her?

The day before Passover Sara returned early from the market with the fish and the meat, the Passover dishes, and the bitter herbs. She was distracted, agitated, perspiring, boiling, her eyes almost popping with strain. After resting a moment, no more than to catch her breath, she remained standing in the middle of the room and looked around at the still-to-be-packed away *khometz* dishes and still-to-be-unpacked Passover plates, the covered little crock of borscht in the corner, the ropes of onions on the wall, the beets and potatoes, the *haroses*—chopped apples—the new grater and the *moror*—bitter herbs—and she wrung her hands, saying to herself, "*Vey iz mir!* How will I be able to put this all in order? How will I clear up this chaos when my head is bursting?"

She began her labors by packing her husband, David, off to work, not allowing him sufficient time to perform the ritual of burning the *khometz*. He rushed through the prayer, "All the *khometz* still in the house," in one breath, tossing the *khometz* spoon and feather duster into the oven, and fleeing from the house as from a living hell without so much as eating breakfast.

"Where are you flying off to, 'express train'?" Sara shouted after him, feeling guilty; she was, after all, a wife. "Eat something! At least have a glass of tea!"

"Never mind! Never mind!" David shouted back and pulled his hat down resolutely on his head to let her know the consequences of being so irritable before Passover.

"When will you be home to eat the last *khometz* meal?" she shouted down the stairs.

"At the usual time!" he answered, unwilling to look up at her.

"Don't forget, you still have to go to the baths, buy the wine, grate the *haroses* . . ."

"I know! I know!" he muttered under his breath, slammed the door, and was gone.

With even more urgency Sara sent her son off to the *gymnasium*, having awakened the poor child from deepest sleep.

"Syomke! Syomkenyu! Syomketchke! Wake up, my sweet! Wake up, my dearest, light of my life! Come on now, bless your heart!"

But Syomke didn't hear. He lay curled up in his pillow, his black locks thrown back, his cheek and ear red. A smile crossed his lips; the good angel was apparently whispering golden dreams into his ear—about what? Likely about something at school . . . His teacher calls on him by his full name, "S-H-A-P-I-R-O S-H-L-Y-O-M-K-E!" His classmates burst out laughing—quite a handle there, Shlyomke, no? But he doesn't care. Why should their laughter bother him when he knows the lesson cold? He stands up and goes at it with confidence in Russian.

"When Aleksander Nevsky died there were was a war against the throne."

"Enough!" the teacher says to him. Syomke doesn't listen and goes on.

"Moscow was founded in the twelfth century . . ."

"What were the events surrounding it?" the teacher asks.

"Prince Ivan Kalita became the chief, a good ruler and very frugal."

His classmates have long ceased laughing. They almost rise from their seats and exchange amazed glances. "What is this Jewboy saying?" They resent Syomke's having captured a grade of five. Two fives. Three fives. A whole slew of fives. Fives without end! But this did not impress his mother at all—it was the day of Passover. She nudged and shook him harder. "Come on now, wake up! Of all times to be dead asleep!"

Syomke stretched himself out full length under the covers, threw his hands over his head, opened his eyes a tiny bit, scowled, and then looked fearfully at his mother. He was just falling into a new dream: he and Volodka are outside playing ball . . . Syomke tosses the ball up on the roof accidentally and so Volodka pulls his hat off for a joke . . . Syomke begs him, "Volodya! Give it back, Volodya!"

"What's he babbling about?" said Sara, looking around. "What Volodya? He's seeing Volodka in his dreams now! May he be far from us—tphoo! Tphoo! Tphoo!"

Syomke started to laugh at himself and said to his mother, "What is it, Mama?"

"What is it, he's asking! Have you forgotten? Today you eat the *khometz* meal early. You still have to go with your father to the baths and get your hair cut. It's Passover day. So hurry, hurry!"

Syomke's cheeks glowed and his eyes shone.

"Ah? Passover? Matzos? Matzo balls?" Then switching to Russian, he said, "I can ask the Four Questions, I can get a grade of five-plus in that!"

"All right, all right. Tomorrow tell me stories in Russian, not today. The child can only speak to me in Russian, may a curse fall on my enemies! Enough now, you must get up! Get dressed! Are you going to get dressed or are you going to keep me from getting on with the Passover?"

Syomke awoke in a happy frame of mind. He wanted to hug and kiss not only his mother but the entire world. It was hard for him to understand why she was in such a bad mood. Why was she so angry? Why was she stuffing him into his trousers? Why was she in such a hurry? In a minute he was all ready. But as if in spite, one boot refused to go on his foot. No matter what, the boot would not budge!

"Why is this happening to me today of all days?" Sara whined, twisting his foot every which way. "Has the boot shrunk or has your foot swollen? What on earth . . . ?"

"Either way, let her find out!" thought Syomke and bent his foot into such a position that even if the boot were three times as big and his mother would push three years running, day and night, it wouldn't go on.

But this trick didn't work for long because his mother looked at him suspiciously, he looked back at her innocently, and she delivered a ringing slap with her right hand to his left cheek.

"That'll teach you!" Sara snapped at him, and immediately her heart melted with pity for the child. She was torn between blaming herself and embracing and kissing the child, but one mustn't give in. A child knows no limits. A child must learn respect. And sure enough, when Syomke was ready, the boot slid on like butter. Ay, was he crying? So, he would cry till he stopped. She did have one regret—she had slapped him too hard. What if his cheek swelled up, poor child?

"Nu? Are you going to wash yourself or not? Come here, I'll help you wash. Put your hands out. Like this. Wash your face yourself. Come here, I'll dry you."

And with soft, gentle, motherly hands Sara wiped his bright face and lovely eyes, which were soon dry of tears. She yearned to kiss his cheek, on which she could still see the outline of her hand, but she held back. A child knows no limits. A child must learn respect . . . And she stood him up to say his morning prayers.

"There'll be plenty of opportunities for skipping your prayers. Don't worry, you won't be late for that! Go on, pray, pray! Hurry, quick!"

He didn't have to be urged to hurry. He could oblige her by finishing his prayers so quickly that before she could say "prayer" he would be finished. No sooner did she turn away for a moment and aha! he was done.

"Finished? So soon? Some praying!" Sara said, forgetting that she herself had been rushing him. She put his lunch in his pocket—go!

Having gotten rid of her son, it was now time to get to work on her daughter. A young lady in the seventh class and soon, God willing, a bride—how does one awaken her? If only she weren't so impertinent . . . Oh, she's getting up by herself. "Betty! Betty?"

"What in heaven's name is going on out there?" a silvery voice was heard from the other room.

"What a way to talk. Is that a way to speak to your mother?"

"How then do you speak to a mother?"

"Betty! I don't have time to sit around and chat with you now. The day isn't standing still. It's Passover day."

"Well, what do you want?"

"What do you want? Why are you talking to me as if I were just anyone?"

"How then do you want me to talk to you?"

This conversation between mother and daughter had thus far been taking place out of sight of each other. But now Betty appeared at the door of her room, bright and glowing, still not dressed, her uncombed hair cascading down her beautiful, marble-white shoulders draped with a clean towel, her breasts modestly covered with her hands. As soon as this girl appeared, the entire room seemed to become illuminated by her presence, brightness and warmth pervaded every corner. A host of angels must have descended and entered with her, singing a song of praise to this goddess of beauty on the Jewish Street. The small room in great chaos was transformed into a corner of the Garden of Eden. Her own mother gazed at her in wonder. "God bless us! Such a treasure!" Sara thought, gazing at her daughter, who brought such beauty into her home. But it was still the day of Passover, so much work to be done, and she couldn't waste time admiring her daughter, half-dressed and uncombed, looking impertinently at her with her brazen smile.

"I would like to know, Betty, what that smile is all about?"

"Did you want me to cry?"

"Bite your tongue! Who said that? On the contrary, one must laugh while one's mother is killing herself, one person all by herself in such a big place, *keyn eyn horeh*—may no evil eye befall you!"

"Who's asking you to? I'm going to get dressed and I'll help you."

"No one asked you! I don't need your help! You'd better get dressed, Betty, and clear out of your room. There's plenty of work here without you!"

"You mean you're sending me away from the house because it's Passover day? You want to get rid of me?"

"Of course. I have so many daughters!"

"You have one daughter and she's one too many for you."

"One daughter . . . but a good one."

"No, a bad one."

"Who said a bad one, a good one?"

Betty nuzzled her mother like a little kitten. "No, Mama, I really want to know. A good one or a bad one?"

"Will you ever stop? I don't have time to joke around with you now! Get dressed and go in good health!"

"Where do you suggest I go? Or doesn't it matter where?"

Sara couldn't take it any more. She was at her wit's end, barely able to control herself. Every minute was an hour, every hour a day. And here she was standing and making jokes! Sara raised her voice to a high pitch.

"Betty! Bet-ty! Don't drive me crazy! Don't make me angry!"

Betty realized she had pushed her mother too far. She lingered another moment at the door, singing quietly to herself, and disappeared into her bedroom. And with her vanished the brightness and warmth. The living room returned to chaos, and poor Sara felt a pang in her heart. Why was she treating her daughter this way? Such a wonderful daughter and such a treasure! And she had the notion to cast all the work aside, to go into her dear daughter's room and tell her, "My precious child, don't be angry at your mother. Sometimes mothers go crazy . . ." But she remembered it was Passover day, so much work to be done, one person all by herself, such a big house, *keyn eyn horeh*. And her heart again became resolute and hard and she didn't care to know whether Betty had already had her tea or not, nor did she want to see what she was wearing. Betty, hat and umbrella in hand, remained standing in the doorway in case her mother wished to say something. Not a chance! It would be a cold day in hell before she, Sara Shapiro, would speak first to her daughter after she had affronted her with her impertinent singing.

When Betty was gone, Sara stood a while listening to her footsteps, appearing to want to say something, when she heard a cough from the side room.

"Aha! He's also waking up? Just what I needed, as if I didn't have enough trouble!"

The person Sara was so upset about didn't make her wait long. He emerged from his room freshly awakened from a good night's sleep, his hair dark and thick. In a deep baritone voice he bade the landlady good morning and casually asked her, with feigned calm, "Where is Berta Davidovna?"

"Go look for her!" Sara snapped, then asked him, "Are you leaving soon or will it take a while before you go?"

Either the roomer didn't hear her or he pretended not to because he didn't answer her. He simply considered the chaos around him, looked over toward the door from which the beautiful Betty had left only moments before, and again asked his landlady, "Has Berta Davidovna woken up yet?"

"She woke up ages ago and is long gone."

"Gone? Where could Berta Davidovna have gone so early?"

"What do you want from my life?" Sara exploded at her roomer. "You see I don't have any time. I'm at my wit's end. It's the day of Passover, one person all by herself, such a big house, *keyn eyn horeh*, and him with his Berta Davidovna! And again Berta Davidovna!"

With kindly, smiling eyes the roomer looked into his landlady's face, turned around, went back to his room, returned with his coat, hat, and walking stick, and whistling a Russian tune, "*Vdol po ulitse shirokoy*—On the wide street the young smithy goes singing," went down the steps and was gone.

"I hope he's not insulted," Sara thought. "My heavens! He's not a child . . . a student and a medalist and a millionaire besides . . . and with God's help a bridegroom too . . . and maybe soon? Oh, let it be so, God above, how does one live to see the day! How does one live to see the day!"

And with all the work still ahead of her and having driven out all the members of the household, Sara sat herself down in a corner, one person by herself, leaning her head in her hands, sighing and swaying back and forth as if in prayer, sinking deeper into her worries, cares, griefs and woes, woes, woes! . . .

"PEOPLE-FLIES"

Once he had fled the house, the "chaos" as Sara Shapiro called it, Rabinovitch hailed a cab and asked to be taken to a certain address. As he rode, he kept whistling a tune:

Vdol po ulitse shirokoy
Molodoi kuznets idyot
On idyot—idyot—
Pyesnyu s'prisvistom payot . . . .

He was in high spirits, pleased with himself, with the fine, warm Passover morning, and, all in all, with how everything was going.

And he had good reason to be pleased, even happy. No small matter, Betty, the lovely, exciting Betty, was his—he knew it for certain, as one knew two times two is four.

The black cat that had crossed their path after their evening at the theater was past history. The clouds that had darkened their sky had long since dispersed, and once again the sun, that bright, golden sun which brightens, warms, and quickens not only the body but the very soul and promises happiness, good fortune, and love, love without end, now smiled down on the young couple.

It was not expressed through words—who needed words? Wasn't it enough—a glance from her beautiful, luminous, intelligent eyes? Wasn't it enough—a playful swipe across the nose, a light slap on the hand, a touch in passing, a prank, a silvery laugh, and a thousand other such little things of which a romance is spun much better than of earnest, ponderous, and silly declarations of love?

Their closeness had evolved spontaneously; they both had approached each other with giant steps. The time was ripe. Only one thing remained, one small step—he had to talk with her father or, better still, with her mother, who was looking forward to this event daily, hourly. Several times he had been on the verge of taking this small step when he reminded himself of the mighty wall that stood between them from birth, and each time he drew back in fear, wracking his brain over this dilemma that he could in no way resolve. Betty was too proud of her Jewishness and expressed herself too sharply about those who "use God for their own ends." Their meeting with Lapidus that evening at the theater and the conversations he had had with her afterward were proof enough that he should never touch on that subject again.

When then does one do? He decided to consult a rabbi in order to put his dilemma before him and seek his advice. He asked the Shapiros, as indirectly as possible, who their rabbi was and where he could be found.

When Sara heard that her roomer was asking about a rabbi, her heart began to pound—he must surely wish to see a crown rabbi who issues marriage certificates and licenses. She explained that in the city there were two grades of crown rabbis: one was a crown rabbi and the other one an assistant crown rabbi.

"There she goes again, running off at the mouth!" David cut her off, as always. "He's asking about a rabbi and you're telling him stories about crown and assistant crown rabbis!"

And David began to clarify the matter for the roomer, in his own way, accompanied by broad gestures, that there were, in fact, several rabbis in the city, among them, two crown rabbis, that is to say, one was a crown rabbi and the other an assistant crown rabbi.

"Did you hear that?" Sara interrupted. "And what was I saying? Not the same?"

"Of course," David said, "but if you had an ounce of brains in your head and a crumb of respect and wouldn't butt in when people are talking and let someone finish what he is saying, you would understand I'm not saying the same thing as you because I'm not a moron, I know what I'm talking about!"

David turned toward the roomer, his back to his wife, and began to explain, with appropriate gestures. "So then, we have a lot of rabbis here. Two of them are considered crown rabbis, that is, one is a crown rabbi and the other is an assistant crown rabbi, and the rest" (here David turned momentarily toward his wife and glared at her) "and the rest are called *clerical* rabbis."

Then he explained, still gesticulating, the difference between civil rabbis and clerical rabbis.

"You are, just between us, a Gentile," David said to the roomer quite frankly, "a real *goy*. You don't have the slightest idea what it's like among Jews. Everything is new to you. You don't even know what selling the *khometz* means, buying back the firstborn son, or immersing the dishes in the ritual bath. Some Jew! One has to chew every little thing up and put it in your mouth!"

Rabinovitch found out from his landlord that among all the rabbis there was one who was a *tzotzke*, as David called him, a crackerjack. The whole city, he said, thought the world of him because he had such outstanding qualities. In addition to being a scholar and an honest Jew, he was learned in worldly matters, fluent in languages, a cultured man and an intellectual. People traveled from all over to see him, he said, those who needed an arbitrator, a lawsuit settled, or simply good advice. That was precisely what our hero needed, and it was to him he asked to be taken that morning, the day of Passover.

He entered a large reception hall crowded with men, women, and children. It could have been a doctor's waiting room but for the fact that in a doctor's waiting room it is absolutely quiet as each patient is silently preoccupied with his own worries. But here there was a loud hubbub as in a marketplace; everyone was speaking at once, oddly distraught and restless. People would leap up from their seats, argue heatedly, and then sink back in their seats, sighing deeply.

"People-flies"—flashed through Rabinovitch's mind. Why flies? He had no idea. But that was the impression these people made on him. And he began to listen to what they were talking about so heatedly. What were they so upset about? And why did they keep sighing? From the few Yiddish words he had picked up at the Shapiros', he could piece together that the crowd was talking about the recently discovered Volodka, whom the gazettes had been writing about, accusing the Jews of having murdered him on account of Passover.

"A tragedy, a libel! A pogrom, a pogrom!" were the words he heard most often in the din, and whenever the word "pogrom" was mentioned, he noticed that on each face appeared an expression of distress, of deep dismay. The women sighed and clasped their children closer to their bosoms.

If Rabinovitch could not feel their distress with his heart, he understood it with his head. Just the day before, in one of those newspapers that love to use polite language in order to hide their true intent, he had read, "We don't wish to make predictions, and we don't wish in any way to provoke one segment of the population against the other, but it appears to us, in fact, we are almost totally convinced, that the justified wrath of the offended population will of necessity overflow during the upcoming Holy Days into a well-deserved Jewish pogrom, if not in a series of pogroms, in order to quell the rage and wreak vengeance for the unfortunate Volodka, whose innocent blood was shed by blind fanatics for the purpose of their Passover *mazzah*."

In a second newspaper he had read a similar article under the misleading headline, "Protect Your Children!" The author of the article was not, heaven forbid, intending any malice toward Jews and was not calling for a pogrom. Only that "as the Jewish Passover is nearing in which Jews cannot manage without Christian blood, as has been proven many times, and most recently in the case of the unfortunate Volodi Chigirinski, it is advised that you keep a close eye on your small child," and so on.

A third periodical expressed itself more openly under a headline in large type: "BLOOD FOR BLOOD!" and called on every respectable Christian who has God in his heart to "take revenge, to settle the score with the Jews for the innocent Vladimir Chigirinski, who was sacrificed on the altar of their sinister fanaticism which they brought out with them from Egypt. And speaking of settling the score, this humble journal finds it imperative to beseech its respectable readers not to vent their wrath on the poor Jews alone, but to start with the magnates, those who have clawed their way to the top, grabbed up the choicest properties and finest mansions of our holy city, and who support with their ill-gotten gains countless *Chassidim, Tsaddikim,* and *Shakhatim* who add Christian blood to their *mazzahs*," and so on, and ended with the words: " 'An eye for an eye!' they say. We say, 'Blood for blood!' "

These were the inflammatory newspaper commentaries the crowd was so heatedly and so intensely talking about. As it appeared to our hero, they weren't simply discussing their import but were debating and quarreling over it. He was amazed at how quickly these people spoke, it seemed a thousand words a minute, and yet how they could understand one another when they were all speaking at the same time. "People-flies," he thought; they buzzed like flies, were weak as flies, and like flies, it seemed, they could be dispersed with a loud shout or a raised hand.

Then suddenly there was silence, and the entire group of men, women, and children rose as one, with rare respect, for a person who now appeared at the door.

He was a man of medium stature, a soft, gentle-appearing person, middle-aged, with a young, translucent skin, possessing large, black, youthful eyes and jet black hair flecked with gray, his sidelocks short and straight. He wore a round, velvet yarmulke on his head and a wide, white, smooth collar, a velvet vest, and a clean, long, black kaftan. His youthful face shone with such intelligence and nobility, and his entire gentle-appearing figure conveyed such tranquility, dignity, and inner discipline, that one instinctively rose and removed one's hat in his presence.

This was that *tzotzke* of a rabbi Shapiro had praised to the skies.

the thirty-sixth chapter

PERHAPS A PROVOCATEUR

Our Popov-Rabinovitch had worked out a plan for seeking the rabbi's advice. He would tell him that he had an acquaintance, a Christian friend, who had fallen in love with a Jewish girl, and the girl with him, and since the girl would not change her religion under any circumstances, his Christian friend was prepared to take on *her* religion. He had come to inquire of the rabbi what his friend had to do, because his friend was totally ignorant of the tenets of the Jewish faith and was, altogether, a nonreligious person.

That was the plan he had in mind when he came to the rabbi. But as soon as he crossed the threshold of the rabbi's study and met him face to face, Rabinovitch abandoned his plan entirely. He was immediately taken with the rabbi's dark, Spanish looks, with his rare serenity and deliberate manner, which from the very first won his complete confidence. He felt that with this man he did not need to play any games or make any pretenses but could speak openly.

And so it was. While resting his chin on one hand and, with the other, leafing through a book, the rabbi listened intently to the young man's confession, allowing him to talk at length. When he had finished, the rabbi sighed as if it had been he who had been speaking all the while, not his guest. Then he shut his book and with a smile, said to the guest, "I'm not going to ask you *who* you are or who the young lady is. The fact that you aren't saying is a sign that you wish to keep it secret. I, alas, cannot help you, nor do I have any advice for you. I regret this with all my heart, young man, and feel very sorry for you."

The guest was stunned: He feels sorry for me?

"I feel terribly sorry for you, young man. There are six million unfortunate, despised, harassed, suffering souls in this country who are so well-thought-of that there are people wracking their brains trying to figure out a way to be rid of them, and you want to become yet another one of them? You want to become the first of the seventh million?"

The guest was taken aback, both by what the rabbi said and by the way he said it: quietly, calmly, with a smile on his lips and in perfect Russian—a strange rabbi! Strange words!

As the visitor remained silent, the rabbi continued speaking, as if he had guessed what he was thinking.

"You're surprised to hear these words from me, from a rabbi? I would presume that if a stranger wishing to convert approached your priest, he would do the same. We are obliged, you know, to open the eyes of the one who comes to us so that he will know exactly what he is doing and where it will lead him. It says in the Torah of Moses—'Do not lead a blind person astray.' "

"But I told you my reason," the guest said and turned red. "I . . . I am in love and she is in love with me. There is no other alternative for me."

"A poor reason for such a serious step. Giving up one's faith requires the most profound inner crisis, in which one ceases to believe in one's own faith and begins believing in another. We, for instance, deplore those converts who do so because of a residence permit, a diploma, for business reasons, or for a woman. Understandably, the last motive is somewhat finer, the psychology of it more noble, but a compromise remains a compromise: it is making a deal with God."

Popov-Rabinovitch could not understand how this calm man sitting across from him could see right through him and read his thoughts like a book. He could not even admit to himself that he hadn't come there because he had valued the Jewish faith or because he had fallen in love with the Jewish people. And as if the rabbi had continued to read his thoughts, after a short pause, he again directed his words to the guest.

"I'm not even speaking of belief. In general, people are not strong on belief these days, our people as well as yours. I am talking about a nation, a people. It's hard to believe you can convince yourself that you, born and raised a Christian, in today's times of bitter racial hatred, can love a Jew, can believe there is no difference between a Jew and a non-Jew."

"To me there is no difference!" Popov interrupted him. "I love this Jewish girl so much that nothing can stand in my way. I don't want to know anything . . ."

"Well, yes, I truly believe what you're saying, and I feel with you with all my heart. Yours is an emotion that knows no bounds and doesn't acknowledge the difference between one people and another. But I must tell you, young man, we have a saying, it's perhaps banal but true, 'You can't love your wife if you don't love your wife's family,' and our family, alas, has never been so hated and humiliated as it has been in recent times. Just look at what we've been through. Look at what they're writing about us in the name of God and in the name of the one who preached about love."

The rabbi reached across and handed his guest a Russian newspaper upon which was emblazoned in large, bold letters, "BLOOD FOR BLOOD!"

The guest glanced at the familiar headline and said, "I read that yesterday. It was written by a man without a drop of justice in him. I doubt if you could find a single respectable Gentile who wouldn't be disgusted by those words. I doubt if you could find many Gentiles who wouldn't know at first glance that it is an untrue story, a myth."

"And yet there are among your brethren thousands upon thousands who do believe it is true, not a myth. Now tell me, as an honest Christian, in all good faith, did it never cross your mind when you first read the wild story of the murdered Chigirinski that perhaps it *was* true? Perhaps Jews did do it for blood for their Passover matzo?"

The eyes that gazed at the guest conveyed that he had no need to hide his thoughts. Therefore he felt no need to deny them or to defend himself. He simply felt it necessary to comment to the rabbi that in that particular instance he could have no doubt at all because no one knew as much about that event as he, as he had been well acquainted with the youngster in question. He knew the youngster, he knew the mother, the stepfather, the whole family. Moreover, he was positive, and he had proof, that the murderer of the Chigirinski boy was none other than his stepfather, who was the only one who had an interest in eliminating that innocent soul.

"You say you knew the boy?" the rabbi asked, excited, in an altogether different tone of voice and with a changed expression. "You say you know the stepfather, the mother, and all the rest of them? You say you have proof? Oh! Young man, young man!" He clasped the guest's hand in both of his. "Oh! Young man, young man!"

The rabbi, whose stately calm until that moment had so taken Popov aback, was suddenly transformed before his eyes, seeming to become another person entirely. What had become of his composure, his pride?

"Is it possible?" the rabbi said to him. "You can't imagine, my young man, what you have just said. You can't realize the importance of what you know. You are in a position to rescue a whole city of Jews from tragedy, and a whole people from a . . . from . . . from . . ."

Out of great emotion, words failed him. The rabbi let go of the young man's hand, sighed deeply, and, regaining his composure, began to paint for the guest an accurate picture of the kind of world-shaking drama that was unfolding, the agitation that was being perpetrated, the source of it, and how grievous it could turn out for Jews. In the guest's eyes the rabbi appeared at that moment to have suddenly shrunken, seeming a foot shorter. His face seemed to have become that of an ordinary Jew, one of those "people-flies" he had just come upon in the large waiting room, buzzing with frightened faces, "A pogrom, a pogrom!" "What is this?" thought Popov. "They're all so terrified of a pogrom! Why are they so afraid of a pogrom? Are they really so . . . so weak? Can they never show any resistance? There are thousands of them here in this city! What a strange people this is! A strange people, a strange people!"

At that moment an inside door opened and on the threshold appeared a middle-aged woman wearing a wig who said something to the rabbi which the guest understood to be a call to dinner. The rabbi answered, "Soon, soon," the door closed, and he spoke to the guest.

"Tell me, young man . . . what did I want to ask you? Yes. How do you know this family? And what proof do you have that . . ."

"Oh! I know them very, very well!" the guest tried to squirm out of answering directly for fear he might inadvertently misspeak and have to mention his landlord, thereby letting the rabbi know he was living at the Shapiros' under a Jewish name, and so he hurriedly changed the subject.

"Tell me, honorable rrabbi" (he pronounced the word harshly, with two hard Russian r's), "tell me, honorable rrabbi, please reply to what I'm going to ask you. I am convinced, and not I alone, but, as I told you, most Christians are convinced, that the whole story of the ritual of Christian blood for Jewish matzo is no more than a myth. I myself had the opportunity to observe how you make matzo and I came to the conclusion that it is no more than a legend made up by fanatics from the past. I would like to know where this legend came from? And why just about Jews? Why not about others?"

The rabbi considered the guest: What kind of young man is this? He is in love with a Jewish girl and is prepared to convert, he observes how we bake matzo, and is convinced, he says, that it's a legend, a libel, and nevertheless asks such questions and, in addition, is personally acquainted with the family of the slain Chigirinski . . . For a split second a thought crossed the rabbi's mind: Could it be that this fellow is a provocateur? But no, his face is too naive, too artless, his eyes and his gaze too honest. No. That's not how a provocateur looks.

And he drove away those troubling thoughts and moved closer to the guest, offering him a cigarette although he himself was not a smoker. The guest thanked him; he was also not a smoker.

the thirty-seventh chapter

A PACK OF BOOKS

"Do you understand now, young man," the rabbi said with a bitter smile, "do you understand why one must not rush into these things? When you ask me where this myth comes from and why it is only about Jews, you justify my previous advice that the serious step you desire to take requires careful consideration. You must first become thoroughly familiar with the "family." How would you feel knowing there are members of her "family" who use human blood? You protest, saying it is false? But I say to you that you are not in touch with your own self. You say that you and most Christians are *convinced* it is a libel, a mere legend, a myth. But in truth you are far from convinced, and that is quite natural, simply because you don't really know us. You know us as well as we know the Chinese. You've simply heard about us. They've filled your heads about Jews having secret sects which practice secret rituals. To take the trouble of reading what has already been repudiated a hundred times, or to take it upon oneself to observe, to research, to acquaint oneself thoroughly with us—there are very few among you who are willing to do so. If you knew us better, you would see how ridiculous these myths are. You would see that we have no secret sects, no secret rituals, that all our virtues and faults are exactly like yours, with one exception. You can reproach us for every sin except one—the sin of shedding blood. For us, not only human blood, but even the blood of a cow or a chicken, is forbidden. When it is necessary to slaughter an animal for food, you would be amazed to know how many restrictive laws there are, how many times it is mentioned that we are forbidden to eat anything with blood in it, to shed blood, even to look at blood. It's a pity I don't have more time now . . . quite a few people are waiting for me . . ." (The rabbi glanced at his watch and the guest jumped up.) "Sit, sit. If it weren't Passover—tonight we celebrate Passover—we could discuss it at greater length. If you wish to know more about this matter, I can be of help to you. I have an extensive library; I can lend you a book by Professor Khvolson. Have you ever heard of him? No?" (The rabbi stood up and walked over to the bookcase.) "I can lend you his book till after the holidays. I can also lend you a few books on ritual. And if you are really interested, I can give you another book by that great scholar and expert on Judaism, Reb Lutostanski. He, you understand, cites Gemara, which is neither here nor there, and introduces laws which are more fiction than fact. And yet our adversaries look to him as a great expert, and even though he has been refuted over and over again for his lies and falsehoods, he is still considered in certain circles to be the greatest authority."

The same private door opened and the bewigged woman reappeared. She and the rabbi exchanged glances and he signaled her with his eyes that he would soon be coming. The guest rose and thanked the rabbi warmly for the books. He now realized that there was not much more he had to say about his reason for coming. The rabbi was right—he was in too much of a rush. This Judaism was too hard a nut to crack so quickly. He had miscalculated; it had, apparently, been much easier for Lapidus to step out of Judaism than for him, Popov, to step into it. This people was too proud of itself, it thought too highly of itself in spite of how badly the world thought of it! What the future would hold, he could not foresee, but now it was time to go.

He picked up the books and began to say good-bye when the rabbi stopped him and said he still had a few minutes to spare.

"So, young man, let us return to our previous discussion. As I understand it, you are acquainted with the family of the slain Chigirinski and you know, you say, that it is the stepfather's work? We think so too. We are positive that it's so. But what's the good of our being positive when there are people who are eager for a pogrom? You yourself have read the agitation filling the press, all of them chanting: ritual murder, ritual murder! . . . Our bad luck that it had to happen before Passover . . . Oh! If only you would be willing to step forward! Have you known these people long?"

Popov-Rabinovitch was again fearful of saying too much and so pretended not to hear the question. Instead, he put a question to the rabbi.

"Just one small question I wanted to ask you, honorable rrabbi. How do you explain the fact that this legend seems to surface only around the time before Passover, and one does find here and there a . . ."

"A 'Passover sacrifice'?" the rabbi completed with his soft-spoken irony. The possibility of this man's being a provocateur again ran through his mind, but not for more than a moment, and a pleasant smile again appeared on his face. "You want to have an explanation. It's an easy one. I can illustrate it with a parable."

And the rabbi, now standing at the door with the guest, calmly and slowly, as was his manner, and with the same smile on his face, gave the parable:

"There once was a marksman, an expert marksman, who performed remarkable feats, truly causing a sensation. How? Every time he shot, he hit the bull's-eye. He never missed. The people wondered: How is it possible for someone to hit the bull's-eye every time and never miss? So they began to watch him very carefully and they found out his secret. First he shot and afterward he placed the bull's-eye over the bullet hole . . . That's the parable. You will find that parable in the books I've given you. I hope you'll come back to see me soon after the holiday. I find very interesting what you have to say about the Chigirinski child, that you knew him and that you know for sure who the murderer is. You could serve the cause of truth at the investigation. It would be a great contribution. I mean, it is your duty as a man and as a Christian."

"Oh! You can be certain . . . Once the investigation begins . . . I give you my word of honor . . . Here's my hand on it."

The rabbi gratefully took his hand. "I believe you. Your eyes tell me that I haven't made a mistake. Would that there were many more like you who wish to know us better."

With a special warmth the rabbi shook his hand and our hero left with his books under his arm, satisfied, excited and happy. He couldn't possibly have dreamed that the pack of books he was carrying was not a pack of books but a pack of troubles.

SARA FINDS A TREASURE

"Look at me! I've been sitting here in a corner, forgetting that it was already Passover!" Sara Shapiro said to herself, jumping up from the chair she was sitting on and taking to her work with such energy and zeal that the dust seemed to fly. Mountains of trash were swept out. Shelves full of books were shaken free of dust and stacks of papers were incinerated.

"Heavens! A house full of students and writers! They all study and they all scribble. Syomke scribbles. Betty scribbles. The roomer scribbles. Into the *khometz* pile it all goes!" Sara said as she tossed handfuls of paper into the stove, not sparing a one. "Who needs all this trash? It just adds to the chaos!" As she was cleaning out, she poked into every nook and cranny, between the drawers, behind the dressers and mirrors, and also examined the roomer's desk drawer, that desk drawer no one could open even though it wasn't locked.

"Maybe he has some *khometz* in there, who can tell?" Sara said to herself, hurling deadly curses at the desk because it wouldn't open, until she finally prevailed: the desk drawer opened and there she found a treasure.

First she found hidden among his papers her daughter's picture. "What's Betty's picture doing here? I suppose she gave it to him secretly so we wouldn't know. Does that mean there is something going on between them?" Her daughter was a bit crazy and insisted that they were not to so much as mention the word "match"! It would be of no help to her. In the end, they would both need to come to her, to the mother, and would reveal the secret that they were in love and that . . . ach, how long could she wait to see the day!

These thoughts were running through the happy mother's mind as she tidied his papers and put the portrait back where she had found it when her eyes fell on a small, unbound book, labeled in large letters, "*Moy Dnevnik*—My Diary."

"His diary?" thought Sara, and leafed through the pages, her heart pounding with joyful anticipation. She would never have read it—what did she care what someone wrote in his diary? But as she had already found Betty's picture hidden there, she felt she had a right to read what he had written in his diary, perhaps something about her daughter. And as her heart had told her, the greatest part of his diary was devoted to her Betty: Today he went for a stroll with Betty . . . Today he talked to Betty . . . Tomorrow he was going to the theater with Betty . . . Betty said . . . Betty laughed . . . Betty asked, Betty was silent, and other such world-shaking events! And she had thought she should find something good!

Sara kept leafing through the book, unable to find anything more meaningful, not one item to suggest something more serious. Here she found an entry describing how he had danced with the *Chaseedim*. "Ah! He must mean the Purim evening spent at Shlomo Familiant's—ha-ha-ha! Then he described how he had watched how they baked matzos . . . "I saw it with my own eyes and am satisfied, quite satisfied to have been right there."

She was unimpressed by what he had written so far. Or with the following entry in his diary: "Tomorrow I am going to see the rabbi and will talk to him about dogma and ritual . . ." What kind of nonsense is this? May I know from evil as I begin to understand what this is all about! Plain nonsense!

Sara put down the diary and was about to shut the drawer when her eye was drawn to a beautiful letter written on red paper. "That must be a letter from Betty," she thought, and opened the envelope—no, it wasn't from Betty. It was apparently written by a woman, but not her Betty. Didn't she know Betty's handwriting? "It must be from the millionairess aunt. It's worth looking at, no? What is the aunt writing him?" Sara would never have read the letter—what did she care what a millionairess aunt wrote to her nephew? But as she had already found her daughter's picture in his desk and as she had read in his diary that he thought constantly of her Betty, it would do no harm if she would allow herself to take a little peek at what the millionairess aunt was writing him, perhaps it was about the match. Maybe it was something she, Sara, should know about. But it wasn't from his aunt! His aunt, as Sara recalled, was called Leah and the letter was signed with a P. The correspondent had ended the letter with, "Your eternal beloved who embraces you and kisses you, Vera P." Who could this Vera P. be who kisses and embraces him and ends her letter with "Your eternal beloved"? A lover perhaps, and an eternal one besides!

After Sara read the letter she was in a state of utter shock. She felt as if someone had slandered everything she held dear, as if her worst enemy had suddenly appeared, reviling her cruelly, or as if she had awakened from a horrible nightmare.

The letter read:

My Dearest,

Your letters to us of late have become so seldom and so brief that we often have worrisome thoughts about you. Father says that you will stop writing altogether soon. Father has lately become even more peevish than ever. He misses you too but will not let anyone see it. You can imagine then, my dearest Grisha, how all of us are looking forward to the holiday. I am counting the days and never cease praying to God that He not forsake you, on the contrary, that things go well for you. I wish you a splendid success! We hope you will make us joyful for the blessed holiday with the good news we are all awaiting, I more than everyone else,

Your eternal beloved, who embraces you and kisses you,

Vera P.

Sara laid the letter back where she had found it, shut the desk drawer, and returned to her chores. But it didn't go as before. Everything seemed to fall from her hands. She barely seemed aware of what she was doing. Her mind was preoccupied with the letter from that Vera P., who kisses him and embraces him. A curse upon her, wherever she is! "Who can she be, this Vera P.?" Sara pondered, stopping her work every now and then to crack her knuckles. "Is it a girl who is in love with him? (It was easy to fall in love with such a handsome young man who graduated with a medal and had an aunt who was a millionairess without children of her own!) What kind of close relationship must she have with him if she writes to him so intimately, and why is she looking forward to seeing him for the holidays? And why is she so attached to him?"

Sara's thoughts wandered, but soon returned:

"Can this be a fiancee? (May my enemies not hear of it!) How could he not have mentioned it all this time? And how could he have the nerve to carry on a romance with my daughter? Two loves? Two fiancees? That would be worse than in Sodom! The heavens themselves would open! That would be the end of the world! No. It can't be! Rabinovitch is not that kind of person . . . It can't be! It can't be!"

Sara took to her work again. She wanted to put it out of her mind but could not. This Vera P. would not leave her alone! "Did you ever hear of something so irksome? If that *shlimazel,* Tumarkin, were here now, she might be able to find out through him who this was. But he had vanished into thin air. What to do? She couldn't ask the roomer about this Vera P. because that would betray the fact that she had been rummaging through his papers. But what could she do? What idea could she come up with to find out who this Vera P. was?

And so the poor mother wracked her brain without coming up with a solution, for even if she had had eighteen heads she could never have guessed that this Vera P. was none other than our hero's sister, Vera Popova.

At first Sara had the idea of taking the letter and showing it to her daughter to find out what she would make of it. Maybe Betty knew about this Vera P. Then she reconsidered and decided she had better not start up with such a sharp-tongued girl. Betty was capable of making quite a fuss with her because she had read other people's letters. Then again, her heart ached for Betty; if she knew as much as she who this Vera P. was, her Passover would be ruined.

"Just what we needed now, a new *shlimazel,* a Vera P.!" Sara thought. Out of great heartache she wished to take it out on her roomer and burn the letter along with the rest of the *khometz.* Would that she had done so. Would that she had burned the letter together with the diary and thereby have spared her roomer the dire consequences that awaited him, as we will soon see.

the thirty-ninth chapter

SYOMKE: THE SCAPEGOAT

As Sara was debating whether or not to remove the letter she had found in her roomer's desk drawer, the doorbell started ringing.

"That must be either the roomer or Betty," thought Sara and ran down to open the door. It was neither the roomer nor Betty but the young Syomke, who was home from *gymnasium* earlier than usual. They had all just been dismissed for Passover, the Jewish as well as the Gentile children, and Syomke should have come home happy and excited. But there he was in tears and disheveled. He burst into a loud, mournful wail.

"God be with you! Syomkenyu, my darling, why are you crying? A bad grade?" the mother asked, ready to wring her hands.

"No. Good grades. All fives."

"So why the tears?"

They had hit him.

"Who?"

His older Gentile classmates. As he was leaving the *gymnasium* after being dismissed, they had thrown him to the ground and had beaten him up, striking him here, and here, and right here . . .

"How terrible! Why? Why did they beat you?"

How should he know! On account of Chigirinski, that's why they said they were beating him!

"For which Chigirinski?"

"For Volodka. They said we murdered him for Passover and drained his blood for our matzo."

And Syomke wailed and sobbed, wiping his eyes with both fists as his mother cracked her knuckles while calling down the most dreadful of disasters upon her enemies' heads. She kept on cursing until the entire household had gathered, first David, then Betty (the roomer arrived last of all) for the final *khometz* meal, which is appropriately eaten in haste on the day of Passover when time is pressing, and when one is also upset over the poor child so badly mistreated through no fault of his own. They felt that a great misfortune was looming ahead. This Volodka and his untimely, horrible death was God's punishment on an entire city of Jews, and more than on anyone else, it was being inflicted on them, on the Shapiros, who happened to be neighbors of that Kirilikha. And now each one was trying to put the blame on the other for encouraging the friendship with Kirilikha and her family.

The first to speak was David Shapiro, who attacked his wife for carrying on friendships with Gentile neighbors. He would have lived here ten years, twenty years, a hundred years without speaking so much as a word to those two drunkards and would have objected to his roomer's studying with their son. What, he said, did we have to do with them? And why did his Syomke have to play games with someone not his equal? These and many more broadsides he directed at his wife and the others as well.

"Finished? Are you through or not?" Sara said to him. "Will you let me get a word in edgewise?"

"Why not? As far as I'm concerned, you can get in ten thousand words."

"If that's so," said Sara, "I have news for you. You are still a Shapiro, a madman, and an 'express train'!"

"Congratulations!" and David bowed deeply.

"Well, congratulations to you too!" Sara answered him, and finished her thought. "If you weren't a Shapiro and a madman and an 'express train,' you would know that the entire friendship with the Kirilikhas came about because of your daughter. As for the plan that the roomer teach the youngster, I'm not positive who suggested it. Seems to me it was actually Rabinovitch himself . . ."

At this moment the roomer arrived, and hearing his name spoken, asked Betty with his eyes what was going on.

"You're mistaken, Mama," Betty spoke up in Russian so that the roomer would understand. "The plan that Rabinovitch help Volodka with his lessons was actually Syomke's idea. Syomke had boasted to Volodka about the "fives" he brought home from the *gymnasium* and Volodka had said that if he had a tutor like Syomke's he too would bring home "fives" from *his* school, and then maybe his stepfather wouldn't beat him so much. So Syomke took pity on him and asked Rabinovitch to study with his friend just half an hour a day. Isn't that the way it happened, Syomke?"

"Why do you need witnesses? We believe you without testimony," said the mother, angry at her daughter for coming to the defense of the roomer and laying the whole blame on poor Syomke when that very morning she had chanced upon that fine letter in the roomer's desk drawer, which had chased all thoughts of the millionairess aunt out of her mind. As if it weren't bad enough that the poor child had been abused, now he would have to defend himself before his crazy father.

And it was just as she had feared. All David needed was someone on whom to vent his rage. He began to needle and nag the "little squirrel," to scold him. "Serves you right! A boy should know whom to be friends with and whom to have pity on. You got what you deserved . . ." And with more such words, the father continued to lambaste the innocent Syomke, who began to cry and sob all over again.

It was apparently fated that this day Syomke should be the scapegoat in the Shapiro household, where the atmosphere was becoming thicker and heavier, as if dark clouds were gathering overhead, the kind of clouds that must end in a storm, in a drenching downpour. Each one in the house sensed it and each one was outraged, most of all, the roomer. When he was told at the *khometz* meal the story of how Syomke had that day been attacked, he pushed his food away. He was idignant! As long as he had been a roomer at the Shapiros they could not remember ever having seen him angry. Always mild and gentle, he suddenly became enraged. His eyes bulged, his face turned red, and his thick, black hair seemed to stand on end, resembling a mane. He looked strange, like a provoked animal.

"I will not keep silent about this!" he thundered. "I'm going right down to the Inspector, to the Director, and raise the roof. I'll turn their *gymnasium* upside down!"

"Shhh . . . Don't run, don't raise the roof, don't overturn the *gymnasium*!" David Shapiro said, touching the roomer's elbow. "Your rushing around and causing an uproar won't accomplish a thing. We're Jews, they're Gentiles, it's a lost cause!"

But the roomer would not allow himself to be calmed.

"What do you mean, it's a lost cause? It's not a lost cause! Something like this can't be taken lying down!"

"Can't be taken lying down! And if you scream, what will you accomplish?" David asked him with a bitter laugh. "You'll just accomplish one thing: the 'little squirrel' will be requested to leave the *gymnasium* and we'll remain without a residence permit. That's what you'll accomplish!"

The roomer looked with astonishment at his landlord as he went on, "You're looking at me in surprise? I know what I'm talking about. Believe me, I know. To you it's a game, whether you have a residence permit or not. If necessary, you can just pick yourself up and go. Whom do you have to answer to? I hate this entire business. I don't want the police to become too interested in me. Enough. I'm sick and tired of it. I've had it up to here with residence permits!"

David Shapiro pointed to his throat. The roomer was speechless. If people have only one thing on their minds—residence permits—what good can come of it? he thought and sat back down. But David Shapiro continued to hold forth. "If we took it to heart, do you hear, every time they beat us and cursed us and dragged us through the mud, we would, nu-nu, spend all our time crying or have to keep shouting 'Sh'ma Yisroel—Hear, O Israel,' while complaining at the top of our lungs that we were being insulted. In the Duma on one day we are accused of things that are even greater insults. Or do you need a greater insult than all the garbage being printed lately about all this sickening blood business?—Tphoo!"

Rabinovitch also wanted to get in a word, but David didn't allow it. Once he got going, there was no stopping him.

"What can you tell me? What advice can you give me? I already know what you'll say. You'll say what they all say—"self-respect," "honor." I know it, believe me, as well as you. You are absolutely right. It's humiliating, especially when they attack a child who is totally without blame, a child who is pure and good. But we mustn't forget that we are Jews and that we live in a bitter time. It will pass, believe me, it will pass. There will come a time when they'll regret it. You'll see! And Syomke? Well, with God's help he will grow up and forget. As I am a Jew, he'll forget. We have a saying, 'It will heal by the time of the wedding.' "

Rabinovitch realized it was no use; he would not change this man's mind. A strange person! A strange people these Jews, with a strange psychology!

"So, enough weeping and wailing, my dear medalist. How long can you go on like this?" Shapiro said to Syomke, who had begun crying again, the tears pouring from his eyes. "Silly boy! God will get even with them for you and for me and for all of us. He is trustworthy, little silly. If He but wants to, it will be done. Get dressed now, my boy, and come along with me to the Alexandrovska and I'll buy you a pair of new boots for the holiday, and from there we'll go down to the wine shop to buy wine for the seder."

When Syomke heard the words "new pair of boots" and "wine for the seder," he became a changed child. He suddenly remembered the smell of new boots for the holiday and the atmosphere of the wine shop from a year ago and from two years ago and from three years ago when he had accompanied his father. He got up slowly and still sobbing, wiped his swollen eyes and red nose with his fingers, and was ready to forget the tears, the blows, and the humiliation. "A child remains a child, bless his heart!" his mother thought, kissing him and, with her apron, helping him wipe from his precious face the last tears which still clung to his long lashes like small drops of dew on a summer morning when the sun is rising. And the father didn't stop talking. He also felt sorry for his son, perhaps no less than the mother, but didn't wish to show it and so submerged that feeling in words.

"Well, then, let's get going!" he said to Syomke, hurrying him on. "Let's get a move on, it's Passover, my boy, and they might buy up all the boots and not leave us a drop of wine for the seder."

the fortieth chapter

WHO IS RIGHT?

The task of installing Passover in the household is not so easy as it seems at first glance, and when there is no extra help, it can be as difficult as parting the Red Sea. And yet Sara Shapiro could boast that she had finished her Passover preparations on time, if not a little early. The sun hadn't yet begun to set. Many servantless housewives like herself were just getting started, whereas her house was fully ready. It was only left to sit down at the seder table. Every corner was spotless, sparkling and shining. The table was newly spread with a snow-white cloth, the candles for the blessing were in the candelabrum, the matzo tray and the wine that David and his son had brought from the wine shop were in their proper places. Even the *moror* and the *haroses* announced their presence with their pungent aroma of freshly grated horseradish.

Sara herself was not yet dressed in her holiday clothes. Standing in the kitchen with her sleeves rolled up, she beat eggs into the matzo meal for the *latkes*—potato pancakes—real Passover *latkes*, which she then fried in goose fat in a large frying pan, *latkes* fit for a king.

David had just arrived from the bathhouse, red as a beet, his sidelocks and whiskers closely clipped as well as his beard. (He wasn't responsible for the beard clipping: the barber had taken it upon himself to even it up for appearances' sake). David went to his room, threw off his everyday clothes, and was donning his holiday garb. At that moment he was trying to put on his starched shirt and new tie. As we all know, David liked to do everything in a hurry, but this time neither the shirt nor the tie was cooperating; they had plenty of time. David became infuriated, ready to rip them apart!

In another room, Betty was creating a new coiffure, which was a pity. To take the hair with which nature had blessed her and to try to force it into some artificial style—feh! But what can one do with fashion? What woman would dare go against the current style?

Only Syomke was already fully dressed in his uniform with the shiny, silver buttons and the brand new Passover boots that served as a cure, a balm to soothe the wounds he had received at the hands of his classmates that morning. The feel of the new boots, their brand new smell, the aroma of the Passover *schmaltz*—goose fat—cooking in his mother's frying pan, and the *Haggadah Shel Pesach*—the Passover Haggadah—which was removed from between the dusty books every Passover, almost made Syomke forget that anyone had so much as laid a finger on him, although if one looked closely, one could see the traces— bluish bruises under his eyes. But with such fine new boots, with the delicious aroma of *latkes* soon to be served wafting in the air, with the seder to look forward to, for which he had memorized the Four Questions, with test grades of "fives" from *gymnasium* in his pocket, and with the beautiful Passover Haggadah before his eyes, was it any wonder that all his wounds were healed? Merely the sight of that Haggadah would be enough to cure all the ills of the world.

The *Haggadah Shel Pesach* in which Syomke had become so absorbed was not your ordinary Haggadah, purchased for a few rubles anywhere. No. This was an old Haggadah that Shapiro had inherited from the true, from the Slaviteh Shapiros, with all thirty-two commentaries, with full-page pictures and illustrations. It deserves mentioning because later this Haggadah would earn the honor of being investigated by police and studied by experts, as we will shortly see in the ensuing chapters of our novel.

In fact, its newly acquired "honor" would have nothing to do with the Haggadah itself. It was a Haggadah like all Haggadahs, containing the Four Questions and the *Avodim Hayinu* and the *L'faykhokh* and the Song of the One Kid." The illustrations are what would make this Haggadah important. True, one could certainly not say the art was outstanding. The artists who had executed the illustrations were not among the best in the world. The Egyptian Pharoah, depicted on the first page, looked more like a butcher than a king. Moses with his staff looked like a Russian, and his brother, Aaron the Kohane—like an Orthodox priest. Joseph had a maidenly face, while Potiphar looked more like a man. Only the Ten Plagues were perfectly depicted: "blood" and "frogs" and "vermin" and the rest were most realistic and natural. The Four Sons, too, were well drawn, and best of all, the "Wise Son." His face exhibited no particular wisdom, but the artist decided to draw him with his finger pointing to his forehead to indicate he was a man of intellect. The Bad Son didn't look evil at all. On the contrary, his face was attractively mild-looking. Luckily, "Bad Son" was printed underneath, or one would certainly have believed he was a saint instead of a villain. The "Simpleton" and the "The One Who Cannot Inquire" were drawn naked as the day they were born, both snub-nosed, heads to the side, and hands held apart as if to say, "What do we know? We are idiots. We don't know anything . . ."

The most exquisite illustration was of the Sacrifice, a drawing of the attempted sacrifice of Isaac, in which Abraham our Patriarch was leading his one and only son Isaac to the sacrificial altar, although one wonders what this sacrificial scene was doing in the middle of a Passover Haggadah? And whatever made the artist depict our first good patriarch as a hooligan wearing satin slippers and silk hose, a large, square, tasseled undergarment worn by orthodox men, and long sidelocks probably not worn in the times of Abraham our Patriarch? And whatever made the artist put in Abraham's hand, not a slaughtering knife, but a Caucasian dagger, with which he was ready to stab the innocent Isaac's throat through and through?

These questions didn't occur to Syomke at all. On the contrary, he thoroughly enjoyed all the pictures, especially—wouldn't you know—the one of the Sacrifice! He thought there could be nothing more wonderful. Syomke remembered from his Pentateuch class how God had wanted to test Abraham and had bade him bring his one and only son to the sacrificial altar, how Abraham had brought him there with firewood and a knife, how Isaac kept asking his father about the lamb, and how, after Abraham bound his son, he raised the knife and was about to cut his throat, when one of God's angels flew down to stay his hand. Syomke's heart, which had been pounding, calmed down, the tears welling in his eyes instantly dried up, and he was greatly relieved that God did not allow such a thing to happen.

While examining that picture, Syomke responded with fresh feelings to what had happened long ago as if it were happening before his eyes: pity for Isaac, fear lest Abraham kill him, and joy when the angel arrived in time to prevent it. He turned the pages, enjoying the old Haggadah with its lovely, rare illustrations. He was beginning to get into a holiday mood, as were the others in the house, except one—the roomer Rabinovitch.

Since the *khometz* meal, Rabonivitch had been sitting in his room reading the blood-libel literature the rabbi had lent him that morning. He read how "Jews needed Christian blood for their Passover matzo." In a word, he was getting acquainted with spurious laws of ritual, stuffing his mind with those infamous, blood-filled trials which took place in Grodno, in Velisz, in Borisov, in Saratov, and in other cities where a dismissed Gentile girl or a converted, noncommissioned officer would be the only experts, the only trusted witnesses of how Jews practice drawing blood from a slain Christian for their Passover matzos, and other such tales, where every page and every line shouted, "Falsehoods and lies! . . . Blackmail . . . Stupidity . . . Provocation!" He stood up, paced back and forth across his room, smoothed his disheveled hair, sat down again, took out the diary from his desk, and wrote the following words: "Today I spent almost all my time on ritual. Today I—" and was interrupted right in the middle of a sentence by a frighteningly loud ringing downstairs. The pen dropped from his fingers. It was the familiar ring heard in that city, as we have noted, only when there is a fire, endangering someone's life, or when there is a house search for Jews.

David Shapiro, who knew more about such ringing than anyone, immediately said "Police!" as he hurriedly threw his kaftan on and started to run down, but Sara stopped him and, as usual, tried to contradict him.

"Why are you running? They're not police. Where did you get the idea it was the police? Seems to me there's never been a house search during the day, only at night."

"With that reasoning you can explain why ducks go barefoot! How do you know it's a police *search*?"

"What else? Do you think they would come on Passover before the seder to wish you a happy holiday?"

"What a woman! She has to show her stupidity in everything! Did you ever hear such nonsense? If I say it's the police, it's the police!"

Apparently those standing at the door didn't have the time to wait till husband and wife settled their differences. The ringing resumed, even louder and more urgently than before, the kind of ringing one thinks will never stop. The landlord and the roomer, each emerging from his room at the same time, ran down the steps together, almost knocking each other over in their haste. Each tried to outrun the other to open the door, and you can imagine what they encountered. *He* had guessed right, not *she*. Of course! What was he, a child? If he says it's the police, it's the police . . .

And David Shapiro, though he looked more dead than alive, still was able to summon the strength to say with a wry laugh to his wife, who had remained standing at the head of the stairs almost in a faint, the half-cooked *latkes* in her hand, "So? Who is right?"

the forty-first chapter

THE FIRST HOUSE SEARCH

Among the uninvited guests who had barged into Shapiro's house David recognized only one: an old friend, a local policeman whom David had more than once had to "pay off," sometimes on special occasions and sometimes just for the sake of friendship. There were times when the Russian spoke to David in the familiar form of address, a sure sign of friendship. Aside from this policeman, however, all the army officers and district officials were strangers. He had the impression that the officials had nothing to do with residence permits. One of them, a bald-headed man with fine, gray eyes and narrow epaulets, looked like a judge. Another young man had an impressive moustache and was an officer of some kind—either in the police or in the army.

Another in Shapiro's shoes would probably not have been bothered at all: so what if a district official was at his door—what difference did it make? But David Shapiro was not that kind of person. As we know, he had cut his teeth on matters having to do with police and residence permits, and so his suspicions were aroused at seeing a district official. What did that one have to do with residence permits?

A third member of the group also looked quite familiar to David. He was a tall, sturdy man with broad shoulders and full lips, wore blue-tinted eyeglasses, and was dressed in civilian clothes. He kept himself in the background, did not speak at all, but every now and then would sidle up to one of the officers, wink meaningfully, and then retreat. "I think I've seen that bird somewhere before. I don't like the looks of him," David thought, and could not remember where he had seen him.

But if David Shapiro didn't know who this man was, his daughter, Betty, and his roomer recognized him immediately as the man with the thick, sensuous lips who had on that night last winter arrested Rabinovitch. And though he was wearing thick, blue glasses, Betty could tell that he never took his eyes off her, a persistent stare she found hard to tolerate. She felt frightened, not knowing of whom, and was trembling, not knowing why. And as that evening at the theater, she exchanged glances with the roomer, as if to ask, "Is that him?" "It's him," the roomer answered with a return look, and smiled as if to tell her she had nothing to fear now.

David Shapiro could boast that, in all his experiences with house checks and police, he had never been so calm and collected as at that moment. His heart beat no faster and he conducted himself coolly with the uninvited guests, not feeling any need to ask questions. He simply folded his hands behind him, smiled slightly, and waited. What's next?

He didn't have to wait long. The more familiar officer approached him, and while the others stood and gazed first at the ceiling, then at the walls, and then at the floor, he informed Shapiro in a friendly manner that they had come to search the premises.

Shapiro looked at the officer quite calmly.

"Search the premises? For what? Have I stolen something?"

"Whether you've stolen something or not," the officer answered, half-friendly, half-officially, "we still have to search the premises. We might find something."

"Ah, with the greatest of pleasure!" Shapiro laughed nervously.

Sara couldn't understand what was striking her husband so funny.

"They want to search the house," David explained to his wife, telling her they were looking for something.

"What are they looking for? Last year's snow?"

"What do you care? Let them look."

During the time the couple was conversing, the man with the blue spectacles winked to the policeman, indicating the locked cupboard. The policeman went over to David as to an old acquaintance and requested the keys to the cupboard.

"Since when do I have keys?" David replied with a laugh. "Keys are *her* business. Sara!" he called to his wife in Yiddish. "Where are the keys? Open the cupboard for them."

"What do you mean open the cupboard for them?" Sara said in a frightened voice. "The matzos are in there!"

"So what if the matzos are in there? Fool, will they eat your matzos?"

"What are you talking about? They won't eat the matzos but they'll make the matzos *khometz* and ruin my whole Passover."

From this conversation, held in Yiddish, the guests could understand only one word, "matzo," which had been repeated many times, and by the frightened look on Sara's face they could surmise that she didn't at all like the idea of opening the cupboard for them. They exchanged knowing glances, as if to say, "The cat knows who ate the canary."

David Shapiro interpreted that glance another way. He imagined they were laughing at his wife for worrying about the matzos and he was prepared to join them in their laughter. He was also a male, and he said to them with a laugh, "All women are the same, heh, heh! She's afraid you'll make her matzos *khometz*, heh, heh!"

In Russian this sounded, as one can imagine, even better.

"*Ona boitsya chto vy nye akhametsovali yeyo matsu, heh-heh!* She's afraid we'll make the matzo *khometsovali*. What does *khometsovali* mean?" they asked Shapiro, who gladly explained to them what it is that makes Passover matzos *khometkz'dik.*

In order for them better to understand, he demonstrated with his hands that, according to his wife's thinking, as soon as they so much as touched the matzos with their "unclean" hands, the matzos would be permanently ruined, nullified, and would have to be thrown out, heh, heh.

It cannot be said that this explanation satisfied them, and the one who looked like an army officer was actually offended. He ordered the policeman to have the cupboard opened. The policeman went over to Shapiro, laid his hand on his shoulder, and spoke now, not as a friend, but harshly and officially, as a policeman: the cupboard had to be opened. And the cupboard was opened.

And ah! What a sight greeted their eyes: the lower three shelves were crammed from top to bottom with white, round, baked matzos that seemed to be inviting everyone to remove them and do with them what it is ordained to do when Passover comes: crumble and break and crack and split them and use them for all the dishes Jews prepare for Passover—matzo balls, *latkes*, blintzes, baked pudding, *farfel*, or simply crumbled and fried in Passover goose fat with an egg.

That was on the lower three shelves. The two upper shelves were also lined with white paper and full to the brim with good things. There a treasure was to be found: large bowls full of eggs, pots of chicken fat, onions, horseradish, pepper and salt, parsnips, apples, plums, raisins, nuts, and oranges. Way back in a corner on top, set apart, all by itself, like an aristocrat, was an unusual earthen vessel, neither a pot nor a jar but more like a crock. It was covered with a white sheet of paper tied with a red satin cord and attached to it was a label on which was inscribed in large handwritten letters: Kosher for Passover.

It was this crock that particularly drew the attention of the police. Slowly, carefully, as if it were something precious, it was removed from the cupboard, and a dialogue between the bald-headed man and the landlord David Shapiro ensued, which we set down verbatim:

"What is this?"

"This is a gift for Passover."

"From whom is this gift for Passover?"

"From my sister."

"Who is your sister?"

"She is a rich woman, I mean, a rich man's wife, I mean, her husband is a rich, pious Jew, I mean, one of the *Chassidim*."

"*Chaseedim?*"

The group exchanged glances. The one with the bald head sighed deeply like a person for whom things are finally falling into place. The officer coughed and tugged at his whiskers. The conversation continued.

"Would it be possible to uncover this crock?"

"Why not? With the greatest of pleasure!" David said, starting to uncover the crock, but Sara lunged toward him with both hands. "Watch what you're doing, you'll spill it . . ."

"What are you so afraid of?" David jumped at her angrily, now becoming irritated by this whole fuss. "What are you so afraid of, I'd like to know? What are you trembling for? What am I going to spill? The precious liquid in there? She's worrying! If they order you to uncover, you have to uncover everything! A house search is not the same as a residence permit check."

"All right, enough is enough!" the policeman cut him off. "You'll have plenty of time to talk together in your Yiddish jargon after we leave. But now, if you don't mind, please uncover the crock!"

David Shapiro slowly untied the red satin cord, removed the white paper, and uncovered the crock. Lying there were perfect, firm, aromatic sour cucumbers, kosher for Passover, steeped in brine, each pickle glistening like a jewel, their aroma wafting through the room announcing their heavenly taste.

ALL'S WELL THAT ENDS WELL

We will not burden our readers with a detailed description of how the rest of the house search was conducted. In short, we can reassure them that it was properly carried out according to all the laws and commandments. Every corner was explored inside the cupboard, above the cupboard, and under the cupboard. They were not reluctant to peer under all the beds and in the kitchen, and even poked their noses into the small crock of Passover borscht, proving to themselves that, in fact, it did smell of beets. All the secular and sacred books were leafed through, even Sara's Yiddish version of the Pentateuch with its women's "Prayers and Pleas." Betty's and Syomke's books and notebooks were examined and put back in their places. Only one book did they find necessary to take with them. That book had been pointed out by the silent one with the blue spectacles. First he had looked through the book himself, paying particular attention to one dog-eared page, and then, pointing out the dog-eared page, he had shown it to the older, bald-headed fellow, who also took a keen interest in the book and signaled to the policeman, who, in his turn, bent over the book, examined it, and coughed as he twirled his moustache. One after another they all examined the book, which seemed to fascinate them.

The book that evoked such a keen interest was none other than that fine old Haggadah with the lovely illustrations Syomke had so enjoyed. The dog-eared page was the one depicting Abraham the Patriarch leading his one and only son, Isaac, to the Sacrifice, which, of all the pictures, had impressed Syomke the most.

"What can they have seen in the Haggadah that excited them so? And why don't they even mention the word—residence permit?" wondered David as he followed them from room to room with the firm steps of a person who knows he is not guilty in any way. When they finally came to Rabinovitch's room, David, without hesitation, announced that this was where his roomer lived, Rabinovitch by name. What had he to fear?

"Here he is, Rabinovitch himself," David indicated with a smile.

"A pleasure!" said the bald-headed fellow, who bowed quite politely to the roomer and asked him what he did.

"I am a dentist," Rabinovitch answered. But Shapiro hurried to correct him, adding that he wasn't a dentist yet but, with God's help, would one day become a dentist, if he were worthy of it.

"Very nice!" the man said with the same polite tone. "Are you studying dentistry in order to obtain a residence permit?"

Rabinovitch imagined he was being made fun of because he needed a *pravozhitelstvo*. He regretted that he had earlier that day at the *khometz* meal ridiculed the Jewish *pravozhitelstvo*. He was about to speak up when his landlord interrupted him. (David was relieved finally to hear the familiar word "*pravozhitelstvo*.")

David, coming to his roomer's defense, felt that an explanation was due. This Rabinovitch was a medalist and it would have been only right for him to be accepted as a student along with all the other students. But since he was one of ours, a Jew, he came under the quota regulation.

Shapiro would have gone on explaining had his acquaintance, the policeman, not given him a warning wink from across the room to be quiet. The others went about their business. In the roomer's quarters they followed the same procedure as in the other rooms: they searched above and under and in the cupboards and did not hesitate to look under the bed. The bald-headed fellow spied some books spread out over the roomer's table and asked him whether they were his dentistry books or other kinds. "Other kinds," Rabinovitch answered him and felt himself reddening. He was worried that they might examine the books and ask him why they dealt with blood and why he was reading them.

As his heart had forewarned him, that was exactly what happened. Not only did the officer interest himself in the books, he summoned the rest of the officers with his eyes and pointed to the books.

Rabinovitch was quite uncomfortable watching them leaf through the blood libel literature that the rabbi had lent him, and, as he had anticipated, they were preparing to gather them up and take them away with them. He tried to protest, "Those books are not mine. They were lent to me for the holiday."

"By whom?"

Rabinovitch realized that the more he said, the worse it would get, and so he remained silent and was relieved when the bald-headed man said to him, "Would you be so kind as to open your desk drawer?"

"With pleasure!" Rabinovitch answered and went to work at it, perhaps sweating a bit because, as we all know, opening the drawer was no easy task. And so that they would not think they would find anything illegal or any forbidden material, he pulled the drawer out altogether and dumped its contents onto the table, as if to say, "There you are, I hope you're satisfied . . ."

Slowly and carefully, as if he were counting checks or bank notes, the bald-headed man made a small pile of smoothed-out papers, nonchalantly scanned a few pages of the diary and, as slowly and carefully, tucked them into his briefcase. Gazing at Rabinovitch with his fine, gray eyes, he found it necessary to apologize for taking his papers and books. He said it would only be for a few days until he had a chance to acquaint himself with them and then he would return them through the police.

"Did they find anything illegal or forbidden among your things?" These were the first words David Shapiro uttered to his roomer after the police squad was finally on the other side of the door and he calculated they were far enough away not to hear, because as brave and coolheaded as David was during the house search, once the officers departed, he reverted to his old self: frightened as a rabbit and scared to death, terrified they might find something among his roomer's possessions that might adversely affect their residence permit.

"They found absolutely nothing illegal," the roomer reassured him, "just a few legitimate books, some unimportant papers, and a letter from my sister."

"You have a sister?" Sara Shapiro asked him with surprise.

"Of course I have a sister. Didn't I tell you?"

"Never. I'm hearing it for the first time. What's her name?"

"Again?" interjected Betty. "Isn't it enough they searched his room and took away all his books and papers, do you have to cross-examine him too?"

"What does it matter to you?" the mother cut her off. "Why should you care if he tells me his sister's name? Is it costing you any money?"

"Her name is Vera," said Betty in an impertinent tone. "So? Now are you satisfied?"

"Is that her name, Vera?" Sara said with surprise, looking at the roomer.

"Yes, Vera," he replied. "What of it?"

Sara reddened, and so as not to raise any suspicions by her surprise at the name Vera, she said to her husband, "What do you say to that? He has a sister and her name is Vera!"

"Wonder of wonders! Miracle of miracles!" said David, and looked at his daughter. "What, tell me, is the greater wonder, that Rabinovitch has a sister or that her name is Vera?"

"Neither," Sara tried to wriggle out of her predicament. "I'm just surprised that Betty knows Rabinovitch has a sister named Vera and I don't."

"And I'm just surprised about something else," David said, quite happy that nothing illegal had been found in his roomer's place. "What I'm really surprised at is that winter has come and gone, Passover is here, thank God, and you're still an idiot."

Everyone laughed, including Sara, but no one really knew what Sara was laughing about, no one knew what a heavy weight had been lifted from her heart: since Vera P. was his sister, it was now another story!

And the happy mother sighed with relief, her spirits rose, and her cheeks flushed. Her good holiday mood returned and at that moment she was prepared to forget the house search they had just been through, the police, the humiliation, and all her troubles as she thanked God with all her heart.

David, too, thanked God that the house search had turned out as well as it did, although he could in no way figure out why the house search had taken place at all.

All his cleverness could not explain why they had confiscated the Passover Haggadah. What could they have found in it? What strange things were happening in the world these days!

"Oh well!" David said to himself resignedly, running his hands over his face. "How do they say it: All's well that ends well . . . In the meantime, it's a holiday, time to go to the synagogue and pray."

A HOLIDAY EVE VISIT

A man of haste who did everything hurriedly, David Shapiro had been absorbed by the holiday preparations and then distracted by the police, who had suddenly, the devil knows why, shown up, so that he had totally forgotten the time. He imagined he was running late when in fact it was quite early. The sun was beginning to bid farewell to the city, cheerfully kindling the church spires and the golden heads of the rich old domes. David was in such a hurry that everything he did had to be done three times over because he was all thumbs. He didn't even have time to properly berate the roomer for not accompanying him to the synagogue in honor of Passover.

"I'm not speaking of piety," David barely had time to explain. "I'm far from religious myself. I would just think that a committed Jew like yourself—you do agree with the Zionists, don't you—would hold this holiday dearer than all other holidays."

Without waiting for an answer, he called out to his wife, hurriedly, as was his fashion, "Listen to me, Sara. It's a holiday. It's Passover. I don't want to hear the word 'search' mentioned in this house. I don't want to hear another word about it. Do you hear what I say?"

"I hear, I hear. How can I not hear?"

"No. I mean I want no mention of it. None at all."

"Fine, fine!" said Sara.

"Because a holiday is a holiday," he gave her to understand, gesticulating with his hands.

"A holiday is a holiday," Sara repeated after him, and David ran off to the synagogue, Syomke hard on his heels.

"It's easy for him to say don't talk about it," thought Sara. "Here you suddenly have the police barging in right before the holiday, turning the house upside down, nobody knows why, and he says don't mention it!" Once David left for the synagogue, Sara yearned to discuss the matter with the children, to try to make some sense of this disturbance. Whether she understood it with her head or with her heart, she was convinced that it had to do with Kirilikha's son and she felt she had to talk it over with someone. But there were neighbors, friends, and acquaintances to put up with, who immediately came running from far and wide, one after the other, as if a tragedy had occurred! There were no secrets on the Jewish Street. No sooner did the house search at the Shapiros end and the police depart, than almost the entire neighborhood knew that the Shapiros had had "guests," and people came running excitedly.

"Police right in the middle of the day?"

"And especially on Passover?"

"What can it be?"

Neighbors, close friends, and acquaintances, although in the midst of preparing for the holiday, came rushing over to the Shapiros, if only for a minute, to find out the details. But they had to leave as empty-handed as they came.

"Nothing. Absolutely nothing. Nonsense, I tell you, just checking on the roomer. They were looking for political pamphlets and found nothing. Absolutely nothing."

"Nothing is nothing. Have yourself a good holiday!" the good friends said, and departed.

Having gotten rid of the neighbors, friends, and acquaintances, Sara had new visitors. As had become customary, she had to welcome her wealthy sister-in-law, Toibe Familiant, together with her daughters, the two mam'selles. Dressed in their holiday best, they had condescended to travel from the wealthy part of the city where the Jewish aristocrats lived to their poor relatives for a short visit. Toibe was now, as she called herself in jest, a "grass widow." Her husband, Reb Shlomo Familiant, who went twice a year, Passover and Sukkos, to his *rebbe*, didn't fail to go again this Passover. Leaving his business affairs in the hands of strangers (the *rebbe* was more important), he left home for two or three weeks. One cannot say his wife and children were terribly upset by his leaving. Quite otherwise, when he wasn't home, the members of his family felt freer. The house took on a new appearance. Each felt as if she had cast off a heavy burden, removed a tight shoe, or had taken off her corset. Toibe was delighted that for two or three weeks she wouldn't have to entertain all those *Chassidim* with their "bim-bam's" and wouldn't have to provide them with three hearty meals a day. Her two daughters, the mam'selles, were even more delighted; they could go visiting, talk to men, spend some time with their poor relatives, stay an extra half-hour talking about fashions, theater, and literature, and fill up on a year's worth of laughter.

This Passover evening Toibe herself urged them to dress faster for the visit to their Aunt Sara, and the three of them arrived at the Shapiros just as Sara was blessing the candles. They divided themselves into two groups: the young people and the mothers, each group with its own interests and conversation. The mothers, who hadn't seen one another since Purim, had much to talk about, although that didn't stop Toibe Familiant from indulging in a little sermonizing, this time not about Sara's children, God forbid, but about her roomer, who had remained at home instead of going with David to the synagogue.

"Why is he so irresponsible?" She made a pious face, and with her smooth tongue and her unctuous voice, she began to preach to Sara that one may very well be a student and a medalist and a millionaire and a Jewish patriot or what have you—nevertheless—what is God's is God's and what is man's is man's. Who ever heard of a Jew not going at least once a year to synagogue, if even only for appearances' sake?"

"Oy, Toibenyu, dear heart, how can you say that?" Sara interrupted her. "Don't you know today's young people? You have children yourself."

"Children? What can they say against my children? My young children pray, blessed be His name, every day, and my daughters . . ."

"How can you compare them, Toibenyu, my soul? Your children have a mother and a father, may they live to be a hundred and twenty . . ."

"Eighteen times over no mother and father. What kind of excuse is that? Now is the time for you, Sara darling, to show yourself to be a real mother, it's high time, I say. Or else allow me to speak a few well-chosen words to him, as a good friend."

And Toibe was fully prepared to go over to the roomer and to give him a piece of her mind, as a good friend, but Sara jumped up as if she had been singed and clasped both of Toibe's hands.

"No, Toibenyu, dear heart, my darling! It's not necessary! It isn't necessary yet! The time isn't right, we have to wait a little while, with God's help, after the holiday, just let the holiday be over with. Tell me better, my soul, what's going on in your part of the city? People like to visit you, and you live in such a fine neighborhood. As for me, I was up to my ears with work for Passover, doing it all myself."

"Oy, it's bad news, Sara darling, very bad!"

And Toibe Familiant, swaying back and forth as over a prayer book, relayed to her sister-in-law all that was going on in her part of the city, what people were saying, and how they were worrying that a Jewish massacre might take place, heaven protect us!

"He is all-knowing," Toibe sighed, using a sacred rabbinical phrase, and related to her sister-in-law an event that had recently taken place on the main Gentile avenue.

"You haven't heard about the miracle, Sara dear?"

"No. Tell me about it, my dear, tell me."

"It almost turned out to be a tragedy," said Toibe, settling into her chair. "The Protector of Israel intervened and nothing came of it. Listen to how God runs the world! This morning, at the height of holiday preparations, when everyone was bustling about, running to the market, buying wine, coming home from work—suddenly there was confusion in the street—running, screaming, pandemonium! The whole street swarmed with people, the trams halted, police whistles blew. What was going on? The explanation turned out to be short and sweet. Some important person, a general, not just any general but an adjutant-general, was going for a stroll when he saw a dark-skinned man leading a small child by the hand. The child didn't want to go with him, was crying and sobbing bitter tears as the man pulled him along against his will. The general approached him and asked him what he was doing with the child. The man was silent. Where was he taking the child? The man was silent. Whose child was it? The man was silent. The general didn't hesitate and shouted for the police, "Arrest that Jew, he's kidnapping a Christian child for a Passover sacrifice!"

Sara wrung her hands. "Really? Was it a Christian child? And who was the Jew?"

"Don't rush me, Sara dear. Anyhow, when a general gives an order, you have to follow it. So they took the man and the child by police wagon to the station, the general following in a carriage, the crowd running behind. What a scene, what a tumult, what a to-do: 'A Jew . . . a child . . . a Passover sacrifice . . . a general!' That's all you could hear. A few people dropped the word 'pogrom.' Jewish stores were about to close."

"Oh, my God! How did it end?"

"The end was, nu-nu! The dark-skinned man, it turned out, was actually a Greek, and the child was his own child, and he was crying because he had spotted some oranges which he wanted his father to buy him and the father refused. What does a child need an orange for, do you see?"

"That's all there was to it? The devil with it! Oh, Toibenyu, did you give me a fright!"

"What do you mean, a fright? People were falling in a dead faint and you're saying a fright. A general isn't a nobody, especially an adjutant-general! And whose fault was it? That Russian boy who was found near you. May God in heaven miraculously keep David from being pulled into it . . ."

"David? Why David? What does he have to do with it?"

"Why do you ask, Sara my dear? Who can tell these days? Have you already forgotten the Purim dinner when that Gentile woman barged into our house with that peasant? Don't you remember?"

"The things that occur to you, I daresay, Toibenyu, really, now!" Sara tried to make light of it but wrung her hands and cracked her knuckles tensely, suddenly feeling her blood turn cold. In that moment the question that had been nagging at her heart had been answered. A multitude of dark thoughts, unformed, fragmented yet sorrowful, one more sorrowful than the next, flew through her mind like a storm, like one bad dream after another . . .

And from where the young people were in the next room, one could hear a conversation carried on in Russian, loud and lively. The conversation was interrupted frequently with loud laughter, the roomer's loudest of all.

"What's the matter with him?" Toibe said with a pious face, twisting her lips to the side. "Jews are living in terrible times, they go to synagogue and pray to God that the holiday pass uneventfully, and he—well, apparently there are all kinds of Jews in God's world!"

Obviously, this was not a pleasant thing for her sister-in-law to hear, so Toibe returned to their former conversation about the fears abroad in the city, not sparing the vivid, dark colors with which she painted the situation. But seeing from Sara's face that she was on the verge of tears, Toibe backed off and began to comfort her, telling her the situation was not so bleak as she thought, there was nothing to fear now, and that if anything were to happen, God forbid, it would be during their holiday, that is, after Passover. And in any case, if something were to happen, she, Sara, shouldn't wait too long, and she and her husband and her children and her roomer should move directly to her place. There, thank God, they had nothing to fear. She lived on a street where they were safe. And with that, Toibe Familiant rose and began to leave because they would soon be coming back from the synagogue.

"A happy holiday to you."

"May you have a good year!" Sara replied as she accompanied her rich sister-in-law to the door, though she loved her like a headache, because whenever Toibe visited her, she never failed to rub salt in Sara's wounds that lasted for a whole week. "May you have a good year and have a happy holiday."

"A happy and a *kosher* holiday!" said Toibe, stressing the word "kosher." "A *kosher* Passover to you and to us and to all of Israel and all the Jews of the world, amen and again amen."

the forty-fourth chapter

A BEAUTIFUL NIGHT

Despite Toibe Familiant's protestations, Sara had insisted that Betty and her constant companion, the roomer, accompany her and her daughters part of the way home. "What for? Thank you! We can find our own way," Toibe had objected, but to no avail. Betty had already thrown a light woolen blue shawl over her shoulders and winked at the roomer, who, although still hatless, was ready to join them. Soon all five of them were on their way.

"Ah! What a night! What a sky!" the young people exclaimed as one, taking great pleasure in the magnificent night.

"In honor of the blessed holiday and in honor of the first seder, God has granted His people this lovely night," Toibe proclaimed in Talmudic intonations, and although it was not too light outdoors, it was still possible to make out her pious, self-satisfied face and pursed lips. Toibe Familiant was altogether pleased with the holiday visit she had paid her poor relatives, and for good reason. She had accomplished so much good: she had given sound advice, she had related all the latest news, and had invited her relatives to her house in case of trouble, God forbid. God should truly repay her efforts. She had done more than her share for her relatives. Why just the other day she had sent out Passover contributions all over: to Zaslav and to Dubnow and to Slaviteh, to this one a fiver, to that one a tenner. The Shapiro family was, no complaint intended, rather extensive . . .

Her daughters were also pleased to have spent a pleasant hour with such an interesting young man as their Aunt Sara's roomer and to have had the chance to show off their knowledge of culture and literature, having dropped the names of books they had read or simply heard about. And as it was now the style when Jewish young women got together to speak of Andreyev or of Artsibashev and others, they dropped those names as well as those of Alexander Bloch, Valeri

Bryusov, Andrei Byeli—the entire golden covey of modern Russian literati, until the outspoken Betty could no longer hold her tongue and had to needle her cousins. "How can Jewish girls," she said with a little laugh but in all seriousness, "how can Jewish girls spend an entire afternoon talking and talking about books and authors without so much as mentioning one Jewish book or one Jewish writer, as if we didn't have our own books or authors? How can one not be ashamed?" The Gentile among them (Popov-Rabinovitch), though he confessed he was not familiar with Jewish literature, had to agree with Berta Davidovna. And every time he said the name "Berta Davidovna," one could see their eyes meet, and Familiant's daughters understood that look. In those matters they were experts. "It's a match," the mam'selles thought, sighing as they exchanged glances wordlessly and soon ceased discussing literature. Without anyone realizing it, the subject of conversation changed to lighter matters, bits of gossip and stories about what was going on in town. One of the sisters related the story about the general and the "Passover Sacrifice," which evoked such loud laughter from Betty that her mother called from the other room, "What's going on there?" Inspired by her, both mam'selles also began to laugh, all three showing off their pearly white teeth. The only one not laughing was the roomer, who not only refrained from laughing but looked more like a person who was either angry or embarrassed to hear one of his own being put in a bad light. He didn't want to believe the story and maintained it could not be true. "Either the general wasn't a general or the whole story is a fabrication," he insisted quite seriously. And the more earnestly he spoke, the more Betty laughed. And ah! How her cousins, the Familiant mam'selles, envied her! On the way home with their pious, privileged mother that night, they had to admit to themselves that their poor cousin Betty was living a much better and freer and happier life than they. What good was their money if they couldn't lift their heads in public, couldn't so much as raise their voices? They sighed deeply. Perhaps they really envied her for something else—for her intended. And that he was her intended, of that there was no doubt. They knew. In such matters they were more expert than anyone. One glance into the happy couple's eyes on this starry, beautiful night was enough to convey to the keen observer exactly where matters stood in this romance.

"Why do you need to walk so far, Bertochka? It's chilly out and you're half-naked," her Aunt Toibe said to Betty pleasantly as she was taking her leave, but her remarks were meant as well for the hatless roomer. Once Betty and the roomer had left and she was alone with her daughters, the pious Toibe loosed invectives against the half-naked Betty and the hatless roomer, but she was especially critical of her sister-in-law, who had forgotten that her husband was a Shapiro, one of the true Slaviteh Shapiros!

"Oh, Mama! We've heard that seventy-five thousand times!" her daughters cut her off as they looked back at their fortunate cousin, Betty, walking away hand in hand with the handsome, happy student in that magnificent, festive first night of Passover.

And it was true—that first night of Passover was exceptionally festive and beautiful, with its hundreds of thousands of stars gazing down and pouring out their dark blue light on the happy faces of the young pair who walked hand in hand in measured steps so as to prolong their time together alone. Now the time had come, the time was more than ripe for him to bare his heart, to tell her the whole truth. How long could this go on? God Himself had created this beautiful night so that Rabinovitch could pour out his full heart, so that all that weighed heavily on his soul could be unburdened at last. Everything, everything must be said, everything from beginning to end: how it had all started with a joke and how the joke had turned serious, how he had thought at first he could change her way to his but was now prepared to change his because there was nothing in the world he would not do to win her. He had gradually been preparing her for this confession. She was the only one to whom he had confessed that the whole story of his millionairess aunt was nothing more than a hoax that had to remain a secret for a while longer. She was the only one he had told that he had a father who loved him, but with whom he had serious differences, and a very pious sister named Vera, whom he loved and who would give her life for him. Yet he would have to break with them both because the step he would need to take would be a deathblow to them . . .

What that "step" was, he could not as yet tell Betty, but she gave it her own interpretation, nor could one say that what he told her was pleasing to her. She did not like the battle he would have to wage with his father. What kind of person can this Rabinovitch really be? How does he come by a pious sister? She imagined she knew his father, as if she had met him many times: a bourgeois Jew, a parvenu who considered himself an aristocrat. To make sure Rabinovitch wasn't too impressed with his "aristocracy," Betty once let him know in no uncertain terms that she was the very opposite of her mother. As much as her mother knelt in adoration at the feet of the rich and deified millionaires, so she despised this attitude as a Jew despised pork.

"What do you have against them?" asked Rabinovitch, who enjoyed teasing her, loving to see her sparkling white teeth when she talked.

"I have nothing against them," Betty had answered, "but I hate them. I can't stand those Jewish moneyed 'aristocrats' with their fat bellies, their double chins, their smug expressions, and their blank eyes."

"It's dangerous to fall prey to those sharp teeth!" Rabinovitch had laughed, unable to look his fill of her.

"May God protect you then!" said Betty with a little laugh, yet feeling a bit insulted.

"On the contrary," Rabinovitch had said to her, "I would like to try it . . ."

"Don't. You'll be sorry. My teeth are much too sharp!"

Exactly at those words, Sara had appeared. (Sara always appeared in the nick of time.) Fearful that a quarrel might break out between the "children," she wanted to divert the conversation and so had said to the roomer, "Why do you bother listening to what she says? Don't you know her by now? She's a Shapiro through and through!"

Since that conversation some time had passed, and every day they grew closer and closer to each other. And now, on that lovely night, alone together after Toibe Familiant and her daughters were long gone and no one was around to observe them as they walked hand in hand in silence, their eyes met in the light of the stars and—they themselves didn't know how it happened—their lips met for the first time. Again their eyes met and they began laughing. Suddenly Betty tore her hand from his and began running ahead, he after her, until both of them ran into the house with flushed faces, eyes strangely aglow. Sara noticed their flushed faces and strangely sparkling eyes and said offhandedly, "Is it a nice night out?"

And both answered in the same offhand manner, "A beautiful night! A divine night!"

the forty-fifth chapter

"PACKS OF TROUBLE"

As if it weren't sufficient that each Jew had his own pack of troubles—worry about making a living, residence permits, quotas for schools, and other such honors only a Jew is deemed worthy of, our blessed God presented to the Jews of the city where our extraordinary events take place with yet another pack, this one for all Jews alike, called Chigirinski.

Jews have long been inured to troubles and have often been the target of libels. They have heard it all and seen it all before. But Jews know how to put their troubles aside by pursuing matters closer to their hearts. First there is Passover, the dear, beloved holiday Passover, when Jews carry out the *khometz*, discard their everyday winter clothing and put on all new holiday clothes, and gather in the synagogues, where this year they were treated with the welcome news about their new "pack of troubles" in such detail that it made everyone's blood run cold and ruined the holiday.

Not that they went to the synagogues to hear news. They went to pray, and normally, immediately after services, people would wish one another a good holiday and go home, each to his wife and children, and preside over the seder. But this time, right after prayers, after the orphans had hurriedly chanted the *kaddish* prayer for their dead, each trying to outshout the others in loud lamentation, the synagogue sextons, the rabbis' assistants in all the synagogues, loudly slapped their hands on the lectern to draw the congregation's attention, and announced, half in Hebrew and half in Russian, the following:

"It is proclaimed and declared in the name of the Governor and of all the authorities that the people should not panic or take action as all precautions have been taken to prevent any pogroms . . ."

No sooner did the sexton speak these words in his odd mix of languages than a great hubbub broke out in the synagogue. The congregation all began to speak at the same time so that even a keen-eared bystander would have been hard pressed to say if he could make out any particular words except the few that swept back and forth through the crowd: "blood ritual . . . pogromchiks . . ." The rest was impossible to make out.

When they left the synagogues that first night of Passover, the Jews, these masters of the Passover, didn't hurry home as usual; instead they gathered in small groups and tried to make some sense of this latest announcement, this new "pack of troubles." No one needed to spell out what the announcement meant. Everyone knew what they were dealing with. Although much was written daily in the papers, there were, God bless them, Jews who knew much more. (Do the newspapers write up everything that happens? And what they do write about, aren't they often lies and falsehoods?) Someone in the crowd was describing how that very day there had been a near-riot at a funeral in Sobor when some student stirred up the mourners with a fiery speech so that they were ready to march across town and settle matters with the Jews, as God had apparently commanded them. Luckily the police got wind of it and sent over a few little cossacks on their little horses and, whips in hand, they drove off the rabble, depriving them of their sport, poor things.

"Long live those little cossacks and their blessed whips!" a voice was heard shouting, no one knew whose, as the crowd was large. "Rest assured, if there are no clouds, it won't rain . . ."

"We have a great God!" added an even more optimistic man. "As proof, as soon as they arrested that drunken Gentile who probably murdered the child, he began changing his story and it's likely they've gotten closer to a solution. They just have to find out who the instigators and the perpetrators are who ran the criminal ring."

"They'll find out, don't worry, they'll find out the whole story because heaven and earth have sworn that nothing can be concealed for long in the world and the truth must surface like oil on water."

"We simply must pray to God, that's all," another interjected, this one a pessimist, it seemed. "We have to pray to God and beg Him to make the oil rise to the surface more quickly because their holiday is approaching—you know what I mean—and who knows if a little pogrom might not come out of it, and this time, if there is a pogrom, it will *really* be a pogrom like no other pogrom before it!"

"Bite your tongue!" David Shapiro interrupted. He had been standing to the side the whole time, listening intently to all that was being said. "Didn't you hear what the sexton just announced? Why do Jews have the habit of making the worst of everything and calling troubles down on themselves?"

"Listen here! Did I say there *would* be a pogrom?" the pessimist protested. "I just said that *if* there should be one, it would . . ."

But David Shapiro would hear no more. Angrily he walked away from that cluster of men and walked over to another group to listen from a distance to what *they* had to say. It was the same there. They weren't talking so much about the local "packs of troubles" but were recounting stories of incidents occurring in other cities where Jews had their own troubles.

"You have no idea what's going on in the world when it comes to wild stories!" spoke a young man, a storekeeper from Bakaley with an old face and eyes that laughed as if he were about to relate something about which they would all hold their sides laughing. "Listen to this one that almost happened just before Passover in Heisin. I'm from Heisin and have a brother and sister in Heisin. They discovered in a retired soldier's house four corpses, his wife and three children all slaughtered. And how do you think they were slaughtered? The way you slaughter a chicken or an ox? Feh! Their hands and feet were chopped off, their ears cut off, their eyes gouged out, their bellies slit open . . ."

"Enough with the anatomy—it's turning our stomachs!" the more fastidious among them admonished, spitting in disgust but still listening further.

"There was a great outcry. Who could have dismembered four people right before Passover if not the children of Israel? And they got hold of a Jew, Yenkel Short Sidelocks they called him. Why Yenkel Short Sidelocks? Because this Yenkel Short Sidelocks was a Jewish shopkeeper and that Gentile soldier's wife used to buy from him on credit. The day before, this Yenkel had been seen at the Gentile's place trying to collect his money. It was before Passover and the Gentile neighbors saw him nosing around the house at dusk—in short, that's all they needed. So they hauled Yenkel Short Sidelocks off to the police station looking more dead than alive. 'Tell us, Yenkel, who were the accomplices who helped you pull off this job? And what did you do with so much blood?' Does a wall answer? Yenkel was struck dumb! And, I don't need to tell you what was going on among the Jews in town. I won't go into all the details, but a high magistrate, an expert investigator, came on the scene, took one look at the four corpses and at Yenkel, and then listened to the story of the unfortunate man whose wife and children had been so horribly murdered. The investigator twisted his mouth to the side and turned on the husband of the slain woman and the father of the mutilated creatures: 'All right now, take off your clothes, my fine fellow, and let me take a good look at you. And afterward, be so kind as to show me your attic. Maybe we'll find something there?' What more is there to say? To make a long story short, on his shirt they found red stains, in the attic they found the murder weapons, an axe and a knife, covered with blood. He himself confessed that since he had a mistress whom he wanted to marry and a divorce was difficult to obtain, he had found an easier way to get rid of an unwanted wife. But why did he have to kill the poor children? A good question. I suppose once a person starts cutting, he has to keep on cutting. So we have another question: why did he need to dismember them? The answer is: Passover! . . ."

The crowd heard the Heisin story to the very end, nudging each other with delight at its outcome and animatedly expressing to one another how they felt. Only David Shapiro was dissatisfied with the way Jews were licking their chops

over these scandals, and he stepped over to another circle. There he heard the
same concerns and the same words being bandied about: blood libel, Zamislov-
ski, Purishkevitch, "packs of trouble," and similar tales and anecdotes: in a
small town in Volnya province a Russian servant disappeared for a few hours,
almost precipitating a tragedy; in a village in Chernigov province a little Gentile
girl went clay digging and was buried in a cave-in. The Gentiles of the village
gathered together, got drunk, and were about to make trouble for the Jews when
God performed a miracle and the little girl was dug up, dead but without a sign
of having been bled. Troubles in Bessarabia . . . troubles in Poland . . . troubles
even in Nizhni Novgodor—may the devil take it all!

David spat and wanted to leave for home, but where was that boy of his? His
little *gymnasium* student Syomke had vanished. Where could he be, that imp?
And whom could he ask when everyone was all caught up in "blood libel," for
God's sake? Ask the synagogue sexton? But where could he be? Ah, there he
was, squeezed between two groups, a slightly built, curious-looking Jew with
strangely long arms, his eyes shut, and listening to what the men were saying.
With one ear he was listening to one circle and with the other ear, to a second.
David was irritated.

"Why are you listening to this nonsense?"

"Why not? Am I not a Jew?" the sexton retorted, sounding both surly and
obsequious while fearing to budge lest he miss a word of importance.

"Do you have any idea where my son is?"

"Your son?" repeated the sexton, and darted his eyes around on all sides,
thereby missing the best part of the discussions. But that was the price he had to
pay as part of his job.

It would be a mistake, however, to think that the sexton would drop everything and go searching for the boy for the likes of Shapiro, even if he was one of
the true, Slaviteh Shapiros. Why couldn't he ask the assistant sexton to do that
kind of job? And the sexton did a bit of fast footwork, located the assistant
sexton, a man also with a soul, who also wanted to hear what was being said,
and ordered him sternly, like an officer commanding a solider, "Listen, you, go
help him find his boy, a youngster, a *gymnasium* student. But hurry up, step on
it!" And the sexton himself returned to his groups like a man who had fulfilled
his duty.

The assistant sexton to whom the head sexton had given his stern order was
no youngster himself, but a man the same age as the sexton, with an even fuller
beard than the sexton, but God had endowed him with legs that couldn't walk
of their own accord; they had to be dragged. It was with those blessed legs that
he set off to search for Shapiro's student son among the small fry, where Syomke
was not to be found. Syomke was listening, all ears, to what was engrossing the
crowd. He had stationed himself near a group of old Jews, folded his arms across
his chest, bent his head slightly to the side, like an adult, and listened to all the
stories. He would gaze deeply into each speaker's eyes, not letting a word go by.
But he had completely forgotten that today was Passover and that it was time to
go home, where he would sit down at the seder table and ask his father the Four

Questions. But Syomke had his own questions in place of the old Four Questions he knew by heart. His first question: Why did they beat him up that day in school? His second question: Why every year at Passover time were Jews afraid of a pogrom? His third question: Why was it always Gentiles who made pogroms? His fourth question—but there was his father. When David saw Syomke in that pose, he felt a pang in his heart. The poor child did not have to hear such stories . . .

"Little devil that you are! Must you also have to listen to such things? May heaven protect you!"

Ignoring the fact that Syomke was no longer a small child but a lad wearing a uniform with silver buttons, David took him angrily by the hand and hurried him home, as was his manner.

the forty-sixth chapter

AT THE SEDER

By the time David Shapiro arrived home from the synagogue he was in an expansive mood, as he was every year, greeting the family with the same hearty "Happy holiday!" and, as he did every year, seating himself upon the throne reserved for the head of the household, a true freeborn spirit, an aristocrat who could count in his lineage many generations of Passover "Kings." He conducted the seder with the same zeal as every year and with the same familiar ancient tunes that we have all chanted from generation to generation. True, his face was clouded by an uncustomary look of suppressed sorrow and in his voice could be heard a minor key, an echo of that special Jewish burden symbolized by the name "Chigirinski." But the only one who could notice this was Sara, who now sat to his right, dressed and adorned like a queen and bearing herself truly like a queen. No one would have believed that this was the same Sara who had with her own hands carried out the *khometz*, or, as she called it, the "chaos," from this same room and had by herself with great effort brought in the Passover. Now these same hands were clean and white; a pair of small diamonds sparkled on the old rings she had put on in honor of the holiday. Similar little diamonds sparkled in her old earrings reserved for Passover. But even more sparkling was her still youthful, handsome face, now a bit more worried-looking than usual. It didn't matter. Sara had been bearing a burden of sorrows in her heart since Purim, but she told no one of it because her David hated when anyone spoke of the murdered Volodka. Why should she cause him unnecessary pain? Sara herself would have desired to forget about this festering sore, but her sister-in-law's comments in passing made it impossible. Those few words had cut deeply into her heart, and only after Toibe's departure did Sara remember that among the papers removed from her lodger's room was her daughter's portrait. Her distress was profound! She had entirely forgotten, poor woman! As she gazed upon the glowing, happy face of her daughter sitting close to the even happier roomer, she prayed to God for them, not sure exactly what she was praying for. She prayed that the happiness of the household would not be disrupted at this time when an engagement was imminent and joy should prevail. And that an announcement of an engagement was imminent, there was no doubt in her mind, otherwise why would the "children" be so close with one another? Sara Shapiro knew her daughter very well—wasn't that what a mother was for?—and she also knew the roomer and felt assured that his intentions were honorable. However, today's young folks resented being checked up on. They had time . . .

When David returned from the synagogue, the first thing he did was to ask the roomer to be so kind as to don a hat.

"I know you are a student," David had said, "and a medalist and, I swear, half a Gentile, but one thing has nothing to do with the other. A Jew has to wear a hat at the seder, as God commanded."

Then David seated him at his immediate left, next to Betty—Sara, the Passover Queen, occupied the seat on his right—gave the two young people a Haggadah to share, and said to his daughter in Yiddish, "You'll have to show him everything, what to say and what not to say, because he probably knows as much about the Haggadah as . . ."

Betty translated her father's words for him. Oh! who could be compared to them at that moment? They were sitting close together and sharing one Haggadah. Where were their thoughts? Betty could still feel on her lips the fiery imprint of his kiss, and she imagined that anyone, if they looked hard enough, could see it. She could not for the life of her figure out how it had happened. Who had been the first—he, or she? And what would happen next? With whom would he speak—with her father or her mother? And how would he say it? Or would he want to have his own father come, that parvenu rich man with the fat belly, the double chin, the smug lips, and blank eyes?

"No, that he won't do. He knows that would displease me," thought Betty. As she turned the pages of the Haggadah, her eyes enountered his, which calmed her and conveyed so much, so much! . . .

"Be mine!" she imagined his eyes were telling her, and she answered him with hers, "I am yours . . . I've been yours for so long although you were a mystery to me and I couldn't understand you . . ." Now she felt she understood him and knew him through and through, even his very thoughts at that moment. Ah, happy, foolish Betty! How could she know that this handsome, remarkable young man, with the fine shock of dark hair and Jewish nose, who bore that very Jewish name of Rabinovitch, and who now realized the true fate of being one of the Chosen People for whom quotas and residence permits and other such fine privileges were created, was not Rabinovitch and not a Jew and not one of the

Chosen People but another kind of aristocrat? His forefathers were not the Patriarchs Abraham, Isaac, and Jacob, of whom we are so proud; his claim to aristocracy was merely that his father, a Russian nobleman and a wealthy land-owner, Ivan Ivanovitch Popov, was a distinguished person in high circles, an intimate of the powers that be, with a high rank almost that of a minister. No, Ivan Ivanovitch Popov could not boast that he was a descendant of the Shapiros, the true, Slaviteh Shapiros. But he could boast of the fact that he had one brother who was a governor and another who was a rural district chancellor and that he himself was certainly not a nobody; he was no more nor less than the former T_____ chief provincial magistrate! Now who could have imagined that? Would even our hero himself a year ago have imagined that he would this night be sitting with Jews at a Jewish table celebrating the Jewish Passover seder, joining in the reading of the Haggadah, in which is related the great wonder of the exodus from Egypt, and afterward satisfy his hunger, together with Jews, with the dry crackers he called *mazzah*, the strong, bitter horseradish, the highly seasoned gefilte fish, the plump matzo dumplings? And who would take it upon himself to attempt to put on paper the turbulent sea of feelings and the multi-tude of thoughts our Russian hero was experiencing that night of the Jewish Passover at the Jewish seder table? Just before the holiday he had read in a newspaper a short item from his home town in T_____ province, that on orders of the T_____ governor—his uncle—four hundred fifty Jewish families were going to be expelled in two weeks.

"Four hundred fifty Jewish families," he thought as he looked at the Hagga-dah with Betty. "Four hundred fifty families, about two thousand souls, are being expelled because of my uncle, the governor, and not because they've murdered or robbed anyone. You can't catch four hundred fifty families commit-ting a crime. They are being expelled simply because they are Jews." He pictured them waking up so many families one fine day or one dark night and reading them the order that in the course of two weeks they had to gather all their belongings and betake themselves wherever their feet would carry them, any-where in the Pale. And as this was no easy undertaking for four hundred fifty families to uproot themselves and within two weeks' time move bag and baggage great distances, and as the Jewish people were, according to what he had learned, an excitable people, an intense, buzzing group of people-flies, he could imagine what was going on: men packing, women weeping, children bawling, police on the alert lest, God forbid, a single Jew of the four hundred fifty families might slip away. And four hundred fifty families picked themselves up from the homes they had occupied for perhaps hundreds of years and dragged themselves and their belongings on the trains, ships, and roads of our sprawling great land, an ironic exodus from Egypt in the twentieth century.

As he mused on this, he was reminded of the words of the news account, "according to the order of the T_____ governor." That was his uncle, his father's younger brother, Andrei Ivanovitch Popov, who was not only a superb, fine person with a sympathetic character but a man of liberal ideas. He remem-bered how his uncle, Andrei Ivanovitch, together with his own father, Ivan

Ivanovitch, had once strongly protested and quarreled with their elder brother, the rural district chancellor, Nikolai Ivanovitch, because he had allowed a peasant to be whipped. He remembered how his uncle, Andrei Ivanovitch, had raged and called the other uncle, Nikolai Ivanovitch, a barbarian. How was it possible? Was it possible that the four hundred fifty Jewish families would allow his uncle to do this to them without lifting a finger, without pleading with him to change his mind? Jews loved to plead their causes, loved to send delegations! Where was his uncle's good heart then? Where were his liberal ideas? Everything has turned upside down in people's minds, everyone's gone mad! Something has happened in these times, he thought further, and everything is backward. What used to be wrong and crazy is today acceptable. What used to be entirely unthinkable is today altogether possible. Take that incident with the general the Familiant girls were talking about earlier today. Here you have a general walking along the street—not a shady character or a coach driver or a drifter—but a *general!* So, he sees a Greek dragging a crying child by the hand and that immediately suggests to him that a Jew is taking a Gentile child to be a Passover sacrifice; it cannot be otherwise. Apparently, all of us, from young to old, from soldier to general, from worker to intellectual, from the journals *Double-Headed Eagle* to *Novoye Vremya,* believe that in our great sprawling land, among all our diverse peoples, there is a people called the Jews, and that these Jews, they tell us, are not only worse and more dangerous and more inferior than other people but that they are also such wild fanatics that they use human blood for ritual purposes, especially Christian blood, which they drain from our Christian children in so inhuman a way that one has to go back to barbarians in primitive times for comparison! And these Jews are no small number who have secluded themselves somewhere in a far corner on the other side of the Urals or on the Kovkoz. No. They are several millions of our closest neighbors, with whom we have shared the same territory, breathed the same air, and eaten the same bread for hundreds of years! These are not Chinese or Indians whose beliefs are alien to us and whose history is unkown to us. No. We are completely knowledgeable of their beliefs, which are so close to ours, and their history is for us an open book. If that is so, if an entire people across many generations can misperceive and form such false, strange conceptions about another people with whom they live, one can say, under the same roof, then what can any opinion and belief be worth?

"Do you like it? Do you want to go on?" Betty said to him, and with a teasing laugh she poked his nose with the Haggadah.

"Betty, you're an insolent girl!" her mother reprimanded. "What business is it of yours? Maybe he wants to say the 'Song of Songs' too?"

"Soo . . ." drawled David, who was always doing the opposite of what his wife wanted, even at the Passover seder, "since you seem to know everything, I believe our Rabinovitch will be able to manage without the 'Song of Songs' this year. It's enough he was able to sit all the way through the singing of "One Kid." You can take off your hat, if you like, if it's not too uncomfortable for you."

The roomer stood up from the table together with Betty, removed his hat, which was for him truly a heavy burden, and the two of them sat down off to the side to chat a while or quarrel a bit or tease one another, as was their way. And David sang out in a clear voice the ancient melody of the time-honored "Song of Songs," and Syomke, with his young little voice, sang along with him as Sara beamed with pride.

the forty-seventh chapter

GOOD FRIENDS QUARREL— LOVEBIRDS KISS

Bickering, teasing, contradicting one another—these had become daily fare for our young couple. Often Betty's mother had to intervene in order to make peace between them.

"I never saw children who fight like cats day and night!" she would exclaim. Or:

"Betty! Will you *ever* agree with what he says?" Or:

"Why do you listen to her, Mr. Rabinovitch? Don't you know she's a Shapiro? All the Shapiros love to be contrary, to say the opposite of what anyone else says, it can drive you crazy."

Sara was right. No matter what Rabinovitch said, Betty had to say the opposite. But he also enjoyed contradicting her. Even when he knew she was entirely right, he would contradict her for the sole purpose of seeing her flare up and display her hot temperament and small, sharp teeth.

Characteristically, something like the following would happen. Feeling himself to be comfortably at home with the Shapiros, and noticing that mother and daughter disliked it when David Shapiro boasted of his ancestors, the true, Slaviteh Shapiros, he had once jokingly asked his landlord what exactly was so great about those Slaviteh Shapiros? David had fixed his eyes on the roomer as if he had asked him to defend the greatness of Abraham the Patriarch or Moses.

"What? You've never heard the story about the Slaviteh Shapiros in Vasiltchikov who were persecuted, flogged, and driven out because of a false accusation? How is that possible?" David had exclaimed, and immediately began to relate the tragic tale of two brothers, eminent Torah scholars, one named Reb Shmuel Abba Shapiro and the other Reb Pinkhasl Shapiro. Both had lived in Slaviteh, where they owned a printing shop. It so happened there was an uproar over a false rumor about them, some denunciation. The Vasiltchikov governor ordered that the two be punished by having them run between two lines of soldiers and flogged, as was done in the old days. And as the soldiers, at the orders of their commanding officers, were flogging them, the older brother's yarmulke fell off. Without so much as a glance at the floggers, he bent down, picked up the yarmulke, and put it back on his head as if nothing unusual were going on."

"Is that all?" the roomer had blurted out involuntarily. Betty flared up.

"What more did you want?"

Wishing to defend himself, Rabinovitch had opined that he saw nothing particularly heroic in the incident and that he didn't understand why they were so proud of someone in the family who had been flogged.

Nu-nu. That's all Rabinovitch had to say. He was attacked from both sides. From one side, David Shapiro was fuming, as only he could, asserting that this Rabinovitch had in him the mannerisms and attitudes of a real Gentile, he had not a single drop of Jewish blood in him, and so on. And Betty, from her side, demanded to know which, in his opinion, was more shameful—to be the one whipped or the one who whips? Which was more honorable—having a hanged man in the family or a hangman?

"That's enough! It doesn't take much to get those two going, the father and the daughter!" Sara had broken in and ended it.

Another time Betty and the roomer were having their morning tea while reading the daily paper. Rabinovitch's eye was caught by a foolish but sad episode which would not be news to a Jew because it was an everyday occurrence in the Jewish Pale.

The episode had taken place in a town in the Jewish Pale. The Czar greatly enjoyed having small children dressed up as little soldiers and having them parade in formation. Under the watchful eye of an officer in one *gymnasium,* more than one hundred children had been lined up in the town square, according to the news correspondent, ready to march, a sight that attracted many passersby. The whole town had come out to see and admire the little soldiers. Suddenly the officer sent to instruct them issued a command, *"Yevrey vperyod!*—Jewish children to the front!"

Three little soldiers with Jewish faces from the youngest class stepped forward, and like real soldiers they stood at attention before the teacher and with eager eyes awaited further orders.

"Stupaytye domoi!—Go home!" was the teacher's command, and the three children remained standing as if paralyzed, unable to comprehend.

"Stupaytye domoi!" the stern teacher repeated, and so that they would more easily understand him, he added, "Hershke, Yenkel, Borakh, Tatele, Mamele, go home!" with such mimicking gestures that the whole crowd burst into gleeful laughter and clapping. The three Jewish soldiers, heads bowed, slunk home to loud applause.

"Chort znayet chto!—The devil take it!" Rabinovitch burst out, and flung the paper from him, sprang up, and began pacing the room, running his fingers through his hair and denouncing that brute of an officer who had in him not one ounce of humanity, the stupid masses who were ready to applaud every outrage, as well as that idiot of a correspondent who wrote up in such an idiotic

tone a vile act over which people ought to tear their hair, call down thunder and lightning!

"Lower your voice!" Betty interrupted him. "We've seen worse things than that."

Rabinovitch stood stock still.

"Worse things? There can't be anything worse than that, Berta Davidovna. Just imagine the deep humiliation, Berta Davidovna, the great pity for the three innocent little students of the youngest class—what could have gone through their heads? And the deadly poison poured into the pure hearts of the rest, the Christian children—how could they understand that? And the crowd that applauded like a flock of sheep . . ."

"That flock of sheep," Betty cut in, "had already seen worse things, which they also applauded. They had seen tiny babies ripped in half, thrown from second-story windows with nails hammered into their heads together with smashed pianos and shredded Jewish pillows . . ."

"Ach, Berta Davidovna, how can you compare them? That was a pogrom and this is something else again . . ."

"The same pogrom, Grigori Moiseyevitch, but without a big brass band."

"Fine words, but when you say them, somehow they come out meaning something else. Ach, Berta Davidovna! Berta Davidovna!"

"What is this constant Berta Davidovna, Berta Davidovna?" Betty mimicked him, and he made a face back and asked her, "So, Berta Davidovna! . . ."

Hearing this in the kitchen, Sara thought the children were having a fight; she didn't realize that, when good friends fight, it is like lovebirds kissing, and she ran in frightened. "Sha! What's going on here? What's happened?"

"Nothing's going on," they calmed her. "Nothing's happened."

"So why do I keep hearing Berta Davidovna and again, Berta Davidovna? I would like to know why he's suddenly so full of Berta Davidovnas."

It all ended in laughter, as usual, but it wasn't too long before the children were at one another again, God help us!

When they had gotten up from the seder table, our young couple began to bicker over a matter of principle: Why wouldn't David Shapiro tolerate any talk about "blood ritual"? Why did he start to throw himself about when he heard the words "blood accusation"? Rabinovitch had stated that he couldn't understand why Jews kept quiet about it. As he saw it, Jews all over the world should unite and apply all their energies to protest against such monstrous accusations . . .

"Just the opposite!" Betty cut him off, directly and sharply as always. "Just the opposite! It is not we who should protest, but the honest, respectable Christians, because for them it must be more of a humiliation than it is for us, if you must know. And you say protest! Where does protesting end? You can't say 'God bless you' to everyone's sneeze. Now they're accusing us of using Christian blood in our matzo for Passover. Tomorrow they'll accuse us of swallowing Christian children live on empty stomachs. Will we have to protest against every ridiculous accusation? Will we have to take a stand and deny that, no, we don't swallow Christian children live on empty stomachs? Pooh! Papa is very right not to want to talk about it. It proves he's aristocratic . . ."

"Aristocratic?"

"Why are you smiling like that? Certainly aristocratic! And certainly more aristocratic than that general who saw a Gypsy or a Greek with a crying child and confused, as we say, a short cow with a pear tree, immediately smelling blood because these people have blood on their minds. Human blood . . . Dreaming and awake, all they see is blood and more blood . . . Oh, we don't have to protest and we don't have to deny anything, what we have to do, what we should do, if you ask me, is to come out publicly with a counteraccusation against all of them."

The young pair had become so involved in their discussion that they failed to notice that David Shapiro had completed the "Song of Songs," had risen from the table in the best of moods, and with a rare smile had gone over to the "children" to hear what they were talking about, just as they were discussing the "blood accusation," something he couldn't tolerate. "You, too, discussing the 'blood ritual'? Everybody, everybody with the 'blood ritual,' God help us."

Betty saw that her father was in high spirits, which was rare for him. "Papa, I was just having a little argument with our roomer about you."

"About me? What is there to argue about me?"

"He doesn't understand why you hate to talk about 'blood ritual.' "

David lowered his head, shut his eyes, and said mildly, "Nu, and do you understand why?"

"Of course I understand. I want to explain to him that you are above such ugliness, that you consider it beneath your dignity, that you take it as an insult, that you . . ."

"Te-te-te!" said David, and covered his ears. He hated when others spoke when he preferred to speak himself. "Why so many words? If you really want to know, I'll tell you why. This 'blood ritual,' as you call it, or 'blood accusation,' as it used to be called, cost us, I mean, our family, too dearly. When I hear the words 'blood accusation,' a chill runs through me. I am reminded of what my father, may he rest in peace, told me, that he had heard from his father's father, from the Slaviteh Shapiros, how it happened that a whole town of Jews was almost destroyed. Only a miracle from God saved them. It's a moving story. A fine story, but a short one."

"Tell it, Papa, tell us about the real, Slaviteh Shapiros," Betty said, cozying up to her father, putting her hand on his white robe, and looking coquettishly into his eyes.

In that coquettish glance, as in how she said "Slaviteh Shapiros," one could detect an irony conveying that the story he would tell might be very interesting, but whether it had to do with the Slaviteh Shapiros was another matter. And they all seated themselves around David—Betty and the roomer on one side, Sara and the youngster on the other. Syomke's eyes lit up. For a story he would give you anything, except, of course, his new boots. And David Shapiro began to tell his story that had happened "to their very own family."

A STORY FROM LONG AGO

The story David Shapiro started to tell was quite a good story, and he told it well. However, because the roomer understood about as much Yiddish as a Gentile, David had to recount it in a language in which he was not quite at home. Whenever words failed him, he had to do what his father had done before him: fill in with his hands. At first, Betty tried to assist as translator, but that wouldn't do because David Shapiro could not tolerate anyone else speaking for him. Was he, God forbid, a mute? Whenever the roomer turned to Betty for an explanation, he became furious. "Why are you asking her? What does she know? She knows as much as you and you know as much as she. In these matters, leave it to me and I'll explain it exactly."

This produced merry laughter from the young people, among whom one must count the young Syomke, who was listening to his father's story with the intelligence of an adult. "Bless his heart!" thought Sara, the four glasses of wine having made her a bit tipsy, her cheeks red and her eyes drowsy.

"My great-great-grandfather, that is, my grandfather's grandfather," Shapiro began his story, already gesticulating intensely in case anyone dared interrupt him, which was to him the worst offense, "told how his grandfather, Reb Shmuel Abba, whom the Slaviteh rabbi, Reb Shmuel Abba, was named after, had two children, a son and a daughter. The son was named Pinkhas, after whom was named the Slaviteh Reb Pinkhasl, and the daughter was named Hodel, named after Reb Yisroel Baal Shemtov's daughter, Hodele. And they were bright children. Pinkhas was studying Torah, and Hodel . . ."

". . . was one of the great beauties of her day!" Betty completed the sentence for him, fully expecting to be told by her mother that she was an impertinent girl for interrupting her father. David became angry and said that, since he was being cut off, he would no longer continue his story, upsetting the young Syomke lest his father act on his threat.

"It won't happen again, Papa!" Betty apologized to him, and David, today more forgiving than other times, relented and went on.

"So, the grandfather, Reb Shmuel Abba, had a son and a daughter, was a man of wealth, and was greatly esteemed by the local landowner, not only because he held the lease of the estate, but also because he was a frequent visitor of his. The old landowner enjoyed spending time with him in many ways, playing chess—people from Slaviteh were famous chess players—or simply passing the time of day with him because the old landowner was a friend of Jews and thought very highly of the Shapiros. What does God do? The old landowner had a son, a scoundrel, who amounted to nothing, may the devil take him! All he cared about was riding to the hounds and shooting birds, a fellow who hated Jews as a kosher Jew hates pork.

It happened one fine Saturday afternoon that the old man's daughter, that beauty Hodel, went strolling with her girlfriends. The young landowner saw her and fell madly in love with her right on the spot, and from that moment on she couldn't show her face on the street again. It got to the point where she had to tell the old man, who immediately went off to see the old landowner to tell him he had an idler of a son who only cared for riding to the hounds and shooting birds. Let him stick to his horses, his hounds, and his birds, but leave his daughter alone. After hearing the old man out, the landowner calmed him and promised it would never happen again, and then sent him home. What took place between the landowner and the young man, no one knows, but from then on they no longer saw the wastrel hanging around the grandfather's house, cracking his whip, making eyes, and whistling. What does God do? The old landowner died and, as it is written, a new king arose. It was a new household with new ways which was felt most keenly by the Jews, as we said tonight in the Haggadah—Go ahead, Betty, translate *that* into Russian. What am I saying? It is absolutely impossible to translate that into another language. For instance, I dare you translate 'a new king arose.' No, daughter, listen to me, don't even try, it'll sound ridiculous! Let me tell it, it'll sound a lot better."

David cleared his throat, adjusted the white yarmulke still on his head from the seder which so became his pale face and black little beard that the daughter couldn't contain herself, and said to the roomer, "My father is quite a handsome man, isn't he?"

Those words made Sara's face even more glowing, and she exchanged glances with David to indicate she was pleased with the compliment Betty had given her father. She embraced Syomke and kissed both his cheeks, which were rosy from having drunk the four glasses of wine. David went on.

"To make a long story short, it was before Passover. Jews were baking matzos and were preparing for the holiday. Whoever had the means, had it good, and whoever didn't, was in trouble, as usual. And as is the custom among Jews, when Passover comes around, one has to provide for the poor people, to see to it that they have matzos, that they receive *moes khitim*—charity. And who has to see to it that the poor get *moes khitim?*"

"They get *mosquitos?*" the roomer asked, looking at Betty, who burst into such gales of laughter that the others jumped from their seats.

"Oh, that's too much, just too much!" Betty howled, doubled up with laughter. "To him, *moes khitim* became 'mosquitos,' ha-ha, little insects that bite you, ha-ha-ha!" Everyone, including the roomer, joined Betty in laughter.

"Don't you have the custom of *moes khitim* where you come from?" David asked him. "How is that possible? Strange Jews you have there! Unless there are no poor people where you live. If that's the case, you should be told what *moes khitim* means." And David, gesticulating, told the roomer that *moes khitim* meant you collected money for the poor so they would have matzos for Passover. The poor might die of hunger the rest of the year, it didn't matter, but when Passover came, all Jews had to have matzos. People went from house to house and collected money from every single person. "Now do you see that *moes khitim* doesn't mean mosquitos? So where were we in the story? At the old man's and at the *moes khitim*. They gathered to hold a meeting at his house, where the rabbis, judges, the seven elders of the city, as well as the wealthy shopkeepers were discussing how to raise the *moes khitim*. Poor people in the town were plentiful, God bless them, and money was scarce, so from whom would the money for the *moes khitim* come? This one had an idea, that one had an idea; ideas flew thick and fast, as is usual among our sons of Israel. As they were talking, the door flew open and someone ran in shouting to my great-great-grandfather, 'Reb Shmuel Abba, bad news! A terrible thing has happened in town! A blood accusation!' What was going on? I'll soon tell you: some Gentiles were riding through the forest and found a murdered young girl, slashed to ribbons. They brought her straight to the police station, and the whole town was in a turmoil because, according to the doctor, there was every sign it was the work of Jews, perpetrated in honor of Passover—in a word, it was a ritual murder. Well, can you imagine the panic that the old man and everyone there felt, because as soon as one hears the words ritual murder, whom do you think they blame if not the leaders of the community and the first among them, Reb Shmuel Abba. And what do you think? It took no longer than it takes me to say these words before the police arrived. 'How do you do, Reb Shmuel Abba, please be so kind as to accompany us to the police station for interrogation.' As you can imagine, he almost passed out from fright. He bid farewell to his wife, knowing he was going straight to prison and from prison directly to the Other World, because in those days, a blood accusation wasn't like it is today. Today we have a trial, attorneys, and a sentence. It used to be otherwise. In those days they would torture you, beat you, pull out your veins, burn you with hot irons until the tormented prisoner, in order to stop the agony, would admit to everything they wanted, which would come out as 'He confessed . . . ' In short, my great-great-grandfather made his confession of sins, again bid his wife farewell, and wished to say goodbye to his children, but they were gone. Where were they? His son was in the synagogue studying, but the daughter was nowhere to be found. She hadn't been seen since early morning. Where could she be? But who could think of that, I ask you, when such a calamity had befallen them? In short, when they got to the police station, first they tried to force the old man to confess the entire truth and name those who had murdered the girl and those who had held the instruments to bleed her while she was still alive. He most likely said he knew nothing about this nightmare they had dreamed up, so they clapped him into jail and took to the other wealthy men of the town with the same demands: confess, Jews, whose work was this? The grandmother, the *bubbe*, rushed in to rescue her husband, weeping and wailing, pleading and falling at their feet. But as she passed by the corpse, she threw herself on the body with a scream. 'Hodel! . . . My daughter!!! . . . My child!!! . . . ' And that was the last thing she said, because she fainted again and again and died that very day. Both mother and daughter were buried the following morning, side by side . . ."

"And the grandfather?"

"The grandfather? May he have a happy paradise. He was immediately freed, of course, sat shiva for his wife and daughter. Within a week, they say, his hair turned gray as a dove's, from pain and suffering, but especially from his great humiliation. They found out, much later, you understand, what had happened: it had been the work of the young landowner, may his name be obliterated forever! He had stolen her away from the house early in the morning, taken her to the woods, where she had been raped and then slaughtered. They knew . . . There were witnesses: the coachman, who had driven them, and the forest ranger, who was afraid of testifying against the landowner."

"Well, what happened to the landowner?" Rabinovitch asked, upset. "Did he get away with it? Didn't anyone speak up?"

"Who? Who would start up with a landowner? Who would risk it?"

"How about the Jews? And the old man?" Rabinovitch pressed on, becoming more agitated. David started to become angry.

"The Jews? What could the Jews do in those days? It wasn't like today, when there is a court of law, attorneys, and some justice. After sitting shiva, followed by the obligatory thirty days of mourning—it was right after Passover—there was a sumptuous banquet with much dancing. The town was jubilant, the celebration lasted three days and nights, and the old man was among the revelers."

"The old man too?"

"Why not? He couldn't bring the dead back to life, could he? And if it was God's wish that a whole town of Jews be spared from a blood libel, wasn't it allowable to celebrate? What do you think? What is your opinion?"

The question remained unanswered. The landlord rose from the table with a yawn, ready to go to sleep, Sara and the young lad following. Only Betty and the roomer remained to talk awhile about the tragic story from the past and were soon ready with sharp tongues, as usual, to debate heatedly. Betty waited till Rabinovitch had expressed his views so she could contradict him. Rabinovitch was saying that it reminded him of the story of Jeptha's daughter. Her father's story seemed absurd to him, and he wasn't terribly impressed with those Jews of the past. Betty cut him off and claimed he had as much of a sense of those old-time Jews as a deaf-mute from birth had a sense of Wagner's music.

"But Berta Davidovna!" Rabinovitch was about to protest when Sara came in, dressed for bed, and, turning down the lamps, said, "Enough with the Berta Davidovna! Have you forgotten it's the holiday and we have to wake up early tomorrow?"

And thus on this first night of Passover, each one left for a good night's rest.

HE WRITES LETTERS

That night our hero hardly slept at all. Alone in his little room, he sat and wrote letters, one letter after another.

The first letter was to Betty. It started: "Please don't be surprised, Berta Davidovna, that I am writing you a letter rather than speaking to you directly, because I must first prepare you for what I have to tell you in person. It's about a friend of mine, a close friend, with whom I spent my childhood and with whom I went through all eight classes of the *gymnasium*. My friend's name is Popov. He is a Christian, the son of a wealthy city official in T____province. He doesn't have a mother. She died soon after his birth so that he never knew her. But from his only sister he learned that his mother was a rare beauty, famous throughout the entire province. She took pride in the fact that she had been no more than a poor Gypsy, a singer in a Gypsy chorus. His father had fallen desperately in love with her, and ignoring the fact that his parents and entire family were opposed to their relationship, he married her. He desired to introduce her into the highest social circles, as befits an aristocratic woman (my friend's father was then a chief provincial magistrate, and one brother was a district council head, and another a governor). But the family wouldn't accept her, and let her know at every step who she was and what her origins were. What the poor woman had to suffer is hard to realize—she told no one. But obviously her life was far from sweet. She vowed to take revenge on this family of aristocrats, but how could a poor lonely woman take revenge if not with the one gift nature had granted her—her rare beauty? She encouraged her husband's two brothers, the chancellor and the governor, one after another, to fall in love with her, but so cleverly that one didn't know about the other, and each one had to vie for her love, which she would not return. Though it was supposed to be a secret, it was the talk of the town and the entire province. In short, she created a scandal, playing a game of cat and mouse with her brothers-in-law, setting one against the other, and triumphantly taking revenge upon them as only a wily Gypsy could. Understand, it wasn't easy for her. Her husband found it hard to appreciate her Gypsy machinations; he could not believe in the purity of her soul. Most likely, many ugly scenes were enacted between them. But one thing was clear to my friend— that his mother had been pure and honorable. He was reassured of that by his sister, whom the mother had called to her bedside an hour before her death, had drawn her close to her heart, kissed her, and said, 'Pray to God for your mother. Her body is pure and her soul honorable . . . ' This made a lasting impression on my friend's sister so that she vowed to pray for her mother's soul for as long as she would live, and, foreswearing the liberal upbringing her father had given her, she became so pious that her one goal in life was to enter a convent."

Having written those few pages, he reconsidered. What good were these pretenses, made-up friends, mystifications? Why shouldn't he be direct? Why couldn't he write her his own life story from beginning to end, until the moment when this hoax began, when he, Grigori Popov, changed places with his friend, Hersh Rabinovitch? He had written this long, involved story but still hadn't come to the point; what good was it? He was making a fool of himself. Couldn't he talk directly to her? Could he be hesitating because Betty might not understand him and might end their relationship, especially when he was prepared to . . . ? But here he remembered the battle he would have to wage with his father, his sister, and his whole family. He tore the letter to bits and began writing a long letter to his father, prefacing it by saying that only he would understand him because he alone was able to appreciate the value of a true, pure, sacred love, an allusion to his father's romance with his beautiful Gypsy mother. Only he would understand that every obstacle would be overcome, again alluding to his father's marrying the Gypsy outcast against his parents' wishes.

He finished the letter to his father and was again dissatisfied. He knew full well that his father would forgive him fifty Gypsy women more readily than one Jewish woman. Who better than he knew what a Jew meant to his family? And how did he himself perceive a Jew just a few months ago? And even now? Could he in all honesty say, placing his hand over his heart, that he could possibly know a Jew the way Jews know each other and that he could love a Jewish woman the way a Jew could? Wasn't the rabbi correct in his theory that a Christian cannot love a Jew? The Messiah, for whom the Jewish people are waiting, and who will make all people brothers, has not yet come. And now, on the contrary, is a time of bitter racial hatred, when peoples cannot bear each other's presence or share the planet amicably.

And so the letter to his father suffered the same fate as the other one, and he began to write a letter to his sister, feeling that only to her could he reveal the secret in his heart, and only in her pure, pious soul could his secret find a sympathetic response. She would not refuse to be the helpful intercessor between him and his unpredictable father.

Carefully and slowly he prepared her for the serious step he was about to take. First he fully described the girl with whom he had fallen in love and without whom he could not live. Then he told her that the girl did not come from a wealthy family but had simple, honest parents, which wouldn't be so much of a problem if the girl shared his religion or were at least willing to take on his faith for his sake. The truth was, she was Jewish. There lay before him two choices: either to take his life or to forego the outward forms of his religion.

Having come out and written these words to his sister, he confessed he felt better, as if a heavy weight had been lifted from his heart. He ended his letter by saying she should not think he had forgotten that she was a pious Christian soul. On the contrary, it was *because* of her piety that he assumed she would, with particular zeal, accept his plan of joining with our elder brethren in order to demonstrate to the so-called nonbelieving Jewish people that they were mistaken and that the Messiah had already come.

He read this letter over again and thought, God knows if his sister would understand what he meant by the words "joining with our elder brethren," and "demonstrate to the nonbelievers that the Messiah has already come."

And he also ripped this letter to bits.

the fiftieth chapter

BEFORE THE BATTLE

The first morning of Passover, as Jews were going respectfully to pray in the synagogue, dressed in their holiday best, men in top hats and women in broad-brimmed chapeaus, they were accosted by Gentile youths wearing large caps, hawking newspapers.

"Chigirinski's picture! Jew Passover! Three kopeks!" Aggressively, they pressed the newspapers on the passersby—and Jews bought them. It is difficult to say why, whether it was because the Jews with the top hats didn't want people to know they were Jews or whether they were eager to see the picture of Chigirinski and to read what these clever writers had to say about this Jewish Passover. But it is a fact that most of the anti-Semitic sheets that libel us with Haman's lies and incite pogroms against Jews end up in Jewish hands. The majority of Russian readers of this yellow journalism inside and outside the Jewish Pale are Jews.

The newspaper hawked by the Gentile youths was the famous pogrom newspaper that gave itself the high-sounding name *Double-Headed Eagle*. In itself, the newspaper was mediocre, like all newspapers of its kind: inadequately small, irresponsibly outspoken, vulgar, and foul-mouthed. In honor of the Jewish holiday, it had been cleaned up a bit, increased in size, illustrated with a picture of a dead lad lying stabbed and tortured, and topped with a headline that would move a stone: "Orthodox Russian People! Remember Vladimir Chigirinski! A Boy Tortured by Jews! Protect Your Children! The Seventeenth of March Is Their Passover!"

That filled the first page. Inside the paper was a series of frightfully written pogrom articles couched in the most provocative language. Several were written by the editor himself, who wasn't ashamed to sign his name and priestly title, and others by his equally shameless co-workers, among whom stood out one cretin of a student named Korshunov, a "great expert" on Jewish sects and customs. His list of Jewish sects included *Ashkenazi*, *Sephardim*, and *Chassidim*.

Each sect, claimed this expert, had its method of tricking a Christian child into giving up his blood, which was then distributed to Jews throughout the Diaspora for their Passover crackers.

The victim, our great expert, the student Korshunov, went on, had to be an illegitimate first-born male, no older than thirteen. Since the unfortunate schoolboy, Volodya Chigirinski, was a firstborn male and illegitimate, it was his fate to be sacrificed for the Passover by that Jewish sect in our blessed city.

When the Jews read this outrageous story about this so-called sect, which was probably to be found only on the moon—no sect with so crazy a name and such crazy customs had ever been heard of on his planet—and when they read about the remarkable "crackers," they held their sides with laughter.

"What kind of cracker are they talking about that is baked with the blood of a firstborn, illegitimate boy? Who ever heard of such nonsense!"

"And how would Jews know which Gentile is firstborn or illegitimate?"

"Idiot! If you want to be picky about his being illegitimate, what's the difference if he's firstborn or not? Maybe the firstborn bastard had other bastards born after him, does that then mean he is unfit for the crackers?"

This scholarly exegesis was accompanied by a Talmudic sing-song and a punctuating twist of the thumb so that the crowd was howling with laughter. But they weren't satisfied with that and kept on:

"What good is your splitting hairs about firstborn bastards and crackers? Just read what they say about our sects. It looks like we ourselves don't know what's going on."

"For example?"

"For example, it says here that when a rabbi is performing a marriage, he cuts a hard-boiled egg in two, one half for the bridegroom and the other half for the bride, and dips the egg in ashes mixed with human blood."

"Tphoo! Who says that? That same 'Double-Headed' scholar?"

"With so much wisdom, he is eligible to teach all the Jews of the world. Apparently he can answer every question there is . . ."

"He does . . ."

Thus the Jews made fun of the situation that first day of the holiday as they were going to and from the synagogue, but each in his heart felt like a person who finds out after eating that he had swallowed something revolting. It seemed that all those idiotic hairsplitters and clever, scholarly Korshunovs, and God-fearing priests were singing the same tune: Beat Jews! Completing the Korshunov article was a description of how the day before a divine service had been held in the churches for the soul of the Jew-tortured Volodya Chigirinski. But Jews felt in their hearts that this was not to be taken seriously: they felt insulted, but is that something new? Weren't Jews used to worse troubles?

And so the first day of Passover passed, thank God, calmly. But when *Khol hamoed*, the days falling between the first and last days of Passover, arrived on Thursday of that week, the day before the dreaded Good Friday, one sensed a strange unrest among Jews. They were whispering among themselves, uttering half-sentences in subdued voices, secretly packing their things as if going off for a short stay or a wedding, when one packs minimally, taking only whatever is close at hand, but making sure to include the most precious and necessary articles. And silently, secretly, they carted their belongings to one place—to the neighborhood pawnshop for security.

Two refined rich women met one another there.

"What, Madam, are you doing here so early in the morning?"

"And what, Madam, are *you* doing here so early in the morning?"

"I wish I knew for sure. It seems Jews make trouble for themselves. Do you have any idea what there is to be afraid of?"

"My very words. Why, I ask, does this seem to happen every year? Comes Passover, and they become terrified. I told them, I said, fools, I said, why Passover? If anything's going to happen, I said, why can't it happen in the middle of the year?"

"My very words. It's nothing to get upset over. Still, I didn't want my few pieces of jewelry and silver to be in the house at such a time."

"The same with me. But why did you bring your fur cloak?"

"I have the cloak stored at the pawnbroker every year. Why should I bother to look after my fur pieces myself? I can't stand the smell of naphtha."

"My very thoughts."

And so it went. Within two hours, the approach to the pawnshop had become so packed with Jewish ladies who were worried about their finery, jewelry, and silver and who couldn't stand the smell of naphtha, that the police soon had to be called in to maintain order so that "the Jews wouldn't start a pogrom against themselves." (That was spoken in jest by a policeman, a former student, who had to marry a girl because she had borne him, *keyn eyn horeh*, twins, and so he needed to go to work.)

But if the well-off middle class, whom we today call "petit bourgeois," were worried about their jewelry and fur coats, the upper classes, the Jewish behemoths and leviathans, were saving their *own* skins, which were more precious to them than their jewelry, silver, or fur coats.

Within a few days the governor's administrative office was inundated with applications for passports to go abroad. Journalists were making the most of the situation. "It appears the delicate stomachs of our Jewish upper classes have been upset by their Passover *mazzah* and they have to travel abroad." (So joked a y ̤ng officer, a one-time student, ostracized by his friends because of a scandal that smelled of blackmail. He too had to leave the university and go to work.)

After the very wealthy had abandoned the city, the middle classes, the petit bourgeois, also started to make their way out of the city, without official passports and not abroad to cure their indigestion, but wherever they could manage to go, rather than remain where the air had become polluted and the word "pogrom" was buzzing in one's ears like bees buzzing in peak honey season.

All that remained were the third-class passengers of the great ship called "the city": the small shopkeepers, craftsmen, middlemen, school teachers, and just plain poor people, who took to rescuing themselves, their wives, and children at the last minute. It was the Sabbath, the Sabbath before the last day of the holiday, before Easter Sunday, when it was whispered that the worst slaughter would occur in the city. And because it was the Sabbath and travel by train was forbidden, they came up with the idea (when is a Jew lacking in ideas?) that they should hurry to the boats. They swarmed down to the riverside and besieged the ticket window, each one fighting to be first until, here too, the police had to intercede so that "the Jews wouldn't start a pogrom against themselves." And when the Sabbath was over and night fell, the night before Easter Sunday, the city looked as if before a battle, after the first shot has been heard and the hot breath of the enemy is felt in the city. All the streets leading to the train station were flooded with Jews. Men, women, and children were lined up in the station to buy tickets. And as it was impossible to reach the ticket window, they made themselves comfortable in the meantime, sitting on the ground and absolutely refusing to go back to the city, even though they were assured that a delegation had met with the governor.

"Let the rich folks celebrate!" the poor people replied bitterly, unaware that the rich were long since gone. The golden behemoths and leviathans were at that moment arriving in Nice, in Taormina, in Monte Carlo and other such quiet corners. At the roulette tables, at the card tables, playing at *trente et quarante* and other such diversions, they would for a while forget all their Jewish problems.

Among those who had rushed to the train station Saturday after dark and spent the night on the street was our Shapiro household. David Shapiro, his wife Sara, his daughter Betty, his young son Syomke and their roomer Popov-Rabinovitch, the son of the former chief provincial magistrate and nephew of the T____governor and district council head.

the fifty-first chapter

WHEREVER THEIR FEET CARRY THEM

As long as the business where David worked remained open, he didn't want to hear about leaving. He would dash home every night, eat hurriedly, as usual, and without a word dash back to work. But when the business suddenly closed one fine Friday morning, the second day of *Khol hamoed*, and the owner and his sons fled the country, our gallant Shapiro suddenly lost his pluck. He came home, drew Sara aside, and whispered in her ear, "Sara, it's bad, very bad. We have to save ourselves and the children . . ."

"God help us!" Sara wrung her hands, "The pogrom has started? I'm shocked!"

"Sha! Don't talk so loud! It hasn't started yet! Who said it had? Try to tell her something. Can you say a word to her? Can you trust her from here to there? As I live!"

Husband and wife quarreled, as was their habit, but this time the row ended with both of them starting to pack. They were relieved that Betty was off somewhere in the city with the roomer. If Syomke overheard them, they would tell him that they were packing for the remaining days of the holiday. But they were not convinced they could deceive Syomke. First of all, what sense would it make to his childish mind that they had to pack for the remaining days of the holiday? Where was it written? And second of all, having overheard in the synagogue on the first day of Passover what Jews were saying about blood accusations and pogroms, he must surely understand what was going on. Certainly he would remember when he was a small child how he had lain in hiding in an attic with his mother while his father and Betty were in Aunt Toibe's attic. For three days and nights, they hadn't known of the others' whereabouts. In short, he would not be fooled. Syomke did know what a pogrom was, thank God, and our young *gymnasium* student also began to pack quietly, so that no one would hear. With a belt from an old uniform, he tied his school texts and all his notebooks together in a bundle. He stuffed the certificate with the grades of fives from the *gymnasium* deep in his pocket and was ready to leave when along came his sister and his tutor, who brought everything to a halt.

"What's going on here? Where are you packing to go?" Betty assailed them, as only she could. "You're running away? Run! I'm not budging!"

Rabinovitch, who saw what was going on, of course agreed with Betty that it was foolish to leave. To begin with, nothing was going to happen, and then, even if it did, there was no need to be afraid. What was there to fear?

"That's easy for *you* to say!" Shapiro said. "What do you know about our Jewish troubles? Tell me, where were you in 1905?"

A discussion then ensued about the year 1905. Everyone had a story to tell, even Rabinovitch; although he stated that there were no Jews in his province, not even one, nevertheless there was still some unrest.

"What, there are no Jews where you come from?" Sara interrupted him. "So where were you? And your aunt? And your sister? Or don't you count yourselves as Jews?"

Rabinovitch realized he had blundered. He tried to correct himself by saying that a few Jewish families didn't amount to very much, when David came to his rescue. He didn't let him continue, preferring to do all the talking, and began describing the horrors and humiliations they had suffered here in this city: how he had taken his daughter to his sister's, to Toibe Familiant's, reckoning to leave her with Toibe's children while he himself returned home. It turned out to be impossible for him to leave, and he had to hide with them in the attic. For three days he didn't know what was happening with Sara and Syomke, who was a small child then.

"And that small child and I were lying in that attic," Sara started to further elaborate the story while "that child," Syomke, also wanted to put in a word about his experience, but his father cut him off—"A little squirrel like you shouldn't fill his mind with such things"—and he continued telling about that time, how the Gentiles avenged themselves on the Jewish community, how in one week they totally destroyed it, and how they did it so cleverly that not a peep was heard from a single little Jew, not a cock crowed in alarm.

Shapiro described this event in a tone conveying to the roomer that the Jews themselves believed they were a weak, insignificant people, yet they did not lose so much as a hair of self-respect over it. On the contrary, it appeared they were proud of their two-thousand-year wanderings, boasted of their long exile that made sheep of heroes and insects of people who weren't ashamed to call themselves "little Jews." "A strange, strange people! . . ."

And so Friday passed. David and Sara Shapiro, together with the young Syomke, were ready to flee along with the other Jews wherever their feet would carry them. But Betty and the roomer held them back. With evening the Sabbath arrived, when it is forbidden to travel, unless by water. All their neighbors, friends, and acquaintances and all the inhabitants of the Jewish Street had made their way to the boats. Why shouldn't they also go by boat? But Betty was stubborn—nothing would convince her to go by boat. Why not? She simply refused. And when Betty says no, you can be sure it's no. Only with pleading, tears, and threats did her mother finally succeed in convincing her they should at the very least leave the Jewish Street, which was so emptied of people on that Sabbath a thief could brazenly walk into any house and carry off everything and no one would be there to say a word. "Since it's the Passover Sabbath, let's pretend we're just stopping by for a visit at Aunt Toibe's," Sara said. But by the time the Shapiros had gathered themselves to go, it had gotten dark. Driving was forbidden and it was a long walk. By the time they arrived at the Familiants' courtyard, exhausted and perspiring, they found the gate locked. They had to ring the bell three times before the gatekeeper appeared, more drunk than sober. When he saw they were Jews, he began to curse them unto their mother's mother's generation. Shapiro became incensed and remonstrated with the gatekeeper—what did he have against his poor dead mother? Finally the roomer, even more incensed, stepped in.

"Why bother arguing with this nobody! I'm going to punch him right in the snout so he'll have a little respect!"

At this the gatekeeper became hot under the collar, stepped up close to Rabinovitch and spat out, "In *your* Yid snout! You say you'll punch me in the snout? One whistle from me and the lot of you will be taken care of but good even before our boys have a good night's sleep so they can be all rested up to teach you a lesson in honor of the holy Easter."

It took no small effort before the Shapiros were able to tear the overexcited roomer away from the drunken gatekeeper, thus avoiding trouble. It was Betty who managed, with one look, to quell the fury of this young man who had in him such un-Jewish ways. "How can a Jew take it upon himself to act like that with a Gentile at a time like this?" Even Betty had to admit he had strange ways about him, some very un-Jewish instincts.

"So? What do we do now? Go back home?"

"My dear, darling daughter, let's take a cab and go to the train station! Everyone's already gone, let's also go. Let's go wherever our feet carry us!" Sara pleaded with her daughter, throwing her arms around her neck and weeping. Finding it hard to look at his wife weeping, David turned away so as to hide the welling up in his own eyes while Syomke began to sob. He was mainly worried about his school texts and notebooks; what if, God forbid . . .

"Don't cry, my child, we have a great God," Sara comforted him and sent her husband to hail two carriages. As they were seating themselves in the carriages, David, Sara, and Syomke in one, and Betty and the roomer in the other, Sara managed to whisper to the roomer before they drove off that she was entrusting to him her dearest treasure, her most precious possession. More than that she could not speak. She was choked with tears.

"Don't worry, *Matushka*, don't worry at all," the roomer calmed her. "I assure you, I guarantee it, with my life, with my very life!"

Those words were uttered with such sincerity, deep feeling, and warmth that the overwrought mother felt completely confident that her daughter would be in safe hands. Still and all, she made sure that her daughter and the roomer drove ahead of them. And so the cortege slowly made its way to the train station, and from there—wherever their feet would carry them.

the fifty-second chapter

PEACE ON EARTH, GOOD WILL TO MEN

The Shapiros were not the only ones who were making their way to the railroad station. They were among many Jews who had on that Sabbath, while it was still daylight, decided to "visit" the station, pretending they were going for a stroll or a drive, awaiting nightfall, when they could board a train and be off.

As they approached the thoroughfare leading to the station, they could see from a distance stretched out before them masses of people—some driving and some on foot—all Jews, the Chosen People, so recently kings and sons of kings at the Passover seder, mostly poor folk, God bless them, with their wives, children, baggage, bundles, pillows, and rags, endless rags. Scattered among them were well-to-do merchants, intellectuals in peaked caps, ladies in ostrich feathers, young girls with parasols, boys in short jackets, and students in white-buttoned uniforms mingling with poor, hungry, elderly, sick, tubercular Jews, pale, exhausted, bedraggled women and their tiny, thinly clad chicks—in short, the entire Jewish quarter, the entire Jewish Pale, the entire Jewish people.

"Where are you pushing? Move back! Yid snouts! Cursed sidelocks! Stupid Passover outfits!" That was the warm welcome proffered them by a voluble traffic policeman wearing white gloves, who stopped their carriage and treated the horses to a clout on the muzzle with his fist. Responding to the warm welcome was our Rabinovitch, who sprang from the carriage and headed straight for the policeman to discuss philology with him—where had he learned such language? Sara, realizing what he was up to, cried out in alarm to her daughter in Yiddish, "Betty! Stop him! Betty! Don't let him talk! He'll get us into trouble!"

It was useless. They had to continue on foot. But how could they walk when before them was such a mass of humanity, God bless them? They would have to wait until the front of the line had gone by the ticket window, when they would be able to move up. Meanwhile, they had to sit down wherever they could on the street in order to have a place for themselves, because behind them the crowd continued to swell.

"What will we do?" Sara asked her husband, looking around on all sides and seeing the growing multitude. David answered her with his customary abruptness, "What will we do? We'll sit down and write books! What a question—what will we do? Everyone is waiting, we'll also wait. Everyone is sitting, we'll also sit."

The Shapiro family found a spot and sat down on the sidewalk, first David, then Sara and her son. The daughter and the roomer continued to stand, eager to stroll about, but as that required stepping over people and sleeping children, they also sat down for a short while until the crowd would thin, each wrapped in his own thoughts.

That night our Popov-Rabinovitch lived through what most do not experience in a year and pondered more than he had pondered his whole life, for what he had witnessed was ten thousand times more than his fantasy could have invented. The pitiful, heartrending scenes of poor mothers in rags with sagging breasts clutching almost naked, hungry babies, the old, sick, tubercular Jews with pale, starved faces, young people with bent backs and frightened eyes, all of them struggling to keep alive, more terrified of the Angel of Death than all the lucky millions in the world—none of this shocked him as much as the fact that all these people considered this a completely ordinary event. And when was this happening? Precisely on the very eve of Easter Sunday, when good Christians stay up all night, joyously preparing to greet the day of resurrection, embracing and kissing one another.

And his thoughts carried him far, far away to his home, to his family. Every year at this time he would visit home, and there, to please his father and even more his pious sister, Vera, he would spend all night with them in church, and the first person he would kiss in the morning was always his sister Vera, who at that time would look reborn, like a saint, like a person not of this world.

His sister, Vera, with her large, black eyes, was a copy of her exquisite Gypsy mother, indeed would resemble nothing more than a madonna on that night. Everything about her bespoke love, infinite love, love for all mankind, and even more so for the poor, the weak, the oppressed and downtrodden; everything aroused in her the spirit of that great holy day proclaiming the message that on this day there was to be "peace on earth and good will to men."

"Oh! Sister, sister!" he thought. "If you were here now, you would see how meaningless the words 'Peace on earth, good will to men' are. If you were here now, you would see how the best and the holiest are being trampled in the dust! And for what reason? For the reason that we don't know, nor do we wish to know, one another . . . Only for the reason that brothers do not wish to know their brothers as brothers . . ."

His thoughts were interrupted by David Shapiro, who had been sitting quiet as a kitten, and who suddenly sighed deeply and exclaimed, "God in heaven! God in Heaven! What will become of your little Jews?!"

His words had a powerful affect on all those around him, startling a family sitting near the Shapiros. This family consisted of a sickly Jew with red, trachoma-afflicted eyes and an emaciated wife, whose flat, thin face strongly resembled a matzo. Three small children clung to her apron as if she might run away at any moment. Next to the woman with the matzo face sat a swarthy youth wearing a once-white suit that might have been new last summer if not two summers ago. Although this swarthy young man sat with his back to David Shapiro, who had not addressed him directly, he nevertheless responded to Shapiro's words in a decided Litvak accent, "Reb Yid! Don't you worry about God's little Jews, is one. And two, I would like to know, what kind of language is 'little Jews'? Why 'little Jews'? Why not 'Jews'?"

David Shapiro flared up and answered the impertinent youth in the same Litvak accent, "Young man! I'm not talking to you, is one. And two, I would like to know, who are you to speak to me in that tone?"

"And who are *you* to speak to *me* in that tone?"

Though David was not particularly in the mood to invoke his family lineage at this time, he still felt he had to show this young Litvak whippersnapper to whom he was speaking.

"You haven't heard of the Slaviteh Shapiros, I suppose, have you?"

"And you haven't heard of the Pinsk Hurvitches, I suppose, have you?"

By this point they were both facing one another. Rabinovitch saw a familiar, energetic, intelligent, pimply face and heard a familiar, cheerful voice, and he exclaimed, "Classmate! Is it you?"

"Classmate! You're here too? Brother!"

And both young men rose from their places and embraced like old friends and, to the amazement of the Shapiros, kissed each other warmly.

This was the youth from Pinsk, one of the thirteen medalists whom Rabinovitch had gotten to know well in prison. The Pinsk youth introduced the emaciated woman with the matzo face as his sister and the sickly young man with the red, trachoma-afflicted eyes as his brother-in-law, the bookbinder.

"My pleasure! My pleasure!" Rabinovitch shook their hands and introduced his friend and his family to Betty and the rest of the Shapiros, and so a congenial acquaintanceship was struck up between the two families.

the fifty-third chapter

A LONG NIGHT

Away from home, everyone is equal. You can be certain that David Shapiro would never have socialized with a common craftsman. What did he, David Shapiro, a true, Slaviteh Shapiro, have to do with a bookbinder? But here, sitting outside the railroad station, waiting their turn, both families became acquainted, although not quite becoming friends. Appropriately, David distanced himself a bit, as if to say, "Acquaintances, fine, why not? But close friends? Never! . . ." The bookbinder sensed this immediately and treated his new acquaintance with deference, carefully watching what he said, turning his head to the side so that his cigarette smoke would not bother him, making sure to cover his mouth when he coughed, and stifling his laughter so it would not be too loud.

But with the wives, it was entirely different. Wives are of a different breed, especially in the midst of a crisis. Whatever was on the bookbinder's wife's heart was poured out to her new friend, Sara Shapiro, who in turn poured her heart out to the bookbinder's wife as to one's own sister. Though the bookbinder's wife was a true Litvak from Pinsk and though she had a face resembling a matzo, Sara would gladly have traded her for her rich, snobbish sister-in-law, Toibe Familiant, and would have thrown in a little extra to seal the bargain. "Imagine the behavior of this rich woman," she exclaimed, "she simply picks herself up, apparently long before the Sabbath, and runs off from the city with her children without so much as telling her own brother! And she considers herself a pious woman."

"Listen to how clever my husband is. He says that a *Chassid* is worse than a run-around (he means his brother-in-law), and of his sister, he says that her piety is a fake even though she is his sister. There is a saying: 'Whatever you cook, that's what you eat.' If it's a saying, it has to be true."

And so Sara poured out her heart to the bookbinder's wife, and the bookbinder's wife, for her part, talked about who she was and where she came from. She herself was a school teacher's daughter, it's true. All his life her father taught school in Pinsk. He wasn't your ordinary school teacher—but a teacher of Gemara, you understand! Did she deserve to be a craftsman's wife? As much as we Jews deserved this new pack of troubles!

"What new pack of troubles?" wondered Sara.

"Pooh! What do you mean what pack of troubles?" the bookbinder's wife responded. "About that bastard whose Gentile stepfather did him in and made it look like a Jewish neighbor murdered him so they could make a pogrom. I'm really surprised you don't know. How come? They already searched the Jewish neighbor's house the day of Passover, but they didn't find anything."

"So it's true," thought Sara. "Everyone knows about the house search. Everyone. But everyone except us knows that it's related to Kirilikha's son, God help me. So David was right in saying we shouldn't have had anything to do with Kirilikha or her son because we have to bear in mind who our equals are."

She pretended to be listening intently to every word the bookbinder's wife was saying, but her thoughts were spinning and blending with the tolling of the bells. From midnight on, all the church bells of the city had been ringing ceaselessly. One could barely hear above the sound, but the bookbinder's wife did not hesitate to raise her voice above it. She insisted on telling at great length all about herself, her father, and her brother, the student.

"Do you see him over there?" she said, pointing at her brother, the youth from Pinsk. "Looks like something of a somebody, doesn't he, maybe a university student? You'd think so, wouldn't you? Pooh! Don't believe it! By right he should have been a student a long time ago. After all, he finished *gymnasium* with a 'mendal.' He has a head on his shoulders, and what a head! Always something cooking in that noodle pot! Pooh! Do you think they give a 'mendal' for nothing? Back home all his teachers were crazy about him. The 'drector' himself didn't know what to do for him! He called in our father once and said to him like this, 'Do you want your Benny (his name is Benny, my brother) to become a somebody, a real somebody, a real professor?' So my father said, 'Pooh! Why a professor? Why isn't he good enough to be a doctor?' So the 'drector' said to him, 'Pooh! If I say a professor, it's a professor! But one thing,' he said, 'one thing—first he has to convert a little bit . . . ' "

"So?" said Sara, who had heard nothing more of the story than the words "convert a little bit," and the bookbinder's wife answered, "Pooh! That's all he had to hear! As soon as my father came home and told him what the 'drector' had said, my Benny jumped up, grabbed his hat, and started to leave. 'Where to?' 'To the "drector." ' 'What'll you do at the "drector"'s'?' 'I'll tell him,' he said, 'that for his brilliant advice he deserves a punch in the nose.' Pooh! What a thing to say! My father finally convinced him not to start up with the 'drector' because if he starts up with the 'drector,' he'll wind up with a big nothing instead of a 'mendal.' And tell me, what, nowadays, is a Jew without a 'mendal'?"

"So?" again asked Sara, who had heard nothing but the last word, mendal.

"Pooh!" the bookbinder's wife said again. "So God helped him win a 'mendal.' Why? So he could help my husband bind books and help me rock the children so he can at least have a place to lay his head so he can spend whole nights studying books so thick that with each one you can crack the brain of the greatest genius."

"Mama! We're going for a little walk, not too far, and we'll be right back," Betty said to her mother, who did not fully grasp what her daughter meant until after Betty, the roomer, and the youth from Pinsk had gone off in the direction of the station. Sara would never have let her precious daughter leave her side at a time like this, but she was so upset by the events of the night, the ringing of the church bells, and her own fears, and in particular by the few words about the "house search" that the bookbinder's wife had mentioned, that she wasn't thinking clearly. Nor could she move from the spot, because her son had throughout been sitting next to his mother on the ground, listening to the bookbinder's wife's Litvak expressions, and watching her lips move in time to the unceasing ringing of the bells: Glin-glin-glon! Glin-glin-glon!—until his eyelids began to droop as he drew closer to his mother, laying his head on her lap and falling deeply asleep to the sound of the bookbinder's wife's voice and the ringing of the bells, as only a child on his mother's lap can enjoy. And he dreamed of women, many, many women, all running to catch a train and making ringing sounds with their lips like bells: Glin-glin-glon! Glin-glin-glon! "God love him," Sara murmured, drew the child closer, and tried in vain to find Betty. Where could she be?

"Do you have any idea what all this ringing is all about?" the bookbinder's wife asked, and receiving no reply, sighed to herself, "Pooh! What a night!"

The bells kept on ringing. But they did not ring in the same way for everyone. In our hero, Rabinovitch, the Christian Popov, the bells summoned quite different feelings, awakening quite different thoughts, stirring memories from the past, when he was still a child. This night, he recalled, he would go to church with his sister, there to stand all night without getting at all tired, as the bells tolled. The priest led the worship service, the choir sang, the congregants prayed devoutly. And he prayed as well, he recalled, though not as much nor as devoutly as his sister. Nevertheless, his heart flew upward along with the sound of the bells, high up to where his young dead mother looked down upon him with her loving, maternal eyes full of infinite sorrow, love, and longing. He moved closer and closer, he recalled, to his sister. Near her, he imagined, was the One who had planted the seed of love among people on earth, the One who had preached brotherhood and compassion to all people on earth. And afterward, he recalled, when it was already full day and he and his sister arrived home, not only awake and refreshed but also rejuvenated, as if reborn after that night, they would find the table laden with delicacies. And their father, always so severe, intimidating, and unpredictable, would now come toward them with a happy face and gentle glance, open his arms wide, and kiss first his sister and then him. After his father, he recalled, he would be embraced by the old Afanasyevna, their wrinkled, stooped old governess, also reborn after that night. And Nikititch, an old servant with trimmed moustache and sideburns, who sniffed tobacco on the sly so his master wouldn't catch him. And Agafea, the housemaid with the too-red face and too-high bosom. And the cook, Alexandra, with her double goiter, and the bashful Fimka, who washed the dishes, and Trishka, the young boy with the short, curly, platinum hair—all kissed one another, he recalled, and all looked as if reborn after that night, as he himself, as his sister, as his father, Ivan Ivanovitch, as his two uncles, Nikolai Ivanovitch and Andrei Ivanovitch, and as the whole Popov family, who had gathered to honor the holy Easter, and as the whole city of T_____, and as the entire Christian Russian land. And how could it enter anyone's head after that holy night to lift so much as a hand, to lay so much as a finger on innocent men, women, and children for the sole reason that they didn't speak the same language and didn't worship with us in our churches? But here were these dregs of humanity—poor, naked, hungry—running wherever their legs would carry them as if from an inferno or a plague. Of whom were they afraid? Were they afraid of *us*? On *this* night of all nights? . . .

These were the ruminations and memories stirred in our hero by the tolling of the church bells that night.

the fifty-fourth chapter

WHEN WILL IT BE DAY?

"Mama! When will it be day? When will the bells stop ringing? When are we going to leave?" With these words the little Syomke awoke, raised his head, and peered into the dark night.

"Sleep, sleep!" Sara said to him, and covered him with her apron. "It will soon be day, God willing. May it be as certain that our exile will end as day will come . . ."

Syomke soon fell back asleep, and Sara kept on searching the darkness for her daughter. "How could she do this to me? What kind of daughter is that! Where is that Betty?" she muttered. Betty had become so caught up in her new acquaintance, who had introduced himself in Yiddish as "Benny Hurvitch from Pinsk," and was so taken with the way he acted toward Rabinovitch and how he spoke to him that she completely forgot telling her mother she would be gone only a short while. She had been walking with both young men further and further in the direction of the station, listening to their conversation, which interested her, but not so much as this fellow who called himself "Benny Hurvitch from Pinsk." He had remained absolutely calm, as if he were a taking a stroll through a park, while Rabinovitch was at the height of his distress over their need to flee: he raged, com-

plaining vehemently that it was a humiliation for a city full of Jews to pick
themselves up and run wherever their legs would carry them and only because a few schemers had taken it into their heads to threaten a pogrom.
This fellow Hurvitch's calm behavior almost drove Rabinovitch out of his
mind. The more Rabinovitch stewed, the more the Pinsk youth provoked
him, making Rabinovitch almost leap out of his skin.

"Listen to me, why are you getting so steamed up? Why are you crying over
the Jewish people?" the lad from Pinsk suddenly asked his comrade, Rabinovitch, looking at him intently. "Let me tell you something. It wouldn't do any
harm if we were to take you and a few half-Jews like you, with your dainty hands,
stuffed pockets, and full bellies, and air out your furniture a bit while breaking a
few of your bones. On account of the likes of you, do you hear, with your
running after and imitating the Gentiles, we end up reaping the reward of anti-
Semitic persecutions and excesses."

Having spoken those words, he halted, as if regretting what he had said, and
began searching his pockets for something to smoke.

"No. On second thought, do you hear, it wouldn't work. If they do beat us,
they will, sadly, beat the poor people, always the scapegoats, while you and your
well-off family, you can be sure, will not be touched by it. Oh yes, how is 'Botka,'
that banker of yours? And how high are his stocks?"

Rabinovitch felt ill at ease, especially with Betty nearby, and wishing to
change the subject, he said to his friend from Pinsk, "You were always a crackpot
and will always be one. I'm not at all surprised at you. I remember how you
behaved in prison. Do you remember that night in the cell?"

"Heh-heh, do I remember? I can give you regards. I was there a second time,"
he said to Rabinovitch as if he were speaking about their favorite resort.

"Do you see what I mean?" Rabinovitch said, looking at Betty. "If he can't
take his own troubles seriously, how can he be moved by the humiliation of a
whole people fleeing as from a wildfire or a plague, who have to lie out here in
the open all night with all their belongings?"

Rabinovitch indicated with his hand the mass of men, women, and children
overflowing the streets around the train station, in the midst of which the three
young people stood deafened by the tolling of the church bells. Betty waited for
Rabinovitch's comrade's response, which was not long in coming. He placed his
hand on Rabinovitch's broad shoulders.

"Mr. Rabinovitch, you deserve a pinch in the cheek, do you hear—you really
understood me. Excellent! You say the humiliation of a people that has to spend
the night in the streets? I don't know for whom it is more humiliating, the
people who must spend the night in the streets or those who brought on this
humiliation, ha-ha-ha."

Amazing! Exactly what Betty was going to say to him, as if he had taken the
words right out of her mouth! But she was not about to agree with this Pinsk
fellow. She wasn't pleased that he had turned out to be right and her Rabinovitch wrong. She felt she had to defend her friend.

"Rabinovitch here is a strange bird, but he isn't to blame; he grew up in a

Gentile city and was never among Jews, so his thinking is a bit odd, as if—I'm afraid to say it—as if there were no Jewish blood flowing through his veins . . ."

She cast a loving glance at Rabinovitch, which was not lost on Hurvitch from Pinsk, but he let her continue. "Do you see what I mean? A Jew growing up among Gentiles has feelings like a Jew but thinks like a Gentile. We've been at odds about that as long as we've known each other." Again her eyes twinkled as she looked at Rabinovitch. "You just heard his complaint, 'How can an entire city of Jews pick itself up and flee to wherever their legs carry them?' Ask him where he was in 1905 when Jews were beaten, their windows shattered, doors broken down, their merchandise looted as we lay hidden in our attics shaking with terror, gritting our teeth, and tearing our hair in fright as little children trembled and mothers had to stuff their mouths to keep them from crying. I saw this with my own eyes and heard it with my own ears and experienced it with my entire being and now this one comes and gives me a lecture because I am fleeing! And who is he? Not a stranger, but almost a brother!! . . ."

Rabinovitch was about to respond to Betty's speech when his friend, Hurvitch from Pinsk, interrupted. He had just finished rolling a cigarette and, smiling as always, said to his friend, "Ech, my dear brother and classmate! What do you expect from this mass of people? Heroism? What do you expect of these poor, weak, down-and-out, miserable, starved creatures? Who are they? Heroes? Maccabees?"

He wanted to smoke the cigarette, but the wind made it impossible, and so he put it away for later and went on, with greater passion, still with the same smile.

"And if you press me, do you hear, I will say to you: Yes! They *are* heroes! Maccabees! Do you see this mass of Jews, these poor, weak, down-and-out, miserable, starved creatures? Each one is a hero, a Maccabee! Don't look at me, my dear Rabinovitch, as if I were a madman. I am not mad! They flee, you say, to the ends of the earth? It isn't the first time! They take flight every year when Passover comes, as did their fathers and their fathers' fathers and as will likely their children and grandchildren—and yet they will remain what they are until . . . until those who pursue them recognize what they are doing. What? You don't like what I'm saying? According to your thinking, these are not heroes. You believe they are cowards. Why are you scowling, Mr. Rabinovitch?"

"Mr. Rabinovitch" wished to reply, but his friend, Hurvitch from Pinsk, was no longer listening. Once he had had his say, he felt satisfied. He lit his rolled cigarette and went on.

"I love to hear how Jews put themselves down, make fun of themselves, find every fault in the world in themselves. They don't wish to understand, these half-Jews, do you hear, that although we have been fleeing and running for hundreds of years, we have not lost our way—and *that* no other people except us has managed. Shameful, you say, my running away? Heh! They chase me—I run, what else can I do? Tomorrow they'll stop chasing—I'll come back. Nothing will happen to me, do you hear, they won't triumph over me! Do you know why? Because I am not a nation, not a government, not a people. I am a thought, I am an idea, nothing more than an idea! . . . You can destroy a nation. You can overthrow a government. You can slaughter, annihilate a people. But an idea? What can you do to an idea?"

And the Pinsk youth named Benny Hurvitch opened his arms wide and thrust out his chest. His intelligent, energetic, dark, pimply face smiled and beamed with the pride of someone who feels himself to be genuinely strong and great and fortunate, or as a hero going to battle, confident of his triumph. But suddenly he craned his neck in an oddly comic way, squinted his eyes, and began to stare intently into the deepness of the night, looking as if he had just spotted someone he knew.

"Aaaah??? Listen to this, our professor is also here?" he drawled loudly, leaving his friend Rabinovitch and Betty, forgetting them as if they had never existed, and made his way toward an old man with a wrinkled, brightly smiling face and a long beard. The old man was sitting on a cement postern, his head to the side, gazing at the sky as if he could see something there.

"What are you looking at, Professor? What do you see there?"

The old man, whom Hurvitch from Pinsk was calling "Professor," turned his brightly smiling face to him as he stroked his long beard.

"What am I looking at? I am looking to find day in the darkness of night . . . ha-ha!" he chuckled old-manishly, still smiling but with a tinge of sadness in his voice. He clasped his beard and continued, "Do you see these gray hairs? Did I need to go through two great pogroms, in the years 1891 and 1905, only to live to an age when I must see with my own eyes the humiliation of my people? Here you have before you a ragtag of a people without a home and without a land, ha-ha!"

He remained silent a while, the same cheerful smile on his face.

"I didn't want to leave my home—what would be, would be! Let them come! Let them take me! Let them do with me what they will! But my children forced me . . . Here you have before you a ragtag of a people that has no home, no corner to call its own, ha-ha . . ."

And it was difficult to know whether the old man was laughing or crying. His face was smiling but his voice was crying . . . The eyes laughed but there were tears in them.

"Who is that old man you called 'Professor'?" Rabinovitch later asked his friend from Pinsk. Amazed that he didn't know, the friend from Pinsk told him, "You don't know who that is? That's our professor, our famous oculist, the greatest eye doctor in this part of the country, if not one of the greatest in the whole country. Yes, *our* professor, do you hear, our sole Jewish professor. But not one of those professors of whom Heine says:

Sixty-six professors—
Fatherland, you are lost! . . .

No! He is one of those rare minds that in another country would be celebrated, and here he runs wherever his legs carry him, ha-ha! He used to lecture at the university, but not for very long, because when it came time to make him a professor, this was over twenty years ago, his professor colleagues suggested, do you hear, that he convert. He replied that unfortunately all he could offer them was himself just as he was, and if they really felt they had to have a Christian, he could recommend his coachman, a true Christian. Well, they voted him down with bitter denunciations. A person, do you hear, who when Passover comes prefers the blood of Christian children to whiskey, shouldn't be allowed to lecture in the temple of learning, should he? Ha-ha-ha . . ."

His wild laughter echoed loudly that remarkable night, which seemed to last forever. But suddenly the bells ceased their tolling, and from somewhere a welcome breeze sprang up announcing to this sprawling mass of Jews that dawn was breaking, and it would not be long, not too long, before day would come.

the fifty-fifth chapter

AFTER THE STORM

And when day finally broke, joy swept through the encamped Jews. Cossacks on horseback began patrolling the streets. On the front pages of the holiday editions of the newspapers large headlines announced a proclamation from the governor in such emphatic language that the Jews realized the storm had passed and they could go home in peace, each to settle beneath his own grape arbor, and beneath his own fig tree.

True, there were several unpleasant incidents and even a few beatings, but these were minor occurrences that any Jew in a time of pogroms would wish no worse upon himself.

On one street they grabbed several Jewish boys, smeared their mouths with pork fat, and let them go. On another street a few windowpanes were shattered, but the vandals were quickly arrested. However, on one side street they accosted a student with a Jewish nose and beat him black and blue. It turned out the student was a convert.

The news that the beaten student was a convert was brought home by David Shapiro one night after the holidays, when all the Jewish stores had opened and Jews were again doing business without fear or favor and declaring they felt "as safe as in the Land of Israel." Evidence that the beaten student was a Jew, David reported as he washed before eating, was that he had the Jewish name of Lapidus.

"Lapidus?!" both Betty and the roomer cried at the same time, springing from their seats and bursting out laughing, and were soon joined in the laughter by David and Sara, the first laughter heard in the house since before Passover.

From the time they had returned from the train station that night neither the Shapiros nor the roomer will ever forget, not a happy expression had been seen, not a lively word had been heard. They had seemed embarrassed to look one another in the eye, as if each had committed some terrible deed too awful to mention.

When they had fled from their home, each had placed the blame on the other. David had blamed Sara, maintaining that he had right off declared it ridiculous to leave, nothing was going to happen. Sara had slapped her thighs, declaring she would not tolerate it, how could a man be so blind— "Betty, why don't you speak up?"—and the father on his part had also called on Betty as witness. "Nu, what do *you* have to say about it?" "Why Betty? Leave Betty alone! Betty knows nothing! Not one thing!" she had cut them off sharply because her heart was already quite heavy: the holiday had started so beautifully for her and had ended so sadly, so ridiculously sad! . . .

But if the Shapiros felt dejected, their roomer, Rabinovitch, felt a thousand times worse. He was full of self-reproach—he could kick himself! Not only was he infuriated and unable to forgive himself for being persuaded to run away by these "people-flies," who quaked at every breeze and behaved like the worst cowards, not only was he carrying a heart full of scorn toward his own brethren, who desecrate their own faith and cast a shadow on their own belief, thereby demeaning their own people by allowing a few lowlife provocateurs to exploit the name of God for their base interests, but he was even more chagrined that the one he dearly loved was growing more distant from him day by day and that the abyss between them was hourly widening and deepening. He could plainly see she would never depart so much as an inch from her Jewishness for his sake. He was afraid that even if he were to break with his past and go completely over to Judaism, a task as hard as lifting a house on one's back, it seemed she would still never forgive him for belonging to the people who for hundreds of years, and even now, had brought on her people so much misery and shame. But now Betty laughed that delightful laugh of hers, flashed her beautiful white teeth, and bestowed on him her lovely, intelligent eyes and knavish smile that had so attracted him at first when he had arrived to rent a room, and all the clouds vanished, all the dark thoughts and troublesome preoccupations disappeared as if they had never existed, and he was prepared at that moment to forget everything in the world and to topple mountains. There was nothing on earth too difficult for him to do for her sake. Nothing on earth could stop him—and today was the day it had to happen. How long could he carry his secret around with him? The hoax had to come to an end sometime. Tonight it must end!

Tonight he would speak to her. No, it would be more proper for him to discuss it with her parents first. He would tell them he was in love with their daughter, and they would then urge him to disclose his secret to her (they would certainly tell him that). He would reveal to Betty, in their presence, the whole truth, and then all four would decide what had to be done. Now we see what can result from a laugh.

No. It had been a long time since it had been as lively in the Shapiros' household as that evening, a long time since they had had such a cheerful supper. They all spoke at once, they all laughed, especially Betty and the roomer. They both explained who Lapidus was, how they had met him in the theater, and their exasperating conversation with him. They also went over all they had been through these last days. What had seemed so tragic before now seemed so comical, involuntarily evoking laughter.

"Thank God," Sara said almost apologetically. "Thank God we can laugh. May God grant that we be able to recount everything with joy."

The Shapiros had long finished eating supper, and the household continued to enjoy the lively conversation. And when the landlord, head to the side, eyes half-asleep, and resting his hand in his vest, rose to retire, the roomer suddenly, quite unexpectedly, stopped him.

"*Gospodin*, Shapiro!" Rabinovitch blurted out but quickly became tongue-tied and coughed nervously. "*Gospodin*, Shapiro, may I, that is, I would like to ask you if you would, that is, if you have a moment, be so kind as to, that is, if I might have a few moments of your time . . . I have something I would like to say to you, I mean, I must speak with you about a very important and serious matter . . ."

Shapiro's sleepy face in an instant became wide awake and alert. He removed his hand from his vest and placed it in his pocket, and looking the roomer over from head to toe, said almost matter-of-factly, "It's rather late. But if you say it's an important and serious matter, then, all right, come let's hear what you have to say . . ."

Of course, David knew full well what this "important and serious matter" was. He had long been anticipating it, but that blighted Passover had interfered.

The happy father was not only satisfied that God had blessed him with such a fine, successful bridegroom for his daughter, but David Shapiro was also particularly pleased that Rabinovitch had approached him before anyone else. "Good breeding shows," Shapiro thought, and lowered his head as if it were weighed down with important matters, and taking long strides, he followed the lodger to his room, a satisfied, a happy, a radiant man.

But if David was satisfied, happy, and radiant, imagine how Sara felt now that she had at last lived to reap this pleasure. Hadn't Sara long ago predicted it would turn out this way? Hadn't she from the first day foreseen that it was a match made in heaven? And what a match it was! What an inevitable match! *Keyn eyn horeh!*—May no evil eye befall it!

These were Sara's thoughts as she began to help Syomke undress for bed, avoiding exchanging glances with her daughter. And the daughter? But let us not speak of the daughter, not a word. Too sacred are those moments when one's beloved becomes tongue-tied and cannot express what he wishes to say; and however banal, however foolish these words might seem to be, words that every young man utters once in his lifetime, nevertheless, to his beloved they sound like the most beautiful music and remain forever in her memory, never ever to be forgotten.

At first Betty had taken a book and seated herself near the lamp, pretending to read. But seeing, or more accurately, *sensing* her mother's loving eyes blessing her, she could stand it no longer. Children do not like it when a mother hovers over them and blesses their every move—the truth is, it is irksome to them! Betty got up, muttered goodnight to her mother, and retired to her room. What transpired there is no longer our business. But little Syomke, who was already acquiring a few Jewish ways and enjoyed sticking his nose in everywhere, even where it didn't belong, wouldn't go to sleep until his mother explained first: what was the secret the tutor had to tell his father in his room? Second: why did Betty turn so red? And: why did she go to her room looking angry?

"All right, time to go to bed! If you know everything now, you will grow old too soon," said Sara in a tone of mock anger, taking off his boots. But one could not so easily fool Syomke. He could see by his mother's eyes and by her sighing that she was somehow very happy and that he could get away with murder. He thought, what can I ask my mother for now? I can get away with anything! . . .

David barely had time to seat himself on the only chair in the room; the roomer just had launched into a long introduction to his important subject; Sara hadn't yet finished undressing Syomke for bed, when from downstairs there was heard a long, loud ringing, that familiar ring only police can allow themselves to make so insistently—and within a minute Shapiro's house was full of familiar and unfamiliar guests—local policemen, state police, and assorted officials— and there ensued another ransacking, in a word, a second house search. And not your ordinary house search, but a full-scale investigation, a thorough interrogation of each one from young to old: Your real Jewish name? How old? With what authority do you reside in this city? Which sect do you belong to: the *Ashkenazis*, the *Sephardim*, the *Chaseedim?* Only then did they come to the main point: What was your relationship to your neighbor, Kirile Khmara? To his wife, Kirilikha? To their son, Vladimir, or Volodka, Chigirinski? Who knew Volodka best? Who played with him and what games did they play? What gifts did he get and who gave them to him? Who taught him for free and for what reason? Who was the last one to see him on the day he died, under what circumstances, at what time of day and where? Every possible question was asked, so that it was very late, in the early hours of the morning, before they took away the landlord, his daughter, his son, and his roomer, Hersh Movshovitch Rabinovitch, the Shklov resident who was studying dentistry, leaving Sara Shapiro alone in the house, pleading, weeping, exhorting them not to abandon her, to take her with them because she would not survive it, she would go mad there! She would take her own life! But it was to no avail.

When they had all left and Sara remained alone with but the four walls around her, she wrung her hands and fell in a faint on the bed.

ON BENDED KNEE

Sara had vowed that as long as she lived she would never again cross the threshold of her too-pious sister-in-law, who had in the middle of the eight days of Passover picked herself up and fled with her children from the pogrom without letting her own brother know. Nevertheless, when she came to, surveyed the chaos wrought in her house, and realized she was all alone, she did not hesitate a moment, once day arrived, to go directly to her rich brother-in-law, who had by now returned from his stay at the rabbi's. But it was too early; Shlomo Familiant and his family were still asleep. Sara's urgent mission was delayed. The only ones awake were the servants, who were cleaning, scouring, sweeping, and putting up the samovars. Sara was barely able to convince them to admit her. The unfortunate mother poured out her heavy heart to the astounded servants, weeping bitter tears and wringing her hands as she related to them the desperate circumstances in which she found herself. When the Familiant daughters heard someone crying, they jumped out of bed, threw something on, and came out to see who it was.

"Oy! Look who it is—Aunt Sara! Why are you standing in the kitchen? Come in, what is it? What's happened?"

"Oy, it's happened!" Sara burst into louder weeping. "They've murdered us all, *vey iz mir*. You uncle and Betty and Syomke and the roomer, woe is me!"

Hearing the word "murdered," both Familiant mam'selles recoiled in horror and immediately roused their parents.

"Quick! Get up! Something terrible has happened—they've murdered Uncle David and Betty and Syomke and their roomer! . . ."

"What is it? What is it? *Sh'ma Yisroel!* . . . —Hear O Israel! . . ."

One can safely say that not since the pious Toibe Familiant had married many years ago had she ever been seen by anyone without her wig. But this time she sprang from the bed, forgetting her wig and, begging your pardon, her false teeth as she threw a shawl over her shoulders and in a panic ran out to her sister-in-law. In tones of lamentation, bursting into tears, she exclaimed, "Woe unto me! My brother! They've murdered my David! What a brother they've murdered!"

"Who said 'murdered'?" Sara embraced her. "Toibenyu, my soul, God be with you! It isn't him they've murdered! It's *me*! They took him away, your brother, they took him away to the police station! Him and both children and the roomer—my life is ruined!"

Shlomo Familiant, who was not a person to be rushed, took his time donning his robe, put on his house slippers, and with a grand gesture greeted Sara, modesty dictating that he not look directly at her with his nearsighted eyes.

"What-what-what? What's going on here?" He entered the room grandly, as was his style, thrusting out his belly and avoiding looking the others in the eye. When he learned what the situation was, he first heaped blame on his poor sister-in-law and gave her a dressing down, as only a wealthy Jew can when speaking to a poor relative.

"Your involvements!" Shlomo Familiant flared, pacing back and forth, hands clasped behind him, enjoying the sound of his own voice. "Your affairs! *Gymnasiums!* Police! Gentiles! Comrades! N-nneh!"

Never before had Sara suffered the hard lot of poverty in general and in particular at the hands of wealthy relatives as that morning. It was her bitter lot to have to hear from her brother-in-law, among many unfair accusations, some bitter truths—that "a Jew has to remember he is in exile and mustn't push himself among the Gentiles, not be too friendly with them, not feel too sorry for their poor kids, not study with them *rifmatikes* and *gogrophyes.*" (He was referring to her roomer, who out of sympathy tutored Kirilikha's son for free.) Sara allowed that he was entirely right, right as God Himself. But what good did it do? What does one do? What should she do now? They had to rescue her husband and children from disaster, from a libel! And only *he* could save them!

"First God, then you!"

"I?" said Familiant with false humility, shrugged his shoulders, and placed his hand over his heart. "How can I help?"

"What are you saying?" said Sara tearfully. "You are so well known! You are involved in so many important matters! You do so many favors for absolute strangers! You are such a wise Jew! You are respected by the police! You know the governor personally! . . ."

Shlomo Familiant coughed modestly into his beard hearing so many compliments all at once. But nothing was so pleasing and sweet to him as hearing this last compliment, that he was a personal acquaintance of the governor, though to be completely honest, it wasn't altogether true. He was acquainted, not with the governor, but with the vice-governor, and not "personally," but through his secretary, who had several times accepted generous donations from him for concerts, shows, ballets, and other such things. Reb Shlomo bade his sister-in-law sit and ordered tea, but Sara did not want to hear of any tea or of sitting; her heart was with her near and dear ones. And although she didn't know exactly what they were being accused of or what punishment awaited them, she was convinced that a huge, thick, dark cloud had enveloped her home. She refused to budge from her brother-in-law's side till he had dressed and gone off to "rescue" her husband and children.

But Sara was hardly satisfied with that alone. From the Familiants she rushed to her husband's employer and located the boss and his sons, each one occupied, this one with customers, that one with accounts, the other at the cash register counting money. They kept her waiting until they finally took notice of her.

She felt deeply hurt that people were so matter-of-fact and indifferent, each preoccupied with himself and his personal interests at a time when her husband and children found themselves in mortal danger. The first to respond to her were the clerks. "What can we do for you?" She had to see the boss. "He's sitting over there." Her poor head was so rattled she hadn't noticed him.

Up front at the cash register sat a Jew of sixty with round, silver spectacles and a beard that looked pasted on. That was the boss, the head employer. He spat on his fingertips and counted bills. At last he peered at her through his spectacles. "What can I do for you?" She began to weep and wail, telling him all the details of the great misfortune that had befallen her.

Without interrupting his work, the boss said, "Ah? Another house search? Hmm . . . residence permits? It's a comedy!"

"Pure comedy!" echoed a fashionable gentleman with white shoes, doleful eyes, and thick lips who was standing nearby also counting the money, but with his eyes, while licking his chops like a person whose appetite is increased by seeing another eating.

"Pure comedy!"

This stung Sara to the quick; it was on her that God was pouring out His wrath, it was she who was suffering from this tragedy—and to them it was a comedy! . . . Nevertheless, she was reluctant to give them what they deserved. They were, after all, the bosses, the ones who provided bread, even though for that crust of bread her David was ruining his health. Where could one find on this planet such a madman as her David, a man who would commit himself heart and soul to his work, as if he were living for their sake? She restrained herself as much as she was able and quietly explained that it might very well be a comedy, a pure, laughable comedy, but in the meantime she was being bled dry at the thought that they had arrested her husband and her two children, the most precious things she had (she forgot at that moment about her roomer). It wasn't a house search and it wasn't about residence permits. Then why? For what reason? If only it *were* residence permits, she too would think it laughable as they did and would perhaps also say it was a comedy. But this time it wasn't residence permits, no. This time it was a different problem, a blasphemy, a libel, their neighbor's son, the Russian Volodka, who had been found murdered before Passover . . .

"So? . . ."

And both of them, the boss who was counting the money and the fashionable gentleman with the white shoes and thick lips who was helping him count it with his eyes, interrupted their work and began to question the bookkeeper's wife further, on all the circumstances from start to finish. And after the bookkeeper's wife related all the details, the boss removed his eyeglasses, and somehow the money, which he hadn't finished counting, disappeared from sight. He spoke first to the fashionable gentleman and then to his bookkeeper's wife. "Feh! It's a sorry situation, do you hear! An ugly situation! A very, very ugly situation!"

The fashionable gentleman with the white shoes and thick lips leaned on the table, crossed his ankles, and, fingering the thin, gold chain that hung across his vest (also white, like his shoes), muttered in agreement that it was indeed a sorry situation, an ugly situation!

All this talk about a sorry situation and an ugly situation did not ease Sara's pain by so much as a hair—she herself knew that quite well. Why else was she pleading with them not to push the matter aside but to see that something was done to help her out of this terrible tragedy, this awful libel that had befallen her! And a fresh wave of weeping overcame her.

"Not to you alone, but to all of us, to all the Jewish people has this tragedy befallen," said the boss, and summoned all his family, the sons and sons-in-law, and told them how their bookkeeper, Shapiro, and his children had been taken away and how they suspected him of murdering that Volodka Chigirinski! "What do you say to that?"

Sara Shapiro was amazed to see how the boss and his sons, clerks, and even the customers, absolute strangers, crowded together, all talking about her tragedy. But not a one of them made so much as a move to run, to search out, to protest, to rescue her husband and children. No! On the contrary, she saw them dismissing it with a wave of the hand. Others were making light of the whole matter. "Ha-ha-ha!—Idiots!" one of them said, and another contradicted him, "Villains, not idiots!" "I say idiots!" the first one shouted, laughing, and the other one refused to let him have the last word. "Villains, not idiots!" One shouted "Idiots!" the other, "Villains!" but what good did it do *her*? And Sara again tearfully pleaded with them, "God Almighty, Jews, have mercy! Save us!" They were moved by her weeping and comforted her, telling her she was a woman and didn't understand; it was nothing more than nonsense, it wasn't worth wasting one's time on it. It was no more than a humiliation. How could they suspect us Jews of such a thing nowadays when we have railroad trains and telephones and phonographs and cinemas, ha-ha-ha.

"Take my advice, Madam, go home and be calm," the boss himself said to her, peering at her through his round spectacles, which he had put on again. "Madam! Don't worry, do you hear? It's nothing at all, it's ridiculous, it's a mockery, nothing will come of it. It's ludicrous! They know your husband, they know your children. What? It seems to me they haven't harmed so much as a fly, never mind a person! It's just a plot of the pogromist Black Hundreds. They weren't too happy with the results of this Passover's pogrom, so they think they can stir something up this way. But they're wasting their time! A lie doesn't go very far! Nothing will happen. Nothing! They'll question them and they'll let them free. *I* tell you this. *I*! I guarantee nothing will happen . . . Nothing but the humiliation! Humiliation for yourself and humiliation for the world . . . The humiliation is worse than anything else! . . ."

Nothing could convince Sara that the humiliation was worse than her misfortune. Never mind the humiliation. She could live with the humiliation. Just let them bring back her husband and her children! And she couldn't stop weeping and wailing and keening and wringing her hands and dashing from one person to the other seeking help, pleading piteously on bended knee. She should go home? How could she go home? She could sooner go to purgatory, to the netherworld!

"God, God, God! Why are You silent, God?"

And God is merciful and compassionate. He does not allow Jewish tears to go unanswered. He looked down from His tent on high, heard the voice of this poor, downtrodden woman, and quickly came to her aid, as we shall soon see in the following chapters of our novel.

the fifty-seventh chapter

SYOMKE A WITNESS

The first one to be returned was Syomke. They delivered him by coach, escorted by a policeman without any of the others.

"Syomenyu! Syometchke! Syomenyuntchikl! Bless your soul! Where is your father? Where is Betty? Where is the roomer?"

Each word was punctuated with a kiss, on the cheek, on the lips, on the eyes. The child pulled away from his mother's embrace. "Enough, Mama, let go of me, oh, you're suffocating me!"

And Syomke related to his mother how they had taken him, what they had asked him, and what he had answered, accompanying his account with appropriate gestures, like an adult.

Right after they had arrested them, Syomke recounted, they were placed in three separate carriages: his father in one, the roomer in another, and himself and Betty in a third. A man with the blue eyeglasses and Betty sat in the front seat while he and two police officers were seated opposite them, and in this way they drove and drove for a long time. Then they stopped, and he was put in a different carriage by another officer who separated him from his sister and the one with the blue eyeglasses. Again they drove and drove for a long time. Then he was taken to a huge brick building, all lit up, where he was led into a separate little room. He was seated on a long, smooth, hard bench, left alone, and told to lie down on the bench and go to sleep. But how can anyone sleep without pillows? Nevertheless, he lay down on the bench and waited for what seemed like forever until he must have fallen asleep because when he woke up it was broad daylight and standing near him was an officer, not the same one as before, but a different one, who led him to a large room with the Czar's portrait on the wall. Seated in the room was a man with large whiskers and epaulettes, and another man without whiskers but with a shock of hair on his head that hung down and shook as he wrote. The one with the epaulettes questioned him while the one with the shock of hair wrote down every word, and at each word that he wrote, the hair shook. He was questioned about everything—his name, his age, where he went to school, his father's name, his mother's name, his sister's, and the roomer's—everything, everything. Then the man asked him if he know Kirilikha, her husband, and their Volodka. What games did he play with Volodka and when did he play with him last, did Volodka ever come to their house, what did his mother or father give him to eat or drink. What toys did they give him, and many, many more questions like that.

"So what did you say?" his mother asked, wringing her hands and all the while gazing lovingly at the child, so proud of his grownup behavior. "He's exactly like his father."

"What could I say?" Syomke answered, gesturing with his hands. "I told them the truth—my name, my age, where I go to school, that I knew Kirilikha and her husband very well and Volodka really well, we were good friends, but I was never in their house, that we used to play a game of horse and buggy, and the last time we played together was before Purim. Also Volodka was never in our house and Papa never saw him, but the roomer knew him better than anyone because he studied with him. So, then they began to question me all about the roomer."

"So?"

"So, nothing. I told them the truth, that the roomer didn't know him either, and he never would have studied with him if I hadn't told my sister that Kirilikha had a son named Volodka who had a stepfather who beat him when he was drunk and that this Volodka went to school but had no one to help him do his homework—I told them everything, everything. And how I and my sister told the roomer about Volodka who wanted to study but didn't have anyone to help him, and how his stepfather beat him, and how the roomer began to go there to help him with his lessons . . ."

"Is that all?"

"What more do you want? Then they began to question me about the roomer again. They wanted to know what he had to say about Volodka."

"So?"

"So, I told them the whole truth, that the roomer praised Volodka very highly and said he was a good boy who had a 'Jewish head' on his shoulders."

Sara, still worried and upset, could not help but smile. "Those were the very words you used, 'a Jewish head'?"

"What else? Would I make up something like that?" Syomke said proudly, as his father would. "Then they questioned me about what the roomer was whispering to Papa before Passover and what he was doing at the foundry where they baked matzo. And what did we eat at the seder."

"What we ate?" Sara jerked back in surprise.

"They questioned me about everything and I told them everything I know, the whole truth: what the roomer was whispering about with Papa I didn't know, but I did know that the roomer was at the foundry baking matzo, and on Passover at the seder, I said, we ate a lot of good things. We ate, I told them, matzos, bitter herbs, and parsley, potatoes and eggs and fish and meat and latkes and dumplings and pancakes . . ."

Sara could no longer contain herself. She clasped the child and hugged and kissed him. "What a clever child!"

Syomke was also quite pleased with himself and with his grownup way of speaking. He kept remembering more and more details, interrupting himself to relate them to his mother. "Wait! I forgot to tell you, Mama, that they asked me about blood."

"About blood, *vey iz mir?*" exclaimed Sara fearfully.

"Yes, about blood. What we did on Passover or before Passover with the blood?"

"With what blood?" asked Sara, wringing her hands.

"How do I know what blood? I'm asking *you* that," Syomke replied, spreading his hands apart like an adult.

"So what did you tell them?"

"What could I tell them? I told them I didn't know about any blood."

"So what did they say?"

"What could they say? Don't be afraid, they said to me, tell us, tell us, we won't say anything about it."

"So what did you tell them?"

"What could I tell them? I told them I didn't know what to tell them."

"So what did they say?"

Syomke became angry, exactly like his father; moreover, the poor child was starved. He hadn't had a bite of food in his mouth since the night before. He began to shout, as his father would when he became angry at his mother. "*They* said! *You* said! It's a story without an end! And I want to eat!"

"Oh, my God!" Sara jumped up and ran to the cupboard to find something to feed the child. At that very moment David arrived. Sara didn't know what to do first: feed the child, be happy and thank God that her husband had also been freed, or worry that her daughter wasn't there yet. She was barely able to get the words out, "Where is Betty? And where is the roomer?"

"What do you mean? Aren't they here yet?" David asked, looking around the room. "And I thought they had come home long ago."

*　*　*

What a pity! David had raced home so happy, so eager, as if he were carrying with him the best of good news. But the fact that the children were not yet home disturbed him.

Sara gazed at him and thanked God silently that her husband had returned in so happy a frame of mind. Should she tell him what kind of night and morning she had had or should she first ask him what had happened to him?

He didn't let her think too long. He washed his hands and face thoroughly as if he had come from a cemetery or a funeral.

"What a night! What a morning! What a nuisance! Volodka! Chigirinski! Who would have dreamed it!"

And David began to recount what he had lived through that night. "What a night! What a morning!" It was too bad Betty and the roomer weren't there. If they had been there, he could have told the story with joy and in great detail. But now he made it short. He jumped up every few minutes, interrupting himself, looked out the window—and went on with the story.

the fifty-eighth chapter

DAVID SHAPIRO—A HERO

From the moment he had been arrested, he was not concerned at all—so David Shapiro started his account, and one might certainly believe him (whom would he wish to impress—his wife?). He knew for certain that his arrest was ridiculous, nonsensical, a waste of time, not worth a sniff of tobacco.

We recall how Shapiro had behaved like a hero, a true hero during the first house search on the eve of Passover. David Shapiro was utterly convinced that today's world was not the same as it once was; once a Jew had no recourse, but today there were laws and courts, justice, a Duma, and newspapers. "Say what you will, it is not like before, not like the past." And, even if he were the cowardly sort, he needn't be afraid. What did he have to fear when he knew in his heart he was innocent as a lamb? Let them make seventeen house searches, let them arrest him eighteen times, let the gazettes write all they please, let the dogs howl "blood ritual" all they want, who cares? "If you don't eat garlic, your breath won't smell. Isn't that so?"

These were the very words he spoke to his interrogators. He was not intimidated in the least; he had nothing to fear. Quite otherwise, he confronted them with such resolve and spoke with such assurance, accompanying his statements with gestures accentuating his growing anger, that it seemed *he* were accusing them, not they him.

"What are you after?" he shouted at them when they informed him of their suspicions. "You're looking to find a blood ritual? Forget it, it won't work! First of all, we don't have blood rituals. You people made all that up! And second of all, you're wasting your time—it's not the olden days. Nowadays you can't force me to say what *you* want me to say or sign what *you've* written. That was all possible a hundred years ago, but not now. Now we have laws and trials and a public prosecutor—"

"Leave the law and the public prosecutor for later," they cut him off midsentence. "Better tell us everything you know about how your neighbor's stepson, Volodka Chigirinski, was killed."

"What neighbor? What stepson?" Shapiro flared up again. "I don't know any

Volodkas! I don't know any Chigirinskis. Please leave me alone! You want to send me in jail? Send me! You want to make me a victim? Make! I'm not afraid, because I'm innocent. I tell you again, and I'll say it ten thousand more times, that I never laid eyes on Volodka Chigirinski! I only know I have a neighbor named Kirile and that he had a stepson Volodka."

"Aha! So you do know that there was a Volodka?" they interrupted him, and thought they had caught him with his own words.

"Of course I know. Why shouldn't I know?" Shapiro answered them with a laugh. "So what? I know Kirile had a stepson, Volodka, whom he used to beat black and blue; not all the time, only when he was drunk. And more than that, I know nothing. But n-o-t-h-i-n-g!"

David closed the subject with an abrupt gesture as if he were cutting the subject short with a knife. Later he would boast that only because he, Shapiro, had dealt so firmly with them did they let him go. He wasn't aware that he should have been grateful to the "little squirrel," Syomke, who had so naively come to his rescue by stating several times that his father didn't know Volodka at all. Only he, Syomke, knew him, as did the tutor, their roomer, Hersh Moiseyevitch Rabinovitch . . .

He also had to give some thanks to Kirilikha herself and to her husband, who had both volunteered that the Jew Shapiro never had anything to do with their Volodka and it was possible Shapiro didn't even know him. But his wife did know the child, and not so much she as her children, and not so much Shapiro's children as their tutor, "*Ut tut molodai, tchornai zhidek*—him, that young, dark-haired Jew-boy, . . ." who had studied with their Volodka for free.

Thus Kirilikha and her husband implicated Shapiro's roomer, Volodka's free tutor, thereby sparing the Shapiros and their children.

But more than anyone else, Shapiro had to thank the roomer himself, our Rabinovitch. No sooner was he arrested and taken to be interrogated, something he had long been anticipating, than he immediately realized after the first two or three questions where matters were headed. He concluded they were probably considering his landlord, Shapiro, as the prime suspect, and not wishing to wait till they proceeded with the questioning, he decided to make an important statement. He informed the prosecutor that if they tried to implicate Shapiro or any members of his household in Chigirinski's death, they were on the wrong track. Who the real murderer was—only he, Rabinovitch, knew, and no one else. He had known it for some time and had long had in mind submitting a statement to clarify the matter, but had waited to find out whether the investigation itself might expose the truth. Realizing now that this would not happen, he decided that he was obliged to tell all he knew. The problem was that he had not slept all night and his nerves were frayed, and so he requested that they allow him to sleep first, to rest his nerves, and then he would, with a clearer head and calmer spirit, tell them facts that would amaze them. The prosecutor, who had been taking the testimony, rubbed his hands together with pleasure. His face gleamed and his eyes sparkled with a special gratitude to the young man who handled himself so nobly and intelligently. He ordered that Rabinovitch be taken to a separate, clean cell and be allowed to rest all day, as long as his heart desired. Also the best food and drink should be served him. This young man was not to be treated like an ordinary prisoner. As for Shapiro, all they asked of him was his signature and that he not leave the city.

"I will give you a thousand signatures," Shapiro said, happy at being freed and proud that only a man like himself, David Shapiro, with his sharp and clever tongue, could so quickly slip out of their hands.

"Another in my place," he boasted to his wife, "would have been sitting in jail awhile until he would have heard the words 'Go home,' and that's because I have absolutely no fear whatsoever of the police. In any case, so long as I'm certain I'm innocent, what do I have to be afraid of? Right?"

"Right, right," Sara answered as she, like David, kept looking out the window and cracking her knuckles, "You're absolutely right, what else is there to say? You're absolutely right. But why on earth isn't Betty home yet? And why are they detaining the roomer so long?"

"Who told you they're detaining him?" said David bravely while his heart pounded, not so much for the roomer as for his daughter. "I'll tell you exactly what happened and then you yourself will see that, thank God, I know what I'm talking about. As for the roomer, there is absolutely nothing to worry about. Rabinovitch is a young man with a very cool head. He could, believe me, have gone from there to his dental school or have met with eighteen different friends and got to talking."

"Yes, but Betty, God help us!"

"Again! You're starting to get upset again?" David scolded her while he could barely contain himself.

"What do you think?" he said to Sara a bit later with a change in his voice. "Maybe I should run over to my sister's? Maybe she's there?"

"That crazy she isn't!" Sara answered him, not to enrage her husband, God forbid, but simply because her understanding of human nature told her that after such a night, if her daughter didn't come home but went to her Aunt Toibe, she would be out of her mind. But David could not abide having a wife who always contradicted him, always said the opposite. To spite her, he decided to go over to his sister's to show Sara that he would return with their daughter.

"What will you say then?"

"What will I say? I just pray that from your mouth into God's ears!" said Sara, and David ran out of the house, Sara following close behind him. And so the poor distraught parents spent the day running all over town, from place to place, drawing upon friendships, old debts, seeking information, offering bribes, banging on doors their ancestors had never dreamed of, speaking with the kinds of people they wouldn't have thought of speaking to in their wildest dreams. They were exhausted. Sara was so hoarse she could not make a sound. They spent the entire day searching and chasing from one police station to the next, from one administrative office to another, until, unnoticed, it had turned dark. What did they find out? They found out that their roomer had been transferred, under heavy guard, to prison, and of their daughter—no one knew what to say. Unheard of! No one could tell them what had happened to their daughter or where she was.

Where was Betty?

the fifty-ninth chapter

IN THE WOLF'S JAWS

"Here——we——are," the man with the blue eyeglasses and thick, sensuous lips announced to Betty Shapiro, drawing out the words as, after a long, winding drive through many streets, he led her into a dimly lit room, locked the door from the inside, and hid the key in his pocket.

The room called forth in her a sense of doom and foreboding. She realized he had taken her somewhere other than where he had said, and every limb started to feel numb.

She had felt doomed from the first moment she sat down next to this creature in the carriage. An even greater sense of foreboding had come over her when they removed Syomke in the middle of the journey and transferred him to another carriage.

"Where is he going?" she had spread her hands out questioningly in the dark. The man with the dark eyeglasses had calmed her, saying they would all be together soon. But after both police officers sitting opposite her mysteriously disappeared, she had wanted to cry out, but again he had calmed her and requested that she step out of the carriage because they had arrived at their destination. He had led her into the room and stood face to face with her. Oh! She knew she was lost! Lost!

As she looked around the room, she imagined she saw eerie, frightening shadows scrambling up the walls, trembling, dancing on the ceiling. Where had they brought her? Why had she allowed herself to be taken there? Why hadn't she cried for help? Now it was hopeless. She was lost! Lost!

Suddenly, as if by magic, the entire room was bathed in bright light and assumed a different appearance. The shadows that had climbed up the walls and danced on the ceiling had fled, and the light that took their place was a stark, blinding light.

"Girl, you are lost! You are lost!" every corner of the brightly lit room seemed to be saying to her.

With one glance she took in the whole room, the furniture, the doors, the windows, the telephone on the wall. Her first thought was to scream out as loudly as she could; then she realized it wouldn't work. But she would defend herself somehow. How, she had no idea, but she would.

Her glance fell on the table, where she could see nothing with which to defend herself, except possibly the inkstand with its two heavy crystal inkwells. A clout on the head with one of those two inkwells might bash in someone's head . . .

"Sit down," he said to her, bringing a chair over to the table for her and seating himself opposite her. He removed his dark blue glasses and she recognized the gaze of his reddish, heavy-lidded eyes from the night of the "roundup"—and a chill ran through her body.

But she put up a brave front and was determined to show him she had no fear of him, none whatsoever. She looked him straight in the eye and asked him where she was, where her father was, where they had taken her brother, and where their roomer was. Why weren't they all together?

He did not return her forthright gaze but told her to be calm, nothing would happen to them. They would simply be asked one at a time the necessary questions, and then they would determine who was guilty. The guilty person would be sent off where he deserved to be, and whoever was not guilty would then be released. But in the meantime, they would have to be patient for a night, they would all be confined separately so that they could not talk to each other.

They could not talk to each other? Was this all a dream? Was this really happening? Whom were they accusing of such a horrendous crime? Could it be her father, who had never even laid eyes on Volodka? Were they all being accused of Volodka's death? Was this the ritual murder the newspapers were so full of? And *they* were the ritual murderers? It would be something to laugh at if not for this man who remained sitting with her behind the locked door.

The man removed a silver cigarette holder, lit a cigarette, and glanced at Betty. Seeing that she was trembling, he tried to calm her; he wished to be gentlemanly with her, but it didn't suit his coarse, heavily bearded face; he wished to smile at her, but a smile did not befit his thick, sensuous lips; he wished to speak softly, but his gruff voice, sounding as if he were talking in a barrel, contained not one soft tone in it. He said to her that as long as he was involved she had nothing to fear. She must know that if not for him she would not be there now . . . She had *him* to thank for it.

It was all the same to her, Betty said, pretending to be quite calm, but her shaky voice betrayed her—it was all the same to her wherever she was. Her eyes took careful note of his every move. He rose, straightened up and sat down again, drew on the cigarette, and characteristically, without looking directly at her, said, Oh, no! How was it possible that someone like herself would be placed together with all the other prisoners? How could he allow such a . . . such a . . . words failed him. From the corner of his eye he stole a look at her and tapped off the ash from the cigarette with his index finger. His crude face looked oddly pained and a twisted smile crossed his thick lips. He coughed, moved a little closer to her, saying this was not all he could do for her. For her he was prepared to do a great deal more, things he wouldn't do for anyone else for all the money in the world. He wasn't bragging to her but was telling her the truth, the real truth. She must know that all the threads of this tangled matter were in his hands alone and that he could for her sake tie and untie, knot and unravel them as he wished, so that this whole affair could take a different turn.

And he demonstrated with his hand how, if he wished, he could "tie and untie, knot and unravel" the threads, and edged himself closer to her.

Betty summoned all her strength. She felt her heart would leap out of her body at any moment, and she wanted to call him by the name he deserved, but she contained her rage. Softly and deliberately as was possible, but with venom in her voice, she said to him that she did not see what she had done to deserve his putting forth so much effort on her behalf, to tie and untie, knot and unravel, as he had said.

Plain and simple, because he was smitten with her! Plain and simple, because since he had first seen her that night of the "roundup"—surely she remembered—he could not rest! He saw her in his dreams and when he was awake. He knew she was afraid of him—everyone was afraid of him. They hated him. He knew all too well he was hated because he was a secret agent, an informer. As if a secret agent didn't have a soul, as if an informer couldn't love like other men.

With his finger he extinguished the cigarette on the table and inched closer to the girl, who never took her eyes off him. He glanced at her from the corner of his eye, and their eyes met. Every ounce of rage and hatred and disgust her heart could afford were poured into that look. With the steeliness of a cat lying in ambush and measuring its leap, Betty waited and calculated her next move should he throw himself on her. What would she do? But perhaps it would not come to that. Perhaps she could stretch out the time with casual conversation until the night passed and day came. And so she distracted him with words, one after another: she asked him to tell her, first, what kind of affair this was for which he held all the strings in his hand. Second, if he was, as he said, so devoted to her, perhaps he would be so kind as to explain to her in what way he could alter the direction of the affair.

Oh, better not to ask. The affair was a very ugly one and smelled of Siberia, if not worse, for her and her father—for all of them. But if she would only trust him, he would see to it that the wheel turned in the right direction. All she had to do was ask.

He stood up. Betty immediately stood too. He moved close to her, clasped his hands behind him, and stared searchingly into her eyes, the same twisted smile on his lips. Betty never took her eyes off him. What did he mean, all she had to do was ask? What did he expect her to ask, she wondered, and tried to move back a step. But before she could move, he had clasped her in his arms . . .

* * *

Where does one find the words or the palette to describe what our heroine lived through at that moment when she realized she was in the grip of this man? They were not arms she felt holding her, but iron bands her strength had no power to fight off. It was not a human face she saw before her, but that of an animal. She knew she could expect no mercy, no pity, or any human feeling from him. Pleading would be of no avail. Talking would be useless. As would calling for help. That was clear to her from the first. She understood it with her head and felt it with every part of her body. But she also knew something else. Suddenly—was something happening? Did the earth beneath their feet open and swallow them? Did the ceiling split in two and collapse together with the walls? Did a miracle happen? Did people discover that in this room a young soul was struggling in the unclean grip of an evil person with unholy designs, and did they come running to her rescue while there was still time?

No. The ground did not open, the ceiling did not split open, people did not come running to her rescue. Miracles don't happen, there are no heroes. But where did this noisy ringing come from that she now heard? It was the telephone on the wall ringing, long and loud. The ringing broke through the silence of the night as if sounding an alarm, speaking, she could swear, with a human voice saying in clear words, "Quick-quick! Quick-quick!" Was she imagining it? Was it her overwrought nerves? In any case, she felt the iron bands gripping her so mercilessly suddenly loosen and release her. In one leap he was at the wall, holding the telephone receiver to his ear:

"Who is it? . . . Ha? Yes? . . . It's me . . . Me . . . I'm on my way! This minute! . . ."

In the twinkling of an eye the man pulled himself together, his demeanor and appearance entirely transformed. He let her go and hurried out, shouting to someone, "To the police station! To the police station!"

Was it then not a miracle, and was she not saved? Who was on the telephone? What had happened? That Betty did not know, or care to know.

She only knew one thing: she had been spared.

the sixtieth chapter

HELIOTROPE AND IODOFORM

Betty's soul was revived when she realized that the creature with the blue glasses and thick lips was no longer present. Nothing worse could happen now. They could take her wherever they wished, so long as that person was not around.

True, the room into which they had brought her was not overly cheerful. The room smelled of something sour and moldy; one needed to descend several steps to enter it; it was like a cellar. The room was suffused with a gray, smoky, half-light shed by a small lamp on the other side of the door shining through a tiny transom. This weak light proved barely adequate to reveal that the only furnishings in the room were a small table and several long, small, wooden benches hard by the walls. There was no thought of sleep. She could not allow herself to close her eyes. She felt fortunate to have been left alone; as if on guard duty, she sat alertly, her only wish that day come soon. She listened to every sound. A mouse running past, a breeze blowing in from outside—and she was instantly on her feet, convinced it was someone coming for her. When it was quiet again, she sat back in her place and again began to strain to hear the slightest noise in the stillness of that night.

Suddenly she was startled by the loud voices of many people and the sound of many feet. A strange, hoarse, strident woman's voice was outshouting everyone, hurling curses and heaping on someone's head choice phrases of abuse that Betty had surely never heard till now. The shouting, the sound of feet on stairs, and the loud woman's voice drew closer and closer, seeming to be coming down from above. Soon they were right at her door, which suddenly burst open. The woman, who hadn't stopped shouting and cursing like a man, was forcefully thrown into the room by several pairs of male hands.

The door slammed shut and was locked from the outside. The woman who had been thrown in lay on the ground a while, then, drawing herself up on one bare elbow, she looked around on all sides. Aware that she was not alone, she got up slowly, shakily, and approached Betty, examining her face closely. Betty returned the close scrutiny. Despite the poor lighting, she could still make out before her a woman with heavily rouged cheeks, fine but garishly bleached, curly hair under a sorry, crumpled, shabby hat that hid a low, pimply forehead under which peered small, dull eyes with sparse eyebrows. A stiff corset stuffed with cotton thrust up and exposed her slack breasts. Her appearance, her scratchy voice, and hoarse laugh attested to the fact that this woman was not in the best of health. This did not surprise our Betty so much as the smell that issued from her. It was an odd mingling of heliotrope and iodoform, and it was difficult to distinguish which of the two scents was the stronger as each seemed to vie for precedence, sometimes the perfume winning out, other times, the medicinal odor.

After she looked Betty over from head to toe, the odoriferous woman said to her in a friendly tone, "So, my little dove, also from the 'street'?"

And without waiting for a reply, she laughed her hoarse laugh that ended in a crackle as she spat out a mannish oath. She asked Betty if she had a cigarette. No, Betty didn't have a cigarette. She didn't smoke. The odoriferous lady burst out laughing in her hoarse voice. "A fine how-do-you-do! You don't smoke! What kind of streetwalker are you?" She seated herself on the bench next to Betty and confided in her, as in a sister, that she could get along without bread and without sleep and even without whiskey, but without a cigarette—not a chance! But if Betty thought the woman really didn't have any cigarettes, she was mistaken. She wished her captors as many pimples on their tongues as she had cigarettes in her reticule, but they had taken it away, those fiends, may they suffer the cramps of the damned.

The blessing ended, as usual, in a vehement oath and a hoarse cackle. She suddenly became serious and turned her painted face to Betty.

"You been in the business long, my little dove?" And without waiting for an answer, she began talking about herself. She had been in the business a long time, since she was sixteen, not even sixteen. If she wanted, she would tell her how she started.

And without waiting for a reply, she proceeded to tell Betty the long tale of how she had begun.

It was the usual story, one of those oft-told tales of events that happen over and over again in thousands and thousands of variations, filling the world with thousands upon thousands of victimized, unfortunate, sickly souls, crippled, oppressed, and abandoned.

It was the usual story, or rather, a whole series of stories, a long chain of woes, persecutions, intrigues, denunciations, victims, and above all—evil! A sea, a world of evil! And she related it in such a vulgar, licentious tone, with such piquant curses and with so many obscenities, that another in Betty's place would have been consumed with shame and covered her ears in order not to hear. But our heroine was not one of those girls who believe, or want others to believe, that they don't know about these matters and begin blushing when they hear language spoken only among men. Betty had not grown up among the angels; but she had not heard a hundredth part of the human meanness, evil, and malevolence that she heard that night from this lost, abandoned woman, who wasn't so much complaining as simply relating in vivid detail all she had endured till that day at the hands of the "devils and demons" (so she called every creature possessing a beard), who pursued and tormented her and didn't allow her to walk the streets in peace. What did they have against her? It was an outrage! Thousands of hooligans and murderers roamed the streets freely. She herself knew of a gang of ne'er-do-wells, crooks and thieves who not so long ago strangled a thirteen-year-old boy because they were afraid he would sequeal on them. Did anyone take notice about what they were up to? Did anyone give so much as a peep? And if a poor girl goes out on the street, trying to pick up a few pennies to keep body and soul together—aha! she's the one they notice!

The poor woman went on pouring out her tale of woe, cursing her bad luck and all the injustices visited upon her. She did not forget to pepper her harangue with blessings on their ancestors. And each of the devils and demons, thieves and bandits received his share.

But more than any of the others, this poor, inflamed woman let out her rage on a young man named Makar Zherebtchik. She repeated that name about twenty times, if not more. Makar Zherebtchik—he was the hero and villain of her tale. He was her lover, the one for whom she had sacrificed herself, for whom she had sold herself on the street so he could have enough money to run around with debauched women—may they all rot in Hell! . . . Still, she would forgive him, the scoundrel, let him run around with loose women all he wants! But why did he have to fool around with other men's wives? And what wives! Wives whose husbands are involved in thievery, hooliganism, confidence rackets! He thinks he'll get away with strangling a young boy and stabbing him all over so his body ended up looking like a sieve. Just let him try to run around with other men's wives again, she would get even! Look here, she had plenty of goods on him and his pals: she still had the schoolbag belonging to the strangled boy hidden in a safe place.

Betty was more preoccupied with the lot of this poor lost soul than in listening to her stories. She was reflecting on life and on this unfortunate creature who had no sense of self-worth, whose dearest wish was satisfied with a cigarette, and whose terrible stories she could relate so cold-bloodedly. But then she began listening more intently to the horrible story about the strangled young boy that had a striking resemblance to the story of Kirilikha's murdered son—each story dealt with a stepson and a drunken stepfather who dealt in stolen goods. She very much wanted to ask this poor lost soul the name of the strangled youth, but as she had not spoken a single word to her all night, she didn't know how to initiate this conversation, especially when her companion never stopped talking for so much as a moment, her words never ceasing. One story followed another, one more horrible and hateful than the other. Betty hadn't noticed how the night had slipped away until she heard the clinking of keys and the scraping of the door, which suddenly opened wide. A bright streak of daylight forced itself into that pit from the cool outside, and the streetwalker for the first time clearly saw the girl with whom she had spent almost the entire night and to whom she had poured out her heart. She was amazed: so young, so pretty, and so fresh—she had never met her like on the "street"! She became even more amazed when she heard how the girl talked to the police.

When the police officer entered the room and ordered her to accompany him, Betty stood up and declared very firmly that she refused to leave that place alone with him; she would rather die!

At first, he couldn't understand exactly what she meant. Betty explained that if he wished her to go, he would have to call for a second policeman to accompany them or she would refuse to move from the spot; they would have to use force.

"Bravo! What a girl! What a clever girl!" the streetwalker cried, and burst into her hoarse laughter. "That's the way to deal with these rogues! Bravo!"

When Betty was seated between two guards in the droshky, she still imagined she smelled the mingled aromas of heliotrope and iodoform, which did not leave her the rest of the day.

THE STOCK EXCHANGE SEETHES LIKE AN INFERNO

With lightning speed the telegraph wires spread the astounding news to every corner of the country that "at last they have succeeded in identifying the murderer of the Christian youth Vladimir Chigirinski. The murderer is a Jew, a young man studying dentistry . . ."

"The criminal," the dispatch went on, "has not yet confessed nor has he named his accomplices, but all the evidence points to him. There is no doubt that he had at least three accomplices and that the crime was perpetrated for religious purposes . . ."

That was the first bombshell, the first telegraph dispatch pounced on by those newspapers who know how to sensationalize the news and spread it on thick for their readers.

Jews everywhere, accustomed to this libel for generations, outwardly dismissed the fuss and ridiculed the whole affair, claiming the gazettes had invented it to boost circulation, but in their hearts they were worried: "As if we didn't have enough trouble, we didn't need this too!"

But if Jews elsewhere tried to dismiss the matter, the Jews in the city where the criminal was found were in a state of shock, sunk in humiliation and hiding a feeling of terror in their hearts. And more than any other place it affected the city's predominantly Jewish Stock Exchange, which was rocked to the foundations by the news: it boiled like a cauldron, seethed like an inferno.

The ordinary person not familiar with the Stock Exchange and its participants, when passing by the Exchange and seeing the knot of brokers screaming at one another and the excited speculators sitting with worried faces around the white tables, sunk deep in discussion, might imagine that these people have nothing more on their minds and don't speak of anything except money and promissory notes and shares of stock, the current rate of exchange, the price of sugar, sand, and sugar cane, wheat, barley, and lumber, and other such terms, not caring a whit if the world outside is turned upside down.

Wrong, very wrong! More than three-quarters of the time at the Exchange is taken up with news. Should something new occur in the world or in the city—be it the defeat of an entire squadron by Tsusima or a wealthy wedding; be it a big pogrom in Shedlitz or a small bankruptcy in town; be it the largest earthquake in Messina or a bad joke made by the town millionaire, the king of the Stock Exchange, about his mistress—all these news items are first given currency at the Stock Exchange. Here everything is considered with care, analyzed, weighed, evaluated, and assigned its worth. And as the world is vast and news arrives almost every hour, there is never a day when the Stock Exchange is not seething and does not have its "hero of the day."

This time the hero of the day was the dentist Rabinovitch. At the Stock Exchange no other name was heard but the name Rabinovitch. Wherever two people came together, he was the third: "Rabinovitch! Rabinovitch! . . . Which Rabinovitch! . . . From which Rabinovitches? . . ." One broker was certain he was of the Odessa Rabinovitches, another that he was from Krementchug; one insisted he was from neither Odessa nor Krementchug, but from Bobroisk, a Litvak at that. But another claimed that he knew a broker named Katz who said he knew that dentist Rabinovitch intimately. So bring over this Katz!

Katz was not among your more successful brokers, but one of those who rubbed up against the biggest brokers, managing to connive a deal with this one or that one. Like a bird, he would grab up the crumbs that dropped from the tables of the great wealthy leviathans of the Stock Exchange. For the most part, small-time brokers like Katz were to be found milling around outside the Stock Exchange, and seldom, very seldom, were they to be found inside the Stock Exchange, seated at the white tables in the cafe. Occasionally they would have to sneak in to use the men's room, getting past the official stationed outside, who cast a wary eye on them and threatened to remove them from the precincts of the Exchange if they didn't clear out.

Katz was a slightly built man with short legs, which earned him the diminutive of Ketzele. "Tell me, Ketzele, is it true what we hear, that you are an intimate friend of this dentist Rabinovitch?"

"What a question! Am I an intimate friend!" responded Ketzele, and was pleased that big brokers were talking to him as an equal, on familiar terms. They asked him to sit down.

"What will you have? Tea or coffee?"

"It doesn't matter," said Ketzele, and seated himself quite smugly at a white table, smoothing his little beard and moustache and giving a slight cough.

He was in seventh heaven. He felt that now, at that moment, the hero of the day was himself, Katz.

"So tell us, Mr. Katz" (for now he was no longer Ketzele, but Katz), "have you known this dentist, this Rabinovitch, long? Who is he? Where is he from? Drink, why aren't you drinking?"

"Easy! Not everything at once!" said Katz, tossing four cubes of sugar into his cup of coffee, like a person accustomed to drinking his coffee sweet. "I have known him a long time, one could say since the beginning of winter. But we first became close friends around Chanukah time." Suddenly Ketzele broke into laughter as if remembering a funny incident. "Heh-heh-heh! How many times did we play a game of *Stukelke* or *Bantshuk* or *Tertle-mertle*? Guess how many? Try!"

Ketzele looked around at the crowd of brokers and speculators to see what kind of impression he was making on them, and, sipping the sweetened coffee, he went on.

"To play cards with him, I tell you, you had to take your life in your hands! In

Stukelke, for instance, he would always knock. In *Bantshuk,* no matter how full the pot, it didn't bother him. He would win, no matter what! And in *Tertle-mertle,* he was impossible. Less than a ruble a card he wouldn't hear of, and sometimes it was two rubles a card! And three rubles a card! And even a five spot a card was possible! Talk about money—tphoo!"

Ketzele was quite pleased with the effect his words were having on the Stock Exchange and was ready to relate even greater exploits performed by the dentist Rabinovitch at cards, but they cut him off.

"Good, good. But where does he get all this money?"

Ketzele burst out in a staccato laugh, "Heh-heh-heh!"

"As I am a Jew, that's a good question. Where does he get all this money? He's loaded, a millionaire! I mean, he himself doesn't have much money. But he has an aunt, a millionairess, who has, it's safe to say, a cool two and a half million, in Siberia . . ."

"In Siberia?"

"I'm just saying Siberia. I mean in some distant Russian province, God knows where. That's why he only talks Russian and not a word of Yiddish. He really doesn't understand a word of Yiddish, not one single word! Still, that has nothing to do with anything. He's quite a young man! He graduated with a gold medal, he's studying to be a dentist, and he's in love with his landlord's daughter. Shapiro is the landlord's name. This Shapiro is a bookkeeper and not especially bright. Just your ordinary, average Jew, no great brain but no fool either, heh-heh-heh! But has he a daughter! What a girl! Nu, nu!" Here Ketzele kissed the tips of his fingers, drained the last of his coffee and with his tongue, licked clean his wet moustache.

The Stock Exchange denizens enjoy listening to a good story, but they love to delve a bit further into it, consider it from every angle, and analyze it carefully. Something about Ketzele's story seemed unbelievable; it didn't make sense. Think about it: a Jew comes from Siberia, has an aunt with two and a half million—let's give half away and drop another third into the ocean, and you'll still have enough left. So he arrives with a gold medal and is studying dentistry and plays *Stukelke* and *Tertle-mertle* with Ketzele. And on top of that, he falls in love with the poor daughter of a bookkeeper. Say what you will, it's too . . . too . . . too . . .

Too what—they couldn't say. But from their comments Ketzele could gather that the group wasn't altogether satisfied. His face took on the fawning expression it assumed when he was proposing a business deal that wasn't going anywhere. He wished to improve the impression he was making and said to them pleadingly, "I don't know exactly what's bothering you. You have no reason to doubt me. How do they say, '*Za tshto kupil, za to prodol*'—I'm only telling you what I know, what I heard, and beyond that—I wasn't inside his head and I didn't count his money, so why are you doubting me?"

Ketzele was wasting his time; no one was listening. They were all talking among themselves, and not so much talking as arguing, quarreling, and insulting one another. It turned out that there were quite a few others who knew Rabinovitch intimately. They didn't really know him, but they had seen him many times with that girl, Shapiro's daughter, at the theater, at the circus, at the cinema, or strolling together down the street. And the girl's father, Shapiro, they all knew. Wasn't Shlomo Familiant a close relative of his, in fact his brother-in-law? Wasn't Shapiro's wife Shlomo Familiant's sister?

"You mean to say that that this Shapiro and Familiant's wife are brother and sister."

"Let it be that way. But what does that have to do with the dentist Rabinovitch?"

"Listen, the dentist Rabinovitch is Shapiro's roomer, and this Shapiro is the father of that beautiful girl, and they don't live far from Chigirinski's mother, Kirilikha is her name, and this Shapiro, the beauty's father, has a young son who is a *gymnasium* student in the third year, a boy of about twelve or thirteen, who knew and used to play with Kirilikha's son, Volodya Chigirinski. Now do you understand where this is heading?"

"So what? And ducks go barefoot," another cut him off.

"And geese don't wear prayer shawls," another added.

"Go speak to fools! Hear me out to the end," the first man continued, trying to explain what he meant. "Listen to what's involved here: this Rabinovitch was tutoring Shapiro's young student and this student who knew Volodka and played with him must have come home one time and asked his tutor, the dentist Rabinovitch, a favor. Since Volodka was a poor boy and didn't have a tutor, and his stepfather, the Gentile Kirile Khmara, beat him when he was drunk, could he, the dentist Rabinovitch, study with his friend Volodka without payment. Now do you see what I'm getting at?"

The brokers understood, but they were not fully satisfied. On the contrary, their appetites were just whetted, no more. If the dentist Rabinovitch was such a fine fellow and good enough to undertake to study with a poor Gentile boy without pay and only out of pity, does it follow that he murdered him? Is that reason to arrest a Jew and throw him in prison? Where is the sense in that?

"To whom are you complaining, to me?" said one of the brokers with a knavish look, a man with thick eyebrows.

"Be quiet! I wasn't even thinking of you!" answered another broker, a young man with a hoarse voice and a red face, who liked to grab hold of people to get their attention.

"If you weren't thinking of me," the one with the thick brows said menacingly, "maybe you had one of my partners in mind?"

"Jews are being bled white," interrupted another, not a broker but a speculator with brown gloves, who held his head to the side, "and all you have in mind is to insult each other."

Both brokers, the graspy young man and the one with the thick brows, turned toward each other, preparing to apologize.

"So, where were we now with our Rabinovitch?"

And the discussion continued with even more intensity and heat.

THE "CRIMINAL" AT THE INTERROGATION

Although many were disturbed and distressed over the "criminal's" detention, the "criminal" himself showed not a sign that he was upset or worried.

It was remarkable how calm and self-possessed the dentist Rabinovitch held himself when, after a good night's sleep and a decent meal, he was brought before the investigators and was again interrogated about the murdered child, Vladimir Chigirinski.

Oh! He knew a lot, quite a lot about this tragic fact, and he repeated what he had told them that morning: he himself had considered coming forward with a declaration but had delayed intervening into the inquiry unless it proved necessary. In the first place, he didn't want to be an informer or play the role of a spy, and in the second place, as he had stated that morning, he reasoned that the investigation itself would turn up the truth. Now, seeing that they had released the parents of the murdered boy and had involved extraneous people like Shapiro and his children, who were totally innocent, he regretted having been silent. He admitted it lay on his conscience . . .

So began Popov-Rabinovitch in his normally rich baritone voice that was now pitched a bit too high and echoed too loudly through the large, high-ceilinged, empty hall that contained no more than a long, cloth-covered table, several tall chairs with carved arms, and long, polished benches against the walls. But in spite of his brash tone, the criminal's words, particularly the last ones, when he avowed that "it lay on his conscience," made a good impression on the investigatory panel made up of three men. The first was the same man who had questioned him earlier that morning, a man full of energy, with thick, spiky, short, very dark hair and a black pince-nez. The energy spoke out in his keen, penetrating eyes, his sharp voice, and in his every movement. When he talked, he liked to draw out each word, accentuating almost every second or third word, underlining it while half-shutting his eyes. He was the chief investigator.

The second was fair-complexioned and still a young man, but completely bald, without a trace of hair on his head. His high, shiny, bulging forehead made him look as if he had, not one head, but two. The especially thick lenses in his gold eyeglass frames almost completely obscured his eyes. He was a candidate-investigator.

And the third was a tall youth with spurs on his boots, high color in his cheeks, an elegant officer with gold braid on his shoulders and the lively face of a person who means to live the good life. The entire time he behaved like a visitor with no role in the inquiry, who had come out of great curiosity about the proceedings and the accused. All three appeared to be pleased with the demeanor of this "intelligent criminal."

After again questioning him and writing down his name, age, birthplace, employment, and other formalities, the chief investigator, with the energetic face and black pince-nez, requested in a very friendly tone that Rabinovitch tell them the whole story, from beginning to end, unhurriedly, with every detail, no matter how trivial, how it had all happened, naming names of all those who had participated in the murder, for what purpose, and so forth.

After that introduction, all three moved closer to the table and readied themselves to hear out the interesting explanation the criminal had promised to give them that morning when he had assured them that "they would be amazed."

The accused was also more than pleased that they were prepared to hear him out, as it seemed, attentively. He was especially pleased that his account would undoubtedly lead to the release of the innocent Shapiros, who might even receive an apology for having been suspected. He was also pleased that he would be helping set the investigation on the right path to uncover the real murderers of the poor Volodka. For these reasons he proceeded to give his explanation cheerfully, willingly. But in his own mind he wasn't sure where to start: from the moment that Volodka had disappeared? Or when he had become apprehensive and suspicious upon reading the newspaper articles accusing the Jews of having murdered Volodka Chigirinski for their Passover matzos? He considered saying a few words, in general, about these senseless blood accusations that were long overdue for the dustheap. But he reconsidered, deciding he would leave that for the end. For now, he would tell them the story from the very beginning, how he had first met the young boy, Volodka Chigirinski, and how his parents, miserable, uneducated people, had looked askance at him, suspicious as to why he, an unknown dental student, had offered to study with their child without pay. He would never forget that comical scene when he had entered Volodka's home for the first time and had encountered his stepfather, Kirile Khmara, testy and nasty, like a man who had just sobered up and was angry at the whole world. "What do you want here?" the sobered-up Khmara pounced on him. "I happened to hear you have a boy named Volodka, who wants to study and doesn't have anyone with whom . . ." Kirile became even angrier: "What business is that of yours?"

Rabinovitch almost doubled up with laughter telling how Kirilikha arrived soon after and, hearing the discussion, remained standing in the middle of the room, frightened, not comprehending what he wanted of her Volodka. The chief investigator suddenly cut him off.

"Would you kindly clarify first for us exactly how it came about that it was *this* Volodka Chigirinski you sought out? Why was *he* selected and not another? Who chose *him*? Who pointed *him* out to you?"

Here Rabinovitch remained standing, with a confused smile on his lips. It was obvious he didn't understand what was being asked of him. What did they mean by "selected"?

The chief investigator, sensing that the accused was bewildered and perplexed, again proposed that he be so kind as to relate exactly how it came about that he had visited *this* particular boy, Volodka Chigirinski.

"How did it happen? It was very simple!" And the accused told the story of how one fine morning he was approached by his student, Shapiro's son, a *gymnasium* student in the third year, the very one who was just yesterday detained together with his father. The young student, Shapiro, had a friend, Volodka, a poor neighbor boy who wanted to study and didn't have anyone with whom to do so, and the young Shapiro had suggested that he, Rabinovitch, give Volodka a lesson just once or twice a week, without charge, of course, because Volodka's stepfather would not want to spend any money on him.

"And so you *immediately* agreed, right there and then, and you *immediately* got up and *immediately* went over to Volodka's house?"

The accused apparently was slow in grasping the irony in these words and answered naively that he didn't get up *immediately*. Only after the Shapiro boy had suggested it to him several times and had asked his sister and mother to persuade him to do it for his student's sake did he agree, but only on the condition that this Volodka would come to him for the lesson rather than he go there.

"What was your *intention* in that?"

Again the accused appeared perplexed, and the senior man again repeated, "What was your *intention* in insisting so absolutely that Volodka come to *you* to study, not you to *him?*"

He had no particular intention, the accused told them naively and forthrightly, without guile. It was simply more convenient for him to study with Volodka in the Shapiro's house, and that was all there was to it.

"More convenient, you say? Ha . . . Perhaps more suitable and more *useful? . . .*" the interrogator asked pointedly, stressing the word "useful" as he exchanged meaningful glances with his two colleagues.

"It might have been more useful," the accused conceded, again forthrightly, without guile, and continued to relate further how Volodka wasn't allowed to come to him because the elder Shapiro, who did not know Volodka, was not to know anything about this arrangement. Consequently, he, Rabinovitch, had to consent to go to Volodka's house for his lessons. And when he arrived there the first time—

But here the accused was again interrupted. "Tell us, when your student was talking to you about Volodka, were you aware that this Volodka was a Christian child?"

"What's the difference?" the accused answered with astonishment. "Christian or not, he was a poor boy who wanted to study. Why shouldn't he be helped?"

"We are not here to discuss philosophy with you . . . We are simply asking you to answer us truthfully what we ask you: *Did you know at that moment that Volodka Chigirinski was a Christian, or didn't you?*"

For the first time one could hear in those words some annoyance.

The accused thought a moment and allowed that he had known it.

The one with the black pince-nez winked at the one with the thick eyeglasses, indicating that he was to write all that down. As he wrote, the accused observed him, not understanding why it was necessary to record that answer.

"So, please go on, we're listening," the senior investigator continued with a soft, friendly tone, deciding that now they would hear him out without interruption.

Again the three moved closer to the table, prepared to listen attentively for the real "explanation" the "criminal" had promised to give. The criminal didn't wait long to be asked, and with candor and rare calm undertook to tell everything he knew about this "dreadful mystery."

the sixty-third chapter

"IS THAT ALL?"

"If the mountain doesn't come to Mohammed, Mohammed goes to the mountain," the accused began his story confidently, his account flowing as smoothly and easily as water. He related how he began his visits to Volodka's home, how at first he didn't notice anything particularly unusual except that, in the beginning, Volodka's mother, and even more so, his stepfather, Kirile Khmara, behaved in an unfriendly manner toward their unpaid tutor; they looked upon him, he imagined, with suspicion and wariness.

"Why would they be suspicious of you?" the chief investigator couldn't help interrupting.

He had no idea. Perhaps they suspected him of being an undercover agent of the police? He recalled that during the first lessons the stepfather made sure to stand close by his stepson, always listening in case the tutor might speak to him of other matters.

"Is it true you once expressed to Chigirinski's stepfather, to the Gentile Kirile Khmara, that if he would put his stepson in your Jewish hands, you could make better use of him than he could?"

Rabinovitch did not recall saying that. He only remembered frequently praising his student to his stepfather, saying that Volodka had a talent for learning. And that was true. Volodka continued to exhibit such aptitude for learning that he quickly became very fond of the boy. But Volodka seemed to him a frightened child and a bit preoccupied, one of those children who live in their own secret worlds and whose souls seem oppressed. But he, Rabinovitch, hadn't the slightest intention of intruding into this secret little world. To him Volodka was a poor student who needed help with his lessons and no more. He had heard from

Shapiro's children that Volodka was always in trouble with Kirile Khmara and that he was very frequently beaten by his stepfather. But that wasn't his concern either. One time he found himself an unwilling witness to an unpleasant scene. The young Shapiro once tore into the house, exclaiming, "They're killing Volodka!" All three of them—he, Shapiro's wife and daughter—quickly ran over to their neighbor's and rescued the unfortunate Volodka barely alive from his stepfather's grip. From that time on, his student, Volodka, became more trusting of him.

"And you brought him gifts often?" the senior member interjected.

Gifts? No, but he did occasionally bring him books that belonged to his Jewish student, who no longer needed them, and that Volodka could use.

"And you never gave him money?" the investigator asked pointedly.

"No, I don't believe I ever did . . ."

"Remind yourself, maybe you once did? Didn't you once give him a silver coin to buy a ball to play with?"

The accused reminded himself. "Ach, yes. True. That once did happen."

"Why are you hiding facts?"

The accused looked bewildered. "Facts?" He had considered it so trivial that he hadn't felt it deserved mentioning, especially since it had nothing whatsoever to do with the case.

"Let us decide whether or not it pertains to the case," the investigator said in a sharp tone. "Just be so kind as to tell us everything, and don't omit *any* facts, even trivial ones."

At this the accused became bewildered and forgot what he was saying. He reddened to the ears, which might have appeared as evidence that he wished to conceal something, that he had been caught in a lie and didn't know how to get out of it. Three pairs of eyes were observing him so intently that he began to perspire. The senior of the three came to his aid.

"You were telling us how you *bought* your way into your student's trust. And so, what *came of that?*"

"Nothing at all came of that," the accused said, and returned to his story. One time, he was sure it was in the middle of winter, he arrived to find the student Volodka in tears. "What is it, Volodka, did they beat you?" "No, worse." "What could be worse?" "They want to kill me . . ." "Who wants to kill you?" "*They* want to kill me . . ." "Nonsense! Where did you get that idea?" And Volodka told him a story he would now briefly relate:

Volodka's stepfather dealt in stolen goods. He himself didn't steal, others did it for him, a whole gang of thieves. At night they went to work, and whatever they stole was brought to Kirile Khmara's house, where he would find a place to hide it. Volodka didn't know where the stepfather hid the stolen goods. Many police searches had failed to uncover anything. But one time he noticed a well-dressed gentleman with blue-tinted eyeglasses standing on the street not far from their house holding a scaramouch puppet in his hand and cracking nuts, one nut after another. The gentleman saw Volodka looking at him and said, "Do you want some?" and gave him a handful of nuts. Another time he saw the same gentleman with the blue glasses standing in the same spot and holding the same scaramouch puppet. This time he was chewing candies. Seeing Volodka watching him, he said, "Do you want some?" and handed him a piece of candy. The third time he saw Volodka, he called him over, handed him a coin and said to him, "Here, go buy yourself whatever you want, you're a good boy. Tell me, aren't you Kirile Khmara's stepson? I know you. Your stepfather deals in stolen goods, but he hides the stuff so that not even the devil himself can find it. If you were a smart lad, you would overhear what your stepfather says to his gang and would look around to see where they hide the stolen goods. You don't have to be afraid of anything. Your mother won't be harmed, and when they arrest your stepfather it will be better for you. You'll be beaten less." When he came home, Volodka began to think it over. What should he do? Should he tell his mother? And he did tell his mother, in confidence, you understand, but the foolish Kirilikha told her husband. He became enraged and wanted to beat Volodka, but his mother interceded. A night or two later, Volodka was lying on the earthen floor in his little corner pretending to sleep when he overheard a discussion in which his stepfather was telling the gang of thieves about the gentleman with the blue glasses and was asking them for advice. "What should we do with the little bastard?" Bastard—that meant him, Volodka; his stepfather never called him by any other name. Volodka kept pretending to sleep and heard one of the gang say that they had to get rid of the little bastard. Who it was that said those words he couldn't exactly say, but the words "get rid of" he heard for certain. Whatever else was said he could not hear because his mother came in and they stopped talking. From that time on, Volodka told him, he was not sure of his life. Every night when he went to bed, as soon as he shut his eyes, he would imagine they were coming at him with a knife and slitting his throat, or they were chopping off his head with a sharp axe.

Naturally, Rabinovitch made light of it and reassured the boy as much as he could. Volodka apparently soon forgot the incident, because he went back to his studies. But Rabinovitch did not forget the incident. As soon as Volodka disappeared and his mother, Kirilikha, came to the Shapiros looking for her lost son, he immediately told her where to go and for whom to ask. He, Rabinovitch, was not of the opinion that it was conclusively the stepfather's work, as others reasoned—something to do with an inheritance coming to Volodka. Kirile Khmara had certainly played a significant role in this bloody matter, but surely the gang of thieves with whom Kirile Khmara was in cahoots were also involved, and it was among them, as he saw it, that they should look for the real criminals, because they were interested in eliminating the unfortunate Volodka Chigirinski, who, they imagined, was a threat to them. He was positive that if they were to make a thorough search, they would find every last one of them.

"Is that all?" the senior investigator declared after exchanging glances with his colleagues, who had patiently heard out the overlong and uninteresting story artfully invented by the criminal to fit the facts.

The criminal himself was rather satisfied at how straightforwardly he had given his statement. He was, however, a bit surprised at the chief investigator's comment, "Is that all?" What else did they want? It wasn't till later that he realized the true import of those words, when, after leading him out and in a few minutes bringing him back, they began grilling him in earnest.

the sixty-fourth chapter

HE STUMBLES

When they led the accused back to the continuing interrogation, he noticed a slight change. On the green-covered table there now appeared four separate groups of items:

(1) The bundle of books that had been confiscated from him at Passover.

(2) All his papers, letters, and notes tied with a green ribbon.

(3) The small, fat book labeled "My Diary."

(4) An old prayer book with a greasy, black cover and a yellowed, rotted spine.

The accused could have sworn he was seeing this old book for the first time in his life. He looked at all these objects with intense curiosity as well as at the faces of the investigators, who now appeared more confident than before. "What's going on here? . . ." he wondered to himself.

Slowly and carefully, the bundle of writings was untied. They removed and read the letter from his sister, Vera P., in which she wrote him that she "never stopped praying to God that things go smoothly for him, that he should gladden their hearts for the blessed holiday with good news, to which they all looked forward."

The question was posed to him: First, who was this Vera P. who kept *praying* to God? And second, what kind of *news* were they all looking forward to hearing for the *blessed holiday?*

These words were drawled and underlined for emphasis as all eyes strained to see how the accused would react. Calmly and with a smile on his lips, the criminal explained that the news they were all looking forward to hearing was no more than a telegram from him that he, Rabinovitch, was coming home for Passover.

"Nothing more than that?"

Nothing more than a letter saying he was coming home for Passover.

"Just a moment ago you said a *telegram,* now it's a *letter?*"

A letter or a telegram, it's all the same.

"It's not always the same. When *everyone* is looking forward to *good news* and they *pray to God* that things *go smoothly,* a telegram is more appropriate than a letter. But let's put that aside and return to the contents of this letter. You say that the news they are *all* looking forward to having to do with the *blessed* holiday is no more than your coming home. Let us say that is so. But one wonders: who are the *all* who are looking forward to your coming home?"

The accused attempted to clarify that *all* meant the whole family.

"Then it would say, 'the whole family.' The meaning of these words can be construed quite differently here, in ways that might not be in your interest to reveal."

The accused apparently was not happy with their poking around in his sister's letter and tried to take another tack to disentangle himself. He explained to them that they need not seek any hidden meaning in that innocent letter as neither he nor the writer of the letter was carrying on any political agitation, nor did they deal in contraband.

"That's very good," the one with the black pince-nez answered, "very good that you aren't carrying on any *political* agitation or dealing in *contraband*. But it would be much better if you would be a little more forthcoming and tell us who this woman, or this *man*, is who writes you letters under the name 'Vera P.' "

Here Rabinovitch felt ill, quite ill. Not because three pairs of eyes at that moment bored through and through him, but for another reason that bothered him: to tell them the truth and to reveal the secret that Vera P. was Vera Popova, his sister, the daughter of the former T—— provincial governor, a pious Christian who prayed for her brother to come home and nothing more, would mean to suddenly cast off the mask before the agreed-upon time and put an end to this hoax that had gone a bit too far. He was not yet ready to do so, either for himself or for his friend, the real Rabinovitch, whom he might get into deep trouble, while he himself could be severely punished for signing a false name and carrying a false passport and documents. And above all—this was the crux of the matter!—his romance with Shapiro's daughter, which had started as nothing more than a lark, a simple flirtation between a boy and a girl, had now gone far and had developed into something serious. He could not imagine what would happen to either of them were he to bring it all to an end at the very outset, in the very fervor of their friendship that was blossoming into a passionate love affair . . . No! Come what may—he would not say who it was. *He could not say.*

"You *cannot* say? Or you don't *want* to say?"

The accused felt it was one and the same thing. He stated that each person had the right to protect his own self-interests.

"Quite right," the interrogator with the black pince-nez said curtly, and continued his line of questioning energetically. "Quite right. Every person has the right to protect his own self-interests. But when it pertains to the investigation, it must not be deterred from the truth. For our purposes, there is no longer a place for one's *own interests* and *secrets*. Be so kind as to tell us precisely who the person is who wrote to you under the female name of Vera P.? Where does he live? And what is his occupation?

The accused could barely hold in his laughter. Whatever gave them the idea that Vera P. was a "he," not a "she"? He couldn't see the bearing his sister Vera and her letter had on the investigation. And why shouldn't he be able to have his secrets? He stood firm. No, he could not say.

"Write it down!" the older one motioned to the younger, the one with the bulging forehead and thick lenses, who dutifully wrote it down. The accused watched him writing it down conscientiously as if his words had some special importance, but he had not the slightest idea in the world why this was so.

But he was not allowed to muse too long on this matter. The one with the black pince-nez put the letter back into the bundle, tied it all together with the same green ribbon, stood up, turned to the bundle of books, removed one book after another, called out each title, and addressed the accused energetically but amiably as before, asking him to explain why he had collected this *literature* about the so-called *Blood Ritual?*

The accused, relieved that they had let him off the subject of his sister's letter, began quite sincerely and candidly to tell the whole truth. Soon after they had found Volodka Chigirinski murdered, certain newspapers had begun a sharp campaign about Jews using Christian blood for their Passover *mazzah.* He had become interested in learning about the history and literature of the matter called "blood ritual," and so he had borrowed this pack of books from an acquaintance to read during the holidays and to return afterward.

"Up to that time you knew nothing about this so-called ritual?"

The accused didn't notice how ironically that question was phrased and replied ingenuously that he knew almost nothing at all about it.

"*Almost?* How can one understand the word '*almost*'?"

He explained that "almost" meant that he knew Jews used Christian blood— he meant to say, he had heard . . .

You just said very clearly that you *knew* Jews used Christian blood, and now you're saying that you *heard* . . . Tell us where you heard it."

Where he had heard it? He had read about it in the papers . . .

"Before you said you *knew,* then you said you *heard,* now you're saying you *read* it in the papers . . . Would you be so kind as to name the *acquaintance* who *lent* you this literature?"

Here he again felt ill. To identify the rabbi who had been so kind to him and had lent him these books would be to repay a favor with a disservice. He had no idea what could be in those books; since Passover eve he had had time to scan no more than a few of them, at most several pages. He decided to concoct a lie and an unshakable one at that: these books had been lent to him by an acquaintance whose name he had forgotten and who had left town—he didn't know where, and he didn't know whether or not he would return.

He had made this up in order to be rid, once and for all, of the pack of books because he was sensing that the further he went, the more he was stumbling; the more he talked, the more his tongue was getting him into trouble. And moreover, everything he said was being written down. Why, he wondered, were they writing it all down, and for what purpose were they so interested in the books? Why was it necessary? And what did they have to do with the reason he was brought here? Why didn't they get back to the real question of Volodka Chigirinski's death and to the statement he had made today?

The accused wiped the sweat from his forehead and looked at the investigators, who were conversing quietly among themselves. The books were tied back together and returned to their box, and in their place appeared the small, fat book with the label "My Diary." Rabinovitch wondered whether they were going to probe into his diary as they just had into his sister's letter? But what else was in the diary other than his feelings about his beloved? And what would he tell them if they were to probe into his soul: Who is this Betty and what is she to you?

Our poor criminal was sadly mistaken. It was more likely this diary would furnish the investigators with many more important things than all his entries about his beloved . . .

the sixty-fifth chapter

THE DEEPER INTO THE WOODS, THE THICKER THE TREES

"Tell us, Rabinovitch, is this your diary?"

Rabinovitch, who had already recognized the familiar, fat little book, nevertheless leafed through it and declared that, yes, it was his diary.

The senior investigator with the energetic face adjusted his black pince-nez and asked the accused to be so kind as to clarify why he had written in his diary the following entry, which he then read in his customary slow manner, stressing almost every word:

"'HOORAH! TODAY I WENT TO SEE THEM BAKE MATZOS! I MYSELF WAS PRESENT TO SEE IT AND AM DELIGHTED, VERY DELIGHTED, THAT I WAS PRESENT' . . . Perhaps you can tell us exactly what you did there at the *mazzah* ceremony and why you were so delighted to have been present?"

The accused did not immediately answer the question. He felt he ought first to give some introductory account of the agitation carried on recently in the newspapers, claiming that Jews used Christian blood in their *mazzah* for Passover. But they interrupted him before he got well under way and advised him not to involve himself in any irrelevant speculations and to answer immediately, briefly and to the point, the questions put to him: *What did he do at the* mazzah *ceremony* and why was he so happy that he *himself* was *present?*

Briefly and to the point, he answered that he had attended the ceremony only to observe how they baked this bread that had such an ancient historic past surrounded with so terrible a legend. He was delighted that he had had the opportunity to see for himself how this *mazzah* was prepared, and once and for all to disprove the ugly stories about the so-called blood ritual.

Rabinovitch was quite pleased with his fine, crisp response. Yet at the same time he was surprised to hear the older man say to the younger, "Written down?" "Written down," was the answer. The older one continued.

"In your diary you go on," he drew out the words, " 'TOMORROW I GO TO THE RABBI . . . I WILL SPEAK WITH HIM ABOUT DOGMA AND ABOUT RI-TU-AL.' " He drew out the last word as he folded his arms across his chest, leaned back in his chair, half shut his eyes, and waited for a reply. The other two also waited to hear what he would say. He didn't let them wait long, explaining that since he didn't feel sufficiently competent in religious dogma, he had wished to discuss the matter with an authority.

"You aren't *sufficiently competent* in religious dogma?" the elder man interrupted, looking at his colleagues with wonderment. "You spend time with those who call themselves *Chasseedim* and still aren't sufficiently competent? How can that be, I ask you? Right here you yourself say in your diary" (reading), 'YESTERDAY I SPENT THE EVENING WITH *CHASSIDIM*.' Who are these *Chassidim*, as you call them? What sect do they belong to?"

Rabinovitch did not lose heart and explained very calmly what the word *Chassidim* meant. He said that as far as he knew, *Chassidim* were not a sect at all, that Jews have never had sects.

"If that is so, how come they all have different dances? Here in your diary you write" (reading) "I DANCED WITH ALL THE *CHASSIDIM* THEIR *CHASSIDIM* DANCE.' What do you mean by a *Chassidim* dance?"

"It's an ordinary dance," he gave them to understand. "You drink a few glasses of whiskey and feel happy. Whoever can sing, sings. Whoever can't sing, claps his hands and the others stamp their feet."

"Where was this and in what place did you become acquainted with this sect and can you name these people?"

Our hero, whose calm had returned and who had been speaking confidently, again became rattled and speechless. To identify Shapiro's brother-in-law, in whose home he had so joyfully celebrated the Purim feast, would be to drag in innocent people who had no idea what was involved. And he tried to get around it: since this had happened so long ago, it seemed it was midwinter, he had forgotten.

With a sarcastic smile the senior investigator listened carefully and cast a glance at his colleagues. "A pity that you have such a short memory—you could remember so many interesting things. For instance, here you say in your diary, at the very end," and he read, " 'TODAY I SPENT ALMOST THE WHOLE DAY ON THE BLOOD RITUAL . . . TODAY I WAS . . .' Try to remember exactly the word you were going to write after 'was.' "

The accused leaned over and carefully scrutinized the book, as did the investigators. No, he could not remember at all the word he was going to write next.

"Really?" the head of the investigation sighed deeply. "Really? You can't remember? Perhaps this illustration will jog your memory." And with these words he placed before him the old prayer book with the greasy covers and rotted spine, opened it to a dog-eared page, and pointed to an illustration depicting an elderly man with a beard and sidelocks, wearing a ritual undergarment worn by orthodox Jews. He was holding a Caucasian dagger and was about to slit the throat of a naked lad lying bound and docile as a lamb, as if he were saying, "Go ahead, kill me, cut me, stab me, do what you wish to me."

The prayer book was our David Shapiro's old, familiar Haggadah, inherited from the true, Slaviteh Shapiros, and the illustration depicted how our patriarch, Abraham, was about to sacrifice his one and only son, Isaac, on the altar. Our young *gymnasium* student, Syomke, we recall, had been excited by this illustration on Passover eve, just before the house search. Rabinovitch was seeing it for the first time in his life. He leaned over the old prayer book and looked into it with deep concentration, totally befuddled. He had not the slightest notion what this was all about! The investigators also leaned over the book, looked from the illustration to the criminal and at one another, trying to assess what impression the illustration was making on him and what he would say. The illustration elicited no reaction whatsoever from the accused other than his continued puzzlement; he was totally unable to comprehend this apparent caricature. If he was a Gentile, why was he wearing the religious undergarment and long sidelocks? And where did this prayer book come from? And what did it have to do with him? And how did it pertain to the investigation and, moreover, to the murdered Volodka?

After several long moments of silence and exchanging of glances, he was asked to explain the significance of this "symbol." What should it mean to them?

The criminal confessed that he did not know what it was. He had never seen it.

"Never?"

"Never."

"Perhaps you would be so kind as to read a few lines from the text, perhaps it will become clearer to you?"

He would do it with pleasure, but . . . He found himself reddening without knowing why. He had to confess that he could not read the text.

"Why not?"

Because it was written in Yiddish and he couldn't read Yiddish.

All three were astounded.

"You cannot read Yiddish?"

No. Not read, nor write, nor speak it . . .

If he were to be a freak with seven fingers on each hand and foot, they could not have been more amazed than they were at these last words. How was it possible that a Jew who studied "ritual," dogma, and *Kabbalah*, participated in the *mazzah* ceremony, and danced with *Chasseedim* had the impertinence to say he did not understand Yiddish, nor could he read, write, or speak it? Here was a real scoundrel! With him they would be led a merry chase . . .

The senior man stood up, adjusted his pince-nez, and bade the younger man write down the following words: "The accused claims he does not know Yiddish. He cannot read, write, or speak it."

For the first time, Rabinovitch heard himself referred to as "the *accused*." Of what were they accusing him? Could they be suspecting him, along with the Shapiros, of ritual murder?! He felt he had gotten himself into a difficult predicament for which he was himself responsible. He could see the beginning of a tragicomedy that he himself had created. But he wasn't bothered at all because, in truth, there was nothing to worry about when all he needed to do was say one word, tell them his *real name,* and this entire tragicomedy would be dispelled like so much smoke. But he was not yet ready to do that. There was time enough for that. First it was necessary to see what would happen. Was it possible they could build a case against him on the basis of such laughable, flimsy evidence? Could they throw out his entire deposition, accurate and complete in every detail, offered voluntarily to aid the investigation and rescue the innocent Shapiros? And hadn't his lucid account opened their eyes? Or did they think he had made up the entire story from whole cloth in order to deceive them?

He looked at the three investigators. Can it be possible that people with sound judgment can be so misled? Can these clearly intelligent, decent, honest people, whose intentions are no more than to discover the truth, refuse to open their eyes, to awaken from a nightmare perverting their judgment about the myth of "blood ritual" and finally see the naked truth, and to be convinced, as he had been convinced, that it was no more than a fantasy, a misconception carrying over from generation to generation, a falsehood, an outrageous calumny?

These were our hero's thoughts at that moment as he stood there, no longer hearing what was going on around him. He didn't hear the lecture the senior investigator found it necessary to deliver to the criminal at the end of the interrogation in a soft, warm tone, advising him to *stop playing games.* By confessing to the crime and by identifying the implicated sect, he would be doing a favor for his fellow believers. The world would find out once and for all who the real criminals were, and they would stop accusing the entire Jewish people of needing Christian blood for Passover.

"How come we don't renounce *our* own sects and sect members?" he ended his moving lecture, which was altogether wasted. The criminal insisted that what he had told them about this terrible mystery was the only truth, and he knew of no other truth because there *was only one truth.* He was not the least frightened, and his face showed no change when he was informed that he was being sent to prison for his own sake so that he could think it over and, in his isolation, might reconsider whether it would not be wiser in the end, in behalf of his own interests and in the interests of justice, to confess, not to his *imagined* truth, but to the *real* truth about what he knew concerning this "terrible mystery," as he called it . . .

A "NERVOUS FEVER"

Betty herself could not say what had happened to her the morning following that awful night she had lived through. It had all passed over her like a storm, washing over her like a long, troubled dream.

She seemed to remember having been moved from one place to another. People were speaking to her, questioning her. She was trying to answer them. Amid a babble of voices, faces hovered around her. And the more kindly the faces, the more soothing the talk, the more she was reminded of that past night that had charged her heart full of pain and agony, ready at any moment to burst out in words or tears. But neither words nor tears came. A lump was lodged in her throat, her heart shrank, and instead of finding release through tears, she was suddenly struck with fits of laughter. She collapsed onto the first chair and burst out laughing.

She laughed and laughed, loud and long, until finally the laughter turned into mournful weeping.

But the tears provided no release. On the contrary, the more she wept, the more she felt suffocated, the more something seemed to press against her heart and constrict her spirit. The greater her desire to control herself, the more she was impelled to scream, tear her hair, beat her head with her fists.

"The girl is deranged, we have to tie her down!" said one of the men who had brought her there. Earlier that morning he had noticed that the girl was not altogether in her right mind.

He described in detail how that very morning she had attacked him for coming to get her by himself and how she had demanded that he return with another man because she refused to go with him alone—they would have to kill her first. Well, it was clear as day that the girl was deranged and had to be constrained. He was prepared to do whatever he was told, no matter what.

"It's you who are deranged!" a pleasant-sounding voice was heard.

Who had said that?

It was, she seemed to remember, an older man with a very genial appearance, with kind, gray eyes. He was dressed, she vaguely recalled, in a yellow summer-weight uniform, from which peeked a snow-white shirt and a pair of white hands. This was the man who had made the strongest impression on her, with his personable way of speaking, with his humane way of dealing with her, and with the warm gaze of his honest, fine, gray eyes. She did not know why, but she felt herself to be in the presence of a true *human being* who would understand her if she told him what she had lived through last night.

And she wanted to begin to tell him, to speak, but she could not. Impossible, she could not speak!

The man stood up, held her hand, took her pulse, smoothed her forehead and hair. He urged her to calm down. Who was this man in whose words were so much compassion and sympathy? A father might speak to a child in this manner, or a brother to a sister.

"Can't you see what the matter is with this girl? Call the doctor. The doctor!" . . .

. . . .

. . . .

And after that? What happened after that?

She must try to remember . . . remember everything. It was dark . . . A long, difficult, dark, dark night . . . Strange colors, strange shapes, strange figures. Somehow they were circling oddly around an object lying wrapped in a sheet. She was certain it was Kirilikha's son, Volodka, dead, stabbed, the very same as she had seen him when he was found near her house, murdered.

And strange cries, strange smells, a mixture of heliotrope and iodoform. A pair of kind, gray eyes were looking at her, but they were obscured by dark blue spectacles. The blueness of the glasses faded into a lighter shade, and in their place appeared yellow dots, spinning, bouncing, and shimmering before her eyes. And the mingled smells of heliotrope and iodoform seemed to penetrate into her bones. A long, sharp ringing, like that of a telephone, pierced the stillness of the night and deafened her ears. The ringing, she imagined, was screaming out, "Faster-faster! Faster-faster!" And a whistle was heard after the ringing, a long, drawn-out whistle ending in a deep sigh and a moan . . . "The girl is deranged," she heard them say. "The girl is deranged, we have to restrain her!" And the honest, fine, gray eyes didn't stop looking at her compassionately, and the fine, white hands didn't stop smoothing her forehead and hair.

Whose eyes could they be, so kind, so gray? Could they be *his*? Whose hands could that be? So fine and so white? Could they be *his*? Could this be her beloved, her intended, her chosen one?

"My darling! Where did you get such gray eyes? And when did you start wearing eyeglasses, blue eyeglasses? You are a mystery . . . A mystery . . ."

And again she heard a long, loud ringing like a telephone tearing through the quiet of the night and deafening her ears with its cry, "Faster-faster! Faster-faster!" And again Volodka in the white sheet, stabbed to death. And again, "The girl is deranged!" And again a whistle, a long, drawn-out whistle ending in a deep sigh and a moan. Who was sighing so? Who was groaning? Who was cracking her knuckles? Could it be her mother? Why did she smell so?

"Mama! Mamanyu! You smell . . . Do you know of what?"

"Of what, daughter?"

"Heliotrope and iodoform."

"Of what, my child? You're imagining it."

"Why is my throat so dry? Mama! Mamanyu! Why am I dying of thirst? Why don't they give me some water? Just a little water, even a drop of water???"

And here she felt as if a part of her being was breaking away, spinning off at great speed, floating away from her as the rest of her floated back and disappeared deeper and deeper into the abyss.

. . . .

. . . .

What was happening to our Betty? Apparently her too-strained nerves had shattered; an agonized spirit had collapsed. The doctors called it a "nervous fever." If all went well, it would resolve itself after a feverish illness, which itself was not serious so long as the fever broke without involving the brain, God forbid. That, the doctors said, would not be good . . .

The doctors anticipated that she would recover her health completely. But their role as doctors was limited to monitoring her temperature. What else could doctors really do? Nothing. Only Nature, or God—whichever name you preferred—could help. Certainly we can rely on *Him*. Needless to say, He would not commit an injustice. At least Betty knew that was how her mother saw things. And, incidentally, where was her mother at a time like this! Sara Shapiro, who had no more than one daughter and one son, two children, two bright stars, as precious as two eyes, would not remain silent if her daughter were not saved.

the sixty-seventh chapter

A MOTHER

There is a popular saying that is almost accepted as Scripture: "A person can be weaker than a blade of straw and stronger than iron." Sara Shapiro was a perfect example. How this mother could have persevered without going out of her mind was a miracle. "This alone proves there is a God in heaven," she said again and again. But what were all the woes she had already suffered compared with her suffering that night when they took away her David and her two children? And then that following day, when her daughter had vanished as if into thin air! How could she have vanished? How was it possible? But there it was. Everyone else had been accounted for. Her David and Syomke had been freed. They had sent the roomer to prison. And Betty? Betty was nowhere. All their friends and acquaintances, all their neighbors kept coming in and out of the house, inquiring, "Your daughter still isn't back?"

Strange people! They could see for themselves that she wasn't back. Why did they have to rub salt into her wounds? "Why are you sitting here? Why don't you do something? Why aren't you running to the police?" they would upbraid her.

Thank you for the good advice! Hadn't she been running around all day, from sunrise on, from one precinct to the next, beating on doors, but no one would tell her a thing! Some wouldn't even speak to her, some sent her off elsewhere, and others simply laughed at her, ridiculing her. It didn't help that her husband was, as he boasted, "in" with some of the authorities. It didn't help that her rich brother-in-law, Familiant, had pull with the governor. It didn't help that her husband's boss and his sons were fully prepared to do whatever was necessary on her behalf. "When it comes to saving a life, nothing else matters . . . ," so the boss himself said, adding, "Whatever it costs, we must find the missing girl." But Sara was wasting her time and energy. The authorities told her it was better not to interfere, not to get involved in such matters, as if there were some intrigue taking place, a mystery hidden behind a thick veil.

The only thing she was able to find out was that they had brought the girl to one of the precincts very late at night, if not early in the morning. One wondered where had she been until that time. And where was she taken then? "Better not to get involved in such matters."

But the power of political influence is nothing to sneeze at, and when a Jew says he is willing to pay "whatever it costs," you can be certain he can topple walls to find out everything he needs to know. They did find out, quite late at night, that the detained Shapiro girl had early in the morning been taken to a hospital. "What's this? How come the Shapiro girl, a healthy, strong, young girl, was taken to a hospital?" Apparently when she was first brought in to be interrogated, she was strong and healthy, answering every question appropriately and to the point, but suddenly she had burst out laughing and crying in such a manner that they had to call in the doctor. The doctor said she was ill and had to be taken to the hospital, and that's where they took her. "Is that the whole story?" "That's the whole story."

*   *   *

It was in the dead of night when this news was brought to the Shapiros. One of the boss's sons himself delivered this information. David Shapiro was not at home (he was running all over the city to various administrative offices with his brother-in-law, Familiant). Sara was at home alone. When she heard her daughter had been taken to the hospital, she broke into tears, sobbing loudly. She immediately rushed out to hail a carriage, and together with the bearer of the tidings, asked to be taken directly to the hospital.

"What hospital?" the driver asked, turning his head to his passengers.

She hadn't the least idea.

Sara and the messenger exchanged glances. Neither one knew which hospital. "What kind of person are you, for pity's sake? Why didn't you ask?" It hadn't occurred to him.

They raced from one hospital to another. "In heaven's name," Sara pleaded, "have pity on me! Tell me where my daughter is! Her name is Betty, Berta Davidovna Shapiro!" And they did have pity on the distraught mother, and after many telephone calls they ascertained that her daughter, under the name of Basya Davidova Shapiro, was to be found in the Jewish hospital.

"Praise God! Let it be Basya Davidova—so long as my child has been found." And the happy mother went off to the Jewish hospital, where yet another problem awaited her. They wouldn't allow her to see her daughter. It was too late, against the rules! "What do you mean against the rules? Am I not the mother?" She could be the mother seventeen times over—if it was against the rules, it was against the rules. "Come back tomorrow."

"God in heaven! What kind of world is this? What kind of people are these? Where is their compassion? Where is God?" Luckily she caught sight of their family doctor, the one who refused to bargain over his fee but accepted whatever they were willing to pay him. She could not have been happier had she seen her dead father standing there. She ran up to him excitedly. "Thank God you are here! God Himself sent you! My child, my Betty, is in here sick and they won't let me see her. Who ever heard of such a thing? A mother! It's worse than Sodom!"

"Shhh!" the doctor tried to calm her. "Stop shouting! Stop making such an uproar!"

How could she keep from shouting and making an uproar when her child, her Betty . . .

"Your child, your Betty, I know, I know. I've just come from seeing her. She's not well, but in no danger, and it isn't necessary to shout. Your daughter isn't out on the street, she's in a proper hospital. This isn't a public hospital where anyone can come and go as he wishes. Tomorrow morning you can come back and they'll let you in. Now they can't. Do you understand what I'm saying to you?"

"I understand. Why shouldn't I understand? But you have to have God in your heart and be in my shoes. I am a mother, after all. My God! What kind of a world is this, what kind of people are these who don't let a mother at least take a look at her child even from a distance? Is it possible that you're like all the rest, you, our family doctor, a kind friend who knows my daughter, who knows us all intimately? If you can say such things, it's the end of the world!"

The kind doctor removed his glasses and put them on again. He grumbled, grabbed his hat, and flung it back on the table. He called her a nuisance, a pain, a harridan. It was to no avail. In the end, this nuisance, this pain, this harridan prevailed. He turned back, took her by the hand, and quietly, on tiptoe, led her to the room where her daughter lay. He pointed out the bed to her and then forcibly pulled her away.

"Well, now are you satisfied? Enough! Now you can go home."

"Are you out of your mind? How can I go home now when my daughter is lying here in the hospital? What am I—a mother or a stranger? I must know what the matter is, what sickness she has."

"I'm telling you, it isn't serious. The worst that can happen is that she might have a very high fever."

"A very high fever? God help her! How awful!"

"Shhh! Again you're making a racket? Why am I being punished this way with this nuisance? Do you want them to chase you out of here?"

"Chase me out? For what reason? Because I'm a mother and want to know what's happening to my child? And who is saying this? Our family doctor! A kind man! A Jew like the rest of us! Give me your handshake as assurance and then I'll believe my child isn't in any danger."

Again the doctor removed his glasses and put them on again. Again he flung his hat on the table, but he finally shook her hand as assurance that her daughter was not in any danger and that he, on his part, would do what he could. He visited the hospital twice a day. What more could she want? Just one small thing: that they allow her to sleep there, anywhere at all, on the floor, if need be, so long as it was near her child.

It was of no avail. The kind doctor had to persuade the hospital administration to allow this nuisance to sleep there overnight, anywhere at all, in any corner, it would be his responsibility. He snatched his hat and was almost out the door, ready to flee, when Sara Shapiro again took him by the hand. "After all, you aren't like all the rest. You're our family doctor, a Jew, and a kind person. All other doctors should envy you . . ."

"Nuisance! What more do you want?"

"I want you to do me a favor. Since you're driving into the city anyhow, would you mind dropping by our house and telling my husband that our daughter is in the hospital and that she isn't, God forbid, in any danger, and that I am near her and that he, David, should take care of Syomke and tell my brother-in-law, Familiant, and everyone else that they should be sure to . . ."

"Good God! Where do such mothers come from?" The doctor grabbed his head in his hands and fled as if from a wildfire, Sara fast on his heels. She had forgotten to ask him one more small favor. Could he tell her husband, David, to be sure to—

But the doctor no longer heard anything. He had pulled his hat down over his ears, stepped into his old, delapidated cab awaiting him and . . . Away!

SARA'S MIGHTY GOD

The "sisters" who tend the sick in hospitals and do whatever is necessary for them are a wonder to behold. But how can one compare even those devoted sisters to a mother? Only a mother would take it upon herself to sit day and night with the patient, never shutting her eyes. Only a mother knows what the patient needs, her every like and dislike. Only a mother can adjust and smooth out the pillows so that they are perfectly placed. Eighteen sisters, each one with eighteen heads, could never discern at a glance what the patient desires.

All this everyone at the hospital realized. The doctors reluctantly conceded that the ill Shapiro girl could be allowed to have her mother at her side, not only during the day, but all night as well, and that she didn't need any additional help.

Sara Shapiro quickly assumed all the caretaking duties. She learned how to walk on tiptoe as quietly as the sisters and to mark the temperature chart as expertly as they. She learned to administer the medications at the right time as well as any sister in the world. There was no danger of her missing the time by so much as a split second! Was she not a mother? Hadn't she always administered medications to her own children when they were small? But the doctors were worried that once the patient revived, saw her mother, and began talking to her about family matters, it might upset the girl and cause a relapse. It was the family doctor who took it upon himself to handle this problem. A family doctor is a very special person; you can talk freely to him. He alerted the mother to the fact that once the patient began to improve she had to be very careful about what she said. She should only inform her daughter about where she was, a little at a time, without allowing herself to be drawn into discussions about home and the arrests.

"Do you understand what we're telling you?"

"I understood, why shouldn't I understand? Am I not a mother?"

"Mother or no mother," the doctor told her, "you're a woman, and a woman doesn't know when to stop talking. That's an established fact . . ."

The doctor did not convince her. Sara replied in a tactful way that there were plenty of doctors who *also* never stopped talking. Did he understand what *she* meant? We assume so, but he did not appear to be offended. Why should he be? Hadn't he known Betty since she was a tiny child? And how many times had he saved Syomke's life? And hadn't he treated her David for years on end? And hadn't he put up with quite a bit at Sara's hands? For every necessary visit, there were three that were a waste. But he made those unnecessary calls as willingly as he accepted whatever the patient could afford. Still and all, he was perceived on the Jewish Street as someone who had put away quite a sizable bundle in the bank. How much, they didn't know, but enough. Never mind that he wore an old-fashioned cloak that made him look like a windmill with two sails as he flew from house to house. Never mind that he wore a strange-looking hat, more like a battle helmet, never mind that he splashed about in worn-out galoshes. Money, you can be sure, had to be very much on his mind. Otherwise, why would he spend so much time at the Stock Exchange, trading in stocks and buying lottery tickets? A poor doctor doesn't drive around in his own carriage, even though it was delapidated and listing to one side. The horse was lame on one foot, ancient, exhausted, its bones visible. But it was still better than nothing. How would it have looked if the doctor had to go everywhere on foot? On the Jewish Street, where so many poor people lived, he was very much in demand, very popular, and very much beloved. His only fault was that he had a bit of a temper and didn't really believe in medicines. Did you ever hear of a doctor who made fun of other doctors and said of them that they were all worthless? A strange person! You had to plead with him for a prescription. "At least write a prescription for something, anything at all!"

"What should I prescribe? Aggravation? Poverty? Headaches?"

"No thanks. We don't need aggravation. Poverty we have, and let our enemies have headaches. Just write a prescription."

And the poor man had to write a prescription—he had no choice. He hesitated and hated to do it, saying the prescription was not worth the paper it was written on. The most important cure was fresh air, a good diet, milk . . .

"And money, where does one get money for that, Doctor?"

But our doctor wasn't listening. He had put on his hat and was already seated in his old, delapidated carriage drawn by the ancient, exhausted horse and . . . Away!

That's the kind of doctor who was Sara Shapiro's ally in the hospital. If not for him, they would have sent her packing long ago because, between you and me, she got under everyone's skin. She never missed the opportunity to plead for just one thing more to save her child, to try one more remedy, one more pill. She knew, God willing, that her daughter would get well because she had a mighty God and He would not take her precious child from her. Nonetheless, a person had to do whatever she could.

Sara Shapiro intruded herself into every aspect of the treatment. She demanded to know what was being prescribed for the patient and for what purpose. How come her niece, who had also been in bed with a high fever, was given a powder, not a medicinal mixture, not every three hours but every hour, and not a teaspoonful but a tablespoonful?

Her ally, the family doctor, was beside himself. He swore by his Jewishness that if she continued to interfere in these matters that were reserved for doctors he would never again set foot at her daughter's bed, no matter how sick she was!

It did no good. Sara turned a deaf ear. She knew full well that he visited her daughter, not only twice a day when he made rounds, but, if he had the time, he was at her side three and even four times a day, and was prepared to sacrifice his life for her daughter's sake. Even his colleagues, who loved to backbite and scoff behind each others' backs like common gossips, said among themselves that their colleague was behaving toward the Shapiros more intimately than is usual for a family doctor. This was accompanied by a wink to indicate he was an old bachelor.

They called Sara Shapiro "the mother-in-law." And she did treat her family doctor exactly as if she were his mother-in-law: she sent him to her home with all kinds of essential information and dealt with him as one would a family member.

Several times he brought her husband, David, in his carriage (he was going there anyhow—would it cost him extra?) and sometimes he brought her Syomke (a child, what difference did it make if he came along?).

The doctor was really delighted when Betty's health returned and she began to feel better. Once and for all he would be rid of her mother, this nuisance, this harridan, this weight around his neck!

But it didn't happen that fast. Betty's recuperation took longer than expected. It began to look as if she would not be able to get out of bed and be discharged from the hospital as soon as he had thought. Still, Sara was grateful to God. But until the mother had finally heard the words "She's passed the crisis!"—until she had been reassured by the doctors that the danger was over, she had not shed a tear. They had cautioned her not to disturb her daughter. But now the tears poured from her eyes as she sat, naturally, in a corner, so that her daughter wouldn't see her. And after she had had a good cry and wiped her eyes, the doctor declared angrily, as was his manner, "So? Now do you believe your daughter will be well?"

"With God's blessed help!" Sara answered him with tearful eyes, and confessed that next to God, she had relied on him. She knew she had a mighty God, a powerful God!

"Now you can certainly go home."

"Again the same old song? Again home? I would like to know why I, a mother, always seem to be in the way? Am I crowding anybody? Whose place am I taking away? Whose bread am I eating?"

"Sha! Enough! Let there be an end to it! It's impossible to tell you anything!" said the doctor, escaping from this nuisance, waving his hands as if chasing away a bee, but as they approached her daughter's bed, it was impossible to tell they had just been arguing. Their faces glowed, their eyes shone, and they smiled down at the ailing Betty as if she were a small, moody child who had just awakened from sleep, her eyes still half-shut, so that one could not tell in what mood she had awakened.

"HE'S ALIVE! HE'S ALIVE!"

Like the dawning of a summer day—so was Betty's awakening from her long illness. The first face she recognized was her mother's, in which were reflected at that moment many different emotions: fear, happiness, love, devotion, compassion, gratitude. As each emotion vied for expression, it made her appear so comical that the patient could not help but smile at her with her eyes and say just the one word, "Mama . . ."

Imagine the depth of meaning in that word. How many times had the patient uttered that word in her delirium? A hundred would be too little. But the meaning didn't lie in the word itself, but in the tone, in the voice, and especially in the look. It was a special look. And the elated mother couldn't believe her ears or her eyes. Her heart was ready to burst with joy, her eyes filled, and, lighter than a feather, she stood up and on tiptoe went over to Betty's bedside, leaned over her daughter, and barely whispered, "Is there something you want, Betty?"

Is there anything on earth Betty might have wanted that Sara would not have granted her? Heaven itself? No question. Walk a hundred miles? Dig through a mountain of earth with her bare hands? Demean herself and go begging, hand outstretched, weeping for her daughter's sake? Do you think she would hesitate even a moment? If you do, you don't know Sara Shapiro! When the doctor had prescribed *wine*, a good wine, "Kaiser wine," for the patient, Sara had sent for her husband to come immediately to the hospital where he was urgently needed. When he arrived, she drew him off in a corner and confided something to him in secret. The pair talked together long and earnestly, about what, we do not know, but that day there appeared a bottle of wine, nothing but the best "Kaiser wine," brought by their wealthy sister-in-law, Toibe Familiant herself, who arrived in her own carriage. She reprimanded her sister-in-law for sending intermediaries when she needed something. Why couldn't she ask her herself, "Toibenyu, I need a bottle of wine," or "Toibenyu, I need a jar of jam"? When had she denied her anything? "And especially now, when it's a matter of *pikaukh nefesh*—the saving of a life!" The well-to-do, pious woman threw in the Hebrew phrase, pursed her lips in a bittersweet little smile, while assuming so saintly and pious a mien that one would imagine she could, without any difficulty, ascend directly to Heaven.

The other face Betty recognized was that of the family doctor. But where was her father? And why didn't this room look familiar? Where was she? Why was it so brightly lit?

"Shhhh!" the doctor said to her, putting a finger to his lips. "You mustn't talk yet. You mustn't think of anything. You must simply lie quietly, nothing else."

It was easy for him to say—lie quietly, don't talk, don't think—when she so wanted to know where she was and what was wrong with her. She wasn't at home—that she could see. She was ill—that she could feel, but why was she here? How had it happened? She shut her eyes and began to recollect, bit by bit, everything she had lived through. Gradually she realized where she was and began to recognize other familiar faces. Now her father had arrived, but only for a moment because he had no time; he was not his own person. And there was her little brother, Syomke, who had been brought by the doctor in his carriage. "What fun driving in the doctor's carriage!" he said. "But I have to leave soon since the doctor can't stay long." And even her Aunt Toibe and her daughters had come to find out how she was feeling, but hadn't been allowed to stay more than a few minutes and hadn't been allowed to speak so much as a word to her except "How are you? Are you feeling better?" Despite all these familiar faces at her bedside there was one missing, and that one was no less dear to her, perhaps dearer, than all the others. And she didn't understand why the others had come and not he. Where was he? Whom could she ask? How could she ask? She waited for someone to mention his name. She looked deeply into each one's eyes for any hint, but they neither mentioned his name nor betrayed anything with their eyes. How was it possible he wouldn't be there near her or that he would be less concerned about her illness than the others? Could he have gone home? Or was he ill? No, they would have told her. But she could see they weren't speaking about him, no one was uttering his name, as if they had agreed ahead of time, as if they were afraid to speak the truth. What could that truth be? Understandably, she assumed the worst. She imagined what she could not dare say, what she was afraid to even think about.

When the family doctor arrived, she thought she might find something out from him.

"So, how did we sleep?" said the doctor, perfunctorily taking the patient's pulse. There ensued the usual exchange about temperature, about appetite, and about which medications to take and which to stop taking. But the patient saw by the doctor's eyes that neither the temperature nor the medications were important. Her temperature was normal and medications were no longer necessary.

"We'll soon start to think about your discharge from the hospital and going home," said the doctor, who loved to use the word "we." "And we won't go straight home, but first to a dacha, to a house in the country. There we'll quickly get well and recuperate fully."

Betty didn't appreciate being spoken to like a little child who was being tricked and manipulated. She felt they were keeping a secret from her, they were hiding something from her which she mustn't know. The mother could see her daughter was not satisfied. She was being moody, oh, so moody, and looked ready to jump out of her skin. The mother wished somehow to pacify her, to reassure her.

"Do you know, Betty, who asked about you?" the mother said soon after the doctor left, but immediately regretted her comment because she saw Betty red-

den as if every drop of blood in her body had risen to her face. Who else would
be asking about her if not "he"? Betty didn't want her mother to see she was
excited, and put on a calm face. "Who?" But Sara knew full well what kind of
calm it was and cursed herself for what she had said, wishing she had first asked
the doctor for advice. Of course, he would be absolutely furious if he found out.
But having begun, it was too late to retreat. She had to go on.

"How many times do you think he came to ask about you, to find out how
you were feeling, that *shlimazel?*"

"What *shlimazel?*" asked Betty with a lowered voice, looking at her mother to
see whether her face would betray whom she was speaking about.

"That young Litvak with the pimply face," Sara lied with a little smile. "You
must remember him, the bookbinder's brother-in-law. We met his family that
awful night during Passover, outside the railroad station."

Enough description, she knew who he was. It was the young man from Pinsk,
their roomer's friend. She had become excited for nothing. She was hoping to
hear another name but couldn't bring it to her lips, it was too painful. The poor
mother realized that her daughter wasn't listening to what she was saying. She
knew full well *who* her Betty was thinking about and *who* she was hoping would
appear. A mother's eye sees. A mother's heart feels. And what would she do if
Betty were to ask, "Where is the roomer?" What would the poor mother tell her?
How long could they go on avoiding the subject? If not today, then tomorrow,
sooner or later she would have to learn the whole truth. Rather than find out
from someone else, it would be better that she be the one to tell her. But she
didn't know where to begin, even though she had given it a great deal of thought
since her daughter had begun to revive and had asked the advice of her David,
the family doctor, and her sister-in-law, Toibe Familiant. All had agreed it was
too risky to say so much as a word about him unless she herself were to raise the
question, and even then it wasn't necessary to tell her the whole truth. She had
to be duped into believing he had gone home for a visit and would soon return.
But Sara understood better than all of them that it would do no good to make
up any lies because Betty was not so easily deceived. She decided she must
become as indirect as a diplomat right then and there, and said offhandedly,
"May God not punish me for these words, but it seems to me that the more
money one has, the more inconsiderate one is. What good are millions if you
don't have a drop of compassion? I'm talking about his aunt, the millionairess,
that's who I mean."

Betty's heart leaped into her mouth but she waited to hear more. Sara wiped
her lips and continued, "Why on earth is she holding on to her millions? Isn't
life dearer than millions? Will she be able to take it with her to the Other
World?"

"Yes, he's gone," the thought flew through Betty's mind, and she felt she
would faint, but she gathered her strength as well as she was able in order to
hear everything out to the end, to the very end.

"If you ask me," Sara went on, "if I had a million and my heir were accused of
a terrible libel, I would come flying to him the very next day and I would throw

money away hand over fist, wherever it would help. Ten thousand would be nothing. Fifty thousand, nothing. And I would this very minute put up bail. What does fifty thousand mean when you think of what's at stake? And even if it were a hundred thousand, why not? What does your Aunt Toibe say? 'Pikuakh nefesh—the saving of a life!' They take a completely innocent human being and make him out to be a criminal, a murderer."

Betty felt the weight of a thousand pounds lift from her heart. Thank God—he's alive! The color began to return to her cheeks and in the wink of an eye she realized what the real situation was. She desperately wanted to draw more information out of her mother, to find out everything that had happened. And her mother did tell her everything, a little at a time, but instead of being overwhelmed by the news as Sara had feared, Betty began to laugh for the first time since she had emerged from her delirium. Her face glowed and her eyes took on their old fire and glint.

The ecstatic mother imagined it was not her daughter who was laughing but all the good angels in heaven. God Himself was laughing. "Keyn eyn horeh! May nothing bad happen! Tfu-tfu-tfu!" To her daughter she exclaimed, "Betty! You're laughing! And why not? Who else should laugh? Imagine, Rabinovitch a criminal! A murderer! Ha-ha!"

But Betty did not answer her. Betty was absorbed in one thought, "He's alive! He's alive!" and a thousand gardens bloomed before her eyes and a thousand birds sang in unison, "He's alive! He's alive!"

PART TWO

POSTE RESTANTE

The reader will no doubt remember how our hoaxsters, the Gentile Grisha Popov and the Jew Hershke Rabinovitch, after they had agreed to switch identities, drove off in the same carriage after leaving the jubilant graduation celebration. They went straight to their rooms to discuss the details of their plan and to exchange vital facts about each other in order to play perfectly the new roles they would be assuming for the next year.

Within half a day they had worked out the entire plan, taking great pains to thoroughly check over the personal documents they would need to exchange. It was all organized with the greatest care. It only remained for the Gentile Popov, now called Rabinovitch, to travel to the large university city located in the very heart of the Jewish Pale, where as a medalist he would easily be accepted into the university. There he would have the opportunity to learn about Jewishness from the inside. The Jew Rabinovitch, now called Popov, would make his way to the large Russian city located at the very heart of the country, and as a Gentile he would most certainly be accepted at the university as befits Popov's son. And best of all, it would all look kosher in everyone's eyes.

Since the Gentile Popov and the Jew Rabinovitch remained in regular contact with their families through letters, it would also be necessary to keep those at home deceived. The Popovs had to be reassured that their Grisha was studying at the central Russian city, while the Rabinovitches had to believe their Hershl was studying in the city of the Jewish Pale. But that was precisely the problem—how would it be possible to manage the deception when instead of Grigori Popov it was Hersh Rabinovitch who was studying in the Russian city, and in the city of the Jewish Pale instead of the Jew Rabinovitch it was the Gentile Popov who was living there? For a difficult problem a clever Jew has a way of finding a solution. So it was Rabinovitch who came up with the idea that the letters Rabinovitch (the fake, not the real one) would write home, he would first send to his friend, the real Rabinovitch, in the Russian city, who would then send them on to the Popovs. And the letters the real Rabinovitch would write home would be sent to the fake Rabinovitch in the Jewish Pale, and from there they would be sent on to the Rabinovitches. For Popov's mail, the same would apply but in reverse.

However, one question remained: sometimes the unexpected happens. When young students write letters to one another, the letters sometimes fall into the wrong hands.

"What's to be done?" asked the pretend Rabinovitch of the real one, looking directly into his eyes.

"What's to be done?" the real Rabinovitch echoed, grasping his chin as if it already had the small beard that would some day grow there. "I'll tell you what's to be done. With God's help, when you get there and are settled in, kindly write your family that they not send you any letters in your name because there are three Popovs at your university, and just your luck, they all have the first name Grisha. Understood? And I will write to my people that at my university in the Jewish Pale there are as many Rabinovitches as there are stray dogs, and therefore I must ask them to send all mail *poste restante,* to be held at the Post Office. Understood?"

"Bravo, Hershke!" cried Popov, delighted with this brainstorm. "What Talmudic finesse, I must say!"

"Talmudic or not," the true Rabinovitch said, "it is a brainstorm. We must confound things so that no one can ever be sure who is writing to whom. No address, no Popov, no Rabinovitch; just *poste restante,* our initials only and let them try to find us out! Understood?"

"Entirely, Hershke," the pretend Rabinovitch said to the real Rabinovitch. "Let us embrace!" And both friends embraced each other warmly.

*   *   *

Indeed this brainstorm was highly successful. The mail traveled back and forth without a hitch. The Popovs from T_____province wrote their letters to their Grisha *poste restante* in the Russian city and the Rabinovitches sent their letters to their Hershl in the large city of the Jewish Pale, also *poste restante.* The Post Office, all business, did its double duty altogether faithfully, delivering the letters twice from one to the other, back and forth, *poste restante.* And it would surely have continued in this manner uninterruptedly all year as they had planned. Not a soul would have known until the designated time when they would resume their own identities and it was finally over! But suddenly something went amiss, as if a cog had slipped, bringing the entire machinery to a halt.

What had happened?

A trifle. The real Rabinovitch, studying under the name of Popov in the Russian city, stopped receiving letters from his friend, the real Popov, enrolled as the dental student Rabinovitch in the large city of the Jewish Pale. It did no good to send registered letters. It did no good to send wires. The pretend Rabinovitch apparently didn't want to reply, and the true Rabinovitch almost went out of his mind. And as if for spite, the Popovs were lately bombarding their Grisha with letters, all of which Hershke forwarded faithfully *poste restante* to his friend Grisha in the Jewish Pale—and there they remained unclaimed at the Post Office along with all the other letters that the Rabinovitches had sent *poste restante* to their Hershl, complaining that no matter how hard they tried, they simply couldn't understand why they hadn't received any answers to their letters. They wrote, "Perhaps you are ill, God forbid, in which case you could ask someone else to write a letter for you or send a telegram and someone would come running to help you, even though it isn't that easy to leave the business at the height of the season and go traveling to your city, where they don't allow a Jew to stay overnight . . . If you are not ill, what else can it be? Have you gotten in some sort of trouble, heaven forbid? Hardly likely. You're not that sort of person, although we cannot for the life of us understand your request that we write to you *poste restante* and only *poste restante!* You should know, Hershl, we will wait one more week, no more than one week. And if, God forbid, that week passes and we still haven't heard from you, then one of us, your father or I, will have to go there and find out for ourselves what's going on with you."

This letter was written by his older brother, Abraham-Leib Rabinovitch, a newlywed young man with a fine beard, who worked together with his father in a business near the train station. Before this letter was posted, they were already preparing for the trip but were spared the trouble and expense. The very same day that his letter was sent out, the newlywed Abraham-Leib with the little beard and his father, Reb Moshe Rabinovitch, were arrested and taken to prison. The whole town was in an uproar, in a state of shock.

"How can it be? Reb Moshe Rabinovitch isn't the kind of Jew who deals in stolen goods, and his Abraham-Leib isn't the kind of young man to get mixed up in these matters like some other folks. What can it mean?"

the seventy-first chapter

REB MOSHE RABINOVITCH SETS OUT TO RESCUE HIS SON

Even before Reb Moshe Rabinovitch and his older son, Abraham-Leib, were released from prison, the whole town knew the story behind their arrest. There was an uproar.

The townspeople had found out about it from the newspapers, which had finally published the name and identity of the ritual murderer. Earlier they had simply referred to "a Jewish dental student." Now they said plainly that he was a resident of Shklov studying dentistry, whose name was Hersh Movshovitch Rabinovitch. There could be no doubt who it was.

How the town carried on! So much news in so small a town! Where once the town lay quiet and dreamy, now suddenly it possessed its own Dreyfus! Imagine! But how could anyone take a story like that seriously in this day and age? It was laughable. Still and all, it was a shame for the Gentile world! A shame for Europe! A shame for themselves! "In these modern times, when even a town like ours has a railroad and a movie house . . ."

"Who's talking about a movie house, blockhead? What's so great about a movie house? We're talking about airplanes and dirigibles and he throws in movie houses!"

"All right, you can boast about your airplanes and dirigibles—still and all it's a pity on our poor Rabinovitches—what a libel!"

"If a Jew is in for trouble, it will come down his chimney after him!"

"In the meanwhile they've arrested one Jew there, and two Jews here. A catastrophe!"

"Nonsense! I'll bet you anything they'll free all three of them soon. May the Messiah come as quickly."

The townspeople were right on the mark. In time, they did release all three. You could not expect them to vouch for the release of the Jew who was held elsewhere, but the father and his elder son were released on the third day. They had merely questioned them, searched them carefully, and confiscated a pack of letters, all the letters their Hershl had written to them, and they were told they could leave. As soon as they were released, Reb Moshe Rabinovitch consulted with his family, friends, and knowledgeable people about what was to be done next. It was decided that he must rescue his son. But how to do it? No one knew. But if a Jew is drowning, he has no choice.

The poor father wasted no time. After again discussing the matter with a few more knowledgeable people (by this time amounting to the entire town), he packed his suitcase and set out for the big city, putting himself in God's hands and giving no thought to the fact that a Jew was not allowed to stay there overnight. What did it matter that knowledgeable people encouraged and consoled him? Whatever God had in store for him, that would be his lot. Can one believe that a Jew couldn't spend even one day there? Take a city like St. Petersburg, where a Jew is definitely not kosher. Nevertheless, people bless St. Petersburg because there is no other city in the world like St. Petersburg for a Jew. Or take Moscow, for example. What could be bigger than Moscow? Yet a Jew there is in deep trouble! A terrible place, that Moscow! But trouble or no trouble, one could wish for as many hundreds of rubles as there are Jews going in and out of Moscow day after day. A Jew is obliged to do what he can and God has to help . . .

Reb Moshe Rabinovitch was going, one could almost say, to his martyrdom. The poor man even forgot his passport. No small matter, a father setting out to rescue his child! And because he was a man of the old world, he brought along his elder son, Abraham-Leib, who was, as they say, a man of the world. He could hold his own with the smartest Gentile. Although Abraham-Leib hadn't graduated from the *gymnasium* or won a medal as his younger brother, Hershl, had, and he himself would concede his inferiority on some technical subjects, when it came to mastery of language, he would yield to no one, not even Reb Hershl himself. And if you were to insist, he was perhaps better. Never mind that Abraham-Leib looked like an innocent steeped in narrow piety and religious fervor. You may be sure that even as a youngster he knew his Russian literature and could recite all of Kirpitchnikov and Galakhov by heart. But he had no luck. His father absolutely refused to allow him to go to the *gymnasium*, even though he was older than Hershl by more than a year. His father swore that he had not wanted his Hershl to go to the *gymnasium*, but what choice did he have when that little scoundrel, as the father good-humoredly called him, had run away from home to another city? For a long time no one knew what had become of his offspring. Much later they found out from the little scoundrel himself, that he was trying to enroll in the *gymnasium* and had already taken the examination and done quite well. Alas, there was no vacancy. But the rascal wrote that they were not to worry about him, he would keep on trying until he was admitted, but under no circumstances would he be coming back home. You might well ask, what could a father who loved his son have done, especially with a gifted boy who succeeded in whatever he applied himself to?

So recounted the father, Reb Moshe Rabinovitch, an ordinary, honest Jew who owned a modest shipping business near the train depot. We can understand from his father's tale that his son, Hershl, struggled, starved, and froze more than his share while waiting for an opening, until he was finally admitted to one of the middle-level *gymnasium* classes in some distant city deep in Russia (in T_____province), where hardly any Jews exist. There he found a relative on his mother's side, a craftsman with a residence permit, who registered him as his own. Hershl was admitted into the school, where he studied, toiled, tutored students, and, with some help from his father, completed *gymnasium* with the ease befitting such a rascal.

When the father himself boasted without shame how he, Reb Moshe Rabinovitch, an orthodox Jew, had a son who was almost like a Gentile, he would shrug, saying there was nothing to be done about it in these modern times. But thank God he hadn't cast off all that was Jewish, like some others nowadays. On the contrary, whenever his Hershl did come home for a holiday and accompanied his father to the synagogue, his chanting before the congregation of the *haftaruh*—the lesson—was a rare treat, the rascal. What can a gifted person not do?

So the father consoled himself and occasionally sent his son whatever he could, but secretly, so that the elder son, Abraham-Leib, would not be jealous. But Abraham-Leib did know of it and was highly displeased, frequently disguising his displeasure because one could not go against a father. Honoring one's father is, after all, no small matter. He would merely allow himself to grumble occasionally in passing that he, Abraham-Leib, could see no advantage these days for a Jew to be educated. It was all the same, *gymnasium* or no *gymnasium*. Quite otherwise, a Jew with a *gymnasium* education was a thousand times more unkosher than a Jew without a *gymnasium* education. And let us suppose he has completed *gymnasium*—then what? And between us, let us suppose he has even completed university too. So? What next? Pch—nothing would come of it. He would be the same Hershke, but a thousand times worse, because Hershke without a diploma was to them still Hershke, but once he earned a diploma he would no longer wish to be called Hershke, but Grisha or Grigori, and when a Hershke acts like a Grisha, or a Grigori, that they won't tolerate, do them what you will!

The truth in these words was mixed with not a little envy. His younger brother was studying while he, Abraham-Leib, only a year older, and who knew all of Kirpitchnikov and Galakhov by heart, had to be a shipper at the railroad. He had to hold his hat in his hand, not only for the head of the station, but even for the night watchman, the Gentile in felt boots who had the temerity to speak to Abraham-Leib with the familiar "ty." The "ty" would not have been so offensive, but that oaf decided to call him "Chalamizer." "Chalamizer" was the oaf's version of Chaim-Lazer, even though he was named neither Chaim nor Lazer but Abraham-Leib. But try to explain things to a boor! If you're a Jew and have two names, they automatically call you "Chalamizer." *What* a people!

When the news arrived from the great city in the Jewish Pale that Hershl had not been admitted to the university but was studying dentistry, Abraham-Leib was secretly pleased, because he had known from the very beginning that it would work out like that. How else could it be? You think a medal is what counts?—it can be a silver medal, a gold medal, a diamond medal! "Yidele, liedele, where are you pushing yourself with your fiddele?" . . .

The older Rabinovitch, so pious a Jew that they called him Reb Moshe, insisted on boasting to everyone about his Hershl. "You know that little scoundrel? Well, now he's a student. Not a university student, but studying to be a dentist. But what's the difference, a university student or a dental student? You should see the letters he writes!" A short time later the father said, "Just imagine, that little scoundrel has already started earning money so that he says he doesn't need his father's help any more. On the contrary, he wants to repay his old debts, that little devil! How about that scamp! He sends money home every month, sometimes a fifty, sometimes a hundred. So, what do you have to say now about your brother, eh, Abraham-Leib? Why are you so quiet?"

What could Abraham-Leib say? First of all, he had never said anything bad about his brother, and second of all, if you pressed him for an answer, Abraham-Leib would still say it was too early to tell. There was a long way to go yet. If a person earns a little one month, it still doesn't prove anything. Also, how could he contradict his father? After all, honor thy father . . .

At first, Abraham-Leib felt a wave of fear when his brother suddenly stopped sending the fifties and hundreds. His letters also ceased. "That means our bigshot is already too important to write us a letter once in a while, peh!" Abraham-Leib once remarked in his father's hearing, but he immediately regretted it as he couldn't bear to witness his father's anguish as he went around like a shadow of himself, unable to find any comfort. Much later Abraham-Leib himself also began quietly to worry about what might have befallen his brother. "What can you expect from these young whippersnappers nowadays. Maybe he's gone over to 'them'? May that never happen! Father wouldn't survive it . . ." thought Abraham-Leib, and felt devastated by the very thought.

Imagine how he felt once they found out what a catastrophe had befallen his brother. He waited impatiently for his father to allow him to accompany him. He had already informed his father how much he wanted to go. Everyone in the town assumed that, if they had to go, they would go together, father and son.

Common sense dictated it. And when they boarded the train, the whole town came down to bid the Rabinovitches farewell and to wish them success, reminding Abraham-Leib a hundred times over that he was a clever young man who could write them everything, extensively and often. And with God's help, if there were good news, he should not be stingy but send a telegram.

"Remember, Abraham-Leib, don't forget, lots of postcards and send a telegram."

"Good, good. May it work out well." And they could swear that Abraham-Leib surreptitiously wiped away a tear.

The locomotive whistle blew, smoke puffed from the chimney, the wheels began to turn, and the railroad cars snaked along one after another. From the train window peered two gloomy faces: one of an older man with a beard and a shawl around his neck, the other, of a young man with a white dickey and early signs of a little beard. Poor Reb Moshe and his elder son, Abraham-Leib—what God had against them no one knew. A minute later and they were no longer to be seen. Jews with downcast faces still hung back along the tracks, waving to the travelers, shouting after them from the distance. One could hear fragmentary phrases and sentences, "Have a good trip! . . . Postcards! . . . Succeed! . . . Send a telegram! . . ."

the seventy-second chapter

HAVING THE RIGHT FAMILY NAME

For our other hero, the real Rabinovitch, things went a great deal better than for his friend, the real Popov. For him, the false Popov, it was a success from the very first moment.

It goes without saying that he was immediately admitted to the university without question. It took but one look at his credentials to realize what his family origins were. Coming from the right family is no small matter. His father's name, Ivan Ivanovitch Popov, was well known in that city.

There were a few bad moments when he submitted his papers at the university. The documents were not in the best order; the photograph attached to his diploma was somehow not quite as it should be according to the university registrar, but the family name Popov was so impressive that the registrar bit his tongue for having had so much as a moment's suspicion. He swiftly folded up the diploma and covered it with other documents as if he wanted to hide his own mistake and to banish any inappropriate thought.

That was the first step our pretend Popov took, which almost sank him and from which he emerged safely.

The other step was more perilous than the first. As he was accustomed to the necessity of earning extra income by tutoring students, and as he wished to ease his father's burden, he decided to seek out a few students in that wealthy Russian city who could pay high fees. But instead of putting an ad in the papers, he had the bright idea of going to see the rector of the university to ask him to keep him in mind if anyone were to inquire after a tutor.

He was received by the rector, an older man with sideburns that were long out of style, in a kind and friendly manner. After listening to the student's request, the older man with the sideburns peered at him oddly, as if trying to convince himself that the person speaking to him was the one he thought it was and not another. His lower lip hung down in a strange way. The pretend Popov with his Jewish quickness gathered immediately from this look and from the sagging lip that he must seem outlandish to the rector and that his request must appear to him to be out of place. How was it possible that Popov's son should be asking for students to tutor? He quickly attempted to correct his mistake and began to explain to the rector that he had promised he would not accept his father's help for one year. But then he realized the rector might, God forbid, check with his father, that is to say, with his friend's father, something that would not do at all, to put it mildly, and so he felt it necessary to correct that as well by confiding to the rector in the strictest of confidence—not a soul must know, even his father, how and from what source he wished to support himself during the year. It was for him a kind of sport, a bet he was telling only him, the rector, about and no one else.

This story did seem outlandish to the rector, but the genial face of the student, his fine demeanor, his sincere and candid manner, and especially the fact that in front of him was seated Ivan Ivanovitch Popov's son (again the family name)—all this caused the gullible rector to suspend reason and overlook the obvious as he chuckled, a sign that he was rather pleased with this ruse. Nevertheless, he found it necessary to comment in a mildly chiding tone that, although it was certainly very considerate on his part to wish to spare his father any expense and to show he could be self-sufficient, especially when he had given his word, and a word must be kept, that was as it should be, one must not forget that there were hundreds of poor students who did not have well-to-do-fathers like Ivan Ivanovitch Popov, who lived from tutoring students and had no other source of support than their own earning power, and to give Popov's son students to tutor would simply be the same as taking the last bit of food out of a poor student's mouth, and this a young man like himself could not, in good conscience, ask. But as Popov had already given his word, and one's word must be kept, he promised that should anyone ask for someone like himself as a tutor, he would keep him in mind.

What the rector meant by the words "someone like himself," the student did not understand, but after the warm squeeze of the hand and the clap on the back as he was accompanied to the door, he did feel reassured that if the right student were to come along, he, Popov, would be the first candidate.

And so it was. Hardly a week had passed before our Rabinovitch-Popov was called to the rector's office, asked to be seated, and again given a long lecture about how it wasn't fair to take work away from poor students who didn't have any support other than their own earning power, to take the last bit of food from their mouths and to give it away to a young man like Ivan Ivanovitch's son. The fact that he, Popov, had given his word to his father to be self-sufficient for one year would not have mattered very much to the rector had not, through a coincidence, a remarkable circumstance arisen. There lived in the city a very wealthy landowner from a distinguished family, a certain Feoktist Fedoseyitch Bardo-Brodovski, who was seeking a student-tutor who was himself well-born, from a respectable house, someone he, the rector himself, could vouch for, could guarantee would be appropriate for his children so that they would not fall into the wrong hands. In view of this unusual request, the rector could no longer reckon with the fact that many poor students were also hoping for such an opportunity. When it came to guarantees, when it was specified that children be protected from all extremes, there was no room for pity, fairness, and other such feelings.

When the rector concluded, he went over to the desk and wrote down a few words.

"Here you have my calling card, young man, go take the position and the best of luck to you. May you both be pleased with one another and may I not regret my recommendation. And as for your request that this be kept a secret from your father and from anyone else," the rector said as he rose, "you can trust me. As I have already given you my word that it would remain a secret between us alone, you may rest assured it will remain so."

With those words the rector led the young Popov from his office and found it necessary to remind him again that even though it wasn't altogether fair at a time when many poor students who had no other means of support . . .

And so forth and so on.

the seventy-third chapter

HE FINDS HIMSELF IN MARBLE HALLS

With trembling hand and pounding heart the student Rabinovitch-Popov rang the bell in the magnificent entryway leading into a mansion on one of the wealthiest streets of that wealthy Russian city. What a house! Who lived in it? How should he conduct himself with them? How would he find himself feeling? And above all—was he not playing with fire? Wouldn't his eyes give him away, his nose, his accent? Perhaps this wasn't the best plan after all. It was too impressive a house. It was all too much for him! He hadn't aimed this high. "Think it over, Hershl, maybe there's still time to get out of here . . ." But it was too late, for responding to his ring was a tall, liveried butler with a white, smooth-shaven, soft face. The butler took the measure of the student with one look from top to bottom, accepted the rector's calling card from him, led him into a luxurious foyer, and asked him to wait while he, the tall butler, disappeared up the sweeping, rounded stairs. This gave the student time to take in this unusually beautiful foyer with its gleaming yellow marble columns, painted high glass ceiling, opulent furniture, precious paintings on the walls, bronze and marble statues, expensively bound books, journals and illustrations on the table, as well as other fine objects and antiques. What amazed him most was not so much the wealth and beauty and brilliance of this entry hall, but its expanse, its spaciousness, its aura of permanence and comfort, its peacefulness, and, particularly, the assured, secure spirit hovering in the air, letting one know that the owners not only must feel comfort and pleasure here, but felt safe, confident, and fully at ease in their own home. These feelings only a Jew can best appreciate, because no matter how wealthy a Jew might be, no matter how firmly he might be established, no matter how broad his influence, no matter how loudly he might proclaim his success, he still must feel as if he were a guest at a hotel or a wayfarer at an inn, and if this were not his own fate, it would surely be the fate of his children or, if he were lucky, of his grandchildren, wherever they might end up.

"Feoktist Fedoseyitch bids you join him," the clean-shaven butler broke into his thoughts and led him up the broad, yellow, marble staircase, through a series of mirrored rooms, one larger and more spacious and more beautiful and more luxurious than the next, and into a magnificent, tastefully furnished study with the most expensive carpets and softest divans, muffling the sound of one's every footstep.

The first thing that met his eyes was a huge, smooth-haired, steel-colored hound lying stretched out in the middle of the study floor, snoozing with one eye shut, his snout nestled between his front paws, while the other eye, red and threatening, glared in an angry and melancholy manner at the newly arrived stranger. The dog apparently was not prepared to extend a warm welcome befitting the guest, a student who came with high recommendations and an impressive family name. That was immediately evident from the menacing growling and grumbling that emanated from the dog's throat, a sort of "Grrrr" that might have been no more than a sound conveying "Welcome to you, Mr. Jew, come on in, nice to see you!" . . .

The new guest, however, interpreted it differently as cold fear struck his heart. We are not ashamed to admit that our second hero, Grigori Popov, really Hersh Rabinovitch, had inherited from his ancestors an inexplicable antipathy toward, or rather a dreadful fear of, dogs. Where this came from, we do not know. Perhaps it was because his forefathers, the elder Rabinovitches, were people who served the local landowner, who would tease them by setting his dogs on them whenever one of them would enter his courtyard, not for the dogs to tear them apart, but for the sake of entertaining his guests as they looked down from the balcony. But that is no more than conjecture; we do not wish to engage in such speculations. We leave it to those who occupy themselves with these matters to explain it properly. I simply wish to state the fact that our Hershl Popov did not like dogs. He believed, along with his co-religionists, that a dog was no more than a dog and to rely on its canine good will was folly. And so upon entering the study he remained stock-still, looking at the master of the household, who sat hidden behind a newspaper in a far corner of the room while keeping a watchful eye on this huge dog that was still deliberating which kind of welcome to give the hesitant guest. At this point, the master of the household spoke to the dog in German.

"Glyuk! *Blaybst ruhig!*—Be quiet!"

Why the dog deserved to be spoken to in German is a good question; nevertheless, as soon as he heard those three words from his master, the dog's demeanor changed. His open red eye still glared at the newly arrived young man, but the growling ceased. He proceeded to lick himself, allowed the guest to pass, then remained lying calm and quiet in his place as if to say, "This time you can thank your lucky stars, but next time, we'll see . . ."

His host had in the meantime put aside his newspaper, raised himself from the large armchair in which he sat, greeted the guest with an outstretched large, white hand, bade him come closer, and indicated a nearby chair as he himself sat down again. In the most cordial manner he initiated this first conversation with the student, giving the student an opportunity to observe his host.

He was a massively built man, almost too large, too heavy, sluggish in his movements, but for all that, a pleasant, sympathetic person. His face was not what one would call attractive: the cheeks seemed swollen, the beard parted, half whipped to the right and half to the left, his teeth looking as if they had been removed and not put back in their original order. Yet, this man need speak only a few words to win one over and inspire love without one's realizing why. One sensed in him a human being who, despite his wealth and size, was at heart simple and small as a child. What sincerity and openness! He said directly what he felt. In addition, he possessed a generous heart, a generous soul, a generous hand, which was immediately evident from the first moment one met him. He enchanted the student, Popov, with the benevolence and kindness with which he treated him. Apparently the student also made the best impression on his host because he did not spend much time talking about how many hours a day he wished him to tutor his children or how much he would be paid for it. He simply told the student frankly that since a man like Mikhal Mikhalitch (the name of the rector) was vouching for him, he considered any further discussion unnecessary, especially as it was now teatime and they had to go to the table.

With these words the massively built host rose from his deep, overstuffed chair, took the tutor by the arm, and led him to the table, accompanied, of course, by the huge hound that had bounded to its feet and now seemed to Popov like some large, untamed animal. This animal decided to thoroughly sniff the new tutor all over to find out what he smelled like and so honored him by shoving his damp cold snout into his hands. He was eager to thrust his damp cold snout into his face as well, but his master winked at him and again said in German, "Glyuk, *blaybst ruhig* . . ."

The family had already gathered at the table. The new tutor was dazzled as he was introduced by his new employer to the members of the household. There were so many different faces before him with so many different names. But of all the faces, that of the mistress of the household impressed him the most. She was a stunning woman whose eyes, encountered but once, would return forever in one's dreams. Nadezhda Feodorovna was the name he repeated to himself over and over so as not to forget it. Most of the names of the others at the table went in one ear and out the other. Of all the other names he also remembered Fetya and Seryozha—those were his new pupils; one was in the first level, the other in the third. After that came such other names as Monsieur Dubois, the French teacher, a fop with a pale face, black eyes, and a bizarrely curled moustache the likes of which had never been seen since the world was created and people curled their moustaches. Next was Herr Frisch, a German with gray eyes and with enough red color in his cheeks to provide rouge for three women. After the German came Miss Tockton, an Englishwoman with bony shoulders and abrupt gestures. There followed an assortment of Russian names, masculine and feminine, that Popov did not even try to remember. He wondered whether he would ever learn all these names by heart.

*   *   *

That same night our Rabinovitch-Popov sat in a neat, attractive room, writing two letters. One letter was to his father, for whom he concocted two big lies: that God had sent him jobs in two wealthy Jewish homes, from which he hoped to save a good amount of money. Starting the following month he planned to send money home in order to pay off the debt he owed his father. About his admission to the university, he hoped he would be able to write about that after Saturday, as the quotas had not yet been decided.

The second letter, mailed together with the one described above, was sent to his friend, the real Popov, living in the city of the Jewish Pale, to whom he bared his heart, telling the entire story about how he had managed to gain access into the highest levels of society by unwittingly taking advantage of his friend's name, something he deeply regretted. He felt as if he had robbed someone . . . but it was too late. It had happened of itself, he was not responsible for it. He ended the letter with these words:

> . . . and be sure to write me what is happening with you. Have you been accepted yet? I must know so I can stop stringing my father along. I hate having to make up one story after another. I'm already up to my neck in lies. But I'm not complaining. I hope, dear Grisha, it hasn't gone any worse for you than it has for me at this

beginning of our extraordinary hoax, and I hope, dear God, you won't regret the role you've agreed to play in this comedy we've undertaken. Speaking for myself, I predict I will not regret that I am no longer called Hershke, but,

Grisha

Whether this prediction of our Rabinovitch-Popov was fulfilled or not, we will soon learn.

the seventy-fourth chapter

AND HE IS FEELING NOT BAD AT ALL

In this mansion, among all his fresh acquaintances, the new tutor felt at first as if he were in a forest, or as if he had just arrived in a strange, large, busy city with unfamiliar streets, houses, and people. Although he was surrounded by people, he felt lonesome, a person entirely alone with his thoughts and feelings. There were moments when he regretted the whole affair, was disenchanted with the hoax, with the comedy he was playing, missing his home being with Jews. And then there were moments when he went around intoxicated. He imagined he was the hero of one of those beautiful tales he had heard as a schoolboy in which he was magically transported to a golden palace where there was prepared for his pleasure the best of everything. Those who dwelt there were not ordinary people, but knights, counts, and dukes, and he himself was the prince for whom all this had been created. But one thing was lacking: the princess whom he had to free from this enchanted castle . . . And he began to laugh at his childish fantasies and ridiculed himself for his juvenile thoughts that refused to be banished but crept back into his head where they insisted on weaving these golden, magical dreams.

All this was before he had become acquainted with what was going on around him, before he had awakened himself, leaving behind the world of unreality for the real world, abandoning the realm of fantasy for actuality. He quickly came down to earth and began to feel more and more at home, soon mastering everyone's name as everyone knew his. After the second day he was no longer thought of merely as a tutor, but as Grigori Ivanovitch, a member of this large, odd family. And these people did seem odd to him because they behaved toward one another at the same time as strangers yet intimates, distant yet close,

friendly yet indifferent to each other's life circumstances. Observing these people and their relationships to one another with his keen Jewish eyes, our pretend
Popov had to admit that these were people, not only of another religion and
nationality, but entirely different in their psychology, which was altogether alien
to him. He compared them with his own people and wondered how it would be
if these people were Jews. From the oldest to the youngest they would already
have known who he was, whether or not he had parents, sisters, or brothers, and
what their lives were like. And he certainly would have known who they were
and what they were like, each individual's biography. He was puzzled by these
people who gathered together several times a day at the same table, chatting so
warmly and conversing so amiably, and laughing so heartily, yet once they arose
from the table, each returned to his own corner, each to his own task, once
again strangers and as distant from one another as east and west. How each of
them could convey such generosity of spirit, serenity, confidence, security, and
unruffled contentment! Ach! How fortunate it seemed to him these people must
be, yet they themselves did not realize their good fortune, as a small child might
remain unaware, or as a healthy adult may not appreciate that he is healthy.
Unbidden, there came to mind thoughts of his own people, the pursued, the
cast out, the lamentable and wretched, impoverished and dejected, terrified of a
fly, unsure of life and limb, chosen by God yet superfluous to humankind,
precious only to each other and worthless to the rest of the world. But be gone!
Be gone dark thoughts! As he now found himself among those who were fortunate, free, confident and secure, let him be like them—if not forever, at least for
a short time. As he had succeeded in being accepted in these marble halls and
had entered this Garden of Eden—be it a stranger's Garden of Eden, be it for
but a brief time—let him also enjoy the taste, even if for a short time, of what it
is like when one is not a Jew. How would it be not to be afraid that at any
moment, any second, they will let you know who you really are and that at any
second they will call you by your right name?

The new tutor not only became familiar with this grand house and felt quite
at home with the people in it, he also became comrades with the dog, who now
felt so comfortable with him that every time the dog greeted him he would jump
up on him, yelp gleefully, and lick him with pleasure. The servants also became
fond of Master Grigori Ivanovitch because he did not put on airs like the others
in the house, had no aristocratic pretensions, and was hardly ever to be heard—
a strange master! . . .

But more than the rest, his two young students, Fetya and Seryozha, adored
him and became attached to him. Eagerly they left the French teacher, Monsieur Dubois, the German Herr Frisch, or the English Miss Tockton and awaited
Grigori Ivanovitch and his Russian lessons, which were frequently attended by
Nadezhda Feodorovna, and occasionally, by Feoktist Fedoseyitch himself,
pleased that the children were fond of their Russian teacher, who hadn't deceived them and hadn't embarrassed the rector.

"Grigori Ivanovitch, are we going to play lawn tennis?" his young pupils once
asked him after class. "Let's go," Grigori Ivanovitch answered, and followed

them onto the grounds to play lawn tennis. But Grigori Ivanovitch Popov had momentarily forgotten that Hershl Rabinovitch knew as much about lawn tennis as a rooster about the affairs of men. Ask him to hold a racket, what a serve or a stroke was, a game, or a set, a double fault, or other such terms that are used in playing lawn tennis. It was all Greek to him, gibberish. He caught himself in time and said to his students, "Do you know what, children? You play alone today. I have a bit of a headache . . ."

"Grigori Ivanovitch! Are you good at horseback riding?" his students asked another time.

"Why do you want to know?"

"Because we were just talking about our horses. You'll surely join us this summer at our country place and we can go riding together."

Grigori Ivanovitch remembered that Hershl Rabinovitch not only was no horseman, he was ashamed to say he was afraid of getting close to a horse.

"Sasha is an excellent rider!" said his students, who much preferred a horse to a book and who would much rather go riding than to sit at their lessons.

Poor Grigori Ivanovitch had to maintain his imposture and tell a new lie, that he was a good horseman.

"If that's so," one of the boys exclaimed, "you can ride all day with Sasha. Sasha loves to ride."

Grigori Ivanovitch already knew who this Sasha was—it was their older sister, who was studying at an exclusive boarding school and who would soon be coming home for vacation. They were all looking forward to this and were preparing to welcome her like a princess. Not a teatime passed without hearing the name "Sasha" over and over—Sasha likes this and Sasha doesn't like that. "Who is this Sasha they talk about so much? What does she look like?" he thought to himself. He had once seen her picture; she was the image of her mother, especially her mother's eyes. He had to admit the picture amazed him in two ways: first, he had the feeling that she looked familiar, that he had met her somewhere, and second, she reminded him of that princess who had graced the magic tales and golden dreams of his childhood imagination . . .

"This is my daughter," the mistress of the house, Nadezhda Feodorovna, pointed out with maternal pride. "She's coming home for Christmas."

"For Christmas?" he echoed, comparing her eyes to the daughter's, exact replicas. But where had he seen her before? Could it have been in a dream? Without intending to, he began to look forward to Christmas along with the rest of the household.

"When do we have Christmas?" he wondered, and remembered that the word "we" was out of place. What business did Hershl Rabinovitch have with Christmas? With Christmas eve? And he sat down to write a letter to his friend, the real Grigori Ivanovitch Popov, from whom he kept no secrets and to whom he poured out his heart as one would to a brother:

"Curse me, dear Grisha! Scold me! Call me anything you like! I deserve it because I am a base person, a vile person! Imagine, there are moments when I

am so overwhelmed, I forget who I am and what I am, and I am happy to forget
it, *want* to forget it! . . .

Another time he wrote him in a happy, humorous vein:

" . . . Aren't you a fool, Grisha, to be upset about trivialities like the troubles
you must tolerate for being Jewish. You want to solve national problems and
other prosaic matters when my dream princess will be arriving soon. But don't
you worry about me. I am not you. I will not play with fire like you. Forgive me—
I can't write too much today. I hurry to mail this and will rush right home. We
will then be off in three sleds—three swift troikas—to go meet her. This is
living!"

the seventy-fifth chapter

IN THREE TROIKAS

It was a true Russian winter morning. The frost singed the skin
and bit at the nostrils. The white, newly fallen snow sparkled and crunched.
Three swift teams of horses, each a troika, were pulling three wide sleds, in
Russian called "sprawlers" because these sleds were so wide and roomy that
one could sit in them and spread one's legs out full length. The middle
horse of Hershke's troika, ears laid back, strained at the shaft as the two side
horses, one's head turned right, the other's, left, pranced wildly, kicking up
clouds of snow with their hooves. The many little bells with which they were
bedecked tinkled their silvery tune, and the driver, a Russian with a broad
bottom and combed beard, instead of whipping the horses on, allowed the
reins to hang loose and clicked with his tongue, "Steady now, steady now."
Those who lay sprawled out in the sleds, wrapped snuggly in fox and sable
blankets, could barely catch their breaths, crying out, "Vanka! Hold me
tight!" That was the Russian troika. Only a Russian can truly savor and
appreciate it.

Our pretend Popov, sitting among the others sprawled out in his wide, roomy
sled, the troika flying like an arrow from a bow, did not experience its true
Russian flavor. His thoughts were elsewhere, far from where he found himself.
Half an hour earlier he had picked up a packet of letters at the post office from
his friend, Grisha, in which there was a letter from his elder brother, Abraham-
Leib, who had the habit of writing mainly about gloomy matters that sent the
reader into a funk for the rest of the day.

We offer a portion of that letter as an illustration:

. . . also be advised, dear brother, that of the money you sent Father, there is not a
trace left. It was necessary to supplement your sum with another fifty to send our
brother-in-law, Velvel the *shlimazel,* because the authorities have investigated him
and decided that he did not qualify under the residential edict and they sent him
packing with his three little children, nor would it serve to take hat in hand and go
begging from house to house. Our sister, Feyge-Leah, must also periodically be sent a
few rubles. And in addition, she is not in good health; she writes that she needs a
consultation desperately. If she had the wherewithal, she writes, she would travel to
you so you could accompany her to a specialist. She says that where you live, there
are famous specialists. But we urged her to remain home because to travel to you
involves not only expenses but means returning by the tiresome, slow train. Also be
advised, dear brother, that business now is really down and God has granted us a
station master—may God take his soul, a Haman of the worst sort! He hates Jews
like poison—but where do they love Jews? The wonderful news we hear about Jews
nowadays, blessed be His name, I don't need to write you. You know it without my
telling you. Also, dear brother, Father wants to remind you again, that on the
seventh day of the month of Shevat, we have the *yahrtzayt*—commemoration—of
our mother, may she rest in peace, so please don't forget to say *kaddish*—the prayer
for the dead. You may be only half a student, a dentist, but even if you were a full
student and even a full doctor, still and all, it makes no difference, *yahrtzayt* is
yahrtzayt. . . .

Strange! Whenever he received a letter from his elder brother, he felt sick at
heart. Abraham-Leib had a terrible way with a letter—he was a bird of ill omen:
you would never hear any good news from him. His father's letters were far
gentler and more pleasant to read. Laced with rabbinical Hebrew, he would
write:

To my dear son, Tzvi Hersh, may his light shine forever!
    With my fondest regards, as is the custom, I wish to let you know that we are all
perfectly well and healthy, blessed be His name. As for the shipping business, I let
you know that it is not any better than a year ago. The One Above, blessed be His
name, will show us the right way. The mud this year is worse than you can imagine
and transport is terribly expensive. But heaven forbid, don't worry. The Blessed One
will provide good weather and we pray in the future that everything will improve for
us and for all of the people of Israel. May we only hear good and comforting news, of
peace and long life.
    From me, your father, the one who seeks your welfare and sends regards and
hopes for success,

                                    Moshe Bar Tzvi Hersh Rabinovitch

True, these letters filled with Hebrew were not that cheerful, and the news
that the father wrote him was not that much better or happier than his
brother's, but the tone was somehow different. Why did Abraham-Leib need to
remind him that he had to say *kaddish* in memory of his mother's *yahrtzayt* the
seventh day of Shevat? More than anything else, he was upset by the news that
his sister was ill and might be visiting him. How would it look, he thought, if she

were to arrive and find, instead of him, his friend Grisha?! He broke out in a cold sweat at the thought. He would have to write a long letter home insisting that none of them should dare come as no Jew was allowed to stay over night. Would it ever be possible, he thought, riding in the sled, to be left alone so he could say he had lived at least one year like a human being, without fear of tomorrow, without thought of a residence permit, and without humiliation dogging every step?

Humiliation was fresh in his memory from the time he started at the *gymnasium*, before he had become close friends with the real Grisha Popov. He remembered how he had been tormented. His name, Hershke, provoked such merriment, as if God knows what humor lay in that name. The teacher himself loved to poke fun at his name. All the other students were called upon by their family names, but he was called upon by both his names: Hershke Rabinovitch (Rabinovitch alone was not enough!). Only the laziest did not box him across the nose, pull his ear, poke him in the ribs, hit him on the back of the neck and across the shoulders, or set out a foot to trip him, or lay him out flat on the ground and smear pork fat over his lips. It was the smearing of pork fat on his lips that actually sealed his friendship with Grisha Popov. It so happened that Grisha Popov chanced upon the scene of the "Jewboy" Hershke lying on the courtyard ground of the *gymnasium* as a large group of boys stood over him shouting, "Let's have the pork fat! Pork fat! Let's rub it into his kisser!" With one loud whoop, Grisha Popov, whom they all knew and respected, dispersed the entire gang, rescued the "Jewboy" Hershke from their clutches and chastised the troublemakers as well. "Aren't you ashamed to force someone to do something his religion forbids him to do?"

That was the first time. The second time his friend Grisha rescued him from a far worse fate. Besides being a "Jewboy," Hershke was at the top of his class. His classmates knew they had to turn to Hershke whenever there was a stiff exam. Hershke knew everything. "Listen here, Hershke, how come I can't get the answers no matter what I do?" Or, "Here, Hershke, write down the answer, but make sure no one will know it's yours . . ."

Before a test he was besieged by them. And at the exam itself they almost tore him apart. This particular time, the faculty had given the class an examination that no one but Hershke could complete. Understandably, all eyes were turned toward the "Jewboy" Hershke. At first they only stared hard at him and winked to get his attention. Then they began to signal him with their fingers, or whispered and made odd sounds with their lips. Then they began to pass twisted bits of paper notes up to him. Hershke tried to satisfy everyone to the best of his ability. First, he took care of his friend, Grisha Popov, and after that, the others. The examination would have gone as smoothly as any other examination had not the devil himself interfered. Something happened for which no one was to blame.

As if our Hershke were cursed by fate, God had sent him a classmate, one

Kotyelnikov, already of marriageable age, who had been left back in the same grade for the second year. He could not seem to advance on his own at all. He had to be dragged forward by his ears. And since this Kotyelnikov was bigger, the teacher seated him in the back of the hall where he would not disturb the younger students. As a result, his twisted paper note reached Hershke late. Neither winking nor coughing nor shuffling his feet did any good—his note didn't come back soon enough. In a rage, he scribbled a new note but was too impatient to pass it along. He angrily flung the note directly at Hershke and hit the director smack in the beard instead. The director, wasting no time, picked up the note, straightened it out, and to his astonishment read these words:

LOUSY JEWBOY! YOU GAVE EVERYONE ELSE IN THE CLASS THE AN-
SWERS EXCEPT ME. JUST YOU WAIT, I'LL BREAK EVERY BONE IN YOUR
BODY!

KOTYELNIKOV

A dreadful scandal ensued. The whole class was punished, the teacher received a blot on his record, and the Jew—well, one can imagine. He was, after all, the guilty party. Rabinovitch would surely have been expelled from the *gymnasium* had it not been for his friend, Ivan Ivanovitch Popov's son. Miraculously the scandal was quashed and forgotten, not a trace left of it. Apparently, having the right name was no small matter, and family status carried weight.

But this was neither the only nor the last trial that our true Rabinovitch had to endure before he graduated from the *gymnasium*. There were many other ordeals he had to suffer before receiving his diploma and the medal, of which he was never certain until the end: would he get it or not? "And where did it get him, that medal?" he thought. The result was that they slammed the door to the university right in the pretend Rabinovitch's face even with his medal. He was politely told to please enroll as a dental student. If not, Reb Hersh Bar Moshe, you can put one foot in front of the other and march straight back to Shklov province . . .

And the pretend Popov was reminded of his friend, the real Popov, and of the letters he wrote about his troubles and he thought, 'Well, Grishutchka? Now do you know what it's like to be a Jew? I'll bet you've learned your lesson, and, if you don't change your mind before this year is out, you will learn not to play such games any more.'

These were the thoughts of our Rabinovitch-Popov as he lay sprawled out in the wide sled, only snapping out of them when all three troikas pulled up to a halt in front of the train station and the entire family poured out, Feoktist Fedoseyitch Bardo-Brodovski, his children, and all the teachers, the hound, Glyuk, leading the way.

THE POWER OF A NAME

In the same three capacious sleds drawn by the same three spirited troikas, the family Bardo-Brodovski sped off from the train station toward home, their newly arrived, long-awaited guest in their midst.

The first to announce the news that Sasha had arrived was none other than Glyuk, whose keen sense of smell detected Sasha from the moment her dainty foot stepped on the platform from the first-class car. Glyuk's joy knew no bounds. He expressed his happiness rapturously with much yelping and barking and hurtling himself clumsily between Sasha and her parents, until Feoktist Fedoseyitch had to remind him several times, "Glyuk! *Blaybst Ruhig*" . . . But it was useless. How could Glyuk be calm when this most welcome guest had suddenly arrived as unexpectedly as if dropped from the sky? *They* were lucky, *they* knew Sasha was coming; *they* had received a telegram the day before, *they* were lucky to know the very hour and minute when she would be arriving. But Glyuk? How could he know that he would at that moment be picking up the familiar scent of his dear friend Sasha, the same Sasha he had always loved as long as he could remember and who had always loved him? It was Sasha who had fed Glyuk big pieces of chocolate. It was Sasha who had petted him, stroked him, tickled him, and stolen kisses when Glyuk was still such a small puppy he could walk under the table. It was Sasha who had taught him a whole repertoire of tricks no other dog could boast of. Why would anyone have been surprised that, after she had left, Glyuk had gone around for days on end in a state of confusion? His canine mind could in no way comprehend what had become of the one who had pampered him, fussed over him, and played with him more than all the others. Glyuk had sniffed in every corner of the house searching for her. He had become downcast and almost stopped eating. Lying on the floor, with his snout buried in his forepaws, he would often see Sasha in his dreams, and his canine heart would weep silently. He could not tell anyone of his sorrow, nor did anyone have it in his power to comfort him. Was it any wonder that Glyuk was now so elated that he was almost beside himself? Was it any wonder he was nipping at his own paws for joy, rolling on the ground and leaping as if he wanted to jump out of his skin?

Glyuk's joy was even greater when he saw that his friend recognized him and had not forgotten him, as he had not forgotten her. She had remained devoted to him as he had to her. Oh, dearest, dearest! Now he was leaping almost higher than her head. Now he was stretching himself out full length on the ground before her! Now he was licking the tips of her fragrant little shoes! Now he sprang up and somersaulted three times, yelping, as if to say, "Why are you humans so calm when we have such a guest, such a beloved guest—Sasha!"

But none of the humans paid any attention at all to the dog; they were all preoccupied with the guest. Each one looked her over carefully and told Sasha that in the short period of time she had been away she was greatly changed, had grown up, become prettier. Sasha's cheeks, which were always like rosebuds in May, blossomed at the compliment, "Hasn't she become prettier?" Sasha herself knew she was pretty. Nevertheless, it was always pleasant for a girl to hear it again. She greeted each one of them as one greets an old friend, bestowing a word, a laugh, a joke, a comment, or a smile. But when she was introduced to the new tutor, Grigori Ivanovitch Popov, she barely accorded him a glance from her lovely eyes—but it was a searching glance which took him in from head to toe, and then she quietly asked her mother, "A Georgian?"

"No, dear, not a Georgian, but a Russian, named Popov," her mother answered, also quietly, and Sasha resumed her chattering, laughing loudly and joking as she joined her parents in their sled, the rest of the family and entourage following behind as the three troikas galloped back home.

"So that's Sasha, eh?" mused the tutor Popov, who was so taken aback that he had not even had time to look her over properly.

He was not taken aback so much by her beauty, which far exceeded her portrait, as by the fact that he could have sworn he had seen her somewhere before, but he could not remember where or when . . .

All the way back he did not stop thinking about the newly arrived Sasha: how would it be if he were the real Popov? But he couldn't keep his thoughts from veering off to the letter he had received that day from his older brother, reminding him when he was supposed to commemorate the anniversary of his mother's death, informing him of his brother-in-law, whom the authorities were throwing out of his home, and of his sister, who was planning to come for a consultation with a specialist. He couldn't help but feel resentment at all those "happy" bits of news from home. He was not allowed to put out of his mind for even so much as a moment these troubling images of which they kept reminding him lest he forget.

But that he himself wished to forget troubled him even more. Why should he wish to forget what was happening at home? How could he permit himself to forget that he was a guest here for only a short while? How could he permit himself to forget, when he and his friend, Grisha, had arranged what was no more than a trivial hoax soon to end with the new year? No matter how seriously it was still taken by the true Popov, the hoax no longer made any sense to him, the false Popov. On the contrary, this free, open, secure, happy life among these fortunate, self-assured people might bring him to the point where returning to his former Jewish life would be a thousand times more difficult and unbearable than before. What good was this hoax to him? Why did he need this jest? What good could possibly come of it? But the image of the newly arrived Sasha kept reappearing as he felt a flow of warmth in his heart, like that of a man who has been deep in thought and is suddenly reminded of something that is very dear and close to him about which he has forgotten.

Having arrived home from the railroad station, the family gathered at the table, where Sasha was the center of attention. All eyes were on Sasha, everyone listened to Sasha, everyone turned toward Sasha. And Sasha managed to do many things at the same time: she talked, listened, ate, laughed, questioned everyone and answered everyone without fail while granting Glyuk a pat on the head with her tiny hand, whispering affectionately to him, as one might to a child, while pursing her lips, *"Dusya!*—My sweet!"

Glyuk was obviously pleased with her attentions and kept restlessly inching closer and closer to the guest, likely feeling that Sasha had come home for his sake alone. The hound was so insistent, he had to be taken by the ears and unceremoniously ushered from the room. But it took no longer than it does to write these words before Glyuk was again lying next to Sasha's small feet, now quiet and chastened, but glancing sideways a bit resentfully, as if to say, "It's about time they knew I wasn't one of those dogs that needs to be ushered out by the ears . . ."

Not only Sasha but the rest of the family were also carrying on a lively conversation. Each member of the family had something to say. Even Fetya and Seryozha had stories to tell. The only one not speaking was the Russian tutor, Grigori Ivanovitch Popov. As always, he observed what the others were doing, and even more, listened to what they had to say. As always, he was impressed and envied them, not so much for their wealth or their style as for their unforced vivacity, openness of spirit, serenity, confidence, security, and ease. Could a Jew ever feel this way, even the wealthiest, the most fortunate Jew? Perhaps a long time ago, he thought, his ancestors might have felt like this in their own land, on their own soil, perhaps in King Solomon's days.

But where had he seen this Sasha before? How much she resembled her mother, like two peas in a pod, especially the eyes. And how the name "Sasha" suited her.

The name "Sasha" occupied the highest place in his thoughts. A strange warmth flowed through his heart and through every part of his body whenever someone mentioned or he himself thought of the name "Sasha." That name, he imagined, rang with a special sound. It was a musical name, "Sa-sha."

The power of a name!

the seventy-seventh chapter

FLEETING HAPPINESS

With Sasha's homecoming, the Bardo-Brodovskis' household reached new heights of liveliness.

A series of festival days went by: first Christmas, then New Year's, then Baptism Day—for each holiday Sasha herself planned the events in which she included the whole jolly company of teachers, governesses, and, naturally, Hersh Rabinovitch-Popov among them.

How could he keep himself aloof from that fellowship when Sasha herself had invited him, granting him a look from her wonderfully beautiful eyes and laughing in so playful and lively a fashion that he would have given his life for another of those looks.

In short, it was all such lighthearted, mischievous fun that from the very first day everyone was drawn in. Even a grande dame like Nadezhda Feodorovna and even the heavy-set, awkward, burly Feoktist Fedoseyitch found themselves behaving foolishly along with the rest, engaging in childish games and repeating silly tricks. In this happy household adults frolicked like little children, enjoyed themselves like little children, and were as happy as little children.

For our hero, Rabinovitch, who continued artfully playing the role of Grisha Popov, it was all astoundingly new. He could never have imagined his father, Reb Moshe Rabinovitch, taking time to dance or play hide-and-seek and other games with his children in the middle of the day. He could never have imagined any Jew being so happy, allowing himself for no special reason in the world to break out into laughter and make a fool of himself. Never, not even during Purim or Simkhas Torah, those holidays when one is *supposed* to be joyful, when Jews become drunk, could he remember his father allowing himself to become overly joyful. On the contrary, he remembered him, after a few glasses of wine, going off by himself in a corner with a worried look on his face, or perhaps even breaking into tears—he did not know for what reason. Was it because of the destruction of the Temple in Jerusalem centuries ago, or because his own father, whom he always referred to as a "remarkable Jew," had died over thirty years ago?

Having now been drawn into this household, amidst all this happy confusion that went on for weeks on end, the false Popov felt his breath taken away, the ground spinning beneath him. He began to forget he was a Jew. Into the bargain, he found himself among people in a household where he expected that Jews were reviled, yet the word "Jew" was never so much as spoken, as if these people did not know there existed in the world something called a Jew.

Once only did he happen to hear this word mentioned, and it shook him to the core. It was in the midst of the winter holidays. "Tatiana's Day," it was called. Sasha had planned an outing in the Russian style with swift troikas to go shooting or hunting or to go off to the ravine where young people from the city gathered to have a good time. But it so happened that Tatiana's Day fell on the seventh day of Shavat, the very day Hershl Rabinovitch had yahrtzayt for his mother and about which his brother had been nagging him in almost every letter. In the three years since his mother's death, he had never missed going to the synagogue to say kaddish on her yahrtzayt, not out of piety, but because he had promised his father to do so and because he had very much loved his mother. She was the only one he had missed and wished to be with when he came home on vacation every year. An unusual bond, a touching devotion had existed between mother and son. When he would arrive home, he would not leave his mother's side, as if wishing to make amends for the pain he had caused her when he had run away from home to study, causing the poor woman to turn prematurely old and gray. She could not comprehend how it was possible for her child, her Hershl, to pick himself up and fly off like a bird without a word to his mother. She had never berated him for it, but he himself realized what a sin he had committed against her and wished to atone for it. And he succeeded; his mother forgave him after his first return home. She had no need to mention it. Between them words were not necessary. Couldn't he tell by her smiling face and moist eyes? His mother's dying wish, conveyed to him by his father, that her Hershl vow to say *kaddish* for her, was hence especially meaningful.

A few days before the *yahrtzayt*, he had risen early and, hiding his face behind his large collar lest he run into a Jewish student who might know him, slipped into the synagogue and told the sexton that he would be having a *yahrtzayt* soon and requested that he set out the proper candle. All the while his teeth were chattering with fear. He imagined the sexton, a short Jew with full, red cheeks and a long, white beard who reminded one of these decorative gnomes found in gardens, was looking at him in an oddly suspicious way, as if he were an apostate or a convert but, in any case, not a Jew.

"Who are you, where do you live, and whose *yahrtzayt* is it?" the little sexton with the long beard asked, holding his head to the side and looking him up and down.

"What difference does it make?" Rabinovitch-Popov answered impatiently, glancing around to make sure they were alone.

"You don't want to say, you don't have to!" the gnome sexton said with a dismissive gesture of the hands and a shake of his beard. He then commenced to lock up the synagogue with great haste as if expecting thieves.

How could he have forseen that Tatiana's Day would fall right on the very same day as the *yahrtzayt* and that Sasha would get it into her head to send for the Russian tutor, Grigori Ivanovitch, informing him that the whole household would be going on a big outing that day?

There was no way poor Grigori Ivanovitch could get out of it, although he insisted he could not go. Of no avail was his excuse that as Tatiana's Day was also a university holiday, he had to spend it with his student friends. Sasha would not hear of any excuses. With her tiny hand she covered his mouth so he could not speak, all the while gazing at him and laughing so charmingly that he forgot the *yahrtzayt*, the vow, his mother in the *other* world, his father in *this* world, and even himself, and, of course, he surrendered.

But this is not the point of the story. It happened that as Sasha was convincing him not to forgo their merry company, another person, quite inadvertently, came out with a banal remark, a joke that was, as a matter of fact, often made in Russian society without intending to insult anyone in particular.

The joke was a lame one: "The merrier the company, the sadder the Yid."

The group laughed at the joke while our hero's blood turned cold: first, because of the word "Yid" itself, the painfulness of which can only be felt by a Jew. This word can be uttered by the finest Gentile with the best of intentions; nevertheless, it is perceived as a deep insult because it conveys unintentionally that you are a member of an inferior race. And second, he imagined that the one who said it did mean something by it. It had been spoken by the only person in the household he thought of as an enemy, who had appeared the very day following Sasha's homecoming.

He was a young officer, an aristocrat no less, a count with a hyphenated name, Shirei-Nyepyatov, and he was not called "Count," but "Pierre," shortened from Pyotr Mikhailovitch. It is difficult to say why, but this Pierre made the worst impression on our hero. He liked neither the demeanor of this "little officer," stiff as a ramrod, nor his smoothly combed hair parted in the middle, nor his pink, fresh, smooth little cheeks, nor his tiny, pointed moustache, nor his constantly smiling little eyes. Nor did he like the way he expressed himself, though Pierre's remark was typically Russian. He imagined that everything Pierre said was contrived, banal, and shallow, and whatever witticism he might utter was irksome. Perhaps this was because, except for Sasha, everyone in the house treated this Pierre like an exalted, highly esteemed, and most welcome guest. The servants stood stiffly and uncomfortably before him, and at his slightest glance fell all over themselves to accommodate him.

But what surprised and painfully disappointed the tutor Popov was the respect the refined, the good Nadezhda Feodorovna accorded this Pierre, being more attentive and friendly toward him than anyone else. "Can this be a possible match? . . . If not right now, maybe in the future . . . Yes, that's clear as day . . ." decided the student Popov, and developed a hatred toward this "little officer." He found himself incapable of looking at his well-scrubbed face with its thin eyebrows; he could not bear to listen to his high-pitched voice and shrill laughter. And the "little officer," for his part, instinctively (a heart knows a heart) had little liking for this dark-complexioned student, or, as he called him, "that eastern person."

Although everyone had to admit that Grigori Ivanovitch had a very likable appearance, Pierre had dubbed him with that name because he did have more Georgian, Armenian, or Greek features than those of a true Russian. Where would a Russian get *those* eyes and *that* nose!

"What? Is that true, Grigori Ivanovitch?" said Sasha, gazing at him warmly and laughing so kindheartedly that even if he *were* a Georgian, an Armenian, or a Greek, even if he looked like the devil himself, he would have been content to have her gaze at him that way and laugh.

What chagrined him most was that the idea of his being an "eastern person" came from no other than Pierre and that Pierre had spoken the word "person," he imagined, with a Yiddish accent. He felt his heart skip a beat. Did he really have such a Jewish appearance? Did he really speak Russian with a Yiddish accent? Could this "little officer" be ever so slightly suspicious of him?

That is why he was so unsettled when he heard the banal remark and the word "Yid" for the first time in the house. But his fear was unwarranted; Pierre was totally oblivious of him and couldn't care less about Jews, like everyone else in that house, which distressed the false Popov even more. It is not pleasant at all when you realize someone does not so much as notice you, does not give you a thought, as if you did not exist. On the other hand, Rabinovitch was terribly curious to know what opinion *they* did hold of Jews in this house. Even more, he wanted to know what she, Sasha, thought. He himself did not wish to bring the subject up—much too delicate. He preferred to stand at a distance as an outsider and listen to what they were saying. But as if out of spite, nothing was ever said about it, till by chance that comment was made. Only then did he have a good opportunity to convince himself how Jews were perceived, how Jews were thought of, and of what little worth the people God had chosen and blessed with the name "Jew" had. In the meantime, as he expressed it in one of his letters to his friend, the real Popov, he could, unhindered, "drink of that sweet cup called life . . ."

It was, to be sure, fleeting happiness.

the seventy-eighth chapter

THE PRINCESS

With Sasha's departure, the holidays came to an end and the daily routines resumed.

True, life didn't change all that much—the same house as before, comfortable and satisfying, the same large compatible group of people at the table. It was all as before, but there was no longer the same spirited liveliness. One felt something missing. Someone had left.

That "someone" was Sasha.

Nonetheless, when she had left, our Rabinovitch-Popov noticed that not a tear was shed, not a sigh was heard. If someone in this household did go around in a state of distraction, unable to find a spot for himself, it was none other than Glyuk.

It was heartbreaking to witness the dog's suffering. In his anguish, he sought out the Russian tutor in his room, where he stretched himself out on the floor, his eyes full of longing, as if wordlessly saying, "She's gone, gone again! . . ." And the Jew, who no longer had any fear of the dog, lowered himself alongside Glyuk and stroked his warm, smooth, steel-colored fur, comforting him. "I know how you feel, Glyuk, I know for whom you are longing. It's all right, there's someone else in this house who misses her too . . ."

Our Hersh was once again reliving in his mind all the happy moments of the last few weeks that had flown by like a dream for him, like one of those wondrous magical tales he had heard as a child when he was studying in *kheder*. No one knew where these tales came from or whose imagination had created them. Perhaps they were born right there in that gloomy classroom. They were usually told in the time between the afternoon and evening prayers, when the rabbi had gone off to the synagogue and it was pitch-dark in the schoolroom. The young students would huddle in a corner like little sheep and would listen intently as one of the older boys with large, thoughtful eyes began speaking quietly and soothingly, like running water:

"What kind of story do you want me to tell you today, children? If you like, I'll tell you a story about a princess from the land of Offir. The land of Offir should be familiar to you from the passages we just studied. The land is far, far away on the other side of the impassable river of the Sambatyon, beyond the legendary mountains of darkness. There, as you know, live the remnant of the ten lost tribes. God had blessed them so that they would not ever know sickness, misfortune, evil decrees, poverty, or any other woes. That's why they are all wealthy and money is as plentiful as rubbish. The streets are paved with the most expensive jewels, called jacinth; no one even pays attention to pearls because they are as common to them as hay is to us. But then something happened: their king, from the tribe of Levi, died, leaving two sons and a beautiful daughter. The sons could not agree on how to divide the inheritance. Both wanted to ascend the throne to rule. For a long time they waged war against each other and shed much blood. One fine morning the ten tribes, after talking it over, took the brothers captive, bound them hand and foot, and asked: 'What shall we do with two brothers for whom the world is too small to live in together?' An answer came: 'We must send them to heaven. Maybe there they will have more room. Let us find a tall tree and hang them from it.' That is what they did and peace reigned. From that time on they didn't have a king. What was to be done with their sister, the princess? One called out: 'You don't know what to do? I'll tell you! Take her far, far away to an island in the middle of the ocean. Let her live there to the ripe old age of a hundred and twenty years and let them not say of us that we shed innocent blood.' And that is what they did. They took the princess far, far away to an island in the middle of the ocean, built for her a palace of pure crystal covered with fine gold, and left her full chests of riches. 'Here remain. Eat, drink, and may it go well with you.' She did remain there, that beautiful princess, all alone on the island in the middle of the ocean, waiting to be rescued by someone who might have lost his way and landed on her island. He would take her back to the land of Offir, marry her, seat her on her father's throne, where she would rule over the ten tribes.

"In the meantime something else happened: a great rabbi and miracle worker of our region learned from a holy spirit about the outrage the ten tribes had committed against their king by hanging his two sons and, above all, against the beautiful, innocent princess. He sent for one of the finest young men studying in the synagogue and said to him: 'What is your name?' The young man told him thus and so. The great rabbi said: 'Listen well, my child, to what I will ask of you. What if someone were to tell you to go on the other side of the Sambatyon, beyond the mountains of darkness to the land of Offir, where the remnant of the ten tribes are living without a king to rule over them—what would you say to that?' The youth pondered in silence, a sign that he agreed. The miracle worker said to him again: 'And you know the law. You must first cross the ocean and find an island on which stands a gold-covered crystal palace. A beautiful princess lives in that palace waiting to be rescued.' Again the youth was silent, a sign that he agreed to this too. The miracle worker went on: 'And as soon as you bring her to the land of Offir, you will wed her according to the Laws of Moses and Israel. What do you say to that?' The youth turned red with embarrassment, a sign that he wasn't refusing. The miracle worker then said 'In that case, my child, here is my staff and my shawl and my alms box. Go and be successful . . .' Where to go, he did not tell him, and to ask was not fitting. When such a person says go—you go, especially when he gives you his staff and his shawl and his alms box . . .

"And here the real story begins—how the youth made his way, the misfortunes he had to endure, his adventures along the way, and the miracles performed by the holy man's staff, shawl, and alms box, each miracle in its own time, serving its own purpose. And it was still a long way to reach the princess."

It appeared that the young boy with the thoughtful eyes who was telling the interesting story about the princess would be a while in reaching her even if he were to tell the story for a year straight, which was too bad, as the rabbi would soon return and Hershl really wanted to know what was going to happen to the young man. Would he reach the beautiful princess? He imagined he would, and his own fantasy filled in the rest. He pictured the faraway island in the middle of the ocean, the gold-roofed crystal palace, and the beautiful princess in such sharp and vivid detail that he felt he knew her as well as he knew himself. He even knew what kind of eyes she had, what kind of hair, how she was dressed, her voice, her words, her laugh—everything, everything. And he imagined himself to be that young man who had gone off to seek the beautiful princess. They were fated for one another and they would go off together across the ocean back to the land of Offir, where they would arrive safely and would be married according to the Laws of Moses and Israel. What amazed him about this story was that the beautiful princess he had pictured in his mind had now materialized as a real, living person in the form of Sasha.

The fact that he had known this girl before seeing her almost drove him mad, and he became a fatalist, beginning to believe in the most impossible things. He allowed his fantasy to carry him further and further, transporting him ecstatically to paradise, where he envisioned the most beautiful and brightest images. And he asked himself, "Can it be possible that those dreams I dreamed so long ago are coming true?" But no, he did not want to think about it now. He did not want to know what *might* be, what *could* be, he was content with what had already happened.

And what had happened? This is what had happened.

*   *   *

One evening they were all playing one of their games. As part of the game, he happened to be seated at the far end of a room, not alone, but paired off with Sasha, a chair next to a chair. In another room sat all the rest of the group, as their part of the game. It was the first time he had ever sat so close to her. He could hear her breathing. He could smell her perfume. But he sat as calmly as he could. He tried to pretend that sitting so close to her made no difference. It was no more than a game they were playing.

"Grigori Ivanovitch, why are you so glum? I don't like glum people, I like cheerful people," Sasha said straightforwardly, without a trace of irony, without a bit of coquetry, but candidly, because Sasha really did like it when people were cheerful.

"You are carrying a burden in your heart," she added seriously, granting him one of those glances of her lovely eyes for which he was prepared to die. But he restrained himself. "How did you know I was carrying a burden in my heart?" "How? Don't you know I'm good at reading another's thoughts like a book?" Sasha answered loudly, bending over and laughing her happy, resonant laugh that both gladdened and made one feel sad, that made one wish to laugh or cry because her laugh could be a good-natured laugh issuing from a generous heart or, when she desired, it could convey something entirely different. How could he be sure she wasn't laughing in derision or out of a wish to ridicule? But no, let her laugh. Let her laugh!

And something else happened.

It was a cold, snowy winter night. The city was enveloped in white. The family Bardo-Brodovski was walking rather than riding home from the theater. They had grown tired of going by sled. At the theater they had sat in three loges. In one loge sat the father, mother, daughter, and Pierre, and in the other two loges, the teaching staff, including Grigori Ivanovitch Popov-Rabinovitch. But his heart was in the first loge. He was in agony. Not only was *he* not sitting there, but the "little officer," whom he could not bear to look at, was sitting right next to her. He was barely able to sit through to the end and was happy when Pierre left with a group of officers for his club. The family Bardo-Brodovski sent the horses home and proceeded by foot over the hard, frozen snow two by two. In front, wrapped in sables, walked Feoktist Fedoseyitch with his Nadezhda Feodorovna, behind them the teachers and governesses and, taking up the rear, Sasha and the Russian tutor. Sasha kept chattering and giggling, and the tutor listened more than he spoke.

"How do you like the count?" she said suddenly, grasping his arm, as was her way, while changing her tone abruptly from the greatest gaiety to the greatest seriousness.

"What count?"

Sasha raised her eyes to look at him and they stopped walking for a moment.

But at this point one of those in front joined them and the conversation was interrupted.

Was Pierre really a count? It had never occurred to him. Of course, that explained a good deal. The parents loved their daughter, they wanted to see to it that she married well, and therefore they had to match her up with a nothing of an officer because he was an aristocrat, a count. If her heart didn't desire the count, her parents wouldn't hear of it. That's the way it has always been and that's the way it is likely always to be . . . an old story, as old as the world!

* * *

That same night, the pretend Popov wrote a letter to his friend, the real Popov, and as always, poured out his full heart to him. Without being specific and without identifying people by name (Grisha Popov also wrote to him in the same circumspect way), he confessed that now he realized he had been a fool when he had warned him, Grisha, that he was playing with fire, that he was involving himself with someone not of his own kind. Now he saw how foolish it was for the brain to command the heart, for reason to dictate to the emotions. He ended his letter:

> . . . Do you remember, Grisha, how I once told you about a princess, a great beauty, whom I knew and who dominated my feelings for years even though I had never seen her? Well, I have met her in real life. Do you know what I will tell you, Grisha? Life is not as ugly as I had thought. Being alive is worthwhile. Life is worthwhile, it's worthwhile, it's worthwhile! . . .

the seventy-ninth chapter

HIS STOCK RISES

That year the winter was cold and long, longer than any other year—but time did not stand still. The weeks passed, and the calendar, page by page, moved closer and closer to Easter.

The family Bardo-Brodovski counted off the seven weeks of Lent and, along with all the staff and servants, went to confession, as is the custom of the Russian Orthodox. Only one member of the household failed to go, and that was the Russian tutor, who fortunately was able to get out of this religious observance thanks to the fact that, in general, things had been going very smoothly for him. He was unaware of how high his stock had risen in this house.

Besides being genuinely liked by everyone, from the youngest to the eldest
("Such a young man is a rarity among today's students," Feoktist Fedoseyitch
had said. "Such a pleasant young man," Nadezhda Feodorovna had added),
luck was on his side. It so happened that Feoktist Fedoseyitch had bumped into
the rector of the university at a ball, where he thanked the rector for having
recommended the tutor.

"A fine young man, very fine. I am pleased. Very pleased!" said Feoktist
Fedoseyitch, warmly squeezing the rector's hand. The rector almost melted with
delight at having been of service to a good friend.

"You have good instincts when it comes to people," Bardo-Brodovski granted
him a compliment, and again squeezed his hand, ready now to be done with
him. But the rector was so taken with the compliment that he took his arm,
drew him closer, and, with a smile that spread to his sideburns, asked, "But do
you know who this student is?"

"Who?"

"I will tell you, but on one condition: give me your word it will remain between us. I myself gave my word. It is—you understand what I'm saying—a dare,
a bet . . . a secret, a family secret . . . ." And with his smile now engaging his
entire face and speaking quietly, intimately, the rector revealed the secret. When
they parted the rector again reminded him that it had to remain between them
because he had given his word and "a word has to be kept."

You understand, Feoktist Fedoseyitch did not tell the secret to anyone except
his wife, and Nadezhda Feodorovna confided the secret only to her daughter,
the daughter told the count, and the count told all his friends and officers at the
club, finishing his news with "If not for this information, I would have bet a
thousand to one that he was a Yid . . . Who would have guessed he's a real
Popov, one of those Popovs who—"

"Does he play Baccarrat?"

"Who the devil knows!"

"If he does, bring him around . . ."

* * *

Rabinovitch-Popov was not mistaken when his heart told him that the
count, Pierre, was being considered as a future husband. Everyone in the
household knew it, but no one spoke of it. And if they did speak of it, it was
in total secrecy and not before the children. Only the parents desired this
match to be made. But the match was even more desired by Pierre's parents,
the old count, Lieutenant-General Mikhail Andreyitch Shirei-Nyepyotov, still
a robust cavalier who wore spurs and had a thick, gray moustache, and his
wife, Yulia Vladimirovna, an old ruin and spiritualist who was stone deaf and
had to use an ear trumpet.

The two old folks adored Sasha and had no fonder hope than having her as
Pierre's bride. Not immediately, of course: Sasha was still too young, and
Pierre had yet to establish his career, which he would in due time accomplish.
In the meanwhile it was necessary for the children to get to know one another

better. As soon as Sasha came home for the holidays, the old count gave
Pierre official leave from service for a bit of a "rest." And though Pierre was
not that eager to drag himself home (it was far livelier at headquarters), when
his father gave an order, he had to obey. Although Pierre was an only son,
very much pampered by his mother, his father was a strict military man of the
old school and believed in discipline. He had only to write his son three
words: "Come for Christmas"—and he had come. Now it was approaching
Easter and he would write, "Come for Easter," and he would come. And as at
Christmas, Pierre would likely spend most of Easter at the Bardo-Brodovskis'
rather than at home. The general's old wife, Yulia Vladimirovna, would, as
always, wish avidly to show off her handsome, pampered boy, the lone survi-
vor of three, who had remained close, faithful, and obedient. He would come
home for Easter, would kiss her and go off to his fiancee. She would not see
him again and she would be content to pray to God for both of them. Ah, the
poor old woman was mistaken. She thought that Pierre was as eager for the
match as she, his old mother, who adored Sasha. She thought that Pierre was
attending Sasha day and night, never going to his club, never playing Baccarrat. How could she guess that the old general was secretly paying his own and
his son's debts from her estate? If the truth be known, the old general himself
was not above gambling at cards, though he never played at his son's table—
God forbid! He was, after all, of the old school and believed in strict discipline . . . The old man played Baccarat, but with his old colleagues.

     After this aside, it will be easy to understand why the Russian tutor was
looking forward to Sasha's homecoming at Easter far more than her fiance,
Pierre. The tutor was not merely looking forward to her arrival, he was counting
the weeks and days and hours. With every page torn from the calendar, a weight
was lifted from his heart as the day drew closer to . . . to what? Don't bother to
ask him, for he himself did not know, he himself had no idea what was happening to him. He would open his right-hand desk drawer, remove an ordinary
unbound book from it, and place it under his pillow before going to sleep. But
before placing it under his pillow, he would first press it to his heart, then to his
lips, and kiss it passionately. Then he would slip it under his pillow.

     What was happening to our Hershl Rabinovitch? Had he gone out of his
mind? And what sort of book was he kissing and placing under his pillow?

     It was *Anna Karenina,* the famous novel by Tolstoy. Imagine! And not only
because it was the famous novel by the great Leo Tolstoy, but also for another
reason: this very novel had been brought home by Sasha. Traveling home for
Christmas, she had been reading this novel. Sasha had been reading this same
novel. Do you understand? Sasha's hands had held this very book. Her fingers
had turned these very pages. her thoughts had been absorbed with the ideas
Tolstoy had put in this very book. Her heart had felt the joys and sufferings of
the heroine, Anna Karenina, and now he had that book in his possession. She
herself had given it to him. He had asked her for it and she had given it to him.
Shall we not allow him this pleasure? You will say it's foolish. But which of you,

when you were young and in love—try to remember—which of you did not kiss the handkerchief, the glove, or the flower your beloved had accidentally dropped?

You will say it is a form of idolatry? But it is sweet, sweet idolatry . . .

Moreover, he knew that Sasha was as aware of what was in his heart as the idol is aware of who is bowing down before it, and yet he was ready, were he not ashamed to do so, to take the book, Sasha's book, raise it on high like an idol and proceed to prostrate himself before it, and heaven forbid that she ever learn he had done so. No one would ever know that Hershl Rabinovitch, now called Grigori Popov, was so dangerously smitten that he actually worshipped an idol . . .

the eightieth chapter

HE CANNOT SLEEP

Who knows what other foolishness our false Popov would have perpetrated if he had been allowed to follow his own way and had not been diverted, from the one side by his older brother, the melancholy Abraham-Leib Rabinovitch, with his too frequent and overly depressing news from home, and from the other side by his friend, the true Popov, with his naïve, almost childlike discussions and hair-splitting nonsensical disputations.

It was as if the two had conspired to make his life miserable: his brother with his unending tidings of new woes, oppressions, and persecutions of Jews and with his polite insinuations about modern young people who "for the sake of a uniform with gold buttons are prepared to renounce their parents, God, everything," and his friend, Grisha, with his frequent philosophizing about "the eternal problems of the eternal people . . ."

His brother wrote him about a Jewish *gymnasium* student, a poor widow's son from a small nearby town, who, in order to get into the university, had converted secretly so that his widowed mother would be spared the knowledge of it. How would she have been able to withstand the humiliation?

"Fine!" wrote Abraham-Leib Rabinovitch in his letter, "so he's gone over to the other side! To the Jewish people he's as good as dead. Whoever has to say *kaddish* over him or tear his clothing in mourning, or shed a tear for him will have to suffer for it. But if that weren't enough, that fine young man convinces his younger sister, a nice young woman and a *gymnasium* student herself, to become a midwife. But she doesn't have a residence permit and they were about to expel her from the city. So her brother, as a true friend, suggests that she do as he did, but she doesn't want to. She has pity, she says, on her mother, an old, sick woman who might not survive the news, God forbid. The devoted brother thinks it over and tells her that if she doesn't do as he suggests, he will immediately send off a letter to their mother and confess what he has done . . . To make a long story short, he changed her mind. A girl, what did she know? What do you think happened next? No sooner did she do as he had said than she regretted it, and bitter quarrels broke out between brother and sister. Maybe she said something to him and he answered, a word here, a word there—in short, she went and poisoned herself. The poor sick, widowed mother came running, found out the entire truth, retured home, and without any further ado dropped dead on the spot."

"So, what do you say, Hershl, to your kind of young people?" Abraham-Leib's letter ended. "So, is it worth it? Find out about this clever fellow. His name is Lapidus. He's blond and is something of a distant relative of ours: his mother and our brother-in-law Velvel-the-*shlimazel*'s mother were second cousins."

Naturally, Hershl didn't answer his brother's letter, but the brother would not drop the matter. In every letter he repeated again and again the same story and asked him if he had yet met that fine relative, Lapidus. What did he look like? And what did he say? Abraham-Leib nagged him until finally Hershl had to answer him. He begged him to stop pestering him about this devil-knows-what-kind-of-relative, this Lapidus, whom he had never heard of! He ended his letter a bit softer with "He's not the first, and he won't be the last. No tragedy, one less Jew . . ."

But in his heart this story nagged at him. What ever made that Lapidus drag his sister into it? Above all, what was so important about having her becoming a midwife? Weren't there enough midwives already? Midwives and dentists were as plentiful as stars and sand!

He intentionally steered his thoughts to another subject in order to avoid thinking about the main point—what Lapidus had done. But his conversion burrowed into his mind and didn't allow him to sleep.

By comparison, his letters from his friend Grisha were like a dessert. Apparently the real Popov was undertaking a serious study of the Jewish question from all sides. He was always coming up with new ideas, or so he thought.

The real Popov could not fathom at all what kind of people the Jews really were. They had not a drop of ambition in them, allowed themselves to be trodden down, spat upon and insulted at every step. They stubbornly insisted on remaining Jews, hoping that in time a Messiah would eliminate all their problems and liberate them, their children, and grandchildren from their exile in one fell swoop.

"Wouldn't it be a thousand times easier," the letter went on, "for you to liberate yourselves of your own free will, change your odd dress and outward appearance and enrich our country with a few million talented, useful citizens, enjoying equal rights? Instead you insist on going down the same miserable path you have been on for a hundred years. Whom are you trying to impress with your stubborness? What are you trying to prove?"

To this the real Rabinovitch replied as every Jew would when they heard that refrain about "liberation." "Don't worry too much about us. Jews have survived worse problems and they will continue to."

Then the false Rabinovitch took a new tack. He liked Doctor Herzl's idea. "Zion" was the only way out for the Jews. To renew the ancient Jewish nation with a state on its original soil in the land of their ancestors—what could be finer and nobler and more practical? But he didn't understand, he wrote, why this exalted program had not yet been embraced by Jews all over the world. He did not understand why, instead of striving for an independent life, Jews sacrificed themselves over such foolishnesses as a gold medal or a diploma.

"Is it possible," he ended his letter to his friend, "that you are not in your heart a Zionist? If that is so, what kind of Jew are you? Oh! If I were you! If I were a real, not a pretend, Rabinovitch, I would place myself at the very forefront of such a movement and would inculcate this sacred idea, first in the young students, and then in the rest of the people. Oh! I would show the world what Jews are made of and what Jews can accomplish!"

To this he received the following reply from the true Rabinovitch:

> My dear Grisha!
>   From your latest letter it is plain to see you have come under the influence of Zionist friends. But I must discourage you, my dear friend, and tell you the truth. Your friends are fools if they believe that Zion is the only way for my unfortunate brethren. It only demonstrates that they are overzealous patriots, but they do not comprehend that this people is not the same as all other people. Sociology teaches us that a people is defined by three elements: a land, a state, and a language. Our people has managed to exist without a land and without a state for hundreds of years. Do you know why? Because we have no land and no state. We are not afraid of anyone. What can they do to us? Take away the land we don't possess? Destroy the state we don't have? We are, if you want to know, an extraterritorial people, a people without the external trappings of nationhood. We are pure spirit, pure idea—and an idea lives forever. Don't worry about our destruction, do you understand me?

This is what he wrote to Grisha, but in his heart he felt it was no more than an empty show, no more than rhetoric. If he were the kind of Jew his friend Grisha imagined, he would not need to wait for his friend, the Gentile, to remind him of Zion. It seemed both comical and humiliating.

And he spent his nights lying on his soft bedding in his luxuriously furnished room, covered with a silk blanket, tossing and turning. He could not sleep.

Perhaps you have a cure for such insomnia?

AN UNEXPECTED DISCUSSION

Winter had long passed.

The beloved Easter holiday, to which Rabinovitch-Popov was so looking forward, was fast approaching, and she who reigned over his sweetest dreams was once again home.

The Bardo-Brodovski house revived, and Glyuk, the dog, was once again crazy with joy and rapture. What was going on in that house! Baking and cooking, cleaning and polishing; bag after bag was arriving from the market as preparations were underway for the happy, blessed holiday. Everyone's face shone, everyone's eyes glowed, and more than anyone's, Sasha's. Her voice rang louder and clearer, her laughter resounded more than anyone else's. Sasha had brought home countless gifts. Most of them were, of course, for her little brothers, Fetya and Seryozha—a whole arsenal of toy cannons, pistols, and soldiers as well as telephones, gramophones, photography equipment, and airplanes.

For the teaching staff, she brought something special for each one: for one a golden egg, for another a cigar holder, a medallion, a silk scarf in the latest style, and for the Russian tutor all the works of Tolstoy richly bound. Grigori Ivanovitch was a devotee of Tolstoy. For the servants she brought a storeful of haberdashery and yard goods, not forgetting a one, and oh! what joy, what laughter when she distributed the gifts! As usual, in the midst of these festivities was the rambunctious Glyuk. Although he had received no more gift from the special guest than a pat on the head, he was happier than anyone and exhibited his joy more than all of them, for which he was rewarded with being unceremoniously escorted out by the ears.

In short, the house once again took on the same atmosphere as the previous winter when Sasha had come home from school, and there ensued once again the same lively, happy festive days with their multitude of games, excursions, music, dance, recreations, and other diversions. But where was the Russian tutor? Where was Grigori Ivanovitch? Why wasn't he to be seen? He would only join them at the table, downcast, barely speaking, and forcing an occasional smile, but it was plain to see he was restless and uneasy. No sooner did people get up from the table than he was gone. No. Something was amiss with him.

. . . .

However much the pretend Popov tried to forget Jews and Jewishness, however hard he tried to separate himself from his Jewish world, however much effort he exerted to forget that the "Jewish exile" did exist, from which a Jew could never be free anywhere, except after death, his efforts to forget that reality were in vain and utterly wasted once the news of the blood libel surfaced on the front pages of the press . . .

The truth is, the real Hershl Rabinovitch had never for a moment stopped being a Rabinovitch. Like every Jew who takes a Russian newspaper in hand and whose eyes immediately seek out the word "Jew," so Hershl Rabinovitch-Popov would daily scan the pages for that magic word. Whenever he would find it, his heart would pound, but he would force his eyes to skip over it until he could return to that word when no one was looking, and he would secretly read everything that was written about Jews. It was all old, familiar, oft-repeated news about Jewish quotas, Jewish deportations, Jewish expulsions, Jewish restrictions in the army, in schools, in jurisprudence, and so on and so forth—all those things to which Jews have long been accustomed and on which Gentiles battened.

He was experiencing the pain of one who had been reviled, but he was determined to cover it up and forget about it. He could do nothing about it, nor would taking it to heart make things easier, especially since he had constantly to wear a mask and be afraid of revealing his identity and thus betraying the secret.

When he had first read the horrible account of what had happened to the Gentile boy in the large city of the Pale and the suspicion that it was the work of Jews, he felt some slight shame, but no more. As a Jew, he knew of the delusion, the barbaric folly called *"alilas-dom,"* or blood accusation, with which they had been slandering his brethren for years. But he also knew that Jews laughed it off because *as Jews they knew what a ridiculous, misguided falsehood this was.*

The only thing that troubled him was the fact that this deed had happened in the very city where his friend Grisha Popov lived under his, Rabinovitch's, name. He noted to himself that when he next wrote Grisha a letter he would ask him about this matter. But when it came time to write, he forgot all about it.

Imagine then how stunned he was when he was reminded of this story by no other than Feoktist Fedoseyitch Bardo-Brodovski!

Feoktist Fedoseyitch, who hated talking about politics, especially at the table, one time allowed himself at tea time to touch on this story, but in the same tone he would have used if he were talking about a horse who had taken first prize, or a new athlete who was coming from London, or a dirigible that had passed over the city, or something else having to do with sport. But by his tone it was clear that he himself, as well as the rest sitting around the table, were convinced that the story was absolutely true.

The only one who exhibited the least doubt was the French teacher, Monsieur Dubois, but his German colleague, Herr Frisch, quite earnestly and with a broad smile dimpling his shiny red cheeks explained to him that Russian Jews were not at all like French or German Jews and that Russian, especially Polish, Jews were so uncivilized that they still needed a Passover sacrifice. He ended his explanation with a wink to his colleague, "Gregoire Ifanofish," and expected that he, as a Russian student, would know it better than all of them.

Grigori Ivanovitch, who was already sitting on hot coals, felt his anger rising to the boiling point and he vented his bitter heart on the German's head. He did not speak directly to him but posed a general question: How was it possible that modern, civilized European people could still believe such wild, foolish, long-outdated nonsense reeking of the moldy past, of medieval fanaticism, of boorish ignorance? How could people bring to their lips words that were a disgrace in a respectable house for respectable people to hear and a sin, a crime, to repeat in front of young children?

Those unexpected, impassioned words spoken by the Russian student who suddenly came to the defense of the Jews shocked the entire household, and more than anyone, Feoktist Fedoseyitch, who fixed his gaze on the Russian tutor.

"Seems like such a quiet young man," he mused, "so modest, and suddenly, what sharp teeth! And over what? Over Jews . . . Strange!" Fetya and Seryozha also stared at him in bewilderment: what was going on with their teacher? They had never seen him like that. And even Glyuk, who had been lying at the student's feet and certainly did not understand what was going on, sensed that his new friend was agitated. He got up, stretched, and moved on to someone else. And so all those at the table became involved in this unexpected discussion. Almost all of them agreed with the German. The only one siding with Grigori Ivanovitch was the Frenchman, Monsieur Dubois, charmed by the Russian tutor's hot temperament, and the good Nadezhda Feodorovna, who, wishing to keep peace, supported the Russian tutor, but in such a way that the German would not come out altogether in the wrong, said, "I feel that Grigori Ivanovitch is correct. To persecute people for having a different belief is not honorable. But," she turned to the Russian tutor, "I would like to know one thing, Grigori Ivanovitch. Do you know them *personally*, these Jews? Do you know even one Jew? Ach! They must be dreadful . . ."

Had three buckets of cold water been poured over him, they could not have more quickly cooled off the heated student than did those several soft, naive words of the good Nadezhda Feodorovna. What could he answer her? "I can't say. Of course, I really don't know any Jews—how would I know any? But I am well acquainted with their history and their literature and I have never come across so much as a word, a hint, or a trace of what they are babbling about."

He felt himself seething within and his voice trembled, but he kept himself as controlled as possible, speaking calmly and with the smile of a disinterested observer, a passerby who had seen a disservice done and was pained by it. But he felt that his words were excessive and unappreciated. Perhaps he should not have said anything at all. And he deeply regretted having started up with that German, the devil take him! But to his defense came none other than the German himself, who spoke in his broken, incorrect Russian.

"Very well said, Nadezhda Feodorovna, and very well said, too, Gregoire Ifanofish." The German pronounced his approval and asked permission to relate an anecdote. And though it had little pertinence to the subject being discussed and though the anecdote itself was shallow, evoking more of a yawn than a smile, it was a good remedy for smoothing over and helping to forget the unexpected discussion.

SHE IS AFRAID OF THEM

The inhabitants of the house did not return to this disagreeable discussion till Sasha came home for Easter. And it was the German teacher, Herr Frisch, who brought up the story at the table, indicating that "Gregoire Ifanofish" was of the opinion that the account in the newspapers of the ritual murder was no more than a myth—ho-ho-ho!

"Who says so?" asked Pierre, who had appeared on the second day after Sasha's arrival and was sitting at the table on Sasha's left.

"I say so!" said Grigori Ivanovitch loudly because he was sitting at a distance from Pierre and wanted to be sure he was heard. He was determined once and for all to speak up and express fully what had been building up in his heart since he had arrived and that was such a hellish torture for him. Let the chips fall where they may! How long could he keep silent? It was time to speak out! It was high time to open their eyes, to show this smug, lucky, self-confident household that it was criminal to dismiss with a wave of the hand an entire people who were trembling, bleeding, wrestling with the Angel of Death and who desired only to live and to be accepted as equals. Above all, he was most anxious to show up this "little officer," whose face revolted him. He wanted to prove to all of them, and especially to Sasha, what an ignoramus he was, this glib, polished count with his aristocratic posturing. He had long been waiting for an opportunity to put him up against the wall. But Pierre didn't appear eager to take on this "dark student" who had the temperament of a Georgian and the face of a Yid or an Armenian, though he was Popov's son. Pierre did not so much as honor him with a glance and leaned over to Sasha, who had heard the tutor's "I say so!" and showed interest. She turned to the student and said, "Grigori Ivanovitch, what are you talking about?"

Grigori Ivanovitch brightened, felt a strange warmth, and his heart began to pound. That was exactly what he had wanted, to hear *her* opinion—that alone was worth everything. He felt that in her he would find a sympathetic supporter, friend, and ally. He was certain that this fine, gentle soul would sooner side with him than with that vacuous count, who had nothing in his head but thoughts of dressing up, standing erect like a yardstick, and jingling his spurs—ach, how he hated him!

Grigori Ivanovitch leaned as far forward toward Sasha as he could and, enunciating each word as calmly and confidently as possible, said to her, "We are speaking about Jews, Alexandra Feoktistovna, about Jews and about . . ."

"Oh, no! No! Don't speak about those . . . those . . . I'm afraid of them!"

And Sasha threw her head back and shook both hands as one shakes off something disgusting, but it looked so childishly naive and so charming that the entire table broke into laughter. The first to laugh was Monsieur Dubois, who understood the least of what was going on, but the loudest laugh belonged to the German teacher, Herr Frisch. He threw his head back, the veins bulging in his fat neck, and his shiny face, already flushed from too much beer, became even more florid. One feared that, with his complexion, he might suffer a stroke.

. . . .

As Grigori Ivanovitch rose from the table with the others, he felt a rushing in his head, and a veil seemed to cover his eyes. Sasha's words rang in his ears, *"Don't talk about them—I am afraid of them!"*

She was afraid of them? . . . And her mother, the good Nadezhda Feodorovna had once said, *"They must be dreadful!"* Ach, what an abyss! What a deep gulf between human beings when such good, refined souls as these two could express themselves in that way! These were good, gentle souls who could not bear to hear a mean word, who turned away from an angry face! He looked from mother to daughter and from daughter to mother and was reminded of something he himself had witnessed a while back. Each of them had removed jewelry—the mother two diamond rings and the daughter a precious bracelet—and had given them to Pierre to bring to his father, the old count, who was collecting donations for the hungry.

"What would they say," he thought, "these two good, gentle souls, if they knew how many hungry, desolate, dejected, humiliated, and abandoned people were to be found in their very midst, who have starved all their lives yearning for a crust of bread? And not only yearning for a dry crust, but yearning for simple dignity; they yearned for a kind word, for a ray of sunshine, a little fresh air, a bit of education, if only the Russian alphabet, the basic Russian alphabet. . . ."

And he remembered another incident he had witnessed.

It was some time ago, at the beginning of the winter. They were all ice-skating. He was standing to the side observing Sasha skating with the French teacher with his curled moustache, with the German teacher, Herr Frisch, with his shiny red cheeks, and with Pierre, whom he could not stand. Glyuk was also on the ice—how could there be a happy outing without Glyuk? Suddenly they heard a loud racket. Screams mingled with the yelping of dogs. Someone fainted. It took a good two minutes before they could make out what was happening. A minor tragedy was being played out before them.

The main actor in this tragedy was Glyuk. There were other actors as well, other dogs but much smaller than he. There was one dog in particular, an appealing, high-strung little animal, one of those aristocratic rare breeds for whom some hire a special caretaker and who might be bathed in champagne. It had white, silky fur, black, angry little eyes, shaky legs, and the face of a monkey, its tiny lower teeth protruding. You can imagine how much one must pay for such a prize. A fight had broken out among the dogs and they had bitten one another badly. Glyuk had inflicted such serious injury on this tiny aristocrat that it had barely came out of it alive. Glyuk himself hadn't counted on that happening. By the way he was standing and licking himself, and by the odd look in his eyes, he seemed to be saying, "Maybe I did something foolish, but it's too late now." The mistress of the injured little dog, a Russian official's daughter, fainted, and Sasha, who was holding the injured dog, was tearfully and silently sobbing. Later, when she told her mother what had happened, one could see tears in the eyes of both.

What made him remember this story now? His eyes sought out Sasha and he saw her standing at the piano with the Frenchman, who was asking her to play something, but she demurred. How would it be, Rabinovitch-Popov wondered, what effect would it have if he were to take her aside to speak no more than a few words to her? He would beg her pardon for not speaking before—he had not been able—but now he had to tell her the whole truth, now he would divulge a secret, and only to her, to no one else—*he was one of those of whom she was afraid* . . . But there she was, coming toward him with her bright, happy face and friendly smile.

"Grigori Ivanovitch, let's play a game of Trik-trak."

the eighty-third chapter

ONE SHOCK AFTER ANOTHER

Where was his good sense? Where were his eyes? Where was he looking and what was he seeing?

He realized that whatever had happened until now was no more than a dream, a fairy tale about a princess from the land of Offir.

He realized he had been peering through a thick, iron gate into a strange garden where, through dense, magnificent trees and beautiful, fragrant flowers one could barely discern the outline of a splendid palace. All the rest, how the palace and the happy people living in it looked, was a figment of an imagination that had made it possible for him to picture a beautiful princess who reigned over him in the land of Offir.

He realized that but for the fortunate happenstance that had led to the exposure of their true feelings, thus opening his eyes and making him aware of how he stood with them, he might have gone too far, have been carried away to the point from which it would not have been easy to return. He blamed no one but himself.

In no way could he forgive himself for behaving like a child from the very first day he had stepped into this strange world, for instead of using this opportunity to defend his brethren, as a loyal son of his people would, spreading light and driving away shadows, he had stood by like a disinterested observer, had sat as a guest without burning anyone with the fire of his words, without poisoning anyone with the venom of his bloodied soul. And even when he had tried to speak up, he had quickly regretted it, afraid they might be suspicious of his true motives and who he really was.

He could not forgive himself that, at the same time he was deceiving strangers who believed in him, he was also deceiving his own family, writing them one falsehood after another, each greater than the one before. He lied to his old, gullible father, telling him not to be offended because he couldn't come home for the holidays; in the dental school where he was studying, Passover time was the busiest time of all. He was not to be upset because he had arranged to attend both seders in two fine homes, the best families in the city, and he should rest assured that not a crumb of *khometz* would, God forbid, pass his lips. Oh! If the simple, honest Reb Moshe Rabinovitch had only known *what* his son had eaten this Passover, *where* his son had been on Good Friday and on Easter Sunday when the churchbells were ringing, or on the following morning when he had exchanged kisses with everyone, from the stout Feoktist Fedoseyitch to the tall, clean-shaven butler—and all this for what? On account of a schoolboy's prank, on account of a dream, on account of a fabled princess from the land of Offir. But you must forgive him—he had already paid for his sins many times over. Fate had seen to it that with every day the fires of hell grew higher and hotter, each day bringing him a new surprise, one disaster after another, one shock after another, one bombshell greater than the next.

The newspapers entertained him daily with still another item of news and still another editorial on the famous blood ritual in the large city in the Pale. These fine items of information, as bitter as they were to him, he could have swallowed and forgotten. But God sent him a good friend, the German Herr Frisch, who was habitually intrigued by sensational newspaper reports of all sorts of crimes. He always brought the same ugly story up at the table, directing his comments to the head of the household in his broken Russian: "What do you think, Fuktist Fedoseytch, about the terrible ritual murder?"

Feoktist Fedoseyitch, who much preferred to talk about happier things, either remained silent or changed the subject. But the tutor's other good friend, Pierre, egged the German on, saying he was convinced that soon enough they would expose the whole Yid network that had spread across the land and perpetrated "such things."

"Ach! How good it would be," thought Rabinovitch-Popov, "to hurl this round wine flask in his face, to punch him, to maim his well-scrubbed face, to poke out an eye, to split his skull in two!"

"Grigori Ivanovitch!" He heard from the other end of the table Sasha's voice, which sounded like music to his ears. "Grigori Ivanovitch! What's the matter with you? What's eating you? You look like someone who, for the life of him, cannot remember what he dreamed last night . . ."

All of them laughed, Grigori too, but what he was feeling while doing so, only he and God knew.

On top of it all, the news arrived that, in the city where the "ritual murder" had taken place, they were expecting "a merry time" and that Jews were fleeing. It had been a long time since he had seen that wonderful euphemism or read the word "pogrom" in print anywhere.

In the vestibule of the Bardo-Brodovskis, piles of newspapers and journals from many countries and in many languages lay strewn about. Each resident came and took the one he or she wanted. There he found the French Monsieur Dubois, the German Herr Frisch, and the English Miss Tokton, each with a suitable newspaper. Sasha was there as well, dressed for a stroll but leafing through the illustrated pages of several journals.

It was a lovely morning, one of those beautiful early days at Passover time.

He wanted to put down his paper but could not. He read: "THERE IS TALK HERE OF A POGROM. JEWS ARE FLEEING BY THE THOUSANDS. FEAR IS RAMPANT . . ." An image came to his mind that he had not forgotten nor would ever forget:

—A small shtetl . . . the beginning of winter . . . he, a bar-mitzvah-aged boy, secretly memorizing geography . . . his older brother, Abraham-Leib, also a bright lad, constantly bringing news from the city: "Jews are talking . . . Jews are fleeing . . . they say it will definitely happen . . . it's probably already started . . ." "What should we do?" "We must flee." "Where to?" "Wherever our eyes take us . . ." They started negotiating a plan. Abraham-Leib suggested that both sisters go to the station master's, he and his father to the priest's, and the mother and Hershl to the police commissioner's, or rather, the police commissioner's wife, a fine Gentile woman who had offered sanctuary. But the mother refused to go. "Do you think I am out of my mind? Am I going to entrust my daughters to the station master?" Abraham-Leib, who was always agreeable, said, "If that's the case, let mother and Hershl go to the station master's, both sisters to the priest's, and father and I to the police commissioner's wife." Again the mother said, "Oh, sure, I'm about to fly off with my daughters to the priest!" Agreeing as always, Abraham-Leib said, "If that's the case, let's change the plan: father and I to the station master's, mother and Hershl to the priest, and the sisters to the commissioner's wife . . ."

In the end, neither the station master nor the priest nor the police commissioner's wife took them in—they were already full up. All of them, the father, mother, and children, were taken in by a Gentile neighbor, who locked them in a stable where they could hear everything that was happening in the town.

He remembered Abraham-Leib angrily pacing like a caged animal, bitterly complaining, in his usual quiet manner, about how he had been imprisoned. He should have stayed home where at least he could have bashed someone on the head with a wooden stave. "One for one, a death for a death!" Abraham-Leib declared, and his mother silenced him and begged him to take pity, if not on her, at least on the other children. The father prayed quietly all night . . . In a far corner of the stable someone was lying and groaning heavily, not only "Oy!" but "Oh!" or "Oho!"—groaning and then seeming to revive, "Oh! . . . Oho! . . . Oh! . . ." He imagined it had to be an old man with a long white beard, with a yellowed wrinkled face, toothless, lips sagging, eyes glazed over, a sick person, critically ill and perhaps, he thought with dread, even dying . . . Listening to his father's quiet praying and to the unknown person's groans—"Oh! Oho! Oh!"—our Hershl finally fell asleep. His mother had scraped together some rotted straw and laid it under his head and had covered him with her shawl. When he awoke, it was broad daylight, and he saw that the one who had been groaning in such an odd manner, alternately suffering and reviving, was not an old, dying man but a vagrant. "And this is where my father was praying?" he then thought. "Praying the whole night!"

. . . .

Shall we go for a stroll?" he heard a familiar voice say. He startled and saw Sasha putting her gloves on her small hands.

"Pardon! I was so deep in thought about politics I forgot you were here."

the eighty-fourth chapter

THE DEPARTURE

The worst blow of all came when Grigori Ivanovitch Popov found out *who* the suspect was in the case of the so-called "blood ritual."

That happened one morning when his colleague, the German Herr Frisch, a broad smile lighting up his chubby, red face, accosted him with a newspaper in his hand and in tortured Russian smugly informed "Herr Gregoire Ifanofish" that they had already caught the murderer and that he was, in fact, an educated person, a dentist named Rabinovitch (he accented the second syllable).

Grigori Ivanovitch had to find a chair on which to sit down or he would have keeled over. He took the newspaper from the German and read the account from beginning to end, not once but twice. He controlled himself. He did not speak a word, showed no reaction. On the contrary, he felt a strange lightness in the head and a rare clarity of thought. Suddenly it became clear why he had not heard from his friend Grisha in so long a time. His head filled with plans on how to rescue his innocent friend from this entanglement. It was not only his duty, but from the article he realized that also he was the only one who could save him . . .

It was plain he had to go as soon as possible to the city where his unfortunate friend was imprisoned, to see for himself what had to be done. In order to leave, he would first need permission from the university. He wasted no time; not waiting for morning tea, he hurried to the university, his feet fairly flying over the ground.

Now it was also clear why he had not heard any news from home. How would they react when they read that same report! And what would they be thinking in Grisha's home after not receiving letters from him for so long? But perhaps Grisha himself had informed his father, Ivan Ivanovitch, where he was and what was happening to him. But no—he knew Grisha. Grisha would never betray him. Ach, but who knew what was really going on there! Who knew how much his poor friend was suffering! Who knew what was going through his Gentile mind and what he might blunder into saying? No, it was essential to go there, the sooner the better . . .

When he arrived at the university administrative office to request permission to leave, he was informed that the rector needed to see him urgently. Him? Why urgently? Could it be about the same matter? And he hurried to the rector's office.

On the way, he caught a few words exchanged between two Jewish students he knew but from whom he had kept himself distant, fearing they might sniff out who he was. The two were reading a newspaper, but when they spied Popov they hid the newspaper, and one said to the other in Yiddish, which he heard quite distinctly, "Don't say anything, it's a disgrace before that Gentile."

He knew very well what the two were talking about. For the first time, he truly wished to stop right there with those two fellow students to exchange a few words, especially in Yiddish, about this strange affair that was in truth "a disgrace before a Gentile." A disgrace and a deep-seated ache! Perhaps he could learn more news from them. What was being written? What was being said? What were people thinking? Who else but a Jew would know how foolish this was? Foolish and bitter . . . When Jews spoke together it became a bit easier to bear. But he resisted the urge and passed them, maintaining an outwardly calm manner without looking in their direction.

He then came across a group of half-Jewish students, former Jews, who were also whispering among themselves, but upon seeing Popov they too suddenly fell silent. He could have sworn they were also discussing that same affair. He felt his face burning with shame to see even these, who had torn themselves away from Jewish life and were living in their own little world, even these, whom he deeply despised as a Gentile despises a Jew, even these, who appeared in his eyes to be nothing more than provocateurs, nevertheless interested themselves in this event, which blackened the name of all Jews and made them hideous in the eyes of other peoples. And only he, the false Grigori Ivanovitch Popov, in reality Hershl Bar Moshe Rabinovitch, had kept himself at a distance like a bystander, as if he were not involved. Until today he had been living in his golden dreams, had been building castles in the air, fantasying about a princess from the land of Offir, serving idols at a time when his friend, the real Popov, was suffering for Jews, was a sacrificial lamb for another's people. "You deserve to be whipped, Hershl, to be hanged . . ."

* * *

The rector greeted him with the same open friendliness as always. He invited him to be seated, said he was glad to see him looking so well and hoped every-thing was in the best order. Thank God he had not brought up *that* subject. But then he rose, went over to the table and picked up a telegram, opened it, and read aloud that his father, Ivan Ivanovitch Popov, was asking about his son, Grigori, how he was, where he was living, and why he hadn't written.

"Understand, my dear friend," the rector said to him, stroking his sideburns while he looked closely at him, "that your father doesn't know where you live is easy to understand—a bet, ha-ha, no small matter. But that you haven't written, that's not right, young man. That's already . . . eh-eh-eh."

The student felt his mouth run dry. He coughed nervously as he spoke. "Did you answer him?"

"Well, of course! I answered yesterday, by telegram, naturally."

The student's knee began to tremble.

"By telegram? Wha-what did it say?"

The rector burst out laughing.

"What? Ha-ha! That you were well and strong, may we all be so. And I gave him your address, but just your address and no more. What he needs to know, let him know, but what is a secret must remain a secret, ha-ha. A promise is sacred. Ah, yes, we understand one another, young man, eh?"

So that was all? A great weight was lifted from his shoulders. And if that were the case, he did wisely in preparing himself to leave. He left with his permission in hand and returned home where yet another surprise awaited him.

"You have a telegram," he was greeted at the door by the tall, clean-shaven butler, who looked more like a governor than a doorman, and who handed him a telegram on a small silver tray. It was the first correspondence the Russian tutor had received in all the time he had been there.

The telegram was from Grisha Popov's sister and consisted entirely of three words: "ARRIVING BY EXPRESS. VERA."

Within half an hour the entire household knew that Grigori Ivanovitch had received a telegram and was going home. What was in the telegram no one tried to ask him, but by his rushing to pack and by his ashen face, it was plain to see that something terrible must have happened. They all sympathized with him, even those who didn't think highly of him. His blood enemy, Pierre, suddenly warmed to him, became soft as dough, offering him a cigar and asking solici-tously, "Are you leaving us?"

"I'm not leaving," he answered pointedly, "I'm just going home . . ."

That meant: "Don't be too happy, my dear count—we'll meet again."

The person who displayed the most concern about his departure was Madam Bardo-Brodovski. It was evident that the good Nadezhda Feodorovna truly pit-ied him. She deeply regretted that the tutor was leaving, if only for a short while.

"Sasha," she called to her daughter, who had just emerged from her room, "Grigori Ivanovitch is quitting us."

"Impossible! It can't be!" she exclaimed, granting him a look with her rare, beautiful eyes, for which he was prepared to forget all about his friend's sister on her way there, to forget his duty to his friend and, on the spot, right there in front of her mother, throw himself at her feet, kiss the ground she stood on, and confess the truth, the whole truth, let the chips fall where they may! They were both such good, gentle, devoted people that they would forgive him for not entrusting to them the secret that he was one of those they feared. They would understand that he was not responsible for having been condemned from birth to be ostracized from human society, a source of fear for those who have a false idea of what he was . . . that he was not guilty for the sin of his ancestors, who had the audacity to kindle the first light of divinity in the world and provide mankind with the first Book telling them what was good and what was bad.

"It can't be!" Sasha said again, and her mother explained that he was not leaving for good but for a few days—he had received a telegram.

"That's another story!" Sasha drew out the words and began laughing merrily. He imagined the world was laughing along with her, and he no longer heard what was going on around him. People were swirling about, many familiar faces, many familiar voices, and he was shaking everyone's hand. Fetya and Seryozha were throwing their arms around his neck. The dog also wanted to kiss him. "Glyuk! *Blaybst ruhig* . . ." Feoktist Fedoseyitch commanded, and with his huge hand he pulled him off by the collar, but the dog insisted that he wanted to sit in his friend's carriage. It would do no good, they would have to lock him in the house, let him scratch with his paws at the door to his heart's desire. The good Nadezhda Feodorovna bade a motherly farewell to the tutor, making the sign of the cross over him.

Too many people had gathered to see him off, too much commotion. He could not be alone with Sasha to say at least one word, just one word . . . Not until they were outside, when they were preoccupied with the dog, was it possible to stand close enough to Sasha to be able to say a few words to her.

"Good-bye—we may never see each other again . . ." And he imagined he saw her bright face cloud over and her bright eyes shudder beneath her lovely, thick brows. When Pierre came over at that moment to ask her something, he imagined she did not respond. "Serves him right!" he gloated. That "little officer" would regret it when he, Grigori Ivanovitch, would be gone because Sasha would pine away, a shadow of her former self, and not a soul would know for whom she was longing . . .

. . . .

"Dreaming once again? Fantasies once again? Once again the princess from the land of Offir?" he interrupted his own thoughts while sitting in the carriage racing to catch the train as quickly as Feoktist Fedoseyitch's spirited horses could get him to the station.

Within half an hour he was on the train that, instead of carrying him to T———, where the Bardo-Brodovskis imagined he was going, was taking him to the large city in the Pale to rescue his friend, the true Grigori Ivanovitch Popov.

the eighty-fifth chapter

THOU ART OUR BROTHER

The closer Reb Moshe Rabinovitch and his older son, Abraham-Leib, drew to the large city, the more often they heard Jews talking about that "pack of trouble" and the unfortunate *shlimazel* of a dentist held in isolation, not a living soul allowed to see him.

When father and son, who throughout the journey kept quietly to themselves in a corner, heard those words, they perked up their ears, hoping to hear more. But they would learn nothing new beyond the words "*shlimazel* dentist," "unfortunate victim," and other such epithets; they imagined people were making light of the situation, which distressed them greatly because they could not see what there was to laugh about.

More than anyone, they were infuriated by a redheaded Jew of small stature, a man with thick lips who spoke as if he were nibbling at something and laughed constantly, his eyes tearing with laughter. He had this complaint:

"No. I must say this. If only they had arrested a real Jew, you know, a Jew with sidelocks, but here we have a dentist, a complete Gentile who doesn't know a word of Yiddish. He can't tell a star from a crucifix. Oh, my sides are bursting!"

Father and son exchanged glances. Were they talking about their Hershl? How was it possible? Their Hershl didn't know a word of Yiddish, "couldn't tell a star from a crucifix"? Luckily his father was sitting next to him, for had Abraham-Leib been alone, a good fight might have broken out then and there. Abraham-Leib was a hot-tempered young man. As it was, he kept straining toward the redheaded Jew with the thick, nibbling lips, but the father held him back with a tug at the sleeve, "Sit!" And the poor young man had to sit in misery listening to all that poppycock, all lies and falsehoods. What could he do? He had to obey his father.

But they soon arrived, thank God. The passengers began collecting their baggage; only the Jews exited anxiously, breathing heavily, as one does before an examination, a conscription, or a trial. Some fingered their pockets, some their passports, others straightened their caps, carefully tucking their sidelocks behind their ears, doing everything possible not to affront anyone with their Jewishness.

But our Rabinovitches knew nothing yet of this kind of anxiety. They had not yet fully tasted the flavor of being in exile. Yes, they had heard that Jews were being driven out of this city, that there were roundups and Jews were sent back home by train within twenty-four hours of arrival, and other such fine things, but the difference between hearing about something and experiencing it is great. And as they were first-time travelers, they had eagerly hurried out and were among the first to rush from the train headlong into the great tide of the large city, almost deafened by the enormous din and bustle that engulfed them like an inferno.

"Where do we go first?" the father asked his son as he was jostled from all sides.

"Where do we go?" the son answered with the same words, and found himself face-to-face with a horse's muzzle and almost lost his footing. "Do you know what, Father, to the devil with all of this, let's take a cab."

"Where to?"

"First let's sit down and then we'll see where to."

"Maybe you're right," the father agreed.

Easy enough to say "take a cab," but they had lost their place in line and had been swept up in the tide of people and carried farther and farther away. Our poor small-town travelers were almost the very last and had to plead for a cab. And so, at the end of a long line of carriages, buses, coaches, and droshkies, one could see two Jews, one elderly with a full beard, the other young with a hint of a beard, all hunched up and bounced about in an old, lopsided droshky drawn by an ancient, emaciated, white horse. Had it not been in this large, glorious city where a Jew needs a residence permit, one would surely have thought they were being driven by a Jewish coachman. And especially if one had looked at the coachman from the front, not from behind, it would have become immediately apparent he was a Jew, not a Gentile. And if he had known this, Reb Moshe Rabinovitch would not have had to stumble over words in a language in which he was weak, and his son, Abraham-Leib, would not have needed to show how much of Kirpitchnikov's grammar he knew. After a half-hour of bouncing them about, the driver asked his passengers, in Russian, where they wished to be taken. Abraham-Leib told him in Russian to go directly to the dental school. The driver half-turned his head toward him and said, "There are two dental schools." But Abraham-Leib quickly cut him off and corrected his grammar, telling him that he had used a feminine article with a masculine noun.

For the first time during the trip the coachman turned full-face to his passengers and they saw before them—God in heaven!—a Jew! His eyes were Jewish, so was his nose, and so was his curly Jewish beard. But he was all decked out in a uniform complete with a Russian greatcoat cinched by a wide belt. Atop his head sat a typical smooth black Russian shako like a noodlepot. If not for the uniform he could have been mistaken for a sexton in their small shtetl synagogue rather than a coachman in this large, noisy Russian city.

"I could swear," the father said a minute later to the son, "that our driver is a Jew and not a Gentile."

"Let me try a few words on him and we'll soon know whether or not he's a

Jew," the son answered, turning to the driver, but he did not know precisely how to phrase his comment. To ask the driver straight out, "Are you one of ours?" would be too vulgar. To ask politely, "Permit me to ask your nationality," would be a bit much for a mere coachman, but the driver spared him the trouble. He again turned full-face to his passengers and spoke to them directly in Yiddish.

"You're going to a dental school? We have two or three of them here. Give me a name or an address so I'll know where to go, understand?"

"God bless you!" cried Reb Moshe Rabinovitch, delighted that the driver was Jewish. "So you're one of us? Why didn't you say so before? *Sholom aleichem!*"

He shook the driver's rough-skinned, calloused hand, which smelled of horses and resin, and Abraham-Leib, on his part, also extended a hand to him.

"Thou art our brother. *Sholom aleichem*—peace unto you."

"*Aleichem v'al bneichem!*—Unto you and unto your children!" the driver responded, now almost completely facing them, his black helmet pushed back revealing black curly hair on his sweaty, wrinkled forehead. The passengers questioned the driver thoroughly about who he was, where he came from, and how long he had been working at this job, and the driver in turn questioned them about who they were, where they were from, and what they were doing there.

Who they were and where from they gladly told him, but what they were doing they deemed imprudent to tell him. To say to a Jew "*sholom aleichem*"—well, why not? But to get involved with a coachman in personal matters—watch out!

"Maybe some business?" said the driver, trying not to pry, but attempting to make small talk.

"Maybe some business," they allowed.

"And maybe to the doctor?" the driver tried again.

"Maybe to the doctor," they both replied, thinking they were finished with him. But it turned out he wanted to know which doctor and for what illness.

The passengers realized they would not so quickly be rid of him, and so they decided they had better tell him the truth. Why play games? He was a Jew, just like them, what did they have to fear from him? And perhaps they might learn something from him. They didn't even know in which dental school their Hershl was studying or on which street he lived. Who would have guessed that this driver (a Jew, after all, is not a Gentile) would be so fully informed about the sad story of the blood ritual. He not only knew their Hershl but also knew well the people with whom he lived because he had driven them places as many times as he had hairs in his beard. At Passover, who had brought them to the factory to bake matzos and took them back home if not he and with this very horse?

"A fine young man, may I have a son like that! Is that really your own relative, poor boy? Giddyap!"

"God bless you!" the old man cried. "Then why are we wasting our time going to ask about him at the dental school? You can take us straight to where he lives."

"Of course I can take you straight there, why not? Giddyap! Do you mean you want to see him? I'm afraid you're wasting your time. I heard tell they don't let anyone at all see him. They're afraid someone might bribe the guards and that he'll escape because he's very rich!"

Both men looked at one another, and the older one said to the driver, "God bless you! Who did you say was very rich?"

"He, the one who is sitting in prison. You say he's a relative? He's very rich, they say—Giddyap! He himself is not rich, but they say he has very rich relatives, millionaires—Giddyap! We're almost there. Do you see that high wall there? In the second or third courtyard is where a Jew named Shapiro lives, a fine man, his wife, a God-fearing woman, and their charmer of a daughter, who is now staying at a dacha—Giddyap! But explain to me, please, you know better than I do, I'm a simple Jew, a coachman, and my coachman's mind can't figure something out: a young man studying to be a dentist, a respectable young man who can't speak a word of Yiddish? . . ."

Both passengers exchanged glances again, and the elder one asked, "Who did you say can't speak a word of Yiddish?"

"That very same relative of yours. What is he, a nephew, a cousin? A distant cousin? Whoa! Here we are. Do you see that bell? Pull the cord and they'll open the gate. You don't know how? Let me . . . How much do you owe me? This is my rate. You have no more baggage? . . . When do you figure, with God's help, to go back? . . . You yourselves don't know when? Nu, I understand, how would you know? If you need to go somewhere, please tell her, Madam Shapiro, she knows me, I used to drive her to visit her daughter at the hospital. Here is where I can be found most of the time, on the Jewish Street. A Jewish droshky should be found on the Jewish Street. As you yourself say, we are brethren. When you began talking to me in Russian, what did you think I was? A Russky? Ha-ha! The uniform is to blame. A fellow has to cover up the Jew in him so they won't recognize him—what can we do? We're on their turf, they're not on ours. Do you want the change, or are you giving me a tip? Long life to you! May God help you, may you succeed in whatever you wish. You're surprised I know what you're doing? I am, after all, as you yourselves said, 'thy brother . . .' and a good one!"

the eighty-sixth chapter

VISITORS

As if Sara Shapiro's tired shoulders were not burdened enough, God sent her two visitors—the roomer's father and brother, Reb Moshe Rabinovitch and his elder son, Abraham-Leib, or, as his young wife called him, Abraham-Leibush. (We will henceforth refer to him as Abraham-Leibush for her sake.)

The tall, slender father with deeply set worried eyes beneath a pale, wrinkled brow appeared delicate and frail. Each breath seemed to cost him great effort. Softly and pleasantly, he would intone "God bless you" whenever he spoke to someone. The son, a newlywed with a hint of a fine beard, was a strong, healthy, fine-looking young man, but quite gloomy and a bit impertinent; his father was more afraid of him than he of his father, or rather, both had a healthy respect for one another. The son did not blow his nose into a handkerchief as most people do, but with one finger pressed to a nostril he would empty his nose, the mark of an aggressive young man.

The visitors arrived at the Shapiros' house at noon, when David Shapiro usually came home for lunch, ate hurriedly, and ran back to work because "his time was not his own."

Of late, David Shapiro had grown accustomed to having strangers, newspaper correspondents and others, barge in to pester him about his roomer, the unfortunate dentist, who had gotten himself arrested. At first, David was pleased that people were interested in his roomer and wished to hear what he, David, had to say of the misfortune; but as time went by, it had become a nuisance, and he had to chase people from the door. If Sara had not intervened, there would have been ugly scenes.

When these two new strangers arrived, David almost sent them packing after the first *sholom aleichem*.

"*Aleichem sholom*," David answered curtly. "What's on your mind?"

"You had a roomer living with you—" the newly arrived visitors began, but David cut them off and completed the sentence.

"The dentist Rabinovitch? With me, with me. But what is it to you? Why do you have to know? And what good will it do you once you know? And who can benefit from it? Jews always like to poke around."

After this polite welcome both visitors remained standing wordlessly, at a loss to know what to do next. The son was eager to return the fine welcome as only he could, but the father held him back with a tug at the sleeve, and the feisty Abraham-Leibush turned aside to blow his nose hard with one finger while Reb Moshe Rabinovitch addressed himself to Shapiro gently but with a rueful smile.

"God bless you! If you would ask us our names and find out who we are first, you would spare yourself some needless aggravation."

"Very true," interrupted Sara, who had been standing nearby holding a platter of chopped herring and shredded onions made with vinegar and spices. The delicious, zesty aroma of the tangy herring permeated the entire apartment, so stimulating the appetites of the visitors that Abraham-Leibush swallowed loudly. "The man is absolutely right, absolutely! First find out who they are and why they've come, and then you can show off your temper."

Another time, Sara would not have gotten away with openly contradicting her husband, a true Shapiro, but this time he felt a bit guilty for lashing out at these strangers without even knowing their names, and he continued speaking to them but in a softer tone of voice.

"Well, who are you and why are you asking about the dentist, Rabinovitch, and where are you from?"

The older man lowered his head and said quietly, "The dentist Rabinovitch is my son and I am his father. This one here is also my son, the older one, the older brother of your roomer . . ."

Now it was the Shapiros who were speechless. As long as their roomer had been with them, they had never heard him mention that he had a father or a brother. They only knew of a wealthy aunt, a childless millionairess, and a sister named Vera. Other than that they knew of no other close or distant relatives. And suddenly standing before them a father and a brother! In her state of shock Sara did not know what to do with the platter of chopped herring, whether to lay it on the table or to take it back to the kitchen. David forgot that his "time was not his own" and, his eyes blinking nervously, he addressed the roomer's father.

"Pardon me . . . what was I saying? Yes. So, you say your son, Rabinovitch, is your dentist, I mean, that the dentist is your son? We had no idea, no idea at all that your son had a father . . ."

"God bless you," the elder man said with the same rueful smile, "every son has a father . . ."

"Well, yes, of course," David Shapiro felt his face flush, "certainly so, what else? I didn't mean that. I meant, you understand . . ."

"Never mind. Why do we need to go into that!" Sara broke in again, quickly depositing the herring on the table. "Tell me, my dear sir, what is your name?"

"My name? It is Moshe, Moshe Rabinovitch," and glanced at his son.

"Reb Moshe Rabinovitch," the son corrected him, and blew his nose.

"Well, of course!" Sara replied, "That fits—his name was Grigori Moiseyevitch . . ."

The elder man again lowered his eyes and spoke quietly.

"What did you say—Grigori Moiseyevitch? At home we called him Hershl and here he becomes Grigori, that rascal. At home I'm called Moshe, my passport says Movshe, and here I've become a Moiseyevitch! Modern children! Can better be expected?"

Sara was much more taken with her roomer's father than with the brother. She hurriedly offered both of them chairs. David as well became as attentive to the guests as if he had already asked them several times to be seated and had been refused.

"Sit, why don't you sit down?"

Both visitors seated themselves and began to question their hosts about their Hershl. How had it all happened and why had such a God's punishment befallen them? They in turn related what they had been through, how they had not received a letter for so long and thought they would go out of their minds with worry, how they had been arrested, questioned, and searched and detained for two days. Only after their release had they learned from the newspapers the true extent of the calamity—that the dentist who had been arrested was their own Hershl! And so they had come here to rescue him. Imagine, in a big city, with so many wealthy Jews, millionaires, how could they remain silent and allow a man to be locked up in prison on such a trumped up charge? How was it possible?

"Who would have thought," Abraham-Leibush added, "that something like this could happen in this day and age—a time of progress and civilization!"

"And I tell you, it's all stuff and nonsense! Listen, they arrested me too and put me through the same business as you and it's nothing more than nonsense, pure nonsense! A joke!" This was David Shapiro's opportunity to boast about how he had conducted himself, from the time he was first arrested to the present day. He told them all about the searches, the arrests, how many times they had dragged him before the interrogator, what they had asked him, and how he had stood up to them. What did he have to fear? "If you don't eat garlic, you can't smell of it . . ." He ended his narration, as always, with "The whole affair isn't worth this much," and he indicated the tip of his finger. "They'll hold him awhile and they'll let him go, in the name of God."

"Amen, may it be so!" Sara interjected. "Your words into God's ear! Meanwhile, your boy is locked up, that poor, delicate boy, so well brought up. They won't let a soul near him. You can't bring him food, he can't write a letter, can't smoke a cigarette. Who knows why? A person is doomed to suffer in this world . . ."

Sara brushed away a tear as the poor father wept on one side of her, his son on the other. They wiped their eyes and again bewilderedly asked one another how this could have happened. Where did it all start? Both Shapiros, speaking almost simultaneously, quickly related the story of their neighbor's stepson, who had been a friend of their Syomke, a brilliant *gymnasium* student, who would soon be coming home for lunch. They told them how their roomer, Rabinovitch, who had been tutoring Syomke, had also tutored the neighbor's stepson, not for money, God forbid—why did he need money?—but because of Syomke and Betty, their daughter, who was now convalescing at a dacha—a pity they couldn't see her, she was quite a girl, their Betty! . . .

"God bless you both!" the elder visitor interrupted. "You said my son didn't need money and was tutoring as a favor? What about those two wealthy homes where he was giving lessons?"

"What homes? What lessons?" said David Shapiro, and returned to his own story.

The visitors exchanged glances in amazement: What was it with these people? When they were traveling in the train they had heard these unbelievable stories about their Hershl, that he didn't know "a star from a crucifix," and now they were hearing that he didn't have any well-paying pupils in this city. What was going on? And the host, Shapiro—once he started talking about himself, it was impossible to stop him.

"Maybe that's enough now!" David finally stopped himself. "I have to go to work. My time, you understand, is not my own, I'm only an employee," he said to the visitors, and then to his wife, "Why don't you invite our guests to the table, they must be hungry. You know what they say, 'Don't dance before you eat and never ignore the belly.' Right?"

"Certainly. As long as a person lives. But this isn't an inn, God bless you!" exclaimed the father, and looked at the son to see whether or not he should accept the invitation.

"We came here for a purpose," said the son, not budging from his chair, an indication that he agreed they should stay for dinner.

"You don't need to worry," Sara said, turning to set two more places. "You won't be any extra trouble. The herring is ready, dinner is cooking. If two can eat, so can four. Go, David, wash up and call the guests in."

"Be so kind," David said to them, indicating the washstand, and washed first, as is the custom for the host. "Please make yourselves at home."

"God bless you!" the father said hesitantly as he stood up and continued to look at his son. "We don't even know one another properly. We don't even know who you are or how to call you."

"Nonsense!" said the host, muttering the prayer for the washing of the hands in haste, as usual, winking to his wife to warn her that she had better not say anything during his silent prayer that he would want to say. He made the prayer over the bread hurriedly so that he would be able to speak again. "Nonsense! Now we know very well who you are. Your son was not only our roomer but our friend, closer than most friends, one can say a devoted friend who had made a place for himself in all of our hearts, truly a beloved person! And who we are— you will soon know. I will just say one word: 'SLAVITEH.' Have you ever heard of Slaviteh?" David look at their faces searchingly.

"God bless you!" said the father, now washed and chewing a piece of the ritual bread with salt. "What Jew has not heard of Slaviteh?" And the son, still drying his hands and not permitted to speak yet, communicated with his eyes, "Pss . . . nu . . . oh . . . nu . . . Slaviteh!"

Before Abraham-Leibush sat down to the table, he again blew his nose with one finger, and the host and his guests dug right into the chopped herring and fried spiced onions, whose aroma wafted deliciously and temptingly throughout the apartment.

the eighty-seventh chapter

ONE SURPRISE AFTER ANOTHER

Once their host began to regale his two guests with his background, they felt honor bound to listen to his account of his impressive lineage. Though their hearts were elsewhere and it was not easy for them to tolerate other people's stories while their minds were preoccupied with their unfortunate

Hershl, it would have been disrespectful not to hear him out while sitting at his table.

"You mean to say you are from Slaviteh?" Reb Moshe Rabinovitch said, and both father and son looked at Shapiro as if what he was telling them was immediately relevant to their concerns and for which express purpose they had come.

David Shapiro began to chuckle like someone about to amaze the world with the revelation of his identity but at a loss to know where to begin.

"Have you ever heard the name Shapiro? Well, I know you've heard it . . ." And he swallowed his food hurriedly, brushed the crumbs from his beard, and blurted out, "Why drag it out and torture people? In short, I am from the true, the only Slaviteh Shapiros . . ." And David looked steadily at his guests in order to see what impact the name Shapiro was making on them.

That name should have made a greater impact on the guests than it did, and it is very possible that it would indeed have impressed them as Shapiro had desired had not Sara interfered—a woman remains a woman!—and begun playing her little tricks. Sara, who in the meantime had served the meal, wanted to know "only one thing": since the tragedy, how come no one had heard so much as a word nor seen any trace of that aunt, nor could anyone tell that she even cared that her nephew was being held in prison and might, God forbid, be there for who knows how long?

"I can't understand," she concluded, "what kind of aunt she can be. Don't be offended by my speaking so frankly, but she must not be made of flesh and blood, but of stone or iron . . ."

While Sara was speaking, the father and son looked at one another, and when she finished, Reb Moshe Rabinovitch stopped eating and said to her, "God bless you! What aunt are you talking about?"

"What do you mean what aunt?" said Sara. "About what aunt could I be talking? Naturally, about the rich aunt, the widow, the millionairess."

"What rich aunt? What kind of millionairess? What widow?" the father said, looking at the son, who added his few words:

"What are you talking about?" and he leaned over and blew his nose.

This did make an impact. David entirely forgot about his famous lineage and looked at his wife.

"'What do you mean?" Sara said to the guests in a higher-pitched voice. "What do you mean? Your Rabinovitch doesn't have a childless millionairess aunt for whom he is the only heir, may she live to be a hundred and twenty years?"

The father and son stopped eating and laid their forks down.

"That can't possibly be!" said the father, and the son added in Hebrew, "*Lo haya v'lo nivra!*—It is not and never was!"

"And never had one?" Sara asked, embarrassed to look at her husband.

"God bless you! What you mean never? He does have an aunt. Two aunts, three aunts, lots of aunts, but all of them are poor, not one a millionairess."

"Who told you such a crazy fairy tale?" added the son.

"He himself, your brother," Sara said, now quite upset.

"With those exact words, he told you, 'I have an aunt a millionairess'?" Abraham-Leibush asked again. Here Sara lashed out at him.

"Why are you grilling me like an interrogator, asking me what exact words he used? You know very well those couldn't be his exact words because your brother doesn't speak our language . . ."

"Then what language does my brother speak?" said Abraham-Leibush, glancing at his father.

"What is there to be ashamed of?" David broke in. "Nowadays there are enough such young people among us. Don't worry, your son isn't the only one who doesn't understand a word of Yiddish."

"My Hershl, you say, doesn't understand a word of Yiddish?" exclaimed the father, never taking his eyes off his son's face.

"Who told you such a bald-faced lie?" added Abraham-Leibush.

"A bald-faced lie? He himself, your brother told us, now do you know who?" Sara couldn't contain herself and was ready to tear apart this brash young man to whom she had taken an instantaneous dislike from the very first. "Or maybe you think we're making it up? You must know we aren't liars. Everyone knows who we are!"

Abraham-Leibush did not respond, but blew his nose with one finger. It was the elder Rabinovitch who replied.

"God bless you!" he said, and withdrew a thick wallet from his breast pocket. "A young man who doesn't speak a word of Yiddish doesn't write letters like these in our mother tongue . . . It's a pity I can't show you how he writes the sacred tongue, but we had a house search, and they confiscated everything from this wallet, including his handwritten, Hebrew letters, all in beautifully expressed Hebrew."

David and Sara gaped in astonishment, unable to believe their ears. What was this? A dream? Witchcraft? But they had to be respectful. No matter what, guests had to be encouraged to eat.

"Why don't you eat?" the host said to them in a sour tone, and the hostess added, "Eat, eat. One thing has nothing to do with the other."

"God bless you!" said the elder Rabinovitch, a bit put out that his son was being accused of not understanding Yiddish. "A fine story but a short one! You should hear how my Hershl recited *kaddish* for his mother, how he can polish off a *maftir* or a portion from the Prophets when he comes home for the holidays, or how he reads the Haggadah at the Passover seder . . ."

"The Haggadah at the Passover seder?" exclaimed David Shapiro, almost choking on his food. He looked disbelievingly at Sara and felt sick to his stomach.

Sara did not so much as touch her supper. All she kept thinking about was the millionairess aunt. That meant that her roomer, of whom she had thought the world, was a plain liar . . . God in heaven! Why did he have to make up such a crazy lie? "Sha, now we'll find out for sure," she said to herself, and turned toward the father (she hated the son and didn't want to have anything to do with him).

"Didn't you have a brother-in-law who was named Abraham and his father was called Abraham too? Abraham Abramovitch?"

"God bless you!" the elder man exclaimed. "How is it possible among Jews for a father and son to have the same name?"

"That's for Gentiles," the son added. "They can have a father named Ivan and the son also Ivan."

"We know that without your telling us," said Sara, unwilling to grant him so much as a glance. She preferred speaking to the father.

"Answer this for me, please. How many children do you have?"

"What business is it of yours?" an irritated David pounced on her. "Are you an interrogator or what?"

"Don't get so upset. Maybe I know what I'm doing," Sara cut him off as she again addressed the elder guest. 'I just want to know if you have a daughter Vera?"

"I? A daughter Vera? I have two daughters, may they be well, and they both have Jewish names, not Gentile ones. One is called Shifra, and she is, God bless her, quite poor, and the other is called Sara-Leah, and she is also not well-off and is, into the bargain, not well and needs an operation desperately . . ."

Sara remained even more troubled. It appeared that not only was he a liar but a swindler as well, because if he didn't have a sister Vera, who then was this Vera P? Or maybe he once did have a sister who died? There was still a spark of hope as she again directed a question to the elder man.

"Is it possible that you once did have a daughter named Vera, or Dvora, or . . .?"

"Sara! Will you ever stop this nonsense?" David assailed her loudly. "Did you ever see how a woman gets something into her head? What's the big difference, Vera or Dvora or Sosi or Dvosi? Better serve dessert so we can say grace. You know very well my time isn't my own, I have to go."

With a deep sigh Sara rose from the table, set out a small pitcher of water on a dish, and thought to herself: "It's just lucky Betty isn't here . . ." David poured some water over his fingertips and pushed the pitcher toward the guests.

"Gentlemen, let us pray!"

The guests began to sway in prayer, joining their host.

"Blessed be the name of the Lord henceforth and forever . . ."

"With the consent of our masters and our sages and honored guests seated here let us bless God whose food we have eaten."

"Blessed be our God whose food we have eaten and through whose goodness we live," the guests concluded in a sing-song, and, with the same melody, the three continued chanting the prayer, swaying back and forth, each one praying in his own way. The host ran through the prayer so rapidly that three locomotives couldn't catch up to him; Rabinovitch, the father, on the other hand, prayed slowly, enunciating each word carefully as if he were counting beans or stringing pearls, while his son, Abraham-Leibush, muttered under his breath in a little falsetto so that one didn't know for sure whether he was praying or simply singing a little tune. But the three kept glancing at one another, picking at their teeth, each one preoccupied with his own thoughts.

the eighty-eighth chapter

BRIBERY MONEY

Whoever thought Reb Moshe Rabinovitch had come to this large city to rescue his son with empty pockets would be very much in error. True, he did not bring any huge amounts. Nevertheless, he had been able to accumulate enough money for expenses with the help of a few friends and through his own resources. He had pawned his watch and his elder son's used watch of fifty-six-carat gold. Abraham-Leibush had been reluctant to part with this watch because it was a wedding gift from his bride. But in view of the town's eagerness to support them in their plight, "the ransoming of prisoners"—he had no choice. He took off the watch with its chain (not of pure gold, but of richly gilded silver) and surrendered it to his father.

Still and all, they managed to bring enough money for bribes, something only a man as respected and valued in his community as Reb Moshe Rabinovitch could have achieved. The shtetl rabbi had written a warm letter of introduction to the rabbi of the large city in eloquent, flowery language penned in a fine hand and in an excellent Hebrew, qualities rare in a shtetl rabbi.

He started his letter by offering a hundred blessings and a thousand good wishes to his colleague and to all Israel, may it be those in that city, may it be those in all the cities in the world wherever the children of Israel dwelt.

He then went on to pour out an apologia. How could a mere worm such as himself have the temerity to dare approach someone of his greatness, a veritable mountain, a mighty column reaching to the clouds on which all of Israel leaned? But as they were dealing with a matter of vital concern to all of Judaism, it had strengthened and emboldened him, and so on and so on . . . , Only then did he get to the matter at hand, depicting in every possible coloration the woes and persecutions Jews had suffered until that very day as long as they had been a people. No, this was not a letter but a sea of fiery rhetoric, a true masterpiece filling three pages that would move a stone. Best of all was the brilliant ending: "POUND ON THE DOORS OF OUR GREAT AND MIGHTY! AWAKEN MERCY IN THEIR FLESH! ISRAEL IS NOT BEREFT OF WEALTHY PEO-PLE WITH GOOD HEARTS! FREE THE PRISONERS AND TO THOSE

CHAINED, SAY: GET THEE UP! SHED HUMILIATION FROM OUR
PEOPLE AND MAY THE MOUTHS OF OUR ENEMIES AND FOES BE
STOPPED UP—Amen!"

Quite a letter. But before our Rabinovitches could get down to their task,
before they were able to make the necessary contacts in that tumultuous city,
they had to find a place to stay. David Shapiro assisted them in their search for
lodgings. But it did not go as easily as they had expected. In all the lodgings that
Shapiro took them to they were asked for documents even before they crossed
the threshold. Unfortunately, they could produce no documents. Not only did
they lack those documents especially created for Jews, called residence permits,
they had in their rush to leave failed to take along even an ordinary passport,
black on white, that every person must carry when he travels. What was to be
done? They had the choice of sleeping in the streets under God's sky or turning
around and going back home.

But among Jews there is always a solution. They were able to find a good
person, a poor Jew (poor people are always and everywhere more compassionate), who offered them a room, bed, and table and all he had for nothing, not so
much as a groshen. He said he wasn't running an inn, he wasn't making a living
from renting rooms. He made his living from something else. Reb David Shapiro
knew him; he was always at the Stock Exchange. Sometimes something worked
out, sometimes it didn't, but one managed . . .

This was our old acquaintance, Katz, whom we met in the Stock Exchange
cafe. Everyone called him "Ketzele" because he was a small man with short
legs.

Ketzele encountered the visitors as they were standing with Shapiro, who had
taken some extra time to help them find lodgings even though "his time was not
his own." He did not mind the few minutes he was losing but he was unhappy
with them over the documents and was berating them for it: "Even if you were
to chop my head off, I can't begin to comprehend how it's possible for mature
people, men with beards, to leave home without so much as a single legal
document, without a written piece of paper, and whereto? To this city of all
cities, where a Jew is in mortal danger!"

Both Rabinovitches themselves conceded it had been a foolish oversight to
have left without the proper papers, but they tried to explain their mistake,
saying their heads had been in such a whirl it was lucky they hadn't left themselves at home, never mind their passports. What had not gone on at their
departure! The entire town had been in an uproar!

Very fine. But David Shapiro did not want to hear any excuses.

"I don't care if your heads were whirling about seventeen times over and there
were eighteen uproars, a Jew has to remember that there is a law and there are
checkups . . ."

At that very moment, as if out of nowhere, Ketzele materialized.

"What's the matter? What's the problem? Can something be done? And who
are these men? Not from hereabouts? Where from? *Sholom aleichem* to you."

Any other time, Ketzele would not have been tolerated by David Shapiro: a

Jew walks by, let him go in good health, he doesn't need to stick his nose in where it isn't needed. But this time, pushed to the limit by his guests, David was relieved to have a third person intervene. Let someone else know what kind of crazy people there are in the world who are oblivious to laws and checkups and who think everything has to be prepared beforehand for their convenience—lodgings, residence permits, you name it . . . !

David Shapiro was waving his arms about so vehemently that he caught Ketzele right in the nose, accidentally of course. It was no one's fault he had such short legs and his nose was at exactly the same level as another's arm. Ketzele moved off a bit and said to Shapiro, "So, are you through? If so, can I also get a word in, eh?"

"Who said you couldn't? Even eighteen thousand words, but the most important thing is not to talk too long because I don't have time, my time isn't my own."

David Shapiro had not been counting on getting rid of his unpleasant guests so easily. Be a prophet and know that Ketzele, a poor wretch of a Jew who ran around trying to scrape up a few pennies, would suddenly become such a hospitable host.

"With pleasure," cried Shapiro. "Wonderful, but what about that other problem?"

"What other problem?" Ketzele asked naively. "You mean the bedbugs?"

"What bedbugs!" David waved his hands, "What bedbugs are you talking about! Who's thinking about bedbugs? What I'm talking about is the police. What if there's a roundup, God forbid? These men don't have permits."

Ketzele started to laugh. "Heh-heh-heh! What are you talking about? What police? What roundups? Peh! I've been living in the same place eight years with my wife and children, God bless them, *keyn eyn horeh*, and a mother-in-law into the bargain, without any residence permit—and nothing has happened! If a person always worries about such things, what kind of life would it be? Who cares? Roundups and police or noodles and onions—it's all the same to me—come on!"

"Fine!" said Shapiro to Ketzele. "If it's all right with you, it's all right with me," and to the guests he said, "Now don't forget to keep in touch and be well. We have lots, lots more to talk about! Don't take me wrong, but there's something not quite right with your story. It's all mixed up. Please forgive me for saying that, but it's all tangled up . . ."

Shapiro demonstrated with his hands how things were mixed up and entangled.

"God bless you!" Reb Moshe Rabinovitch said, plainly and pleasantly. "To us it's quite straightforward. It seems to me, nothing could be more straightforward," and he made a straightforward gesture with his hand.

"Maybe it's mixed up and tangled to *you*, I'm sure," added Abraham-Leibush impertinently, turning his head and blowing his nose.

"What an insolent young man!" Shapiro thought later on, after the guests and Ketzele had left. "Nothing at all like his brother. And the father? In my life I would never have said that this was our roomer's father! And where does he suddenly get a father from? It sounds very fishy to me . . ."

Do not think this thought had just occurred to him. Back home he had had the same thought, but his wife had addled his brain. When a woman starts mixing in . . . ! He felt the urge to turn back, to catch up with Ketzele and the guests, and to speak plainly and openly to them: "Tell me, Jews, are you perhaps mixed up with those crooks who falsely claim to have lost property in a fire and try to cheat others by making them pay for it? Those things have been known to happen!" But he had second thoughts: they could discuss it another time, there was no hurry. He would have another chance to talk to them, they would not run off before morning.

And David Shapiro went his way with hurried steps, energetically shrugging his shoulders and gesticualting with his hands and swinging his cane in the air like a windmill.

the eighty-ninth chapter

KETZELE—A HOSPITABLE HOST

There was no need for Ketzele to exaggerate the spaciousness of the accommodations and how well things were run in his household. Why did he have to boast? Was he asking payment of them? Here were these poor Jews searching for a place to spend the night, why shouldn't he put them up? Was he not a fellow Jew? And especially when a tragedy had befallen them, a misfortune that was not theirs alone but that of all Jews.

So reasoned Ketzele as he led the guests God had sent him to his dwelling.

"True, I am not wealthy, not even a man of means, why should I lie? Rich people live much nicer and more luxuriously. What is there to say? We don't serve pheasant or drink champagne. A piece of bread, if you can get it, and some meat are nothing to complain about. What else does one need?"

Ketzele paused, caught his breath, and continued, the guests in tow.

The main thing, he went on, was that his home was quiet, thank God, he had well-behaved children, and a wife who was nobody's fool, one could even say she was quite intelligent, someone you could exchange a word or two with, took after her mother, who also lived with him. His mother-in-law was a jewel of a woman, had once been a somebody, even well-to-do, quite well-to-do, you might say rich, had owned her own house, silverware, and, of course, jewelry and a fine wardrobe. She had pearls, a whole neckfull, her own horses, three of them, a carriage with a driver in front and a driver in back, and was gen-er-ous!

This was rattled off in one breath by Ketzele, who himself felt that he was overdoing it. Why he needed to do it only God knew, but you can rest assured that he had no ulterior motive other than to boast to strangers, something all people love to do. And perhaps his profession was to blame—a person who makes his livelihood on the Stock Exchange, a Jewish broker at that, is always hoping for some business to come his way. Who could tell? The way he figured it, here were two Jews who had come to the city over the sort of matter that is world-shaking, and though they didn't look like rich people, he remembered that their son, the dentist who was in prison, had this rich aunt, a millionairess, they said, and she might show up one of these days. Maybe, anything was possible, there might be a little profit in it. How? Such things have been known to happen: a Jew comes to town from who-knows-where selling fur, goes over to the Stock Exchange, talks to this one, to that one—one thing leads to an-other—he goes house hunting, buys a house, and in the meantime brokers are making money. It was just a shame he had boasted so much about his apartment and about his family. Soon they would see for themselves. Whatever led him to invent things that never were and never could be? A tongue is like a young horse—let it loose and it will carry you off God-knows-where!

Ketzele mopped his sweaty brow with his kaftan and gazed intently into the guests' eyes, trying to discern their thoughts, but their eyes did not express any doubts about him. On the contrary, it appeared that everything he was saying was taken as holy writ. "Small-town Jews," he thought. "Where does this classy dentist fit in with them? He probably didn't grow up at home but with his millionairess aunt. I must ask them about it."

To Ketzele's delight, his theory was confirmed because the guests themselves said that their Hershl had grown up mainly away from home, not with them. Ketzele was pleased with himself, which made him all the more talkative, and he wondered aloud about their son's match. It turned out they knew nothing about it.

"What match?" they both asked simultaneously.

Ketzele took this to mean that the Shapiros were hiding the fact that they might soon be in-laws. If that were the case, it would be scandalous! Imagine, first the Shapiros were boasting to one and all that their daughter and the dentist were engaged, and now that he was in the hoosegow, they were keeping their mouths shut. "Feh, not nice, not nice at all! Really a disgrace, if you want my opinion. If that's the case, it would serve them right to be punished for being hypocrites!"

And Ketzele gave over to his guests the whole story about how the Shapiros (really very fine people, he wasn't criticizing them—what did he have against them?—but as the subject had come up . . .), how these Shapiros had gone after their roomer as one goes fishing for a fat pike, anxious to net him for their daughter—"a very fine girl, one can say, and educated, maybe a bit too edu-cated, and anything too much is no good . . ."

Ketzele glanced over at the two men and kept on prattling.

"It's likely he was taken in by all of them, the father, the mother, and even the daughter, with all kinds of wiles, but apparently it didn't work. The young man eventually looked around and realized—he was no fool—that she was a pretty girl, but a pretty face isn't everything. And let's not fool ourselves—what's his big hurry? Someone like him won't miss out if he waits till later. Ah, and supposing he said a blessing over the bread without first washing his hands, hee-hee, I don't mean anything serious, I just mean a kiss in the dark, after all, a pretty girl, hee-hee . . . Watch your step here," Ketzele cautioned them as he and his guests descended into a low cellar down rickety, wooden stairs. "It's pitch dark here and slippery into the bargain! I tell you, they never put on a light for you! They say they're afraid of fire, but I spit in their faces—they're just scrimping on kerosene for three groshen. Three plagues upon them! When several families are living in one hole-in-the-wall, can you expect anything to work? Each one expects someone else to take care of things, and you have nothing but aggravation. Sha! What's all this screaming about? Quiet! Shut up! Leave your silly women's arguments for another time! Don't you see we have guests?"

This was spoken to three women, one of whom was Ketzele's wife, a bedraggled woman. The second was her mother, an old hag wearing a black kerchief from which strayed unkempt gray hair, and the third was a woman with a bird-like face and rotten teeth, a harridan with a terrible temper.

Considering the heat of the discussion and the earsplitting racket, one might have been convinced that the women were close to blows, but it was no more than a to-do over a roasted chicken gizzard that the cat might have dragged off. But the woman with the bird-like face, a neighbor of Ketzele's, was insisting that it wasn't a cat who had done the deed but a Ketzele, and not one Ketzele but three Ketzeles. She was referring to three small, half-naked children who, like little mice, were peeking out from behind the stove, hiding their hands behind them and enjoying the spectacle God had provided for them. Best of all was seeing their grandmother, the old hag, who normally cursed them and barked at them and scuffed them and swatted them ten times a day, suddenly coming to their defense, proclaiming that "even the Czar doesn't have such golden children like my grandchildren. They're not children. They're angels! How can a woman have the nerve to think up such things or bring herself to say them?"

When Ketzele entered with the guests, the old woman adjusted her black kerchief, Ketzele's wife wiped her sagging lips, and the neighbor with the bird-like face instantaneously vanished, no one noticed how.

"Come here, scamps," Ketzele commanded the children. "Say hello to the guests and they'll give you a few pennies." But the scamps could live without the pennies and refused to say hello to the guests. They were apparently ashamed because they weren't properly dressed. They looked at one another and all three burst out laughing.

"Not a bit of respect for strangers, shame on you! Wait-wait, I'll pay you later for this," the father vowed, called his wife and mother-in-law to the side, and whispered something in their ears. Then he turned to the guests.

"What would you like to do first? Rest up? You must be exhausted from the trip. Maybe you'd like to lie down right here on the sofa, or—sha!—maybe in the bed? Esther, for now I'll give them your bed, at night we'll figure something else out . . ."

How a man with a wife, a mother-in-law, and three children could invite guests when he possessed, all told, one bed and a broken-down sofa the guests did not allow themselves to question. First of all, they were pleased that in that terrifying city they had finally found a place to lay their heads, and second of all, they were not the fastidious kind. Above all, they had not come all that way for pleasure, more's the pity.

The guests had been quite upset upon arriving at Ketzele's house, furious at that Jew from Slaviteh who had told them outlandish things about their Hershl one had to be crazy to believe: that he supposedly had an aunt who was a millionairess and a sister named Vera and that he could not speak a word of Yiddish—ridiculous! Had they been in better spirits they would have laughed! But most of all they were vexed by what this diminutive man had told them about a match. Had they tricked their Hershl into a marriage trap? Kissing in the dark . . . feh! Disgusting! Now it all made sense. Now they understood what was going on. "Some sharpster, that Shapiro, all the time bragging about being from Slaviteh! And his wife, also a pain, along with that tricky daughter of theirs—a fine family for you!"

By comparison, the tiny Ketzele was far more respectable in their eyes. Imagine, a poor Jew, one might even say impoverished, who didn't know them at all; nevertheless, he went out of his way, made his house available to them, and gave up a whole day on account of them even though, as he himself said, he was a busy man and had a thousand business deals awaiting him on the Stock Exchange. "Don't think for a minute they're important: fantasies, a waste of time, telegrams from Petersburg, exchange rates, this thing and that, they won't run away. I would much rather spend a few hours with you talking about the matter that brought you to this city. I know this city like the palm of my hand. I know everyone in this city and what they're like better than anyone, especially the big wheels. Them, do you hear, you have to know. Oy, do you have to know them . . ."

And Ketzele did not leave his guests' sides all day and most of the night as he described in copious detail the great size of his city and its "big wheels," endowing them with three or four times their financial worth, not begrudging them a few millions, and relating tales of their generosity and the favors they had done and were doing and wished to do and were planning to do for Jews. "So, how can you complain about our affluent Jews and say they aren't helping the poor folk?"

The guests' mouths dropped and their ears perked up as they sat and listened to Ketzele's stories, their eyes riveted on him. Their hearts opened up to him and they sighed quietly because, if what he was saying were true, there might be some hope. The man spoke so earnestly and so convincingly. Everything he said was so simple and straightforward that it did not occur to them to wonder whether he might not be exaggerating.

There was no greater cynic than Abraham-Leibush, a man who had once expressed in a letter to his brother, Hershl, the opinion that the great Leo Tolstoy was no more than flesh and blood. Notwithstanding, late into the night, lying in great discomfort on the broken-down sofa and fighting off the bedbugs, Abraham-Leibush thought, "Let's see, what can we make of this? Let's say that half of what this Jew says we can throw in the ocean and from the remaining half we can toss another half away, there's still enough left over. But God in heaven, how long before morning comes and we can escape alive from this hellhole and really get down to work!"

the ninetieth chapter

ABRAHAM-LEIBUSH DEMONSTRATES HOW MUCH HE KNOWS

Who would have thought that, during the very night the Rabinovitches were staying at Ketzele's, the authorities would get it into their heads to conduct a house search on the very street and select the very cellar apartment where Ketzele had settled his family and had invited guests to spend the night?

Our poor guests were sound asleep, probably dreaming about the influential citizens of the city and how these "big shots" had taken up their Hershl's cause and were working on his behalf, using all their clout. They were sure that at any minute they would be setting their Hershl free in good health, when suddenly they were rudely awakened and required to show their papers.

True, to Ketzele a house search was as natural as whiskey to a soldier. How many times had it been stamped in red ink on his passport that he had to leave within twenty-four hours, and how many times had he left and returned the very next day! And even when they had threatened to ship him out with a prisoner's convoy the next time, he was not frightened. What did he care when he was from nearby Vasilevke and could go back and forth from there three times in one day if necessary?

Ketzele had so frustrated the authorities that they had once asked him, "What can we do to be rid of you?" To which Ketzele replied quite earnestly that there was but one solution: they should put in writing, black on white, that he had permission to remain permanently, and that would be the end of it.

Another time they had picked him up in the street and shouted at him, "You again? What can we do so we never see your face again?" "Cover your eyes—" replied Ketzele coolly.

Another anecdote about him making the rounds of the Stock Exchange (the Stock Exchange loved such anecdotes) was that Ketzele had presented a certificate to the chief of police stating he was a craftsman and so was entitled to a residence permit. "What is your craft?" "I know," he said, "how to make ink." "How to make ink," said the chief of police, "that I also know." "Well, that's why you have a residence permit, your excellency . . ."

But we believe these are no more than stories. One cannot imagine the authorities with nothing better to do with their time than to engage in repartee, and with a Jew no less. Furthermore, it is an insult to those who make it their business to ensure that people do not, God forbid, overstep the limits of justice and legality. One should not think that all cities are alike or that anyone can come and go as he pleases and settle himself wherever he wishes on God's earth freely and openly according to his whim. A person is not a bird who can say: "The sky is mine." A person is not a dog whom one can stop on the street and ask, "Tell me, Reb Dog, who are you?"

In short, there was a search of Jewish homes that night. They collected Ketzele together with his household and his two guests and delivered the guests to the proper place, where they began having a go at them.

"Who are you?"

"We are Jews."

"Where do you Jews come from?"

"From wherever."

"Do you have the necessary 'black on white'?"

"No, we forgot to take them . . ."

Had they at least been willing to say where they came from—but no! It turned out they gave the name of some place called Shklov as their home. The consequence was that they would have to be shipped by convoy to Shklov—of all out-of-the-way places!

That would have been bad enough, but when they searched the young Rabinovitch, Abraham-Leibush, they found a thick packet that contained the bribery money and the letter from their shtetl rabbi to the city rabbi.

"What is this packet you have here, brother?"

"It's a letter."

"A letter? Hm . . . Why such a thick heavy letter? Maybe it means there's money somewhere in there?"

The one who said this was apparently quite a jokester. He examined the packet from all sides and hefted it in his hands as if estimating its weight. It might very well be that had Abraham-Leibush been able to think up a lie, saying it was a business letter, it would have ended in a wisecrack and that would have been the end of it. "Who wants to mess with Jews or with their writing? It's bad enough having to deal with them at all!" But Abraham-Leibush was not that kind of person. He felt he was in a bind: to tell or not tell? If he did tell, they would want to know what was in the letter. If he didn't tell, God knows what they would think: fake checks, contraband, stolen goods! That he didn't need. And so he decided to tell the truth, the whole truth. Oh, the truth, the holy truth! There is nothing better on earth than the truth. With the truth you can go all over the wide world, head held high from one end to the other. With the truth the Torah was given to Moses on Mount Sinai. I ask you, why should a young man like Abraham-Leibush Rabinovitch be afraid to tell the truth about who they were and for what reason they had come? Was it a great secret what had happened to their Hershl, how they had grabbed him, accused him of a blood libel, a pure invention, and thrown him in prison with thieves, vandals, and hooligans, a delicate, pampered boy who was terrified of a dog, who had never harmed a fly?

It was with those very words that Abraham-Leibush harangued them, giving them a lesson they would long remember, demonstrating how much he knew. Hadn't he memorized all of Kirpitchnikov and Galakhov, and hadn't he read all of Pushkin, Turgenev, and Tolstoy from cover to cover?

It is difficult to say exactly why—whether he wanted to explain the reason for the letter they had found or whether he simply wished to exhibit how well versed he was in Tolstoy, but Abraham-Leibush became so worked up by the very end that he burst out with this complaint: "What are we to do? Are we to wait politely until someone has compassion and says a kind word to us? Blessed are those that help themselves. Did your big shots help us at all? Did your great Leo Tolstoy take up our cause? Did he even once come out with a good word for Jews?"

"Right. Everything you say is right. You're right as God Himself. So what is this letter about? From whom to whom?"

Abraham-Leibush wiped the sweat from his face.

"Who is this letter from? From our rabbi to your rabbi, that is, the rabbi of our town writing to the rabbi of your city."

"Aha. What, can you tell me, is your rabbi writing to our rabbi?"

"What is he writing? He's writing not badly at all. It's something worth reading. Here, let me translate the letter for you if you like."

And Abraham-Leibush wasted no time and translated the rabbi's letter for them. Not word for word, needless to say. That was not possible. How can you translate such fine, expressive language into Russian? But the main contents, the gist of the letter, he could tell them. What was there to be afraid of? It wasn't political, there were no secrets. He finished with the following words:

"It's clear as day. In our Talmud it is written that because of a wagon peg a great city like Betar was destroyed. But a blood libel with no basis in fact, that besmirches an entire people, that defiles them by taking a man who is completely innocent and that accuses him of such nonsense, is a mad crime, a shame to have to mention it at the beginning of the twentieth century, in the very epoch of progress and civilization, when people are talking of peace over the entire world. As the prophet said, 'And they shall beat their swords into plowshares and their spears into pruning hooks . . .'"

Who knows where Abraham-Leibush's tongue would have taken him if they had not cut him off in the middle of his oration and asked him with a knavish smile to pardon them and remain in the room awhile and then they would expedite his trip together with his father to where they came from, all the way to Shklov . . .

Despite this news, Abraham-Leibush did not in the least lose courage. He felt quite satisfied that he had at least spoken up and had said what every Jew thinks and is in every Jew's heart. It had not occurred to him that he had stirred up a hornet's nest that would erupt as soon as they translated the rabbi's letter exactly into pure Russian, word for word, and would come to the passage: "Pound on the doors of our great and mighty! Free the prisoners and to those chained, say: Get thee up . . ." Do we need Pharisees to pass judgment? It was clear enough who the prisoners were and who were those chained . . .

* * *

But in addition to entangling himself and his father in an ugly situation and complicating their efforts to free the prisoner, the loquacious Abraham-Leibush had also dragged the poor author of that finely written letter, the rabbi of their shtetl, into the tragic affair. An order came down stating that this Jew also be called for questioning and made to testify about whom he was referring to by "our great and mighty" whose "doors were to be pounded on"? And what did he mean by the words, "Israel is not lacking in wealthy people with good hearts"? Didn't this hint at the existence of some secret organization, and if so, where were its roots? Who was funding it and what were the names of the people at the top? These and more questions they put to the rabbi, whose Hebrew was so beautifully written that it was difficult to believe a rabbi from a small shtetl could have composed the letter.

Understandably, at first the small-town rabbi was frightened out of his wits and could not utter a word. He was articulate only on paper and had a knack for writing fine letters but not for speaking, especially in Russian. But later, when he had calmed down, he followed the same path as Abraham-Leibush—with the truth. There is no better way on earth than the truth. With the truth you can go all over the world from end to end, head held high. With the truth the holy Torah was given to Moses on Mount Sinai. And although the rabbi was not as good with words as Abraham-Leibush (he had never studied Kirpitchnikov or Galakhov, nor had he read Leo Tolstoy's books), he had other qualities—a directness of speech and a guileless face, and his eyes were so ingenuous that it was impossible to doubt that what he said was what he truly believed. As if to God on high, he bared his soul and spoke the entire truth: "Since this tragedy has befallen us, a blood libel that affects all of Israel; and since this Moshe Rabinovitch is a modest Jew, an honest man who has no enemies in his town, a man whose children are honest and would never bother a fly; and since in the great city where his son sits in prison there are to be found important people, rich and powerful, who are relied on by the officials; and since in that city there is, they say, an influential rabbi, a very wise man with a reputation of renown; and since, as everyone knows, the blood libel has been disavowed time after time by kings, tsars, and popes in Rome; and since . . ."

"Stop! I beg your pardon, Herr Rabiner, yours is a story without an end. Until this thing gets worked out completely and until the Rabinovitches are shipped home and the three of you are called before the interrogators, it might not be a bad idea if you would do us the favor of remaining here behind bars . . ."

One can easily imagine what went on in that small shtetl when, instead of the postcards and telegrams that they were looking forward to receiving from the big city, they learned that the Rabinovitches were being shipped home, and to top it, their rabbi had been arrested and put in prison. Why, they didn't know . . .

the ninety-first chapter

A NEW CONVERT

Although the pretend Popov was a fantasist and a dreamer with a vivid imagination about princesses from the land of Offir, he abandoned his fantasies almost as soon as they began. Like a true child of his people when put to the test, he sobered up quickly once he remembered what life was really like for a Jew. He realized his worth once he removed the uniform of a Grigori Popov and donned the clothing of a Hersh Rabinovitch.

It was quite otherwise with the real Popov, who was masquerading as a Rabinovitch. The truth is that a new convert is more fanatic than a born believer. While eager to see how it would all end and stubborn as only a Gentile can be (the moment he gave his word, that was it), and sworn to maintain his Jewishness for the duration of the agreed term, he had taken into his head the fatalistic idea that the hoax he and his Jewish comrade had undertaken was no mere accident. It was fated that he, the Gentile Popov, should become a martyr, a Christian atonement for the suffering the Jewish people had endured as a universal scapegoat. "Who knows," he thought. "Who knows, maybe I am an emissary. Perhaps it is ordained that because I, a Christian, am accused of such a crime, the world will finally open its eyes and see the madness of it and once and for all put an end to this historic nightmare called ritual murder."

One could not tell from his appearance that he was a martyr or that he was suffering and in agony. He looked hale and hearty, had a good appetite, slept well. His thick head of hair had grown longer and thicker, and he had allowed his beard to grow in, very much suiting his pale, clear face, which had become paler from lack of sun and air, rendering his appearance even more Semitic.

It was astonishing how calmly and patiently he bore up under the investiga-

tion, with what pride he conducted himself at the hearing, and with what obstinacy he maintained his views. Having said the word "no," it was a waste of time
repeating the question or trying to catch him in a contradiction. Nothing frightened him. He firmly believed that he who sought the truth would find the truth.
He was positive, moreover, that his friends, the Shapiros, were not idle and were
doing their best to uncover the truth.

When he thought of the Shapiros, he would feel a pang in his heart. "What is
happening to Betty? Where is she? Is she thinking of me?" And he would also
think about home, his real home: "How is my father? What must he be thinking
when he hasn't received a letter from me in so long? And my sister, Vera? But
most likely my friend, Hershke, has taken care of everything. A Jewish head, the
devil take it, he'll think of something!"

He had not the faintest idea that the clouds hovering over his head were
thickening from day to day and that his plight was day to day worsening. Aside
from all the obvious indications that things were not going in his favor, there
were three more factors that weighed against him.

One—the fact that he stubbornly maintained he did not understand a word
of Yiddish. A different story was told by the letters that had been confiscated
from his father's house and been shown to experts. The accused not only understood and wrote Yiddish but possessed perfect fluency in the ancient Hebrew
language. That was one.

Two— the rabbi's letter they had found in his older brother's pocket. Was that
not evidence that a communal crime had been perpetrated involving more than
just one person? If that were not the case, why were the Jews so anxious to free
just him? Are they short of Jewish criminals in prison? Why didn't the Jews come
running to the defense of other Jewish criminals? That was two.

Three—the janitor of the house where the dentist Rabinovitch lived.
When they began questioning the janitor regarding what he knew about the
roomer who lived with the Jew Shapiro, he stated he had nothing to say
against him. The accused was a quiet fellow, meticulous, had about him the
manner of a bourgeois, liked to give orders but always paid well for each
service and gave him a larger New Year's gift than anyone else. There was
nothing he could hold against him. The only thing that puzzled the janitor,
something that really upset him, was a frequent visitor to the roomer, a very
suspicious-looking man, an edgy Yid with black, curly hair and black, shifty
eyes. This little Jew, the janitor noticed, used to steal in to see the Shapiros'
roomer after dark and would occasionally stay with him until long after it
became light, having spent the night there. Naturally, he, the janitor, protested, complaining he could not permit that when according to regulations
it behooved him as janitor to record the documents of every single person
entering his building. Who had to answer to the police about all his residents and everyone else if not the janitor? From that time on, the suspicious person with the black, shifty eyes vanished, and he never saw him
again.

When they questioned the accused about the identity of that suspicious person with the black, shifty eyes who used to steal in to visit him and what he did there all those nights, Rabinovitch at first tried to deny it, saying he did not know what they were talking about, that no suspicious people with shifty eyes had ever come to see him and that he had never had anything to do with robbers or criminals. But later they put on the witness stand David Shapiro, who, as was his way, blurted out the truth ("If you don't eat garlic, your mouth won't smell"). The visitor was the roomer's friend, a *shlimazel,* whose name he didn't remember; he just knew he was a fiery Zionist and very poor. Rabinovitch had to admit that it was true, he did have a friend with the name of Tumarkin who was a fanatic believer in Zionism, which was, it seemed to him, far from a crime. But what had become of this Tumarkin he did not know. (That Tumarkin was one of the thirteen who had not been admitted to the university Rabinovitch did not wish to say. Why drag in others?)

Rabinovitch also admitted that he had carried on long debates and discussions about nationalism, Zionism, and other such subjects with Tumarkin and that he, Rabinovitch, had learned a great deal from him, becoming a bit of a Zionist himself. But because Tumarkin had neither a residence permit nor the money to pay off the police, he had frequently invited him to spend the night with him, but only out of pity. What the janitor had said, that Tumarkin used to steal in or that he had protested, was pure invention. Tumarkin used to walk right in and the janitor used to receive from him, Rabinovitch, a gratuity every time.

That it had not been himself, but the landlord, Shapiro, who had bribed the janitor Rabinovitch did not mention. Why should he? It didn't really matter. Of course, the janitor swore up and down before God that he was clean and clear, if not may he drop dead on the spot. Rest assured, the janitor received more than a slap on the wrist; he was severely chastised and lost his job. Nevertheless, he was counted as a witness against the accused, who did not realize he was sinking deeper and deeper . . .

It was no wonder, then, that the prisoner's situation became even more dire and restrictive. Though they had kept the criminal entirely cut off from the outside world, now, especially after all the testimony about the rabbi's letter, proving without a shadow of a doubt that they wished to free the bird from the cage, they made sure that no one could have so much as a glimmer of hope of reaching him. His daily regimen became much harsher than before. They reduced his already short time for walking outside to the absolute minimum. But that did not bother him at all. He promised himself to bear up resolutely under his ordeal for the sake of the truth, no matter what the outcome! And he would certainly have survived this test as well, not losing heart for a moment while maintaining his exalted standards till the end, had not something happened to convince the authorities that not only was he the real offender but also a sly culprit who would use any ruse to slip out of the hands of justice.

THE GREAT TEST

One day when they had led the prisoners out for a walk in the courtyard, Rabinovitch noticed another Jewish prisoner who was wearing the gray smock of a sentenced convict. The man, he thought, was looking at him in a strange way and was winking at him. It was plain he wished to say something to him but was afraid of the guard. After two attempts, the prisoner could not contain himself any longer and spoke to him from a distance in Yiddish heavily laced with Russian.

"You are the Rabinovitch they suspect of ritual murder? If so, I can give you regards from Miss Shapiro. Before they arrested me and put me in prison we were together in the Jewish hospital."

The Jew wanted to say more but the guard gave him a strong warning with the butt of his rifle and led him off to his cell.

From this, Popov-Rabinovitch understood only the few Russian words: "*obvinyayet*—suspect," "*ritualnoye ubistvo*—ritual murder," "Miss Shapiro," "*ostrog*—prison," "*yevreyskaya bolnitza*—Jewish hospital," but that was enough for him to spend three sleepless nights.

It was as clear as day to him that they suspected Mam'selle Shapiro of ritual murder. They had put her in prison and from there into the Jewish hospital—what else could it mean? And which Miss Shapiro could the prisoner be talking about if not David Shapiro's daughter? Not only had they accused Betty of the same ritual murder and put her in prison, but she had doubtless fallen ill from her suffering and now found herself in a hospital.

He understood now why none of the Shapiros had visited him all the time he had been in prison. Every prisoner had a visitor at least once a week, if only for a few minutes, but not he. Why was he worse than the others? It could only be that she was very ill, and who knows, perhaps worse than ill.

He sprang up from his prison cot and paced about with long strides in his little cell. Thousands of thoughts, one darker and more disturbing than the next, passed through his mind as he felt his head exploding. He suddenly had the desire to tear down the entire building, to put an end to it all.

If the one for whose sake he had withstood so much was no more, for whose sake he had been bearing up so well, and for whom he was prepared to sacrifice his career, his very life, then what good was this mockery to him? Was he truly obliged to sacrifice himself for a truth that was there for everyone to see but to which they turned a blind eye? Let it all go to the devil then! No later than tomorrow morning he would send word that he wished to reveal something that would totally illuminate and change the case . . .

Of course, the following morning he regretted his decision and thoroughly berated himself: "A person shouldn't be a coward. A promise must be kept." At night, when the shadows had gathered and a funereal stillness reigned over the prison, only occasionally interrupted by the clanking of iron chains or the foot-falls of wooden soles on cobblestones, or the spitting of a restless sentry pacing back and forth outside, he was again assailed by thousands of thoughts that did not allow him to sleep.

He tossed from side to side or lay with half-closed eyes, seeing himself as a Gentile, as the fortunate Grisha Popov in his own home, on the wealthy estate of his aristocratic father, where everything was so comfortable, luxurious and overflowing, bright and warm, agreeable and good . . .

And he imagined what it would be like if he were still his old self. Where would he be now? He would now have finished his first year at school. He would have been preparing to go home for vacation, to his father's estate, "Blagos-vetlovo," where they usually spent the summers.

Blagosvetlovo—the most beautiful, the most wonderful spot on earth to spend the summer! His father, Ivan Ivanovitch, his sister, Vera, and he himself loved Blagosvetlovo more than all their other estates in T——— province. That was where all the Popovs, the entire family, all of Grisha's uncles and aunts and their children, gathered when summer came, and not just the family, but other landowners from all about, and there began a round of social events—endless lunches, picnics, hunting, fishing, racing, excursions.

That was for the adults. For them, for the young folk, it was like living in paradise: months and months of vacation, swimming with friends three times a day in the Sazhelka River, criss-crossing it back and forth. Marvelous! And boating with cousins who were still children but acted like grown-up "mam'selles." That was the place where young boys became young men and young girls became young ladies, where the first stirrings of puppy love awak-ened, where the first awkward, intense romances were carried on, which began with innocent, childish games and ended harmlessly . . . and oh! How he would love to be there now! He was being put to a great, a difficult test! . . .

He sprang up from his hard prison cot and paced the four cubits of his tiny cell back and forth with long strides several times, lay back down again on his hard bed, and eyes half-closed, transported himself back to his dear, beloved home, to when he was still a *gymnasium* student and his beloved sister was eagerly awaiting his arrival.

It was infinitely pleasant at this time to think about his sister, Vera, and about both of them as young children, playing childhood games, ensconced in an English carriage that he himself drove, or riding on swift horses, flying across field and meadow.

All about it is green, flat as far as the eye can see, and bright with sun. The wheat fields and meadows stretch out endlessly. Like ocean waves the still un-ripe wheat sways back and forth. Like people from the East praying to God, the trees in the woods rock to and fro. Like a band of motley musicians, birds sing, storks peck, locusts buzz, flies hum. Nearby a stream rushes and snakes its way downhill, then quietly murmuring far off near the mill it lets loose with a roar and drops precipitously, boiling, bubbling, splashing, foaming. "Let me! Let me! Let me!" one imagines the water saying as it runs down and pulls along with it everything in its path. At the mill the two stop.

Vera and he dismount, and the miller's wife, a short peasant woman wearing a tall headdress comes toward them, bows low to the ground, and offers them a pitcher of ice-cold milk.

How does the miller's wife know they are parched? The miller's wife does not own a glass, and she offers no other utensil, so they must drink directly from the pitcher.

"You drink first, Vera, you're older."

"No, Grisha, you drink first, you're more deserving."

"No, Vera, you."

"No, Grisha, you." And how they laugh and laugh!

A great, a difficult test! . . .

He opened his half-shut eyes and remembered where he was. He sprang up from his hard prison cot, paced again with long strides the four cubits of his narrow cell—where was he? What was he doing there? How had he allowed this to happen? Why was he being put to such a great test? For whose sins was he atoning? There had to be an end to it! He had to put an end to all this!

But how? Was it possible that now, after he had suffered so long, he could suddenly take it upon himself to rip off his mask: "Look—I am not who you think . . ."? And, about the word he had given? Was it possible that he, Popov, would be the first to break his promise? Was it possible that he, the Gentile Popov, would not be able to withstand the test that any weak, downtrodden Jew had withstood for so long, for hundreds and hundreds of years? "Grisha, you should be deeply ashamed of yourself!"

He grabbed his head at the temples and felt that if he had to spend one more night like this, they would have to take him to another place, an insane asylum.

Under strict guard, with swords bared, they led the accused, Hersh Movshovitch Rabinovitch, to the house of justice for renewed interrogation.

He had declared that he wished to disclose to the judges something completely new, something that had serious bearing on the case . . .

the ninety-third chapter

"A JEWISH STORY"

As he was led through the streets in the fresh air, feeling the bright rays of the warm summer sun and seeing ordinary people bustling about, our hero's mind cleared, and he began to have second thoughts about his firm conviction to divulge the whole truth about who he was.

But the very same fresh air and bright rays of the warm summer sun and the very appearance of people convinced the prisoner that he had to divulge his true identity all the sooner in order to attain the freedom for which he suddenly so strongly yearned.

With open mouth, he gulped the fresh, delicious air, filling his healthy lungs, from which it coursed to all his young, healthy limbs, and all at once he felt alive, he felt that life was truly a very good thing, a delight, a joy, as if this were something new to him, as if he had never felt this before. Was it possible that within an hour or less he would be a free man like all the people he saw around him now? Was it possible that this very day he would be able to go wherever he pleased, travel wherever he wanted, do anything he wished?

He would immediately hail a carriage and ask to be taken directly to *that* street, would stop at *that* house, and ring *that* bell. No sooner would he be up the stairs than he would ask, "What is the matter with Berta Davidovna?" But who knows whom he would encounter first and what he would find out? He felt a chill go through his body, and for a moment his earlier elation about being alive and life being a delight and a joy was disturbed.

Never before had the accused walked with so resolute a stride, and never before had he held his head as high with pride as now. He was positive this would be the last time he would be coming there, the last visit he would be making to the Department of Justice.

With a slight bow he entered the spacious, brightly lit office, where every detail was so familiar to him and so monotonously unchanged that it had become tedious. The investigators were the same as always, but this day their faces appeared to him more cheerful than usual. He imagined they were now anticipating hearing something new and important. He thought they looked different somehow, as if they were dressed up on his account. But for all that, they were not hurrying or displaying any particular eagerness and were as cold and indifferent toward him as always. The senior person said to him casually, "So, what new information do you have for us?"

They began shuffling their papers and whispering among themselves about other matters, but he observed, nevertheless, how intent and eager they were to hear what he had to say. He pictured how their faces would look when they would hear what he had to disclose. But how should he begin? Should he get to the point directly, without beating around the bush—"Know, my dear sirs, that before you stands not a Jew, Hersh Movshovitch Rabinovitch, but a Gentile, Grigori Ivanovitch Popov"? It could make a strong impression but might not have the effect he wanted. No, he would not set forth everything at once, he would feed them a spoonful every half-hour; little by little he would lift the veil from their eyes, and they would realize what a mistake they had made. As for the question why he had not done so till now—well, he had not wanted to. What could they do to him? At worst, what could happen? They could punish him for assuming a false identity and using false documents, but that was not a great crime, and in addition he was not, remember, just anybody. He was still Ivan Ivanovitch Popov's son. Let him write one word to his father, send one telegram, and that would put an end to all the haggling!

With these thoughts, his courage revived and he began feeling more at ease, more so than ever, and he addressed his inquisitors in teasing hints and questions as if he were not the accused, not a prisoner, but a friendly colleague of theirs.

"Is it new information you want from me?" the accused began quite confidently with a calm smile on his lips. "What you will soon hear from me will assuredly be news, astonishing news! But before I begin, I must take the liberty of asking you something." He took a few steps back, clasped his hands behind him, and took on a pose as if he were about to perform a trick, like standing on his head or walking on his hands. "What would happen, let's say, if you were to find out right now, that . . . that I am not who you think I am?"

These words did have a definite effect. With perplexed eyes, they stared at him and considered the young man carefully as if to prove to themselves whether he was who they thought he was.

"Exactly what do you mean to say?" one asked him, and the accused began to speak again, with even greater boldness and pride.

"What I mean to say is—what if you were to find out, let's say, if I were to prove to you that you are not dealing with a Jew accused of murdering a Gentile boy for ritual purposes—pure nonsense—but, in fact, you have before you a Gentile who hails from nobility?"

Having blurted out those words in one breath and in the same tone, his voice sounding as if it were a stranger's, the accused drew a deep breath and paused. He wanted to see what impression his statement had made. But it was difficult to say what kind of effect it had. In any case, it was not the one he expected because, after a brief pause during which they exchanged glances, they stated that it would be hard to say what would happen but it was not pertinent to raise hypothetical questions about irrelevant matters. They had not brought *him* here for that purpose, nor were *they* there for that reason. It would be far better if he were to get to the point, without tricks, without jokes, without speaking in circles, and say what he had to say.

The accused was abashed. "Perhaps they're right," he thought. "Why make all these introductions? Better to get right to it." Another thought came to him: "Maybe quit altogether? There's still enough time to reconsider. You can still turn back, Grisha! Don't bring shame on yourself. You've suffered so much, put up with so much, and you're so close to the end and you couldn't hang on, you gave in!?" Spitefully the sun's golden rays shone in through the window, darting mischievously up the walls, onto the ceiling

and down again, playing upon the serious faces of the well-dressed gentlemen. And from time to time, through the half-open windows, the tumultuous sounds rushed in from outside and one could hear the distant rumble of
iron-shod wheels over the cobbled streets of the great, lively city. Everything
cried out, attested to being alive. Everything called out to him: Be free, alive,
out here, where priceless freedom awaits you. No, he could no longer be
expected to master himself! He took a few steps toward the table, put both
hands in his pockets and spoke quietly but with the assured tone of a person
who knows his true worth.

"You force me to tell you directly without any further introduction, and so I
will comply and tell you straight out that you have been misled. You believe I am
a Jew and that my name is Rabinovitch, but at last I must open your eyes and
tell you the truth. You see before you a Gentile and a nobleman, a true nobleman, whose father is a former provincial governor, whose uncle is a district
councilman and another uncle a governor."

"And you yourself are the Prince of Portugal?" the senior investigator cut him
off, and the others burst out laughing.

He had not counted on that reaction at all. He had expected any other
outcome but ridicule! They considered him a buffoon!

This reaction was so unexpected that he was left speechless. He stared at his
inquisitors with astonished eyes as if asking them, "Am I crazy or are you trying
to drive me crazy?" They had stopped laughing, realizing how the accused's face
had become transformed.

"We understood you, Rabinovitch," one of them said, giving him a penetrating look. "We understood quite well what you meant, but we must tell you
frankly that it won't work. You've made up a poor alibi. You've concocted an
unconvincing story."

"It's a *Jewish* story," another added, drawing out the word "Jewish."

"Not convincing," a third one reproved him in a surprisingly friendly tone,
"not convincing and not clever. We thought you were a lot smarter."

Rabinovitch heard what each said, standing before them, stunned and
confused. Had he been slapped in the face he would not have felt more
thoroughly chastised. He tried to consider carefully what they were saying to
him; he concentrated on the words "a *Jewish* story" . . . "Why did they seem
so pleased that it was a story, and a Jewish one at that?" he wondered, and
he had the urge to laugh but held it in and again asserted that it was not a
story although it might appear like one. But how would it be if he were able
to convince them that what he had said was true? How would it be if he
gave them the opportunity to prove it to themselves with a telegram, just
one telegram to his father, who was—he assured them again—a Gentile and
a nobleman and a former provincial head whose two brothers were also high
officials. "You're repeating yourself," they interrupted him, rang a bell, and
ordered the accused be led off to a side room until they deliberated on the
matter and then they would call him back.

the ninety-fourth chapter

AN EXPERT OPINION

Later, when they had brought the accused back to the office, the interrogators were gone. Leaning on an elbow at the window, sitting and peering outside with worried eyes, was someone who was entirely new to him.

He was an older man, not in uniform, personable and seemingly ordinary. The only thing one was struck by was his unusually high, broad forehead and the melancholy look of his large, worried eyes.

As soon as they led the accused in, this older, dignified man stood up, walked toward him and offered him a large, warm hand. He signaled to the guard to leave and bade the prisoner to sit as he seated himself opposite him, and with a light sigh and mournful voice, as if about to complain about some pain, he spoke slowly.

"Your name is Rabinovitch? That derives from the word *rabbin* and gives testimony that your parents are descended from rabbis, a generation of rabbis, scholars . . ."

This was said gently, softly, as if he were speaking to himself. As he spoke, his eyes never left the young man, his gaze seeming to penetrate deeply into the very heart and soul.

"Who is this person?" Rabinovitch wondered as he looked intently at him and listened as he spoke his gentle, soft words, moving easily from subject to subject so that gradually what he was saying became more and more interesting.

Like a person walking on thin ice, feeling his way carefully step by step before setting a foot down, the older man felt his way in order to determine what might interest this young man. He ranged over many subjects and issues until he touched on the point that moved the accused most of all.

It was the accursed "ritual question." Whenever the innocent accused talked about it, he boiled with rage. He was embarrassed that people still believed in its existence among Jews and at the same time he was upset that he had been within a hairbreadth of believing it himself. "This man has apparently been sent to sniff out something about this horrible, ugly legend," he thought, and promised himself not to say a word. He was thoroughly sick and tired of it all. "Always ritual murder and more ritual murder!" But the man spoke about it so thoughtfully and so persuasively that he could not keep his promise and blurted out almost insolently that he did not understand how an intelligent person could speak about such a matter in a serious tone.

"I don't understand," he said, fire in his voice, "how they aren't ashamed to drag out of the old archives an accusation that has been lying around and gathering mountains of dust for hundreds of years and concoct a case out of it."

It had been some time since Popov-Rabinovitch had had the opportunity to speak so freely, and he let himself go.

The elderly man with the high forehead heard him out completely, and cleverly remained silent, looking very deeply into his eyes, seeming to nod his head in agreement and from time to time adding a word. And when Rabinovitch stopped raging, he responded. He spoke pleasantly and unhurriedly, in his quiet, mournful voice.

"You are absolutely correct, young man, absolutely . . . It is truly nonsense and one must certainly be thoroughly irreligious and a simpleton to accuse an entire people, a nation with an ancient culture, of such a wild, barbaric custom that is for you no more than a remnant of the past. But then again, to deny it entirely and say there doesn't exist among you a sect that . . ."

The words "among you" forced the accused to drop his eyes and, now somewhat more controlled and with less ardor, he replied to this dignified man that, if there did exist among Jews such a sect, how come there was not to be found any evidence of it in their rich literature?

The elderly man heard out the young man, who spoke so logically and competently, not betraying any sign of abnormality. Only one thing was surprising: why did he always speak of the Jews in the third person, "they"? Why didn't he say *our* literature? Why *their* literature? He put the thought aside and said to the young man that what the literature had to say about sects and its members was not so simple as one might think, not everyone could boast that he was clear about it. He himself, for example, had been studying this literature for many years, and yet he was far from believing that he had plumbed its depths. He had not only studied the literature but he had also done various researches on the sect members themselves. He had written many papers on the subject as well as published entire books.

"Who is this person?" Rabinovitch thought again. "He seems like an agreeable enough old codger, well educated and a scholar. He's published books on the subject. It would be good to read those books, to learn his opinion on this tragic question. I would also like to find out who he is. He looks like a professor, or maybe a doctor of psychiatry . . ."

The thought that this was a professor, a psychiatrist, caught on with him firmly and would not be dispelled: "Is it possible he's a professor? Is it possible he's a doctor? Then what is he doing here? What is the significance of this conversation? Do they think I'm crazy?"

And he began to recall, step by step, everything he had done that day, from the first thing in the morning until now. It seemed to him it was all a normal, lucid person would do. He went over what he had said and felt he had not uttered anything questionable, save, perhaps, that he had told them his true identity. And he began to look upon this person, not with curiosity, but with fear. A professor . . . A doctor . . . A psychiatrist! Did that mean they were thinking he was ill, mentally ill? Since when? Might it have been the result of his new plan? Could they be interpreting his confessing who he was as a delusion and seeing him as a madman? That would mean all his efforts had been in vain, in vain the desire prematurely to tear away the mask.

"Don't be offended at what I will ask you," he turned to the elder man, who gazed at him with worried eyes.

"Ask."

"Are you a doctor?"

"A doctor."

"Of psychiatry?"

"Of psychiatry."

"Are you thinking that maybe I'm . . . not in my right mind?"

"Not at all."

"He doesn't want to tell me the truth," he thought, looking intently at the doctor while the doctor returned his intent look. He had another question to ask, but the man rose and again extended his large, warm hand.

"We will likely see each other again . . ."

The sun was already bidding farewell to the summer day, setting ablaze the golden church spires as the same prison escort, with bared swords, led the criminal back to his cell. One could not tell from his face that he had fallen in his own self-esteem. He still held his head high and walked with confidence. Only from his slightly more furrowed brow was it possible to tell that he was deep in thought. What was he thinking about? About the truth that once and for all had to rise like oil on water? About the bitter cup that he was forced to drain to the very last drop? About the blow he had suffered that day? Was he disappointed that he had not succeeded in attaining his release from prison? Or, quite the opposite, was he pleased that it had worked out so that he would have to uphold Jewishness till the end?

*   *   *

To the substantial accumulation of documents that had thus far been gathered concerning the murder of Volodya Chigirinski was added another document, an expert opinion written by a famous professor of psychiatry. In this deposition, for which the professor of psychiatry had sat up all night composing what amounted to an entire treatise in the cause of science and justice, he expounded a profound and novel theory about the psychology of all those who belong to sects: "Whereas it is possible to observe in all other sect members— for example, among Christian sect members—signs of madness, the fanatic Jewish sect members who use Christian blood are for the most part normally developed people with a healthy understanding and strong will . . ." Then the professor of psychiatry presented a long list of citations from the greatest scholars in the field, such as Lambrozo, Krafft-Ebbing, Wundt, Charcot, and others. He concluded his expert opinion with the statement that, on the basis of his long, probing interview with the accused and on the basis of the evidence provided by his intrinsically Jewish physiognomy, from the Semitic shape of his head and from his style of reacting and speaking, it was his profound conviction that the criminal was spiritually as well as physically healthy and strong. His efforts to convince others that he was not a Jew but a Christian nobleman who came from people of very high rank must under no circumstances be diagnosed as an illness called paranoid grandiosity, but was simply the simulation of a criminal who wanted others to believe he was insane.

"With this kind of criminal," the professor of psychiatry concluded his severe expert opinion, "one must be very cautious . . ."

the ninety-fifth chapter

BETTY GOES TO A DACHA

When the danger had passed and Betty began to come to herself again, improving from day to day, the doctors decided that the patient should be discharged from the hospital, not for home, where things might unsettle her and cause a relapse, but for a place situated out in the country air, in the woods near a village. In a word—she needed a dacha.

When she heard the word "dacha," Sara Shapiro thought, "It's easy for them to say a dacha. First of all, who can afford a dacha? And second of all, let us suppose we were able to come up with the money—the Jew has yet to be born who cannot somehow lay his hands on money necessary for his health—there was still another problem. Residence permits! Not every Jew can be sick outside the Pale. For that you must have pull. *They* consider it a privilege: you either have to be dead or filthy rich. Take my brother-in-law, Shlomo Familiant—he could be sick wherever he pleased because he had money. But he had no intention of being sick. Only the poor become sick. For that we have a God who runs His world with benevolence. He probably knows what He is doing. Who is there to contradict Him?"

Sara did not keep these thoughts to herself; she was quite outspoken, both with the family doctor—one could say anything one wished to him—and to her husband—with him one could certainly speak plainly. Why not tell him bluntly to go straight to his rich sister and tell her thus-and-so, we must rescue a child, save her life. What then? Was she not also deserving? Where was it written that his sister's daughters must bathe in butter and honey while her daughter was so sick that doctors said she needed complete rest as one needed life itself?

"What do you want? For me to go begging to my sister?" David shouted angrily at her, but this time his anger was of no avail. Sara was not intimidated. So long as it had to do with the life and health of her Betty, her husband could rant and rave all he wished; he could get as angry as he liked and she would still remind him again and again until he would capitulate, go to his sister and prevail upon her to come herself and beg on bended knee that Betty come to her dacha.

And sure enough, one afternoon when Betty was dozing in her hospital bed, her mother sitting at her side with some handwork, the door opened and in the doorway appeared Toibe Familiant's wig and diamond earrings. Sara immediately got up and signaled to her sister-in-law that her daughter was asleep and drew her into the corridor, where the following conversation took place:

"Do you know, Sara'le darling, why I've come to see you in the hospital?"

Sara put on an uncomprehending face: "How should I know? What am I, a prophetess?"

"I came to see you in the hospital because . . . David told me that the doctors say, *l'maan hashem*, without fail, your daughter needs to go to a dacha. So I talked it over with my Shlomo and my Shlomo said, what was there to talk about? *Im ertza hashem*, if it please God, as soon as your Betty is on her feet and the One Above will help and she can leave the hospital, he could send the carriage for her and take her straight to our dacha."

Sara's heart swelled almost to bursting, but she still played dumb.

"What are you talking about, Toibenyu? In order for Betty to get well, she has to have a separate room. She has to be taken care of. I'm telling you, it's a trouble and a bother."

"You speak such nonsense, Sara'le, may God not punish me for these words! What trouble? No trouble at all and no bother at all. Not even this much! And about a separate room, I'm surprised at you. You know very well that I have, *keyn eyn horeh*, enough rooms. You don't have to worry about that. May the One Above only allow her to arrive safely, even this very day."

Sara still hesitated.

"You forget, Toibenyu, my soul, that there is still one problem—a residence permit."

"Really now, please forgive me, but that's a foolish thing for you to say. You know very well that if my Shlomo says she should come, then he's thought of that too. My Shlomo is no child, as God is great!"

Sara was so moved that she began to speak to her sister-in-law more openly.

"Maybe you're right, Toibenyu, my heart, but to you I can talk as to my own sister. If it were entirely up to me, there would be no problem. On my part, I will never, ever forget this. But you know my Betty, may she have many years ahead of her. Why should I deny it, it's terrible—she's so moody. Oh, what a moody girl! She can suddenly turn stubborn. When she says no, nothing can be done! And especially now . . ."

The rich sister-in-law was fast becoming insulted: you try to do a poor relative a favor and *she's* hesitating. She made a pious face.

"Oy, Sara'le darling, God, blessed be He, shouldn't punish me, I don't want, God forbid, to rub salt into your wounds. You have a heavy heart, poor thing, what is there to say? But I must tell you the truth, like a real sister. The One Above loves the truth. You aren't handling this correctly and you aren't doing the right thing. Look, I too am a mother, may it be till a hundred and twenty

years. I also have children, may they live and be well, and I do everything to see
that they follow the path of righteousness."

"How can you compare yourself to me, Toibe'nyu? I only have one precious
daughter, and you, *keyn eyn horeh*, may they be well and strong . . ."

But the pious sister-in-law wouldn't let her finish. She had something to say
and she was going to say it. "Eh! Sara'le darling, you should say that? You
yourself know very well, as it says in the holy books, children and good deeds are
a gift from God, the more the better. And if you have ten fingers, and one, God
forbid, hurts, believe me, it hurts as much as if you had one finger."

The conversation between the two mothers went on in whispers behind the
door for a long time. When Sara came back, Betty demanded to know what she
was whispering about for so long with her Aunt Toibe. Sara tried to wiggle out of
it by lying but it didn't work, she had to tell her the whole truth, saying first that
if God had granted her a rich aunt and a generous uncle who spent the whole
summer at a dacha, and there was no problem about a residence permit because
her Uncle Shlomo had connections with the police . . .

And so on. Sara thought that Betty was ready to go but it turned out that
Betty wanted nothing to do with any rich aunts or generous uncles or dachas or
police or residence permits.

"Sha, if you say no, let it be no," said Sara, wiping her lips. "Do you know
what? I told her myself, your Aunt Toibe, as God is my witness, that it wouldn't
work. My child, do you think anyone would force you? Sha! Forget it! Don't
even think about it. It's forgotten!"

But it wasn't true. How could she, a mother, forget, when the doctors had
warned that her daughter needed a complete rest to save her life? "Complete
rest," they had said. "She has to have fresh air, out in the pine forests." So,
could she be silent? Although she was embittered by her capricious daughter,
who would not hear of a dacha, she diplomatically approached their family
doctor and began to convince him about how necessary it was for her child to
have a complete rest.

"Complete rest," she emphasized with hand gestures, "is what is essential to
air out one's intestines the way one airs out rooms with an open window, or, for
example . . ."

"God almighty!" the doctor clasped his bald head. "What kind of woman are
you? You want to tell *me* what 'complete rest' is and what your daughter needs?
It seems it was *I* who told *you* a thousand times that your daughter needs a
dacha as one needs life."

"You told me that? What good did it do that you told *me*? You convinced *me*
long ago. Better convince *her*, my daughter, then you can boast."

The doctor did not answer her. He spread out his hands and in the end
promised her he would do what he could, he would speak to her daughter and
try to convince her. "What else do you want from me?"

"*I* from *you*?" said Sara. "What should I want from you? Have we signed a
contract, or something? Did you ever hear such a thing, what do *I* want from
him? Well, if that isn't too much!"

The doctor squinted at her with one eye. This woman was going too far now. At another time she would have received a good talking to from him. He wouldn't have let her get away with it, but now, he was in a sorry state. He had no idea exactly what was happening to him; he had the feeling it was time he ended his bachelorhood. It was high time he got married, and to this very woman's daughter. Terrible! Since this girl had become ill and he had been treating her, the feeling had grown in him day by day that she was the one for him. As many patients as he had cared for in his life, it had never happened that he had felt the way he was feeling now. He had imagined when Betty was critically ill that if she were to die he would not know what he would do with himself. But as she began to recover, he responded not as if she were a patient but as if she were close to him, like a sister, much more than a sister. No, not for nothing did his colleagues make fun of him, calling him "bridegroom," and Sara, "mother-in-law" behind his back.

Had Sara noticed this too? It seemed that way to him. He felt the mother knew he was enamored of her daughter and that was why she was so presumptuous with him, in fact, a bit too presumptuous. And he put up with it in order that his patient recover completely and that he be able to speak openly. But to whom? He was afraid to think about it. But when he considered that first he would have to speak to that woman, her mother, he almost broke out in a fever at the thought. He gave her his hand on it that he would speak to her daughter about a dacha, he would speak without fail, but not today. Today it was too late. Tomorrow!

"Tomorrow is tomorrow," Sara answered. "Am I saying it must be today? Is anyone chasing you? The town isn't burning down and the summer has a long way to go."

A day passed and then another. The doctor came twice a day, visited for two hours, but no one heard him say so much as a word about a dacha. Sara reminded him before he left, but politely: "Didn't you promise me something?" The doctor remained standing, rubbing his bald head.

"What did I promise?" the doctor said.

"Slap your forehead, maybe you'll remember."

The doctor suddenly remembered and swore that he had completely forgotten, as today was Friday. Sara replied that anyone who could forget from Wednesday to Friday needed to knot his handkerchief as a reminder.

But Sara's efforts and all her diplomatic wiles were for naught. Betty listened to the doctor's words about a dacha, about fresh air and a pine forest, as she lay on her bed and looked with glassy eyes at the ceiling as if it were written there what her answer should be. Why? What good was a dacha, fresh air, a pine forest? Why live when he was no longer there?

Sara saw by her daughter's eyes that her efforts were in vain—it was a lost cause. Betty would not go to her Aunt Toibe's dacha, and she signaled the doctor to be silent, not to say any more.

But when the time is ripe, sometimes things fall into place. No one knows how these things happen. One fine morning, Betty woke up and informed her mother she was going to her Aunt Toibe's dacha.

This was soon after she had learned from her mother herself the good news that Rabinovitch was alive and in prison.

the ninety-sixth chapter

"I REALLY DIDN'T NEED THAT"

The first thing Betty did after she found out that Rabinovitch was alive and in prison was to throw herself into the task of reading through all the newspapers and periodicals, old and new, during the time she had been ill. In half a day she had digested all the published accounts of the discovery of Volodya's body. And in her mind she quickly formed a plan for finding the real murderers and freeing her beloved from imprisonment. This now became her sole desire, the aim and meaning of her life. The plan appeared to her to be simple and easy to carry out. She remembered the dreadful night she had spent together with that miserable lost soul who reeked of heliotrope and iodoform, who had filled her ear with horrid tales. She recalled what she had been told about the street woman's lover, whose name she had now forgotten. According to what the woman had begun to relate, he must be one of those who had murdered Kirilikha's son. She was as certain of this as she was of being alive. The problem was that she had forgotten and could in no way recollect either the name of that poor woman or the name of her lover. That night it had not occurred to her that she could one day make use of the information told her by a woman of the streets. Most of what she had said had gone in one ear and out the other, but one thing stuck in her mind and that was the name of the village from which they came, and that village was the very one where her Uncle Familiant had his dacha. An ordinary coincidence, but anything was possible. Who could tell? That was Betty's reasoning for suddenly consenting to go to her Aunt Toibe's dacha. Her mother was in seventh heaven. It was nothing to sneeze at, this opportunity for a full recovery and a complete rest, among family and without costing anything!

Imagine how Sara Shapiro wept when she had to separate from her daughter. Even if she were going to be with family, it was still not home, still not under her mother's eye. And after she had beseeched God . . . beloved Father! Why was her rich brother-in-law, Shlomo Familiant, too stingy to invite them all to the country? Couldn't he put them all up at the dacha? Why not? Didn't her David need a rest? And wouldn't it do Syomke a world of good to play in the open fields or in the green woods instead of broiling in the sun and breathing in the dust of the Jewish Street?

"O, God Almighty, God Almighty!" Sara lamented, in the way of women when they bare their hearts to God as to a close friend. "I'm not telling You what to do, whom to give to and whom not to give to. If You give one a little and another a full plate, or even one everything and the other nothing—You must know what You're doing, that's why You're something of a Creator of the World, as my sister-in-law says, and You run Your little world as You see fit. But if I were the one who was blessed, I would do more for my poor relatives than my rich sister-in-law, who locks up her bread and pinches the servants, just so long as she puts the Torah scrolls on a decorative mantel and prays to You every day from her fat prayer book. May You not punish me for these words, dear God, but since she can't hear me, it won't do her any harm . . .

*   *   *

Sara told her daughter at least twenty times how to behave at her rich Aunt Toibe's dacha, especially to be careful not to exert herself, but to eat and drink and rest, above all, rest!

"Rest! Rest!" mimicked the little Syomke, who then received a slap for being insolent, even though he was an only son. But Syomke took the slap in stride because soon he and his sister would be off to the dacha.

Betty was supposed to have gone in her Uncle Shlomo's carriage, which was to have come after her, but since the doctor had warned that she had to be careful during the journey and had offered to accompany her, and since the doctor had his own carriage, it remained that the three of them would go, Betty and the doctor with Syomke as chaperone. That was exactly what his mother had told him: "You go too, with the doctor, Syomke, and you can be the chaperone." Syomke was certainly happy to hear this news even though his young mind could not comprehend the reason for a chaperone when his sister was traveling with a doctor. And why did his sister suddenly turn red, and why did the doctor, he had noticed, lower his eyes at the words his mother had said? Also, along the way, Syomke could not understand why both of them were silent.

When the doctor returned from the dacha, he brought Syomke home with him and delivered to Madam Shapiro a message from her daughter telling her what a lovely dacha it was, what a beautiful woods, and what healthy air. And the people!

"What a welcome they gave us, Madam Shapiro!"

"The devil take them," Madam Shapiro interjected. "*They* need to be thanked? They can't afford it? They haven't got enough?"

"Don't say that, Madam Shapiro," the doctor tried to calm her. "Nowadays—"

"What are you telling me, nowadays? Nowadays should a sister allow a brother, and especially a brother like my David, to slave for strangers while her husband is stuffed to the gills with business? Is it beyond his means, a wealthy Jew like that? May both of us, you and I, make as much as he spends in a year."

The doctor drew back offended.

"Hold on, Madam! Why are you making me a partner in this? How do you know how much I make? Maybe I'm not as rich as your Shlomo Familiant, but I can't complain."

"May God grant you three times as much!" Sara cut him off. "Whoever begrudges you, let him not have anything."

"We're not talking about that," said the doctor, who wished to turn the conversation in a different direction. "We're talking about something else." He crumpled his hat in his hands, rubbed his bald head, and didn't know where to begin. He moved a little closer to Madam Shapiro and said, "Hmm . . . Understand, Madam, I wanted to speak to you about something else. It's like this: I have known your daughter since she was this big" (he put his hand close to the ground) "and always looked on her as a child, a little girl . . . Now, when she became sick . . ."

"May it never happen again," Sara corrected him.

"May it never happen again. When she became sick, I, may it never happen again, came every day, twice a day, three times a day, may it never happen again . . ."

"What a strange person you are!" Sara interrupted him. "How many times did I ask you to write down the number of visits you made, and you got all puffed up and were furious at me . . ."

"A disaster, not a woman!" thought the doctor, mopping his bald head with a red handkerchief. He sprang up and quickly sat down again.

"No! Not that, Madam! You didn't understand me, I mean you *misunder-*stood me. I have never spoken to you and am now not speaking to you and will never speak to you about visits."

"Yes, well, I know you accept whatever we give you. I've talked it over with my husband and . . ."

"Hol-hold on, Madam!" the doctor raised his voice. "Let me finish. I'm not talking about that. I don't want any money from you. I told you that, it seems to me, many times!" In exasperation the doctor removed his spectacles as Sara said calmly, "If it's not about money, what are you going on about?"

Those words impelled the doctor out of his seat. He quickly put on his spectacles and his hat and, laughing bitterly, cried out in a voice in which one could hear tears.

"What a peculiar woman you are! Do you hear? You are a peculiar woman. A person comes to you about a serious matter, about a matter that is perhaps very important to him, and you speak to him as if you were speaking to a . . . to . . . to a servant or to a coachman or I don't know to whom . . . !"

Out of control and livid with anger, the doctor slammed the door and left in a huff. Sara remained seated, looking out the window, and saw him hunched over with his hat pulled down over his eyes. He jumped into his broken-down little carriage and signaled the driver to go, never looking back.

"A crazy doctor! A good person but crazy," thought Sara, not understanding what had made him crazy and what he had wanted to say that was so vital to him. She was ready to heap curses on his head when she thought, "What do I have against him? It was enough that he put my daughter back on her feet (first God, then him), enough that he doesn't want any money and was so gentlemanly and took the trouble at his age to personally deliver my Betty to her uncle's dacha in his carriage and to bring back a message from her. So why did I receive him so coldly, not even offering him a glass of tea? But whose fault is it when my mind is so addled that I couldn't even listen properly to what he was trying to tell me? Maybe the *shlimazel* was trying to tell me something important?"

"I really didn't need that!" Sara comforted herself, and stopped thinking about the doctor. Her thoughts carried her off somewhere else.

She had enough to think about.

the ninety-seventh chapter

COOLED OFF

As is the way with most rich relatives like the Familiants, Betty was at first a most welcome guest. They could not do enough for her. All, from the youngest to the oldest, danced attention upon her. Her Aunt Toibe could not have pampered her more, constantly complaining that Betty ate too little. "You call that eating! I don't know what she lives on!" And her daughters, the "mam'selles," were simply delighted to have their cousin with them, a new person to talk to freely about literature, such as Artsibashev's latest novel. And even the father himself, Reb Shlomo Familiant, who was, needless to say, a thoroughgoing *Chassid* with a broad *tallis kotn*, the ample required undergarment whose fringes peeped from beneath his fully cut satin vest with its massive gold watch chain—even that Jew exhibited a special friendliness and warmth to Betty beyond the ordinary.

After having done her the favor of registering her as his daughter and bribing the police—he was a Familiant and a Jew who was influential with the authorities—and after assuring her that she could have a better rest there than at home, he himself took the trouble to escort her to her room. And when with his nearsighted eyes he spotted a towel on the floor, he raised a hue and cry, called together the servants, and dressed them down thoroughly. Then as he led her into the garden and showed her the path through the woods and where one could put up a hammock to rest in the shade, he noticed an empty glass on the table (so nearsighted and he saw everything!), and he again raised a fuss and showed what a strict master he was—a generous host but a demanding master.

But as time went on, the Familiants' hospitality, as with most rich relatives, slowly began to diminish and fade, to cool off along with the end of summer.

The first to show her disenchantment was her Aunt Toibe. The aunt could not abide the fact that her niece did not make the blessing on the Sabbath candles. "What does one thing have to do with the other?" the pious aunt complained. "You can be the most educated woman with seven degrees and, still, what belongs to God belongs to God and what to man to man." Look at her own daughters, also educated young women, who read Russian books and could even speak French, dance and play instruments too, but when it comes to the Sabbath, what does one thing have to do with the other? That's why they were Jewish daughters.

She did not fault Betty herself. That was the way she was brought up. Why was she to blame? The one she faulted was her mother. "How does a mother, David Shapiro's wife, bring up a child not to know the most necessary things a Jewish daughter has to know? No wonder the Messiah hasn't come and Jews suffer in exile," the aunt concluded with a pious face, her lips pursed tightly.

It should be noted that all these misgivings were aired by the religious Toibe Familiant only to her children and servants. She was afraid of openly confronting Betty, and not so much afraid of Betty as of her husband. Shlomo Familiant thought the world of his little niece, which vexed his wife considerably. It rankled her when he came to her defense and interfered at the table, insisting she be served more food. At the table, she, Toibe, was the mistress who knew who should be served and how much. What right did a man have to interfere in such matters, especially a *Chassid?* "If you're a *Chassid,* take care of your *Chassidim,* sing songs with them Friday night at dinner or dance with them after dinner, but stop looking into your little niece's dish and worrying about whether or not she's drunk her milk today."

It was silly; Toibe herself knew it was silly, but, like most wives who are suspicious that their husbands are looking where they shouldn't, she suffered great pain and did not sleep nights. And it was no secret that her husband suffered no less on account of her and also slept poorly. And over what exactly?

Betty had always been her uncle's favorite. He called her by her Yiddish name, Basya. And not just Basya, but Basya'ke, drawn out. When she was a child, he used to pinch her cheeks, not kiss her, but pinch her hard, leaving marks, but he would pay her a coin for every pinch so she would not cry. Later, when she was more grown up, he still liked to pinch her cheeks, and right where the dimple showed when she laughed (so nearsighted and yet saw everything!). But once she was fully grown, she did not let herself be pinched anymore. What an impertinent girl—impossible! In this matter, Aunt Toibe had interfered, coming to the defense of her niece: "What kind of craziness is this pinching, making her black and blue? It's a pity on the poor creature!" She couldn't bear to see it.

From that time on, he stopped pinching his niece, but when he caught sight of her, he would gaze at her with half-shut eyes (the man *was* nearsighted!) and sigh. "Hm . . . *keyn eyn horeh!*" he would think. "Just yester-day, it seems, she was a child, and all of a sudden—a woman!" And especially now, after her illness, he could not have his fill of looking at her, amazed at how she had suddenly become more mature, prettier, and blos-somed and ripened—a woman and a beauty at that, and what a beauty! "Ach-ach-ach-ach-ach!" he sighed deeply, and tossed and turned in his bed, unable to shut an eye. Thoughts, thoughts, and more thoughts—a terrible punishment! And not only in bed, but in the morning, right in the middle of his prayers, he could not rid himself of these thoughts. No sooner did he don his *tallis* and *tefillin* (he had gotten that far with a pure mind), when his niece, the beauty, would suddenly pop into his consciousness, and again, thoughts, thoughts, and more thoughts . . . He would stand facing the wall, cover his eyes with his hand, and begin swaying back and forth rapidly in agitation, praying so fervently that the walls rang with it! If a person is strong, he can suppress his urges.

And his dreams! What does one do with troubling dreams when one sleeps like a corpse and has no control over oneself? Ever since his beautiful niece was in his home, his nights were disturbed by tangled dreams he could neither understand nor account for. Luckily, Reb Shlomo Familiant was no simpleton and was acquainted with the biblical portion—*v'khalomos shav yedabrin*—dreams are nonsense. Imagine what this Jew dreams about.

He dreams he has become a widower (God forbid, may it not ever happen to anyone!) His Toibe has died, may she have a bright Paradise, and the poor man is sitting shiva and crying, the tears pouring down his face as he studies the Book of Job . . . The thirty days of mourning pass and the man has not a thought of remarrying . . . But there are matchmakers in this world and they are breaking his door down, driving him wild: You must, they say, get married. You mustn't, they say, be alone, after all, a man like yourself . . . Go ahead, ask the rabbi, they say, and he will also tell you, you must quickly get married and to your own niece—first, they say, because she is unmarried, and second, because she is one of your own family and is poor, and so, it's a *mitzvah* as well as righting a wrong. As the Gemara says, *v'khol hamikayim nefesh akhas*—whoever helps sustain life . . .

"God be with you, Shlomo, why are you groaning so?" Toibe finally roused him, and though it was hours till day, neither of them could go back to sleep. Toibe began complaining about their niece, saying she wasn't conducting herself properly and that she was sorry she had taken her in. "For what possible rea-son?" asked Shlomo, peering at her with his nearsighted eyes and remembering his horrible dream.

"For what possible reason?" answered Toibe, who looked in her white night-gown like an old nurse who hadn't slept in three nights. "It isn't proper for a girl who is one of us to behave this way, to be so cozy with strange men, go for strolls with them in the woods, tell secrets and whisper with them, and more things like that. In her mother's house she can do whatever she pleases, but not here. We have grown daughters. What kind of lesson, for God's sake, can they learn from such carryings-on and from such behavior, God, blessed be He, shouldn't pun-ish me for these words?"

These "strange men" the pious Toibe was referring to were, first of all, the doctor, who came once a week to visit Betty, supposedly to find out how she was doing. "So? Make up your mind—if you're a doctor, hear her out, write a pre-scription, and go home in good health. Why do you have to sit and chatter for three hours on end, who knows what about, and who cares?"

But at least he was a doctor, how do they say, a healer of the sick, a friend of the family's, bringing news from home every Sunday. But what is this other young *shlimazel* doing here, what does David's daughter have to do with some half-student who can't even afford a decent pair of boots? What secrets does she have to whisper about that she has to go into the woods with a strange boy?

For almost a week Toibe hadn't stopped nagging and gnawing at her husband with her pious words about this poor young man, the half-student, who came to visit Betty and took her out to the woods to whisper in secret. And not only was Toibe constantly talking about him, he was also on her daughters' tongues. They were furious at him and at their cousin, fuming and whispering between them-selves. When Betty would come in, they would suddenly become silent, ex-change knowing glances and give little coughs, so that Betty would need to have been an idiot not to realize it was about her.

Who was this impoverished young man, the half-student, who had so stirred up the Familiants at the dacha and had caused such a cooling off toward their poor relative, Betty?

He was none other than the young man from Pinsk, Rabinovitch's old friend and associate from among the thirteen medalists who had not been deemed worthy, as the Pinsk youth had put it, of entering the "temple of learning," and was therefore at loose ends, wandering about, along with all those other Jews who know the bitter taste of residence permit laws.

the ninety-eighth chapter

BENNY HURVITCH

It was an oppressively hot summer day, one of those days when everything seems to be dozing lethargically under the burning sky, when one longs for a cool breeze, for a pond, for some ice, when every creature seeks the shade in which to hide itself from the unmerciful sun, which broils and bakes and drips with fire.

Sleepily still, as if in deep thought, the old, venerable forest, thick with tall pines, lay spread out, its floor covered with green, fragrant needles. This was the only spot where one could survive the unbearable heat of that blistering hot summer day. There, attached to trees, hung three woven hammocks, in which reclined in various positions three lovely girls: two of them were Toibe Familiant's daughters, the Jewish young ladies, reading Russian books, and the third was their cousin, Betty.

All three were fanning themselves vigorously because the heat was exhausting. The two sisters were in no mood to discuss literature with Betty, which ordinarily would never have tired them. Betty was content to be left to her own thoughts, a state in which of late she was happy to find herself. Suddenly she was informed that a young man in a white tunic was asking to see her.

"A young man in a white tunic? Who can it be?" asked Betty, turning her head to her cousins and sitting up.

"Why do you need to guess? If a young man is asking for you, receive him. Tell him to come out here," her cousins said as they sat up and straightened their hair.

Betty obeyed them, and no sooner did the young man with a broad smile on his open, freckled face approach than Betty immediately recognized him to be Rabinovitch's friend, to whom Rabinovitch had introduced her one time in the streets during the night of terror. Her face flooded with color. She became as excited to see him as if she had seen Rabinovitch himself.

Betty remembered that her mother had told her that he had visited her several times in the hospital to ask after her health but she had forgotten. Her thoughts from that time till the present were preoccupied with only one person, and that one person excluded all others from her mind. She was, therefore, feeling guilty toward him and wished to welcome him as befits a special guest. "Don't bother. I hate formalities, empty-minded conventions. I'm a simple man. I'm satisfied to sit down with you right here on God's earth under God's sky."

Without a second thought, he tossed his hat on the ground and seated himself under a tree next to Betty, clasped his knees, and spoke to her as to an intimate friend in his broad Litvak dialect.

"So tell me, my dear, how are you and what do you hear from your boyfriend, my half-Gentile comrade whose only claim to Jewishness is his name?"

Betty blushed deeper and wished to change the subject. She had not spoken a word to her cousins about Rabinovitch, had not so much as mentioned his name. They figured it was because the doctor had said over and over again not to speak about anything that might upset her, and they respected that. Betty was at a loss to know how to redirect the conversation and so she jumped upon the fact that she had forgotten to introduce her cousins to the guest. She introduced them by name and wanted to introduce her guest by name, as politeness required, but she had forgotten it.

The guest came to her aid: "Hurvitch, Benny Hurvitch," he introduced himself without standing up and without bowing, greatly displeasing the mam'selles. They became noticeably unhappy. But the guest was apparently quite pleased with himself and in great good humor as usual. He noticed the sisters exchanging frowns, and he said to them, "I can see my name means nothing to you, so let me mention the city from which I hail. Pinsk is the name of the city—have you ever heard of Pinsk? Well, I am one of the Pinsk Hurvitches, one of the *real,* Pinsk Hurvitches!"

Saying this, he glanced at Betty and saw by her face that she understood he was mimicking her father, David Shapiro, one of the real, Slaviteh Shapiros, and both burst out laughing.

This Hurvitch from Pinsk was making an unusually good impression on Betty. A cheerful, talkative fellow who laughed at his own jokes with so much evident enjoyment that it was catching.

They all soon fell into a conversation, including the Familiant sisters, who had quickly forgiven the guest his inelegant introduction. Their spirits lifted as they turned the discussion to modern literature, Artsibashev, and so on. But Hurvitch from Pinsk cut them off rudely.

"Tell me something, my dear girls. Why are you talking to me in Russian? Certainly my name, Benny Hurvitch, doesn't convey that I am, God forbid, a Gentile. Can you see the sign of the cross on my face? Forgive me for saying so, but it does seem to me you are Jewish children. If your faces don't give you away, then the way you speak Russian certainly does. So why don't you answer me in Yiddish?"

The poor Familiant mam'selles were totally unnerved. Never before had they met such a rude person. Imagine a young man allowing himself to speak that way. And they began to defend themselves: was Yiddish really a language? Did "jargon" have a grammar?

But Benny Hurvitch from Pinsk did not let them get away with such reasoning and said to them, laughing good-naturedly, "Yiddish isn't a language? 'Jargon,' you say, and doesn't have a grammar? Shame on you! Listen to what I say. First of all, Yiddish *is* a language like any other. Pity I don't have the time to get deeper into it to prove to you how wrong you are. Second of all, and please listen carefully to me, the fact that you aren't speaking Yiddish is not because it doesn't have a grammar—you can obviously get along without a grammar. You're not speaking Yiddish because you are slaves to the fashion of the times and do what everybody else is doing. Listen, do you really think that if you speak Russian they won't know who you are, ha-ha-ha! We resent it when the world thinks of us as inferior, ridicules us and shames us everywhere. Listen, how can we expect strangers to give us respect when we ourselves step on our own toes and spit in our own faces?"

The mam'selles were stunned speechless.

"A fine intellectual!" they thought. "Some gentleman! Goes around in shabby clothes and talks like an old gossip, with 'my dears' and 'listen to me,' like a *yenta* or Nekhama, the old lady who sells us chickens, geese, and ducks. It's a disgrace to be in the company of such a person, a disgrace!"

This would have been tolerable, had not Benny Hurvitch from Pinsk turned to Betty, as if they weren't there, and said to her in his Litvak dialect, "Did you know, my dear, I came here just to see you? Listen, I must talk to you about an important matter, very important, but just between us."

Both Familiant girls jumped up from their hammocks as if scalded and were about to leave in a huff without a farewell, leaving their cousin alone with her fine cavalier who did not know how to behave properly in the company of intelligent young ladies, but Betty stopped them by making sure to get up first and ask their forgiveness. She would spend a little time with her guest not far off in the woods and would soon come back.

This was for the mam'selles a final blow. They became infuriated at their cousin who now seemed to be rubbing it in. And they went off to their mother to inquire further whether she knew who this shabby *shlimazel* was who called himself by the name of Benny Hurvitch and boasted that he was from Pinsk, from the true, Pinsk Hurvitches.

Betty and her guest followed a narrow path between two rows of pine trees, which oozed sap and resin because of the heat, making the air redolent with fresh turpentine. When the pair had gone just far enough into the woods so that they could not be overheard, Benny Hurvitch from Pinsk immediately came to the point, and in his hearty voice and cheerful tone told Betty a story that raised her spirits to the skies. It was like a dream to her, a tale from a thousand and one nights, which reminded her of the miracles and wonders of the fabulous tales of Sherlock Holmes and Nat Pinkerton.

the ninety-ninth chapter

SHERLOCK HOLMES OR NAT PINKERTON

"Listen, I myself am a stubborn Jew," Benny Hurvitch from Pinsk began to tell Betty his story in his heavy Litvak dialect as they strolled in the woods. He took such long strides with his long legs that he had to stop every few minutes to allow her to catch up. "Out of sheer stubbornness I live here in this city, where a Jew must get himself a residence permit. Listen, *they* want me to live in Pinsk, and just because that's what *they* want, I want to live here—let's see them do something about that! And I *must* live here because all the books I need for my studies are found here. Let them insist on a residence permit till they're blue in the face, it will do them no good. I have to do what I have to do, no matter what! And I feel that sooner or later I'll win out in the end. Listen, I have so man ew ideas and inventions in my head that if they would allow me

into that "temple of learning" and provide me with everything I need—a laboratory with instruments and paraphernalia—I would turn the world upside down!
Maybe you'll laugh at me, you'll think I'm a dreamer or altogether crazy, but I
really believe I'm on to something that will make it unnecessary for people to
fight over a piece of bread like dogs. It's a new synthetic food that not only
would cost less than bread and meat and vegetables and not only hold its own
with all of these, but also would be a mixture that anyone could make with his
own hands. Are you hungry? Sit yourself down, take this little machine out of
your pocket, press here, crank there—presto—supper!"

The "pressing here" and "cranking there" he demonstrated with gestures as
seriously as if the "little machine" were right there in his hands.

"How I came upon this discovery and what problems I had to overcome until
I was able to obtain the necessary means to do the first tests and chemical
experiments and how many experiments still need to be undertaken in order to
develop the right combination is a long story, and I'm afraid you won't understand me. I'm not saying I have this thing ready at hand—I'm not that crazy.
I'm just saying that I think I'm on the right track. There were plenty before me
who cracked their heads on these universal problems, and maybe it will also be
my fate to crack my head, that I don't know. Maybe yes and maybe no. But if my
work succeeds you can appreciate what value I place on their residence permits,
damn them! Imagine what a sensation this discovery would cause and how the
world would then look, do you hear, if everyone were well fed, if there were no
more hunger, no more misery, no class struggle, no economic theories, no
Lumpenproletariat—an end to all problems!"

All the while he was talking, his eyes sparkled so brightly with triumph and his
freckled face shone so with happiness that Betty involuntarily stared at this odd
young man who had momentarily paused to mop the perspiration from his
broad forehead with the hem of his faded, creased, white tunic. She could not
help but notice that this discoverer of synthetic food, who would make the world
happy, was wearing a sorry tunic, long begging to be washed, ironed, and
mended.

"So, I am a stubborn Jew, as I told you, and live without a residence permit in
a city where I'm supposed to have one and I do what I want—I study. But listen,
since a belly can't live on theories, on stubbornness, or on a residence permit,
until the synthetic food becomes a reality, you have to fill it up, devil take it, so
it will leave you in peace. What can a Jew like Benny Hurvitch from Pinsk do?
He tutors students, you hear, and Gentile ones at that, the kind of Gentiles who
are thick with the police. How do they say?—'In a kosher pot you'll find a
kosher spoon!' But you may ask: Where do the police come in? What have I to
do with police? Wonder of wonders! Just because I *don't* have a residence permit
and have to look out for the police, I was helped all the more, in a roundabout
way. How? I thought it over and said to myself: 'Your head is on the chopping
block as it is, Benny, what have you got to lose? Try to win them over with
kindness. Why should you always be at war with everyone?' So I said to one of
them, face to face, 'Listen, Gentile, to what I will tell you. The story,' I said, 'is

this: money,' I said, 'I can't give you, and you,' I said, 'are a person who needs to
be on the take. I need to pay you off,' I said, 'but how? If, I said, you have
children and you want your children to learn something, I am prepared,' I said,
'to teach them one hour a day, and I promise you that, even if they're dunces,
I'll turn them into scholars, distinguished Torah scholars.' "

"Those were my very words, but why go on and on? The Gentile looked me up
and down, and I must have been to his liking. He said to me: 'Come to my
house at such and such a time and we'll talk.' Do you hear that? Of course, I
didn't waste any time and came exactly to the minute and found there, listen to
this, children, one after another—and real dunces! But if a person is destined, it
really goes well for him, and by word of mouth one job led to another, but this
time for money, until I came across this Gentile, a higher up, who had been
given the boot. Why did they give him the boot? Over an intrigue: they dug and
dug around him until they buried him—well, not exactly buried, that isn't the
main point of the story. That's just hearsay. The point is that I appealed to this
Gentile, and listen to this, he liked me so much that he trusted me with a
confidence, something that has a great deal to do with you."

Betty startled and he imagined she turned somewhat pale.

"With me?"

But Benny Hurvitch from Pinsk quickly reassured her.

"If not you directly, then indirectly, with your . . . well, with your friend, let
us say, with my half-Gentile comrade, who is suffering for all Israel."

Betty exhaled and Benny Hurvitch from Pinsk continued.

"To make a long story short, this higher up who wanted to climb the ladder to
go still higher, as soon as they caught him and gave him the sack, decided to
take revenge, as we say, 'An eye for an eye . . .' He vowed, 'Revenge!' He swore
he would bury those who had buried him, but how? It's quite a story, just listen:
This higher up I'm telling you about was one of those whose task it was to
investigate robberies and robbers. Their minds are focused only on things that
have to do with the commandment 'Thou shalt not steal,' and since he was an
expert in these matters, they assigned him a large number of thefts committed
by a band of infamous thieves and swindlers. He undertook to investigate those
thefts one by one, to weed out and prosecute the criminals and put them in the
clink. Luckily, he succeeded because he was diligent and thorough.

"Listen, he frequented countless taverns, thieves' dens, and rat holes, became
intimate with robbers, bandits, and hooligans, learned their argot, drank whiskey
with them, joined them in their crimes of robbing, breaking in, and other things,
even went so far as having himself arrested with them for the sole purpose of
learning more of their secrets about other thefts and crimes. Had he been allowed to carry it out to the end, he would probably have gotten a promotion,
risen higher and higher in the ranks, and would in time have become famous, a
kind of Sherlock Holmes or Nat Pinkerton. But what happened? It was a real
tragedy, do you hear. He was suddenly stopped dead in his tracks! He was at the
very point, he said, of winding up the whole case, and the devil got into him, he
said, and he got involved in this new case where he ran into this Gentile, young

but already a veteran thief. Under the influence of a glass of liquor, this Gentile admitted to a whole string of thefts, assorted crimes, and murders, among them, the murder of the young Gentile, Volodka, who became a celebrity because of us Jews! And until then, you must know, our Gentile was positive, like so many other Gentiles, that Volodka's death was the work of Jews in honor of Passover, because he was convinced even to this day that we eat chicken all year just like everyone else, but when Passover comes, it is our custom to swallow small Gentile boys . . . what can you do? So having come upon this new case, our Sherlock Holmes, or Nat Pinkerton, thought it over and decided to spit on all the other thefts and crimes and to put all his energy into pursuing this new case. He didn't take his eyes off this Gentile, became very friendly with him, real bosom buddies, and began little by little to extract information from him, a spoonful every day, until finally he found out all there was to know—the whole kit and caboodle. Just listen to this. It was a whole gang, and in the middle of it all, a woman, *cherchez la femme.* No, not just one woman, but two, three women. Volodka had boasted to his mother that some stranger, an official, was giving him candies in return for information—and that one was—listen to this—none other than our Sherlock Holmes, or Nat Pinkerton, the official who had been given the sack. And when he realized that he might have been an unwitting accomplice in the murder of Volodka, he was all the more impelled to quickly uncover the entire conspiracy. He says he would certainly have succeeded in doing so, and in the most spectacular way, had he not been fired, out of the blue. Right in the middle of his work! He had no idea why! Just a little bit more time, and the whole case, he said, would have been served up on a platter. He was lacking, he said, only two things: first, the Gentile mind of our Sherlock Holmes couldn't figure out why there were forty-nine stab wounds on the little Gentile's body. The number forty-nine, he said, upset him. He had heard that for Jews it was a Kabbalistic number. According to the Kabbalah, he said, Jews must draw blood from forty-nine wounds.

"I burst out laughing, do you hear, and said to him, 'Listen to me, Gentile, leave the Kabbalah out of this. You know from Kabbalah, as I know from drawing blood from forty-nine wounds. But one thing surprises me about you, I said, you are a Gentile with energy and common sense, almost a Sherlock Holmes, I said, or at least a Nat Pinkerton. You can see plainly that this is a victim, not of Jews, but of your own thieves and hooligans who finished off Volodka for their own purposes and put the blame on Jews so they wouldn't be suspected. Why didn't the thought enter your head that the gang intentionally stabbed the boy forty-nine times after the murder in order to delude you and other Pinkertons like yourself, who know about as much about our Kabbalah as I know about Mars?' He stopped and thought it over, my Sherlock Holmes, and said to me, 'What you say is all very possible, although you can't convince me that you can get along without our blood on Passover . . .' 'A curse on his head!' I thought, but he went on to say, 'I'll tell you the whole truth. Something else is bothering me: I was afraid to rely on this young crook's word. What a thief brags about under the influence of alcohol is nothing much to go on. To uncover something big you need, he said, reliable proof, some hard evidence in your hand, what jurists call "corpus delicti." ' . . . And in order to get such evidence, my Sherlock Holmes thought it over and came up with a brilliant ruse, like a true Pinkerton. He said to the thief that he didn't believe him, it was an utter lie, just boasting, and that was all there was to it. That one swore up and down that it was true, but he still wouldn't believe him. He played so long on his vanity that the young hood was ready to roll up his sleeves and punch our Pinkerton in the nose to teach him a lesson.

"The long and the short of it is, listen to this, he gave his word he would produce some evidence, some proof that could not be refuted. 'Where is your proof?' He couldn't, he said, produce it right there on the spot. He would bring it to him tomorrow or the day after tomorrow. He didn't have it, his former wife had it, a Gentile woman with whom he had had a fight. 'What's her name?' 'I can tell you everything but that. Forget it!' 'What is the evidence? Can't you at least tell me that?' 'It's a satchel with books and school lessons that the young Volodka was carrying the morning they did him in.'

"It was just then that my Sherlock Holmes met his downfall. Soon after, the young crook vanished and the *corpus delicti*, Volodka's satchel with the books and school lessons, some Gentile woman had whose name he still did not know. But he was searching for her and felt he was sure to find her, even if he had to look for her at the ends of the earth, unless he were to die first. And I believe him. Do you know why? Because he isn't doing this out of love but out of hatred. There is no better motive, do you hear me, than hatred, and no more terrible weapon than revenge. But how do we say it?—Let it be a Cossack, as long as it's a remedy . . ."

the hundredth chapter

BETTY GETS DOWN TO WORK

From the very first, the way this Benny Hurvitch from Pinsk talked appealed to Betty. He spoke with every part of his body; his eyes sparkled, his face flushed as he lowered his head, while his hands moved up and down like a woman blessing the Sabbath candles. At every opportunity, he laughed in a loud, resonant voice that echoed through the woods. No wonder Betty heard him out so intently, not wishing to interrupt him, especially as his story became more and more pertinent to her. And as her interest grew, so did her confidence and her good feeling toward this young man. She was reminded of her first meeting with him that night of the great terror when they had fled together with other Jews wherever their feet would carry them. She was reminded of the exchange he had had at that time with Rabinovitch, and she recalled that even then he had seemed to be very likable. She remembered comparing them. It struck her that this young man, who called himself Benny Hurvitch from Pinsk, was perhaps a good head taller than Rabinovitch. She was quite disappointed, she remembered, that he was taller. Not superior—no, she wasn't saying that—but taller, perhaps more mature, more genuine, and a warmer person than the other . . .

"God Himself has sent him here," Betty thought as she listened to his tale, afraid to miss a single word. Everything, every word was important to her, and no one could appreciate it as much as she because no one else knew what she knew. She and none other had had the rare privilege of spending a night in prison with the one whom this "Sherlock Holmes" was now seeking and could not find. This was the poor lost soul who smelled of heliotrope and iodoform and from whom Betty had heard so many dreadful stories. In the possession of that lost soul was to be found the key to the mystery, the essential clue, the *corpus delicti* needed for the trial—the satchel of books and school lessons belonging to the murdered Volodka. Once obtained, and the gang of thieves put away, it would spell the end of the blood libel and the accusation of ritual murder, it would all be over and Rabinovitch would go free! No, Betty could no longer hold herself back. She reached out with both hands to the genial Hurvitch from Pinsk and bestowed upon him a look of her beautiful eyes that Rabinovitch could never resist and said to him, "The story you've just told me, though you tell it as if it is all about 'Sherlock Holmes' or 'Nat Pinkerton,' is of enormous interest to me, really to us all! You cannot imagine what could come out of this. I don't have enough words to express to you how grateful I am for your . . . for your visit."

"Grateful for my visit?" Benny Hurvitch said, taking her in with a kindly, ironic look as a father would look at a child, or an older brother at a naive, foolish younger sister, and he burst into his fresh, healthy, resonant laugh, which echoed far into the woods. "Listen, I return half the thanks to you. My comrade may be closer to you than I, but he is still a Jew locked up behind thick walls. He isn't the only one in prison. Listen to me, together with him in prison are all our millions of Jews, as many of us as are in this country, and we are all being accused as he is of something that is a disgrace even to have to answer for. So why all this gratitude and these clichés we Jews dismiss as fancy talk?"

"You don't understand me," Betty tried to explain. "To me your story had a particular interest. The wife of that young thief, the one they're looking for and can't find, I know a way . . ."

But here Betty caught herself and did not wish to go further, as there were several plans unfolding in her head about how to get down to work on the matter. Above all, it would be necessary to find out the name of the woman—that wasn't difficult. Since she and Betty had both been arrested at the same time that awful night, her name must be entered together with her own. Someone would have to requisition the records. Only a high-ranking official or someone who used to be one could do that. But how could she give this information to Hurvitch when she had no inclination to reveal that she had once been in prison? Her vain, proud nature wouldn't allow it. Perhaps he would start questioning her about matters she herself wished to forget. But neither could she remain silent. It was high time to get down to the real work! Now the time had come when she had to and could *do* something. In a moment she had formulated a plan in her mind, a wonderful plan she could not tell anyone. She again spoke to him and moved a bit closer, granting him one of those irresistible looks that Rabinovitch would even now have given half his life for, if not all of it.

"Listen, I have a favor to ask you . . ."

Benny Hurvitch thrust both hands into the pockets of his faded white tunic and took her in with that ironic, friendly look and responded merrily in several different languages.

"A favor? Name it, tell me what it is, for instance, *par exemple, nafshiklad, naprimiere,* anything."

Betty backed off a bit. She was thinking: "What kind of person is this? Here he was just talking with such fire about such lofty matters, brilliant inventions and ideas, and now he makes himself into a simpleton, talks like a clown, and at a time when we are speaking about a serious matter that even he says the honor of all Jews depends on." She was not loath to tell him openly and rather sharply that she hated puns and that she enjoyed joking when it was appropriate, but she simply could not understand how one could laugh and be so cheerful at a time when a friend was in prison, as he himself had said, locked behind thick walls . . .

"You don't understand how one can be cheerful? Listen, just to look at you makes one feel good despite oneself . . . But sha! Peace!" he said to her, noting that she was becoming even angrier, and he extended his large hand, stained with the dye of some chemical mixture. "Sha! I beg you, please, let's make peace! We don't dare quarrel. We must be friends . . . All right? Forgiven? Now tell me what favor I can do for you and I pledge to you half my kingdom . . ."

Betty realized it was impossible to remain angry at this man for long. From the moment he had said "Peace," her heart softened toward him and she said to him a bit capriciously, as was her style, with a little smile, "Really, you're in luck. I should, as a matter of fact, be very angry with you, but since you've brought me such good news today, I'll forgive you this time. The favor I want to ask of you is this: I want you to introduce me to that . . . that . . ."

Benny Hurvitch came to her rescue.

"To my Sherlock Holmes? What for?"

He gave her his kindly, mocking look and waited.

Should she tell him why? Should she go into how she had once spent a night in prison together with a street woman? No, that she wouldn't do! Under no circumstances! And she tried to wriggle out of it.

"Just like this . . . I mean, it wouldn't do any harm if I were to have a little talk with him . . ."

"What for?"

Betty began to get angry. "Just like a Litvak!" she thought. She cut him off as only she could do, imitating his dialect.

"What for? What business is it of yours? What for? If I say I want to meet him, I probably know what for! Do I need to give you an accounting?"

But Benny Hurvitch was not one of those easily cowed men. He stood his ground and looked her right in the eye.

"An accounting, you say? Why do I need an accounting from you? Listen, you can believe me that I can get along without your accounting. You don't want to tell me, you don't have to. I promise you I can do whatever you wish! I don't need your accounting!"

Betty felt she had stepped on his toes. This person was friendly, spoke so gently and warmly that one felt good in his company, involuntarily. She wished to placate him, and said softly: "Taste a few of these fragrant cherries from this tree. Do believe me, it isn't out of sheer curiosity. There's a good reason for it. I'm no Sherlock Holmes or Nat Pinkerton. Nevertheless, I'm in a position to assist your acquaintance in finding that woman. In a word, I can be useful. So, I beg you to introduce me to him."

All the while Betty was speaking, Benny Hurvitch from Pinsk stood with his hands in the pockets of his faded, short white tunic, looked at her and thought: "What a firebrand! She'll twist someone like Rabinovitch around her little finger! But he's no fool either, that Rabinovitch."

"Why are you looking at me like that?" Betty suddenly grabbed his hand, scattering the cherries.

"Why am I looking at you? Listen, I was wondering how we can get the cat to swim across the river. How will you work it, my dear, so that it will come off smoothly and cleverly? For instance" (and here he launched into the sing-song of a *yeshiva* student), should you go out of your way to meet him—too much respect for such a Gentile—or should he come to you? It wouldn't be fitting for your rich, religious relatives, as I can see. So the question remains: how do we get the cat to cross the river?"

"Well, yes, how do we get the cat across?" Betty echoed his words, and felt guilty toward this young man who was in truth so good-hearted. She wanted all the more to appease him, but he had already forgotten the slight as he spoke to her amiably, in his resonant, energetic voice and suddenly gave himself a smack on the forehead.

"Wait, do you know what? Listen, Sunday is the day that everyone in the city goes out to the dachas to cool off and get some fresh air. I'll tell my Gentile, 'Listen, Gentile, there's someone'—I won't tell him who, just some-one—'who wants to meet you and has some important secret information to tell you about a certain matter,' and I'm positive, do you hear, that the Gentile will run out here, because he's so involved in this case that he'll go to the ends of the earth for it. And I'll bring him to this very spot . . . no, I'll arrive with him on the two-thirty train at the station, where you'll wait for us, and from there the three of us can walk in the field across from the station or through the woods on the opposite side. And you can tell him all the secrets you have and, listen, I won't disturb you. Do you like my plan?"

What a question, did she like his plan! Betty was in seventh heaven: she would really be getting down to work. *She* would be helping to locate the main clue, *she* would be helping to solve the mystery, *she* would be helping to free her innocent friend. And whom did she have to thank? This Benny Hurvitch from Pinsk. "A strange person, but a generous heart and a sincere soul," thought Betty as she parted from him warmly, again and again pressing his large, calloused, stained hand as they went their separate ways—he to the train station in town and she to her wealthy relatives at the dacha, satisfied and happy that the time had come when she could get to work and put an end to what others, complete strangers, had started. It was more than even she herself had hoped for. And the whole world suddenly took on a new aspect in her eyes. Where had this lovely, gloriously attired woods been until now? Why had she not smelled the rare aroma that filled this earthly paradise till now? Where had all these multitudes of birds and flying things been till now? Why had she not heard their singing and whistling, twittering, buzzing and humming till now? And the sky—had it always been as blue and infinitely deep as now? Who would now say that life was a sad, foolish jest? . . .

*   *   *

When Betty arrived home at the dacha, flushed with the heat and happy from the successful day, revealed by the gleam in her lovely eyes and the color in her cheeks, she encountered her Aunt Toibe, who greeted her with a cold look and with her lips more tightly pursed than ever.

"Where have you been so long? They've been searching all over for you, in every corner of the woods. Your uncle was frantic and was about to harness the horses to the carriage to go looking for you in town. You modern girls, you go off with some young man in the woods, may the blessed God not punish me for these words, I don't like to say anything bad about anyone, heaven forbid!"

As her pious aunt was berating her as if she were reciting from her prayer book, her daughters, the intellectual mam'selles, pretended to be so deeply absorbed in their books that they didn't hear their mother's invective. But one could see by their pinched noses that they were in a huff about their little cousin. But what did Betty care, when no later than the coming Sunday she would be meeting with a person who had in his hands the key to the mystery upon which depended not only her happiness but the honor of her people, of an entire people?

SENDING THE FOX TO GUARD THE CHICKEN COOP

The visit from the roomer's relatives, the Rabinovitches, as expected, caused an upheaval in the Shapiro household. David Shapiro declared that he had from the very beginning had his doubts about the roomer, that he was not what he seemed. And it was all *her* fault, he complained, indicating his wife. If not for *her*, a charlatan like that would long have seen the other side of his door.

"Since when did he become a charlatan?" Sara tried to contradict her husband, but she knew he was right, bless his soul, he was right! As highly as she had regarded the roomer, so low had he now fallen in her estimation, to the point of revulsion. He could keep his millionairess aunt, together with his large inheritance. Where was it written that a Jew needed a rich aunt to leave him money? How many Jews were there in the world who managed just fine without rich aunts? What really stuck in her throat was this "sister," Vera. According to his father and brother, he had no sister named Vera, so who was this beauty who wrote him love letters, devil take her, and signed them "Vera P."?

And another thing Sara could not begin to understand: why did he have to pretend he didn't understand a word of Yiddish? What kind of perverse joke was that? And all those other stories of his were also obviously made out of whole cloth, intended to deceive everyone, to bring misfortune to her daughter and, who knows, maybe end by leaving her a grass widow?

Sara was reminded of those dreadful tales she had heard about young men, clever operators, supposedly from Byelorussia, who would come to town ostensibly to find brides, would dandy themselves up to attract women, pretend to fall in love with them, and carry off the best girls, the devil knows where. She felt a chill pass over her body. God knows what could have happened to her child if this Volodka blood libel had not happened. Now just one thing remained—to open her daughter's eyes, to let her learn who this rascal was. But how could it be done when the doctors had warned a hundred times over that she had to be allowed to recuperate and no word was to be said about matters that might upset her?

Sara spent a good deal of time considering all kinds of alternatives and finally chose the best way and the best person to carry it out. This was none other than the doctor himself, the family doctor.

"First, he's a doctor, and who knows as well as a doctor how to talk to a patient so it won't do him any harm? And second, he's our family doctor, and he says he's devoted to her—so now let him prove his devotion. No, we could find no better emissary than he."

Sara Shapiro wasted no time and took the trouble to go herself to the doctor's home.

When he saw who his visitor was, the doctor became a bit confused and scratched his bald pate, which shone like a polished samovar. He made short work of his poor patients, giving one a salve for his back and pushing another out the door: "Good, good! Next time I'll write you a prescription!" And he eagerly opened the door of his office and called in Sara Shapiro.

"Sit, Madam, what good news do you have for me?"

They sat down together uncomfortably, as if forced to sit on hot coals. Sara's eyes began to dart about the doctor's office, which was cluttered with piles of old books, mounds of dust, papers, instruments, a few worn cuffs thrown into a heap, everything all helter-skelter. Like a typical, meticulous Jewish housewife, she couldn't help remark about the mess his office was in, "worse than a disorderly bathhouse."

"Listen to me. You need to get married," she tossed off lightly, to get the conversation started. But the doctor interpreted it quite differently and his face flushed deeply. Large beads of perspiration stood out on his shiny pate. He removed his glasses and quickly replaced them.

"You are certainly right, Madam. I've been thinking about that a long time, I mean, not too long, I just started to think about it . . ."

"Look at him with his bald head," Sara said to herself. "Finally decided to think about it! It would almost be time for him to bring children to the wedding canopy and he's just starting to think!"

"I was planning to ask your advice about it," the doctor went on, and had difficulty breathing.

"What's there to give advice about?" Sara interrupted him, and inundated him with words, as was her style, giving him countless examples of friends who had married too early or who had married too late and finished by saying, "If I had my way, I would rather marry earlier than later because since the world began it's never happened that anyone who married too early regretted it."

The doctor wanted to answer her, "First of all, Madam, . . ." but all he got out were the four words, "First of all, Madam," as the "Madam" didn't allow him to finish his sentence. She assured him she knew better than he what he was going to say, but it was nonsense, there were no exceptions, that's how God created the world—that was it. And she immediately turned to the matter for which she had come.

"Since you are our family doctor and a good friend of my child, my Betty, whom you say you've known since she was this high" (Sara placed her hand close to the floor and the doctor put on a serious face and felt his heart was almost bursting), "I have a favor to ask you."

And she related to him at length the story about the visit of their roomer's father and brother, from whom they had found out so many fine things about this Rabinovitch, who, begging your pardon, turned out to be a liar, a trickster, a foolish braggart. There's no aunt, no millions, no inheritance, all a fairy tale; the cow jumped over the moon and laid an egg . . .

The doctor, who could barely sit still in his chair for joy, had to use all his strength not to leap up. He felt his heart swelling, and a rosy flush spread across his cheeks, his excitement making it impossible for him to say a word. He sprang up, removed his glasses, and exclaimed to her, "Madam, listen to what I will tell you. I don't need to boast to you and I don't want to say anything bad about anyone, but I swear that I knew it would happen this way. I knew it as surely as I live! For instance, do you remember the first time when I was called to see him after the first house search? What did I tell you then, Madam?"

The doctor put on his glasses and sat down.

"What did you tell me?" the "Madam" asked, and stared at him like a Cossack caught stealing.

"I told you, I told you honestly right away that he was an odd Jew."

"Is that all?" Sara said, and leaned back in her chair. "A mute wouldn't say in a year what you just said in a minute."

"No. I knew," the doctor insisted on her understanding him, but Sara wouldn't let him speak.

"You knew? My husband also says he knew. You're all prophets in hindsight."

"Per-permit me, Madam . . ."

"What's this permit me, permit me! What are you talking about! Do you think there was anything between them, God forbid? Not a thing! Nothing at all!"

The doctor was satisfied that there had been nothing between them but was still a bit uneasy.

"I know it was nothing . . . What *could* there have been between them?"

Sara looked at him.

"Are you out of your mind? What do you mean, what *could* there have been between them? Only talk, that's all. What else could there have been?"

The doctor removed his glasses and put them right back on again: So it appears it had gone quite far . . . He said to her, "They talked? What do you mean?"

"Why not? Is there something wrong with that?"

"Wrong, you say? What a strange woman you are. How does one come to the other? Your Betty is a Jewish daughter and the other one is a . . . a . . . who knows what?"

"Well, yes, of course, now you're all sages! All wise men! Afterward, in hindsight, a blind person can see, a deaf person can hear, and a mute can talk . . ."

For some time they circled around this same point, not understanding one another. Sara deluged him with words, not allowing him to open his mouth, until they finally came to the reason for her coming: she wanted him to help her remove that man from her daughter's heart. It was difficult for her to know how to put it, one had to be a mother to understand her. In short, as he usually drove out to visit her every Sunday, he should speak to her about the roomer, he should tell her he was really a poor *shlimazel* who was sitting in prison for another's sins, a scapegoat for all of Israel. But he was also—she should excuse him for saying it—worthless, a liar, a deceiver, an empty windbag. At the same time, he was to tell her the story about his relatives, but a little at a time, not all at once, and cleverly, carefully, because with her Betty you had to be well prepared if you wanted to discuss a serious matter. "She's some Betty!" she said to him with a sigh, standing at the door, still not allowing him to speak. She told him again and again how to deal with Betty, carefully and guardedly!

Sara Shapiro was content that she had succeeded in choosing the right emissary, and even if he wasn't so terribly crafty, he was still an honest man, better than most, and his words would carry some weight with her Betty.

It didn't occur to the happy mother that she was inadvertantly sending the fox to guard the chicken coop. Had she given it more thought, she would have seen by the doctor's glowing face and by his eyes, which now shone with a different gleam and appeared younger than usual, that he seemed to have become suddenly more youthful now that he had been assigned this pleasant task. He was already preparing the way he would talk to Mam'selle Shapiro. Gradually he would open her eyes to this scoundrel, this adventurer. After that, he would casually, politely, quite calmly but diplomatically say a few words on his own behalf. When he wanted to, he could be very calm. He would tell her why he had not spoken to her until now. He would say he had not wished to stand between her and the other, who was younger than he and perhaps had finer qualities than he. That was what he had once thought. But now, as it had turned out, the young had to take lessons from their elders . . . Now, as it had turned out, he was little more than a rascal, an adventurer, a rake, a scoundrel, a real charlatan who led people to believe he was the wealthy heir of a millionairess aunt, entirely false, and who pretended he didn't know a star from a crucifix, acted as if he didn't understand a word of Yiddish. He had been leading everybody around by the nose, the devil only knows why, perhaps just to confuse everyone. If that were the case, then someone like that deserved— who-knows-what! Calm, polite, dignified, without any ulterior motive, he, if he so wished, could do it. Now it was necessary to prepare, to pull oneself together.

After boiling himself some water on a small alcohol burner all bachelors possess, he sharpened his straight razor on the leather strop that had hung on the same door frame for years and that shone like his bald pate. He locked himself in his office, shaved, and donned his best suit, inspected his image in the cracked mirror and had to admit that, even though he was no youngster, he still had a solid look about him. In any case, there were many older bachelors than himself, and even his bald head was not such a catastrophe. Nowadays there were many marriageable young men, real gentlemen and scholars with naked scalps, without a trace of hair, absolutely none! He smoothed out what little growth remained, a reminder that this man once did have a full head of hair. He got rid of the last patient, who had managed to squeeze himself in, insisting that the Herr Doktor kindly see him and prescribe something for him.

"Prescribe something for you! This is what I'll prescribe!" The doctor waved his cane with the ivory handle that was once white but with time had turned yellow. "I told you, it seems to me, twenty thousand times, that Sunday afternoon I don't see any patients, no matter what! I can be a person like everyone else half a day a week, can't I?"

He ordered the horses harnessed to his worn, broken-down, little carriage, donned his hat, straightened his back, drew himself up like a bridegroom, and set out, optimistic and cheerful, like a person on his way to a sure thing.

the hundred-second chapter

SHE RECOGNIZES HIM!

From afar, the train station resembled a bouquet of many-colored flowers as the ladies from the dachas in their Sunday finery came out to greet their guests arriving from the big city. Some were awaiting their husbands or friends who were certain to arrive, others for guests who might arrive, and others had come only out of curiosity to see whoever might arrive. They were dressed up in summery country styles, low-cut and a bit unbuttoned. There was no stinting on silk fabric, multicolored ribbons, and the most expensive lace, while white, red, green, and yellow parasols bobbed in the crowd—a bouquet of human flowers.

Since early morning on this special Sunday Betty Shapiro had been dressed from head to toe in white: a white batiste frock with white lace, a little white hat, small white gloves, a white parasol, and even white shoes. Her outfit was not the most expensive to be found, most likely the cheapest Sara Shapiro could afford to buy her. Nonetheless, it fit her so charmingly, so flatteringly, and so suited her perfect figure and beautiful face, flushed with excitement under her thick, hastily rolled-up tresses and her large, clear, intelligent eyes under full, soft brows—that everything she wore that lovely, bright, summery morning sparkled, shimmered, and sang. As one looked at her, comparisons to the Song of Songs involuntarily suggested themselves, like morning star, Shulamit, rose of Sharon, lily of the valley.

Betty did not mention she was going anywhere and hid her excitement so that no one could tell. But when the Familiants had gone off for their rest after lunch and the mam'selles left with their books and hammocks for the woods, Betty held off for an hour and then quietly slipped out of her room, passed through the garden, and from there hurried down the path to the station. She arrived in time to witness how the entire bouquet of human flowers moved from the steps toward the incoming train, out of which streamed, singly, the arriving passengers carrying large suitcases, baskets, and rucksacks. A bustle of excited welcoming ensued.

From the distance, Betty spotted the Pinsk youth, Benny Hurvitch, by his faded, yellow-white tunic and his freckled, open, smiling face as he stepped from the train. She also noticed another person following him from the train, a tall big-boned man wearing a wide-brimmed, white straw hat that made it impossible to see his face.

Benny Hurvitch left the man with the wide-brimmed hat standing near the steps while he ran quickly with his long legs straight to Mam'selle Shapiro and greeted her with his usual cheerfulness.

"*Mazel tov*, I brought you this rare bird you asked to see, the official who was so ignominiously fired. He still doesn't know who was responsible for ruining him, poor fellow. Where do you want to speak to him, or to put it more elegantly, where does the Mam'selle wish to *rendezvous* with him?"

The good humor in Hurvitch's speech made Betty laugh, and she pointed to a lane of young trees on the right with green benches on either side that ascended the hill. The lane led to a fountain decorated with a young, nude angel holding a flute spouting water. There they would be able to sit and talk.

"Ho-ho! Nothing could be better!" Hurvitch gave his approval, pursing his lips. "A true earthly paradise! The greatest poet, do you hear, could not have invented a more romantic place for a *rendezvous* between a Jewish Shulamit and a Gentile Sherlock Holmes, or Nat Pinkerton, ha-ha! Please be so kind and sit down a moment. I'll go after my Gentile."

With those words the merry Hurvitch from Pinsk ran down the steps to his acquaintance while Betty seated herself on one of the green benches next to the fountain graced by the statue spouting water. She hadn't noticed that the crowd had in the meantime thinned out, the tumult had abated, and the human bouquet had melted in the sun like freshly fallen snow. In a few minutes not a soul remained on the platform except for a few porters and janitors who were collecting the remaining freight—a pair of chairs packed in straw, a child's cradle, a bicycle, and other such items. Among them the stationmaster was walking about with a red hat pulled down to the tips of his protruding ears and shoved forward over his drawn, tubercular face. Both hands were stuffed in the pockets of his heavy overcoat though it was still warm out. He gazed skyward in appreciation of the clear, blue sky and the kindly, warm sun.

The youth from Pinsk quickly reappeared, and behind him, the big-boned man with the wide-brimmed white hat from under which one could clearly make out black or dark blue spectacles with shiny, round, convex lenses—spectacles that were designed for the purpose of hiding the eyes. Dark eyeglasses had never been pleasant for Betty to look at, but more so since the encounter with that person who wore exactly the same glasses. Remembering him, Betty lost the good mood Hurvitch had just instilled with his constantly cheerful face and odd, lively expressions. And the person with the wide-brimmed hat, even before he approached her and even before Hurvitch introduced him, removed his hat—and at once Betty had to grasp the railing of the bench she was sitting on in order not to fall over.

SHE HAD RECOGNIZED HIM!

In a split second, in the wink of an eye, she relived all that she had endured that night she could never forget. What should she do? Get up and run away? No, there was no time for that, no chance, no strength to get up and no words to utter. How could she not have asked beforehand exactly who he was? Hurvitch had told her he was a former high official, now stripped of his job. She herself should have guessed who it must be, it was easy to figure out. But what good did it do her now? It was too late—it was *he!* . . . Now *he* was her ally, and through him they would have to protect and clear the name of her beloved and the honor of them all, of her entire people. Could there be a more bitter irony?

No less astonished, apparently, was he. It seemed he also recognized her immediately because as he stood holding in his hand the hat he had just removed, his body froze and his face changed expressions several times in an instant, taking on a different appearance. This man had the ability to alter his physiognomy at will. If you see him today, you will not be sure you will see him tomorrow looking exactly the same as he had the day before.

But this time he had so lost hold of himself that he did not know what expression to assume. On the way there, he had in vain asked Hurvitch time and time again to tell him who the person was who wanted to meet him. He had made the trip without enthusiasm and, had not this wily Jew, for whom he felt an odd fondness and trust, seduced him with his charming speech, he probably would not have come. This Jewish fellow had teased him, saying he was a coward, he was afraid of going with him. *He* a coward? *He* afraid of going with him? *He* who had knocked around with hooligans, thieves, and murderers, afraid of a Jew? And he inquired no further, proceeding entirely in the dark—and now whom did he meet!

Never would he have dreamed that it would be this girl, this "Venus of the Jewish Street," whom he had pursued in vain and because of whom he had forfeited his career! He was positive of that although no one had said it in so many words, but he knew. Right after that very night, intrigue upon intrigue had been plotted against him, a veritable campaign, until finally they had succeeded in bringing him down. He knew they wanted to destroy him altogether, but they didn't have enough evidence because the girl herself apparently did not wish to press charges. How many times had he thought about her, wondering where she was, how she was? Then he had heard that she was ill, in the hospital, even that she had died. Then they told him it was untrue—and here she was! So *she* was the one who wanted to meet with him to talk about the matter for which he was now prepared to give his life in order to take revenge on his bloody friends! Surely, if a hole had opened in the earth at that moment, he would gladly have leaped into it!

It is hard to say what exactly this person was feeling during those few trying minutes: Embarrassment? Regret? What people call pangs of conscience? Self-hatred or hatred of others? Or all of these at once? Who can know what goes on in another's soul, and especially in the darkest corners of the soul of one who has been stripped of his dignity, who has more than one transgression on his conscience, but who, out of a desire for revenge and for other personal reasons, suddenly becomes a penitent?

the hundred-third chapter

A CLOWN!

But if Betty and the former official were astonished, their go-between, Benny Hurvitch from Pinsk, was much more astonished than they. "Well," he thought, "*she's* a girl—a delicate thing, a fragile being a strong wind can blow away. But the Gentile, what's happening to *his* strength, to *his* tongue? What's struck him dumb? There he is, standing like a bewildered bridegroom—we've got to shake them up a bit!" And he was fully prepared to take on the role of facilitator, first to introduce them, as was only polite, to set them on the right path, and then to leave them on their own. But Betty could tell by his eyes what he was thinking, and before he could open his mouth, she anticipated him. She marshaled all her strength, stood up, took two steps forward, and spoke as firmly to the man as possible, although her voice trembled and her cheeks flushed.

"Don't take offense, we will not introduce ourselves by name, as is customary—it isn't necessary. We have more important things to do. We're meeting for the first time" (she stressed the word "first") "and probably the last. We won't waste any time because we have little of it to spare, only a few minutes. I must go from here to another town, where I live with my sister" (she looked meaningfully at Benny Hurvitch). "Let's get right down to business."

She sat down on the the bench and motioned for him to sit near her. The man first removed his hat and looked for a spot to place it and couldn't seem to find one for the longest time. It was plain to see the man was still disconcerted and had not yet calmed down. Then he seated himself, still wordlessly. But by the look through his dark blue spectacles at the young man from Pinsk, it was obvious he was furious at him for misleading him in this way. And as if Betty had guessed his thoughts or simply wished to begin the conversation quickly and in some way to defend Hurvitch, she said to the man with a smile that cost her dearly, "Our friend Hurvitch has misled you. He told you that a *man* was waiting here to meet you and wanted to speak to you. And in the end you find out it's a . . . girl. That was my doing. I told him to do that."

The last words were spoken with such pride, and Betty lifted her head so high and gestured so magnanimously, that one might have thought a queen were speaking to her subject, to whom she had lowered herself for his sake.

"Say, I'm beginning to like this girl. She's one of my kind," Benny Hurvitch from Pinsk thought. "She's a little bit crazy. Why does she need to make up all those lies? But maybe that's part of her strategy—who cares!" And as he hadn't been invited to sit, he surmised that they could do very well without him. And perhaps it was a secret from him. Or perhaps he should preoccupy himself with his own thoughts. Whatever the case, he unobtrusively removed himself, stepped off to the side, leaned with both arms on the vine-covered fence, and, deep in thought, quietly hummed a Pinsk song, tapping his foot in time:

> Comes a *goy* into a little bar,
> Into a little bar,
> Drinks to the dregs, wants a bottle more,
> A bottle more.
> Oy! Drinking suits a *goy*!
> Drinking is his
> Steady business,
> 'Cause he is a *goy* . . .

> Comes a Jew into a little *shul*,
> A little *shul*,
> Sits and studies a Talmudic rule,
> A Talmudic rule.
> Oy! Study suits a Jew!
> Study is his
> Steady business,
> 'Cause he is a Jew . . .

Betty was so absorbed in her discussion with the person that she hardly noticed the young man from Pinsk. In as few words as possible she wanted to convey the most important information to the former official. She said, "I know everything. This Hurvitch has told me everything he heard from you about Volodya Chigirinski's death. You must forgive him for telling a stranger a secret without your permission. He told only me and no one else. And it's a good thing he told me. It doesn't interest me any less, and perhaps more, than it does you. That's one thing. And another is that you cannot imagine how useful I can be to you. When I tell you exactly how I can be useful to you, you will realize that the thief who boasted about possessing evidence, Volodka's school bag with the papers and class lessons . . . I've already forgotten his name . . ."

"Makar Zherebtchik," the man with the blue glasses blurted out, and seemed quickly to regret having done so because he wanted to say something else, but Betty interrupted him. She was delighted that she had been reminded of something she had not until that moment been able to bring to mind.

"Yes, yes, that was his name. Did he tell you, this Makar Zherebtchik, that he had a lover, a wife, some girl who has the satchel? It's true. I can vouch that it's true. I know her, that girl, and it was from her that I heard it."

This was spoken with the same pride and with the same magnanimous gesture of the hand. And now the man with the blue glasses was visibly elated.

"You know her personally? She herself told you that?"

"She herself . . . I've just forgotten what her name is. But that isn't hard to find out, and it's easier for you than for someone else. You must remember. And if you don't remember, you can find out from the records that on that particular night . . . on that night, when we . . . when you . . ."

This was no longer spoken with the same pride as before. And the man with the dark eyeglasses understood what night the girl was speaking of and why she was having trouble articulating it, and he had the desire to apologize to her, to beg her to forget what had happened.

At that moment he took on the countenance of an honest penitent who had been caught in a transgression, or a *kheder* boy whose teacher was letting him know he was on to him. He took his wide-brimmed hat and nervously began to turn it in his hands before beginning to speak: "Forget, I beg you, forget what happened . . . I was a . . ." Betty was afraid that with one word he might bring back what had happened. She tossed back her head and made an odd motion with her hand, as if she were pushing something away from herself, and told him sternly not to dare speak so much as a word about what had happened! (She looked around on all sides.) If he really wanted to obtain the key to what he was seeking, there was no need for him even to mention that. (She looked around again.) They had never met before, or else she would get up and leave immediately, and he would never see her again as he had not seen her until now!

The girl's tone of voice was familiar to him. Now, hearing her words and seeing her passionate expression and burning eyes, he realized that he was in the presence of the firm will of a person hard to break or overcome. He lowered his head, drew in his shoulders like a turtle, and became quiet as a kitten, listening docilely to everything Betty continued to say hurriedly. She told him everything she had heard from that woman about Makar Zherebtchik and about the hold she had over him—the satchel of books belonging to the murdered Volodka. All that remained now was to obtain her name, and that was very simple, Betty said, because that night (she looked around) they were the only two in prison. And once they knew her name, it would not be difficult to find her, especially since, if she wasn't mistaken, she lived not too far from here, if not in this very town.

When Betty had finished, the man with the dark blue spectacles, who was sitting as if on pins and needles, barely controlling himself as he took in her words, afraid to interrupt her, stood up, sat back down again, and took on another face and was almost unrecognizable. A smile appeared on his thick, fleshy lips, he raised his head and held it a bit to the side, clasped his hands behind his back, and, jiggling one leg up and down, he spoke to Betty.

"May I say a word? You have no idea what you've done by calling me here and telling me this. You've put such a trump card in my hand" (saying this he motioned with his hand, thereby causing the sun to reflect off the diamond in his gold ring, which Betty recognized) "that before you turn around, that whole gang will be right here" (he indicated his bosom pocket). "I don't even need to look up that woman's name in the records" (he smoothed his knees with both hands), "since, if she is the one who was in prison that night, it can be none other than Masha Tcherepkova . . . Ach, Mashka, Mashka," he said as if to himself, and shook his head, stood up straight, and grabbed his hat.

"Now everything is clear," he said half to himself, "everything in all ways . . . One intrigue on top of another intrigue" (he crossed one finger over another). "First I must get to her, then to him, and if that doesn't work out, I have another and yet another who'll talk. One will put the blame on the next, that one on a third. Ach, you fool!" he cried, slapping himself in the head. "Where were your brains? If I'd known earlier . . . that it was Mashka! . . . Listen to me," he said to Betty, now with another demeanor, with the face of a real Sherlock Holmes, or Nat Pinkerton: "Mark my words, in no more than a week, at the most, two, your 'Rrabenovetch' will be free!"

He spoke the name Rabinovitch with two hard *r*'s and two *e*'s, and what sweetness, what music Betty heard in that word! She no longer had any doubt that this person had in the palm of his hand the entire knotted affair and that he alone was the one who could unravel it, that he was the one who would expose the real criminals and that it was fated through him and no one else that the innocent prisoner would be freed and the whole world learn the pure, honest, absolute truth. What could be better, brighter, and more beautiful than the truth? That thought was to her so delightful that she imagined she could already see it all before her eyes. And this beautiful, bright world became to her even more beautiful and bright, as she herself was, and the sun was shining differently, and even this person with the dark blue glasses and the thick, fleshy lips no longer appeared to her as frightening as he had seemed before. She was almost prepared to forgive him his conduct of the past—all forgotten, forgotten, forgotten! . . .

"Mr. Hurvitch," she called out joyously in her silvery voice. "Where are you? Come here, we have good news for you."

Hurvitch from Pinsk was leaning on the ivy-covered fence, deep in thought, humming to himself his Pinsk song with the melody he himself invented, tapping to the beat of the music:

> Comes the drunkard home to his wife,
> Home to his wife,
> Beats her up within an inch of her life,
> An inch of her life.
> Oy! Drinking suits a *goy*,
> Beating the missus
> His steady business,
> 'Cause he is a *goy*.
>
> Comes a Jew into a little *shul*.
> A little *shul*,
> Mutters a prayer and a *kiddush'l*,
> A *kiddush'l*.
> Oy! Pious is a Jew!
> Praying is his

Steady business
'Cause he is a Jew . . .

"Mr. Hurvitch," Betty called to him again, "What are you doing there? Why are you suddenly singing? Come here and you'll hear something interesting."

"Here I am—I'm ready," Hurvitch from Pinsk replied in his cheerful way, and with two or three strides of his long legs he was there, looking at Betty and taking great pleasure in her happy, smiling face.

"I have good news for you," she said to him, and her eyes were laughing, beaming and shining like two sparkling diamonds in the sun. "I can tell you the good news that in two weeks he will be free!"

Betty anticipated that, once Hurvitch from Pinsk heard this news, he would surely be beside himself with excitement and want to know all about it. But how surprised she was when he didn't ask anything further but simply gave her a *mazel tov* and hoped they would always hear nothing but good things and triumphs for all of Israel. And stretching out his neck like a rooster, he finished off with a chant, as if he were at a circumcision when the crowd is growing tipsy:

"*V-naa-mar a-men*—And we say Amen!"

"Why this clowning?" thought Betty, and looked him over angrily, but it bothered him not one whit! He spun around and faced the man with the dark eyeglasses and declared to him cheerfully, half in Russian, half in Yiddish, "*Itak,* that is, *dyele v'shlyape?*—So, we're finished? *Ochen rad!*—I'm very glad! But listen, *Goy, nye pora li nam na lyevo krugom i hashiveynu nazad?*—It's time to leave, return and go left, around and back."

"A clown!" Betty decided, and on her way home from her *rendezvous* she enjoyed a good laugh. She could not remember the time when she had had so delicious, sweet, and healthy a laugh—and all to herself.

the hundred-fourth chapter

THE SUFFERING OF THE DAMNED

The greater the distance he traveled from the Russian heartland and the nearer he drew to the Jewish Pale on his way to rescue his friend, the more the real Rabinovitch felt at home, the more he felt his Jewish identity, the Jewish hurt and Jewish exile. And the more he felt that way, the more gratified and relieved he was. He had come to his senses in time and could rectify his mistaken readiness to divest himself entirely of his Jewishness because of a sweet, seductive dream about a princess. And he was even more relieved to be on his way to rescue not only a friend from disaster, but also a large group of people from an ugly libel, and an even larger group of people from committing, if not a historic crime, then a historic mistake. It was clear as day to him that he had but to arrive and tell the proper authorities the truth, that the real Hersh Rabinovitch was himself and that the other one was a Popov, a Gentile friend of his with whom he had, as a hoax, in sheer jest, switched identities—what more would they need? The whole affair would be resolved, the doors would open, and his friend, Grisha, would leave a free man—and an end to the blood libel, an end to the unseemly bacchanalia the press had stirred up, and an end to the bloody hoax!

His heart beating happily, our Rabinovitch-Popov began his journey, but his happiness did not last long. His good mood was quickly destroyed by all the printed matter, the "provisions," with which he had supplied himself for the journey, all the rightist and leftist newspapers and tabloids. As soon as he seated himself in the train next to a window, he began looking through his "provisions," searching to see what had been written about the ritual crime and about the criminal, the dentist, Hersh Rabinovitch. He didn't have to search long. The papers, almost without exception, were filled with the case, and most of the newspapers, besides giving the bare facts, added their fine, venomous articles about the great Jewish people, who wanted to suck the world dry of blood, demanding reason and justice from the court because "if we Jews rely on the wrath of the Russian people," they warned, "it will be much worse, they will demand blood for blood . . ."

Still and all, it did not trouble him that these bloody incitements printed by some of the ultra-patriotic newspapers blew out of all proportion the case of the imprisoned dentist, Rabinovitch, making of it a *cause célèbre*, a kind of Dreyfus affair. From their tone it was plain that these articles were written by hired hands who traded on know-nothing patriotism and were jumping out of their skins with eagerness to outdo one another in calumny, malice, ignorance, and gall. These self-styled experts, he knew, had their place in the scheme of things, and one knew their true worth. Opposing these shrill voices, he consoled himself, was a good portion of the more sensible community that thought quite otherwise and that was ready from time to time to raise its voice, to speak seriously and truthfully and come out publicly with passion against the destructive agitation and show that they were more ashamed of the accusers than of the accused. And as proof, there in the midst of all this deadly poison spread over page after page, he came across protests against the new libel, with hundreds of signatures of famous people—scholars, writers, professors, jurists, and priests, and his Jewish heart was delighted and found a modicum of satisfaction in that.

He was much more troubled and pained by what people everywhere were saying, the conversations and discussions he had overheard, first sitting in third class, among ordinary people, and then in second class, among so-called intellectuals.

The crowd in third class consisted of tradesmen, workers, and plain Russian youths, boys who wore their shirts over their trousers, affected trimmed, round caps, long, silver chains around their necks, and heavy, copper signet rings on their thick fingers with dirty nails. These youths, who were not in the least interested in politics or, above all, in the world at large, would jump off the train at whatever station, large or small, in order to grab a glass of beer or a shot of whisky, but not a one bought a newspaper. "Those lucky fellows!" though Rabinovitch-Popov, and truly envied them for being ignorant of libels and incitements, for not needing to justify themselves and have to have others come to their defense with protests and signatures. But where did this new character come from, a half-baked intellectual with a pimply face and a runny eye? He had seated himself, not at a window but in the center of the car in the semidark, slouched over, and had begun reading a newspaper out loud as the other passengers listened.

Rabinovitch-Popov could not make out what he was reading, but when the man with the runny eye ended, a discussion started up among the passengers. The two or three words he was able to catch conveyed to him that they were talking about the matter for which he was on his way to the Jewish Pale, and he began listening more attentively. The discussion went in circles, one example supporting another, and he kept hearing that fine word "Yid" spoken with a variety of connotations and intimations.

So ignorant and ludicrous was this discussion that he decided to move a bit closer in order to hear better. Slowly inching from seat to seat, the unknown student moved closer to the group of passengers. Once he was among them, he could not help but join in, first with a word, then with another, until, without intending it, he had joined the discussion, not with all of them, but with the half-baked intellectual with the runny eye. Finally he pushed him to the wall, wanting him to say how he knew Jews so well. Oh! He knew them very well! No, the student wanted to know just one thing: had he ever seen a Jew? It turned out that the half-baked intellectual had never seen a Jew because in his village there were no Jews. There once was one but he was driven out long ago, before he was born. But since he read the papers—in his district they got all the papers and he was the district correspondent—he had read up so much about Jews that he felt he knew them thoroughly.

Here the student changed his demeanor and gave the district correspondent a good scolding. How shocked he was when one of the passengers who was sitting exactly opposite him, head held in his hands, elbows on his knees, looked directly at him and, barely voicing his words, suddenly inquired of the speaker in an agreeable tone, naive and serious, in pure, deep Russian speech, using the familiar form.

"Tell us, my dear man, are you not yourself a Yid?"

This seemed to delight the crowd. To a man, they erupted in loud laughter. The poor student, Rabinovitch-Popov, turned red and could no longer speak. At the next stop, he paid a supplement to the ticket vendor and moved himself over to a second-class car.

But when it is so fated, trouble follows at one's heels. He was lucky enough to discover in the second-class car a group of real intellectuals right in the middle of a heated argument about the upcoming blood libel trial of the Jewish dentist, Rabinovitch. As they were now nearer the Pale, there were among these intellectual passengers several Jews, perhaps more Jews than Gentiles. They were arguing both sides of the case so passionately and heaping such invective and venom on one another that anyone would have thought they would come to blows.

More fired up than all the others was a Jewish young man with a blond moustache and wearing a jeweled stickpin in an elegant green cravat. He was mightily upset, his normally pale lips now completely bloodless, and his hands were trembling.

"I'll tell you what!" the distraught young man with the jeweled stickpin said to the opposition, leaping up and grabbing his side pocket, "I have here a thousand rubles in cash that I will give to this little Father" (he pointed to an elderly priest with a decent face), "and you put up a hundred, just a hundred, for whatever charity you choose, for a hospital, for the Red Cross, it's your choice, that the court will find the accused innocent. Aha, that shut you up, didn't it?"

Except for the elderly priest, who kept calmer than the rest of them, the already agitated crowd became even more agitated at this challenge, and the atmosphere turned ugly.

"You probably know something," said one of the opposite side, with a good-natured little laugh on his full, moist lips, exposing his healthy, white teeth. "Maybe you know someone who is paying off the jurors, like some of *your* people, who tried to bribe the professors so they would say the accused was insane. Or like the dentist's father, who tried to buy off the guards to help the prisoner escape the other day."

The young man with the blond moustache sprang up and, with hands held tightly behind him and eyes bulging, lunged at the accuser. "Do you know what you get for such talk? Do you know?!"

Luckily, one of the Jewish opposition interceded and sat the young man down in his seat, or else an ugly scene might have ensued in which the worst injury most likely would have been suffered by none other than the young man with the blond moustache and jeweled stickpin in his elegant green cravat for throwing around thousands.

"Where does so much poisonous hatred of one human being for another come from? These people seem ready to tear each other limb from limb. If they could only be calm, without fixed opinions and without the need to prove how right they were, if they would only listen to one another and discover the real truth instead of tearing each other's hair out, these people would hold their sides and laugh so hard that their laughter would echo throughout the world!"

So thought the real Rabinovitch, who had in the meantime inadvertently learned of news, strange news, that was for him not good tidings. What is called *khibet-hakeyver*—"the suffering of the damned"—was nothing compared to what he was already suffering and what lay in store for him to suffer in this difficult mission he had taken upon himself—to extricate his comrade from quicksand and his people from a new libel.

A VINDICTIVE APOSTATE

Arriving in the big city of the Pale, our Rabinovitch-Popov paused to look around the busy station as every passenger arriving for the first time in a new place does. The first thing that caught his eye was the kiosk where newspapers and magazines were sold. He went over to the kiosk and asked for the latest editions of the three newspapers published in the city, and, as his heart had told him, he immediately found what he was looking for, and a great deal more. On the very front page, under a screaming headline, "NEW AS-TOUNDING DISCOVERY IN CHIGIRINSKI'S DEATH," he saw a long editorial full of spite and venom against those who wanted to defend the imprisoned criminal, against those who were struggling to prove with all kinds of Jewish wiles and Talmudic casuistry that the dentist Rabinovitch was entirely innocent, poor fellow, a scapegoat for the sins of others. "It will be interesting to hear," the writer of the editorial concluded, "what they will say now, these same bought-off Jew lovers, now that a former Jew has come forward openly, with a clean conscience before God, and swears that he knows for a fact and can prove it, as two and two make four, that fanatic Jews use Christian blood for Passover and that it is not a fabrication or old wives' tale, not an ancient legend, but a fact that all Jews know about but that no one has the courage to admit."

The second newspaper, apparently a liberal one, also had an editorial, but under another headline: "PSYCHOPATH, OR VINDICTIVE APOSTATE?" This editorial was written with no less spite about some traitor convert, a student, who wasn't satisfied that he had, for personal reasons, changed his religion, but now had to come out with a letter that was the work of either a psychopath or a vindictive apostate.

The passenger became so caught up in this news that he completely forgot his purpose for coming. He sat down in the first-class dining room to read further in the newspapers about this stunning news. He found in all three papers a letter to the editor written in the same style. We report it here word for word:

Esteemed Editor!

Permit me through your respected newspaper to make public the information that I today submitted to the prosecutor of the local circuit court. As I am a faithful son of the people to whom I now have the honor of belonging and a devoted servant to our beloved fatherland, and desiring to cast new light on the truth that is being so diligently sought in the death of the unfortunate child, Volodya Chigirinski, I beg to be called as a witness at this trial, which I hope to illuminate with my factual testimony and with my confession before God. Having been born of Jewish parents and a Jew for over twenty years, I know all their secret rites and can with certainty swear before God that the ancient, primitive rite of using Christian blood for the Passover matzos is still practiced to this day by the majority of religious Jewish fanatics all over the world. I know how great a risk I am taking in speaking out against a people that can take revenge against its foes and lets nothing stand in the way of its revenge, but my dedication to the pure, naked truth and my devotion to my country, which must remain dearer to us than life itself, forces me to sacrifice myself and say openly and before the entire world what I heard countless times from my late father—he was a sexton in the synagogue—and from my rabbi, who is also long dead: to spill blood, or at least to witness the spilling of blood, is beloved of God. Whoever doubts this is urged to ask a Jew to invite him, if they will allow him in, to attend his sons's circumcision on the seventh day after his birth and let him observe carefully what is done and what is said and how delighted the people are when they see the blood that is spilled and is then sucked up by the eldest and most respected guests. And should a Jew not allow his son to be circumcised on the seventh day after his birth, they will stone him, or at best, excommunicate him for the rest of his life. No Jewish daughter would marry such a son and he would not be allowed into any Jewish community. I hope, if I am called to testify at the trial, to have a great deal to say about these religious fanatics and about the so-called sect of *Chassidim*, as well as the newer, no-less-dangerous sect of Zionists. I ask all Russian newspapers to print my letter.

Student Lapidus

Student Lapidus? Why, wasn't that the fellow his older brother, Abraham-Leib, had written him about, the one whose widowed mother and brother-in-law Velvel-the-*shlimazel's* mother were second cousins—or some other complicated kinship? Out of sheer pain, Rabinovitch began to laugh. On the *seventh day* we now circumcise our children, ha-ha! And someone like *that* uses *such* "facts" to testify against an entire people? And there are those who believe this, or who pretend to believe it? No! How did our people ever produce such a creature? That's what makes it so sad! And he could not forgive himself for having spent all that time so serenely, so comfortably, among strangers, without being aware of the hell that was wreaking havoc in the Jewish world! *He* was dreaming of princesses! *He* was dreaming of the land of Offir! A disgrace! A shame!

Beside himself with heartache, he gathered up the pile of newspapers, hailed a cab, and asked to be taken to the center of the city.

the hundred-sixth chapter

AMONG HIS OWN

From the moment our second hero set foot in the city that first day, he realized he had been greatly mistaken in believing that, the moment he arrived, his friend would be rescued from his predicament. Of course, visiting his friend in prison was out of the question. He soon saw that it would be as possible to do that as it would to bring the prisoner to his hotel. As it happened, the officials to whom he directed himself were suspicious of him and considered him to be some kind of adventurer intent on deceiving them, probably someone paid off by Jews. Luckily his documents were in good order, otherwise his face might have betrayed his Jewishness.

After wasting the entire morning running from one administrative office to another, exhausted and hungry, he entered the first large cafe he saw, ordered lunch at the counter, and was barely able to find an empty seat at a table, so packed was it with Jews. As he looked around to get his bearings, he realized he was at last among his own.

This was the Stock Exchange cafe described before. The crowd was all worked up over something, and heated discussions were in full swing. A few were running from one table to another in a dither. As the visitor began to listen in, he heard the name Lapidus and knew immediately what the excitement was all about.

It had been a long time since he had been among Jews and heard a Yiddish word spoken, and so he found it pleasant to be among his own. It was pleasant to be in the midst of this Jewish noise and commotion, even pleasant to be sharing the pain they were feeling no less than he. He also very much wanted to hear what they were saying. An ancient Jewish instinct was aroused in him, and with it, the ancient Jewish past. He was among his own, together as Jews, sharing and sharing alike what one knew and thought and meant.

He noticed that, more than anyone, a short-legged Jew was jumping out of his skin with eagerness to be heard. He stood on tiptoe and kept bouncing up and down.

"Lapidus? Let me, I'll tell you who this Lapidus is!"

The little Jew who was so anxious to tell about Lapidus was Katz, or Ketzele, our old friend, the impoverished broker whom everyone knew and who knew everyone.

"Do you know Lapidus?" one of them took mercy on Ketzele.

"Do I know him!" said Ketzele, wiping the perspiration from his brow. "There's knowing and there's really knowing. I used to know his father, and his father's father I knew, he was an honest Jew, his father, but even more than his father was his father's father."

"Leave his father's father out of this, Ketzele! Just tell us about him, if you know anything at all."

"If I know anything at all?" said Ketzele. Pleased that things were finally going his way, he was speaking and everyone was listening to him. "He's a regular scoundrel, that Lapidus! He was going to marry the daughter of a friend of mine, David Shapiro's girl, the one who was the fiancee of the dentist, poor Rabinovitch, while he was still their roomer."

"Don't believe a word of it! Ketzele will tell you stories!" one of the brokers interrupted, a blond man with very white teeth and gold-rimmed eyeglasses. "He wasn't going to marry Shapiro's daughter, it never even occurred to him, because

David Shapiro has no money, only a pretty daughter, and he was looking for money. If you ask me, I'll tell you, I know better, he wanted to marry my partner's daughter, Berele Greenberg's. Berele Greenberg has both virtues—a pretty daughter and a big dowry—but they turned him down and so he's letting out his anger on all Jews. Do you understand?"

"It could be," poor Ketzele tried to work himself back into the spotlight. "It could very well be that he wanted to marry Berele Greenberg's daughter too. But about David Shapiro, whom I'm telling you about, I know for sure, because you all know I've always been a steady visitor there, even during the time that *shlimazel* Rabinovitch was their roomer."

"With Rabinovitch you also said you were inseparable, and it turns out it was just another story."

And thus was Ketzele ousted from the spotlight, and no one wanted to listen to him any more. His place was taken by the blond broker with the white teeth and gold-rimmed eyeglasses. Popov, or Rabinovitch, who was sitting at his table, felt sorry for Ketzele but also wanted to make his acquaintance after hearing him say he knew the dentist Rabinovitch. He beckoned him over with his finger, offered him a cigarette, asked him to sit down, and invited him to have a glass of tea. Ketzele accepted the cigarette and did not refuse the tea, but on the contrary, acquiesced with the greatest pleasure. He was pleased that he had found at least one gentleman.

"Where does the young man come from? Not from these parts?" Ketzele asked him, drawing his chair closer and looking searchingly into his eyes. "I could swear you look familiar to me. Where have we met?"

"No, you don't know me, I'm a Litvak from Lithuania," the real Rabinovitch replied, pleased with himself that he could still speak Yiddish so well. "Tell me something. You just said that you knew the dentist Rabinovitch and the girl he was going to marry. Can you tell me whatever you know about that?"

"Whatever I know?" said Ketzele with a chuckle, and moved closer to the tea that had been served him. "Oy, my dear friend, if I were to tell you whatever I know, there would be little left of the day and the night and another day and night. But if you want me to tell you, I'll tell you; if that's what you want, I'm agreeable. So now, whom do you want me to tell you about—the dentist himself? Or his fiancee? Or his father and brother?"

"You know his father and brother, too?" Rabinovitch asked, astonished.

"I wish I didn't know them," said Ketzele, sipping his tea. "Because of those two *shlimazèls* who came without passports, without money, practically without a shirt on their backs, I also suffered from the honor of residence permits. But that wasn't so bad. It says somewhere that Jews were meant to suffer in this world because of official documents. What I'm asking is this: what in the devil drove them to come to our officials with a letter from their rabbi written to our wealthy Jewish citizens asking them to collect ransom money, to make every effort to try, with God's help, to clear the innocent victim of the blood libel?"

One can imagine how our Rabinovitch felt when he received this news about his family. But he kept himself under control, and as calmly as possible asked, "So, what came of this?"

"What could come of it? Nothing," said Ketzele, sipping his tea with pleasure. "They added the letter to the case documents, and the Rabinovitches were politely asked to kindly betake themselves back to Mohilev, or Shklov, the devil knows where they come from, and it's likely that all three of them, the Rabinovitches and that genius of a rabbi, were clapped in jail. Now, if God finds us worthy, we'll have two packs of troubles on our backs, or, better said, a scab on top of a boil. But listen! What's going on here? What are the police doing here? A roundup right in the middle of the day? I can't believe this! They're going to send me off to Vasilkov by convoy again, I just got back the other week, didn't even get a chance to rest my legs, may Pharaoh's plagues and Job's woes befall them, *yihey shmai raba*—may His great name be blessed, amen."

In a split second the Stock Exchange cafe was besieged with police. All the doors and windows were shut and the search began. Those who could produce a permit from the chief of police, indicating they had permission to reside there, had their names written down and one by one were led out the door, while those who could not produce a permit were taken respectfully to the precinct office—there they would see what was to be done with them.

Among those led away were Ketzele and his unknown friend, who had treated him so kindly, offered him a cigarette and tea, and had dealt with him as no one else in the cafe ever had.

the hundred-seventh chapter

AN UNEXPECTED FINALE

Even in this city, where people had become accustomed to roundups and searches since the sixth day of Creation, the roundup right in the middle of the day was a source of enormous astonishment and called out a flood of talk, rumors, and stories. In truth, however, it was an ordinary event, it could not be more ordinary. The police had long had their eye on this Stock Exchange cafe, which was always full of Stock Exchange people, all Jews. They knew it was the right place to pick up a sizable number of illegal "goods." But that morning, apparently because of the to-do over the apostate Lapidus's letter, there was an even bigger crowd, providing the police with more "goods" than it had bargained for. Among those arrested, our second hero, the real Rabinovitch, was paid scant attention by the police during the commotion although, according to his documents, he was a legitimate Gentile and son of Gentiles by the name of

Grigori Ivanovitch Popov. Together with the broker Ketzele, and many others like him, he was kept cooling his heels all day until they would get around to examining their documents. He had the opportunity to find out from Ketzele many more particulars about the dentist Rabinovitch, about his father, his brother, and about his former fiancee, who had been arrested and so badly treated that the poor girl had become ill and was now recuperating at the dacha of a rich uncle, who was desperately seeking a husband for her, offering a large dowry to marry her off quickly in order to cover up her shame. Ketzele's imagination ran away with him as he carried on with one more fanciful and frightening tale after another until he was interrupted and told the prisoners were being called before the police commissioner.

The police commissioner, who that day was not in a good mood, looked over the papers of the captured "goods," and when he saw among them a document with the name of a nobleman, Popov, he became enraged and roared out, "Which one is Popov? How did he get here?"

"I am Popov!" The real Rabinovitch stepped forward, walked up close to the examiner, and said quietly that he had something most important to tell him but only on condition it would be between the two of them. The police commissioner was annoyed: what was all this about secrets? Nonetheless, he ordered the room cleared, and in the twinkling of an eye no one remained but the two of them. The police commissioner studied the person before him carefully. It seemed to him he had a strange face, strange eyes. But his face expressed nothing other than his readiness to confide something. Rabinovitch had decided to bare the entire truth, with one word to make an end to this tragicomedy that was becoming more tangled from day to day, dragging in more people and beginning to take on the character of a fantastic, unbelievable novel. He had no idea to whom or how or in what form he should make his shocking revelation, but as it had worked out that he had been mistakenly arrested like all the other Jews and brought to the precinct office, he had decided to make a clean breast of it. He blurted out to the commissioner, "I must inform you that before you stands not a Gentile and not a nobleman, Grigori Ivanovitch Popov, but a Jew and ordinary citizen, Hersh Movshovitch Rabinovitch, the same Rabinovitch who is sitting in your prison and is accused of murdering the Gentile boy, Vladimir Chigirinski, for Jewish matzo on Passover."

When he finished what he had to say, he felt as if a stone had been lifted from his heart, and in his mind's eye he pictured a scene, a sequence of scenes. They would soon free the real Popov, and after him, his father, brother, and the town rabbi. And he imagined the excitement and uproar that would erupt in this city and all over the world, the articles the newspapers would write about this epic, about the tragicomedy that would be called "THE BLOODY HOAX." At the very worst, they would arrest Rabinovitch for not having a residence permit, or both of them, the real Popov and the real Rabinovitch, would be tried for having switched identities and lived for almost a year under false names. But what was that compared to the suffering this hoax had caused and could continue to cause? The one thing that had held him back a little was that he had not maintained his Jewishness and would be the first to break the solemn oath not to reveal their secret before the end of the year. But that was foolish. A bet that had brought so much unhappiness and had given rise to so much unnecessary grief and woe was not a bet. One mustn't play with fire.

How stunned he was to see that his confession caused no stir at all. On the contrary, it had the opposite effect. The police commissioner simply looked him over from head to toe and said nothing. He felt he was dealing with a madman who had taken a crazy idea into his head. There are all kinds of crazy people in the world.

Seeing that the police commissioner was not responding, Rabinovitch reasoned that he was too stunned by his revelation. He paused a moment and said, "Well? Why don't you arrest me? Or do you want to arrange a face-to-face meeting between me and the other Rabinovitch in the prison!"

That irked the commissioner.

"No face-to-face meeting! Get out of here and quit babbling nonsense! If you repeat this once more, they'll arrest you, not as a criminal but as an insane person, and they'll send you off to an asylum."

Rabinovitch opened his mouth to speak, to clarify his story for him, but the police commissioner became furious.

"Get out of here, I tell you! As if we don't have enough trouble day in and day out with these Jews, now we have to put up with psychopaths and maniacs! Go, get out of here!"

With those words the police commissioner threw his documents in his face and rang for the officers to bring in the rest of the crowd, and poor Rabinovitch had to gather up his papers in humiliation and leave.

Our Rabinovitch had not at all counted on this kind of finale. All his plans were in shambles, and his coming to the city, it turned out, was a complete waste of time. What should he do now? Go higher? Submit a statement to the state prosecutor? But what if they didn't believe him and considered him to be a psychopath, a maniac, or a madman? It was entirely possible that they would, without hesitation, as the commissioner had said, send him off to an insane asylum and then all would be lost. No! He had to find another way. Only one person could help—his friend Grisha's father, Ivan Ivanovitch Popov. How could he get him to come to the city? By telegram? By letter? That wouldn't work. Better to go himself to Grisha's father's home, the sooner the better, and there open his eyes and explain how this hoax, which had started off so merrily, so comically, was about to end in a sorry, hideous tragedy, becoming finally a stupid, bloody hoax. He could tear himself limb from limb!

*   *   *

That very day, before nightfall, an express train carried our second hero, the real Rabinovitch, from the large city in the Jewish Pale to the Russian city of T_____, where resided his friend Grisha's father, the nobleman and former provincial governor, Ivan Ivanovitch Popov.

AL D'ATEYFET —"HE WHO DROWNS OTHERS . . ."

Benny Hurvitch from Pinsk had become so frequent a visitor at the Familiants' dacha that as soon as the servants spotted from a distance his faded white tunic with the wide sleeves, they immediately informed the Mam'selle Shapiro that her young man had arrived, all the while barely stifling their laughter. The servants laughed while the Madam, Toibe Familiant, simmered like a hot kettle, furious at her niece, a poor girl who was behaving like a princess, without an ounce of respect for her rich aunt, for wealth, for expensive pearls, gold, silver, and diamonds, wasting her time in the woods with a down-at-the heels youth who strutted proudly about as if he were a somebody. And she was even more aggrieved because her husband, that *Chassid*, Reb Shlomo Familiant, instead of siding with her, Toibe, out of sheer spite supported his niece through thick and thin. Whatever she did was good in his eyes, and even this poor young man pleased him. He had spoken with the young man several times and had been quite taken by him. He knew everything, Shlomo said. There was not a Jewish tome among our holy volumes that this young man from Pinsk was not well versed in. He was, he said, a Torah scholar, a genius, one who could be a great rabbi. Ha-ha! A fine rabbi, without a hat and his face clean-shaven!

Shlomo was saying all this to Toibe spitefully because he knew she didn't approve of their niece and disliked this impertinent young man. Whenever Hurvitch would come to visit, he would greet her in a way that seemed to her mocking. He would say, "Good morning, Auntie." What kind of an aunt was she to him? Everyone called her "Madam," but this one got it into his head to call her "Aunt," and not just "Aunt," but "Auntie"! "The nerve of that Litvak! Ach, of what value is age nowadays? May the good Lord above protect and defend His beloved people, Israel here and everywhere, today and forever— Amen."

Her daughters, the mam'selles, were no less critical, upset at their cousin for carrying on with this Hurvitch as if he were her closest confidant. Whenever he would come, she would not permit him to become more friendly with them. She would sit with him alone in the garden or stroll with him in the woods—secrets, of course!

When Betty's mother learned from her sister-in-law that her daughter was not behaving properly—she wasn't, God forbid, saying bad things about her, she was merely saying she wasn't behaving properly—Sara came to visit for a few hours, apparently dropping in to see whether Betty was homesick, but taking the opportunity to have a talk with her sister-in-law, in passing, about this new shlimazel who had wormed his way into Betty's life. Betty, Sara said, needed to understand that it didn't bother her at all that she had befriended someone like this shlimazel from Pinsk, though his brother-in-law, the bookbinder, was no find for the likes of the Slaviteh Shapiros. What was the problem then? But Sara was by no means criticizing Betty. She was only saying that one had to think of appearances and how one was seen by others, and when one was the guest of a rich uncle, one had to know that—

That was as far as Sara got. She was going no further because her daughter had stopped her in her tracks, and she became reluctant to say anything about her daughter's affairs. She no longer wished to comment even about the roomer to her, although she had originally come to talk to her daughter about him. Oy, that roomer was God's punishment and enough said. Aside from being a burden for all of Israel, it was her own burden as well. It was she, Sara, who had the lion's share of the worry. It would have been far better had she broken an arm or a leg that morning before she had rented him the room.

And did she really know where matters stood in all this? One could be driven mad by the talk one heard. Here come these two Jews calling themselves Rabinovitch, claiming to be the father and brother of the roomer and making him out to be a liar and a falsifier. Then it turns out not to be true at all! They're two ordinary rogues who have come to trick them out of money by calling themselves Rabinovitch and carrying false letters and papers from some rabbis. How did learn she about this? From Katz. The two had spent the night at Katz's and he had seen those letters and papers, and he said they had boasted to him about them. They had also grilled him about the local well-off Jews. Katz swore that even if she had learned all this from an apostate, it would be God's truth. How would a good Jew like himself make this all up! And so it turned out they were the real liars! She had immediately taken a dislike to them, especially the younger one, who blew his nose with one finger.

And if that were the case, why was she going through all the trouble of sending the doctor to forewarn Betty about Rabinovitch? That's all she needed! It was lucky the doctor was by nature a procrastinator, although a very fine person otherwise, and had put off talking to Betty for another time. Now she had no use at all for him. She herself would do the talking. But how can one talk when the other won't listen? Besides, it seemed Betty had lately gone out of her mind, God help us. It was a heartache and an embarrassment to her mother, a shame for others! Toibe wasn't claiming that Betty was a bad child, God forbid. She was only saying that she was so totally absorbed in her own affairs that she wasn't eating or drinking.

"I'll give you an example, a for instance. Take this young man from Pinsk, may the One Above not punish me for these words. He comes here almost every day, every day, and as soon as he comes, they fly off into the woods and whisper together: shu-shu-shu, shu-shu-shu! Right now they've been in the woods more than an hour. Ask them about what. Why do they need to keep secrets when it isn't a secret anymore? Everyone knows what they're talking about. They're talking about him, about that Rabinovitch. All well and good, freeing prisoners is certainly a big *mitzvah,* but to sacrifice your life for someone else is not required anywhere in the holy books, unless the person is deathly ill, and that we call *pikuakh nefesh*—saving a life. And talking about the match, first of all, it's a big question mark about whether it *is* a match. Don't take what I'm saying so openly to you the wrong way. All the Shapiros are like that—we don't like to mince words. And second of all, I'll tell you, my dear, the whole world may know that your poor Rabinovitch is innocent as a lamb, the scapegoat for all of Israel; nevertheless, he has a stain on him, may the One Above not punish me for these words. A man—we should be preserved and protected, one mustn't sin— who has been sitting in prison so long, say what you will, Sara darling, you may even be angry at me—he's not someone suitable for my David . . . Take a little preserves, I beg you."

"Thank you, Toibenyu, I took some already," answered Sara, barely able to sit still, eager to see whether her daughter had returned from the woods with the Pinsk *shlimazel.* "Who's talking about such things at this time, Toibenyu, *lyube'nyu?* Who even has it in mind? That's not what we're talking about. We're talking about something else. And you say—"

At that point Betty arrived, agitated and visibly upset, abruptly ending the long discussion between the women.

Sara wasn't saying a word to her daughter—she knew her too well. At such times, she knew it was better not to bother her.

"Won't you have some preserves," asked her Aunt Toibe with a friendly little smile on her pursed lips. But Betty's wordless thanks were accompanied by a glance that told her not to offer her any more preserves. Betty said to her mother, "It's a good thing you've come, Mama, we're going home."

No amount of questioning about why she needed to go home nor pleas to remain at least a few more weeks were of any avail. Aunt Toibe went through the motions of sincere protest, saying that when her uncle came from the city and found out, it would be like the darkness over Egypt, and he would be right! But in her heart Toibe was so elated she felt like dancing. She was worried that, God forbid, her husband might show up and make a fuss about his niece's leaving. What else would you expect of him?

"Do me one favor," Toibe requested of her sister-in-law, sounding as if her very life depended on it. "At least do me the favor of taking home half a jar of preserves!"

Without waiting to hear any protest, she immediately poured half the preserves into another jar. When Toibe noticed that one half was larger than the other, she quickly put the larger half away in her cupboard and forced the smaller half into her sister-in-law's hands. Sara had no idea what this was all about, why she was being saddled with this jar of preserves. She had no need of it. Only later, when she and her daughter were sitting in the train going home, did Sara examine the jar of preserves and fling it out the open window with such force one would think it were the source of all her misfortunes and heartaches.

*   *   *

Standing statue-like in a corner of the train and gazing out the window, hands folded behind her, Betty watched the trees, fields, small houses, and telegraph poles appear and disappear as quickly as her thoughts, one after another, one after another, and now, on her way home, she relived in her mind all the events that had taken place at the dacha until that day. First, her close relationship with Hurvitch from Pinsk, which from day to day grew closer. She was afraid to admit it, but she imagined that this Hurvitch, notwithstanding some of his strange, clownish ways, was more likable than all the other young men she had ever known. What she liked more than anything else was his remarkable simplicity and unique openness. He was a person who said what he thought and thought what he said. There were no hidden meanings, no diplomatic wiles. At the second visit he had already declared to her in simple words that he had loved her since that night of the terror when the prince (that was what he called his friend, Rabinovitch) had introduced him to her on the street near the railroad station. She knew he was prepared, if she wanted it said in purple prose, "to go through fire and water" for her, to sacrifice his life for her at any time, to have both his hands cut off for her "for whatever was dear to her." By this last he meant, of course, the prince, Rabinovitch, about whom he had not permitted himself to say so much as one bad word, for which she would be eternally grateful.

She was even more grateful that he had never touched upon her feelings for Rabinovitch, as if they never existed, or were altogether natural and understandable, as if Rabinovitch were her brother and he, Hurvitch, their older brother. It was worth observing how this young man took such delight in the good news he would bring from the city about the dismissed official (whose name was never mentioned and for which she was especially grateful). "It's going well, everything is fine, couldn't be better!" This was the news early on. From his smooth, unfurrowed brow she could read from a distance the word "Marvelous!" Under no circumstances did he wish to expose her to the underworld, the "gutter" whence this good news originated, even though Betty insisted on knowing everything. "Listen to me, if you want to know everything, you'll get old quickly," Hurvitch warned her, trying to dismiss the matter with a witticism. But Betty told him she disliked his witticisms, which wasn't true. Betty not only liked his witticisms, she even found his expression "Listen to me," used so frequently, whether it fit or not, particularly charming.

Of course, Betty had her way: she learned about everything, or almost everything. She knew that the fired official had, after much difficulty and effort, like a true Sherlock Holmes or Nat Pinkerton, managed by heroic means to unearth that lost soul, Masha Tcherepkova, and to obtain from her, not only vital information, but also a good deal of important evidence in the form of certain objects and documents. She knew that, thanks to this Masha Tcherepkova, they had arrested two more women who had allegedly taken part in Volodka's death, which both of them vociferously denied, throwing the entire blame on Masha's boyfriend, Makar Zherebtchik, who had disappeared as if swallowed up by the earth. That was the first good news. Then Hurvitch brought the best news of all, that his Sherlock Holmes, or Nat Pinkerton, working behind the scenes through others because he no longer held his previous position, had finally been able to bring about the capture of the boyfriend, Makar Zherebtchik, and have him imprisoned. But even that news was nothing compared to Makar Zherebtchik's then fingering the whole gang of thieves and hooligans who had planned to instigate a Passover pogrom by murdering Volodya Chigirinski and inflicting the forty-nine knife wounds to make it appear like a ritual murder. Makar Zherebtchik had promised to name all the members of the gang who had partici- pated in this apparent cult murder as well as the names of other accomplices and gang leaders. In short, no effort was spared to round up all the criminals. Who could have been as happy as Betty that day? Her joy knew no bounds. After all, it was all that was needed, Betty had thought, even more than was needed. Everything was ready, soon, soon a new light would be thrown on everything, and all that had happened before would automatically be null and void. But suddenly—it was just a few days ago—Hurvitch had arrived with bad news (Betty could tell by his face that he was not bringing good news). What was it? "Listen to me, it's an ugly story—the boyfriend has fled, fled from under the wedding canopy!" Betty was so upset by this news that she let out her bitter heart on Hurvitch's head. She wanted to know one thing—at a time like this, how could a person think of jokes? "Listen to me, you have to be a bit of a philosopher," Hurvitch replied merrily, as was his way, "then you'll be able to see that this little drop of news amounts to a humiliating nothing in this vast world with its seven heavens and its many transformations."

Betty was so irate with this kind of talk that she called him a clown and a bore, left him without a farewell, and was, understandably, unable to sleep all night from remorse for having unnecessarily insulted someone who was so loyal and devoted, heart and soul. She was relieved when she saw him the next morning with his usual happy expression, as if no quarrel had happened between them.

"It's bad, my dear," he said to her, "listen to me, it's very bad, so bad that it would have been bad even for our Patriarchs!"

"I beg you, don't make any more jokes," Betty pleaded with him as one would plead with the devil.

"What does one joke more or less matter, my dear, when one sees the truth walking on foot, bent over with a hunched back, hugging the walls, while false- hood goes riding by, head held high, whistling, and cracking his whip, trampling people in the streets. 'Eh! Make way! Let me through!' "

Still, he comforted her as much as possible, giving her hope that his Sherlock Holmes was still alive—and, "as long as that *goy* is alive, he won't rest till he solves the case." But who could have expected the blow that struck them like a thunderbolt out of the blue—and that was the terrible news Hurvitch had brought her that very day from the city.

"They've arrested, do you hear, our Sherlock Holmes himself and led him off like an ordinary mortal to prison. We still don't know for what marvelous deeds. Apparently our wise men were correct, do you hear, when they said *Al d'ateyfet otfukh,'* which means, 'Because you drowned others, you will be drowned your-self.' Do you get the meaning? Now only one thing is left: we can't allow this to cool off, we have to use all the information, do you hear, and put it all into the hands of a good lawyer, let him make a tasty omelet out of it. If you wish, I'll do it today; I know a good lawyer, he's one of us from Pinsk. He is, do you hear, a prince among lawyers, a man who turns snow into diamonds, has a head on him like a minister of state, and a tongue, do you hear—when he talks, flies drop, and besides that, he's an honest man and won't sell you for two guilden . . ."

"I'm leaving here," Betty said to him with absolute determination in her voice, conveying she would not be contradicted or challenged. "I'm going home. I want you to be in the city tomorrow morning between nine and ten."

"*Slooshayu-s!*—Yessir!" Hurvitch snapped to attention like a soldier, cocked his cap and earned a reprimand—a person ought to know how to act properly, and it was high time to stop behaving like a—

"Like a what?"

"Like a clown."

the hundred-ninth chapter

A PRINCE AMONG LAWYERS

When Betty arrived home from the dacha, a new surprise awaited her. After awakening the following morning, dressing, and then waiting for Hurvitch to arrive, as planned, so they could go together to this "prince among lawyers," she scanned the newspapers, searching for what interested her most— news about the ritual case. How astonished she was to read in a news item that the accused, Hersh Movshovitch Rabinovitch, had just recently been given a copy of the charges against him, which consisted of over two hundred pages, and that the day of trial had been set for the twenty-ninth. And another news item: among the witnesses to be called by the prosecution were to be the Jew, David Shapiro, in whose dwelling the accused had been a roomer, his daughter, and a teen-aged son who had been a friend of the murdered Vlodimir Chigirinski.

Betty was furious at herself for having wasted critical time at the dacha. She believed that if she had been in the city, it would have turned out differently. It was no good to rely on strangers. And whose fault was it if not her mother's, who had foisted that boring doctor on her: "Dacha-dacha! Dacha-dacha!"? And as if they knew she was thinking about them, they both came in, each with his own demand: her mother wanting her to eat something—a chicken liver, an egg, a glass of milk, perhaps some scrambled eggs. And the doctor came simply inquiring after her health although he had seen her last night when she had just arrived home from the dacha. Neither came away unscathed. She brazenly told her mother to leave her alone with her livers and scrambled eggs, she wasn't a goose that needed to be stuffed and fattened up. She had drunk a cup of coffee earlier and that was enough. And she settled up with the doctor, too, but a bit more politely. He noticed the newspaper in her hand and surmised she had read the latest news. He decided right then to take his courage in his hands and reproach her, as an objective bystander who had always wanted to help her see that she wasn't doing the right thing by sacrificing her health on account of a person who . . .

"On account of a *person?*" Betty interrupted him, and cast a look of rage and hatred at him, though she tried hard to say it with a smile. "On account of a *person,* you say? On account of *one* person? You believe he's the only one on trial? You're forgetting that together with him you and all of us are on trial! You're forgetting that . . ."

Betty didn't complete her sentence because at that moment the door opened and in came the one she had been awaiting, Benny Hurvitch from Pinsk. Lively and merry, as always, and after the initial "good morning," he asked Betty whether she had read the good news, and without looking at the doctor, he began pacing back and forth with his long legs, spouting words in his satirical, flowery language. "Best of all, do you hear, I like that they're calling as witnesses the father and his children! And who but the prosecutor himself!"

Noting that he was totally ignored, the doctor grabbed his hat and with a dry "*Adieu!*" left, promising himself he was finished with them all, this was his last visit. How long could he allow himself to be slighted by a girl with a pretty face who had every young man in the world chasing after her!

The doctor's hurried departure apparently made no impression at all upon the young couple. They were preoccupied with something else. Hurvitch did not stop pacing and spouting.

"Lost, do you hear, the cow and the tether, all our work wasted! It's an ugly business, it couldn't be uglier! But to give up—feh! A Jew, do you hear, has to do what's necessary, let God undo it. Man thinks and God winks . . ."

In this vein Benny Hurvitch from Pinsk poured his heart out to her, a heart that from the day of his birth had never lost its boldness. On his way there, he had decided that, since the date of the trial was now set, the accused had to have a lawyer, and so he decided to drop in on his acquaintance, that prince among lawyers who could make diamonds out of snow, who had the head of a minister of state, and when he spoke, flies dropped.

"If we're going to go, let's go!"

"I'm going with you!" Betty said determinedly, with the tone of a queen that suited her truly regal figure and enhanced her special charm. When her mother heard this, she ran into the room, frightened.

"Where are you going?"

"Listen to me, Auntie, with Benny Hurvitch from Pinsk, she's going with me!"

And Benny Hurvitch from Pinsk slapped himself on the chest and looked directly into Sara's eyes with a merry, happy look, as if he were going with Betty to their wedding and not to a lawyer. After Sara Shapiro accompanied them to the door and closed it behind them, she thought, "What a nuisance! That doctor runs off as if from a fire and this Pinsk *shlimazel* is running all over town with her. May it all turn out well in the end!" She sighed deeply and cracked every one of her knuckles.

If a minister of state's head ought to be as large as a bear's and smooth as a noodle board, without a sign of hair, this prince among lawyers, aside from the one fault that he was a Jew from Pinsk, looked not only exactly like a minister of state but also like the definitive minister of state. His head appeared to be even larger because he himself was a spare, thin, fair-skinned man with long, slender legs. And even though he struck a comic figure, he made a forceful impression on Betty. Perhaps it was because Hurvitch had praised him so highly and perhaps because the lawyer maintained that the case against the accused wasn't worth a cigarette butt. Whether or not he could make diamonds out of snow, as Hurvitch had assured her, she did not know. But that he could talk—she was certain from the very first visit because during the entire time they spent with him he was almost the only one to speak. At first he had listened attentively, his eyes shut, to Hurvitch's abbreviated account of the downfall of their Sherlock Holmes, or Nat Pinkerton, and when Hurvitch was through, he sat up as if from sleep, began lighting cigarette after cigarette, not so much smoking them as chewing them between his teeth and lips while swinging his foot and crossing and uncrossing his legs. Once he began talking, he was the sole speaker till the end. He belittled all their previous efforts, their Sherlock Holmes and all his work. He put forth his theory that there were only two ways to proceed. "One way is to prove that the accused is not guilty and the second way is to find the real guilty parties. I am not at all interested in the second way; let others who are obliged to, find criminals, that's what they were paid for. But we must demonstrate again and again and ten more times and a hundred more times that we do not commit ritual murders. And even if people are misled and fixed in their opinions and allow themselves to by hypnotized by others so that they come to believe such outrageous nonsense, we must still provide them with evidence and pound it into their heads that two times two are four and not a sour pickle. Our duty then is to provide that proof. And that is as easy to do as this—"

Saying this, he removed the butt end of a cigarette that had remained unsmoked, or rather, unchewed, and began smoking forthwith a new cigarette. Hurvitch, taking advantage of that pause, said that now nothing more remained but the first way, and that was exactly the reason for their coming to him, to ask him to . . .

"To be his defense lawyer?" he completed the sentence, now chewing on the new cigarette. "It's late, my dear friend, you've come too late."

Betty's heart sank at those words: what did he mean, late? It turned out that they were late because he had already been named from the start as the lawyer for the "criminal," oho-ho!

Betty gave a sigh of relief as the lawyer began to relate how this had come to pass.

"There were, you understand, a series of meetings of our most upright citizens, which is the way we do it, at which many suggestions were put forward. Many argued for hiring the renowned Solovey, the greatest master of them all. I told them you can hire whomever you want, children, but how would it be, my dear friends, if I were to prove to you that we don't need any big shots or Soloveychiks. That the accused will be found innocent is as clear, I said, as the day is long."

Betty was melting with pleasure. This lawyer's every word was for her holy writ. He was no ordinary person talking, but a prophet.

"My system," the lawyer continued smoothly and confidently without pause, as if he were reading from a book, "my system is *persuasion*. I will prove to them that this dentist is as guilty of the crime as I am guilty of the destruction of Rome or Napoleon's downfall in 1812. That's *my* system. And when the subject of ritual murder comes up, I'll give them a lecture that will enlighten them forever. Do you see this!" He indicated a large pile of books, writings, and papers and began to list authors and titles, rattling off entire pages from memory, not so much reading as declaiming with expression and feeling, and so smoothly and sweetly—Ach! Betty would not have tired had he gone on and on and on. But alas, he suddenly stopped, spit out the remaining stub of cigarette, stood up to his full height, glanced quickly at the clock, and asked to be excused, he had to change his clothing and go to the prison, to see that very Rabinovitch.

"In that case," Hurvitch said to him in Yiddish, "I wish you the best of luck, and make sure to give regards, do you hear, from me and this girl . . . Shapiro is her name."

"Shapiro?" The lawyer spun around to face Betty, stretched out a slender, bony, cold hand with its slender, bony, cold fingers, and gazed with pleasure at her pretty, radiant face as if he were just noticing her.

"Shapiro, from the real, the . . . the Slaviteh Shapiros," Hurvitch wanted to say, as David Shapiro would say, but meeting Betty's eyes, kept quiet. The lawyer, catching the look between them, provided his own interpretation.

"Are you trying to tell me that this girl is your fiancee? Then I give you a *mazel tov* and a bravo at the same time. You have good taste."

Hurvitch burst out laughing loudly and exchanged glances with Betty, who blushed deeply as if her face were on fire. At that moment she looked so divinely beautiful, so charming, that both men could not take their eyes off her. The lawyer, himself a bachelor, envied his townsman. Where did he find such a rare flower? But Hurvitch quickly reassured him, saying to him in Yiddish, "She *is* a fiancee, do you hear, unfortunately not mine but another's actually . . ."

"Ach, that's enough!" Betty interrupted in Russian, and asked the lawyer if it were possible at this time to visit with . . .

"With the 'criminal'? Certainly! Now everything is possible. He himself must give notice with whom he wishes to visit, and you, on your part, must apply to the prosecutor. Come see me today around three or four o'clock and I'll take care of everything. You'll be able to see him by tomorrow."

In less than an hour the prince among lawyers was sitting face-to-face with the accused and could not gaze his fill of this young man who appeared fresh and hearty, not at all like a prisoner, except that he was wildly hairy (the entire time in prison he had not shaved or cut his hair). He held himself erect, confident and proud, not at all the depressed Jewish mien or perceptiveness that seeks to discover what really is going on in your heart: "Are you with us or with our enemies?" The lawyer had never seen a Jew with such a broad chest and such sturdy bones—"A solid chap, a pleasure to look at!"

Popov-Rabinovitch, it is true, had never looked better, mainly because he had never felt happier. Not only would he soon be set free—of that there was no doubt, not only would the whole world be shown because of him that the horrible myth of the so-called blood ritual was no more than a fantasy and that an entire people would at last be exonerated from this accusation—but also he had just found out that Betty was alive and well and was being called up as a witness. And above all, this lawyer (what a wonderful, dear man he was!) had delivered fond regards from her and had promised to arrange a *rendezvous* for them—Oh! If he weren't embarrassed, he would embrace and kiss him. And only half an hour earlier, when the lawyer had first come in and introduced himself and said why he had come, Popov-Rabinovitch had not been polite to him. He had thanked him and had said he didn't need a lawyer—he himself had a tongue. Understandably, what he had said was foolish, very foolish. The accused, though he may be the greatest orator, Cicero himself, must have a lawyer at the trial, a defender.

"You must pardon me, a thousand times pardon. I was hotheaded. You are my lawyer, you and no other."

"Better to be angry at first," the lawyer spoke in Yiddish, and the accused asked him, "What does that mean?"

"Ach, I forgot you're a half-Jew," the lawyer caught himself. Their discussion became more and more personal, and when the time came to leave, both of them felt as if they had been good friends for many years.

the hundred-tenth chapter

IVAN IVANOVITCH POPOV

The summer residence of the Popovs, the beautiful, cheerful Blagosvetlova, was this summer not the same as in other years. Ever since the household had moved there from the city, one almost never saw an outsider. Few came visiting, and those who did left without a welcome. If necessary, it was the steward who received them. On those rare occasions when Ivan Ivanovitch left for a few days, he would return, lock himself in his rooms, and would not even ride out to inspect his fields. Every morning the steward would bring him a report and, standing throughout, would inform him of what had happened the previous day. When the steward finally left, it was with relief, because it was exceedingly trying for even a few minutes to put up with Ivan Ivanovitch, who had become increasingly difficult since God's punishment had befallen him, something everyone knew about but no one dared mention.

What was this severe punishment? There were many speculations in the household. In whispers they exchanged bits of news about the lost young man. Some said he was in prison and would be tried. Some insisted he had already been tried and sent away, God knows where. Some feared it was worse than being sent away and crossed themselves. As evidence, they cited the young lady, or, as they called her, the "cloistered one." They felt more sorry for her than for the master. The servants, who always know everything that is going on in every household, if not more, reported that they had seen with their own eyes the young lady on her knees praying for the dead young man. Others recounted how they had heard the father and daughter quarreling, he blaming her for her brother's misfortune because she knew he was going down the wrong path, had kept it from him, and had always come to her brother's defense. One lackey, a handsome youth in a frock coat, had hinted while gazing at himself in the kitchen mirror about an unlikely occurrence, saying he had come upon the young man as he was raising his hand to strike the young lady. But this lie met with shocked protests from all sides and caused an outcry among the servants. Had this lackey in the frock coat not retracted his words, they would have dragged him from the coachman's protective arms, beaten him as a warning not to dare make up such outrageous lies again.

In all this talk, greatly exaggerated of course, there existed a tiny grain of truth. Ivan Ivanovitch had always maintained that his daughter and her brother kept secrets, that she probably knew the reason Grisha wanted letters sent to him *poste restante,* and that she certainly knew why Grisha hadn't come home for Easter. She would not convince him otherwise. His son had been swept away with the tide—of that he was as certain as his name was Ivan Ivanovitch Popov. His son had allowed himself to follow a dangerous path, and if not today, then tomorrow, they would hear news that he had been arrested, if not worse. And who was guilty if not he, Ivan Ivanovitch himself, with his system of raising his children in absolute freedom? Why did he need to raise them away from home, his son at a *gymnasium* in one place, his daughter at an institute in another? Was not his brother, Nikolai, right? He had said that children need to be under a parent's surveillance at all times. Children who grow up without a father and mother are like grass growing without sun. But Ivan Ivanovitch believed that a motherless home was no home at all. Since he had been widowed, his home had become tedious to him. He could not find any solace there; nothing pleased him for long. He did not seek to advance his promising career; by the age of thirty he had already become a governor and there had been a time when he dreamed of a minister's portfolio. The promising, happy Ivan Ivanovitch, who had once loved to give advice and had always been at the center of society, gradually began to neglect himself, to distance himself from people, becoming a melancholy and unpredictable lord of the manor, a stern father to his children and an even stricter master to his tenants, so that his own brothers did not recognize him or understand what was happening to him. The only pleasure he allowed himself was *okhote*—hunting. Hunting was his life. But this summer he had rarely gone out to do even that. Most of the time he would sit at home in his rooms, reading and smoking, smoking and reading, showing up at the dining table gloomy as the night, greeting his daughter coldly, occasionally exchanging a few words with her and never a word about the son, as if he were long dead.

The last time the name Grisha was mentioned was the day before, when Vera had returned from the central Russian city and had brought strange news about her brother: first, that he was an excellent student at the university, comported himself responsibly, and second, that he had been temporarily employed at the very respectable home of people called Bardo-Brodovski, who could not praise him enough, and third, the Bardo-Brodovskis had told her how, before his departure, he had received a telegram that upset him terribly, and he had said he had to go home.

"That's all?"

Ivan Ivanovitch scrutinized his daughter and Vera realized her father did not believe she was telling him the entire truth. Perhaps she knew something more about her brother that she was keeping from him and was afraid of disclosing. She tried to convince him otherwise, swearing by the sacred memory of her dead mother. But that did not placate the angry, overwrought Ivan Ivanovitch. On the contrary, he became even more infuriated because his daughter had invoked the memory of her dead mother, who was surely as dear to him as she was to her. He remained convinced that something more was going on. It didn't make sense—why temporary employment? Why would his son need to be temporarily employed? It was an evasion, a pretext, a subterfuge. Everyone was plotting against him, everyone—his own children, his flesh and blood. And Ivan Ivanovitch rose, slammed the door, went off to his own chambers, locked himself in—and not another word about his son. No more son. Dead.

And what should happen: the steward delivered a message to his master that some young man, a student, had come and wished to speak to him about a most important matter. Ivan Ivanovitch's glare made the steward tremble. He knew very well the rule that he was not to be interrupted, no exceptions. But the student had insisted that the matter he had come about was more vital to Ivan Ivanovitch than to himself. It was urgent that he see him without fail and immediately.

"What does he look like?"

"Like an Armenian, a Georgian, or a Jew."

"His name?"

"He didn't say."

"*Vun!!!*—Out!"

The word "Out!" was uttered so violently that the windows rattled and the steward fled, half-dead, out the door. But Ivan Ivanovitch called him back.

"Let him put what he wants in writing!"

In a few minutes Ivan Ivanovitch was handed a signed envelope containing a note consisting of three words, "*Po dyelu sina*—Concerning your son," and he began to tremble.

"A Georgian or a Jew . . . certainly a comrade . . . a revolutionary, perhaps an anarchist . . . part of some plot to extort money . . . have to be careful, take precautions, a Georgian or a Jew . . . these Jews are everywhere!!!"

When the student (who was the real Rabinovitch, as the reader has no doubt guessed) was led in, the first thing to greet him was a Browning rifle resting on the table with its barrel aimed directly at him. Then he saw his friend Grisha's father, whom he recognized, first, from the portrait he had often seen at his friend's, and second, even if he hadn't seen it, he would have known this was Grisha's father. He had the same honest, benign, sad eyes, though more deeply set than his son's, the same thick, black, but graying hair, and the same deep chest with the broad, slightly raised shoulders. All the gestures, including passing his hand over his hair and the toss of the head, were Grisha's characteristic mannerisms, even the loud, rapid way of speaking—two of a kind.

"Sit. What do you wish to tell me?"

Ivan Ivanovitch indicated a chair at the end of the table as he seated himself at the other end, closer to the loaded Browning, examining the guest with his deep, penetrating eyes as he waited to hear what he had to say. He was positive the visitor would begin by saying he had come to rescue his son from some misfortune . . . and so it was, as he had guessed! The student first looked about to get his bearings and came right to the point, but his voice quivered.

"I have been your Grisha's friend since *gymnasium*" (he mentioned the city). "Your son is in trouble. There are worse troubles, his life isn't in danger, but . . ."

"He's in prison?" Ivan Ivanovitch asked, gesturing with his hand. That was the main thing he wanted to know. The student was surprised and looked at him uneasily.

"You already know he's in prison?"

With his deep-set eyes, Ivan Ivanovitch took in the student and didn't answer, but asked quickly, as was his way, "So, you've come to rescue him?"

Rabinovitch was even more surprised and started to tell him the story of their playful prank that had turned into a bloody hoax.

Ivan Ivanovitch threw his head back, ran his fingers over his hair, leaned back in his chair, exhaled, and again considered his visitor, who was beginning to look to him not so much like an opportunist or a blackmailer but like a madman, a person not in his right mind. The guest apparently surmised this and said, "Ivan Ivanovitch, I see you are looking at me as if I don't know what I'm talking about, but I must relate to you the entire saga, the tragicomedy from beginning to end. It's a long, complicated, tangled story proving how sometimes a foolish trifle can lead to the greatest tragedy. But first of all, you must forgive me for presuming. You must give your word of honor, the best of guarantees because I know my friend, Grisha, and know his father, that what I tell you must not leave these four walls. One word, one wink of an eye can give me away, and they can arrest me on the spot. That would do untold damage to the case and to your son, although, I repeat, he is not in mortal danger. Once they find out the truth, they will in the end release him. That's one thing . . ."

"That's one, and what's the second?" asked Ivan Ivanovitch, who was beginning to resent the audacity of this Jew's demanding of him, of Ivan Ivanovitch Popov, his word of honor. He was eager to hear the point of the story, but the student had the impression he wasn't being believed, he was being laughed at, and so he paused. But Ivan Ivanovitch urged him on.

"And second?"

"And second, I ask you to trust me, because you see before you a person who, besides being your son's friend and comrade, desires nothing more than to right the wrong, the foolish wrong, that two friends committed in a carefree moment at a celebration of close friends. You yourself were once young and probably also made mistakes, but certainly never so stupid a mistake as ours, mine and your son's."

During the entire time they had exchanged identities, the real Rabinovitch had never realized so clearly as now how foolish it had been on both their parts to perpetrate this terrible hoax. And though his comrade carried more of the responsibility than he, because at the time it was Grisha who was intoxicated, not he—still he accepted half of the blame for himself.

The young man's words proved to Ivan Ivanovitch that he was not dealing with a madman, but he still did not know what the student was after. His mind could not comprehend what he meant by their having exchanged identities. What did he mean by a tragicomedy? He wasn't loath to ask him.

"I don't really understand you, young man. I just hear words, 'mistake,' 'hoax,' 'celebration,' 'tragicomedy.' What they mean, I don't understand. Maybe I would understand it better if you would express yourself more clearly. And that you demand my word of honor is laughable. How can I give my word to someone I don't know? You yourself just said you know your friend and his father—if so, you must realize you may say anything you wish. It will go no further."

By the soft tone and the sincere eyes gazing trustingly at him, Rabinovitch saw that his demand had been altogether unnecessary, and he set about quickly to impart his long story, the tragicomedy, as he called it, in all its particulars, from beginning to end, how a foolish prank friends had thought up in a carefree moment had led to a sorrowful, bloody hoax.

Here Rabinovitch had to digress a bit to explain why he called it a bloody hoax. He gave Ivan Ivanovitch a short disquisition about the fact that there were people, even in our progressive times, who believed in the existence of so heinous a thing as *alilas dom*—ritual murder. And this information was not superfluous, because Ivan Ivanovitch afterward admitted that he really hadn't known about such matters. He had read in the newspapers about something having to do with blood, that some Jewish dentist had tricked a Gentile youth into his confidence and had murdered him because of a Jewish holiday, but it had never occurred to him to pay attention—my God, there were plenty of people being slaughtered daily nowadays!

Ivan Ivanovitch learned many amazing things that day from this student, who related, together with the story of his son's woes, his own problems and the suffering he had undergone because of his Jewishness during the best years of his young life and how he had that year been so torn as he tried to be a pretend Gentile treated as an equal among Gentiles. And especially the hell he had gone through during his recent long journey to the large city of the Jewish Pale (he also had to explain the impact on Jews of the Pale), where he had counted on rescuing his friend but had been totally thwarted. Rabinovitch laid out every-thing for his friend's father as he would for his own father.

On Ivan Ivanovitch's face could be discerned the full gamut of emotions he had experienced in the hours that flew by like minutes, so new and deeply absorbing was this young Jew's tale. His words rang with such heartfelt truth, even though he was a Jew . . . The lackey in the frock coat and white tie who had served tea was amazed at how his master seemed to have suddenly taken on a new demeanor during the time he had spent with the student. A different person!

Toward evening of that same day, Ivan Ivanovitch ordered the horses to be harnessed, sent for the steward and gave him orders for the entire week, called in his daughter to inform her that he had important information he could not tell her about yet. It had to do with Grisha . . . (A spark had ignited in his eyes.) It was possible he would soon be bringing him home. He was leaving for a few days . . . He would write . . . He would wire . . .

For the first time in his life, Ivan Ivanovitch sat side-by-side with a Jew. In the first-class compartment in which they sat, he had enough time on the way to learn many amazing new things from his traveling companion, about which, he had to confess, he had had no inkling. An entire world, an unknown world, opened up before him. Still, he was bothered that his traveling companion, though a thoroughly agreeable person, was still and all a Jew.

the hundred-eleventh chapter

IN THE HALLS OF JUSTICE

Not only the long, gray courthouse with the two porticos, but also the street on which it was located was jammed with people. Never before had the Stock Exchange been so empty and deserted as on that morning. Never before had the markets and shops, the offices and banks seen so few patrons as on that morning, as if all interests in the city had ceased except one—the ritual-murder trial, with its hero, the dentist Rabinovitch. From early morning curiosity seekers had been standing for two hours by the clock in the rain, hoping to catch a glimpse of the accused being led in. And as most of this crowd was Jewish, and, as everyone knows, whenever Jews gather they do not like to waste time, they occupied themselves doing something useful, talking—animatedly, intensely, and full of gestures, as is only fitting for Jews. What were they talking about? As usual, about the Jewish "burden," about the trial, and about the dentist over and over again. The talk was exaggerated, peppered with homilies, stories, strongly held opinions, and speculations without end. How much the general public knew what was going on behind the scenes was hard to say. But Jews always know absolutely everything. Jews knew, for instance, of the new witnesses, one of whom was a well-known graduate student, Karshunov, who would swear that he himself saw the dentist Rabinovitch and a swarthy young man with curly hair riding in a cab. At their feet lay a bound-up sack, inside of which something alive was thrashing and squirming. The two Jews were whispering something in Yiddish they couldn't understand, but they did catch one word: "Matzo" . . . The witnesses followed the cab but the Jews spotted them and ordered the driver to go faster. Their cab turned off onto a side street and disappeared down the street where the synagogue was located.

Jews know everything. Jews knew that they had recently rearrested Kirile and Kirilikha after an informer had helped them catch the real criminal, some thief who had already made a confession and named his accomplices. But misfortune struck—the thief had mysteriously disappeared from prison, and the informer, who had dug a hole for the thieves to fall in, was himself imprisoned for a theft.

Jews know everything. The Jews knew that the convert, Lapidus, the spiteful apostate, had reconsidered and was prepared to recant his testimony, to confess that some madness had possessed him, he himself did not know what had happened to him. Now he was prepared to suffer the consequences. "Serves him right!" the Jews exclaimed. "That's what should befall all our enemies!"

Jews know everything. The Jews even knew what the lawyers would be saying and in what order they would be speaking. And many great deeds and exaggerated stories were exchanged, not only about the famous lawyers but also about the prosecutor who had been appointed because he was a renowned specialist in blood ritual matters. For a month he had been studying there on the spot every aspect of the case. He had photographed the entire Jewish Street; he went everywhere, in the shul and even to the place where Jews baked matzos, where he summoned the rabbi for an interview. Many, many more news items were exchanged among them, every miracle and every wonder. There was also much talk about the accused, although no one had seen him. It was said that, in the time he had been sitting in prison, he had grown gray as a mourning dove, and it was likely he had become a bit deranged. But he had recovered; he had written a note recently to his fiancee in Hebrew and had sent it to her through his lawyer.

"What gray hair? What fiancee? Do you mean Shapiro's daughter? It doesn't even begin to be true! She hasn't been his fiancee for a long time. She has a new fiance. Ask me. I know better than all of you. I'm their neighbor and close friend."

Plainly this was spoken by none other than Katz, or Ketzele, as he was called on the Stock Exchange. Perspiring heavily and with a furrowed brow, Ketzele was scurrying about that morning on his short legs from one person to the next, gesticulating wildly with his hands, shoulders, and every limb, never standing still for long in one spot, as if someone had hammered nails into the soles of his shoes or as if the street were paved, not with cobblestones, but with hot coals. Poor Ketzele obeyed the laws of his own nature faithfully and zealously. If you had paid a person the largest sum, he would not have worked so diligently and nimbly. Not only had he known the person in question himself, but had played card games with him countless times and had had the opportunity to befriend his father, who had spent a day and night as a guest in his home and had "talked and talked and talked—" Ketzele would say, and was already on his way. After all, there was so much to do, *keyn eyn horeh*, so many Jews to keep informed . . .

Nor could one say that the crowd consisted only of Jews. There were also many Gentiles who were no less interested in the trial trumpeted ceaselessly in the newspapers day after day, so that it was blown up into a world-shaking event, attracting special correspondents, not only from the capital but also from the greatest foreign cities. Everybody was eager to gain admission to the courtroom, but few were able to do so. One needed tickets to be admitted, and the number was limited because there were many witnesses, correspondents, jurists, and officials who literally besieged the building, pressing against the door, which was still locked and guarded. Much later, coaches began arriving with elegant ladies wearing beautiful chapeaus, female devotees of criminal proceedings, without whom, as everyone knows, there can be no great trial. Soon the approach to the court became more and more congested, and the entryway became impossible. Police appeared, and not a moment too soon, because several incidents broke out among the different classes making up the crowd that could have ended far from happily.

But now the crowd stirred, the sea of heads moved like a wave—the door opened and the lucky ones began to push in one at a time, their way not made any easier by all the shoving and crowding, while the less fortunate had to remain outside the door. No amount of pleading or pushing or fist-fighting helped. They had no choice but to settle for at least standing closer to the door and to thank God the rain had stopped. "A Jew considers it a stroke of luck to have a cool *Tisha B'Av*—Day of Fast . . . ," said philosophically the Jews who had to remain outside.

"Look," they kept joking, "whom you have to envy: the men in the short frock coats and white cravats. They're allowed in, but on the other side of the metal grating. It isn't bad to be a policeman, either. As long as you're a higher up, they let you in."

At that moment a well-appointed carriage drove up, and from it stepped a distinguished gentleman with deep-set eyes and, right behind him, a student with a Jewish appearance. The distinguished man, followed by the student, made his way to the door but was not allowed in and, as it appeared, both were dismayed by the rejection. The distinguished man glanced with his deep-set eyes at the student, and the student was saying something heatedly, gesturing with his hands and appearing very upset.

Understandably, the Jews interpreted this scene in many ways and asked one another who this Gentile was and what was he doing arriving in the same carriage with a Jewish student? Up popped Ketzele.

"You can call me crazy and a madman and whatever you wish, but I'm willing to bet anything that the student is a brother of the accused. I know his elder brother, Abraham-Leibush, and they're as alike as two drops of water! I spent a day and a night with him and observed him very carefully."

"Good, so who then is this Gentile?"

"What's so hard to figure out? It's probably the wealthy landowner who holds the lease on the property Rabinovitch's father lives on," Ketzele said with such aplomb that it didn't occur to anyone to ask him, what lease? Also they were eager to see what would happen with the landowner. Would they let him in? Some said yes, others no. In the meantime, the Gentile was talking something over with the student, who flared up and waved his arms heatedly. Was he giving him advice? Was he telling him what to do? A Jewish head . . . Evidently the Gentile followed his advice and took out of his breast pocket a calling card and handed it to the guard. It took no more than a few minutes before the door opened and the Gentile was ushered inside while the student with the Jewish face was left to pace at the door, agitatedly tugging at his moustache. After a while, he got into the carriage and left.

"See? What did I tell you?" said Ketzele with a triumphant laugh. "That landowner is no ordinary landowner, but probably a count, and he sent his calling card to the official inside—Count So-and-So—and they rolled out the welcome mat for him." And to the Jew he said, "You wait a few minutes while I get them to let you inside. And if it doesn't work out, go back to the hotel and tell them to put up a samovar for you at my expense."

"He knows everything, this Ketzele, like a sage of old."

"Not so much old, as experienced."

"Just like he's reading it from a book."

"An odd man."

"A restless man."

Inside the courtroom it took a while before the crowd seated itself on the closely placed chairs. Each person felt that, no matter where he sat, he might be sitting in a better place, and no matter how much he could see, he felt he might see better. Not only in the courtroom itself, but even on the other side of the grating, where the officials and special guests sat, it was packed solid. These were the jurists, lawyers, and their assistants, all wearing black frock coats, and most of them, whether they needed them or not, carrying large briefcases under their arms. From among these jurists the "prince among lawyers" stood out with his ministerial head and his long, thin legs; the black frock coat and white cravat lent his large, smooth head a particular sheen, and his broad, white forehead gave testimony that this man was a serious thinker who maintained his calm and was prepared to wage war, no matter how strong and how well armed the foe might be. If the foe were strong, he would be stronger. If the foe were well armed, he would be better armed. On his side was the certainty that his accused client was not guilty, on his side was truth and innocence. And who was that lawyer with the leonine head and the fiery black eyes whom all the other lawyers were falling over one another to get near, shaking his hand in such a friendly manner and surrounding him? This was the famous orator-lawyer who had been brought in from the capital, or, as the prince among lawyers called him, the famous Solovey, the greatest big shot of them all. They quickly took their seats on the right side of the room at a long table next to the accused's chair, directly opposite the prosecutor's table.

The prosecutor was also a new face in the hall, having been sent from the capital on special assignment for this important trial. And though he was still a rather young man, a novice, because of his aristocratic lineage (we will soon learn who this was) and the great influence he had, his role in the trial was certain to advance his career. He was a young man whom one could call "distinguished," of elegant bearing, with a fine moustache, an impressive head of closely cropped hair, a smooth speaker with a charismatic voice—in a word, everything needed in order to win the hearts of the aforementioned female devotees.

Gradually the crowd seated itself and calmed down, but it only calmed down completely when the bailiff, an imposing fellow, tall and smooth-shaven, wearing a heavy gold chain around his neck, bellowed in a thunderous voice, "The court is in session." Up above sat the magistrates, one an older man, respectable-looking, with a round face and a grayish goatee and bags under his eyes, who looked exactly like the English King Edward. On either side of him were seated two colleagues, one a tall, slender, sickly-looking man whose shriveled neck stuck out of his gold collar, and the other, a man of Tatar appearance, short and rotund, with a black, wide, closely tonsured head and a broad, kindly face, from which peered a pair of small, mousy eyes. Sitting below the three magistrates, in a long row of chairs by the wall under the Czar's portrait, were various additional observers, high-placed individuals with and without gold pips on their collars.

But the eyes of the public were not drawn to him so much as to the specially appointed young prosecutor with the elegant figure as well as to the special defense lawyer with his leonine head. They were the two heroes—gladiators who would step out into the arena of justice with the might of their fine words and the power of their logic and ability to convince. Both sides, in addition to having previously prepared themselves, filling themselves with facts and opinions from many sources, had brought along with them fat tomes and documents, each with its expert views. One side brought the books of Karl Ecker, Hermann

Beher, August Rolling, and the famous Lyutastanski that proved with irrefutable arguments that Jews could not do without Christian blood for their Passover matzos. And the other side had brought along the books of Professor Delitch, Professor Khvulson, Doctor Frank, a Catholic priest, and Doctor Shtrak, a Lutheran pastor, as well as many other Jewish and Christian authorities that proved with much strong evidence from the Torah itself and with irrefutable arguments from the *Talmud, Kabbalah,* and from historic sources, that all these accusations were false from beginning to end, crude, ignorant, unfounded denunciations and caricatures, thoroughly shot through with venom, libel, intrigue, blackmail, and other such impure motives. What more was there to say? To the general public this was pure spectacle. Before them was an exciting drama to behold, brilliant speaker-gladiators to enjoy. But how could it have appeared to the few fortunate Jews who with great effort and influence had been able to get into the hall? Those who knew the real truth must have been quite disappointed at Phemida, the goddess of justice, who stood with eyes blindfolded, holding a scale in her hand; both sides of the scale were exactly even, not a hair's difference. But how could there be any doubt? Was it still necessary to prove we are not cannibals? One would surmise they imagined they were hearing an oracular voice from on high calling out: "WOE UNTO HIM WHO IS SUSPECTED AND IS GUILTLESS!"

the hundred-twelfth chapter

ONE SURPRISE AFTER ANOTHER

If most of the crowd was fascinated with the famous legal gladiators, with the famous lawyers and the prosecutor, they became completely mesmerized when the presiding judge with the bags under his eyes, who resembled the English King Edward, gave the order to bring in the accused. Some expected to see a sallow being with the face of a vampire and the eyes of a demon. Others expected the opposite: no vampire, no demon, no sallow being, but a dark-complexioned, nervous little Jew with a painted head, a cunning face, and shrewd little eyes. But neither one nor the other was correct. Led in by two soldiers with bared swords was a tall, big-boned young man with an especially handsome, thick growth of beard, fine, thoughtful eyes, and a sympathetic, open face framed by black, soft, unshorn hair. All eyes gazed in astonishment at the accused. Women peered through their lorgnettes: "Ach, who would have thought that someone like *that* could commit *such* a crime!?" The "criminal" did not look like a criminal at all. On his face was not a sign of guilt, anguish, suffering, or the least disturbance. Only the inward look in his fine eyes and the paleness of his skin testified to the fact that this man had endured much, had languished painfully, and had reflected on himself long and hard. For him this day was, if not the finally hoped-for day which he had waited for and looked forward to for so long, then at least the end of the tragicomedy. He felt certain the moment for it had arrived, the historic moment, when it would finally be proved, not only that he was innocent of this blood-ritual murder, but above all that such a crime had never been committed anywhere by Jews. He was relying heavily on the sound understanding and honesty of the judges. He was depending a great deal on his two lawyers—two giants, two lions. If they could not be convincing, who could?! But mostly he was relying on himself, on his own strength, on his firm will, and on the power of the holy truth that must shine through his every word. "There is no greater power in the world than the truth."

These were the thoughts of the accused, who was ready to answer all the questions asked of him. He was even ready with the way he would sum up his case before the judges, allowed him by law. These were carefully chosen words, but high-minded, passionate words straight from the heart, words that seared, penetrated the soul, convinced beyond the shadow of a doubt. He was so eager to speak his piece and to be put on trial that he began to see himself as a sacrifice, a martyr for the Jewish people, and, as an unwilling martyr, he was prepared for any outcome. He did not consider what *any outcome* might mean, but he felt a particular sweetness in contemplating the fate of a martyr, a historical sacrifice for an ancient people. Nevertheless, if he would be judged not guilty, as he was in fact, what a triumph that would be for the truth! What a victory it would be for an entire people, for those who had been persecuted and oppressed, humiliated and belittled, who would have been saved through *him*, through someone who in fact belonged to the oppressors. And his fantasy swept him upward on its gossamer wings and painted for him bright, elaborate, shining images, one more elaborate and more grandiose than the next. God knows where they would have swept him away, entirely forgetful of this world; he could barely remember that there was a beautiful girl called Betty with whom he was in love and whom he would soon be seeing and hearing right there in the courtroom.

He searched for her but could not find her. She had not arrived, nor had any of the witnesses nor the judges for whom he had prepared his moving speech. He only saw before him a sea of faces, all turned toward him, many ladies' hats with fancy feathers and lorgnettes fixed on him. He saw the three magistrates sitting high up with their embroidered collars, and directly opposite them, that fine, young prosecutor with the handsome moustache and closely cropped hair. Who could that be? Why did he look so familiar? He felt a burning sensation in his armpits, and his heart began to hammer in his chest. He looked intently at him. His eyes grew larger: "Could it be . . . ," he thought. "No, it can't be!" He imagined . . . "sometimes people resembled others . . ." "It can't be! It can't be!" At that moment the presiding judge was handed a calling card by a courier entering through the side door. He looked at it carefully and said something to the courier, who then disappeared through the side door. The accused took advantage of that moment and leaned over to his lawyer and whispered in his ear: "Who is that person across from us?" "That's our Angel of Death," the lawyer whispered back in his ear, "the young prosecutor specially sent here for our sake. A tough young man, they say . . . but don't worry about it, we'll take care of him." "Ach, that's not what I mean," the accused was annoyed. "Not that. I mean, what is his name?" "His name? Just a minute." The lawyer quietly asked his colleague with the lion's head and then turned to whisper it to the accused.

"His name is Popov . . . Dmitri Nikolaievitch Popov . . ."

Of course! He had hit it! It was he! Ach, how he had changed! What a sharp-looking official he had turned into! He had always been an elegant young man and a careerist, disciplined and socially adept, but a careerist. "My Mitya will go far," his uncle, Nikolai Ivanovitch, used to boast. And now *he* was standing accused before him! *He* would be trying him. "No! No novel could spring such surprises as life itself could," thought our hero, the real Popov, when he realized he had not been in error and that this was his uncle Nikolai Ivanovitch Popov's eldest son, with whom he had spent many a happy summer day in Blagosvet-lovo, going together to the woods, boating and fishing together on the Sazhelka. True, this was long ago. He, Grisha, was then in the youngest class of his *gymnasium,* and the other was already a student in his first or second year of university. "Have I changed so much that's it's hard to recognize me? How long has it been? Four years, five years, six years?" But here his thoughts were interrupted: the presiding judge, who had previously examined the calling card and was whispering to his two colleagues, gathered together the papers on the table and with a little cough and a pleasant tenor voice initiated the proceedings. He had barely uttered the first three words when from the crowd there rose a tall, most distinguished man with broad, slightly raised shoulders (this was the Gentile who had arrived with the student in the carriage), and holding before him a white sheet of paper folded in four, he proceeded down the aisle with firm steps straight toward the presiding judge, who paused mid-sentence. The crowd did not comprehend what was happening. They saw that the distinguished man who was heading toward the presiding judge with the paper in his hand came to the locked grating, remained standing a while and exchanged glances, first with the prosecutor, then with the accused. This took all together no more than a few seconds because the bailiff stepped up as quietly as if he had been walking on feathers and, following the wordless command of the presiding judge, took the paper from the man's hand and brought it to him. He read it over immediately and showed it to his two colleagues. Each of the three, one after the other, showed noticeable amazement, carefully examined the accused, and, huddling together, quietly but heatedly discussed the matter while the man who had handed them the paper laid one hand on the grating and with the other brushed back his black, silver-streaked hair and waited.

The crowd had no idea or suspicion that unfolding before them was an astonishing drama. This unknown man made no particular impression on anyone except on two people who were not only stunned but, as was plain to see, had also completely lost their composure. One was the prosecutor, who had sprung up from his chair and looked intently at the man, unable to comprehend why he was there and what the paper he had handed over meant, and the other was the accused. The latter remained frozen in his seat, unable to rise, grasping the bars of the grating and feeling as if his eyes would pop out of his head. For a moment he thought it was a hallucination, that an apparition of his father had appeared because he had that night been thinking so much about him. For a moment he thought he might faint . . .

As in a dream he observed everything that was taking place around him. He saw how the paper was passed from hand to hand by the three magistrates until it reached the shocked prosecutor, who fixed his eyes on him and appeared finally to recognize him. Then the presiding judge posed questions to him and he answered—he did not remember how. The room seemed to be spinning around, he felt a ringing in his ears, and his face was burning as if with a hellish fire. Then he suddenly heard, as if from afar, the young prosecutor's resounding voice, and he listened to it as if he were trying to convince himself that it was Mitya speaking, Dmitri Nikolaievitch Popov. From his speech, he could catch only a few words, that "according to Article 549, the case had to be remitted for a new investigation and the accused . . ." The rest he did not hear. Afterward, he remembered the magistrates stood up, the courtroom broke into an uproar, and he was led away, but not by soldiers and not to prison! No more prison!

What then happened in the courtroom and afterward when they learned about the stunning news that the accused, who had spent so long in prison as the dentist Rabinovitch, was not a Jew at all and not a Shklov citizen named Hersh Movshovitch Rabinovitch, but a man of noble birth, a son of the T_____ former provincial governor, and his real name was Grigori Ivanovitch Popov—we leave to the reader to suppose. Many, unfortunately, had a bad day. First, the female devotees, who were left without a performance. The black fellowship of die-hard Jew haters had their downfall, a strange downfall. Some hinted darkly that it didn't add up, it had to be a Jewish trick, nothing more. Others complained it was nervy of a Jew to fool so many people and that the real Rabinovitch and all the Rabinovitches ought to be severely punished. A bad, bitter day was had by the real die-hard Jew haters. But the Jews celebrated and declared a holiday—was it not a miracle to be rid of so heavy a burden in so miraculous a way? The house of mourning had turned into a house of joy. All forgotten! Forgotten, all their troubles, as they ran to one another relating the good news, stopping one another and extolling what God can do. Others embraced. It was no small thing to celebrate—the whole world would now know, in this twentieth century, that Jews were not cannibals! "No, don't say there are no more miracles nowadays or that there is no longer a God in the world!" "Ay, God!" "The Jewish God!" . . .

But more than anyone else, Ketzele was as usual working away, running here and there, and exclaiming loudly, "Well, Jewish children, what did I tell you? Is Katz still a madman? Well?" What the newspapers of all stripes had to say was also not difficult to imagine. The reader is sure to be most interested in knowing what finally happened to the heroes of this extraordinary account. Did they ever find the real perpetrators and their accomplices? Did they receive their just deserts according to law and according to right as they truly deserved? This the reader will learn in the last chapter, in the epilogue to the saga of the bloody hoax.

END OF PART TWO

EPILOGUE

It was a winter evening during one of the eight days of Chanukah. The Shapiros' home was surprisingly neat and prepared for the holiday. The head of the household himself, David Shapiro, was clad in his black, Sabbath gabardine. He had already made the blessing over the Chanukah candles and was ready to welcome the guests, who were not long in arriving at the Shapiros' "for *latkes*." That was only a manner of speaking, "for *latkes*." In reality everyone knew that at the Shapiros' tonight there would be an announcement and a betrothal party. Betty was to be betrothed to some poor but brilliant student. He was called Hurvitch, Benny Hurvitch. "That Hurvitch is not just any Hurvitch. He comes from a distinguished line," boasted David Shapiro. "He comes from the real, the Pinsk Hurvitches, whose lineage goes back to the venerable *Shela Hakadosh*. Now do you know?"

The first to arrive were from the groom's side, the bookbinder and his wife, who had the face of a matzo, both dressed in their Sabbath best. They seated themselves in a corner very humbly. No one had received them. Betty was still in her room and it was beneath David: "A mere worker!" And Sara was in the kitchen with another woman, both of them deeply absorbed in their work—roasting geese, rendering fat, and frying *latkes*. But when the wealthy relatives arrived, the rich sister-in-law, Toibe, and her married daughters and daughter-in-law (the brother-in-law, Reb Shlomo Familiant, was not in town; that very frugal man had allowed himself the luxury of going off to the Rebbe's for Chanukah), and after them, David's boss and his sons, they could no longer be so rude. Sara put on her silk dress and little diamonds and entered the room glowingly to welcome the dear guests as she kissed her wealthy relatives.

"Toibenyu, dear heart, where are your younger daughters?"

"God be with you, Sara'le darling, don't you know that young ladies can't attend betrothal parties?" And there followed several minutes of many good wishes exchanged between them. First Toibe wished that Sara live to see her daughter under the wedding canopy, God willing. "It's time . . . " Then Sara wished Toibe that her unmarried daughters soon have a betrothal party of their own. "It's high time . . . "

"Amen, may it be so," Toibe murmured with a pious face, pretending she didn't notice how her sister-in-law had repaid her, barb for barb, as her eyes searched among the guests for the bride and groom. She spied the groom sitting in a corner playing chess with the doctor, both hatless and both so deeply absorbed in the chessboard that neither noticed what was going on around them. The bride sat apart with an unknown man, also hatless, with a very large head (this was the prince among lawyers).

Betty, it seemed, had never looked more beautiful or more charming than now. She truly shone like the sun, although on her shining face was to be seen a new, careworn wrinkle, a sign of a suppressed melancholy. But that only lent her a special charm. Her Aunt Toibe gazed at her and sighed, but why she sighed was hard to say. Was it because poor girls without a groshen of dowry had bridegrooms while the One Above did not send her young ladies any matches? Or was she upset because most of the men were sitting without hats like Gentiles? Or perhaps it was because, when she looked at Betty, she was reminded that if her Shlomo, the *Chassid,* were there, he would be ogling his little niece with his nearsighted eyes? In a word, poor Aunt Toibe sighed mightily, but who could pay attention to her now when there were so many new guests constantly arriving and each one had to be welcomed? The wealthy relatives were seated at the head of the table next to David's boss with the slicked beard and the round, silver spectacles and his sons and sons-in-law, who smoked so much people could barely see one another. Near them stood the host, David Shapiro, engaging them in conversation. He was telling them, quietly of course, about his future son-in-law, who, although not rich, was the descendant of a great line. "He's a Hurvitch, from the true, Pinsk Hurvitches, who go all the way back to *Shelah Hakadosh.* Ach! His mind, his knowledge, his achievements—the first student among students who, compared to him, are . . . nothing! You should hear him speak! And does he write Hebrew! Knows Gemara by heart! And can he play chess!"

For David, the celebration was spoiled a bit by the groom's brother-in-law, the bookbinder, who sat in a corner as if he were sitting in a hot bath, sweating profusely, his eyes fearfully darting about on all sides, especially when they encountered the rich relatives. The bookbinder's wife with the matzo face attempted several times to start a conversation with Madam Shapiro as an old friend, to remind her of that night when they had spent, may it never happen again, all night in the street, but her husband would not let her. He would repeatedly tug at her elbow, telling her to sit still, as he coughed into his sleeve, "A poor man has to sit humbly among rich folk . . . "

For Sara Shapiro, this celebration had not come easily. She almost had to go on bended knee to her daughter before she would agree to make the announcement. Let there be an end to it! Let people's tongues be silenced. Let them stop whispering about her daughter and the student who spent day and night at their house, never leaving! The poor mother had no idea what temptation her daughter had to withstand, the letters she had received from their former roomer, who had so tragically perpetrated the bloody hoax. Not a soul knew of the contents of these letters, not even Benny Hurvitch, who was her sole confidant. He did know she was receiving letters from someone and was answering them; he even knew who this person was. But to ask her specifically about them, he did not wish to do. No one could expect that of him. That was why he was a Pinsk lad and a Hurvitch. No, he would rather die before showing any sign that he knew what was going on. And that, Betty resented greatly! She yearned to discuss the letters with him, to ask his advice about what to answer. But if he wasn't going to ask any questions, if he pretended not to be interested at all, she was not about to explain things or make apologies. No one could expect that of her. She was Shapiro's daughter, from the real, the Slaviteh Shapiros. For three days she had been overwrought, for three nights had not slept, had cried and cried, washed her face and cried again, no one aware of her anguish. And on the fourth day she had sent off in reply a long, friendly letter in which she poured out her heart, revealed the entire truth, confessed what her feelings had been toward him up until the day of the catastrophe and after that day (for the word "catastrophe" she meant the day of the trial, when it had become known that the Jew, Grigori Moiseyevitch Rabinovitch was really a Gentile, Grigori Iva-novitch Popov . . .). She endeavored to demonstrate to him that what he was desiring would be insanity for them both. She could never cross the boundaries that separated them, out of love for her people, because of whom and for whom she had been persecuted and was prepared to be persecuted in the future—that she had told him many times. It was an instinct one could feel only with one's heart and could not be controlled by reason. And he, too, must not cross those boundaries because it would go against common sense, against nature, and against reason. He had too much integrity to be capable of doing something so questionable . . .

"You have demonstrated such heroism," she ended her letter. "Continue being a hero. Forget that there were other feelings between us besides the feel-ings of pure friendship that will remain with us forever and ever! . . . "

When Grigori Ivanovitch Popov received this letter, it brought on a severe depression. He was prepared to take his life, but finally relented. When he finished fulfilling his punishment for the hoax of assuming a false name and using a false permit and a false diploma, he made peace with his father, entered the university, and it was said he did well. Gradually he awakened from his one-time dreams and entered the mainstream of Russian life. It was to be hoped he would become an enlightened Gentile who had been purified by his Jewish experience. Give us more such Christians, and Judaism will be protected from many unnecessary accusations, vilifications, libels, woes, anguish, evils .

But the one who could not bear the shame was his sister. The good, pious Vera, soon after her brother's homecoming, entered a convent.

* * *

And the real Rabinovitch, like the false Rabinovitch, first had to fulfill his punishment for the same hoax, but it was nothing compared to the sea of troubles awaiting him once he sought to continue his studies. He was deluged with official notifications, full of so many new regulations and so many new restrictions that he had to go abroad "to draw wisdom and knowledge from strange wells . . . " In the final, bitter months of his life, he transported himself in his mind to the magic land of Offir, where he found his princess, who knew nothing about a "bloody hoax" or that he had once been one of its heroes.

THE · END